KEIGH ANDERS

AND THE

BEARS OF BJORN

KEIGH ANDERS

AND THE
BEARS OF BJORN

BOOK I IN THE SON OF EDEN TRILOGY

TORY STELLER

This book is dedicated to my parents, my gold. And to all those in search of their king.
Know that he's not so far off as you imagine.

CONTENTS

GARDEN WALL

QUEENS VEIL FALLS

LAKE GREBE

WARTEN

OLD WATCHTOWER

SUTNI

BJORN

ANDERS HOME

TAOFI

BICKOR

PREDANNOST

BULLHORN
MOUNTAINS

KINGS RIVER

DAWNUS

KINGS ROAD

URSUS MOUNTAINS

VADERKIRK

MODESTA

SENTINEL

THE CURTAIN WALL

THE KINGDOM OF
EDEN

Oftentimes, the most significant day of your life isn't a day from your life at all. It is the lives and choices of countless others that till the soil, knowingly and unknowingly preparing the way for the seed of your life to be planted. Once planted, however, will you grow? Or will the wilting of your life serve only as fuel for the seed that will fight to live and thrive, no matter the soil prepared for it?

PROLOGUE

40-22-14

Massive doors of red cedar and black iron rumbled to life as six muscular male servants in white wool tunics pressed their weight against the towering timbers. No sooner had the two doors parted than twelve men in opulent robes of deep emerald green strode single file, through the gap, into the king's cavernous throne room.

When the last of the robed men cleared the doors, the servants shifted in unspoken unison. Grunting, they grabbed the iron pull bars and threw their weight back toward the brightly lit entrance hall. A deep, creaking groan of protest sounded from each of the doors' enormous metal hinges as their momentum was halted, then reversed.

The men of the Queen's Council glided across the polished granite floors of the vaulted throne room without a word. During feasts, the room was alive, loud with five hundred of the king's chosen guests conversing around tables piled high with choice meats, breads, cheeses, and fruits... but this was no feast. A sullen silence reigned in the empty chamber tonight. Only one table sat before the thrones now. Made from a single slab of a great pine, it was as wide as the height of two men and as long as ten horses. Polished smooth and oiled till it gleamed, the table was surrounded by twenty-two high-backed chairs with black leather wraps and padding, each made from the single enormous white antler of a moose, with legs and arms of bleached elk antler.

The banner of light from the open doors gradually slimmed until it was just a sliver, then, with an ominous boom, the council was shut in. Nine of the councilmen took seats at the far end of the table. Two paced the room, while the last man, hair white with age, walked calmly to the furthest of the room's high arched windows and surveyed the snow falling on the palace courtyards below.

At the head of the room were three thrones, aglow in the warm light of two hundred and forty-two candles—one for each year of the Kingdom of Eden's existence. The center throne, carved from a single block of pure white marble and inlaid with deep veins of gold and silver like sheets of lightning, was the king's. To its left, the ironwood throne of the queen. To its right, several paces removed, was the gold throne of the long-awaited heir.

One of the pacing men strode the length of the table, wringing his hands and muttering to himself. The other walked smoothly in front of the thrones, occasionally stopping to study the gold throne of the heir.

Minutes stretched into an hour this way, with no change but the snow piling up in the windowsills and no sound but the crackling of the torches hung on the walls.

The silence finally broke when a young servant girl entered the room through a small door hidden in the rear wall. She bore a golden tray of ceramic mugs and a pot of hot tea. Placing the tray on the table, she began filling the mugs with the steaming brew. The men at the table accepted their cups with gracious nods and tired smiles, as did the man at the window. The muttering man snatched his from the girl's hand and took a hurried drink, burning his tongue. He slammed the mug down on the table, splattering several of his cohorts with the hot brew. Giving their scowls an apologetic wince, he resumed his pacing.

Lastly, the girl served a mug to the man by the thrones. He was slender as a snake, with dark eyes and oily black hair to match. She approached him cautiously, slowly proffering the mug. At first, he paused, looking down his pointed nose at the thrall—then, with the swiftness of a striking viper, he seized hold of the mug with both hands, clasping the girl's hand down on the handle. His eyes narrowed, lip curling, daring her to resist. A moment later, he straightened, rolling back his shoulders as if just waking. Releasing his grip on the girl, he nodded toward the door, dismissing her.

The thrall girl's eyelids drooped. She stumbled back to the table, spilling the unaccepted tea and nearly falling. Catching the back of the closest chair, she paused to gather herself. The men at the table stared into the bottom of their mugs. None lifted their eyes or offered to aid the girl as she collected her items with trembling hands.

She let go of the chair and stiffened her back. The cords of her neck tightened as she attempted to still her quaking limbs. Taking up her tray, she held its edge tight to her body but was unable to keep the silver spoons from chattering on the thin metal. Her face quickly reddening, she began staggering back toward the door she had entered through. Halfway there, her strength faltered. She crashed to the floor in a heap. The gold tray clanged noisily off the stone floor, sending silver spoons and empty mugs chittering across the polished surface. The din reverberated around the room, echoing loudly off the hard, dark walls before slowly fading back to consuming silence.

The elderly councilman by the window rushed to her assistance. Helping the poor girl back to her feet, he collected her items for her and walked her slowly to her exit.

When the small door clicked shut behind her, the white-haired councilman paced back to his spot at the window. "You shouldn't do that, Slate," he said sternly, addressing the man by the thrones without giving him a glance.

"Whatever do you mean, Absaar?" Slate sneered. "I merely wasn't thirsty. Nerves, you know…"

The men at the table raised their eyes from their mugs.

"You know damn well what you did," insisted Absaar.

"Then say it!" snapped Slate.

"You pulled from the girl!" bellowed Absaar, turning to face Slate. At this, the men at the table hurriedly buried their faces back in their mugs. Even the pacing councilman paused before twitching back into motion.

"That…is a *very*…serious…accusation, my friend." Slate's words dripped with sincerity. "Your proof?"

"You know the king's law."

"Yes, and I wouldn't *dare* break a word of it," crooned Slate. "But as it stands, your accusation is baseless! That is, unless you think the word of a peasant counts for anything. It would be much easier for me to prove you coerced her testimony than it would be for you to prove I've done anything wrong."

He glared back at Absaar. When no rebuttal came, he shrugged and turned his back on the old man, resuming his pacing.

A second later he halted. "For the sake of debate, however, let's just say I did do what you claim. Does the king not deserve us at our very best?" he said, placing an offended hand on his chest. "Or perhaps it's jealousy that fuels your accusation. You would have me hide my abilities from a simple thrall girl? I can assure you, Absaar, even if I had pulled from her, she would never be able to piece together what was happening. You know…simple as they are."

"Please! This has nothing to do with me," spat Absaar, still glowering at Slate. "It's no secret you harbor resentment of the old ways!"

Slate whirled around. "And you seem to forget we live in new times! We have the authority to make the laws, but all you ever seem to want to do is worship the old ones!"

"To find fault in the law is to find fault in the king! Would you question his wisdom?" retorted Absaar. "It's this same spirit of pride that consumes Draiden! It is his ruin!"

"Ruin," sniffed Slate. "If you could call it that. Our enemy now controls all the lands outside of Eden. Rumor is he's discovered a cache of the old weapons of power. Every wandering tribe and band serves his purposes, and we sit here behind our wall. Yes, we are unmoved and unconquerable, but also inflexible and unchanging…all while the powers around us move to undermine our every effort."

At this, the jittery man interjected, "There are many f-f-free peoples outside the b-borders of Eden. S-s-surely…" His eyes flitted around the room, looking for confirmation of his statement. None came.

"Yes, Elric," said Slate, addressing the man as one might a small child. "Many of the land's peoples live under the *illusion* of freedom. They would even tell you they are free from the rule of any king. But they fool only themselves. The day Draiden comes to their gates, they will bend the knee... and he *will* come. His thirst for power will not be satiated until all the earth is under his banner, especially Eden." His dark eyes stared out the window into the distant black of night.

"As long as the king lives, Eden cannot be conquered." Absaar chanted the popular refrain before returning to his silent contemplation at the window.

"Yes, long live the king—but that brings us to the issue at hand tonight," Slate redirected. "Elric, how many males have been born to cane households this month?"

"Only three, in twenty-four births!" squeaked Elric. "And only two more expecting households due by month's end! And who knows if they will bear sons?"

The men at the table began shouting.

"The queen's time wasn't expected for another month!"

"Have the families been notified?"

"Messengers were dispatched this evening," offered Elric.

"It's an old law," piped a round man with rosy cheeks and a bulbous nose. "Are they aware of their duty to the kingdom?"

"Canes will do whatever the kingdom requires of them without question!" shouted a broad-shouldered councilman with bulging arms, who looked more mule than man.

"The point of the Consecrate is to hide the identity of the king's natural-born son, to all but the king himself," stated a councilman with a long black beard. "The law is clear! Only males born to cane families, in the same month as the king's son, will be taken into the Consecrate. How are we to hide his identity if there are so few children of his age? Surely anyone with brains more than a chickens will deduce which one he is, especially if he grows to be anywhere near the size of his father!"

"The *point*," snapped Slate, "of the Consecrate...is to develop character in our future lord...Character that isn't easily fostered in great halls of riches and comfort." He directed a look of utter detestation at the round man, who's rosy cheeks flushed purple as he averted his eyes. "Besides...the king does not have to select his own blood to be his heir. The Consecrate allows him to select an heir on merit. This is why sons of ables and thralls are not included in the Consecrate, and why they are not entrusted with sons of the Consecrate. The heir must be worthy of the throne."

"I know plenty of thralls with more *merit* than the average cane," Absaar grumbled from his place by the window.

Slate shook his head, lip curling.

Elric raised his hand, seeking permission to interject. "P-p-perhaps—all this worry is for nought and the queen will give birth to a daughter?"

The mulish man stood up resolutely. "We must be prepared for an heir. The Consecrate will be formed no matter the number. We will carry out the will of the king!"

"Hear! Hear!" the men chanted, banging their mugs on the table.

"Yes, yes, the wise will of the king," Slate drawled. "But do we *know* the king's will on this issue? Surely he must be informed of the situation and given a chance to change course."

"I informed him earlier today, when it became c-clear the queen would give b-birth..." Elric gulped. "He...he gave me n-n-no word."

Slate swooped to the end of the table, descending on the men like a bird of prey. "The king cannot be expected to have all the answers all at once. This is why we, the Queen's Council, are here tonight. It is our duty to direct the king toward reason, should he seek our advice. He cannot be expected to know everything," said Slate, before muttering to himself, "He can't know *everything*."

"The king's will *is* reason!" barked the strong man.

"Of *course!* Spoken like a true cane." Slate's lip curled. "No one questions your devotion, Damien. In fact, I'm a bit jealous of it myself. But alas, where you received a bull's allotment of brawn, I received the burden of a vast intellect." He locked eyes with Damien. "There will always be a need for multitudes of men who go where they are pointed, but I'd much rather be the one doing the pointing."

Damien bristled. The handle of his mug cracked in his hand as he returned Slate's glare.

Slate was the first to balk. "Now, now, we are all friends here, and of course you are right. The king's will *is* law and the law *is* good." He gave a slight conciliatory bow and turned his back on the table.

BANG!

In the gloom behind the candlelight, two enormous doors flew inward, shoved abruptly open by the paw of a gigantic bear. The powerful beast emerged from the shadows behind two glowing eyes. Its fur, the lustrous dark burgundy of blood, glistened in the candlelight. Long silver guard hairs flecked its neck and shoulders. More than twice the height of a man at its shoulder, it lumbered into the throne room, wagging a head the size of a boulder.

The men of the Queen's Council stood in unison. None flinched or even paid the bear much notice. Their eyes remained fixed on the open doorway.

Breathing loudly, the red bear sauntered around the golden throne and over to the table, nudging Damien with the tip of its massive nose. The round man next to him gave a frightened squeak and inched himself behind his neighbor.

Damien ran a hand up the bear's snout. "Sorry, Gorr...No food on the table tonight." He gave the giant bear a vigorous two-handed rub behind its elbow.

The bear gave a disappointed snort. Throwing his head back toward the front of the room, Gorr took two great bounds and planted himself in the gap between the marble throne of the king and the gold throne of the heir, neatly filling the void. He sat heavily on his haunches and faced the room looking like a giant guard dog.

No one spoke. All eyes still fixed on the doorway. The only sound was the crackle of torches and the rhythmic panting of the giant red bear.

Motion stirred in the shadows beyond the door. The councilmen straightened to attention.

A man strode into the room. Seven feet tall and broad as the door of a house, he wore radiant white pants and a long-sleeved shirt beneath a vest of rich sapphire-blue velvet emblazoned with emblems of gold filigree. His silver-pommeled sword hung at his waist from a belt of gold. The train of his white fur robe swept across the floor behind him.

On his head was a helmet of flawless artistry. Painstaking detail had been taken to give it the look of a natural head, with flowing gold hair and a curling beard. A gold crown with three prominent points topped the helm. The face bore an inscrutable expression, holes for eyes and mouth presenting only black voids behind them.

The king passed through the gap between his bear and his throne, running the fingers of one hand through Gorr's fur before slumping exhaustedly into the marble throne.

Still, no one spoke.

The king stooped forward, elbows on knees. He rested the face of his helm in his palms. Soon his shoulders began to heave, and his breathing became ragged. Gentle sobs sounded from behind the mask.

The men fidgeted nervously but remained silent.

Sitting up straight, the king gathered himself. The tension in the room grew thick. Every man rigid, as though bound by invisible ropes. Slate was bone-white, the blood draining entirely from his face.

When he spoke, the king's voice was mellifluous and warm from inside his golden helm. "Friends!" He stretched his arms wide. "At long last, Eden has an heir to the throne."

The men at the table cheered, roaring shouts of elation. Grinning like children, they hugged each other, slapping one another on the back. Slate called for palace thralls to bring bottles of wine. Toasts to king and kingdom were made. The king inclined his head in reception to each.

As the initial jubilee began to wane, the king motioned for the men to quiet.

Even in this moment of celebration, his voice weighed heavy with authority. "My bride..." His golden face turned to Slate. "*My* queen..." He faced the men at the table again. "...has given birth to—"

His words were cut off as a violent gust of wind rushed through the room, extinguishing the torches on the walls, yet leaving the throne's candles untouched.

Absaar stood in the corner, a black silhouette against the window. His eyes, two pupil-less pearls of white, reflected the flickering candlelight.

He spoke slowly, his voice emanated from the corner where he stood, filling the room with an unnatural thundering that made it seem as though the very air were speaking.

"A way is laid!
A way is open!
Son of Eden,
A child's been chosen!
A father stricken,
Two mothers torn.
Eden's enemy
Will rise once more!
Though this son
Is claimed by three,
In only one
Is his identity.
A hidden one
In sight of all.
For one to rise
One must fall.
The first to ever
But last to enter,
Both joy and anger
His deeds will render
Both, betrayer
And betrayed.
Powerless he'll be
To be saved.
A son so strong
And yet so feeble

Unknowingly leads
The way for evil.
His bow his rescue.
His sword his sight.
His life reclaimed,
But not by might.
Clothed in armor
Not his own.
Our hero stands!
But not alone.
A companion large
And one so small.
Before the end
They'll die for all.
In death
there's life.
Eden's son
Will have a wife
Though who he'll choose
Remains unclear.
She first must prove
Herself sincere.
In his error
He'll be protected.
In righteous aims,
Be rejected.
From his home,
A trail unbeaten,
His feet will take him
Far from Eden.
Power filled
And power from

The force he yields
He's one of one.
One divided
And one united,
Two wars he'll wage
Still young in age.
Though he looks
To be defeated,
He will rise,
Hero of Eden!
His fate is sealed
With this vision!
Which way he'll choose
Remains unwritten."

The pearls of white disappeared. Absaar's eyes closed before he collapsed into a crumpled heap on the floor. As he hit the ground, a second blast of air tore from the corner, extinguishing the candles and plunging the room into sullen blackness. From the darkness, rumbled the heavy bass of a growl deep in Gorr's chest.

CHAPTER 1

TEARS FOR A TEAR

50-2-4

Vvrrrrrrrrrp!

Bjorn's fifteen-year-olds were leaving their daily instruction in the town square when the sudden sound of ripping fabric stopped them in their tracks.

Deacon Wulf, a handsome, tan youth who, though not tall, still managed to look down on nearly everyone, was the first to find his tongue. "Unreal!"

He grinned, pointing at the homely girl desperately trying to cover herself. An exposed nail in one of the wooden dividers that separated the various age groups had ripped a large hole in her homemade patchwork dress, exposing her undergarments.

"Pfft! Even walking is an ugly affair when thralls try it," Deacon laughed.

Being careful to keep his eyes clear of the hole in her skirt, Keigh Anders hustled to the poor girl's side.

"Here, Emerson," he said, taking off the threadbare overshirt he wore to keep himself warm against the chill of early spring. He handed it to Emerson, placing himself between her and the group of jeering teenagers. "Tie this around your waist. It should cover you well enough till you get home."

Emerson reached for the shirt, hands quivering. Her movements were like those of someone caught out too long in the cold: slow and shaky, joints stiff and rigid.

"What's this? Keigh has a new girlfriend?" Deacon cackled, earning him a halfhearted chuckle from a few of the other fifteens. "Guess you're lucky Misselli isn't here to get jealous."

Keigh grit his teeth. He and Emerson were the only two thralls in their age group. Tasked with paying off the debt they owed their "betters," thralls were the lowest class in Eden, regarded as people to whom little respect was owed.

He turned to face their richly clothed mocker. "Maybe I just asked myself, 'What is the last thing Deacon would do?'" Keigh shrugged. "Then it came to me…I should think about someone other than myself."

Deacon sniffed and plucked a hair off his fine black tunic, dropping it contemptuously away from him. "Gets one peek under a girl's skirt, and now he's *thinking about her*…" He sneered at Keigh, giving him the same look he'd given the hair.

The pretty redhead beside Deacon snorted and covered her mouth as she laughed. The rest of the group shuffled uncomfortably.

By now, kids from various age groups were filtering out of their instruction areas, drawn to the scene like ants to a food scrap. Blood rushed to Keigh's face as the murmuring crowd gathered to get a better view. He hoped Deacon wouldn't notice. The last thing he wanted was for Deacon Wulf to think he had actually stung him.

"Why don't you leave, Deacon, before I make you," said Keigh, standing up straight, reminding his opponent that he was bigger than him, even if only just barely.

A broad, perfect white grin broke across the angular features of Deacon's face. "Anders don't tell Wulfs what to do…" He wagged his head at Keigh, adopting the tone of a parent explaining something simple to their young one. "We own you. You and your whole…*worthless*…family. You really think attacking me will help your debt go away any sooner?"

He took a step toward Keigh and ground his feet into the gravel.

"You know what? Why don't you? I might actually enjoy beating you so much I'll be able to convince my father to count it toward your debt."

Keigh glared at Deacon, imagining what his 'better' might look like with a fresh black eye. Several onlookers were now shouting encouragement, egging them on to fight. The pressure in his chest was unbearable. If he didn't punch the smug look off Deacon's face soon, he may just explode.

Keigh tossed his head back, clearing the hair out of his face. Then, quick as a rattlesnake, he lunged.

Just as he was closing in on his enemy, a long, muscular arm hooked him around the chest, stopping his charge.

"Let me go, Tarin!" Keigh shouted, eyes still locked on Deacon's triumphant face. People were laughing. He tried to pry himself free of his friend's grasp, to no avail. While Tarin wasn't the biggest teen in town—that distinction belonged to the massive new kid, Beaudy Besnik—he was the strongest. "Put me down!"

Keigh was about to elbow Tarin in the ribs when his friend released him. Keigh started at Deacon again, but Tarin snagged him by the collar, holding him back.

"Stop, Keigh," said Tarin, exasperated. "You really want to cause more trouble for your family? Your father will kill you."

Keigh stopped trying to pull away. He slapped Tarin's hand off his collar. Tarin was right: his father would be furious if he did anything to invite additional scorn from the Anders family's "better"—Deacon's father, Vicerous Wulf.

Keigh glared at Deacon. Emboldened by the growing crowd of hecklers hoping to witness a fight, Deacon adopted a pouty face and wiped fake tears from his eyes, taunting Keigh to resume.

"Leave! All of you!" Tarin shouted at the onlookers gawking at the scene.

Perhaps fearing the muscular teen may put hands on them next, the group averted their eyes and began wandering away.

Only Deacon lingered. "Someday, Tarin won't be here to save you," he told Keigh. "Come at me like that again, and I'll make sure my father doubles your family's yearly quota."

Keigh opened his mouth to shout, but Tarin stepped between him and Deacon. "Do you ever think if you weren't such an insufferable git sometimes, that maybe, just *maybe*, Keigh wouldn't feel the need to punch your teeth out?"

Tarin was the only one who could talk to Deacon in such a way. Not only was he physically imposing in stature, he was also the only member of the Consecrate in Bjorn other than Deacon. Born the same year and month as the king's son, he and Deacon both had a chance of one day becoming King of Eden. While nobody knew exactly which member of the Consecrate was the king's natural-born son, nearly every one of the boys could give a plausible reason why they believed it was them. Tarin, for example, exhibited the king's large stature, while Deacon's father told anyone who would listen that Deacon bore a remarkable resemblance to the queen with his black hair and tan complexion.

Deacon shook his head at Tarin. "I don't know why you waste your time defending him. The Anders are animals. How many times does he need to lose control before you see the truth of it?" Deacon looked down his nose at Keigh and sniffed derisively. "Rabid animals need to be put down, not put on a leash." Turning on the spot, he stalked away toward the pretty redhead, who stood waiting for him.

Keigh rounded on Tarin. "How can you be friends with him?"

Smiling, Tarin gave Keigh a shove. "You know Deacon wonders how I can possibly be friends with you? He says canes should have no business with thralls except to collect on their debts."

Keigh glowered up at Tarin's still-smiling face. "Nobody's making you be my friend."

"Nobody's making me be your *best* friend..." Tarin teased.

It was common enough knowledge that Keigh's best friend was Misselli Labelle—the blonde firecracker, absent from today's instruction, who had lived next to him his whole life. Truth be told, though, if anyone else could claim the title of being Keigh's best friend, it would be Tarin.

Keigh looked at his tall, handsome friend. Tarin's brilliant white teeth flashed, his skin glowed, his hair shone, his eyes twinkled, his muscles rippled…It was like an artist had been commissioned to sculpt a young king out of pure sunlight and gold. Keigh considered his own light skin, unruly hair, and wiry frame, shaking his head at the unfairness of it all.

Tarin was the tip-top of the social hierarchy among the teens of Bjorn, but despite this, he had never once treated Keigh as anything less than an equal. And it wasn't just Keigh—Tarin was friendly to everyone. Probably a dozen people thought of him as their best friend. Keigh assumed that was exactly what Tarin wanted. It was a skill that would no doubt serve him well if one day he should become king.

Keigh feigned a grateful expression. "Well, thank you for bestowing your kindness upon me."

Tarin rolled his eyes. "Come on, Keigh. How many times do we have to do this? Why is it charity that someone wants to be your friend? Maybe you're just a great guy when you aren't busy feeling bad for yourself."

"Easy for you to say," Keigh snorted. "It wasn't you that put yourself between Emerson and Deacon. It wasn't you being laughed at…Actually, I'm pretty sure you were one of the people laughing!" He pushed an accusing finger into Tarin's chest.

Tarin pulled back, clearly stung by Keigh's rebuke. He didn't respond right away. When he spoke, his words were deliberate and measured. "I didn't laugh at *you*."

Keigh just shook his head. "You don't get it, man."

"You're mad at me 'cause I laughed at Emerson? Come on! Everyone did at first. It was funny. It was just her clothes. She wasn't hurt. Are you telling me that if I had ripped my tunic on a nail today, you wouldn't have laughed?"

"That's different, Tarin, and you know it!"

Keigh pushed past him and took a knee in the gravel in front of where Emerson sat, huddled with her arms around her knees, staring glassy-eyed at the ground.

Tarin hung his head, exhaling heavily. He turned and faced the two thralls next to each other in the dirt. "I'm sorry, Emerson. I didn't think you were hurt."

Emerson raised her eyebrows slightly, acknowledging the apology, but her blank stare remained.

"Look, Keigh, I've got to go. Councilman Slate is out visiting his good friend Vicerous again, and Deacon is no doubt trying to make his case for the throne as we speak." Tarin paused. When Keigh didn't respond, he continued. "I would invite you to come with, but Vicerous...You know how he is. I'm fine with you coming...Just maybe not a good idea..."

"Better get going, then," said Keigh, waving him away.

Tarin nodded, seemingly unsure of what to say, or if he had already said too much. After a few uncomfortable seconds of silence, he turned and jogged toward the main road that led out of the rough-cut timber town of Bjorn, toward the Wulf estate.

Keigh pinched his eyes shut and made a deliberate effort to calm his breathing. He and Tarin rarely argued, but when they did, it was almost always centered around the different lots they had been cast in life. Tarin had seemingly received every good thing, while Keigh had been denied nearly everything due to his family's classification as thralls. He knew it was wrong to be jealous. Tarin was his friend and had treated him with more honor than he could hope to receive from any other member of the upper class. Case in point: the cane Braddock Fortier, Bjorn's battle master, had never so much as made eye contact with Keigh, let alone spoken to him, despite Bjorn being a small town and the two of them often occupying the same spaces.

Canes were the pinnacle of the social structure in Eden. Everyone wanted to be a cane or marry a cane. As much as he resented the gap between canes and thralls, Keigh still dreamed of becoming one, but as a thrall, the normal avenue of doing so was closed to him. Only children of canes and ables could undergo agoge testing to earn the right to apprentice in a desired occupation. If Keigh were given the chance, it would only be because the country was at war.

But war was an unlikely event. Eden was strong, its king untouchable in battle. Canes were the premier fighting soldiers, even without the massive red bears a select few canes paired with. Only Draiden would possibly dare confront them, and all news of him had dried up years ago. He had been reduced to a fairy tale, a boogeyman, a cautionary tale for youngsters. Still, if war came, Keigh would be ready.

Right now, however, there was a teary-eyed, embarrassed girl trying to melt into the earth in front of him. He gulped, not sure of what to say. He would rather face the danger of an attacking warrior than the awkwardness of a sad girl any day.

"Are...are you okay?" he asked.

Emerson nodded. Her face, beet red moments ago, was now blotchy with patches of white and pink.

"Don't worry about Deacon. He's a jerk to everyone," said Keigh, unsure how to console her. "Honestly, I can't stand him. I totally get it if you hate him, too."

Emerson pulled her knees closer and buried her face in the ruffles of her dirty patchwork dress. "I don't hate him," she said, her words muffled.

"You don't?" Keigh asked incredulously. "How can you not? The git just mocked you in front of our whole class. How can you not want to tear him to pieces? He made me want to punch him, and I wasn't even the one he started at!"

Emerson lifted her face and looked at Keigh, tears streaming from her eyes. "Deacon isn't the klutz who ripped their dress...again!" She spread a portion of her dress, displaying numerous patches in the olive-green cloth. "Deacon isn't the one who lost their quill and inkwell for the second time in a month. Deacon isn't the one with crooked teeth and a whiny voice. Deacon isn't the one who screwed up his mother's order at the bakery and cost their family a week's wages—"

"Cause Deacon doesn't have a mother—"

"That's not the point!" burst Emerson. "Deacon isn't the problem. Deacon isn't the screw-up. Deacon isn't the one I hate..." She buried her face in her knees again. "I am."

Keigh sat there, stunned, watching his poor friend's shoulders heave with heavy sobs. "Listen...Deacon used to make me feel like dirt too. He used to actually make me think I was less than him. One day, I realized *he's* dirt, not me. He might have money and good looks, but there's nothing between his ears and nothing beating in his chest. Hating him made me feel better." Keigh hesitated, unsure if anything he was saying was making an impact. "It will help you feel better, too."

Emerson lifted her head. A yellow line of snot under her nose matched the color of her teeth. For the briefest second, Keigh thought she really could do more to not make herself such an easy target for ridicule, but when she spoke, his heart broke.

"I don't need to *start* hating Deacon..." She sniffed, sucking the line of snot back into her nose. "I just want to *stop* hating me." Emerson stared again at the gravel in front of her. "And I will stop...soon."

Keigh wasn't sure what she meant by that. How could someone just stop that kind of hurt on command? What he did understand, what he could relate to, was the intense feeling of defeat radiating from her. He had felt that hopelessness before, many times. Why was it the harmless that always seemed to attract the most harm? To see her now, crushed and sinking lower by the second...it was as if a millstone had been tied around his heart and tossed into Lake Grebe. Its weight pulling him down with her, threatening to suffocate.

"What can I do, Emerson?"

Emerson sniffed again. Shaking her head, she smiled sadly. "There's nothing you can do. I'm the mistake. I'm the problem. So, unless you can make me not be me anymore, there's nothing you can do to help." She caught a sob as it tried to escape her throat, then buried her face once again in her dress.

Keigh slumped from his kneeling position to sit in the dirt next to his fellow thrall. His fellow sufferer. She had just spoken the words out loud that he himself had only ever entertained privately in his lowest moments.

What's so wrong with me? Why do I fail when others succeed? Why am I put down while others are elevated? Am I inferior...A nobody? Is this my inescapable lot in life?

The two of them sat there in the dirt, alone, silent save for the sounds of Emerson's muffled crying. For the first few minutes, Keigh's mind raced for answers...*How can I help? What can I say? How do I fix this?* But after a while, when nothing sufficient occurred to him, he resigned himself to just staying put. If he couldn't bring her out of the pit, he would make sure she didn't have to be down there all alone.

They sat there like that for nearly an hour, listening to the bustle of Bjorn. The world wouldn't stop, not for them. Keigh knew his parents would most likely be upset by his delay, but hopefully they would understand Emerson needed him more than they did right now.

When she finally lifted her face, she flinched. "What are you still doing here?"

Keigh gave her a sympathetic smile. "I thought today...was as good a day as any..." he said, resting a hand on her shoulder. "To spend with a friend."

"A friend?" Emerson blinked. "But we barely ever talk...Don't get me wrong, though," she added, "you've never been unkind to me."

Keigh sighed. He had harbored similar resentments when his own friends had been disappointingly absent in his low moments.

"Well, we should fix that," he said, standing up. Brushing the dust off his backside, he offered Emerson a hand up. "If you'll let me?"

The corners of her mouth lifted slightly, even as her eyes avoided Keigh's. "Okay," she said, reaching up to take his hand. She adjusted his shirt around her waist, positioning it over the hole in her dress.

"Ready to go home?" Keigh asked.

Emerson took a long, slow inhale and nodded. "I wasn't, but...I am now."

She smiled at Keigh, and for the first time in his memory, he saw all her teeth. He had never seen her smile without her making an effort to cover them with her lips or the palm of her hand. There was something beautiful about it. Not her teeth—they were sadly snaggled and yellow with neglect—but the fact that she had the bravery to smile without hiding, presenting herself as she was, not fearing ridicule...That was beautiful. In that moment, he felt lucky to be her friend.

"Shall we go?" he asked.

Emerson nodded, and the two of them set out for home together.

As they made their way down the bustling main road, past the weathered wooden buildings and shops with their wares proudly displayed in foggy glass windows, a commotion broke out behind them.

"Is this how you treat all visitors?" A man wearing a backward tunic, and sandals strapped uncomfortably loose stumbled out of the tavern and into the street, followed closely by the town's battle master, Braddock Fortier.

"Just the ones I don't recognize, asking far too many questions beyond what's proper." Braddock grabbed the man by the collar and began to march him down the dirt road toward Keigh and Emerson.

The man ran a hand through the blonde hair on top of his head. It was styled in a fashion Keigh had not seen before: shaved on the sides and long on top. He flashed a broad, disarming smile at Braddock. A significant chip in one of his front teeth gave the smile an odd charm, usually reserved for young boys trying to hide minor offenses behind their toothless innocence.

"So, it's a crime in this town to ask questions? I only wanted to know where I might find him. How's a man supposed to deliver a message if he can't be told where to find the recipient?"

Braddock continued marching him along. "I don't know you, never seen you, don't trust you. Any message you need to deliver can be given to me and I'll see he receives it."

While Keigh had never seen Braddock display anything he would classify as warmth or good humor, he had also never seen him agitated like he was today. What questions could the man have been asking?

The man tried to slow down, but Braddock shoved him, causing him to stumble in his too-loose sandals. Keigh, dumbfounded by the sudden eventfulness of their normally quiet town, failed to get out of the way before the stranger crashed into him.

The man righted himself and gave Keigh the briefest of looks. While his boyish smile never faltered, his eyes flashed menacingly, as if Keigh were some loathsome pile of excrement he had just stepped in.

Keigh knew the look well. He didn't need more than a second to recognize it. The Wulfs looked at him the same way. At least with the stranger, the look passed quickly and was soon replaced with the previous mischievous twinkle. In Keigh's mind, however, the flash had revealed the man's true character. He was just like every other highborn, high-class, wealthy cane or able: too good to have anything to do with nobody, nothing, Keigh Anders.

Braddock likewise gave Keigh an unexpected look. If nothing else, Braddock Fortier was unflappable. Keigh thought stones could even take a few pointers from the seasoned warrior on the art of remaining unmoved, so when he saw the startled look of surprise contort Braddock's usually cool, indifferent demeanor, he nearly forgot which of the two men was the stranger. But like the blonde man's expression, Braddock's, too, was gone in a second.

"Ah!" said the stranger, addressing Keigh and Emerson with sudden interest. "Perhaps you two might know where I may find—Argh!"

The man yelped as Braddock grabbed the long hair on top of his head and bent his neck painfully backward. "You will not speak to anyone but me! Understood?" barked the brawny battle master. Regaining his hold on the man's collar, Braddock shoved him farther down the street, marching him toward the front gate. The stranger resumed his fruitless appeal to the stoic cane, his charm returning in full as Braddock continued to bark him out of town.

Emerson and Keigh watched the proceedings along with every other stunned citizen in the street. Once the two had disappeared, the street broke out in a frenzy of curious conversations, each person speculating on the business of the stranger. Some of the men from the tavern even began pointing at Keigh excitedly.

Keigh was too curious to care, though. *Who was that man? What message did he need to deliver to someone in Bjorn?* And even more interesting: *Who could he possibly be looking for that people wouldn't tell him where to find them?*

Most messages delivered to Bjorn were messages of general news and going-ons from Eden's capital, Sentinel. The king's own messenger, a mountain of a man named Mannie Raya, delivered those. Mannie was a close friend to Keigh and to the whole Anders family. He, too, was a thrall, even though he served a far more gracious "better" in the king. Messages of a personal or individual nature were either delivered in writing and left at the town's record hall and library with Master Alden, or delivered directly in person by a messenger who knew the intended recipient.

Keigh couldn't blame Braddock, though. The man's job was to protect the people of Bjorn, who were quick to believe the worst of others. It wasn't exactly a good quality, but it had kept them safe. As the old proverb said: *A man with two eyes open defends himself from attack, but it's the man with eyes to his back that is never betrayed.*

Keigh and Emerson excitedly chatted their way past the ramshackle timber structures of Bjorn's main road, through the portcullis in the pointed eighty-foot-high log walls that surrounded the town, and up the gravel road toward the towering Ursus Mountains, whose jagged peaks were still capped in thick layers of snow. As they made their way, their theories about the man and his undelivered message became increasingly conspiratorial.

The two finally stopped at the head of the path leading to Emerson's home.

"I don't know, Emerson—you think he was actually here to deliver gold?" Keigh laughed.

"Well, I don't know either," she shrugged. "But think about it: what besides money, and the idea of losing that money, could cause such secrecy? If he was here to give someone gold, he couldn't outright tell people he was carrying that much wealth, could he?"

"Seems a bit far-fetched to me."

"What if someone in Bjorn has a distant rich relative that just passed away, and their estate is being given to their closest living kin?" Emerson smiled wistfully. "Can you imagine? Poor today, rich as a noble tomorrow." She stared out across the valley, no doubt imagining herself adorned with all the luxuries and comforts of Eden's wealthiest citizens.

Keigh, too, briefly allowed himself to daydream. To be somebody of worth, somebody of value, somebody people listened to and respected...That was the dream. No longer a nobody. No longer a thrall. Wealthy, famous, and loved by all.

He shook his head. That was not reality, and it did no good to waste time imagining a future that would forever be denied him. Reality was that he, a poor thrall shivering in his too-thin shirt, stood across from another poor thrall in a dress ripped, repaired, and reused a hundred times over. Dreams were all they had. Dreams were all they would ever be.

Keigh tossed his head, shaking the last images of grandeur from his mind. "Like I said, it's far-fetched."

"And your theory isn't?" Emerson crossed her arms.

"At least my theory explains why the man was so different," Keigh argued.

"You think he's from outside of Eden?" Emerson shook her head. "Nobody has entered or exited Eden without the king's knowledge for as long as we've been alive...As long as our parents have been alive!"

"It's the only answer that makes sense, though. Did you not see how he was dressed? Like he had never worn a tunic and sandals before." But Keigh knew the chance of the man actually being foreign was also far-fetched. Nobody got into Eden without the king's consent. The only way in or out was through the king's gate in the curtain wall, a five-hundred-foot-tall stone block structure that spanned the width of the valley from the Ursus Mountains of the eastern border to the rugged slopes of the Bullhorn Mountains to the west. The northern border was where the two colossal mountain ranges converged, closing off the verdant glacial valley to anyone who valued their life. Crossing into Eden through either mountain range was suicide to all but the most powerful of legends or the luckiest of fools.

Keigh sighed. "I suppose we'll never know," he said, smiling at Emerson. "Especially if Braddock is the only one who knows anything."

She chuckled. They both knew the tight-lipped nature of their town's battle master.

"I'll see you tomorrow, Emerson. Sit by me during instruction. Me and Misselli will make sure Deacon leaves you alone." He raised his hand in farewell, turning to leave.

"Keigh!" Emerson blurted after him.

Keigh turned to face her again.

She shuffled nervously, her fingers bunching up handfuls of fabric as she pulled at her dress. "Thank you."

Keigh nodded. "No problem, Emerson."

He turned to leave again, but once more, she stopped him. "Keigh!" She tossed her handfuls of dress and held her arms rigid at her sides. "Thank you..." She paused, her mouth moving without sound as she seemed to struggle for words. "Thank you for seeing me. Nobody sees me...and if they do, they certainly never move toward me. I'm a mess. Nobody wants anything to do with a mess...but you stood by me today. You saw the mess and...and..." She sniffed, her eyes wet with tears again. "And you didn't walk away."

Keigh was unsure how to respond. The matter had been a small thing in his mind, but Emerson was acting like he had just saved one of her family members from drowning. "Really, Emerson, it was nothing," he shrugged.

"It wasn't nothing to me." She stared at the ground. "You made me believe, for the first time in a long time, that *I'm* not nothing."

Keigh laughed. "Emerson, you're worth ten Deacons. So whatever that pretentious whelp thinks he's worth, you're worth more."

She lifted her eyes. "You really think so?"

"I know so," he said, glad to see her beginning to smile.

Keigh turned to depart again, but before he had gone four steps, he heard the shuffling sound of Emerson's leather sandals sprinting toward him, and before he could turn, she slammed into the back of him, wrapping her arms tight around his waist.

"I think you're worth ten Deacons, too," she said.

Slowly, cautiously, Keigh put an arm around the homely girl in the patchwork dress and hugged her back.

He wasn't about to admit it, but he also needed to hear those words.

CHAPTER 2

A FAMILIAR FACE

19-139-3

K eigh woke once again to find himself uncovered. He remembered his little sister Jessie waking him during the night as she crawled up onto his straw mattress. The smallest of his three siblings, she never ceased to amaze him with the amount of blanket she apparently needed in order to sleep. Seeing her now, enveloped in his blankets with tufts of her brown hair poking out of every conceivable gap, reminded him of a caterpillar ready to burst from its cocoon, though he doubted that whatever emerged from this cocoon would look anything like a butterfly. Most likely, at this early hour, it would resemble something more like a rabid raccoon, both in appearance and temperament.

Rolling away from the little blanket bandit, he sat upright with a groan. Keigh swung his legs off the log-framed bed and planted his feet on the floor. He flexed his back, trying to wake up his drooping shoulders.

At fifteen, Keigh was not yet a man by Eden's standards, but old enough to pull his own weight. His hair hung down in waving curls to his jawline, framing the tan features of his face. He was a well-built boy—or at least better built than his older brothers, who, like their father Owen, seemed to be unnaturally broad. While his father's wide frame was stacked high and wide with the lean muscle of a man who spent his days in hard labor, his twin brothers, Jotham and Jobey, were stacked high and wide with…well…not muscle. The second youngest of four children, Keigh was a foot taller than his older brothers, but shared the same chocolate-brown hair as all his siblings.

Still sitting on the edge of his bed, he wiped the sleep from his eyes. Moonlight trickled in past the shades, giving everything the appearance of a charcoal sketch: vivid in detail but stealing the warmth that usually characterized the small bedroom he had shared with his brothers for the last fifteen years. As his eyes adjusted to the light, he could see their beds, one on each side of the far end of the room. The log frames flexed downward with each of their long snores, their straw mattresses struggling under their weight. Even if Keigh hadn't been Jessie's favorite, he doubted she could sneak into one of their beds if she tried, let alone pull an inch of blanket out from under their heavy bodies.

The room was as clean as could be expected from three teenage boys. *Tidy* was a better description—it had no obvious clutter, but to anyone giving it more than a passing glance, the room showed the tell-tale signs of numerous messes hastily hidden. Foot wrappings, bootstraps, and shirt sleeves spilled out from under beds. Wicker baskets were unable to close, their lids hung up on whittled walking sticks, fishing poles, and the most recent wooden sparring sword Keigh had yet to break.

Shelves on the walls above each bed held the boys' prized possessions. For Keigh, there was an antler from the first deer he'd ever killed with his bow, and a unique stone he'd found, so clear and smooth that he still maintained it was a diamond. His mother insisted that it couldn't be, for the simple fact that "she would know one when she saw one," which never failed to produce eye-rolls from her boys and giggles from Jessie. He also had a few wooden toy figures of Eden's cane warriors, given to him for various birthdays, as well as the first bow he had ever made by himself, now far too small and frail to be of any use.

Lastly, a family friend had given him a metal sphere the size of a pheasant's egg that admittedly wasn't much to look at, but fascinated Keigh endlessly. It was much too heavy to be any normal metal. Additionally, it had the unique quality of always being cold no matter its surroundings. Once, he'd got it to feel almost room temperature by boiling it in a pot of water for an hour. The small sphere remained that temperature for a week before resuming its usual cool existence. He never had tried to heat it again after his father "promoted" him to "family firewood fetcher" for a month, citing his careless waste of family resources on "childish curiosities."

His brothers' shelves were similarly adorned with items of value or nostalgia—but, upon closer inspection, also contained a half-eaten baked potato and dinner rolls they had pilfered from the table the night before. Most would consider the food scraps waste, but to Jotham and Jobey, those items *were* treasures.

Keigh stretched out his legs. The creak of his bedframe may as well have come from his muscles, tight as they were from the previous day's work in the field. He had not wanted to wake this early, but decided he might need the extra time now. Today he had promised to take Misselli hunting with him. In addition to lessening his chances of making a kill, her presence also meant that he would have to change his route to his hunting grounds. An early start would be necessary if they were to return to town in time for their instruction.

Rising, he slipped into his buckskin pants, wrapped his feet in cloth, laced and tied his rawhide boots, and grabbed a soft cotton shirt on his way out of his room. His lucky hunting jacket would have to stay home. He wasn't going to give Misselli anything to tease him about, least of all the smell of a dirty jacket.

He tiptoed his way across the great room on a well-practiced route, carefully avoiding the floorboards he knew to be squeakers. Gently, he lifted the latch on the thick pine front door, opening it just far enough to slip out. Then, softly, with both hands, he eased it shut. As was his ritual, Keigh turned to face the red bear engraved in the door. Over the years the elements had bleached and dried the wood. Slivers now bristled on the gray pine, giving the bear an aged look. He placed a hand on its head, wordlessly promising to return home safely to his family. Turning again, he hopped over the front steps and out into the brisk morning air of spring.

Gray and lifeless in the early morning light, their wood-plank, thatched-roofed home sat at the foot of the mountains, just below the tree line. A thin curl of smoke rose out of the stone chimney before falling to gently suspend itself just above the ground in a blanket of haze. The farthest farm from town, only untamed wilderness lay uphill of the Anders' house. Downhill, farm buildings appeared as dark islands in a sea of grasses that reflected what little light the crescent moon offered. Black squares of freshly plowed fields checkered the valley. Soon farmers would be planting them with wheat, barley, corn, sugar beets, and potatoes. Below the farms, a calm breeze swept up from the valley floor, carrying the smell of the town's dying cookfires from the night before.

Stopping by the tool shed, Keigh grabbed his bow, carefully lifting it from the cedar chest where he stored it. He unwrapped the shaft's protective coverings, then strung it in a fluid motion perfected over years of practice. It was a far nicer bow than anything he could have made on his own. Shorter than a true longbow yet longer than the short bows favored by the canes, it was a hybrid of sorts. Coupling the power of the long with the speed and maneuverability of the short, it was perfect for hunting.

Giving it to Keigh when he was twelve, his father had told him, "Don't think I am giving you this bow as a toy to be played with and neglected. It was a gift, and the worst thing you can do with a gift is waste it. Now go! Practice! The sooner you get the feel for the weight of it, the sooner I'll be enjoying a hot venison roast with your mother's famous gravy. And…uh…if you happen to hit Mrs. Schaffer, I'll understand," he had added with a wink.

To this day, Keigh still had no idea who had given his father the bow. His father wasn't too proud to accept anything that might help his family, but that didn't mean he wanted to tell the world he had accepted anything he himself couldn't provide, so Keigh didn't ask. Gifts in the Anders family were usually items made by the giver's hand or acts of service one could redeem at a later time.

Once, at a winter festival, his father had given his mother a beautiful thin silver necklace. In his mind he could still see his mother, tiny next to his hulking father, crying and burying her face in his muscle-bound chest. She'd done this at least once a day for a week afterward, stuttering through tears things like "Y-you sh-shouldn't have" and "I d-don't d-deserve you." Each time this happened, his father would give his boys a look as if to say, *Women...* They had chuckled at him, but Keigh knew his mother wasn't hysterical, in fact, he wasn't sure he had ever even seen his mother cry any time other than that.

Keigh paused, taking time to thoughtfully select five arrows from the ones he had recently fletched with the flawless tail feathers of a goose. Opening his pack, he filled it with knives, rope, and grease-soaked wood chips for starting a fire, being sure to remember the dried venison and small loaf of bread his mother had set out for him the night before.

He slung the pack onto his back. Latching the shed door closed behind him, he made to leave—

"Oop!"

He stifled a gasp, surprised. There, barring his path, was Mrs. Schaffer. Of course she was up. Keigh hoped for a split second that she had forgotten their last encounter, but that was a fool's wish.

She cocked her head, staring him down with one golden eye. The eye narrowed, and he knew his fate was sealed. She did remember. In fairness, he had taken far more of her tail feathers than usual, and the unceremonious way in which he'd snatched them off her backside hadn't helped either.

"I'm sorry!" he whispered. "I promise they'll grow back! Just stay quiet, will ya?"

Mrs. Schaffer relaxed her neck, seemingly appeased by his whispered apology.

Keigh breathed a sigh of relief—but suddenly, the fat goose threw open her long white wings and trumpeted a silence-shattering honk. Lowering her head like a spear, she charged Keigh in a shockingly fast waddle for a bird so girthy. She nipped and pecked everything from his heels to his butt as he desperately tried to flee the scene, all hopes of a quiet departure lost.

Mrs. Schaffer shrieked and honked the entire length of her pursuit across the yard. Keigh ran a loop around a mangled tree trunk he used to practice swordsmanship in an attempt to lose her, but the goose raged onward. The attack ended only when Keigh finally hurdled the wooden rail fence in front of his home.

"Was that really necessary?" he fumed through gritted teeth. "Be happy I don't make jerky out of you!"

Mrs. Schaffer folded her wings. Raising her head in dignified fashion, she closed her eyes. Satisfied that she had run him off for good, she sauntered back toward the house, where Keigh now saw candlelight flickering in his parents' window. He would get an earful later, no doubt, but at least his brothers had not witnessed his shameful retreat.

Turning, Keigh found the well-used trail he and Misselli had created between their two homes and set off at a trot across the hillside. The Ursus Mountains loomed above him, black against the pale gray of the early-morning sky. Their jagged snowcapped peaks jutted up from the valley floor like the teeth of some great mythical beast. They were Eden's greatest defense, offering the people refuge from rival states, tribes, and the roving bands of pirates that still pillaged the land.

It was believed that a strong, healthy man could cross the mountains, provided that the weather and wild beasts of the forest allowed it. There were stories of crossings in Eden's history, but they had been made by men of legend. Tales of such men were told with the stories of potents, mages, and other creatures of magic that were used to entertain children during festivals. As Emerson had pointed out the day before, there was only one way into and out of Eden, and that was through the king's gate in the curtain wall.

Keigh started up the last ridge. Soon he could see a thin column of smoke curling lazily upward, then a chimney, followed by the wood-shingled roof of Misselli Labelle's log home. It was a simple structure, as most ables' homes were: rectangular in shape, single-story, with a pair of bedrooms and a great room where the family would gather for meals and stories. Not only were stories told there, they were made in that little house, too.

Keigh couldn't help but smile as he recalled a particularly hot day when they were eleven. Misselli had coaxed him into pranking her older brother. The plan called for Keigh to get up on the roof above the doorway with a bucket of water; Misselli would then call for her brother's help with something in the yard, and when he came outside, he would find himself freshly bathed from above. Only, when the door opened, it was Misselli's father who got doused. Keigh had been so panicked that he'd dropped the bucket, which proceeded to fall directly—and lodge itself firmly—onto the head of Misselli's mother. The last thing he recalled seeing was Misselli rolling in the grass, howling with laughter, while her father struggled to pry the bucket off a frantic, flailing Rita Labelle.

Now, Keigh found Misselli waiting for him, perched atop the gate in the wooden fence outside her home. She had been his closest friend for as long as he could remember. A slender girl with light blonde hair and blue eyes that always seemed to sparkle with pent up excitement even in the most mundane moments. Today she wore a worn-out pair of her brother's old trousers and had her hair tied back in a ponytail.

A thin smile formed on her mouth as Keigh approached. "What are you grinnin' about?" she teased. "Just happy to see me probably, huh? I see you wore a nice shirt too! If I'd have known this was a date, I would have done something nice with my hair." The gate squeaked as she hopped off it and gave Keigh a playful bump with her shoulder.

Keigh rolled his eyes. "Funny. Don't remind me—I usually hunt alone." Still smiling, he returned her shoulder nudge with one of his own. Truth was, he was wearing his only cotton shirt. They had to be traded for with other states, since Eden did not have the required knowledge or craftsmanship to make them. Keigh had gotten his as a birthday present from his family last year and only wore it on rare occasions.

"Yes, yes. Thank you for letting me join you today." Misselli gave a slight curtsy and fell in behind him as he continued his march up the road. "Do you think we will get something?"

"I hope so, but it's a matter of luck with these short morning hunts," Keigh admitted as he rummaged through his pack, looking for his bowstring wax.

"Well, I suppose I can lend you my luck for the day," she said, her thin smile transforming into a full grin.

Keigh was one of the better hunters in town, but his success stemmed from an unusually high level of patience that seemed only to apply to hunting. Given a full day, he was sure to make a kill as an unwary animal came within range of his bow. With morning hunts, he would walk the forest, hoping to jump game as they bedded down after a night of grazing in the river valley.

They walked back down the path single file, Keigh leading as he waxed his bowstring. He made several swats at a bothersome fly that kept landing on his ear before realizing it was just Misselli tickling him with a long stalk of wheatgrass. Caught, she tossed the grass over her head. Raising both arms, she looked back over her shoulder as if she expected to find the real culprit there.

Keigh gave her a feigned look of annoyance. Not until he had turned away did he allow the stupid grin that had been tugging at his cheeks to win out. She may never be a great hunter, but she was always worth having around.

A short way later, he stopped. "Here's where we go in," he said, pointing toward a game trail leading uphill into the trees. "From here we need to be quiet. Follow me and keep your eyes peeled for anything moving. We aren't the only things hunting in here."

Misselli's jaw tightened, cutting off an involuntary squeak. Keigh had never seen anything worse than a solitary mountain lion, but he liked the idea of stirring Misselli's imagination into a frenzy of hungry beasts out to eat them.

Still, she nodded her understanding. Stepping off their trail, they waded into the long grass that fringed the forest.

Keigh led the way, taking the least obstructed path. The forest was an ancient place filled with creatures both new and old. The elders in town would say, *"In the days before the great collapse, the pines grew slow and thin. Now they grow grander than the towers of men!"* It was true, too. None of Bjorn's structures compared to the living giants. Only the old watchtower came anything close to being their match, and it was less than half their height. The thick branches of the pines caught the golden light of the morning sun, casting the forest floor into perpetual dusk. What light did pass all the way to the forest floor landed in bright shining slivers and nuggets.

Weaving deeper into the forest, Keigh held his bow in one hand behind him to avoid any unnecessary damage to the aging weapon. He chose his steps carefully, years of dead vegetation crunching quietly beneath his feet. A slight headwind carried their scent back downhill, away from their would-be prey.

"Can we talk if we get something?" Misselli whispered.

Keigh merely shrugged as if to say, *I don't think I could stop you even if I wanted to.*

They walked another half-mile before coming to a clearing at the end of the ridge. From just inside the shadows of the forest's edge, the entire valley was visible. Past the square plots of crops and homesteads at the base of the mountain, the eighty-foot-tall walls of Bjorn projected high above the valley floor. The sharpened points of their pine trunks gave the town the appearance of a great, bristling porcupine laid down in a bed of grass that covered the valley floor. Farther north, the valley ended abruptly in a ridge of solid stone, called the Garden Wall. Rising up from the valley floor to its snowcapped rim, usually clothed in clouds, the whole of it was visible today in what was now a brilliantly blue sky.

Dozens of white tendrils of water cascaded down its face, coalescing in a high mountain lake before plummeting over the edge as the Queen's Veil. The thousand-foot freefall crashed down into Lake Grebe, churning the large lake's waters into a beautiful aqua blue. Flowing from Lake Grebe, the King's River was a shimmering ribbon of silver meandering the length of Eden.

At the far side of the valley, thousands more waterfalls striped the cliffs of the Bullhorn Mountains' rugged slopes. Hundreds of green tree lines of cottonwood and aspen snaked away from their base, following streams till they emptied their flow into the King's River. At Eden's southern end, the monolithic man-made mountain of stone that was Eden's capital, Sentinel, was barely visible, jutting up behind the impossibly high curtain wall, Eden's only man-made boundary.

Keigh sighed heavily as his eyes rested on Sentinel. Legends lived there. Someday, he would too. Nothing exciting ever happened in Bjorn. Especially for him.

"This is amazing!" Misselli whispered in his ear, cozying up beside him.

Moments like this always made him wonder how he and Misselli could be such good friends. His whole life, he had wanted nothing more than to break out of Bjorn and shed the dry old routine of his life as a thrall. What he sought to escape, Misselli reveled in, always finding new ways to be fascinated and satisfied in the ordinary.

He smiled. He might not see what was so great about today, but it always made him glad to see her happy. Maybe that was why they were friends. She kept him from wallowing in his servitude and he kept her from floating off the ground in ignorant optimism. They balanced each other. He kept her grounded and she kept him going.

Keigh motioned for Misselli to go set up and watch the south end of the clearing. Ten seconds, one loud crack of a breaking branch, and one silently mouthed apology from Misselli later, and she was in position.

Shaking his head, Keigh brushed the morning dew off a large tuft of bear grass before sitting down. From there, he surveyed the northern end of the clearing for any signs of life. He had had success here in the past. Deer would spend the night on the valley floor, grazing on the long, soft grasses before returning to the dark halls of the forest to digest. If he did not fell something in the next hour, they would have to return empty-handed, and the Anders' meals would be no more than a handful of variations of potatoes and barley.

Keigh allowed himself to stretch out, soaking up the morning sun and listening to the birds sing. He whistled the song of a mountain bluebird at a robin perched overhead. The smell of damp earth and crushed pine needles put his mind at ease as he watched the town below come alive in anticipation of a new day's work...

*

Keigh woke with a jolt as something struck his face. A pinecone slowly rolled away from him. He looked up into the branches, wondering if any more of its neighbors were planning on joining the assault on his head, when he heard Misselli hiss. She sat wide-eyed, staring at him, a second pinecone in her hand. Misselli tossed her head in the direction of the clearing. Following her gaze, Keigh saw movement just inside the forest's edge.

What luck was this? He rarely made a kill on his morning hunts, and now he had slept through most of today's hunt and was still in a position to bring home some meat! His mouth watered as he thought of the stew his mother would make that night. He waved for Misselli to follow him as they left the well-lit edge, retreating into the shadows before creeping south to a point where he could likely cross paths with the deer.

They stopped as they heard the breaking of twigs not far from where they stood. Keigh jerked his head toward a nearby bush. Misselli took the cue and concealed herself behind it. Slowly walking backward, he joined her, hiding his own body from view. The sound of such a noisy animal made Keigh hope for an elk. The extra meat would go a long way in feeding his family, whose stockpile of venison was desperately low after winter.

The large pines kept the underbrush in check, giving Keigh an unobstructed alley for shooting. All he had to do now was wait for the deer to step into view.

He pulled an arrow from his pack. Smoothly. Silently. Nocking it, he drew the bow to its full reach. The deer would step into his sight at any moment. His breathing slowed as he readied to release his arrow at first sight of his quarry.

Another twig snapped. Silence. Then, slowly, into his vision stepped a man—a man he recognized.

The man Braddock had unceremoniously escorted out of Bjorn just yesterday...

The stranger.

CHAPTER 3

MESSAGE DELIVERED

43-10-10

Keigh stood still, heart pounding in his throat. Had the man learned where the recipient of his message was? Why was he up here on the mountainside?

Keigh hadn't taken a breath since raising his bow to shoot. The air in his lungs begged for an escape. Releasing it as quietly as he could, he stayed out of sight. He could only hope Misselli had the sense to remain hidden from the man, whom Keigh had now decided was the strangest-looking person he had ever laid eyes on.

He made eye contact with Misselli and pressed a finger to his lips. From his vantage point in the shadows, he studied the stranger.

The blonde hair alone, shaved on the sides and long on top, was enough to confirm the man's identity as the stranger from town. Slightly taller than Keigh, he had a considerable amount more muscle. He had looked uncomfortable, out of place even, dressed awkwardly in the tunic and sandals most of Eden's men favored, but today he wore a pack on his back as well as boots, trousers, and long sleeves, all colored in the same mottled pattern of browns and greens. Strips of green cloth were wrapped around his face, leaving only the top half of his head exposed. This was not a man of Eden—but that wasn't what gave him pause, it was what he carried.

The man held a walking stick, or perhaps it was a staff, as he had yet to touch either end to the ground. Overlapping in the middle, the staff was split into a metal half and a wooden half, the metal half was narrow to its end and its wooden end was bulky and strange shaped.

The hunters sat motionless in the shadows as the man stopped to inspect the forest around him. His gaze lingered in the direction of Bjorn. Keigh smelled the ripe scent of unwashed skin, pungent in the light breeze.

After a moment, the stranger continued his walk up the ridge.

When the man had passed from sight, Keigh knelt in the brush next to where Misselli had concealed herself.

"We should go," she said, peeking nervously around the bush.

"What are you talking about?" Keigh whispered, hardly believing she was willing to walk away from the most interesting thing that had happened to their boring little town in their lifetimes. "Let's follow him! Did you see what he was carrying? What was that?"

"I don't know," Misselli scowled. "Do you think it's the man you told me about yesterday? The one Braddock ran out of town?"

"It's definitely him," Keigh confirmed, watching the man disappear into the trees again.

"Then we should *definitely* go," said Misselli, now pleading. "If Braddock didn't trust him, neither should we."

"I'm not saying we should bake him a cake and have tea with him," said Keigh, exasperated by the amount of time they were wasting while the stranger moved steadily farther away. "I'm just saying we should find out a bit more before going to Braddock with nothing."

Misselli pursed her lips. She stripped one of the bushes' twigs of its needles as she considered Keigh's proposal.

Realizing he had her on the fence, he continued, "What if he's dangerous? The town will need to know."

"That's what I'm afraid of," she admitted, biting her bottom lip and peeking out again to where the man had been. "Keigh, our lessons start soon, but—"

"But what?"

"But...I...I suppose we could follow him for a bit," she relented, giving him a mischievous smile.

"The elders will want to know more than what we just saw," he added, hoping to cement her decision even further, even though it wasn't entirely true. No doubt Braddock would be concerned that the man he had escorted from town the day before had seemingly not got the message—or worse, *had* got the message and was deliberately intruding where he was not welcome. Braddock, and every other adult in Bjorn, would have told Keigh to report it and leave the rest to them...but nothing new or exciting ever happened in Bjorn, least of all to him. And now he, nobody Keigh Anders, was at the forefront of something everyone would be talking about: an outsider in Eden.

He helped Misselli back to her feet. They grinned at each other, the joy of an unexpected adventure plain on their faces.

Setting out, they made their way into the shadows between the massive trees. Picking their way along the man's trail, they were careful not to let their clothing catch on the surrounding foliage. One snapped branch and all secrecy would be lost.

Before long, the trail went cold. The footprints that had at first been so deep in the soft mosses of the forest floor became shallow, then disappeared altogether as they crossed in and out of the shale deposits dotting the hillside.

Keigh had reached the point of giving up. Even though following the man had been his idea, he was not so desperate for adventure that he didn't understand the one thing more dangerous than tracking a stranger through the forest was continuing to track him after losing his trail.

He was turning to tell Misselli this when he smelled it. The man's stench stood apart from the fresh fragrance of the pines. He had a unique musk, unlike any Keigh had ever smelled before.

They were too close. Keigh motioned for Misselli to stop following. Something wasn't right.

"Stay here." Gripping his bow, he removed the arrow from his palm, placing it back on the string. "If I'm not back in five minutes, head straight downhill to town. Find Braddock and tell him about the man and where to find me. He'll know what to do."

Braddock was the first person who should know about the stranger's return. He was a living legend, not just to the people of Bjorn but to all of Eden. If there were anyone more skilled or experienced in combat, Keigh had not heard of them.

Right now, the hunters had become the hunted. After making sure Misselli was hidden from view, he set off again. He crouched low to the ground, determined to reverse their situation.

Keigh knew how dangerous it was to track animals that had the ability to kill. Once, when he was thirteen, he had tracked a wounded black bear into the brush, a choice that nearly cost him his life and left him with four long scars across his left shoulder. As dangerous as a wounded animal was, he knew man was the most dangerous quarry of all.

Moving from shadow to shadow, he was a ghost. His rawhide boots quiet, as he was careful to step in areas the morning sun had not yet reached with its drying touch. By now the man's stench was palpable. Why hadn't Keigh seen him yet? He must be close. Dangerously close. They could not have been more than a few hundred yards behind when they'd started tailing him, and now, Keigh could smell him with every breath.

He crept cautiously into an opening in the trees. Keeping his eyes on the shadows, he hoped he would be able to find the man's trail in the sunlit grass of the clearing.

"Find what you're looking for?" a low voice, smooth as silk, sounded behind him.

Keigh whirled around. Drawing his bow, he brought the arrow up to face the speaker.

"Put the toy down, boy. You have some answering to do."

A section of forest detached itself from the shadows, materializing as the stranger. He stood with his staff pointed at Keigh's chest.

Keigh had never seen someone disappear as this man just had. Mad at himself for letting the outsider get behind him, he lowered his bow but kept the arrow drawn. Stories of strangers in Eden never ended well. While Keigh still wasn't sure where this man had come from, it would be wise to treat him with caution.

The man pulled on the bottom of the cloth covering his mouth to reveal the pink skin of his shaven face. His teeth, white and perfect as a row of pearls, now showed in a confident smile, oddly different from the charismatic grin of the day before. It was clear he took pride in his appearance, if not his scent. Keigh hadn't remembered him smelling so rank in town, but his odor suggested it had been days since he had bathed.

"Start talking, boy, and answer me true now," said the man, flicking the tip of his staff at Keigh. "How long have you been following me?"

"We...we thought you were a deer," Keigh stammered.

Too late, he realized his mistake.

The stranger caught the slip too. "We?" His eyebrows rose. "Now, son, I only see the one of you, so who is this *we* you're talking about?"

Keigh's heart stopped. Struggling, it resumed its bounding tempo. "I...I misspoke—"

"Misspoke? No, not likely. Who's your partner and where are they?" The man's calm voice was betrayed by his eyes as they flicked frantically from shadow to shadow.

"I told you—"

A twig snapped in the shadows behind the man. Grinning, he cocked an eyebrow at Keigh.

Keigh's skin flushed cold. Misselli must have followed him.

Seeing the panic on Keigh's face, the man whirled around, pointing his staff into the shadows.

An explosion shattered the stillness.

The eruption of the man's magic staff left his ears ringing, but Keigh kept his focus. In one fluid motion of adrenaline and instinct, he drew his bow and released an arrow at the stranger.

The man was turning to face Keigh, staff pointed in preparation to cast another blast, when the arrow struck him in the thigh, burying itself in the bone. Cursing, he dropped his staff and cried out in anguish. He fell to the ground, gripping his wounded leg.

There was a flash of movement as Misselli abandoned her place in the trees behind the man. Bending as she ran, she scooped the staff off the ground. Holding it away from her body like one might hold a venomous snake, she sprinted wide-eyed toward Keigh. She curled around to stand behind him and dropped the staff in the grass in front of him, wiping her hands vigorously on the front of her pants.

Keigh had already nocked another arrow and aimed it at the stranger, who lay in the tufts of brown grass, cursing and clutching his thigh.

"The next one ends you!" shouted Keigh. "I dig potatoes for a living and even I know not to turn my back on an armed man."

"*Man...*" A low chuckle emanated from the stranger's throat before it was cut off by a fit of coughing. "Perhaps...we got off on the wrong foot." He sat up, grimacing, still squeezing his leg with both hands. "Maybe we can help each other. I am looking for someone you may know, and I can pay you quite well for his whereabouts."

"Didn't Braddock make it clear yesterday?" Keigh asked. "Tell him your business in Bjorn or get lost. It's not like people with good intentions to be skulking around."

The stranger cocked his head, seemingly confused, but quickly found a response. "Let's just say the nature of my visit is...sensitive." His jaw clenched, his leg clearly racking him with a fresh wave of pain. "I'm afraid...urgh...the message itself is...private."

The man was crippled and cornered. *I may as well get some information,* thought Keigh. "Who are you looking for?"

"A thrall named Keigh—"

Misselli let out a small squeak, her wide eyes widening further.

Me? Who is this man? What could he want from me? Keigh's mind raced with questions before settling on a plan of action.

"Ah! I see your girlfriend knows the man," said the stranger, hardly able to conceal the eagerness in his voice. "Tell me, girl: where can I find him?"

"You don't speak to her," said Keigh firmly, sweeping Misselli further behind him with his elbow.

"My apologies. Would you be so kind as to ask her for me, then?" the man mocked.

"What business do you have with Keigh?" he asked, his eyes never leaving those of the man on the ground.

"You know him too, then!" the man said, sounding more sure of himself. "Excellent. Where can I find him?"

"What is your business with him?" Keigh repeated.

The man gave an agitated wince. "I must give him something. Now where is he?"

"Give it to me, and I will see it delivered," Keigh said, more a statement than an offer.

"Listen!" the man growled through gritted teeth. "I must be the one to deliver it." Pain strained his speech as blood blackened an ever-growing circle of his trousers.

Keigh surveyed him a moment before turning to Misselli, who had been a silent spectator to the exchange. "Go to town and fetch help. My mother will know how to fix him…Also, alert Braddock of our situation. Tell him the stranger from yesterday is back."

Misselli gave a nod as she crept backward through the grass, then turned and sprinted downhill, disappearing into the shadows.

Turning his eyes back to the stranger, Keigh found the man had leaned to the side, resting his weight on one arm.

"I won't be sticking around for her to come back," he grunted as he reached down to pull the arrow from his leg.

"Wait!" Keigh threw a hand up. "You don't want to pull that. You'll increase the bleeding."

"Well, I can't very well walk with it in my leg, now can I?" the man blustered, but despite his protests, he released his grip on the arrow's shaft.

Keigh stepped forward, kneeling beside him. "I'll tie you off above the wound. It will help keep you from bleeding, but I'm not touching the arrow. I want to be able to see your hands at all times."

"I'll sit on the bloody things if you'll just get me fixed so I can be on my way." Lying back, he rested the palms of his hands on his chest for Keigh to see.

Keigh slipped off his pack. Rummaging through its contents, he quickly found a length of rope he had packed in preparation for the day's hunt. The world was a funny place: the rope intended to help harvest a life would now help save the life of a man who, two minutes earlier, had tried to use magic on him. Still, he knew it was the right thing to do. And it was what he *needed* to do. Braddock would not be able to question the man if the outsider died from blood loss before he got there.

Keigh grabbed a bone-handled knife with a short, curved blade to cut the rope to length. Should the man decide to turn on him again, he would be prepared.

Dropping his pack to the side, he looped the rope under the man's leg, several inches above the wound. He pulled the ends tight in opposite directions and tied a knot.

"You'll have to wait for help to arrive before we can remove the arrow," Keigh said, stepping back to a safe distance to view his work.

The man rolled over in preparation to stand up. "Nope," he grunted. "I told you, I'm here to see Keigh. Don't need anyone else knowing nothin'."

"Maybe you should stick around and talk to him before the others get here," Keigh said.

Realization, followed by that same look of menace Keigh had seen the day before, flashed briefly in the man's eyes. His face broke into a broad grin. "Ha! Here I've been, talking to the person I came to see this whole time! But... you're just a boy. He told us you were a threat...but you're nothing more than a skinny little brat!" He laughed, sounding far too similar to Vicerous Wulf for Keigh's liking.

"I'm not the one with an arrow in his leg! Now, what were you sent to deliver?"

"Of course! Good point, young master." The man ran a hand through his hair, slicking it back. Pulling his arms free of the straps, he pulled the pack off his back and set it in his lap. "Come here. Closer, son. I've got it here in my pack."

Keigh took a cautious step toward him. He didn't like the man's tone. He was way too pleased for someone with an arrow sticking out of his leg. Plus, someone had called *him*, Keigh Anders, thrall boy from Bjorn, a threat? What would someone send a person they saw as a threat? Still, his curiosity compelled him.

The man rummaged through his pack. "I'm not seeing it in here. Perhaps your young eyes can find it. Come here, take a look for yourself."

Keigh took another step closer. "What exactly am I supposed to be looking for?"

"Ah! Here it is! Look and see! Here!" The man opened the top of his pack wide and nodded for Keigh to look inside.

Keigh took another step and craned his neck to see down into the bag. "I don't...I'm not seeing...What's in there for me?"

"Death."

"Wait...dea—"

Growling, the man suddenly threw the pack in his face. In the second it took Keigh to deflect it, the man jerked the arrow from his leg, releasing a reservoir of blood. Brandishing the arrow like a dagger, he lunged upward, thrusting its point at Keigh's throat.

Keigh threw his body out of the way, but not quickly enough. The arrow sliced a path in his skin from neck to ear. Pain seared from the wound. He scrambled, trying to stand, furious with himself for dropping his knife. The man's weight fell on his back, pinning him to the ground. Keigh's arms shot out, fingers digging into the soft dirt floor of the forest, reaching, searching for anything he could use as a weapon.

Rolling over, he struck the man across the jaw with the back of his elbow. Undeterred, the outsider's hands closed around his throat, squeezing off the air to his lungs. Keigh swung at his face, striking him again and again.

His perfect white teeth were soon stained with blood, his lips repeatedly smashing against them as Keigh frantically pounded away at the man's sick smile—but still his grip held.

Desperate, Keigh grabbed the man's throat with one hand. Summoning what strength he had left, he tried forcibly lifting the man off of him. To his surprise, his strength held—not only that, but he felt a rush of new energy infuse his arm. Driving up, he tossed the man into the air.

With a *whumpf*, the stranger landed hard on his back. He wheezed, the breath knocked out of him.

Keigh took a massive breath, allowing his lungs to enjoy oxygen for the first time in what seemed like minutes before he scrambled to his feet, determined not to lose this momentary advantage.

He fell on top of the man. Coming down hard, Keigh landed an elbow to his nose. It crunched under his weight. The two of them exchanged blows, Keigh punching the man's thoroughly bloodied face while the man struck at his sides in desperation. Keigh ceased his punching and clutched the man's throat with a vise-like grip, desperate to render him unconscious and end the fight.

Again, a fresh surge of energy infused his arms. Confusion threatened Keigh's resolve. It was like an adrenaline rush, but altogether different.

A look of unadulterated panic crossed the man's face, his eyes wide with fear. Keigh released his grip, as if he had stuck his hands into some unsavory substance.

Capturing the opportunity, the man seized the front of Keigh's shirt, forcefully pulling them together and landing a headbutt that sent flashes of white light across Keigh's vision.

Having stunned Keigh momentarily, the man tossed him to the side. Frantically, he rolled over and pressed himself up.

Keigh reached out and grabbed the stranger's ankle, not wanting him to get his hands back on his weapon, but the man swiftly kicked him square in the face with the heel of his free foot, then dashed to retrieve his staff from the ground where Misselli had dropped it.

Keigh recovered swiftly, unexpected energy propelling him. He closed the gap quickly, coming up right on the man's heels. When the stranger stooped to grab his staff, Keigh kicked out hard with his heel, landing it right on the man's rear, sending him sprawling, over the staff, into the trunk of an enormous pine. The man's head struck the trunk, sending his chin straight down into his chest with a sickening crack.

Immediately the stranger's limbs went limp as old rope, his whole body crumpled in a mound between two of the tree's fingerlike roots.

Keigh stood, panting, not believing what he had just seen, what he had just done. He stared at the sad pile of limbs, waiting, hopeful for any sign of life. He hadn't meant to kill the man...

But after a minute, it was clear the stranger had breathed his last.

Keigh retched and tried to swallow away the sour taste in his mouth. No longer able to bear looking at the crumpled body, he turned his back on it.

Lowering his eyes, he surveyed the freshly churned patch of earth where the two of them had battled. He stepped over the man's staff and stooped to pick up the bone-handled knife he had dropped earlier. As he bent, a searing pain shot through his side where the man had been punching him. Looking to his ribs, he saw his shirt shredded and caked with blood and dirt. The man must have had the arrowhead lodged between his fingers. Luckily, none of the jabs had gone very deep.

Between his torn-up side, cut neck, and bloody nose, Keigh was a mess. Alive, but a mess.

I'm fine, he told himself. *I just need to rest.*

Walking further into the clearing, he found a patch of undisturbed bunchgrass and plopped down. He lay back, cradling his wounded side with his arms. A flower hawk passed directly above him. The large butterfly's ornate wings of black and yellow fluttered, buffeting him with gusts of air as it briefly seemed to consider landing on him. He watched it as it flew off. Its form was clear and crisp, but the scenery around it seemed to be fading.

The world is a funny place, he thought again. How could such fragility and beauty occupy the same space that death and violence had just laid claim to?

A stabbing pain in his side called him back from his wistful contemplation. Back to the disturbing reality of what had just happened. He had entered the woods that morning prepared to take a life, but the life taken wasn't one he had anticipated, and while he was sure he hadn't done anything wrong, he still...

Keigh vomited again.

Questions flooded his brain. *Why did the man know my name? Was he really sent here to kill me? Who could possibly see me as a threat? Where did he come from and what sorcery did he conjure with his staff? Why did grabbing his throat cause me to feel so...so...strong?*

He closed his eyes and let his mind grope for answers, but only managed to birth more questions. *Is Misselli okay? Did she find help? Will she look at me differently after this? How will my parents react?*

Worry struck him, his heart already grappling with guilt and confusion.

Maybe, Keigh thought, *maybe the world isn't quite so funny a place after all.*

CHAPTER 4

EXPLANATIONS

24-33-3

When Keigh next opened his eyes, he was back at home, lying in his own bed. His head throbbed and he was painfully aware of a soreness in his side that had nothing to do with his lumpy straw mattress. Lifting his head off his pillow slightly, he felt a cracking on the skin of his neck. His hand reached for the place he now remembered the stranger had sliced him with his own arrow, and found it caked over with what felt like dried mud.

"Don't pick at that! The poultice won't do any good if you pick it off."

A thin woman with chocolate-brown hair, a gentle face, and kind eyes, sat at the end of his bed, smiling at him.

"Oh! My son! You're awake!" Keigh's mother stood. Swooping to the head of the bed, she placed a kiss on his forehead. "Don't scare me like that!" She crossed her arms disapprovingly. "My beautiful boy, all cut up and bruised!"

"I'm fine," Keigh protested, knowing that any sign of weakness now would result in a downpour of hugs and kisses.

"Of course you are." She smiled warmly. "You're your father's son, after all." She bent low to kiss his forehead one more time before walking to the door, calling back over her shoulder, "The others will want to know you're awake. I'll fetch them and come back with some water and food."

Before his mother disappeared, he saw her nod and smile into the hallway as though answering some unvoiced question. There was an excited squeak and the patter of bare feet on wood. As his mother vanished, Jessie flew into the opening, grabbing the doorframe she spun herself into the room.

"Keigh!" she squealed. Sprinting, she leapt for the bed. In her excitement, she launched herself from too far away. There was a muffled *whump*, as she bounced off the side of the bed, landing on her rear in a fit of giggles. "You're awake!" she piped, frantically scrambling up off the floorboards and onto the bed, where she sat wide-eyed, looking at her big brother.

"I'm fine, bug," he said, winking at her. "How long was I out for?"

"Five whole years!" She sniggered, displaying all ten of her remaining baby teeth. "Just kidding! Only since they brought you back this morning. Felt longer to me, though."

Keigh sat up straight, dried blood and poultices cracking with the bend of his body. What he had wished had been a bad dream had all happened today, just a few hours ago.

He looked to the window. "What time is it? Have you seen Misselli?"

"Nope. No Misselli. We just ate dinner. Braddock is here and he brought his red bear! Also, he brought us meats, biscuits, and sugar rolls! And Mannie is here!" Jessie beamed, obviously proud of delivering the news. Braddock being in their home certainly was news, and they all loved when Mannie visited. "Mr. Braddock is weird," she added, her face transitioning from excited to confused.

Keigh grinned. "What do you mean, *weird?*" Braddock Fortier could be perceived as many things: serious, aloof, cold, scary even, but *weird* was not a word Keigh would have ever associated with the legend of Bjorn.

"Well," Jessie started, "he doesn't talk much, does he? Don't smile either." She frowned. "Are all canes like that? Will you not smile when you're a cane? You'll still talk to me, right?"

When you're a cane. Keigh's heart swelled. It had never once occurred to his little sister that he may never achieve his dream. "Of course I will, bug."

"Will you still be silly with me? Or will you be boring like all the other old people?" she asked, concern still weighing on her little face.

"Hmm…" Keigh hummed, teasing the appearance of deep contemplation. "I think…" He pointed a finger at Jessie, swerving his hand toward her like a goose beak ready to peck. "I think I'll be silly…just as long as I have a seelly little seester to be silly with!" His hand shot out, poking at her, tickling her ribs and sending her into a renewed fit of giggles.

His mother reentered the room, still smiling warmly. "Enough of that." Sabriya grabbed her daughter and sat her up straight, ending the tickle attack. "Your brother needs his rest."

She combed down a rogue tuft of hair on Jessie's head, then busied herself lighting candles in the rapidly darkening room before taking a place against the opposite wall. Next, Keigh's two block-framed brothers made to enter the room at the same time. One at a time was impressive enough; two would never happen. Wedged in the door frame, they struggled to wriggle their way in, holding half-eaten dinner plates aloft, careful not to spill a morsel.

"I thought your siblings should see you before the men start at you with all their questions," said Sabriya, rolling her eyes at the twins as they finally popped free of the door jamb.

"Guy gave you a beating worse than we ever did, huh, little brother?" Jobey gibed, nudging Keigh with the edge of his dinner plate.

"Yeah! I mean, we knew you liked getting beat up, but we're a little offended you went to someone else before coming to us!" Jotham winked at Keigh and took a big bite of a whole sausage he had on the end of a fork.

"For goodness' sake, child, cut your food!" flustered Sabriya. Abruptly, her scowl disappeared. With a gasp, she smacked her palm to her thigh. "Oh no! Keigh, I forgot your dinner. I'll go fix you a plate."

As she moved toward the door, Keigh's hands shot out to his brothers' plates, snatching a sausage from one and a biscuit from the other. "No need, Mom!" he said, taking a quick bite from each before his brothers could register what had happened. They looked at Keigh as though he had punched them in the mouth.

"That was low," Jotham said glumly, Jobey still gaping at his plate in disbelief. "I see our good cheer isn't appreciated here," he sniffed. "Come on, Jobey, if he's fine enough to nick food out of our starving mouths, he's fine enough. Let's go get dessert."

No sooner had his brothers left the room than Jessie's face transformed from adoration to pure horror. "They'll eat them all!" she shrieked, springing from the bed. She scrambled past the large man who had just entered the doorway, calling back over her shoulder, "Love you!"

"Save me some!" Keigh shouted after her.

The floorboards groaned as the man stepped into the room. He had a shaved head and glossy black beard. He wore a simple sleeveless tan linen tunic and rawhide boots like Keigh's. His clothing did little to hide his muscle-bound arms and chest.

"What happened out there?" he asked.

"Your son's been attacked by a beast of a man and it's straight to business with you!" Sabriya chided her husband. "Can't you see he's hurt? Don't you care how he's feeling?"

"Goodness, woman! He knows I care! Don't you, son?" Owen Anders looked to Keigh to back him up.

Keigh nodded, choking down a dry mouthful of biscuit.

"Besides, Anders don't get hurt—they get better," he added, giving Keigh a reassuring pat on the leg. "Braddock! Mannie!" he called, waving for the men to enter. "Please, come in, come in."

The first to enter was Braddock Fortier. He was a stout, handsome man with an aura of being both emotionally and physically carved from stone. Half a head shorter than Keigh's father, he had short, sandy hair and a clean-shaven face. He wore a tunic of slate gray with a thick leather breast and back plate connected by leather lacing at the shoulders and sides. A sword hung from his leather belt. Over it all he wore a cloak of deep crimson that draped over his left shoulder to the back of his knee.

Keigh shifted awkwardly in his bed, suddenly acutely aware of the very un-canely, boyish nature of his room.

Behind Braddock entered Mannie. A close friend and regular visitor to the Anders' home, he seemed to have received all the cheer and good humor that Braddock was missing. A full head taller than Braddock, he had to stoop through the doorway. He wore a loose-fitting, light tan tunic beneath a long-sleeved, earth-brown robe, and leather sandals instead of boots. He had short, wavy hair that covered his ears and an untamed beard.

He smiled fondly at Keigh and nodded his pleasure at seeing him awake and well.

Keigh smiled back. The king's messenger was the closest thing to family he had outside the five members of his immediate household. Like a fun uncle and proud grandpa wrapped in one, Mannie seemed to fill all the gaps in the Anders' broken family tree.

Keigh's room, which was usually crowded with just him and his brothers in it, suddenly felt uncomfortably full. Mannie made his way across the room and sat on the edge of Jobey's bed, while Keigh's father and Braddock stationed themselves on the two sides of Keigh's bed that weren't pressed into the corner.

When everyone had taken their places, it was his father who spoke first. "Son, this is Master Braddock Fortier. I know you know who he is, so I trust you'll answer his questions fully and respectfully...and, for the sake of our family name, you had better answer honest." He nodded for Braddock to begin.

Braddock, who Keigh knew to be a battle-hardened warrior, began in a most unexpected way: humbly.

"I owe you an apology, Keigh. I have already apologized to your parents..." Braddock gave a fleeting glance to Owen and Sabriya, who didn't see or return it. "But I owe you one as well. I knew yesterday that this man was looking for you. As you saw, I escorted him out of town. Followed him nearly back to Vaderkirk before returning home. Thought he was gone. I did not anticipate he would return, least of all after I told him I would be reporting him to the Capital. Figured that alone would scare him into leaving Eden." Braddock took a deep breath and shook his head. "It was an egregious oversight, one that nearly cost you your life. For that, I'm sorry."

The apology was made to Keigh, yet Braddock seemed to look to Owen to receive it, but once again, Keigh's father paid no notice.

"Anyway, enough about my failures. How are you feeling, Keigh?"

"Um...a bit sore, but...fine, sir." Keigh's response was distracted. He was struggling to wrap his brain around Braddock's confirmation that the stranger had in fact been from outside Eden—and, more disturbingly, had been looking specifically for him!

"Beyond your body, how do you feel? I've seen many a young man take their first life in battle, and I know that no two take it the same way. So, I would like to know...how are *you* taking it?" Braddock pried.

"How do you know I killed him?" Keigh asked, more to delay having to answer than anything else. "What if he tripped?"

"You don't have to be a veteran of war to know the difference between the scene of an accident and the scene of a battle." Braddock smiled thinly. "Your father and I were the ones who found you. I can tell you nearly everything that happened physically in that clearing, but what I don't know is what was said and how it's all affecting you now."

"Okay, then what happened?"

"Keigh!" his father barked.

Braddock raised a palm, cutting him off. "It's quite alright, Owen."

He looked down at Keigh, the glint in his eyes giving Keigh the impression Braddock knew he was stalling.

"Correct me if I'm mistaken, but it looks as though it started a bit uphill from where it ended. The largest pool of blood suggests you drew first blood with a well-placed arrow to his thigh. A warning shot, I'm assuming, since I've heard you're quite the skilled marksman with that fine bow of yours. The man spent some time in that spot, judging by the amount of blood there, before he eventually made a move downhill to attack you. The two of you grappled on the ground, where, based on the look of the man's face and the tooth I found in the dirt, you were able to land some impressively solid punches. Then there was a second scuffle a bit further over. How the wrestling match moved from one spot to the other is something you'll have to explain, as there was only one set of tracks on the ground between the two points.

"Here, at the site of the second scuffle, is where I found what was left of your arrow, and based on your shredded side and the lacerations on the man's hand, this is where he landed the blows to your ribs. From there you two got back on your feet, and a short, fast chase later, you pushed or threw him headfirst into the tree, breaking his neck." Braddock exhaled. "Did I get it about right?"

"It was a kick, actually. I kicked him when he tried to pick up his magic staff." Keigh added, "I didn't mean to kill him, you know…"

"So then, since it *was* you who ended his life, how do you feel about it?"

He couldn't avoid answering the question any longer. In truth, he wasn't quite sure how he felt. Part of him understood the innocence of life had been stripped away, and he grieved that, but another part was glad Misselli and the people of Bjorn were rid of this threat to their safety.

So, he answered truthfully, "I'm not sure."

"I expected as much," Braddock admitted. "Life and death, peace and war, punishment and mercy…These things are rarely black and white. I expect it will take some time to process." His body straightened, and he adopted a more businesslike tone. "Now I need you to tell me what was said between you two. In town, the stranger said he had a message to give you, but he wouldn't give it to me to deliver." Braddock's eyes narrowed. "Your friend was able to tell us a little, but by the sounds of it, you sent her away pretty quickly. A wise choice, I might add. Had things gone the other way and you had been killed…"

Keigh's mother gasped.

"You at least gave us a chance to respond to the threat," Braddock finished.

Keigh racked his mind, trying to remember every detail of the encounter. "He…he wanted to know why we were following him…"

"I'd like the answer to that question too!" his father interjected, his scowl deepening the lines of his face. "Seems a fool thing to do! Following a stranger around the woods…He could have killed you! And what's worse, you took Misselli along with you. What if she had been hurt? How would you feel?"

"Owen!" his mother gasped.

"What, Sabriya? It was foolish at best, reckless at worst." Keigh's father turned to look at him, awaiting an answer.

"Misselli thought we should follow him too…" Keigh dropped his eyes, unwilling to meet his father's glare.

There was a pause. Then, in a voice much calmer than Keigh expected, his father said, "Boys make excuses. Men take responsibility."

Immediately, blood rushed to Keigh's face in red-hot shame. "Yes, Father. I thought we should follow the man because he didn't look like he was from Eden. I wanted to know who he was before reporting it back to town. I thought…I thought I was being careful, but he doubled back and got behind me. I'm sorry. It was reckless. Misselli is okay, isn't she?"

"More than okay, I'd say," said Braddock, breaking the tension with a wry smile. "I thought I was going to have a fight on my hands when I told her she would have to wait. Nearly beat my door off its hinges! Didn't even seem afraid Mace might maul her! She was so adamant that I hear her out that instant." He chuckled, admiration for Keigh's friend clear in his face. "She mentioned the man told you he was looking for you…What for? Did he say?"

"He didn't know it was me he was talking to, at least not at first," said Keigh, grateful for the new line of questioning.

"Yes, I noticed he didn't recognize you yesterday when he saw you in town."

Keigh nodded. "He said someone had sent him to find Keigh Anders, that he had something he needed to deliver to him." It felt weird saying it out loud. It was the first time he had really acknowledged the strange fact that the man had been sent to find *him*…sent to *kill* him.

Braddock pressed further. "Did he say what he was meant to deliver or who sent him?"

"No. He said it was sensitive. Didn't say who sent him, only that he had been sent, and that what he had, he could only give to Keigh. Then, when he realized I was Keigh—"

"Wait! How did he know?" Braddock looked alarmed now.

"Well…I sort of told him who I was after Misselli left," Keigh confessed, a fresh wave of embarrassment washing over him as he realized how foolish he had been.

"And how did he react when you told him? Did he give you anything?" Braddock demanded.

"He got...excited. Then he started looking in his bag." Keigh remembered how he had naively lowered his guard and walked right up to the man. "Then he just attacked me. Said...said death was what he had for me..."

At this, everyone in the room shifted uneasily, all eyes looking to Braddock.

"Did he make any mention of a partner or others he was with?"

"No, not at all. He was acting really secretive—he even tried to blast Misselli with his magic staff. Like he didn't want any witnesses."

Mannie interjected for the first time. "There is nothing magic about the staff."

"It's not really a staff at all," added Braddock. "After inspecting the thing myself and hearing Misselli's account of it, I believe the man's weapon is in fact..." He looked at Mannie, who nodded his agreement. "A gun."

The Anders looked at Braddock as though he had suggested the man's weapon were a dragon. Guns were weapons of legend! They had been used in ancient wars, but nobody alive had ever seen one. Stories of the world from before the Great Collapse included accounts of many fantastic technologies and magics. Carriages that transported hundreds of people through the sky like giant metal birds; devices that allowed people to talk with and even see people on the other side of the planet instantly...and guns, the ancient bows that needed no drawing and slung bits of metal through flesh and bone, faster than the eye could see.

"Surely there's a more reasonable explanation, Braddock," Keigh's father objected, though his voice lacked confidence.

"I'm afraid I agree with Braddock's conclusion," said Mannie. "For many years now, rumors have made their way into Eden that Draiden has discovered many of the weapons of power used by our ancestors to destroy the world. Surely, he would not part with one lightly...or cheaply."

"So, you believe this man was sent here by Draiden himself then?" Braddock asked Mannie skeptically.

"No, *that* is unlikely, as I have no reason to believe that Draiden even knows Keigh exists..." Mannie gave Keigh a wink and a smile. "Though I'm glad I do." He continued, "I think the only thing it does confirm about our mystery assassin is that he was very well financed. Which disturbs me even more, for while we know Draiden to be a great evil, great wealth can convince even a decent man to commit the most unspeakable cruelties. I do not know if Keigh's attacker was a decent man corrupted, or corrupt from the start, but we can be sure he was being paid handsomely for his treachery."

"I'm in agreement. Unfortunately for him, his greed cost him his life." Braddock rapped his knuckles on the foot of Keigh's bed. "Keigh, Owen, I have to ask...is there something you aren't telling me? Never in my life has an enemy of Eden broken through our borders, and now that one has...I'm supposed to believe he's here looking for *you*? Anything? I just can't see why a man carrying a weapon worth more than our entire town would come looking for you."

"There is nothing, Fortier," said Owen, keeping his eyes on his son. "No reason the name Keigh Anders should mean anything to anyone outside of this family."

Mannie frowned at Owen's words. Keigh, too, was stung. And he didn't like what Braddock was insinuating. He wasn't a liar.

"You're right, Father," he said. "What could an insignificant thrall like me possibly do to be noticed by wealth? I nearly had to die before Master Fortier set foot in our home."

He surprised himself with the amount of venom in his words. He was sure he had overstepped. This was no way to speak of an elder, especially a cane.

His father glared at him.

"I'm sorry, sir," he blurted, drooping his head. He braced for the tongue-lashing he knew was coming.

There was a pause before Braddock responded, "Had I known my presence was desired—"

"We never shut our door to you, Fortier." Owen cut the cane off, venom in his voice now as well.

Braddock didn't hesitate. "There's more than one way to shut a door, *Anders.*"

The two men exchanged a cold stare before Braddock spoke again.

"I assure you, my absence here has nothing to do with your family's station," he said, speaking to Keigh but once again looking at Owen. "I must be leaving. I will need to send a message immediately to the Capital regarding today's events. They will need to know our border has been breached." Then, without looking at Keigh, he added, "I would like to return for a proper meal with your family on an evening free of duty, if you'll have me."

"Like I said," Owen replied smoothly, "the door's not shut."

Keigh's mother nodded graciously. "Thank you for your swift response in retrieving our son. He's a good boy and means well—"

"Even if he doesn't seem it today," his father finished, shooting Keigh an icy glare.

"Well..." Braddock shuffled, seemingly unsure how to read the room. "I'd better get that overgrown teddy bear of mine back home before that goose of yours pecks her to death." He nodded to Keigh. Turning on his heel, red cloak flaring, he walked out of the room.

Owen shook his head at Keigh before following after Braddock. His mother gave him a sympathetic smile and touched his foot as she left the room. There was a pause as the sounds of their footsteps faded down the hallway to the great room, where Keigh could hear his siblings squabbling over some unknown bit of food.

Keigh and Mannie sat in silence for what couldn't have been more than seconds, but to Keigh it felt like an eternity. What would Mannie have to say about his disrespectful outburst? Keigh was sure if he hadn't been so injured, his own father would have cuffed him on the head for dishonoring the family like he had. It was one thing for his father to have words with a town elder, but Keigh was not yet a man, and disrespect for one's elders was never tolerable—least of all when that elder had just come to your rescue. Keigh would have preferred a beating rather than see the disappointment in his father's face.

Mannie broke the silence. "You know I hate when you talk about yourself like that. How many times have I told you that being a thrall has nothing to do with what you're worth?"

Keigh wished Mannie had thrown something at him instead. Wished he had just walked out like the other men. "I know," he admitted, still not able to lift his eyes from his bedspread.

"Each person in this room tonight would gladly risk their life to protect you. Your words to Braddock were completely uncalled for. Should danger come against you again, he will be the first one to put his life on the line to defend you. Your contempt for yourself and your family's station is not humility. You accused Braddock of being a fool tonight."

"No...No, I didn't!" denied Keigh. "How?"

"By questioning your value, you call into question the judgment of anyone who has ever invested any love or time into you, because only a fool would waste what precious time and love we have on this earth on something worthless." Mannie gave Keigh a sympathetic look. "That's exactly what you're accusing him of."

"I hope you didn't think I was calling you a fool," Keigh said.

Mannie grinned. Jobey's bed gave a grateful creak as the tall messenger stood up and made his way over to tousle Keigh's hair. Leaning low, he whispered, "Not a chance!" He shoved Keigh's head playfully back toward the pillow. "I never forget what you're worth, even if you sometimes do." The thrall gave him a soft punch to the thigh before walking out of the room.

Keigh slumped back down into his covers. He decided at that moment that he would find Braddock the next day and give him a proper apology.

Mannie's head popped back into his open doorway. Keigh jolted back up.

"I'll be walking you to town for your instruction tomorrow. Don't take off without me." He flashed a toothy grin and disappeared again down the hall.

Keigh lay back down. The dried salves and poultices cracked again as he shifted in his bed. He would have gladly taken twice the physical pain if he could have been rid of the chaotic stew of emotions brewing in his chest at that moment: shame, confusion, anger, curiosity, all roiling inside him. Why had he lashed out at Braddock? How could they ask him if he had done something to cause this? Why did someone want him dead? Would it end with just one attempt?

He blew out the candle on the stand next to his bed. *Tomorrow will be a new day,* he told himself. Rolling over onto his back, he let sleep take him.

CHAPTER 5

THE NEWS

45-8-25

The next morning Keigh was up before the sun again. He had slept hard but not long, his mind still racing with unanswered questions and the underlying anxiety of having to face the men he had disrespected.

His first movement of the day felt like he was breaking his body free of ice: every joint, every limb, rigid and stiff with pain. After timidly easing himself out of bed, he paced the room, assessing his limits. He was pleased to find that, while very sore, he seemed to have sustained nothing more than superficial wounds. He continued to stretch and flex his joints. Slowly, gradually, his cut and bruised body loosened up, his pain diminishing to a dull full-body ache.

He put on a pair of wool pants, then gingerly slipped a linen shirt over his head and heavily bandaged torso. There was a single sugar roll on a small plate on his bedside table. Jessie must have saved it for him. While his little sister showed her love in obvious ways, the fact that the roll was still there and hadn't been devoured by one of his mule brothers was their own way of showing Keigh they cared. He smiled at the twin lumps snoring away in their beds on the far side of the room, then hungrily stuffed the roll in his mouth.

Out of habit, he grabbed his wooden sparring sword from the wicker basket by his bed and headed for the door. He was sore and stiff, but he could still practice his footwork for a bit before morning chores.

He crept from his room, following the same safe sequence of sturdy floorboards he did every morning, but before he reached the front door, a calm, deep voice from the shadows stopped him.

"You can give that a rest, son."

Owen Anders was a hardworking man, and it wasn't uncommon for him to be awake before sunrise, but typically by now he would be in the fields or fixing some odd piece of farm equipment. His presence at the dinner table caught Keigh off guard.

"Wha—why are you up? I mean, why are you inside?" Keigh stammered.

"Sleep didn't come easy last night, and I wanted to talk to you before the others got up."

His father patted the table, gesturing for Keigh to take a seat. Keigh sat down across from him and waited.

Owen took a sip of tea from the steaming mug in front of him and shook his head. "For the life of me, I'll never understand your obsession with combat, Keigh. We are thralls. We work for our creditors. We do not fight Eden's battles. Our service to the kingdom is in serving our betters. This is our station in life, and there is honor in it."

His father paused, seemingly waiting for Keigh to assent. When Keigh said nothing, he sighed.

"But...I suppose all your practice probably did have a hand in saving your life yesterday, so I won't ask you to stop. Only today, I'll ask that you put your sword away and rest. It will make your mother happy."

"Yes, Father, of course," Keigh said. Then, hopefully, he asked, "Should I rest from my morning chores as well?"

His father smirked. "Not today. Not ever." Owen chuckled at the look of despair on his son's face.

"Why are you still inside?" Keigh asked, hoping to distract his father from assigning him chores immediately. "I thought you would be out planting by now."

"Well…" His father paused, the smile fading from his face. "I need to deal with your behavior toward Braddock last night."

"I'm sorry, Dad. I know I was out of line. He's an elder, and a cane. A thrall shouldn't speak that way to his betters. I will go and apologize properly, in person, today."

"I expect my children to speak respectfully to everyone, regardless of class or station. Mannie is a thrall too. Do you think I would ever tolerate you speaking to him that way?"

It was a rhetorical question, but Keigh answered anyway. "No, of course not…but I would never do that to Mannie. He has always been good to us."

Owen's lips pursed as he pointed an accusatory finger at his son. "That's the problem, right there!" He smacked the table so loud they both winced and looked down the hall, waiting to see if it had woken anyone.

After a moment, Keigh asked, "What is…?"

"Last night you accused Braddock of never coming around here—something you obviously believe to be a slight toward our family, though you know nothing of what Braddock does for us, this family, this town, this kingdom, every day! Now you sit here and tell me you wouldn't speak disrespectfully to Mannie because *'he's good to us'*…Do you not see what you're doing?"

Keigh shook his head, still confused.

"You justify your behavior toward these men based on what you perceive they've done or not done for you. You mistreat Braddock cause he mistreated you, and you're courteous to Mannie because he's courteous to you. Do you still not see the problem? You are letting other people decide who *you* are! My son will not be a puppet, merely reacting in kind to however he's being treated…or in your case, how he *thinks* he's being treated. I want my son to be good and kind because that's who *he* is…not just because that's how he was treated first."

Keigh's father sat back in his chair with a huff, as though he had just tossed a particularly heavy bale of hay.

"I was wrong to snap at Braddock. I know I was," Keigh said. "But are you saying I have to just lie down and take being treated poorly?"

"Even worse." His father leaned in again. "I want you to be good to 'em."

"What? But that's not fair!" Keigh couldn't believe what he was hearing. "And what's to keep people from just walking all over me, huh?"

"The way others deal with you, son, will be on their head. They will answer for their misdeeds, in this life or the next."

"Answer to who?" Keigh fumed, still indignant.

"The king's law, his judges, officials...Bigger, stronger bullies. It's beside the point! You will not let others dictate who *you* are or how *you* treat them. An eye for an eye and a tooth for a tooth would leave all of Eden blind and starving!" Owen gave a small shake of his head before raising his mug for another sip of tea.

This was ridiculous. Even in as peaceful a town as Bjorn, there was no shortage of troublemakers, gossips, and hecklers. If Keigh did what his father was asking, he would be the biggest fool in town.

He sat stubbornly for a second before responding. "I've seen you lose your temper. And..." He paused, unsure if his next words would get him in more trouble. "And you weren't overly kind to Braddock yesterday either."

Unsure if his father's silence meant he had crossed a line or backed him into a corner, Keigh watched as he seemingly wrestled with how to respond.

When Owen did answer, he was calm and confident. "You're right, son. I have done the wrong thing and been the wrong man more times than you even know." He paused, dipping his head to stare into his lap. "And yes, I let my own issues with Master Fortier affect my behavior toward him."

What was happening? Had Keigh actually won an argument with his father? What "issues" existed between Owen and Braddock? He didn't dare speak for fear of losing his advantage, but he didn't have to wait long before his father continued.

Owen lifted his head and looked at Keigh, unblinking. "But I..." He pointed a thick finger at his own chest. "If *I* do my duty as a father, I'll raise sons to be better men than I am, better men than I'll ever be."

Keigh was stunned, admiration blossoming in his chest. "I...I don't know anyone who's a better man than you," he confessed. It was true: his family was poor, but his father always found ways to help people. One time, Owen had even taken in a traveler for a whole week, letting the man sleep in his room while he and Keigh's mother slept on the floor of the great room. His father would fill the man's plate at meals with food taken from each of their plates, a gesture that had greatly upset Keigh and his brothers.

When the traveler left, Keigh's brothers complained about this. Their father's response had been simple: "Generosity takes sacrifice. The deed is not generous if it costs you nothing." This was the man sitting across the table, demanding his son be better than he was. Keigh didn't think that was possible.

His father smiled at him warmly. "I'm sure there are many, and I know you're on your way to being one of them. I see a lot of me in you, son, and that's not always a good thing." Then, straightening in his chair, he added, "But as long as you live under my roof, it's my responsibility to encourage and nurture the good I see. And..." Owen gave the table three soft knocks with his knuckles. "To discipline the wrong. So, for last night's outburst, you will be trenching out the irrigation canals at the end of the field—"

"But I always do that—"

"—by hand. No shovel. And that's on top of your normal chores. There will be no sword practice or hunting until it's done, you hear? If you apply yourself, you should be able to finish by the end of the week."

"I can barely move!" Keigh protested. "Do you know how bad that will hurt?"

"And why shouldn't it hurt? You sealed your own fate when I saw you sneaking out of here to practice hacking away with that infernal sword of yours!" Owen sniffed. "If you're well enough to swing a sword, you're well enough to dig a ditch." He paused, then wiping the tiredness from his face with a calloused hand he sighed. "You don't have to start today, though. I know your mother wants you to do something about the garden wolves you've been feeding scraps to. We know you like 'em, so we aren't asking you to get rid of them—just move their den farther from your mom's flower garden. They've been digging up the fish skins she buried in there for fertilizer. You should be able to get that done before Mannie comes to fetch you."

"Yes, Father," Keigh said. He was glad he had not received a worse punishment and had no desire to push his luck by debating it further.

"I'm headed out to the field. If I get started now, I should be able to get spuds in the ground on the five acres we tilled yesterday." His father yawned, standing up from the table. Walking to the door, he grabbed an empty burlap bag off the floor. "Give Mannie my best, will ya?" With that, he left for the fields, closing the door behind him.

The sun was now shooting its first rays through the gaps in the mountain peaks on the far side of the valley. Golden bands of light streamed through the windows, illuminating the dark room. Keigh grabbed a piece of jerky from the pantry. Exiting the house, he paused to place his hand on the bear head engraved on the door, then slowly made his way out to the small wooden shed where he kept his bow and grabbed a shovel. Taking note of where his mom's garden was on the side of the house, he walked the hundred feet to where the yard ended and the forest began. Selecting a particularly gnarled pine, he picked a spot between two roots at the base of the trunk and started digging out a deep hollow.

Fifteen minutes later, he reached his hand into the hole. Finding he could no longer touch the back of it, he smiled, satisfied the wolves would take to it. It would be easy to move the pack this time of year. They had just had their pups, and if he could just get his hands on the bunch, the pack would follow Keigh wherever he took them.

He returned the shovel to the shed, where he found Mrs. Schaffer still apparently angry with him. The bird's memory was proving to be as long as her neck. She gave Keigh a bitter hiss and waddled off toward the house.

From there, Keigh made his way over to their barn, where he knew the wolf pack's current den had been dug under the back corner. The barn was a tall, flimsy-looking building whose thin wallboards and corner posts were black and gray with age. Its gambrel roof and walls leaned precariously uphill toward the forest, but as far as he could remember, it had always been that way, and didn't show any signs of falling down soon.

Most people ran garden wolves off their properties or exterminated them entirely, preferring to leave rodent hunting to the family cats, but Keigh liked the wolves and had developed a bond with them over the years. He found that if any of them ever got out of line, all he had to do was grab the troublemaker and pin it with its back to the ground. After that simple display of dominance, the wolf would usually comply.

Coming to the back corner, he saw two of the housecat-sized wolves dragging the prize of their morning hunt, a cottontail rabbit, back to their den. Keigh took a knee next to the mouth of the den as the alpha male and female came up out of the ground to see what was for breakfast. They were followed closely by four yipping, bouncing, fuzzball pups no bigger than field mice. They really were beautiful animals. Most of the pack had coats of silver-and-white hair, but a few were midnight black with blazing yellow eyes or snow white with eyes of soulful gray. There were nearly twenty of the pint-sized dogs in the pack, and most of them were there now.

This is as good a time as any, Keigh thought, giving the pack leaders each a scratch behind the ears. "Don't be mad," he pleaded. Quickly, he scooped the four pups up in his hand.

Immediately the alphas snarled, baring their teeth. Keigh opened his hand, showing the pack that the pups were unharmed.

"You've got to follow me, okay?"

Walking backward with a pup between each of the fingers on his right hand so the wolves could see them, he led the angry pack back up the hill to where he had dug their new den. A single unruly or aggressive wolf was an easy task, but now, facing twenty of them, Keigh wasn't so sure he could fend them off if they all attacked at once. There was strength in numbers. Twenty wild dogs with razor-sharp teeth and claws could easily pose a threat to his life.

He increased his pace. The less time the wolves had to get riled up, the better.

After what seemed like a much farther distance backward than forward, he finally made it to the tree. Careful not to break eye contact with the alphas, he stooped low to the ground and stuck his arm into the hole, depositing the pups in their new home.

With one last snarl, the wolves broke eye contact and dashed into the new den after the pups.

As a gesture of good faith, Keigh went back down the hill and retrieved the pack's morning kill. Tossing it on the ground in front of the new den, he watched as the pack reemerged from the ground to check it out. After a quick sniff, they decided the cottontail was still good. Yipping and howling, they dragged the rabbit underground.

Keigh brushed the dirt and rabbit hair off his palms and watched the pack sniff around their new headquarters. When he was content that the new den would stick, he returned to the barn to fill in the old den.

Right as he was finishing, he looked up to see Mannie enter through the wooden gate below the house. "Glad to see you up and at it already!" Mannie shouted up the hill. His smile as warm as the sunlight radiating off his shoulders. "You ready to go, then?"

"Yeah! Just need to wash up quick and I'm ready," Keigh called back, making his way over to the well. He drew a bucket of water and started scrubbing his arms and hands clean of their morning work. Scooping some of the cold water with his palm, he tossed it onto his head and face, wiping them dry with the front of his shirt.

Before joining Mannie at the front gate, he poked his head back in the front door of his home and called his goodbyes to his mom and sister. Closing the door behind him, Keigh took off down the hill to join Mannie, who had already started walking back down the gravel road toward Bjorn.

"Wait up!" Keigh started to jog after him before deciding it was too painful to be doing that just yet. A minute later, he caught up with the old messenger. "Morning, Mannie," he panted. "You could have waited."

"Waited?" Mannie asked. "What for? My timing is impeccable. Yours, however..." He raised his eyebrows at Keigh.

It was true—Keigh didn't have a great track record of being on time. There was always something interesting that required his attention. In his opinion, the demands of life could wait; they would be there to greet him every morning of his life. But the oddities, the unique interactions with nature, those things that may never repeat themselves…Those were what deserved his attention. So what if it meant being late to the occasional demand?

Keigh smiled guiltily. "Touche, old man."

"Old man. Pfft!" Mannie huffed. "I travel the breadth of Eden every month, yet it's you panting to catch your breath after only a short jog!" The king's messenger grinned and ruffled Keigh's hair. "Ready for another day's instruction? I'll be joining your class today! Also, I'll be informing your instructor why you missed your lesson yesterday, so don't feel the need to explain yourself. I'll be telling them just the parts they need to know, of course. It would be unwise to be spreading stories about a dangerous man in Eden right now, especially when the man in question is no longer a threat to anyone…thanks to you," he finished with a wink.

"Why are you coming to our class today?" Keigh asked, having finally caught his breath.

"That, you will find out at the same time as your classmates. Why don't you tell me what's been happening in Bjorn since I visited last month?"

Keigh spent the walk to town catching Mannie up on all the news he thought was worth telling, which admittedly wasn't much. He liked talking to Mannie. It seemed that Mannie could always find something interesting in what Keigh had to say. Sometimes Keigh would make up stories that he thought were unbearably boring just to see if Mannie would lose interest, but even then, Mannie managed to feign interest. Keigh didn't test him today, though, and when he couldn't think of anything else to tell him, Mannie finished the rest of the walk telling Keigh the new thrall jokes he had heard.

It used to bother Keigh when Mannie made thrall jokes. He didn't really understand why Mannie liked them, since he was a thrall too, until one day Keigh had finally asked him.

"We should never make light of the misery of others," Mannie had explained. "But if you can't make jokes out of the hard things in your own life, they will make a joke out of you." So now the jokes were a regular staple in their conversations.

Before long they had reached Bjorn's primary gateway. Though Eden had not seen open warfare within its borders since the prior King of Eden, King Orvyn, had raised the curtain wall a hundred years ago, all of Eden's settlements were still heavily fortified. Around the entire town, a deep trench had been excavated, fifteen feet deep and fifty feet wide, with a series of dry canals that connected to the King's River. If the town were under siege, the sluice gates at the river could be raised, filling the trench with water. If that obstacle were not enough to keep out an enemy, they would still need to contend with the eighty-foot wall of sharpened pine trunks. Halfway up and all along the length of the wall, narrow slits had been carved from which the canes could shoot arrows mercilessly down on their foes as they sloshed about, bogged down in the water and mud at the base of the wall.

The entry itself was twenty feet high to allow for the passage of the canes' massive red bears, and another twenty feet wide to accommodate the traffic of the town's many wagons and carts. The bottom points of a heavy steel portcullis were exposed like jagged, rusty teeth in a giant mouth. Keigh hadn't seen the gate closed in his entire life, but it was there should the town need it.

On either side of the gate were two towering totem poles carved from mammoth pines much thicker than the ones used to construct Bjorn's walls. Each pole consisted of two figures carved one on top of the other. At the base was the imposing image of a thirty-foot red bear standing on its hind legs, face fixed in an eternal growl. Above each of the bears, a cane was displayed in full armor, standing at attention, a sword held across his chest.

Keigh stared at the totem poles, imagining himself, one day, clothed in armor and ready for battle.

Mannie nudged him playfully out of his daydream. "You'll catch a bug in there if you aren't careful."

Keigh snapped his mouth shut, a little embarrassed to have been caught gaping.

They walked through the gate into Bjorn, where the asymmetrical shops and homes were built into and out of their neighbors like a rookery of birds' nests. The buildings were so intertwined that the second and third stories often had no discernable first floor.

Bjorn's main street was alive with activity as people bustled up and down its length, buying, selling, and haggling. The butcher in his white apron wiped his windows dry of the morning dew, and the blacksmith wheeled out a cart of freshly sharpened plow heads. The town's two bake shops were directly across the street from each other, and the two women who owned them, one of whom was Misselli's mother, Rita, were rather unconvincingly inspecting their storefronts as they attempted to look at their competitor's fresh-baked offerings for the day. Pedestrians came and went, carrying bags of goods or leading various kinds of livestock through the crowd.

"Go ahead and get to your instruction," said Mannie, rolling up the brown sleeves of his cloak and casting a glance up the main street. "I've got some matters I must attend to. I'll join your class before the end." The king's messenger smiled at Keigh and walked back out the front gate.

Keigh set off toward the community grounds at the center of Bjorn, where classes were held for each age group from eight to fifteen.

Bjorn was a quiet farming community. Most of the townsfolk were ables, Eden's non-fighting population, who filled all the roles needed for a prosperous settlement. They were farmers, smiths, millers, weavers, thatchers, carpenters, bakers, and merchants. Representatives of each trade took turns teaching the community's young people about their craft. By their sixteenth year, Eden's youth would have to pick a profession in which to agoge, Eden's formal vocational training.

The highest honor and greatest calling for any young man in Eden, though, was to be a cane, a full-time warrior of Eden. Canes were respected by everyone and compensated directly from the king's riches. They had special armor awarded to them by the queen in what the warriors called the "Queen's Climb." The higher a cane rose in rank, honor, and renown, the more armor they received. Once a cane had received every piece of armor, feats of bravery or skill could earn them a bear's fang etched into their helmet. This allowed people to see just how accomplished a cane was just by looking at the armor they wore—the exception being Braddock Fortier, who, despite being arguably the most accomplished cane in Eden, preferred to wear only the iconic red cloak of a cane over simple leather armor.

Despite the queen's ability to bestow honor and recognition on canes for their merit, the warriors that Edenites held in highest regard were those who received what the queen could never give: a successful pairing with a red bear. Very few were granted an opportunity to pair with a red bear cub. Fewer still successfully matched with one. Hardly any canes settled near town; most lived in or near the Capital, but still, of the dozen or more that did call Bjorn home, Braddock was the only cane Keigh knew with a red bear.

Last of all, and lowest of the classes, were the thralls, Eden's bondservants. Thralls were typically ables who, through vice or bad fortune, had incurred such a high level of debt with another family that the elders deemed it a sum "unpayable." The debtor and his immediate family would then be committed into the service of their "betters" for life or until released from their obligation. The process of submitting a family for service as thralls was a nasty business, and most people made more agreeable arrangements for repayment rather than commit a family to open shame—but unfortunately for Keigh's family, Vicerous Wulf had submitted his father's debt to the elders and had the Anders reclassed as thralls before Keigh had been born.

Even so, life was good today. Keigh had escaped death only twenty-four hours ago and was feeling rather well, all things considered. The sun was shining, Mannie was in town, and today he had instruction, so soon he would see Misselli and his friends.

The community grounds at Bjorn's center were a large, flat track of gravel that had been sectioned off into smaller areas separated by slat wood fences. In addition to hosting merchant caravans, festival gatherings, and memorial fires, this was the area used for the instruction of Bjorn's youth. Keigh's group, the fifteens, were in the section farthest north on the edge of the grounds.

Keigh made his way past the other age groups' sections. Heads turned and gawked at him as he passed. Precious little information from yesterday's events had likely leaked to the townsfolk, but precious little was all they needed to create grand stories, greatly embellished. Keigh wondered just how wild the tales had already become.

Rounding the barriers of his section, he found that all his classmates were already there, huddled around a beautiful blonde girl in a robin's egg–blue wool dress. She was the first to see him. Misselli's face flushed with relief and then filled with happiness as she plowed her way out of the huddle of teens toward him.

"Keigh!" she cried, dashing to the back of the section. Hardly bothering to slow herself, Misselli threw her arms around Keigh's neck, nearly knocking him off his feet. "Are you okay? I've been worried something terrible happened to you! Braddock made me go home and promise to stay away from your house until he spoke to you. None of us has heard a word since!"

There were eleven fifteen-year-olds in Bjorn, and by the looks of it, they had all been discussing Keigh before he showed up. They made their way over to where he stood with Misselli.

Tarin inserted his muscular frame between Misselli and Keigh, wedging them apart. "Okay, Misselli, that's enough crying over Keigh. I'm sure he's fine." He smiled down at Keigh and clapped him on the shoulder. "How did you get that little scratch on your neck, bud? Looks like you got a pair of black eyes too!" Tarin chuckled.

Keigh smiled back good-naturedly. "Learning to walk might be a lifelong activity for me."

"I don't know about that." Tarin looked over his shoulder at a visibly put-off Misselli. "If Misselli is to be believed, and you really shot an intruder in the woods, then had *the* Braddock Fortier pay you a house call...I think that makes you the Bear today!" he said, inclining his head in a subtle bow.

"Finally!" Keigh grinned at his friend. "I feel like you've been the Bear every week since we were twelve." *The Bear* was a title he and Tarin bestowed on each other whenever one of them experienced a victory or accomplished something of note.

"Well then, enjoy today, because it'll be me again before long!"

He wasn't wrong. Tarin was the betting man's pick to be the king's heir. While nobody had ever seen the king's face, it was common knowledge that he was a giant of a man. There were only five boys in Eden's Consecrate. Five boys all born in the same month as the king's son. Five families who'd had to give up their child to be raised in anonymous cane households throughout Eden. Though secrecy was commanded of host families, a lack of family resemblance and preferential treatment had betrayed the identities of all five by now. None more so than Tarin, who towered a foot taller than his mother and four inches taller than his father.

"Misselli said you shot a man in the woods with your bow!" said Theo Pipps, an excited, frail-looking boy with dark brown skin and bright eyes.

"Well…um…sort of, Theo," Keigh said, not wanting to share too much.

"Misselli said the man cast magic at her!" exclaimed Emerson. Keigh noticed a fresh patch in her dirty dress, where it had ripped two days ago.

"There's no such thing as magic, thrall!" snapped Cecilia Giles. With her red hair, slim build, and electric-blue eyes, Cecilia was quite popular with the young men of Bjorn, and she knew it.

"No, it wasn't magic, but it was unnatural," Keigh interceded, trying to soften the blow to Emerson.

"It could have been magic, though!" Addy Osmond, a short girl with thick glasses, piped up. "That is to say, magic does exist…if you believe the stories, that is…" Her initial confidence died off as she spoke.

"You read that in one of your books?" said Cecilia, looking down her nose at Addy. "I suppose you'd believe anything if it were in a book," she scoffed.

"Braddock's got a good idea what happened, and I reckon he's right about it," said Keigh.

Misselli edged her way out from behind Tarin. "Really? What was it? Did he tell you?"

"Yeah…Well, I probably shouldn't…Maybe I can tell you later…" Keigh trailed off. Could he tell them? He hadn't been told he couldn't, but Mannie had made it obvious that he thought it would be best not to share too much.

"Come on, mate! Don't hold out on us now!" encouraged Conrad Hawk, a well-built and well-liked son of a cane. "I mean, you had *the* legend Braddock Fortier in your home, man! That guy doesn't talk to anyone! You gotta tell us what he said!"

But before Keigh could speak, he was cut off by a sneering voice from behind the group. "He can't tell us anything!"

Deacon Wulf, in his black tunic and cloak, stalked closer to where the rest of the fifteens stood gathered around Keigh.

"Would you all like to know why?" His dark eyes darted from person to person, waiting to be challenged.

Kervyn Popplardo, a chubby boy in a spotless tunic, took the bait. "Why not, Deacon?"

"Keigh can't tell us because he's making it all up!" Deacon pointed his accusation at Keigh before following up with Kervyn. "Braddock ever been to your house, Lardo?"

"Well…umm…n-no," stammered Kervyn, apparently regretting engaging with Deacon.

"Thought not." Deacon's lip curled contemptuously. "And you all think if Braddock hasn't visited the wealthiest family in town, that he's making house calls on Keigh Anders?"

Cecilia let out a cackle as the rest of the group lowered their eyes.

Misselli, however, stepped up, placing herself right in Deacon's face. "So you suppose I'm just making it up too, then?" she snapped.

Deacon paused at her challenge, but Cecilia didn't hesitate.

"I think you would. You two haven't got much going for you, do you? I mean, Keigh is obviously a thrall, but my daddy says your family isn't far off from being reclassed as well."

The two girls glared daggers at each other. At this moment, Keigh thought, they were both more frightening than attractive.

"I believe them," came a confident but quiet voice from a massive youth. It was Beaudy Besnik, the newest kid in their class. His family having just relocated to Bjorn a month ago, Keigh had barely heard him speak much more than his own name before.

"So? What's that to me?" spat Deacon, having recovered from the initial surprise of Misselli's challenge. "You're new here, so I'll assume you're ignorant and not just as stupid as you look."

Beaudy recoiled at this, dropping his gaze back to the dirt at his feet.

"Come on now, Deacon, I'm sure it will all get sorted out soon," Tarin interjected coolly.

Keigh looked at his friend incredulously. "So you think we could be lying too?"

"Well, no...I mean...all I'm saying is—this is a stupid thing to argue about," Tarin said, a hint of pleading in his voice.

"And me? You don't believe me either?" Misselli raised her eyebrows at Tarin.

"Yes! Well, of course I believe you!" Tarin rushed to say, obviously annoyed that his attempt at diplomacy hadn't pacified everyone. He avoided eye contact with Deacon, looking to Conrad for help.

"Easy! Easy, everyone," said Conrad, stepping in to assist. "We're all friends here. Keigh, Deacon, you don't have to like each other, but you both need to stop ruining my day." He laughed, clapping Deacon on the shoulder.

Keigh and Deacon gave each other cold looks as if to say *Fine*, just as a middle-aged woman with arms thick as cordwood and hair wrapped tight in a bun walked up behind them, leading a glossy, dark bay horse by the reins.

"Quickly, quickly, take your seats. Today's instruction will be on the thorough and accurate valuing of horses—what to look for and when not to buy. Quickly, now!" Mrs. Feldman waved them forward to their spots on the ground like a mother hen gathering her chicks.

Keigh took his place between Beaudy and Emerson and leaned forward to listen as Mrs. Feldman began in earnest to show the class the finer points of horse health and vitality. Before long, though, Keigh was daydreaming—after all, he would never have the means to purchase a horse anyway. In his mind he went back to the clearing in the woods, trying to remember any details he had forgotten. The stranger's gun and clothes loomed large in his memory, but he felt he had missed something...He replayed the encounter over and over. Nothing seemed to stand out, but at the same time, something didn't fit.

Two hours later, Keigh was pulled out of the survey of his memory as Mannie, in his rough brown cloak, attempted to sneak his gargantuan frame to the front of the section, with zero success. All eyes were trained on the king's messenger. His cheeks flushed red above his scraggly beard and he gave a small nod to Mrs. Feldman to continue her lesson without interruption.

But Mrs. Feldman seemed to have reached a stopping point. She let go of the horse's mouth where she had been peeling back its lips to expose its teeth. "And of course, there's no need to look there if the horse is a gift," she said in conclusion. "Now, class, we have Mr. Mannie Raya here today with a special message from the Capital for you. You will not have instruction again till next Monday. I hope you will all consider working with horses in your future. They really are incredible creatures." She stroked the nose of the dark bay fondly, then nodded to Mannie as she left.

Mannie walked forward, eyes bright as he looked proudly down on Bjorn's fifteens. "Ah! My favorite class in all of Eden! I am thrilled to be the one to share with you this most exciting news!" He clapped his hands in front of his chest, rubbing them together.

Keigh and Tarin caught each other's eyes, raising their eyebrows in mutual curiosity. Any message direct from the Capital to them must be more interesting than the usual announcements of feasts or royal convoys.

"Well then," Mannie started, "you all have nearly completed your instruction on your fifteenth year. Soon you will undergo agoge! I assume you have all considered which practice you wish to pursue?"

Agoge was the four-year vocational apprenticeship that Eden's youth underwent between the ages of sixteen and twenty. Agoge tests were the examinations all fifteen-year-olds participated in at the end of their last year of instruction. The testing for each trade was different, administered by the guild master of the desired craft or those willing to take on an apprentice for the next four years. Only children of canes and ables entered agoge, as thrall teens were required to continue working for their family's betters.

The only two thralls in class, Keigh and Emerson, both deflated a bit sensing Mannie's special message wouldn't apply to them. Their peers, however, were nodding confidently back to Mannie, none more eagerly than Deacon, Tarin, and Conrad. They were the only three of the six boys who met the requirements to apprentice as canes that anyone expected to pursue life as a warrior of Eden. Kervyn was hopelessly out of shape and was poised to inherit his father's thriving trade selling goods from outside Eden. Theo had the fire to be a cane, he simply lacked the size and strength necessary to pass agoge as one. Last of the eligible boys was Beaudy, who, though he was relatively unknown, seemed too quiet and much too round to be interested in a life of conflict and physically demanding training.

"This message is for those who wish to agoge as canes...and, more specifically, only for those who pass their agoge duels." Mannie's eyes locked in on the three boys sitting together. "The king has declared that next year, the Refining shall take place."

The boys shared a brief questioning glance.

"A Refining Trial has not taken place in Eden for twenty years and you wonder why this affects you now?"

The boys shrugged, apparently too proud to outright admit they didn't know what Mannie was getting at.

"Well, while Refining Trials have only ever been for fully fledged and fully trained canes over the age of twenty, the king has declared that this year, because you are the class of the Consecrate, apprentices will be included in next fall's Selection Festival. Should the city elders nominate you, you will go to the Capital for the Refining Trials."

All three boys' jaws fell open, and to Keigh's surprise, so had his own. To be selected for the Refining was the greatest honor a citizen of Eden could receive from their elders, and to *win* the Refining was the greatest honor the king bestowed on any cane. It hadn't happened in Keigh's lifetime, but he had heard the stories. Stories of great canes, heroes of Eden from times long past, whose names would be remembered forever after winning the Refining.

Keigh couldn't help the jealousy that began to gnaw at him. His class, his friends, were going to be given a chance to do something of which he could only dream. Thralls could not attempt agoge as canes, and only canes were selected for the Refining. His gaze lingered on the now excited boys as they clapped each other on the back and shook each other in celebration.

"While the king has opened a way for you, it is up to you to be found worthy of the nomination," Mannie continued. "Your first step will be passing your duels and beginning agoge as canes. The Queen's Council has sent me here today to ensure that it is communicated to you clearly how important it is for you to prepare for your agoge duels. Should you fail at that, the elders will not consider you for the Refining. Within your class, kingdom-wide, are the sons of the Consecrate, and with them are the hopes of an heir worthy of Eden."

At this Tarin sat up a little straighter, puffing out his muscular chest. Deacon smirked and ran his fingers coolly through his jet-black hair. All eyes were on them now. The implication of the Refining now clear, even to them. This wasn't about sorting canes, promoting commanders, or honoring greatness, as Refinings were often thought to be. Eden wasn't in search of a new hero. The king was moving to name his heir.

"I expect nothing but great things from all of you," said Mannie, voice full of heartfelt affection for the kids he had watched grow up. His eyes settled on Deacon, Conrad, and Tarin as his expression became unflinching and serious. "But it is you from whom we will not just expect greatness, but demand it. To whom much is given, much is expected."

The boys' smiles retreated, replaced by looks of grave solemnity.

"Well then. Having delivered that message, I'm afraid my time in Bjorn has come to a close, as I must continue on to deliver this message to the rest of the fifteens in Eden. Practice hard, and I will be back to see you at your duels...and do try to stay out of trouble."

Mannie looked at Keigh, an amused grin on his lips, then strode through the seated students and disappeared around the end of the section fence, leaving the fifteens to themselves again.

A rush of bodies scrambled onto their feet and over to where Deacon and Tarin stood like kings, already looking down at their newest subjects as they fielded a cascade of excited questions.

Keigh didn't join the rush. He thought he was the only one not joining in on the excitement when he felt a hand gently touch his back.

It was Emerson Bardwick. The homely girl with frizzy hair and freckles looked up at him. "I believe you too, you know."

Keigh squinted at her, confused. He had forgotten all about the argument from before class. "Um, er...yeah. Thanks, Emerson. I appreciate that."

She smiled, briefly exposing her crooked yellow teeth before quickly pursing her lips back together in embarrassment. They stood there silently for a second, watching the group surrounding Deacon and Tarin.

"What will you agoge test as?" Keigh asked, turning to face Emerson.

"I'm a thrall like you, remember?"

"I—I'm sorry, Emerson. I wasn't thinking." There were so few thralls in Bjorn that Keigh often forgot he wasn't the only one living with restrictions on his future. "Well, if you *could* test...what would you want to do?"

"Well, um...my mother is a candlemaker, so I suppose I'll do that either way," she said, though Keigh thought he heard her say something about not being able to fail under her breath afterward.

"That's great, Emerson. Is that what you like doing?"

"I...It's..." She seemed to be searching for the right words. "My parents will be happy for the extra help," she submitted halfheartedly.

Unconvinced by her answer, Keigh asked again, "Is that what you *want* to do?"

"If...if I could choose, I suppose I would want to be a weaver." She blushed and pulled nervously at one of the frayed patches on her dress. "But I've never even used a loom. They would never take me."

Keigh didn't like hearing the sadness in her voice. This must be how Mannie felt when Keigh moped about his station in life.

"I think you would make a great weaver," he told her.

Emerson smiled again. "I...You really think so?...Thank you...What will you agoge as?" She winced, having made the same mistake as Keigh. "I mean, what would you do if they let you?" She sniffed, shuffling her feet. "Sorry," she added when Keigh didn't respond immediately.

Keigh looked back over to Tarin and Conrad, talking to each other now that the rest of their class had fallen into smaller groups and side conversations.

"*They*," Keigh said, glowering at the back of Deacon's head. "They will *let* me dig potatoes...so dig potatoes is what I'll do."

"Oh, I didn't mean...I'm sure you..." Emerson's voice trailed off as she shifted uncomfortably.

Sensing her regret at having brought up a sore subject, Keigh tacked on, "But I would like to agoge as a cane if I could."

"If you could what?" asked Misselli as she and Addy walked over. "What are you going to do, Keigh?"

"Nothing. I'm not doing anything. We were just talking about agoge and I told Emerson I would test to apprentice as a cane if I could."

Misselli gave him a sympathetic smile. "You would make a great cane, Keigh Anders...but I guess you'll just have to settle for staying at home, close to your best friend!" She jabbed him in the shoulder playfully, then immediately went wide-eyed, clearly remembering his wounds.

"What do you mean *if* you could? Why can't you agoge as a cane?" Addy asked, bewildered.

"I know I hide it well," Keigh said, gesturing to his clearly used clothing, dirt stains from his morning dig still on his pants. "But I'm a thrall, remember?"

"So? What's that have to do with anything?" Addy said, sounding impatient.

"*Thralls* don't test, Addy. *We*"—Keigh pointed to himself and Emerson—"We have to work at the family trade," he spat, hating the words he was being forced to say.

"Yes, thralls don't usually test, but there is nothing that says thralls *can't* test." Addy crossed her arms, apparently put off by being spoken to as if she didn't know something. Understandably so, too, since Addy did know most things about most things.

"What?" choked Keigh, giving her his undivided attention. "I was told—but I've never heard of one testing..."

71

"Have you never heard stories of Magog the mage? He was a thrall before he became a cane." Addy looked at Misselli and Emerson for confirmation.

"Sure, we've all heard the stories of Magog and his magic, but those are just tall tales meant to teach children life lessons!" Keigh argued.

"You don't believe Magog was real or you don't believe magic is real?" demanded Addy.

"I believe Magog *existed*. I just think stories of his abilities have been blown out of proportion for the sake of legend."

"What do you have to say about Orvyn's armor, then? It's proof magic is real!"

"Orvyn's armor?" Keigh laughed. "Oh, yeah, nothing will convince me quicker that magic is real than a set of armor lost to history. Easy to say things about objects nobody can test." He sighed. "Look—me and Misselli saw something unbelievable yesterday. I, myself, thought I saw magic, but after Braddock explained it to me, I know there was nothing magic about it."

"Orvyn's armor isn't lost." Addy simmered, still seemingly incensed at being doubted. "At least not all of it..."

"What do you mean?" Misselli asked.

"Orvyn's helmet is in Sentinel. Anyone can go see it. *Anyone...*" Her eyes bored into Keigh's. "...can see it's magic."

"Guess I'll believe it when *I* see it," he retorted. "Until then, I'm not staking my hopes on children's bedtime stories. It's not history. It's not proof."

"Fine!" Addy threw her hands in the air, exasperated. "Forget Magog, forget armor, and trust *me*. I've read the king's law multiple times, and there is nothing in there about thralls not being able to undergo agoge."

Keigh knew Addy wasn't lying. The thick glasses that were her token feature were well used. There wasn't a book in Bjorn she hadn't read at least twice—partly because there weren't very many books in Eden at all, but mostly because Addy loved to know everything she could, about anything she could.

"The only thing that might stop you is if your family's better objects to your apprenticeship." Addy's eyes narrowed as she stared angrily over at

Deacon, who was currently basking in the flirtatious advancements of Cecilia Giles. "But even that wouldn't keep you from testing—it would just possibly prevent you from moving forward to an apprenticeship. You don't have to tell your betters you plan to enter agoge duels. You only need to tell the guild master so they can set up a master to test you in that trade."

Keigh's heart was in his throat. Would he actually be allowed to test? A moment ago, he'd wanted to yell at Addy for trying to feed him false hope, but now...now he could hug her till his arms popped off! All these years he had trained with his bow so that he could provide meat for his family. He had spent countless mornings practicing with his crudely fashioned sparring swords on the now badly chipped and worn trunk of his sparring tree. He'd thought he needed to be prepared to defend his family from robbers or wild beasts, but never really believed that his skills might be accepted as his service to the king.

For the first time, he allowed himself to weigh the possibility. Could he actually become a cane?

"You're not actually considering this, are you, Keigh?" asked Misselli nervously.

"Yeah." He beamed at Addy, who smiled back up at him, her heavy glasses smushing her nose and bowing her ears. Hope welled up inside of him as it hadn't in years. The sun suddenly felt warmer, the sky bluer, the air crisper. "Yeah, I am." Keigh turned to Misselli and gave her a confident grin. "*I am going to be a cane!*"

CHAPTER 6

JUST ASKING

Over the next two weeks, the thrill that had filled Keigh's chest when Addy told him he could test to be a cane only grew. His fervor at the prospect of joining the king's warriors was a blaze inside him, fueling him with seemingly boundless energy and focus. So much so that the punishment his father had given him a week to complete was finished in just two long, grueling days, completing all the trenching by hand.

It had been a terribly agonizing task, as his wounds were still fresh and broke open each morning, spoiling his bandages with fresh blood. His usually gentle mother was noticeably flustered by this and lectured Keigh every opportunity she got: *"You will never heal if you keep insisting on working yourself like an ox!"* But Keigh did insist, and that insistence was what bothered his father most. Keigh had not shared with his parents, or anyone other than the girls from class, his intention to submit his name to Braddock for agoge testing as a cane. So, when he began completing his work with a newfound zeal, even his father questioned him.

Halfway into what would end up being a sixteen-hour day of trenching, his father had journeyed out to where Keigh was working. He found Keigh shirtless and shin-deep in mud, straddling the canal, the bandages that wrapped his torso black with dried blood and caked in dirt.

His father handed him a knapsack of dry food and a canteen of water. "You didn't come in for lunch again. Your mother is going to have my head if I don't get you to slow down."

Keigh accepted the knapsack and devoured the contents, not even bothering to wipe his mud-caked hands clean.

His father eyed him quizzically. "What's gotten into you, son? There's no need to delay your healing by slaving away like this."

Mouth full of partially chewed food, Keigh gave the answer he thought would placate his father most: "I just want to get this behind me. I feel terrible for how I spoke to Braddock and I feel like I should serve my punishment before I go and apologize to him."

"So be it, but you had better wash and boil your bandages thoroughly. We don't have any more cloth to spare in wrapping wounds you seem intent on keeping open." He shrugged and left Keigh to finish his labor.

His father had only barely accepted his answer then, so when Keigh began sparring the next day in the evening in addition to his normal morning routine, he wasn't surprised when his father came to him again.

"You worked out your penance for your words to Braddock, and now you're attacking that tree each night like you intend to fight him next. What need have you for training like this?" Owen's eyes narrowed critically, but the smile on his lips betrayed him. "In all my years of growing potatoes I have yet to have one attack me."

Sweating profusely, Keigh took one last hack at the tree before giving his father his full attention. "After fighting the stranger in the woods, I just think I should be better equipped to defend our home," he said, pausing to catch his breath. "And the man did know my name. He might not be the last to come looking for me."

All of this was true. He hadn't fully lied to his father, but it was the prospect of changing his station and becoming a cane that fueled him most.

"Am I some helpless lamb that I would let someone come after my son? I wasn't always a farmer, you know." Owen sighed. "You are safe here, Keigh. Now put that branch down and come inside before your sister has to go to bed. She misses you." Without waiting for a response, he lumbered back down to the little wood-plank house, its weathered thatch roof illuminated by the pink light of the setting sun.

Whether his father had accepted his answers or just conceded that Keigh's determination to practice was not worth arguing about, he questioned Keigh no further. For two weeks, Keigh spent nearly as much time carving himself new sparring swords from fresh-cut branches as he did actually sparring with the tree above his home. After breaking his tenth "sword" in three days, he adjusted to sparring only on air in his morning sessions. With no tree to swing at, he had only his imagination to fight. In those morning hours he slew scores of weapon-wielding warriors. He focused on staying light on his feet, dodging imagined spear thrusts and parrying the blows of invisible swords.

In addition to altering his routine, he also began to make his sparring swords from thicker, greener branches. They were bulky, heavy, and poorly balanced, but it was a better option than breaking dozens of thinner, lighter sticks. After a week of sparring with the heavier swords, his arm acclimated to the new weight. Now, Keigh found himself able to move with similar speed to what he had been doing before.

In the second week, he added practicing with his bow to his daybreak routine. Loosing a hundred shots each morning into a bale of straw, he fired from every position. He even tried shooting while running, but after firing two arrows clean over the bale and into the darkness of the early morning forest, he ceased that particular practice.

Also in the second week, Jessie took to joining him up by the tree. Sitting cross-legged in the dirt and watching Keigh with an awe only achievable by small children, she bobbed her head up, down, side to side, following every movement of Keigh's sword. Some nights she would grab the handle of an old broken sparring sword and try to mirror his movements, shouting with glee, "Who are we fighting now?"

No matter what enemy Keigh described to her, she stayed in the fight. Gritting what few teeth she had, she battered the air behind Keigh with all her might, spinning and swinging with such enthusiasm that she often lost her feet, sending her giggling and rolling in the dirt.

Jessie wasn't his only spectator. The garden wolves regularly stopped and observed what they thought must be a very peculiar sort of dance. Sitting and wagging their tails, tiny tongues hanging from their mouths, they would watch for a minute before trotting off into the woods in search of a meal.

Keigh was glad instruction days for the fifteens had virtually come to an end. In the past two weeks, there had only been two more days of instruction. One day, Mr. Popplardo, Kervyn's dad, had taught them how to properly order, arrange, and fill out a business ledger—a skill that, to no one's surprise, Addy excelled at, but one that Keigh doubted he would ever need. The other lesson had been taught by Beaudy's dad. A thin man, quite unlike his very un-thin son, he had shown the class some of the guiding principles of thatching a roof. That day, Conrad had to hold Keigh back from striking Deacon when Keigh overheard him telling Cecilia and Tarin that Beaudy was far too fat to be on anyone's roof.

Sadly, those two days of instruction were also the only two days he had been able to see Misselli. They usually spent time together in the evenings after their day's work had been completed, but with Keigh's new self-imposed sparring schedule, there had been no other opportunities. Perhaps it was for the best—the two days he had seen Misselli, she had been less pleasant than usual.

Keigh had thought she would be excited for him to test as a cane. They had talked about their dreams hundreds of times in their years of friendship, and Misselli had always affirmed his dream of becoming a cane, just as he had always supported her dream of inheriting her mother's bake shop and raising a family in Bjorn. But now that Keigh's dream had actually become attainable, Misselli had become a steady source of doubt, consistent as the drip of water from a leaky pail. She hadn't missed an opportunity to point out all the dangers of being a cane—and, to Keigh's greater chagrin, the high likelihood that a boy who had never even held a real sword could not pass a dueling test with a full-fledged cane. As unhelpful as it was, though, he thought he at least understood why she was doing it. If Keigh passed his agoge duels and began apprenticing as a cane, he would most likely no longer live with his family, and maybe not even in Bjorn.

The morning of the second Saturday after the attack in the woods, just two short weeks since Addy had given him hope of becoming a cane, Keigh awoke knowing he could not put off the thing he had been dreading any longer. Requests for agoge duels had to be submitted to guild masters before Monday. The last time he had spoken to Bjorn's guild master of canes, he had accused Braddock of not caring about him or his family. Today he would have to ask for Braddock's blessing to agoge as a cane.

Keigh got out of bed before the sun as he always did. He dressed in what he hoped were his most cane-worthy clothes, or at least the ones he hoped were the least likely to say "farmer." Quietly, he crept through the house, grabbing himself a biscuit for the road. Pausing at the front door, he laid his hand on the grizzled bear head before setting off at a trot down the dirt road.

Braddock's home was located on the far side of Bjorn on a flat plot of land along the King's River. It had been constructed from the trunk of a single massive cedar—so massive that Keigh was unsure how they had even gotten the trunk there, unless they had just felled the tree where it stood. He supposed a team of giant red bears could have moved it, but Braddock's bear, Mace, was the only one Keigh had ever seen around Bjorn.

He left the gravel road and approached Braddock's home on a narrow path through the long grass. As he got closer to the house, new details came into view. In the now bright sunlight of early morning, he saw that the exterior surfaces of the great log had been carved with images of various creatures of Eden: red bears, deer, elk, giant moose, birds, and flower hawks, all living underneath the canopy of a sprawling oak tree, whose branches spread out from its trunk at the center to the far ends of the log home. The top quarter of the house, or what would have been the roof of a normal building, was filled with the oak tree's branches. Thousands of intricate carved leaves and limbs filled the space till there was no wood left uncarved. Around the home's three forward-facing windows and single door were carved wide square frames filled with runes that Keigh couldn't decipher.

He slowed his walk. As he drew closer, the ground next to the path changed from the thick, dew-covered green grass of the river valley to black churned-up earth. But Braddock was no farmer, and this earth hadn't been tilled by a plow.

Keigh stumbled on a low spot in the path. He looked down to find himself standing in the giant paw print of a bear. From the back of the pad to the furthest claw mark, it was nearly as long as he was tall. For the first time, and probably too late, he questioned how wise it was to show up to the home of a red bear unannounced and unaccompanied by the bear's cane.

He looked around. Mace was nowhere to be seen. Breathing a sigh of relief, he sprinted the remaining fifty feet to the front door. He hoped that by coming to Braddock's so early he would have a good chance of finding him before his duties pulled him away from home.

He knocked on the hardwood front door and stepped back. Braddock was a trained warrior, and Keigh wasn't sure how he would react to a surprise visitor.

Two deep whumps and a huffing sound, like that of a massive set of bellows blowing, drew his eyes up to the roof. Mace, Braddock's giant, black-furred red bear, had evidently been lying down behind the house and had now stood up. Placing her forepaws on top of the roof, she craned her huge fluffy black head over the top to see who had woken her. Mace had four long white scars on her face, running from the top of her snout to the bottom of her lip, and one of her ears had been split down the middle. She had seen battle before—Keigh knew that without even having to look at her. Stories of Mace and Braddock's exploits were town favorites at festivals. She peered at Keigh with curious golden eyes the size of cymbals, then huffed again, blowing the hair back off of Keigh's face.

The door to the house burst open. Braddock bolted out, nearly knocking Keigh over as he glared daggers over the top of his home. "Down!" he shouted. "Down, Mace!"

The bear's huge eyes widened, like a small child who had just been caught doing something naughty. Mace reared her head back and silently dropped out of view.

Still looking at the empty space where the bear's massive head had just been, Braddock blustered, "Been with me twelve years now and she still thinks I won't notice when some grand behemoth of a bear throws her great muddy paws onto my roof!"

He was dressed in a gray wool tunic and leather sandals. His usual leather breastplate, sword belt, and iconic red cane cloak were missing. Shaking his head as if it would rid him of his frustration, the brawny veteran turned to Keigh and looked him up and down.

"Mr. Anders. Back on your feet, I see." Braddock jerked his head toward the open door. "Come in, then."

Keigh followed him inside and sat down in the wooden armchair offered him in front of a wide stone fireplace built into the wall. The embers of last night's fire still glowed inside. Keigh surveyed the great room. Lit by only the yellow light of its four windows, the room was plain with simple wood furniture and no decorations. Keigh knew well enough that the king paid his soldiers handsomely, yet Braddock's home was no more luxurious than his own. It was clear Bjorn's battle master valued function over form.

Braddock fetched three dry logs from the stack next to the fireplace and deposited them on the embers. Then, pulling up his own chair, he sat and faced Keigh.

"So, is this your way of showing me how easy it is to visit?" he asked, a wry smile on his lips.

The shame of his last words to Braddock washed over Keigh all over again. "Sir, I'm...I'm really sorry for accusing you of not caring about my family. My father reminded me that you've lived your whole life willing to sacrifice for the people of Eden. People like my family. I should never have spoken to you—or anyone—with such disrespect." Keigh stared into the fire, afraid to look at Braddock.

"Your father told you that?" Braddock asked.

Keigh nodded, still too ashamed to turn away from the fire.

"Look at me, Keigh."

He brought his eyes back to face Braddock, and to his surprise, didn't find him scowling.

"Thank you." Braddock paused. Leaning back in his chair, he placed the tips of his fingers together as he examined Keigh. "I am your elder and you owe me respect for that much alone," he said, then hesitated again. "There is a fire in you, Anders. That fire led you to fight a man in the woods when you could have easily fled, and it was that same fire that sparked your inappropriate outburst toward me, a friend—and I assure you, I am a friend. Only one whom you misunderstand."

The two of them sat in silence as Keigh waited for Braddock to continue.

"Look at the fire, Keigh." Braddock pointed to the now blazing logs. "Inside those stones, fire can burn hot and free, giving light and warmth to all who draw near…but if that fire were to burn outside the stones and ignite my furniture or my house, it becomes a danger that must be quenched." He gestured for Keigh to look at him again. "You let your fire burn outside the stones, Keigh. I trust your father quenched that blaze?"

"Yes, sir! I had to dredge the canals at the end of our fields by hand!" Keigh blurted, subconsciously touching the fresh new scars on his ribs. "It was… painful," he added, wincing at the memory of it. "It won't happen again." He lowered his eyes, ashamed to admit to the man who may one day be his commanding officer that he had needed to be punished like a child.

"Well then, I'll consider the matter resolved and behind us. Besides, I'm a bit old in my thinking. I would prefer to earn a person's trust and respect—a task that is admittedly hard to do when interactions are…infrequent." Braddock leaned forward again, placing his hands on his knees. "So, is your apology the sole reason for your visit today?"

It was a question, but Keigh had the suspicion the veteran knew more than he was letting on.

"I hope Mace didn't frighten you too bad," Braddock continued in a softer tone. "She looks dangerous, but I promise you she's no danger to you so long as you're no danger to others."

"She can sense that?"

"Indeed," said Braddock, looking to a back window obscured by the resting bear's black fur. "Better than any man, if you'd believe it."

"Huh..." Keigh, too, looked at the darkened window. He had so many questions, but they would have to wait. He had come here with a purpose; one he would not be distracted from. "Well, sir, I did want to apologize, and I'm sorry I hadn't done that sooner."

He really was sorry, seeing how Braddock had received his apology so graciously. He could have avoided two weeks of anxiety had he just come to the battle master immediately.

Feeling a bit more confident with the apology behind him, he continued, "Is it true, sir, that there are no laws forbidding thralls from being granted an agoge duel?"

He waited for Braddock to laugh at him, to crush his dream with a quick *"No!"*...but he didn't.

Braddock's eyes narrowed, his jaw moving like he was chewing on what to say next. "That *is* true. Though if it happens at all it must be very rare, as no cane I have ever served with grew up a thrall. Why do you ask?"

Keigh could tell by the way he asked that Braddock already knew the answer to that question. "You are Bjorn's guild master of canes. I wish to submit my name to agoge as a cane of Eden."

Braddock's keen expression remained unmoved. "What do your parents think of this?"

Blood rushed to Keigh's cheeks. "I...I haven't told them, sir," he admitted. "I suppose they expect me to continue growing potatoes and hunting for food."

"As noble a pursuit as any, no? To provide for one's family?" It wasn't a statement. Braddock sounded like he was actually asking.

So Keigh answered, "Yeah...I mean, sort of."

Braddock cocked his head. Keigh's mind raced to think of an explanation a cane would want to hear. His hopes of being granted agoge rested on Braddock's acceptance.

"I...I think serving the king is the most noble life an Edenite can live. And canes serve the king."

"Do you believe that in serving the needs of your family you provide no service to the king? Eden was established in the hope that its people would live in freedom. The people outside our boundaries are oppressed by their lord Draiden. Every day you live in Eden is a testament to the king's goodness. Living in the freedom he has won you honors him."

"But my family isn't really free, are we?" Keigh scowled at the fire, not believing Braddock of all people was lecturing him on being content with a quiet life of potato farming.

Braddock pursed his lips, inhaling deeply through his nostrils. "What people do to each other and the wicked ways we elevate ourselves over our neighbors are not a reflection of the king's will for his people."

"Then why doesn't he put a stop to it? My family have been thralls my whole life!" Keigh was trying to keep his head, but the fire inside him was getting dangerously close to spilling out again. He felt like they were just dancing around the inevitable *"No"* Braddock was sure to give his request.

Braddock shook his head. "Our king is not a tyrant, and the law that binds your family is council law, not king's law," he puffed. "The laws concerning debt were intended to prevent bloodshed amongst neighbors, but they have been weaponized by those who have no love for the king or his law, in order that they may garner power and position for themselves through the downfall of others." He spit the words out like so much sour milk. After a brief pause, he continued in a subdued tone, "Your parents made their choice, and so did Vicerous...I'm sorry you've had to live with the consequences."

Keigh felt like Braddock had just pulled a rug out from under him. *What does he mean, my parents made their choice?* Before he could ask, the elder continued.

"Do you know why thrall boys don't agoge to become canes?"

"Probably 'cause they don't know they're allowed to. I just found out two weeks ago when Addy told me."

Braddock rocked back in his chair and smiled a genuine smile for the first time since Keigh had arrived at his home. "Is that Eveleen Osmond's daughter?"

Keigh nodded.

"Did you know Mrs. Osmond received a large endowment from the town when her husband died? And that she spent nearly the whole thing buying Adelaide's glasses? That money could have fed them well for a year! Instead, the love of a mother decided it was better to give sight to her daughter. *That*"—Braddock clapped—"is how the king's people should use their freedom! To give, not to take..."

He paused again, clearly savoring the story he had just told.

"Thrall boys, besides being unaware of their rights to agoge testing, often don't test to be canes because testing can be perilous. No prospective apprentice has ever bested a cane in an agoge duel. Prospects merely hope to survive long enough to be found worthy of further training. Do you know what Tarin, Deacon, and Conrad have been doing every day since they could walk?"

Keigh shrugged.

"Training!" Braddock snapped. "With metal swords and heavy bows! They have been preparing for this moment their entire lives, and even so, they may only barely pass the test!" He paused to take a deep breath, and his face donned an expression of defeat. "Thrall boys have not the resources nor the time to devote to such pursuits. Thrall boys don't undergo agoge as canes because they don't stand a chance. The odds are stacked against them. So instead of embarrassing themselves by getting seriously hurt by a grown cane in front of the whole town, they just continue in their parents' trade." He sighed. "I'm sorry, son, but you're asking me to endorse your own defeat."

Keigh slumped back in his chair, watching particles of dust floating in the columns of light that pierced the room through the open windows. Had all his training been for nothing? For hours and hours he had practiced blocks, thrusts, parries, footwork, complex sequences of attack...and Braddock wasn't even going to let him try? Though perhaps Braddock was right, and he just wasn't ready to go head-to-head with a cane in armed combat. How could he be expected to pass when the boys who had had all the proper training with the right equipment weren't even likely to do so?

Maybe a potato farmer was all he was—all he would ever be. But...he had fought a man. Not only fought, but won!

No. This couldn't be where it ended.

"Sir, I want to try!" Keigh pleaded. "I have to try!"

Braddock's eyebrows lifted. "You would shame yourself in front of the entire town?"

"The greater shame would be in hiding from a fight just because the odds are stacked against me," he challenged.

"Got more Owen in you than I thought," Braddock mumbled to himself before answering Keigh. "Some would call that wisdom," he countered. "A man doesn't just need fire in his veins—he needs a discerning mind to tell him which battles to fight and which ones to avoid."

"Sir, listen. If I go the rest of my life knowing that I could have been a cane, but I chose to take the easy road, I couldn't live with myself." Keigh stood abruptly, nearly knocking over his chair. He locked eyes with Braddock, seeking any sign that he would budge. "Please, sir!"

He stood motionless, waiting, afraid anything more might tip Braddock in the wrong direction. The room was dead silent, yet the pounding of his heart was threatening to deafen him.

Braddock rose slowly from his chair. Taking a step toward Keigh, he reached out to grip him by the shoulders. "I think..." He paused. "I think we should see just how far your fire will carry you." He smiled, but his eyes remained pensive.

"So, I'm in? Seriously?" It was as if someone had thrown a bucket of pitch on the fire burning inside Keigh. Flames of excitement coursed through every cell in his body.

"Well, yes, I suppose so," chuckled Braddock. "Agoge duels will take place in three weeks. I should be able to find a cane willing to take on an apprentice in that time."

"Thank you! Thank you! I'll be ready! I promise!" exclaimed Keigh, struggling to contain his excitement.

Braddock gave a worried sigh. "You had better be. Vicerous will not be happy with me...nor your parents, I should think."

Who cares? Vicerous was never happy. He'd be just as mad if Keigh had asked for an extra mouthful of bread. Keigh was too excited to let the veteran's worries bring him down. He shook Braddock's hand vigorously. Shouting his thanks over his shoulder, he sprinted out the door.

Whump! Keigh ran straight into the side of a napping Mace, knocking him onto his butt. Apparently, she had gotten too warm in the sun on the back side of the house and moved herself to the front. Mace gave a muffled grunt, but didn't move.

"Whoops—sorry, Mace!" Keigh picked himself back up and dusted himself off before sprinting around the sleeping bear and back up the road to his house.

He had been given a chance.

And that was all he needed.

CHAPTER 7

PRICE OF ADMISSION

40-6-21

For the next three weeks, Keigh's life and thoughts were consumed with preparing to pass his agoge duel. He continued to train in the pre-dawn hours before his chores and the twilight hours after work and instruction, but even while at instruction or in the field, his mind was far off, envisioning himself dueling faceless canes, blocking blows, sidestepping thrusts, swinging and slicing at his nameless tester.

His distraction was so bad that Misselli had taken to trying to see how many pebbles and pieces of straw she could put in his hair before he noticed. Most days he left instruction with his head looking like a poor man's scarecrow, a sight that brought his friends no shortage of laughter. Keigh didn't care, though—nothing mattered more to him than passing his duel. He needed to be a cane. Being a potato farmer wasn't an option.

Misselli was the only person Keigh told about his conversation with Braddock. She had congratulated him, but he could tell she was nervous, a fact confirmed by her subtle suggestions that there was no shame in dropping out. One day she even made a surprisingly persuasive argument for farmers being the backbone of Eden, attempting to convince him that someday they would get the honor they deserved from everyone.

Even though he had only told Misselli, Keigh was pretty sure Braddock had told his father. On the third evening after he'd spoken to Braddock, his father had come out to the sparring tree and wordlessly deposited two big armfuls of fresh branches newly carved into sparring swords. He'd given Keigh a nod of understanding before trudging back down the hill to the house.

His father didn't keep the news to himself, however. His mother had begun fussing over him with renewed vigor, hugging him twice as long and twice as hard every time she saw him. She had also begun insisting Keigh eat seconds of everything at mealtime—a side effect he didn't mind so much, but one that caused his brothers great distress, since it meant less food for them to smuggle back to their room for nighttime snacking.

The only person in the house unaffected by the news seemed to be Jessie, who continued to spend her evenings gawking in wonder at Keigh as he attacked the old chinked-up sparring tree. She must have been seeing the imaginary enemies too, as she clapped and cheered anytime Keigh ducked or dodged an invisible attack. Some of the garden wolves even became so accustomed to her presence that they would lay across her lap and whine for belly scratches, which Jessie gladly gave them.

On the last day before the agoge duels, Keigh's class had instruction. He had not wanted to go, but at his parents' insistence, he attended. Mrs. Feldman had just finished a particularly monotonous two-hour lecture on proper fence maintenance when Keigh once again found himself shaking a mess of straw and pebbles out of his hair, to the delight of his classmates.

"I think I set a new personal record today!" Misselli bragged, smiling and wrinkling her nose at him. "Not sure why you have to shake it all out, though. I thought you looked nice like that."

"Don't worry, *Missy*, I never get all of it." He knew she hated when he called her *Missy*. "Last week, one of your pebbles fell into my soup while I was eating, and I nearly broke a tooth on it."

"Just trying to make you tough like me, friend!" She gave a squinty grin and flexed a bicep at Keigh, using her free hand to push the sausage-link-sized muscle up to twice its normal height. Despite her thin frame and beautiful appearance, Keigh knew Misselli was much tougher than she let on. Growing up, they had wrestled many times, and he had always been impressed with how scrappy she was. One time she had even beaten Keigh by forcing him to tap out when she had hooked a finger inside his mouth and threatened to rip it out. Keigh rubbed his cheek at the memory of it. She might be a dirty fighter, but she was a fighter nonetheless.

"Careful with that thing, Misselli! You'll poke someone's eye out!" Tarin laughed, making his way over to where they stood. The rest of their class followed in his wake like a school of perch after a worm on a hook.

"You're just jealous," said Misselli, giving Tarin a playful shove. "Can't stand the thought of a girl tougher than you!"

Cecilia gave Misselli an appalled look, as if to say, *Who would want that?*

Tarin shoved her back. "A thought I'll never have to think, since there are no girls tougher than me!"

Conrad laughed. "Ha! Go tell that to Mrs. Feldman. You nearly wet yourself when she snapped at you for talking out of turn today."

They laughed at Tarin as he glared daggers at his traitorous friend.

"Why are you scared of Mrs. Feldman?" asked Beaudy, his innocent question bringing about a fresh round of laughter.

"I'm not scared of her, *Beaudy*," scoffed Tarin, "but I was with Deacon when he shot one of her horses with a blunt-tipped practice arrow once. Deacon could be the future king, but Mrs. Feldman couldn't care less. She ran him down and beat his backside to burger with his own arrow! A woman like that shouldn't be crossed," he said, absentmindedly putting a hand to his own backside.

"You guys ready for your agoge duels tomorrow?" asked Kervyn, directing the question at Conrad and Tarin. Deacon had not come to a single instruction ever since Braddock had granted him a duel. "The town hasn't been this excited for a testing in our lifetime! Everyone's going to be there!"

"I'm ready," Tarin said. "I got paired with Braddock for the swordsmanship portion. I should be alright. Conrad is the one who should be worried. He's paired with Chogan Bald Head!"

"He'll be fine," shrugged Conrad. "I've sparred with him before. He's a good teacher."

"Yeah, he'll be fine, right up until he hears me chanting *Baldy* at him from the crowd!" Misselli laughed. "That oughta put him in a foul mood for ya."

Conrad's confidence visibly melted off his face. "You wouldn't do that to a cane, it's disrespectful."

"Better make it a good fight then, Conrad. I'll do anything to watch a good duel," she said, looking serious. The group laughed again, but Keigh knew it was no idle threat. Misselli was fully capable of kicking a hornet's nest and tossing it off on someone if she thought it might be funny.

"Ha, ha. Very funny. What are you entering agoge as? A jester?" Conrad poked back.

Misselli straightened herself indignantly. "Actually, I'm going to continue my mother's practice as a baker, so I won't be testing. I'm quite happy with the life I have…" She paused. "Even if some of us want to leave what they have for greener pastures elsewhere."

Even though her eyes never left Conrad, Keigh knew that last part was directed solely at him.

"Yeesh, Misselli, tell us all how you really feel," chortled Tarin, clearly sensing the need to ease the tension. "We'll still be around. I wouldn't leave Bjorn forever, not as long as you're still here."

Misselli blushed. It was no secret that Tarin fancied her, as he hinted at it regularly in small flirtations. She handled them alright, but they always made Keigh feel uncomfortable. He wasn't sure he liked his best friends flirting, albeit one-sided as it was.

He changed the topic. "Do you guys know who Deacon got paired with?"

"My dad said he heard Vicerous asked to test him, but Braddock wouldn't hear it," said Kervyn, pausing just long enough to be sure he had everyone's attention. There were few things he enjoyed more than knowing the latest gossip, especially if he was the only one to know it. "Said the integrity of the whole test would be compromised if he let Deacon be tested by his own father. I guess Vicerous was pretty furious about it too. Pulled Deacon from instruction and started making him train like mad." Kervyn shook his head and patted his own overly round tummy, as if the most concerning part of his news was the idea that Vicerous Wulf could force someone to exercise.

"There's plenty enough canes in Eden that enjoy testing kids in agoge duels," Tarin said. "It's always kind of a massacre, isn't it? Canes get to show off their skill and us young bucks just have to show enough competency to pass. I'm sure Braddock will have no problem finding a cane to test Deacon. Not exactly a secret that he's one of the Consecrate, is it?" He puffed his chest out slightly, as if to emphasize that he too was included in that most important group.

"I know I would sign up to beat up on him," said Keigh, a smile curling his lips as he relished the idea.

"Ah, but alas, you can't, my thrall friend." Tarin threw an arm around Keigh in mock condolence, patting him on the chest with his free hand. "It wouldn't end well for you anyway, bud. I've sparred with Deacon and he's really quite good. People say his father is the most skilled swordsman in all of Eden."

"Not better than Braddock!" Theo contended.

Tarin shrugged. "Braddock is the more accomplished and decorated cane, but on pure swordsmanship…Vicerous Wulf has no equal."

Deacon has trained his whole life with the most skilled swordsman in Eden and his own father is nervous he won't pass his duel, Keigh thought. *How am I supposed to survive tomorrow?*

He talked a bit longer with his friends, promising to see them all tomorrow at the duels, before setting off for home with Misselli. Along the way, Misselli made one final attempt to get him to back out of his duel, but when he was unyielding, she changed the subject, asking Keigh instead if she could bake him something special for tomorrow morning.

Keigh walked her all the way to her home as usual. They said their goodbyes and she promised to be there tomorrow, cheering him on. He left her standing by the weathered wood gate and set out on the familiar dirt trail the two of them had forged over their many years of friendship.

Halfway home, he stopped. The tall late-spring grasses, in greens and yellows, bent and bowed in unison as a gentle breeze pushed them in waves. Copious amounts of balsamroot flowers, still in bloom, had turned their bright faces, rimmed in long canary-yellow petals, toward the setting sun. The amber light of a dying day set the whole valley on fire with warm color.

"Keigh." He heard the faint sound of his name interwoven in the rustle of the grass. "Keigh!" The breeze carried it to him, this time stronger. "Keigh! Wait!" He turned and looked back down the trail.

Misselli's silvery-blonde hair came into view, bobbing as she ran toward him. Her simple driftwood-colored dress bunched up in her hands as she sprinted after him.

Something's wrong, Keigh thought, dashing back to meet her.

"What's happened?" he asked urgently as they reached each other. He looked past her, hoping to locate the source of her panic.

Misselli bent over. Resting her hands on her knees, her chest and back heaved as she struggled to catch her breath. "Wha—what are you...What are you going to do?"

"What's happened, Misselli?" Keigh asked frantically. "Is everything okay?"

She lifted her head, her sky-blue eyes searching his. "What are you going to do, Keigh?"

"About what?" he asked. Her question confused him.

"When you pass your test tomorrow! What are you going to do? What happens next?" she asked again, pleading for an answer.

"I, uh...Train as a cane, I guess." He shrugged, still confused. "That's *if* I pass...and the odds of that are pretty low, by the sounds of it."

"Don't be stupid, Keigh! You're going to pass! You'll be great—you're great at everything you do..." She trailed off. "There aren't many canes in Bjorn," she added sullenly.

Realization dawned on him. *She doesn't want me to leave!*

"Even if I have to leave Bjorn for my training, I'll still come back. We'll still see each other," he said, hoping to ease her fears.

"See each other?" she snapped. "How many times have you left Bjorn in your life?"

The truth was...never. Not once in his whole boring life had he ventured outside of Bjorn and its surrounding farms and forests.

"You expect me to believe Keigh Anders is going to start traveling and taking vacations now? Now that he's finally rid of us and made a name for himself? Face it, Keigh...once you leave, you'll never come back." Her voice quivered, her eyes now glistening with tears unfallen.

How could she do this to him? Right now? Tonight, of all nights! She should be happy for him, not guilting him into a life of digging in the dirt. He was sick and tired of people expecting him to stay put.

"So what? You want me to stay? Just keep my nose in the dirt where I belong?"

Misselli looked taken aback. "What? No! You know that's not true!" She blinked, releasing lines of tears down her face.

"Then what is it?" he barked. "What's so wrong about me doing something with my life?"

"Nothing—"

"Then why can't you be happy for me?" he shouted, cutting her off. "I thought at least *you* would be happy for me! I thought at least *you* would wish me luck..."

They stood there, looking at each other, for what seemed like forever. Keigh fuming. Misselli choking back sobs and shedding silent tears.

Misselli wiped her nose on the back of her hand and swallowed hard. "Good luck, Keigh Anders."

Red-hot shame flushed over him. "Misselli...you know I—"

"Maybe *you* wouldn't notice if you lost your best friend, but *I*...*I* couldn't bear it." Fresh tears began filling her eyes.

"You'll always be my best friend, Misselli! Nothing will change that."

"It already has. Ever since Addy told you that you could test as a cane, you've disappeared! You didn't even have to leave Bjorn to leave me!" Misselli's voice cracked as a mixture of anger and sadness poured out of her. "All you do now is train. All you think about is fighting. For five weeks now we've hardly even talked! At first I thought you just needed space after what happened in the woods, but the longer I've watched, the more I've realized—you aren't hurt!" Her face hardened. "You're obsessed, Keigh. Obsessed with becoming someone else."

"Well, what if I don't like who I am?"

"Well, what if I *do*?"

They each stood their ground. The breeze gentle as it blew across their hard expressions.

"You wouldn't understand," Keigh said. "You're not a thrall. I'm nothing! My family is nothing! Becoming a cane is the first real chance, and maybe the only chance, I'll ever have at being *something*."

Misselli dried her face with the front of her dress. "I see."

"What? Admit it! There's nothing here for me!" he said, hating how pathetic he sounded.

They paused again, nothing but the sound of field crickets and the rustle of grass between them. Then Misselli slowly, silently walked toward him until she was standing only a handbreadth away. They stood there like that for another long minute: Misselli facing his chest as he looked down at the top of her head, neither one of them sure of what to say next. Then she leaned into him, embracing him gently.

Before Keigh could react or hug her back, she pulled herself away.

"You're something to me, Keigh," she said softly. "And I'm here...and I'll still be here, whenever you decide that I'm more than nothing to you."

Her words cut like knives, straight to his heart. The pain of her accusation left him speechless.

Maybe she got tired of waiting, or maybe she was afraid of what he might say next, but when he didn't respond, she placed her hands on top of his shoulders. Pushing herself up on her tiptoes, she brushed his cheek with a kiss as soft as flower petals and whispered in his ear, "Good luck tomorrow." She lowered herself back down and withdrew with two slow steps backward. "Tomorrow, people will begin to see in you what I've always known."

"What's that?"

Misselli smiled sorrowfully. "Goodnight, Keigh," she said, then turned and walked away.

He stood there, cemented to the ground where she had left him, watching her go—not sure whether to run her down or let her leave, whether to apologize or explain himself. She was gone before he had gotten any closer to deciding.

His mind remained fixed on Misselli for the rest of the evening. It was the first time in weeks he had spent more than a moment thinking of anything but his impending duels.

Would winning his duel really mean losing her?

CHAPTER 8

DUEL DAY

42-14-28

The next morning, Keigh awoke at his usual hour. What was unusual was the sound of voices coming from the great room. His dad, typically the only other person in the house to wake as early as Keigh, was as quiet as he was and rarely lingered inside, not when there was work to be done outside. Keigh quickly slipped on a tunic and made his way down the hall to investigate.

Still dark outside, the great room was warmly lit with a dozen candles, and there, sitting at the dining table, was his whole family and Mannie.

Jessie bounced up from her seat on the worn wooden bench and raced across the room to wrap herself around Keigh's legs. "Brother!"

"Morning, sis. What's all this about?" Keigh asked the smiling faces at the table.

"Just thought you'd like your favorite breakfast," his mother said sweetly, before adding a far less sweet, "while you still have teeth to chew it."

"Now, now, Sabriya. That's our son, remember? And if he's got any of your fight in him, it'll be the other guy's teeth in the dirt today! Come, son. Sit down and eat something." His father patted the open space on the bench between himself and Mannie.

Keigh waddled over to the table, Jessie giggling, her arms still tied around his legs. He pried her off and plopped down next to his father.

"Bran muffins with raisins." His mother set a plate of hot muffins in front of him. "And Mannie has generously brought us some butter."

"Got to fuel like a champion if you're going to fight like a champion." Mannie winked at Keigh. "Makes all your internals work smooth as butter! That's where the saying comes from, you know." He tapped Keigh's knee with the back of his hand and gave a slight flick of his head toward Keigh's mother, who was rolling her eyes at them.

"So, when were you going to tell us?" asked Jobey. His twin brothers smirked at him from across the table.

"I didn't really tell anyone." Keigh's thoughts instantly returned to Misselli, the one person he had told. He plucked one of the hot muffins off the plate in front of him. "Plus, I could tell Mom and Dad knew, so I figured they would tell you."

"What! When did you know?" Jotham hollered, redirecting the twins' collective indignation toward their parents.

"And why didn't you tell us we could agoge as canes?" Jobey protested.

"If I thought they would let you two lumps test using a fork and spoon as weapons, I would have had Braddock sign you up the day you turned fifteen," Owen said coolly.

Jotham and Jobey glowered back at their laughing family, mouths too full of muffin to respond.

Mannie set a hand on Keigh's shoulder. "You nervous, bud?"

Keigh's mouth was also full of muffin. He gave a slight nod and shrugged.

"Don't be." Mannie's face softened, looking like a proud older brother. "You've got excellent genes and you've been raised by the best."

Keigh's parents seemed uncomfortable with the flattery but gave Mannie gracious smiles regardless.

"Thanks," said Keigh, not really confident good genes and nice parents were what he was going to need today. "Will you all be coming to watch?"

he asked. He had been so aware of the large number of people coming to spectate that he had given little thought to whether *his* people would be there.

"Yes, son, we wouldn't miss it," his mother said, setting another muffin on his plate.

"Even Jessie?"

Jessie tore her eyes off Keigh and looked frantically at their mother, as if she hadn't even considered the possibility that they might not take her to town with them.

"Yes, even Jessie." Their father ruffled Jessie's hair with a strong hand and pulled her in close to his side, squeezing her in a one-armed hug. "You'd just better keep your feet today! I'm afraid if you get knocked down, your tester might find himself having to fight two Anders."

"Win or lose, we are all in your corner," Mannie told Keigh reassuringly. "Good luck today, Keigh. I will be there to cheer you on, but for now, I must be going. There is news from the Capital that I must deliver to Cato before we can partake in the day's festivities. I will see you all shortly."

With that he cleared his plate from the table, thanked Keigh's parents, waved goodbye, and walked out into the soft glow of dawn.

Keigh ate another two muffins while his siblings grilled him about the day, from his preparation to what he thought his own chances of passing were. Finishing his breakfast, he thanked his parents for the food and went back to his room to get dressed.

Today he needed to be light and fast. He considered wearing a tunic like the canes did, but he didn't like the idea of fighting with his legs uncovered, and even though his leather sandals were his lightest option, he didn't like the idea of getting his feet smashed either. In the end he opted for the buckskin pants and light leather boots that he always wore hunting. He looked through a few shirts before pulling out the soft cotton one. It was shredded and torn on one side where the stranger had attempted to stab him, the stain of his blood now burgundy after washing, coloring one whole side of the shirt beneath the armpit.

It had been five weeks since the man had attacked Keigh and Misselli. He still thought about the encounter daily, while the others who knew about it seemed to have forgotten it entirely. Whether they thought the idea of someone being sent to kill him was too unbelievable or just too uncomfortable, nobody but Misselli had brought it up to him again. He resolved to ask Braddock for an update the next time he saw him.

Keigh slipped the damaged and stained cotton shirt over his head. His mother would surely be embarrassed by his choice, but the shirt gave him an odd confidence. Just seeing it reminded him that he had fought and won before...that he could fight and win again.

Keigh made his way back out to the great room, where he patiently fielded his mother's objections to his shirt. To his relief, his father seconded his stance and his mother begrudgingly relented. *One fight won,* he thought as he scampered out of the house and retrieved his bow and arrows from the shed.

Mrs. Schaffer gave him a nasty look, like she did every time she saw her old tail feathers sticking out of his quiver. He gave the angry bird a wide berth. *And one fight avoided,* he thought, making his way back across the dew-covered yard to the front door. The wooden bear head was warm to the touch from the morning sun. He rested his palm on it before opening the door.

Win or lose, I'll be back.

"Are you all coming to town with me? Or are you coming down later?" Keigh shouted into the house. "The bow skills are being tested first."

"No, you run on ahead," his father's voice called back. "Your mother is fixing up Jessie's hair and I don't want your brothers lurking around the bake shops any longer than they have to."

Keigh called out his goodbyes and set off down the dirt road to town on his own, carrying only his bow and quiver.

At the front gate to Bjorn sat Mace, staring at one of the massive bears carved into the totem poles that framed the town's entrance. She looked as though she thought it may in fact be a real bear, just pretending to be a wooden pole. Around Mace, a crowd of people stood gawking at her. Keigh didn't blame them. No matter how many times he saw Mace, he always marveled at her. She never caused trouble and was treated by most like the town mascot, but Keigh knew she was much more than an overgrown puppy or novelty. The stories of her and Braddock's career were not fantasy; they were real. And if the stories were real, then Mace was not an animal to be trifled with.

Kervyn had been right: people were extra excited about this year's agoge duels. Even at this early hour, a crowd of people was spilling out of Bjorn's front gate. Men and women greeted each other, jovially catching up with news of their families and retelling favorite stories of previous years' duels.

Keigh made his way through the gate, slipping between groups of people. The townsfolk seemed to notice him more than usual today. Usually, he felt invisible among the older ables and canes, but not today. People liked to have the inside scoop on the duels before they started, and the thrall boy from up the hill, carrying a bow and arrows into town, was certainly a scoop.

All of main street's merchants and shops were already conducting business and people were filing in and out of their open doors. As Keigh looked up the street, he spotted Misselli standing in front of her mother's bakery, her blonde hair woven into a single braid that extended halfway down her back. She craned her head, attempting to look over and around people. Keigh was sure she was looking for him.

Not wanting to risk another emotional conversation that would distract him from the task at hand, he slipped down an alleyway and started up the deserted corridor at the rear of the buildings. This would get him most of the way to the community grounds unseen. He strode quickly up the alleyway as far as he could go, then, navigating a slight jaunt in his path, he rounded the corner—and found two people pressed against the wall in the dark between the buildings.

Cecilia and Deacon were wrapped around each other like a couple of eels. At the sound of Keigh's footsteps, they pulled their faces apart. Cecilia pursed her lips as she took a step back from Deacon, combing her long auburn hair straight with her fingers where Deacon's had tangled it. Deacon glared at him.

"Kervyn told us you'd been training extra hard, but I didn't know this was what he meant," Keigh scoffed.

"Deacon doesn't need extra training! He's the best of his age!" Cecilia gushed. She moved to kiss Deacon's cheek, but Deacon shoved her away, his eyes still boring into Keigh.

"You can't fault Cecilia for recognizing a winner, Anders. You're just jealous 'cause you know that no self-respecting female would ever be caught dead kissing a thrall!"

"If Cecilia is your idea of a self-respecting female, then I'm glad for it."

Cecilia sniffed her displeasure at Keigh and looked to Deacon to defend her.

"Wait a second, Anders..." Deacon had just noticed Keigh's bow and quiver. "Is someone playing with you?" His lips spread into a smirk. "Aww, Anders! Did you think you were included when Mannie said the boys in our class could agoge as canes?" He laughed. "No, no, no, Keigh. You see, he meant boys with standing...boys who are actually worth something."

"Guess you must not have heard him properly yourself," Keigh said. "Braddock has granted me a duel and I'm here to test."

Deacon's confident demeanor faltered, but only slightly. "Thralls don't agoge. They're bound to their family's debt."

Now Keigh was smirking. "See, Deacon, I thought that too—but guess what I found out? There is no law preventing me from testing. Only entitled prats like you, thinking they run the world."

"My father will never allow it!"

"Good! You two can cry about it together. I was worried you were going to have to sulk alone."

"Laugh all you want, Anders." Deacon straightened his black cloak and smoothed his raven hair with a pass of his hand. "Even if you are testing today, they won't be testing us to see how fast we can dig a potato. You're going to have to actually fight with your hands. Your smart mouth won't save you!"

He gave Keigh one last scowl, then turned and shoved his way past Cecilia, disappearing around the corner. Cecilia gave Keigh a disgusted shake of her head before chasing after him.

Those two deserve each other, Keigh thought as he watched them leave.

He finished making his way up to the community grounds using the back alleys. Popping out of the dark gap between the buildings and into the bright sunlight, he studied the grounds. The wood slat fencing that usually sectioned off the large expanse into smaller parcels for classes had been taken down. Rows of wooden benches surrounded the area on three sides. Some of the benches already had eager townsfolk sitting on them so as not to miss out on getting a good seat for the day's events. On the fourth side, at the far end of the grounds, a large, linen-wrapped straw archery target had been placed. A tall, slender man with pointed nose, who looked quite like an arrow himself, stood in front of the target, meticulously painting a series of perfectly circular rings around a bright red bullseye the size of a fist.

Keigh saw Braddock with a small group of men standing to the side, pointing at the gravel, apparently discussing the ground conditions where the duels would take place. Their red cloaks gave the men away as canes.

Keigh strode across the grounds toward the men. As he got closer, he recognized one of them as Chogan Bald Head. Chogan was a lean and muscular man with russet-brown skin and dark eyes. Keigh's father had told him once that Chogan was descended from people who had inhabited the land since the dawn of history. Ironically, Chogan Bald Head wasn't bald at all; in fact, he may have been the least bald man in Bjorn. His dark gray hair, braided and beaded, extended past the small of his back.

On Braddock's other side stood Cecilia and Kervyn's fathers, Victor Giles and Crispin Popplardo, as well as one cane Keigh didn't recognize. As he approached the men, Braddock waved him over to join them.

"Good! You brought your own bow. You'll shoot best with one you're accustomed to. Here, let's take a look at it." Braddock extended a hand.

Keigh handed him the bow and remained silent while the men assessed it.

"Men, this is Keigh Anders, Owen's son," Braddock introduced him. "He will be participating in today's agoge duels. Keigh, I believe you already know Mr. Popplardo and Mr. Giles? They have children your age, if I'm not mistaken."

Victor Giles raised his eyebrows in a mild look of surprise and extended his hand to shake Keigh's. "Owen's son, testing to be a cane." He shook his head. "Hope you can finish what your father started." He turned back to the men. "You know, I always maintained that Owen would have made a great cane. Strong as a bull, he was."

What exactly did my father start? Keigh wondered.

"You know being a cane isn't all about strength, Victor." Crispin Popplardo good-naturedly patted the belly spilling out over his belt. "I always got by on my cunning!" he added, tapping a finger to his temple.

Crispin Popplardo was retired from active service as a cane, like Braddock, but cane was a status a person kept for life, and even though he was now a successful merchant, he still wore the gray tunic, sword belt, and red cloak to festivals and official town functions.

Chogan laughed. "You may be a bit rounder now, but I still remember a Crispin Popplardo the women used to throw themselves at!"

"Oh, they still do," laughed Mr. Popplardo.

"Best not let your wife hear you say that," said Victor out the side of his mouth.

"Don't you men worry about me. While the ladies may have eyes for big Pops, he only has eyes for one woman!"

Seemingly embarrassed with the direction the conversation had turned, Braddock continued with introductions. "Keigh, this is Chogan Bald Head. He will be the one testing Conrad today."

Keigh shook Chogan's hand.

"And this is Zale Woodman." Braddock motioned to the man Keigh hadn't recognized. "He will be testing you."

They shook hands and evaluated each other. Zale had straight, bright orange hair, with light skin and freckles covering his arms. He was built strong and thick like Braddock.

Zale reached out to Braddock for Keigh's bow. He drew it back, flexing the bow as easily as Keigh might flex a willow cane. Then, holding it close to his face, he ran his eyes down the length of it before handing it back to Keigh.

"This is a fine bow. A nice hybrid," he said. His voice was smooth, lacking the rasp of the other men's. "Bit longer than my short bow, but it's got a nice pull to it. Maple core and bison horn?" he asked, looking over the bow at Keigh.

"Uh...I don't—I'm not sure." Keigh had never thought about what his bow was made from.

"Yew and mountain goat, if I remember correctly. The sinew and leather handle wrap are both bison," said Mr. Popplardo, eying the bow suspiciously. "Sold one near identical to this, few years back." He held out a hand for the weapon and went from eyeing the bow to eyeing Keigh. "But there is no way this is that bow. Just from the same tribe, I imagine. They reside just southeast of Eden. Their bows are excellent! Wouldn't sell them if they weren't! Thought I was the only merchant who carried them." He shrugged and handed the bow back to Keigh.

"And your blade?" Zale proffered his hand for Keigh to hand him his sword.

"I...I don't have one, sir." Keigh could feel the blood flooding to his face. His family was too poor to have bought him a sword and he was too proud to ask for one from someone else.

"No sword?" Zale scoffed. The men looked alarmed. "What on earth have you been practicing with?"

"I've been carving my own sparring swords from branches, sir," said Keigh, unable to look him in the eye.

The men looked at him like he was a fish that had just decided to go for a walk on land.

Braddock was the first to recover himself. "I have an extra," he offered. "It used to be my primary blade, but it's still in good shape. It will serve you well. I'm afraid you will have to wait until I have an opportunity to go and retrieve it, though." He gave Keigh a sympathetic look. "Blast! I don't know why I assumed Owen would have given you his sword."

"It's okay. Our family has never had a sword," said Keigh, still wondering why these men kept speaking about his family as if they were canes and not thralls.

The men looked at each other, confused, as if the idea of a family without a sword were unheard of.

"I'm sorry, Keigh," Braddock said. "I should have made sure you were equipped for this."

This was what Keigh had feared. This was why he had rushed through town to find Braddock. He had hoped to be able to acclimate himself to the feel of a metal blade in the hours before his duel, but now it looked as though the first time he would ever hold a steel blade would be minutes, if not seconds, before he had to wield it in combat.

"It's not your fault. I'll be fine," Keigh said, trying to convince himself as much as the men. "It was a privilege meeting you." He nodded to each in turn. "I'm going to go try and find Tarin before we start."

The men wished him luck, and Keigh darted back toward the main street. He found Tarin a few hundred feet down from the grounds. Tarin, Deacon, and Conrad were each surrounded by their own individual clusters of people pushing their way forward to shake their hands and wish them luck. Not wanting to be a part of the fray, Keigh stood back and watched as his classmates, each looking like a proud robin with chests puffed out, tried to decide which of their wide-mouthed chicks to feed next.

Before long, Theo and Beaudy walked by on their way to the grounds. Keigh found their friendship endlessly amusing. Theo, short, thin, quick, and dark-skinned, was fiery and loved to debate every topic under the sun. Beaudy, tall, fat, slow, and fair-skinned, was as docile and agreeable as the overstuffed teddy bear he resembled.

"Hey, Keigh! Excited to watch the duels?" Beaudy asked.

"Uh, yeah. Hey, guys," Keigh greeted his friends, still intent on speaking to Tarin.

Theo looked at the bow in Keigh's hand and followed Keigh's gaze back to the boys surrounded by people. "If I didn't know better, I would say Keigh looks like he's about to assassinate Deacon," he laughed.

"Keigh wouldn't kill Deacon…would you, Keigh?" Beaudy asked, not sounding totally sure of himself.

Theo pinched the bridge of his nose and closed his eyes as if praying for patience. "No, Beaudy, he wouldn't," he said, exasperated. "I am curious, though…Why did you bring your bow, Keigh? Morning hunt? Another tangle with a stranger in the woods?" He winked.

"Well, actually…I'm testing today." Keigh smiled weakly, unsure of how they would react.

"No you're not!" exclaimed Theo.

"No, Theo, he is. Didn't you just hear him tell us so?"

Theo just shook his head, not even looking at Beaudy. "How? Yeesh, you've got guts going to Braddock and asking him to let a poor farm kid play with the big boys!"

Keigh shrugged. "He wasn't too keen on it, but he's letting me try. I think he feels bad for me," he admitted to himself as much as them.

"Okay then!" Theo clapped a hand on Keigh's shoulder. "Beaudy and I were gonna cheer for Tarin, since he's the least pompous of our highbred friends…"

He cast a glance of mild contempt toward their classmates. Conrad and Tarin were now pretending to knight a row of excited children while Deacon fielded the attention of their mothers. Keigh couldn't help but laugh at the miserable look on Cecilia's face as she watched Deacon, looking like a dog who'd just had her bone stolen.

"…but now we've got one of us to cheer for!" said Theo, bringing his eyes back to Keigh. "Mind if I tell the others? Or is this some sort of secret?"

"Go ahead. I don't mind. Misselli already knows, but that's about it."

"I'm sure she does," Theo said with a wry smile. "Suppose the odds of her not knowing what you're up to, or the other way around, are about the same as the odds of Beaudy not finishing his dinner."

"Always gotta finish!" Beaudy said. "Can't waste food. Not when there's people starvin'."

"Absolutely, bud." Theo gave Beaudy an understanding pat on the tummy, then shot Keigh a look as if to say, *See my point?* Then his eyes flicked over Keigh's shoulder, and he grinned. "We should get going. Good luck out there!"

"Why we gotta go? Misselli just got here!" Beaudy protested.

Theo dragged the giant boy off. Beaudy waving his goodbye, a look of longing on his face as they disappeared into the crowd.

"Boo!" said Misselli, poking her head over Keigh's shoulder.

Keigh's heart leapt into his throat and he turned around to see his friend smiling sweetly at him, holding out a small canvas bread bag.

"Mom let me have enough sugar to make you a small loaf of the pumpkin bread you like."

"Uh...thanks," Keigh said awkwardly. How could she be so normal? She was acting as if last night's argument never happened! *Girls,* he thought. But it didn't matter—he was happy she didn't seem to want to bring it up again. He took the small bag from her hands and nodded appreciatively. " And uh, thank your mom for me too."

Misselli clasped her hands behind her back, rocking heel to toe. "So...are you excited?"

Was this a trap? Yesterday's blowup had started with an innocent question too. If he said yes, would she be mad that he was eager to move on? If he said no, would she beg him to drop out?

"I...I'm not sure," he said truthfully, and to his relief, she seemed to accept the answer.

"Makes sense." She paused, swaying a bit where she stood. When Keigh didn't respond, she added, "I'm excited for you."

"Seriously?" That was not what he had expected her to say. "Why?"

"I meant everything I said last night, Keigh. But as much as I don't want things to change, I do..." She winced slightly, as though each word were costing her precious coin to say. "I *do* want you to be happy, and I hope you get it—happiness, that is—wherever you find it."

Keigh's mind raced. What was he supposed to say to that? A battle erupted in his chest like two wild animals fighting to the death. On one side, deep love and appreciation for his best friend was welling up inside him, but on the other, he was furious that she was making him question the path he had chosen to pursue.

In the end, neither animal won, and he sputtered incoherently, "I, uh—you...I'm not—this is—it's not—"

Misselli grinned and cut off his stammering. "I never did hang out with you for your silver tongue. Just be glad you won't be asked to duel anyone with words today." She punched him airily in the chest. "Do you know who you'll be facing yet?"

"Uh, yeah. A cane named Zale Woodman. He's nice—"

"He's nice?" she scoffed, cutting him off. "Here I was concerned this guy was going to try to chop your head off, but now I'm concerned the two of you are gonna run off and become best friends!"

Keigh chuckled. "No, there's no chance of that happening."

They stood there, just smiling at each other for a minute.

"I...um...I should get up to the grounds." Keigh pointed after the mass of people filing their way toward the town center. "The archery testing will be starting soon, and I want to move around a bit before things get going... Thanks, Misselli."

Unsure of what to do next, he stepped forward and gave her a quick side hug, holding the loaf and bow in his free hand.

"See you up there?" he asked as he backpedaled his way toward the testing grounds.

Misselli didn't say a word. She just nodded, her playful grin now an understanding smile.

CHAPTER 9

A HAND UP

23-40-29

As Keigh walked toward what he hoped wouldn't be his death, he found himself alongside Tarin and Conrad. The two had managed to detach themselves from the throng of admirers and well-wishers and were also making their way up to the grounds.

"What's with the bow, bud? Morning hunt?" Tarin asked, throwing a brawny arm around Keigh's neck.

"No, actually." Keigh winced as Tarin squeezed his neck with a flex of his bicep. "I'm testing today too."

Tarin released him and stopped in the street to look at Keigh. After a second, he nodded. "Good. Good for you, Keigh. I'm proud of you, man."

Conrad's only response was to furrow his brow and shake his head as if to say, *It's your funeral.*

Tarin threw his arm back around Keigh's neck and they walked the rest of the distance to the grounds together; the whole way Tarin telling Keigh and Conrad all about strategy and poise in a voice loud enough for all the people on the road to hear. When they got to the grounds, they wished each other luck, then split up to get themselves ready for the task ahead.

Keigh made his way to a corner where he could set up and stretch without having to be out in the center where Tarin, Conrad, and Deacon had placed themselves on display. As he stretched, the benches filled with people laughing and talking excitedly. Many pantomimed shooting bows or swinging swords. Occasionally he would catch people noticing him and pointing him out to their neighbors.

More people kept flooding into the grounds off the main street. Rows of people lined up, standing behind those seated on the benches. *The whole town must be here,* Keigh thought, his mouth going suddenly dry. *Probably even people from outside of Bjorn!* Watching as the crowd continued to pack itself in, he guessed there must be at least two thousand spectators there to watch the duels...to watch *him.*

The sound of a horn blasted out over the din of the crowd. Keigh got to his feet and dusted himself off. All eyes were looking back toward the main road. Over the mass of people, he could see Mace lumbering her way up to the testing grounds. When she got to the edge of the crowd, she sat down heavily on her haunches, her head still ten feet above the upturned faces of the tallest spectators. In front of her, the crowd parted, and a stream of red-cloaked canes and former canes strode into the arena. They arrayed themselves shoulder-to-shoulder along the edge adjacent to the archery target, where they stood at rigid attention.

Behind the canes, three men in loose tunics entered through the gap in the crowd. The first was Mannie, his bright eyes searching the grounds until they landed on Keigh where he stood in the corner. A toothy grin flashed behind his scraggly beard.

Behind Mannie walked a small man with short gray hair and long silver goatee, his face puckered in a self-satisfied way as he nodded and smiled indiscriminately at people in the crowd. Last to enter was an old man with a long, wild hair and beard, both white as clouds. He walked with the assistance of a gnarled and polished walking staff.

These last two were town elders. Braddock was the third of three that governed Bjorn. The elders' main civil function was to act as the town's judges during disputes, making sure that both the king's law and council law were followed. In Bjorn, that meant the elders spent most of their time deciding on community irrigation projects and assigning grazing schedules for the town's livestock owners, though Keigh's father had told him they had the power to serve as the King's Word in times of crisis. Keigh guessed that Mannie must be filling in for Braddock, since Braddock was testing Tarin today.

The three men took their places in front of the canes. A horn blasted again, and the crowd went silent.

"Those who would agoge as canes of Eden, present yourselves!" bellowed the man with the white hair, in a voice much stronger and louder than Keigh thought possible for one so old.

At the command, Tarin, Deacon, and Conrad hustled to align themselves in a row in front of the elders. Caught off guard and a bit dumbfounded, Keigh realized he was watching and not responding. His body snapped into motion. So forceful was his reaction that his feet spun out in the loose gravel, causing him to fall flat on his face in a cloud of dust.

A burble of laughter from the crowd filled the silence. Embarrassed, Keigh picked himself up and sprinted over to where his peers already stood. A second later, he stood shoulder to shoulder with Tarin across from Mannie. At his arrival, the laughter transitioned to a low, curious rumble as people pointed at him with looks of confusion.

Behind Mannie, Keigh saw the one face he had feared he would see today. Vicerous Wulf gaped at him in disbelief, which quickly evolved into unmistakable disdain and contempt for the rebellious thrall boy before him. He glowered at Keigh from where he stood with the other canes.

He can be mad, Keigh thought. *He just needs to stay quiet.*

Taking his eyes off Vicerous, he looked for friendlier faces. He soon found his family sitting on a front-row bench. Jessie, sitting on his mother's lap, enthusiastically waved her little hands at him.

"Canes! Claim your student!" belted the old man.

Four canes detached themselves from the row of red cloaks and made their way around the elders to their testees. Zale took his place behind Keigh,

Braddock behind Tarin, Chogan behind Conrad, and behind Deacon, a cane so hairy he appeared more bear than human.

"Today you test for the right to train as canes! Should you be found acceptable, you will be given the privilege of entering the brotherhood. A brotherhood bonded in blood spilled and strengthened in blood spilled. A duty and reward. You will rise to Eden's highest civilian station! King be with you!"

The elderly man bowed his head toward them as the people of Bjorn echoed in unison, "King be with you!"

A horn blasted and the crowd was silenced again.

The small man with silver hair stepped forward and threw his arms wide in welcome. "Congratulations, young men, on your acceptance into today's duels!" The man beamed at Keigh's three classmates, his eyes stopping short of Keigh.

Keigh's heart was pounding. Every eye other than the one elder's seemed to be fixed on him where he stood, exposed. He didn't like this much attention and found himself embarrassed by his torn and stained shirt. *I must look like a cow in the kitchen to these people. A mutt among purebreds.*

Keigh stole a quick glance back toward his family. Nothing but pure, unadulterated pride on their faces, except for his brothers, who looked to also have some raspberry preserve on their chins. He took a deep breath and heard Misselli's words to him again:

Don't be stupid, Keigh. You're going to pass. You'll be great.

"Okay, Keigh, don't be stupid," he repeated under his breath.

"What?" Tarin whispered.

Keigh just shook his head and committed his attention to the small man as he explained how the archery testing would proceed.

"Canes will shoot first. Students must copy the shot of their cane, placing their arrows as near as, or closer to, the mark. If a student meets or exceeds the placement of their cane's shot, they will receive a point. If the student fails to achieve a placement closer to the mark, their cane will receive a point. The test ends when either one reaches ten points. To pass, students must score no less than five points before their cane reaches ten." The small man clapped his hands and rubbed them together eagerly. "First up! Zale Woodman and Keigh Anders!"

The crowd erupted. All their pent-up excitement bursting out in joyous applause. The competitions they had been waiting for were about to begin.

The elders and canes that were not paired with a student sat cross-legged in the dirt where they had been standing, while the canes of Keigh's peers led them back to sit on the ground in front of the crowd at the far end, facing the target.

As they separated, Keigh overheard Deacon say to Conrad in a voice loud enough for everyone to hear, "Bet it's over in ten shots!"

There'll be a shot headed your way if it is, he thought, grinding his teeth as he followed Zale out to the center of the grounds.

"Watch closely. You don't want to embarrass yourself now," Zale said in a hushed voice, gesturing for Keigh to stand behind him. Then, in a loud voice, he called out to the quiet crowd, "Bullseye!"

Zale raised his bow, holding the target in sight for five seconds before he loosed his arrow. It zipped through the air, striking the top of the bullseye with a thud.

The crowd cheered. Zale smiled and motioned for Keigh to step up and fire from exactly where he had just stood.

Keigh stepped forward, out of the sunlight and into the jagged shadow cast across the testing grounds by Bjorn's outer wall. Its serrated points sharp as the teeth of some shadow demon.

You will not swallow me. I will be free of you.

Keigh pulled an arrow from his quiver and nocked it on his bowstring. The townsfolk quieted. He raised his bow and aligned his sight. *Twang!* He released the string, sending Mrs. Schaffer's white tailfeathers speeding toward the target.

Thud! The arrow buried itself in the bullseye's right lower edge.

"Point, Woodman!" exclaimed the small silver-haired man with a grin.

What! He isn't even going to measure? Keigh felt his shot had at least met that of Zale's, if not exceeded it.

The crowd clapped politely. A girl of about twelve ran to the target and pulled out their arrows, sprinting them back to their owners. Keigh took his arrow from her, biting his lip to keep from cursing.

"Not bad, kid, but you'll have to do better than that. Not everyone loves a dog in the house," Zale said, brushing him aside and nocking an arrow for his next shot. "Quick draw! Bullseye!"

He rolled his shoulders back, then suddenly raised his bow and fired in one smooth motion. *Thud!* The arrow struck the nine ring, just outside the bullseye.

Keigh stepped up, taking Zale's place again and nocked his arrow. He took a long, deep inhale, then exhaled. Raising his bow quickly, he let the arrow fly.

It thudded into the eight ring, an inch outside Zale's arrow.

"Point, Woodman!" the small man cried, his gloating grin smug enough to punch. Again, the crowd responded with polite applause.

This happened six more times: Zale taking a shot from a new angle or at a new target, and Keigh's arrow coming up just short of the mark to beat.

Keigh lay down on his left side in the same place from which Zale had just fired his shot. Zale's arrow had missed its mark, landing in the seven ring when the declared target had been the four. Keigh took a deep breath and drew the string back on his bow. Then he heard Deacon's voice break the silence.

"He'll probably win this one, as comfortable in the dirt as he is."

A gurgle of laughter from the crowd emboldened Deacon to speak again.

"When he lies down like that, I can't really tell where the dirt ends and Keigh begins!"

Another burble of laughter.

It took every fiber of self-control Keigh had to keep from rolling over and firing his arrow right at Deacon's pompous face. *Focus, Keigh. He wants you to fail. He expects you to fail...You must not fail!*

He clenched his jaw and took a deep breath. *Ziiippp!* His arrow thudded into the five ring, two rings closer to the target than Zale's.

The crowd erupted in a deafening roar. Keigh could hardly hear the small man when he shouted, "Point, Anders!"

He got up off the ground and looked to his parents. His mother whistled while also trying to gather Jessie back to her lap from where she was attempting to do cartwheels with reckless abandon in the dirt in front of their bench. His father was exuberantly talking with a man behind him while pointing to his own chest. Keigh thought he could see him mouthing the words, *That's my son!*

Zale smiled patronizingly at him and stepped back up to the line. "Even a blind squirrel finds a nut now and again."

"Apparently a blind squirrel can find a feast," Keigh finally retorted minutes later, speaking over the clamor of applause after scoring his seventh straight point in a row on the confounded cane.

"Feeling confident, are you, boy?" Zale sneered at him. "One last shot? Winner gets two points and the win?"

"I'm not scared. Call your shot!" Keigh *wasn't* scared. He had passed the test. Now he was shooting for respect.

Woodman smirked and strode over to the small man. He whispered something in his ear. The elder nodded and called over the girl from retrieving arrows, murmuring an instruction to her. Her eyes widened, then, without comment, dashed into the crowd and disappeared.

The small man got to his feet and quieted the crowd, who were still raucous from Keigh's last point. "The duelers have agreed to one final shot worth two points! Winner of the next shot wins the duel!"

The crowd roared their approval. Amid the noise, Keigh heard a subdued chant: *Let's go, Keigh! Let's go, Keigh!*

He soon found its source. Usually quiet, Emerson and Addy were conducting his classmates, minus Misselli and Cecilia, in the chant. Even Tarin and Conrad were mouthing along with them from where they sat with their canes.

Then the crowd began to point and chatter excitedly as the girl came back with a small wicker cage.

The small man called for silence again. "The final shot..." He paused for effect as the crowd looked eagerly toward the basket. "The final shot will be the first to land a kill shot on...a garden wolf!"

The crowd went wild.

Keigh's stomach dropped.

Never had he witnessed an agoge duel where the duelers had fired at anything but the straw target. He knew garden wolves were no more loved than rats in Bjorn, but he liked the little dogs, and the idea of shooting an animal that was tethered down was repugnant to him.

The girl opened the basket and tied a cord around the toy-sized dog, then tied the other end to a leg of the target stand. The diminutive white wolf struggled against its tether for a minute before sitting down to wag its tail happily and whip its head back and forth, curiously taking in its new surroundings.

"Contestants will quick-draw fire at the same time, on my signal!" the small man called. "Step up to the line!"

"Got the stomach for this, kid?" Zale scoffed.

Keigh didn't answer. What would he do? What could he do? He couldn't shoot the wolf, nor could he bow out without shaming himself and his family. He nocked an arrow and stood next to Zale.

"Ready..."

The wolf's blue eyes connected with his.

I have to do something! I could try to—no, that's impossible...but what else is there?

"Fire!"

His brief moment of indecision cost him. Zale's bow was up, releasing his shot half a second before Keigh.

That half-second was the longest of Keigh's life. It was as if the world had stopped and everything around him became fluid. The air, the light, the sound, even the people were all some shade of blue liquid. Despite the hallucination, his purpose remained crystal clear. He had to stop Zale.

As he raised his bow, he envisioned his arrow accomplishing its mission, aided and guided by the blue fluid between him and his target.

Hoping beyond hope to do the impossible, Keigh fired his shot.

The arrow flew from his bow with unearthly speed, chasing after Zale's. He watched the white goose feathers of his arrow gaining on the black-fletched tail of his opponent's.

No more than five feet in front of the wolf, Keigh's arrow hit Woodman's mid-shaft, sending both arrows careening off course, just narrowly missing the dog.

The crowd gasped and began talking and arguing excitedly. Had Keigh's arrow hit Zale's by chance? Or had he done the impossible and shot his opponent's arrow out of the air? Not even Keigh knew. That had been his one desperate wish, his one hopeless goal, but there was no way...

His sister seemed to be the first to recover from the initial shock of what they had just witnessed. "Great shot, Keigh! Woooohooooo!" Jessie screamed. A child's intuition. She would credit her brother with intending to save the helpless pup.

Pockets of onlookers started cheering and clapping their approval.

Accident or dumb luck, Keigh didn't care. He was elated! He allowed himself to grin as he looked down the field at the garden wolf, tongue out, happily wagging its tail, totally oblivious to the fate it had just narrowly escaped.

But as he watched, the black shaft of an arrow sprouted from the animal's chest.

The force of its impact lifted the dog off the ground, flinging it onto its back. The wolf gave a piercing whimper, then lay still.

A collective gasp went up from the crowd. Keigh threw his bow down and whirled on his opponent, fists clenched.

"Check your temper, child," Zale said dismissively, refusing to even look at him. He nodded to the small man.

The elder shook himself, removing the look of open-mouthed shock that had been plastered on his face. Clamping his jaw shut, he raised his hands for silence. "Point...and victory...Woodman!"

While the pronouncement was loud, it lacked the same enthusiasm as before. The mass of stunned onlookers clapped, just a few at first, before everyone eventually submitted to decorum and applauded politely for the winner.

Keigh snatched his bow up out of the dust and stomped back to take a seat next to Tarin and Braddock. Both nodded in acknowledgment of his passing of the test, and Tarin gave him a quick thumbs-up. Zale followed, wordlessly taking a seat behind him, next to Braddock.

"Next competitors! Conrad Hawk and Chogan Bald Head!"

At hearing Chogan's name, his daydream of beating Zale to a pulp with a sword was interrupted as he remembered Misselli's threat to taunt the man into a rage. He wondered where she was now, if she had seen him test. Surveying the crowd, he didn't see her.

The next three tests took place without incident, the only abnormality being when Tarin launched an arrow clean out of the grounds while trying to replicate a particularly difficult running shot that Braddock had plunged into the target's center. In the end, all four of the boys passed their archery testing. Conrad had scored just enough with a final count of five to ten. Deacon posted a ten-to-seven victory over his cane, and Tarin scored a cool seven to Braddock's ten.

When the archery was finished, three men disassembled the target and hauled it out of the arena. People from the back of the crowd rushed to fill in the empty end of the field, surrounding the clearing entirely.

The small man rose to his feet and the horn blasted again silencing the people. "Congratulations to you, young men, on passing the first portion of your testing! You will now be tested on your swordsmanship. Canes have been instructed to test your competency with a blade and will duel with progressive skill, technique, and strength until they feel they've reached the limits of your ability. When your cane withdraws and sheds his cloak, you will duel until you submit, relent, or until blood is drawn. You will test with real blades, and once the duel portion has started, the risk of serious bodily harm, even death, is possible."

The four boys stiffened, and a visible ripple passed through the crowd as the reality of their undertaking set in.

"Should you not accept the risk, the time to withdraw is now."

The crowd watched, mute, as the boys met the gazes of their elders with steely resolve.

"Good. Then we shall begin without delay! Students will be tested in the reverse order of their archery tests. First competitors! Tarin Conri and Braddock Fortier!"

For the next hour, Keigh watched as his peers dueled their canes—an hour of roars, screams, and gasps as swords clashed and clanged in their deadly dances.

Braddock had been methodical with Tarin, spending nearly twenty minutes on his skill progression. It may have been because Tarin possessed a depth of skill that took that long to plumb, though. Keigh had been fascinated watching the two swordsmen. They moved around each other like two bull elk weighing the sight of their opponents' antlers before violent clashes of lethal points.

However, five minutes after Braddock shed his cloak and initiated the open duel portion of the test, it was over. Braddock's full prowess as a defensive swordsman was on display as he easily danced around Tarin's powerful swings and stabs. The older man never even took an offensive, seemingly content to parry his opponent's attacks—until, in one eccentric lunge, Tarin overextended himself. Braddock deftly placed a four-inch gash on his shoulder. Having drawn blood, the duel was over, and both combatants took their seats to wild applause.

The hairy cane ended his skill progression early when Deacon took an inappropriately violent swing at his head instead of demonstrating the basic overhead split he was supposed to. The crowd had gasped at this breach of etiquette and the cane had thrown off his cloak. The two battled for nearly ten minutes. Deacon had been very impressive, much to Keigh's dismay, but in the end, he had lost his footing and submitted when he found the hairy cane's sword point pressed against his throat.

Chogan and Conrad's test went as scripted, spending ten minutes progressively displaying Conrad's control of the blade before dueling for another seven or so, the battle coming to an end when Chogan put a gash in Conrad's thigh—not coincidentally, Keigh thought, less than a minute after a familiar voice shouted from the throng, "What are you waiting for, Baldy?"

Keigh smiled, knowing that somewhere in the crowd, Misselli had just had her mother's hand clamped tight over her mouth.

The end of Conrad's duel jolted him back to reality with a gush of nervous anticipation. There would be no more spectating. He was up.

The stress did have one beneficial side effect: he was hyper-aware of himself—every beat of his heart, the tingling of his legs as blood rushed back into them, the hairs on his arms standing on end, a bead of sweat rolling down the small of his back. Even his sight seemed clearer: vivid and bright, colors vibrant as he watched Conrad walk off the field supported by Chogan. Only his hearing seemed to have diminished, the roar of the crowd drowned out by his own voice in his head.

This is it. This is your moment. Prove yourself. Show them you're something.

A tug on his arm pulled him back to the present. "Keigh! Wake up! Pay attention!"

Keigh turned to see Braddock standing behind him.

"Here," Braddock said, shoving the hilt of a sword into his hand. "I wasn't able to go retrieve my extra, so you'll have to use mine. Be careful with it. I don't want to see you cut your own foot off."

"Thanks! I—I won't!"

Keigh lifted the blade. It was light! Lighter than any of the thick green branches he had been sparring with. He moved it through the air experimentally. And balanced! The blade felt like a natural extension of his body. Weighted perfectly, it was as though he had simply grown an extra two-and-a-half feet of arm. He gripped the handle with both hands and, to his delight, found just enough room for both between the hilt and silver pommel.

"Let's go," Zale said, shoving him toward the center of the clearing.

"And our last competitors! Zale Woodman and Keigh—"

The small man was cut off mid-sentence. A scuffle had broken out behind the elders. It appeared that three of the canes were trying to hold down one of their own.

"Enough!" Vicerous Wulf bellowed, tearing himself free of the grip of a stunned Victor Giles and Crispin Popplardo. His glossy blonde hair askew, Vicerous' normally handsome face glared contemptuously at the men before turning his ire to the field.

"What is the meaning of this?" the small man demanded.

"The boy is my bondservant, and I demand he be removed from testing! He—" Vicerous jabbed a finger toward Keigh. "He was entered into today's duels without my knowledge and without my consent!"

The small elder looked to Braddock to dispute the claim. Braddock rose from his place behind Tarin and calmly strode toward the men.

"By entering today's agoge testing, Keigh has not broken any laws, king's or council's." He projected his voice for everyone to hear, flexing his authority as Bjorn's battle master and town elder. "Neither I nor Keigh need *your* consent, as he is not *your* son."

Vicerous' mouth opened to respond, but Braddock rushed to speak over him.

"AND! As you seem to forget—not your property!"

"Then, as no laws have been circumvented..." The small elder paused and looked to the white-haired elder, who nodded in confirmation. "It is the elders' ruling that the boy not be prohibited from testing."

"Then I demand to be the one to test him!" Vicerous spat.

"The boy has been assigned a cane already," said Braddock. "A tester who has already completed the first half of today's duels."

"If he were a competent cane, the boy would never have passed." Vicerous refused to even look at Zale, continuing to glare at Braddock. "I demand to test him!"

"You have no grounds to demand such a thing so long as the boy has a willing cane to test him."

"Zale! Relinquish your position to me!" Vicerous commanded. "Bow out or it will be *your* debt I seek to settle!"

The offended look on Zale's face vanished as some unspoken meaning passed between the men. In its place, a look of nervous understanding washed his ruddy cheeks pale. Turning a look of disdain onto Keigh, he snorted. "The boy obviously lacks the spine for combat. You'd be doing me a favor."

With that, he retrieved his bow and quiver and walked off the field.

Vicerous's smile was wicked. Like a mountain lion cornering a fawn, he drew his sword and stalked out to where Keigh stood waiting.

"You measure yourself, Vicerous!" The strong voice of Owen Anders boomed out from the crowd. Keigh's mother pulled at the crook of his elbow, urging him to be silent. "That's my son you're after! Anything happens to him and you'll have me to deal with!"

"We both know that's not true," sneered Vicerous. "Plus, you already have dealt with me, Owen Anders! Or have you so soon forgotten? I don't think you want to go back on your end lest I fail to keep mine! Now sit back down and watch me deal with the boy."

Owen's jaw clenched, corded muscles in his neck bulging as he sat back down. His nostrils flared in barely contained rage.

"W-well then..." the small man stammered, rapidly trying to regain composure. "It will be...dueling swords...Keigh Anders and Vicerous Wulf!"

The crowd gave a muddled applause and quickly quieted, tense in anticipation of the day's newly personal last duel.

All nervousness had left Keigh, it had been suddenly and violently replaced by white-hot anger. Nothing was left but his need to punish the man who had just publicly shamed his father.

His grip on Braddock's sword tightened. Readying himself for the skill progression, he worked his feet through the loose gravel to the compact ground below, securing his footing.

Vicerous lined up across from him and set his feet. Then, in a voice low enough for only Keigh to hear, he hissed, "The elders may have let you play pretend today, but they have no intention of letting you train as a cane. You're nothing more than a charity, a mild curiosity of bored men." He looked down his sharp nose at Keigh. "I'm going to do you a favor and remind you of who you are…who you'll *always* be."

Vicerous stood tall and raised his blade to the ready.

"Your very existence is a mistake…A mistake I fix. Today."

Now it wasn't just anger for his father. Deep personal loathing filled Keigh. Vicerous had touched his basest fear, and Keigh hated him for it.

"I just hope your son's pitiful footwork was inherited from his father," he retorted.

"Funny. Truly," Vicerous drawled, a thin smile stretching his lips. "Mmm… Yes, Deacon did tell me about your smart mouth…but the time for talk is over." He reached back and, grasping hold of his cloak, tore it off and threw it on the ground.

The townspeople gasped in shock. There would be no skill progression, only a duel. A fight Keigh knew would end in blood.

With a snarl, Vicerous lunged.

Keigh's arm moved instinctually across his body, parrying the thrust to the cold ring of steel on steel. He was elated. He hadn't even thought of what to do—his body had just reacted as if it were the most natural thing in the world!

Vicerous looked shocked at the blocked attack as well. Gathering himself quickly, he brought his sword around in a large, arching, vertical chop, wiping the bemused grin off Keigh's face.

Keigh's body once again reacted instinctively. He brought his blade up horizontally above his head and caught the full force of Vicerous's blow.

He blocked the next six of Vicerous's strikes with an aptitude that hid his inexperience. He was giving ground, but Vicerous had yet to come close to touching him with his blade.

The crowd, previously stunned silent, began stirring to life as it became evident the duel would be a fight, not an execution.

Keigh blocked another swing at his side. Spinning around, he reversed the field. He had seen this before, a thousand times over, in his mind's eye. Vicerous was just another attacking monster he'd fought in his yard each morning for the last five weeks.

Now let's see if he plays the role of stump too.

With a grunt, he lunged at Vicerous in an offensive, seeing him as the hacked and haggard sparring tree he had beat on for years. High, low, side to side, he maneuvered his opponent. Then, feigning a blow to Vicerous's thigh with the sword in his right hand, he stepped forward hard with his left foot, driving all of his body weight into his left fist. A loud crack sounded as his knuckles struck Vicerous under the chin and sent him flailing backward.

The crowd gasped. The sound of hundreds of muttering voices filled the air, undoubtedly debating the merits of what they had just witnessed take place in a duel of blades.

Vicerous put a hand to his mouth and viewed the blood on his fingers with disgust.

"You're bleeding, old man! Duel's over!" Keigh announced.

The two elders and Mannie looked at each other, apparently unsure of what to do.

"Ready to call it quits so soon?" Vicerous spit crimson onto the earth. "Guess I should've expected you would pull some sort of underhanded beggar trick like that."

The small man spoke up. "By rule, the duel is—"

"Ready your sword!" Keigh shouted at Vicerous, cutting the elder off.

The crowd roared. Vicerous smiled, blood staining his flawless white teeth.

"Good boy."

Then, with a growl, he threw himself back at Keigh, raining down blow after blow in an attempt to cleave his skull.

From there on, they battled, their swords a silver blur as they slashed and cut at each other. Each took turns attacking until their opponent maneuvered them into a defensive position. On and on they dueled to the raucous cheers of the crowd: every dodge a gasp, every chop a cry, every change in position a roar.

Forty minutes in and Keigh was drenched in sweat. His skin glistened, stretched tight over flexed muscles as he found himself once again on the defensive, parrying a new onslaught of blows. He was losing ground and losing strength. He was growing faint with dehydration and fatigue. He struggled to stop Vicerous's attacks. Each time he blocked the cane, his own blade nearly rebounded back into his body.

He caught a stab from Vicerous, and before he knew it Vicerous had twisted his blade around in a tight corkscrew, catching the hilt of his sword and pulling the handle out of his sweaty palm. Keigh watched his only weapon spin through the air away from him. The blade slid to a stop in a cloud of dust.

Whump! Seizing on Keigh's momentary distraction, Vicerous kicked him in the chest so hard he was lifted off his feet and sent flying backward.

A collective groan went up from the crowd as Keigh landed hard on his back in front of the elders.

Keigh closed his eyes and awaited the final blow. He was done. Finished. Even if he still had his sword, his arms were lead, his feet boulders. He breathed out, feeling the shadow of his opponent fall upon his face. *At least... at least I showed them...showed them all...I'm more...more than nothing.*

"Move aside, old man!"

Keigh opened his eyes and stared straight up into the sky, panting. The silhouette of a man stood above him.

"Do you want to keep fighting?" the silhouette asked him gently.

"Till...the...bitter end," Keigh gasped.

"Then take my arm and rise." The silhouette offered him a hand up.

"I said move aside, thrall!" bellowed Vicerous.

Keigh reached out and clasped the forearm of his helper, desperate for relief. Immediately he felt his arm infused with liquid fire. The same feeling he'd had in the woods the day he had fought the stranger poured into him, filling him with strength like a waterfall filling a bucket.

The man pulled him up onto his feet and Keigh looked straight into the smiling face of Mannie.

He leaned down to whisper in Keigh's ear, "The butter seems to be working." Withdrawing with a wink, he added, "but you probably still want to go grab your sword."

"Right..."

"Left, actually, I think." Mannie jerked his head subtly in the direction of the sword. "Good luck!" He smiled and released Keigh, then slumped back down next to the elders.

"Done delaying?" Vicerous sneered. Leaping at Keigh, he swung his sword down in a massive chop.

Keigh sidestepped the attack with ease. Vicerous's blade shot shards of gravel at the crowd as its tip buried in the ground.

Keigh felt fresh and new. Everything was crisp and clear. All his senses as quick and alert as when they'd first started, only now, he felt strong. Maybe even stronger than ever.

He ducked the blade as Vicerous took a backhanded swipe at him. *I need to find my sword!* Getting his bearings, he spotted it in the dirt behind Vicerous, right where Mannie had indicated.

Left it is, he confirmed to himself.

Vicerous launched another stab at him. Keigh nimbly sidestepped the point of the sword and punched the back of Vicerous's wrist, causing him to over-rotate. Keigh dove past his opponent's rear as the furious cane rebounded with another vicious backhanded swipe. The blade whistled through the air, inches above Keigh's head.

He hit the ground in a roll and popped up next to his sword. Swiftly, he picked it up out of the dirt. The dust absorbing the sweat off his hand giving him a sure grip on the handle.

"More tricks," came Vicerous's voice. "Must have learned those from your mother."

"Vicerous!" Owen Anders bellowed.

Vicerous shook his head as if trying to rid himself of some annoying gnat. "Enough!"

Keigh and Vicerous ran at each other. Sparks flew as their blades collided between them. There was a flurry of cuts, swipes, chops, and hacks as both fighters sought to strike a winning blow.

Then, summoning all his newfound strength, Keigh gripped his sword with both hands and swung it with all his might.

Their blades collided between them, and with a resounding *PING*—

Both swords shattered.

The people surrounding them collectively inhaled. Both combatants paused to stare in shock at the severed remains of the swords in their hands.

If Vicerous didn't kill him, now Braddock surely would. Keigh threw the ruined sword to the side and clenched his fists, raising them toward Vicerous.

"That was foolish," Vicerous laughed. Bearing his blood stained teeth, he spun the handle of his shattered sword in his hand. Ten inches of its blade still intact.

He swung at Keigh, attempting to cut his throat.

Keigh ducked the slash. Dropping to a knee, he lunged forward, popping up behind Vicerous. Without taking time to turn around, Keigh launched his elbow back with all his might.

CRACK! The point of his elbow smashed into the back of Vicerous's skull.

The sword handle dropped from Vicerous's limp hand. His unconscious body swayed then tipped, falling to the earth like the trunk of a cut pine, landing motionless in a puff of dust.

Silence rang through the common grounds. Keigh feared the blood pounding in his temples had caused him to go deaf until he heard the distant twitter of a bird. He looked to the elders for some clue, anything that might tell him it was over.

The small man and Mannie began talking frantically to each other, but the white-haired elder sat motionless, his steely blue eyes fixed on

Keigh, searching. Keigh expected to see shock, alarm, surprise, or even disappointment in the old man's face, but instead it appeared as though he was merely studying Keigh with intense curiosity.

The small man jumped up and scurried over to Vicerous Wulf's limp form. He gave Keigh a dismissive glance as he passed and knelt next to the still body. He felt Vicerous's throat, then touched the back of his head.

Raising three crimson fingers, the small man presented them to the crowd. "Blood has been drawn!"

"Twice now!" his father shouted, to a murmur of agreement.

"Victory..." The small man hesitated, giving Keigh a quick contemptuous study. "Victory, Keigh Anders."

The crowd erupted. Roaring and screaming, they rushed the field. Leading the pack was his father, who wrapped Keigh in a bear hug and lifted him up, seating him on his shoulder. The throng started chanting his name, no longer just his classmates but hundreds, thousands, of people: *"Anders! Anders! Anders!"*

From where he was perched on his father's shoulder, Keigh sought out the people he loved. His mother stood smile-crying with little Jessie in front of her, bouncing about, snarling and punching the air. Beaudy had lifted Theo onto his own shoulder; both boys gave him a sharp salute. Tarin still stood with Braddock—both men had their arms crossed and seemed to be processing what they had just seen. Emerson and Addy had locked hands and were dancing around in a circle. Mannie had made his way to the center and stood next to Keigh's father. He squeezed Keigh's leg, his face beaming with pride as he gave his token wink.

Then, Keigh saw her. Standing alone, outside the teeming mass of cheering townsfolk. His best friend. In her robin's egg–blue dress, she was a patch of clear sky on a cloudy day...but there were raindrops falling from this blue sky.

Tears streamed down Misselli's face. Her lips were trembling. For a moment, it was as if they were the only two people in town, both trapped by the gaze of the other. Then, with a shake of her head, Misselli turned and walked away, disappearing from Keigh's sight to the sound of:

"Anders! Anders! Anders!"

CHAPTER 10

A NOTHING NO MORE

20-25-27

The hours after his duel with Vicerous were a blur. Deacon had quietly collected his father, the pair limping off together to lick their wounds and, no doubt, curse his name. Keigh stayed in the arena for an hour afterward, shaking hands and meeting people he had seen a thousand times but who had never before spoken a word to him. Names flew at him like a flurry of leaves in the wind, each one lost as it mixed with a hundred others. He would never remember theirs, but they would all remember his.

Keigh Anders. He had done it! He, a simple thrall, a potato farmer, had passed his agoge testing and won his duel. Old men and women, gray haired and wrinkled, were all repeating some variation of *"Never in my life..."* or *"Never would I have thought I'd see the day..."*

Even Braddock had acknowledged the achievement, though with not nearly as much reverence, stating simply, "I suppose there is a first time for everything."

Keigh had just been relieved that he didn't bring up the topic of his now ruined sword—a topic he knew Braddock had not forgotten, since he had watched the man walk about the clearing, scooping up the pieces of the shattered weapon like a father lifting his injured infant child.

His classmates, minus Misselli, Cecilia, and those who had just competed, had enthusiastically dubbed him *King Keigh*. They laughed as they gave him sarcastic bows. Theo and Beaudy had even treated him to a spirited reenactment of the fight—one that didn't quite make it to the grand finale, as Theo accidentally smacked Beaudy in the face, bringing the large boy to tears and the reenactment to a close.

Keigh's family and Mannie waited patiently for him, and when the last congratulations and well wishes had been shared, they made their way home. On the way, Keigh saw Cecilia's red hair, bright as a torch, down a dusky alleyway. He was shocked to see not Deacon, but Tarin entwined in her tentacles this time—a sight he had difficulty processing. On one hand, he was a bit disappointed in his friend's bad taste, but on the other, he found himself feeling grateful it had not been Misselli's blonde hair down that alley.

For the next week he took every opportunity he could to go into town. Finishing his work as fast as he could each day, he would ask his parents if they needed anything he could fetch for them, and when he couldn't disguise it as an errand, he would just make up some urgent matter he needed to attend to. In reality, he just liked being seen. For the first time in his life, people recognized him, knew his name, and wanted to hear what he had to say.

It turned out that he had quite a bit to say, too. People asked his opinion on things now—things he had no experience with and no expertise in, but it didn't matter; he always had an answer. From weather predictions to his preference in clothing, people seemed to want any excuse to talk to him. One woman had even told him she had named her cat after him, a gesture he was flattered by, but not too excited about.

Truthfully, recognition wasn't the only reason he had been eager to visit town each day. He liked the praise. In fact, he loved it. But still, ever since his victory, he had wanted to spend time with his best friend. All the recognition in the world would not scratch that itch. He needed to see Misselli.

The weeks leading up to the duel had stolen all his time with training. Now that his testing was behind him, he just wanted to return to spending his evenings doing nothing special, with the one who knew him best. The problem was, he was pretty sure she didn't want to see him, and he wasn't about to let her know he wanted to see her.

That ruled out going straight to her house. Instead, he had opted for casually stopping by her mother's bakery each day, hoping to find her there under the cover of it being a chance encounter.

He had never had a problem communicating with Misselli before. He'd once thought he knew her better than anyone, but ever since her breakdown on the trail, he'd found her to be more riddle than answer. Crossing blades with Vicerous had been easy compared to this. With Vicerous, everything was clear: the man had hurt his family and needed to be beat. Keigh had stepped into that fight willing and eager, knowing the mission. But with Misselli...he was terrified.

Swords made sense, dueling made sense, work made sense—everything in his life seemed to make sense at the moment except this *one* girl. Did she expect him to stay in Bjorn now that he had passed his agoge duels? Did she think things would never change? Were they still friends? Were they more than friends? Further complicating things was his increasing realization that he didn't really know how he felt about things either, so even if Misselli were to give him all the answers he wanted from her, he would still be left to deal with the quagmire of competing desires in his own heart.

Keigh opened the door to Rita Labelle's bakery. A wall of warm air, thick with the sweet smell of fresh-baked bread, caused his already queasy stomach to rumble uncomfortably. Keeping his mind on the mission, he walked past the tables of loaves and sweet breads, shiny with honey glaze, heading for the back, hoping today would be the day Misselli had joined her mother at work.

Keigh pushed through the double swinging doors separating the kitchen from the sales floor and found Mrs. Labelle kneading a lump of dough.

"Ah, Keigh! In town again? I swear, I've seen you in my shop more times this week than the rest of your young life combined!" Rita Labelle used her forearms to clear the few strands of hair out of her face that had escaped the tight bun atop her head. "Care for a pinch of sugar bun dough?" She pinched off a piece of the dough in her hands and tossed it to Keigh.

"Uh, sure, thanks." He caught the small ball of dough and popped it in his mouth. "Is Misselli here—ugh!" Keigh grimaced as he spit the dough back into his hand. "What is this?"

Mrs. Labelle laughed. "Got ya! It's sourdough!" She took her eyes off Keigh and returned to kneading. Her tone became somber. "I find sour things to be much *more* sour when sweet is expected. Do you agree? That something otherwise good can taste vile if only a person's expectations are elsewhere?"

"Pretty sure I would never like sourdough." Keigh scowled at the slimy bit of dough he still held awkwardly in his palm.

"Child, your brain is dough!" she said, shaking her head impatiently. "I'm not talking about water and flour! I'm trying to teach you something about life."

"I'm sorry..." Keigh deposited the ball of dough in a rubbish bin and wiped his palm dry on his tunic. "What are we talking about?" He had expected riddles from Misselli, not her mother.

"We are talking about you and my daughter." Rita threw a pinch of flour on the counter. "She talks to me, Keigh. I know things between you two have been...different...for a while now."

"Yeah...different is a good word for it."

"I won't tell you anything Misselli has said to me. If the time comes when she feels like sharing those things with you, then that conversation will be her choice. But I do want to tell you..." Mrs. Labelle paused her kneading and looked at Keigh with a soft sigh. "You're like a son to me, Keigh."

Keigh shifted uncomfortably. Mrs. Labelle already had a son. Misselli's older brother Baylor had been a high achiever, a fact that led Misselli to think he could walk on water when they were younger. Then, when Baylor had passed his agoge duels to train as a cane, he had left for the Capital. Shortly after, the family had received a letter from him saying he had been given a special assignment by the king. Nobody had seen or heard from him since.

Mrs. Labelle continued, "What I'm trying to tell you, what I want you to know—while Misselli isn't quite ready to..." She paused, looking up at the ceiling as if she would find words there. "My daughter likes sourdough. She's very happy with sourdough, and will eat it gladly if she has to, for the rest of her life. Only...she had her heart set on sugar buns. She was hoping for sugar buns and got sourdough." She looked back at Keigh. "Does that make sense?"

It didn't.

"Are you missing an ingredient for sugar buns? I could help you, if it would make Misselli happy."

Mrs. Labelle gave a heavy sigh. "You sweet, sweet, simple boy." She shook her head and plopped the ball of dough down on the counter. "How did I ever raise a son—"

Her face brightened as she looked over Keigh's shoulder.

"Oh! Hi, sweetheart! Look who popped in to see you!"

Keigh turned around to see Misselli halfway through the double swinging doors. Blood was quickly flooding to her lightly freckled cheeks. She looked like a rose going into full bloom before their eyes.

"Mother," Misselli said through tight lips. "I think you have a customer out front."

"I don't hear anyone—"

"MOM. I'm quite *sure* you have a customer...*out front.*"

"Out front? OH! *Out front*, out front!" Mrs. Labelle winked. "Yes, of course. I'll go attend to them." She rose from her seat and brushed the flour off her lap. "Good seeing you, Keigh."

She smiled gently and walked past him, planting an unappreciated kiss on Misselli's forehead as she made her way to the front.

"Hey..." Keigh greeted Misselli, desperately hoping to figure out the thing about sourdough before saying too much. Misselli could be a handful when she was hungry.

Misselli entered the kitchen, leaving the swinging doors flapping behind her. "Mom says you've been coming in looking for me a bunch this week." She paced past him like a cat deciding if a person's leg was safe to approach.

"Well, I uh...I wouldn't say a bunch—like, what's a bunch?" Keigh gulped. "But yeah, I hoped I would, uh, catch you while I was, uh, already in town... You know. Doing other stuff."

He tried to play it cool, but Misselli wasn't buying it.

"Okay, Mr. Hometown Hero. Been busy, have you?" She was smiling, but her words had bite to them.

"Yeah—I mean, a bit...Not too busy to come see you...obviously," he stammered.

"You know where I live." Misselli sat back on the counter, seemingly enjoying his nervousness.

"Yes, of course...but, you know...evening chores."

"Evening chores?"

"And earthquakes." He grinned at his friend.

Misselli laughed, her face relaxing. "Earthquakes?"

"Yeah, they're supposed to be really bad this time of year."

"We've literally never had an earthquake."

"Well, don't you think we're about due then?"

They stood there, grinning at each other, like a couple of children waiting for the punchline of their favorite joke to drop.

Misselli broke the impasse. "You were amazing...in your duels, that is." She smiled reassuringly. "I could hardly watch, I was so scared, but from what I did see...you're going to make a great cane."

Her smile seemed to retreat back into her as she spoke the final words. Abruptly, she changed topics, shifting to an upbeat demeanor.

"You may have been busy with earthquakes, but I've been busy too!"

Keigh breathed a sigh of relief. "Oh yeah? With what?"

"I've spent the last week tracking down everyone from class and asking them if they want to start a club."

"A *club*?"

"Ugh...that's exactly what Tarin said. Call it whatever you want to call it, I don't care," she pressed on excitedly. "Now that everyone's agoge testing is done and we're all starting our apprenticeships, I thought we should have something where we could all still get together! Maybe not all the time, but as often as we can spare." She looked at Keigh, clearly waiting for him to reciprocate her level of excitement for the idea.

"I don't know, Misselli…" He watched her wilt at the doubt in his voice. He paused before adding, "I'm kidding! I think it's a great idea."

Misselli sprang back to life. "Really? So you'll come?"

Keigh laughed at her as she nearly came off her feet in her excitement. "Of course I'll come! On one condition, though…"

Misselli was suddenly nervous again. "What's that?"

"We have to come up with a better word than *club*."

She smiled and shook her head. "Keigh Anders, you're going to wish Vicerous Wulf *had* killed you if you don't stop toying with me."

Keigh gave her a puzzled look in mock indignation. "I think, if we are keeping score, you've messed with me waaaaay more than I've messed with you."

Misselli tilted her head, her lips twitching. "You're right. I am winning, aren't I?"

*

Saturday came, and with it, the *club's* first hangout. They had agreed to meet at the rope swing on the pond down by the Muellers' farm for an afternoon of swimming. Keigh had rushed to finish his morning chores and arrived at the pond to find most of the group already there.

"'Bout time you got here!" Tarin called at him from a plank nailed between two trees, fifteen feet above the ground. He held the knotted rope of the swing in his hands. "Nobody else will go off the high board with me."

He gave Misselli an accusing look, then jumped off the plank. The rope swung him in a long arc out over the water. At the peak of his rise, Tarin thrust himself up with his arms. Letting go of the rope, he tucked his knees to his chest, backflipping into the water twenty feet below.

The girls sitting at the water's edge in their wool swim dresses clapped as Tarin's head resurfaced. Water flew in a golden arc as he threw back his thick brown hair.

Conrad and Kervyn walked up on either side of Keigh. "I swear, he just gets out of bed good at stuff," Conrad said, never taking his eyes off Tarin's tall, athletic frame as he moved out of the water into the short grass surrounding the pond.

"You can't do a backflip off the rope, Conrad?" Keigh teased.

Conrad snorted. "Kervyn's closer to landing a backflip flat-footed than I am to pulling one off on the rope," he said, nodding at their plump friend.

"Don't doubt me, Conrad. I may land one someday. Been practicin', ya know." Kervyn struck a heroic pose with his fists on his hips.

They laughed as Tarin made his way across the green grass toward them.

"You're up, Keigh! Think you can do that?" Tarin tossed his head toward the water, indicating the backflip he had just performed.

"I'll go off the high board, but I'm not trying any backflips today."

"Surely the mighty *Keigh Anders* can do a little flip into some nice gentle water!" said Tarin.

"Yeah, Keigh! I wanna see you do a flip too!" Misselli piled on, skipping up to the boys, knowing better than anyone that Keigh was no fan of heights.

"Going off the high board is enough thrill for me, thanks," he said, smiling sardonically at Misselli.

"King Keigh!" Theo called out from behind them as he and Beaudy arrived.

"Hey, guys," Keigh responded, noting the sour look on Tarin's face.

"The *king* can't be convinced to try a simple backflip!" said Tarin.

"Well now, that's not very brave, Keigh." Theo gave him a look of mock disappointment and shrugged. "Might have to change my allegiance if that's true."

"Most important quality in a king is backflipping, you know," said Misselli.

"Don't worry, Keigh, I can't do a backflip either," said Beaudy, as if he were confessing a shocking secret to the group.

"Thanks, Beaudy." Keigh smiled, putting a appreciative hand on Beaudy's shoulder. "I had no idea."

"Well, I'm going again," said Tarin, taking off toward the tree. "Conrad! Grab the rope for me!"

The other boys dashed to follow. Keigh watched them as they raced toward the water. He laughed as Beaudy feigned an elegant dive only to purposefully bellyflop, splashing a still bone-dry Theo with cold water.

"You getting in?" Misselli asked, pulling Keigh's arm toward the water.

"One sec, I want to say hi to Addy and Emerson."

"Okay! Holler if you see any turtles." Misselli grinned, her dimples deepening, and took off to join the boys.

Keigh made his way down to the pond's edge where the two girls sat, soaking their feet in the clear water. He plopped down on the bank next to Addy.

"Hey, guys! What have you been doing since instruction ended?"

Addy, still wearing her thick glasses, squinted at him. "Oh, hi, Keigh! I agoged to be a scribe and I passed! They're going to let me apprentice here in Bjorn, with Master Alden!" she squealed with excitement. "He said he's never had anyone request to agoge as a scribe before, and even so, he said my reading and writing skills were as good as most of the seasoned scribes he's ever worked with!"

"That's awesome, Addy! You'll be great." Keigh beamed at her, squinting as the sun reflected off her thick lenses into his face. "What about you, Emerson?"

While most of the girls wore the typical short, sleeveless swim dresses common in Eden, Emerson wore a saggy, sage-green wool dress with long sleeves that made her look like a shriveled-up, dried-out watermelon. "I...I'm just going to help my ma with her candle-making." She smiled weakly at him, keeping her lips pressed together.

"Didn't you even try as a weaver?" Keigh asked, remembering that had been her dream.

"No." Emerson sighed, dropping her eyes back to her feet kicking slowly in the water. "I just couldn't risk it."

"Risk what?" Keigh didn't see the danger in making clothes.

"Being rejected, Keigh!" she snapped. "I just...I just didn't want one more person telling me I'm not good enough."

Addy put a hand on Emerson's back, comforting her friend. Keigh's mouth was paralyzed. He hadn't expected the conversation to take such a personal turn.

Addy broke the silence. "I know how you feel, Em. I was scared to ask for agoge too, and I didn't even have betters to worry about."

Keigh shook his head. "But Addy, you know there's no law saying thralls can't agoge. It's because of you that I went and asked Braddock to test."

It was Emerson who responded. "It's not a matter of can or can't, Keigh! It's living in a world where you feel like you're nothing and you're treated like nothing! And you can survive that world as long as you can convince yourself it's all in your head. The last thing you want is someone to confirm it. To be evaluated and tested, and have someone conclude definitively, *you aren't good enough*…" Emerson hung her head. "It's better to just stay in our family trades."

Keigh was stunned. Emerson had just described how he had always felt, only she had made her case for remaining a nothing, something he had never considered. All his life he had wanted nothing more than to prove those voices in his head wrong. That he could be something more than just a thrall, just a potato farmer.

"I tested, and it was the best decision I've ever made," he offered, hoping she could see their situation wasn't hopeless.

Emerson slapped her thighs with her palms. "You gambled, Keigh! And you won. Good for you." She shook her head. "But seriously, Keigh, I'm not you. I'm not a fighter…Life's hard enough without putting myself in more positions to lose." She kicked a foot up in frustration, splashing herself in the face. She didn't even bother to wipe herself dry.

"I…I didn't mean to…I'm sorry," Keigh sputtered.

Emerson lifted her gaze and smiled at him with her crooked yellow teeth. "Don't be sorry. We are proud of you." She nudged Addy. "When you won your duel…we all felt like we won. We felt like you were fighting for us, for the nothings, 'cause you were a nothing too—"

A look of horror crossed her face as she blushed cherry-red.

"I'm sorry—oh my—I didn't mean to say—you're not a nothing…" She paused. "Not to us."

The two girls smiled at him, bobbing their heads in agreement, Addy's glasses smushing her nose so far down they nearly fell off her face.

"Thanks, guys," Keigh said, appreciation welling up inside him. Somehow, of all the praise and compliments he had received in the week since dueling

Vicerous, this simple acknowledgment from the two people in his class who best knew what his life was like...It meant more to him than anything else had. "You know, neither of you are a nothing to me, either."

"We know." Addy raised her head high. "We're your favorites, huh?" She grinned, winking one of her magnified eyes.

Keigh smiled back. "Today you are, for sure!"

"Just don't forget about us now that you're famous," teased Emerson.

"Yeah, it's kind of wild, huh?" Keigh scratched his head, frizzing his hair. "You know, someone told me I'm the first thrall to ever pass their agoge duels as a cane."

Addy shook her head at him. "No, Keigh, you're not just the first thrall to pass—you're the first novice of any class to ever best a cane in an agoge duel! Master Alden told me so! They keep records of every cane from agoge duels onward, and no novice has ever *won*."

"And you beat him twice," murmured Emerson, smirking at her own reflection in the water.

"Hey! Are you going to get in or what?" Tarin called to Keigh from the water. "We're going to do chicken fights and Beaudy wants to sit on your shoulders!"

Keigh looked over to where his friends were splashing each other underneath the rope swing, allowing gratitude to flow through him like he hadn't felt in a long time. At that moment, he thought, even if he hadn't passed his duels, even if he were still just a thrall, just a potato farmer, he would be lucky—lucky to have these friends.

He looked to the girls next to him. "Mind if I go join the guys?"

"Go ahead! Just don't ask us to get in. The water is still too cold!" Addy shook herself in a shiver nearly losing her glasses again.

Keigh laughed. "Okay, I won't." He stood up to leave, then paused. "Thank you. You guys are really great. I hope you keep coming to...whatever these hangouts of Misselli's are."

"Misselli's hangouts?" Emerson looked at him questioningly. "She told us this was your idea!"

Addy nodded in agreement.

"Of course she did," he said, rolling his eyes. He didn't care how Misselli had gotten them to come; he was just glad they had. He looked at Misselli, who was impatiently waving at him to get in the water. "If it was my idea, then it's the best one I've had in a while."

With that, he shed his shirt and dove into the water.

*

Keigh and the boys did chicken fights for the next hour, mainly due to Tarin's insistence that they couldn't quit till he had won one. Keigh was as surprised as everyone that the muscular pairing of Conrad and Tarin couldn't beat Theo and Beaudy, no matter how they stacked themselves. Keigh was not surprised, however, that he and Kervyn failed to win any of the fights. While Kervyn loved fun and games as much as anyone, he had no stomach for contentious competition.

After an hour, Beaudy and Theo remained unbeaten. Beaudy's mountain of flesh proved too much for any of the boys to sink, let alone budge. Plus, fighting tiny Theo off his perch was like trying to take hold of a mad badger.

Exhausted and soaking, the boys flopped onto the sun-soaked grass on the edge of the pond.

"You could have won if you'd partnered with me." Misselli flexed her skinny arms in mock intimidation.

"Partnered with which one of us?" Tarin asked.

"Any one of you." She shrugged. "I don't need anything special to beat any one of you limp noodles."

"I personally thought King Keigh would have bested us at least once," said Theo, clapping the back of his hand over his eyes to shield them from the sun. "Seriously, he bested the best blade in Bjorn, maybe all of Eden! I figure he could drown all of us if he had a mind to!"

"Vicerous is old, and he jumped into a duel he wasn't prepared for because he got all flustered that one of his charges wasn't acting right," Tarin dismissed. "Braddock was the real challenge! Did you see him? He's a master with a blade. Even still, it took him five minutes to mark me." He fingered the stitches on his shoulder where Braddock had cut him.

"You were excellent, Tarin, no denying that—but Keigh's duel was one for the ages! They'll be talking about it for years to come I'd wager!" Theo swung an invisible sword through the air above him.

"Keigh's tough, alright," admitted Tarin. "All I'm saying is, there's lots of factors to look at in agoge duels."

"Is that why you never told me I'm the Bear?" Keigh gave Tarin a wry grin, knowing how hard it was for his friend to admit anyone had bested him at anything.

Tarin rolled his eyes, obviously annoyed that Keigh thought he deserved the title. "I told you you were the Bear after you took out that crazy man in the woods, remember?"

"Doesn't hurt to hear it twice," Keigh teased, but his chest tightened. He had been so preoccupied with the duels and distracted by the aftermath that he hadn't thought of the stranger in the woods for weeks.

He touched the scar on his neck, then shook his head, forcing himself to be present. He was safe. Life was good, as good as it had ever been. The intruder was dead.

He returned his attention to Tarin. "We all passed. That's all that matters," he said, attempting to bring relief to his friend's wounded pride.

"Well said, King!" Theo sat up straight and gave Keigh a mock bow.

"*King Keigh*..." scoffed Tarin, just loud enough to be heard.

"That's right, Tarin! Better watch yourself—might have some competition for the throne!" Misselli jibed.

"Pfft! Keigh isn't even part of the Consecrate," huffed Tarin dismissively.

"Maybe the king will hear about him and choose him anyway," Beaudy piped up hopefully.

"We all know you'll be king one day, Tarin. Don't get your swimmies in a bundle," Theo heckled.

"No! You guys think Keigh's better than me!"

"Nobody is saying that, Tarin. Calm down," Keigh said.

"No! They need to see! Head-to-head. Winner is top of the class!"

Keigh didn't feel like arguing with Tarin, but all the same, he didn't like how adamant his friend was that he was better than him. "What are you suggesting? 'Cause I'm not dueling you. I don't even own a sword," he said, earning a laugh from his friends.

"No. Not a duel, something…something else. Something with a clear winner. Like a race or—or a challenge." Tarin's face screwed up as he pondered possible competitions. "I know!" he exclaimed. "We'll climb the old watchtower! First through the upper window wins."

"Deal!" Theo shouted as if he was Keigh's personal representative. The rest of his friends voiced their approval as well.

The last thing Keigh wanted to do was climb a hundred feet off the ground on the outside of a crumbling relic in some silly attempt for Tarin to stroke his own ego. *There has to be a way out of this.*

"The old watchtower is off-limits," he reminded them. "The elders don't want anyone getting hurt up there."

"We'll go after dark, then," Tarin said.

"Name the time!" barked Theo.

"Tonight," said Tarin definitively. "Meet at the tower an hour after sundown!"

Keigh's heart sank as his friends cheered the challenge. There would be no backing out. He would have to climb.

CHAPTER 11

THE CLIMB

43-15-13

Keigh was the last to arrive at the old stone watchtower. Not everyone from the pond had been able to come back out that evening, but Misselli, Theo, Beaudy, Conrad, and Tarin had all returned—and, to Keigh's chagrin, Tarin had brought Deacon with him.

Tarin must have noticed the look of disdain on Keigh's face as he approached. "If you want to be the best, you gotta beat everyone," he said. "Nobody gets to say they would have won if only they'd been there."

Keigh rolled his eyes at Tarin and greeted his friends. Beaudy's small oil lantern bathed their faces in warm light as the group of teens huddled around it. Keigh asked him why he'd brought it when the full moon provided more than enough light for walking, but didn't press further when he noticed Beaudy's eyes taking fearful glances up into the tree line behind the tower. Beaudy wasn't the only one who feared the beasts that stalked the mountain forests at night.

"What does climbing this trash heap even prove?" Deacon asked Tarin, still refusing to acknowledge Keigh's arrival.

"Proves you aren't chicken, for one! And it's an even playing field." Tarin craned his neck to look up at the tower's dilapidated peak. "At our agoge testing we all dueled different men, so who's to say which of us is best when we may have performed better against another cane than our peer did?"

Keigh felt Tarin was deliberately avoiding eye contact with him as he said this last part.

"Why not just duel each other?" asked Conrad.

"Really? And risk Keigh and Deacon killing each other?"

"Fine with me," Keigh and Deacon said in unison, before silencing themselves. Neither of them happy to have shared anything with the other, not even a thought.

"Ugh! Children." Misselli gave them each a disapproving look.

"Exactly my point," Tarin continued. "Listen, the tower is the same for all of us. Same climb, same finish line."

"And you want us all to scramble up that thing together?" Keigh asked, not liking the idea of a bitter Deacon climbing anywhere near him.

"Of course not! We'll all climb separately—"

"Then how are we going to know who was fastest?" Conrad interrupted. "No offense, but I don't think Misselli counting for each of us will really be fair." He glanced casually back and forth between Tarin and Keigh, earning a laugh from Deacon and a fresh scowl from Misselli.

"Yeah, and I don't think we can trust the *King Keigh* fan club to count, either." Deacon nodded at Theo and Beaudy. "That's if Beaudy can even count," he added, laughing at the scowl he had produced on Beaudy's face.

"Nobody is counting," Tarin said in a reassuring voice. "We'll measure who was fastest...using this." He triumphantly pulled a small golden item out of the pocket of his pants.

"Is that a watch?" exclaimed Theo.

"You didn't seriously bring your father's watch out here for this, did you?" Misselli asked.

Tarin shrugged nonchalantly. "It will be fine! He doesn't even know I took it. It will be back on the hearth before he even realizes it's gone."

Even Deacon could barely conceal his shock at seeing the small timepiece. "You would have been safer dueling us. Your dad will kill you if he finds out, Tarin!"

Misselli laughed. "Kill him? My parents would sell me if I took something that valuable! That thing's probably worth more than what my parents make in ten years."

Keigh wasn't overly surprised to see the watch. Tarin sneaking around his parents wasn't anything new, though he didn't usually flaunt his family's wealth like this. He was usually content to let people just gape at how tall, strong, and handsome he was.

"Don't worry about it. It will all be fine," said Tarin, dismissing their concerns with a wave of his hand. "Here, Misselli, you take this." He handed her the gold watch and showed her how to wind it, then nodded to Beaudy and Theo. "You three will take the stairs up to the watchroom. Misselli, you'll give us the go when the second hand..."

Seeing the look of confusion on her face, Tarin pointed to the longest needle as it ticked its way around the watch face.

"...when that needle reaches the twelve at the top. Every tick that hand makes from there is a second. Count those from when we start to when we get our full body through the window. Alright?"

Misselli nodded.

Keigh looked up at the imposing monolith silhouetted by the full moon. The hundred-foot tower had been built just beneath the tree line a mile north of Bjorn. Its height would have been more impressive if it hadn't been built so close to the two-hundred-foot-tall pines of Eden's forests. The tower was primarily made of rough-cut gray granite blocks of various sizes, but hundreds of black wood beams protruded from its exterior, like exposed ribs on a partially eaten carcass. Around its base was a moat, smaller than Bjorn's but full of water from the spring rains.

The tower had been constructed long before Bjorn had been a town. The old folk all had different stories about it, since neither they nor their parents had been alive when the tower was still in use. Some said it had been used by the canes to spot enemies before the curtain wall had been built at Eden's southern border; some said it was for spotting fires in the valley; others said it had been the residence of an eccentric lord of old. Whatever it had been before, it had been off limits all of Keigh's life.

The moat's bridge had long ago deteriorated into nothing. Only the stone piers on either side remained. Working together, the group fetched some manageable logs from the forest. They laid several across the moat, giving them a makeshift bridge to the island.

Once on the other side, they located the door at the base of the tower. Its old, rusted latch was locked, but with one hard kick, Tarin sent the door crashing inward. The locked latch remained fixed to the frame, swinging pathetically from a rusty nail.

"Give us a wave when you get to the top," Tarin instructed the three spectators. "We'll draw straws to determine the order down here." He grabbed Deacon and Conrad, pulling them around the corner to survey the best exterior route to the top.

"Easy enough!" said Theo, pushing Beaudy ahead of him through the open door.

As Misselli moved to follow the light from Beaudy's lantern, Keigh gently grabbed her elbow. "Be careful. Maybe have Beaudy and Theo test the steps before you go up."

"Aw, that's sweet of you," Misselli simpered with mock fragility. "*You* be careful not to fall off the side of this building and die, helping Tarin stroke his ego!" She phrased it like a joke, but Keigh could tell she wasn't happy he was climbing.

"I'll be fine, really," he promised her. "I'll see you at the top, okay?"

She nodded and disappeared inside the building.

Keigh joined the others where they stood pointing out different routes up the side of the tower. There were a few obvious places to avoid. Several of the protruding beams had rotted out on their underside, making them flimsy at best. By the look of it, there would only be two places where they would have to use the stone for leverage. The rest of the climb could be managed using just the beams.

The four boys drew straws. Tarin would go first, then Conrad, Deacon, and lastly, Keigh.

Minutes later Misselli's blonde head poked over the window ledge like a short-haired Rapunzel. "Ready?" she yelled.

"Just give us the signal!" Tarin belted back.

Keigh's heart gave a slight leap as he saw Misselli hold the shiny gold timepiece in front of her face, its polished back glinting in the moonlight as she suspended it over the ground a hundred feet below.

"Hold that inside, would you?" Tarin yelled. He shook his head and said to himself, "Should have let Theo take it...What was I thinking, letting her hold that?"

"Go!" Misselli called from above.

"No warning?" protested Tarin.

"Clock's ticking!" came her reply.

Flustered, Tarin scrambled to start his climb.

Keigh watched in amazement at how easily Tarin's tall frame scaled the side of the building. So easily, in fact, that Keigh started to doubt that this was the first time Tarin had climbed the old tower. Maybe this challenge wasn't as off-the-top-of-his-head as he had made it seem.

In any case, Tarin reached the window and climbed through it with ease. "Four minutes and forty-eight seconds!" he called. "Who's the Bear now? Good luck beating that!"

Keigh shook his head at his cocky friend, then turned to Conrad. "You should probably get ready. Misselli isn't—"

"Go!" Misselli shouted without warning.

Conrad and Deacon both climbed the face of the tower with little issue. Keigh thought Deacon may have even beaten Tarin if he hadn't had to back-track after reaching for one of the decayed beams halfway up. But by the time Keigh's turn came, Tarin still had the fastest time by five seconds.

"Are you ready?" Misselli called down to him.

Keigh grinned. It was a small advantage, but one he was sure Misselli had concocted intentionally. Even now he thought he could hear the distant squabble as the other boys protested her giving him a warning.

"Yeah! I'm ready!" he called back to her.

"Are you sure?"

"Yes! Just give me the go!"

There was silence as they waited for the second hand to hit twelve... then: "Go!"

Keigh took off, throwing himself beam to beam with a recklessness that surprised him. It was like climbing one of the pines in the forest, the pines he had spent his whole childhood climbing. Going up had never been the problem; it was going down that triggered his fear of heights. But he wouldn't have to climb down today—they could take the stairs inside the tower.

His arms, strong from the field, pulled him easily up and onto each successive beam. Keigh grinned. This was just another tree to climb.

As he moved, he noticed several of the beams had gouges in them. Small enough, they would have gone unnoticed if not for the fact that they had been cut deep enough to show the light brown wood that hadn't been exposed to the elements for long. They were confirmation of what he had suspected since seeing Tarin climb. This task had been planned and practiced by his friend before today.

Snorting at Tarin's petty attempt to rig the contest for himself, Keigh pressed on, filled with a new zeal to thwart his friend's underhanded attempt to cheat.

"You've only got two minutes left to get up here if you want to beat Tarin!" called Theo.

In his newfound desire to win, Keigh did what none of the other boys had even attempted: he started skipping beams. With a jump, he could just reach the beams two above him. He was careful to leap for only the ones Tarin had marked, knowing they would hold. He smiled to himself as he imagined the look on Tarin's face when he told the group how he'd known which beams to leap for.

Nearly two minutes later, Keigh pulled himself up and over the window ledge and into the small room with his friends.

Misselli held the watch up to her face. "Four minutes and forty..." She paused for dramatic effect. "...*four* seconds!"

"Yeah, Keigh!" Beaudy grabbed Keigh off the floor and lifted him to his feet.

"Guess this means I'm still the Bear!" Keigh said, prodding Tarin.

Tarin and Deacon were too busy protesting Misselli's timekeeping to answer. Theo goaded them with comments like "Is there anything Keigh can't do?" and "Best in class again!"

Keigh waited for the ruckus to die down so he could have everyone's attention when he brought up the marks on the beams—but right as he was about to call Tarin out, he smelled it.

The unmistakable scent of wood smoke.

"You guys smell that?" Keigh asked.

"Yeah...smells like smoke," Conrad confirmed.

Tarin and Misselli stuck their heads out opposite windows, looking for flames out in the forest or valley, but Deacon saw it first.

"It's in the tower!" Ashen-faced, he pointed to the trapdoor in the floor. Black wisps of smoke were coiling around its edges, like snakes preparing to strike.

"Beaudy, where's your lantern?" Keigh asked, already knowing the answer.

"I left it downstairs so I could climb better."

"You can't climb stairs and hold a lantern?" Tarin asked, sounding annoyed.

"I—well, I need to use the handrail!"

"And you need two hands for that?" Conrad shook his head in disbelief.

"Well...yeah! What if the stairs give way? I'm not going to be able to catch myself with one hand, am I?"

"If a step can't hold you, you think a rail will? Why are we even arguing this? I've got to get out of here!" Tarin started for the window.

"Wait!" called Keigh. "We should try to get down as many flights inside the tower as we can before we get down to too much smoke. Who knows, maybe it's just a smoky straw fire."

The group nodded their agreement. Keigh pulled open the trap door, releasing a small plume of smoke.

"Tarin! You lead the way. I'll bring up the rear and make sure nobody falls or gets left behind."

Tarin didn't need telling twice. He was through the trapdoor in a flash, quickly followed by Conrad, Misselli, Theo, and Beaudy.

"Deacon! We need to go now!" Keigh yelled. Deacon was still standing at the window, apparently contemplating climbing down alone.

"I can't!" Deacon turned around, panic clearly written on his face. "I don't do fire...I—I can't..."

"Come on! We aren't going down to the fire. Just to a lower window."

Deacon shook his head, but his feet moved to the trapdoor. He gave the window one last look of longing, then jumped through the hole in the floor.

Keigh followed Deacon down the ladder and hurried down the stairs to catch the rest of the group. Every two flights of stairs, there was a room with windows to the outside and a door to the next set of steps. Each time they got to a room, Keigh had to pull Deacon from the window and force him to continue down. The smoke was getting thicker at each level, but by keeping their heads low, they were able to keep their breath.

After pulling Deacon out of the second room and onto the fifth flight of stairs, Keigh heard his friends coughing.

Tarin's voice yelled up the stairs. "Go back! There's flames down here!"

Keigh turned back to the room he had just exited, pulling Deacon along with him. When all his friends had spilled back into the room, he slammed the door shut, stopping the relentless billow of smoke pouring through the opening.

"Out the window. It's the only way!" Tarin shot across the room to the window and, without another word, lowered himself over the edge and disappeared.

"What are we going to do?" Theo said, terrified. "There's no way I can climb down! My legs won't reach the beams!"

He was right. His short body would never span the gap between the beams, and neither would Misselli's. There had to be a way to get them down, and fast.

"Conrad, if you go down first, I can take Theo down halfway on my back," Keigh said. "From there, Theo can jump off and you can catch him."

Conrad nodded and wasted no time exiting through the window.

"Jump off?" Theo yelled.

"You'll have to!" Keigh insisted. "Conrad *will* catch you. I can't take the time to go the whole way with you. I have to come back for Misselli!"

"Why doesn't she go before me?" Theo pointed to Misselli. "You know... women first?"

"Because! I'm not going to let go of her!" Keigh barked, not wanting to make eye contact with Misselli for fear she would object to his plan. "Now get on my back and let's go!"

Theo climbed on and locked his arms tightly around Keigh's neck. Keigh couldn't help the grim smile that crossed his lips. This was why Theo had been impossible to dislodge from Beaudy's shoulders during their chicken fights at the pond. He was small, not weak. Keigh only hoped he would let go when the time came, otherwise he was unsure if he would be able to sever the hold Theo had on his neck.

He poked his head out the window. They had descended about halfway down the tower already, leaving another fifty feet to the ground.

We can do this. There's no other option. Nobody is going to die tonight.

He slid his legs over the ledge and lowered himself and Theo down to the first beam. As soon as he let go of the window ledge, the whole world began to spin and shift beneath him. Panicking, he clung to the stone wall, trying to get as much of his body touching it as possible.

Come on, Keigh! You climbed up. You can climb down. No difference.

It was a lie, and he knew it. Going down was so much worse.

"Keep going, Keigh!"

It was Misselli's voice. As long as Theo was on his back, she was trapped in that room. He took a deep breath and swallowed his fear.

Better to fall to my death than live a coward.

Slowly, he lowered himself to the next beam, then the next and the next, until he was descending as quickly as he had climbed up.

CRACK!

The beam beneath him suddenly gave way, sending Keigh and Theo falling back into the darkness. They collided with the next beam down, smashing Theo between Keigh and the wood before pitching them back into thin air.

Falling another level, to the next beam, Keigh struck it square, hitting hard on his chest. But before being caste back into nothingness, Keigh grabbed hold of the beam, clawing desperately into the old wood and halting their descent. Theo's grip nearly broke. His fingers dug bloody furrows into Keigh's collarbones before catching his shoulders.

Keigh felt as if he were about to pass out, like the fall had knocked all the strength out of him. "You've gotta let go!" he told Theo, his hold on the beam slipping. "Conrad will catch you!"

"Jump to me, Theo!" Conrad called from the ground.

"I'm sorry," Theo whispered, releasing his grip on Keigh.

The weight on his back disappeared and he looked down to see Theo freefall the last twenty feet. His body hit squarely between Conrad's outstretched arms. Both boys crumpled to the ground, shaken but okay.

Keigh shook his head, trying to wake himself from his sudden fatigue. *Can't quit now.* Summoning all his willpower, he pulled himself up onto the beam, then, quick as he could, climbed back up to the window he had exited a minute before.

As his head rose above the window ledge, he was already barking orders. "Deacon! Beaudy! Go! I'll take Misselli down with me, behind you!"

"Keigh!"

Misselli's voice was frightened. It took him only a second to see why. Deacon was lying unresponsive on the ground between her and Beaudy. Considerably more smoke was roiling under the door now, filling the top half of the room with its murky haze.

"Keigh!" Misselli's whole body was racked with tremors as she hurriedly tried to communicate what happened. "He just started—started panicking, and—and I think he breathed in too much smoke or, or, or just fainted! But we can't get him to wake up!"

"Beaudy, get going!" Keigh yelled. He pulled himself through the window, his mind racing for what to do with Deacon.

"I...I'll go after Deacon," Beaudy replied weakly.

Keigh didn't have time to argue. They had to move; time was running out.

"Beaudy! I need your sleeve!" He slid down next to Beaudy and began tearing the stitches away at the seams. When he had taken the sleeve off Beaudy's shirt, he tore it again until he had a long strip of linen. "Beaudy, pick Deacon up and put him on my back. Misselli, bring his arms around my neck."

Soon, they had Deacon hanging on Keigh's back, his upper arms tied together around Keigh's neck with Beaudy's sleeve. This would be difficult, but there was no choice.

Panic was starting to touch Keigh. Looking at the smoke-rimmed door again, he realized they had less time than he'd originally hoped. He backed out the window, feeling the full weight of Deacon's limp body hanging from his throat. *I'm not going to be able to breathe!*

He moved with urgency, lowering himself from beam to beam. Every other level he sat down to release the pressure on his throat. Breathing would have been difficult enough even without Deacon's dead weight around his neck. Smoke was now billowing heavily out of the lower windows and crawling up the side of the tower.

Halfway down, he called to Conrad, "You and Tarin are going to have to catch Deacon!"

"Tarin's gone! It's just me and Theo!"

Tarin left? What was he thinking!

He could worry about that later. "Just catch him when I untie his arms! Don't let him land on his head!"

"No promises!" Theo called back.

Keigh pulled the knot in the fabric, releasing Deacon's body into a freefall. He didn't even stop to watch. He had to get back up to Misselli and Beaudy.

A minute later, he pulled himself back over the ledge and into the room to find them lying on the floor, avoiding the cloud of black smoke hanging ominously above them. The floor was hot to the touch. The flames must be right beneath them now.

"Beaudy! You're up! Get out that window!" Keigh pulled the large boy to his feet and waved him toward the window. Reaching back, he took Misselli by the hand and led her, crouching, along behind Beaudy.

When Beaudy got to the window, he stuck his head out and froze.

"Come on, Beaudy! You can do it! Don't look to the ground! Just one beam at a time!" Keigh encouraged, keeping Misselli's head covered with his arm.

"I can't do it, Keigh! It's too high!"

"Just one step at a time! Start by getting your feet up on the ledge, then we can start lowering you down!" Keigh was losing patience, but he knew the feeling Beaudy was battling.

To Keigh's relief, Beaudy moved. He clambered up into the window and sat there, hunched over like a massive owl.

"I can't do it," he said, defeated.

Just as he started to turn back into the room, the door to the stairs fell inward, blasting them with a wave of heat and revealing the flame-filled stairway. Misselli screamed. Beaudy's eyes widened in terror as he froze again, blocking the window. Tongues of fire lapped at the door frame's edges, licking their way into the room.

We don't have time for this!

Keigh knew what he had to do.

He looked at Beaudy's stunned face, the reflection of flames flickering in his wide eyes. "You know how to do a cannonball, Beaudy?"

"Wh-what?"

"I just need you to think *cannonball*, okay? Here, grab my hands."

As soon as Beaudy released his grip on the window frame, Keigh shoved him as hard as he could away from the building, sending the stunned boy hurtling backward into the night.

He climbed up into the window and turned to Misselli. "Get on my back! Let's go."

But before she could move, the floor fell out from under her.

Keigh reached out, snagging her outstretched arm. He pulled her up tight to his chest. Wrapping his arms around her as flames filled the room, he pressed his heels into the ledge and launched them both out into the darkness.

The fall seemed like an eternity. He hoped desperately that he had jumped far enough. Misselli's head pressed to his chest he cradled her body against his, keeping her above him. His body would take the brunt of the fall.

"Hold your breath," he said calmly into her ear. A second later, their bodies collided with the moat in a fantastic splash.

The force of the impact drove the air from his lungs. Every inch of his back seared with pain. He released Misselli, pushing her up toward the surface. Keigh stared after her as she rose through the orange and silver strands of light refracting through the water from fire and moon. His heart rose even as his body sank. *She was safe.* He didn't have the strength to swim his way up. Just as he was about to suck in lungsful of water, his hand touched bottom. Gathering his legs beneath him, he pushed himself up off the bottom with all his remaining strength.

The instant his mouth broke the surface, he gasped, gulping down breath after breath of the cool night air. Desperately, he looked for Beaudy as the patches of white slowly faded from his vision. Had he made it? Had Keigh pushed him far enough out to reach the moat?

Keigh's sight returned just as he located his large friend bobbing in the muddy water next to him. Half of Beaudy's face was bright red. The blood vessels in his right eye had burst, but he was still grinning ear to ear.

"I didn't do the cannonball," was all Keigh heard him say before he was plunged back under the water as Misselli threw her arms around him.

She released him, allowing him to come back up for air. "That was insane!" she crowed. "Incredible! Brave! But absolutely insane! You could have killed us!" She beamed at Keigh, then spit a stream of water playfully at his face before throwing her arms around him again, taking them both under.

He had done it! Theo, Deacon, Beaudy, and Misselli were all safely on the ground.

"Hate to interrupt," Conrad shouted from the bank, "but we have to get out of here." He pointed back toward Bjorn, where a string of lights were working their way up the trail toward the tower.

"We can't be here when they get here! Setting fires is an executable offense!" exclaimed Theo.

Keigh looked at the tower. Resembling an oversized chimney, black smoke billowed out of the top, obscuring the moon's light. Its windows glowed orange as the flames consumed the stone building's wooden guts.

"Quick, then—we need to take cover in the forest. We can work our way around the fire crew and get back to our homes unseen." Keigh pointed for his friends to go.

"What about Deacon?" Misselli groaned, looking at his still unconscious form on the ground as they crawled out of the moat onto the muddy bank.

"I'll carry Deacon. You guys get going."

Misselli squeezed his hand and took off after the other three.

Keigh swam back across the moat. He pulled Deacon down into the water, away from the burning building, toward the forest. When he had swum them across, he looked up to see Misselli vanish into the trees behind Beaudy, Theo, and Conrad. Relief filled him. *They made it.*

"Now we just gotta get you up there," he said, looking at Deacon, a matt of pond weeds plastered to his enemy's unconscious face.

Scooping Deacon's body up in his arms, he took off as fast as he could stagger toward the tree line. His arms were lead. His legs, heavy as tree trunks. He had given everything to getting his friends out of the tower and now struggled to even reach the pace of a fast walk.

Halfway to the edge of the forest, he felt the ground shudder and a low rumble filled the air.

Keigh looked down the tree line to see Mace pounding up the hill toward him, breathing in rough growls, her massive paws thudding the ground with all her weight.

He wasn't going to make it. Not with Deacon. The red bear would spot him long before he made the cover of the forest. But he couldn't just leave Deacon lying there. It wouldn't be right to abandon him. Plus, there was zero chance Deacon wouldn't give them all up to save his own skin.

Once again, Keigh knew what he had to do.

Going swiftly to the nearest bush, he stashed Deacon behind it, covering him with as many pine needles as he could rake up. Rising to his feet, he took one last look at the forest. He could just make out Misselli in the firelight. She waved for him to join them in the shadows. He shook his head at her and waved her on.

Turning back toward the blaze, he started to run back to the tower.

Mace intercepted him right as he reached the moat. As she lowered her head, her white scars and teeth caught the light of the fire, sending her already menacing appearance to a new level of terrifying. Her lip curled as she gave Keigh a warning growl.

"You got someone up there, Mace?" Braddock's voice called from down the path.

Braddock was the last person Keigh wanted to see right now. The man who had let him test as a cane, taken a chance on him, who had lent him his sword and defended him to Vicerous. The man who had shown him grace when Keigh had insulted him…

This is going to hurt, he thought.

Mace stared at him intently, no longer snarling or growling.

A minute later, Braddock arrived, closely followed by Victor Giles, Chogan Bald Head, and a small contingent of men from town, brandishing buckets.

Braddock seemed ready to explode when he saw Keigh backed up against the moat where Mace had cornered him, but after a swift look at his red bear, the fire in his eyes seemed to diminish a bit. "Explain yourself!" he demanded.

"I didn't mean to…It was an accident," Keigh said, shuffling his feet.

Braddock belted orders to the men carrying buckets, then returned his attention to Keigh. The warrior grabbed him by the shoulders and began pelting him with questions. "What happened here? Why are you even up here? Who else is here?"

"Nobody!" Keigh blurted, a little too eagerly. "It's just me, sir. A man in town told me nobody had ever been able to climb the old watchtower, and… and I came up here to prove I could." Keigh hung his head, unable to look Braddock in the eye as he lied. He just had to keep the men's attention on himself so they wouldn't go searching up the hill where Deacon lay hidden. If they found him, all his friends would be revealed.

"So, you decided to light the tower on fire, then?" Braddock asked disbelievingly.

"No, sir. I left my lantern at the base while I climbed, and, well..." Keigh clenched his fists, suddenly angry at how careless Beaudy had been. "It must have fallen over."

"Your lantern?"

Keigh nodded.

Braddock's eyes narrowed at Keigh, then began looking around the ground.

The same man who had been able to tell him nearly every detail of his fight with the stranger in the woods, based upon nothing but what he could see in the dirt, was now investigating the scene where seven people had been no less than ten minutes ago.

The battle master's eyes lingered on the log bridge they had thrown together. "You bring these logs down here by yourself then? Two of them are pretty big."

"Yes, sir. I didn't want to have to get wet crossing the moat."

"Strange, I don't see any drag marks on the ground and..." Braddock pointed at Keigh's soaking wet clothes. "And what...you just decided to get in anyway after going through all the hard work of building yourself a bridge?"

"No, sir. I had to jump for the moat when I saw the tower was on fire, sir."

"Do you wish to explain why I see multiple sets of footprints in the mud here?" Braddock pointed to a small footprint Keigh knew must be Misselli's.

Keigh didn't like how much information Braddock was getting from the scene. He had to force the point. "I don't know! Sir. There must have been people up here before me. I came up here tonight to prove I could climb the tower. I accidentally lit the fire. Nobody else was here. Nobody made me do it." Keigh took a deep breath, attempting to calm himself. "So will you be taking me in or am I free to go?"

Braddock considered him pensively, seemingly unsure of how to respond to his confession. "Okay, I believe you," he said, but Keigh saw his eyes dart up the hill to the tree line. Braddock turned to his fellow canes. "Victor, please keep watch on Mr. Anders while I assist the others in quenching this fire." Then he strode over to Keigh and whispered in his ear, "You sure this is how you want to do this?"

"I was the *only* one here," Keigh repeated clearly.

Stepping back, Braddock gave a short sigh. "Very well, then. Tomorrow you will stand trial before the elders of Bjorn for the mishandling of fire, the destruction of kingdom grounds, and endangering the people of Eden. The punishment for these crimes may be as much as death and no less than five lashes with the cat o' nine tails."

Keigh met Braddock's gaze without flinching. For a moment, the two of them stared at each other. Finally, the cane nodded in understanding and walked away.

As soon as he left, Victor Giles placed a hand on Keigh's shoulder. The cane's eyes watched the blaze, but Keigh's settled on a narrow footprint in the mud. Misselli's footprint.

CHAPTER 12

THE FALL

23-53-5

Keigh's eyes popped open at the sound of voices outside the door. He hadn't been sleeping, in fact, he hadn't slept at all that night. Victor Giles had left him to wait on a hard wooden bench inside Bjorn's town hall, his feet and hands tied. Sleep wouldn't come for him...couldn't come for him. Not because he wasn't tired—he was tired, more tired than he had been since fighting the stranger in the woods. It wasn't even the uncomfortable bench that kept him awake.

It was fear. Fear that at any moment the door would open and he would see his friends marched in, captured as he had been. Fear of his impending trial, fear of punishment—those had been put on hold as his mind conjured images of his friends being hunted down, bound, and dragged in for questioning. So far, though, he remained alone. Early morning light illuminated the town hall's tall windows. Keigh was pretty sure that if they had caught any of his friends in their escape, it would have been during the night. *They must be safe at home by now.*

He lifted his head to see what the commotion outside was about. Suddenly, the door flew open. Keigh's heart jolted to a stop as his father burst into the room.

"You can't go in there!" an unfamiliar voice protested.

"He's my son! You won't keep me from him!"

Keigh sat up straight on the bench as his father barreled across the room toward him.

"Are you hurt?" Owen asked him earnestly.

"I'm fine," said Keigh, attempting to rub blood back into the arm he'd been lying on.

Owen cursed under his breath. "What were you thinking, climbing the tower? You know it's off limits! It always has been! Did one of your friends put you up to this?"

Keigh didn't know how to read his father. The man was a storm of mixed emotions. His voice was full of anger, disbelief, and even fear as he pelted Keigh with questions.

Keigh shook his head. There wasn't any explanation his father would accept. At least none that wouldn't implicate his friends.

"Braddock was up at the house first thing this morning." Owen began pacing, floorboards creaking under his bulk. "He came to tell me *my* son had been taken in for mishandling fire and destruction of kingdom grounds!" He squeezed his eyes shut. "Just be grateful your mother and siblings weren't up to hear him."

Keigh's stomach, already knots, cinched tighter. He had been so preoccupied with making sure his friends were protected, he hadn't even stopped to think how the charges would shame his family.

"I'm sorry," was all he could say, watching his father fume.

"Why? Just tell me why you did it, Keigh," Owen pleaded. "What more do you have to prove? Your mother and I didn't object when you submitted yourself to agoge as a cane, *even* though we knew you could get hurt. We wanted you to have the opportunity to do something you could be proud of... and you did. You *did* do something to be proud of!"

He knelt in front of Keigh and rested a meaty hand on his son's knee.

"I can't tell you how many people have praised me this week for what you did in your duels. I thought you were happy. I thought you just needed to show people you had more to offer than growing crops…" Owen shot back to his feet. "Never did I think my son was just hell bent on getting attention! Well, now you've got it, Keigh! Everyone is going to see you now. Are you happy?" He turned away, apparently too angry to look at Keigh.

"I…I never wanted to embarrass you, or the family." Tears filled Keigh's eyes as he imagined his mother's face upon hearing the news that her son was a criminal.

"Embarrass?" His father turned and knelt in front of him again. Anger still blazed in his eyes, but his voice was tender. "You think I'm mad because you embarrassed us? Son, I can take any and all the shame this world can throw at a man! I've taken on more shame in my life than you'll ever know. I'm not angry because of what you've done to me. I'm angry that the people I love most are going to be hurt. I'm angry your mother's heart will break for the son she loves. I'm angry your brothers will become embittered against a younger brother they looked up to. I'm angry at the fear that will fill your sweet little sister when her hero is broken and beaten for his own failures…I'm angry that my *son* is going to suffer, and I can't do anything to stop it." Owen took a long breath. "Mostly, though, I'm angry at myself. I have failed as a father if my son doesn't feel like he's enough…that my son would feel so unseen and unloved that he would resort to putting his own life at risk, just to prove to the world that he mattered."

Tears poured down Keigh's face. This was so much worse than being yelled at, so much worse than being punished. His father's words hurt because they were true. His family would suffer, and it was all his fault. Why had he let Tarin goad him into climbing the tower? Why couldn't passing his agoge duels have been enough? Why had he let Misselli come anywhere near his recklessness?

"I don't know what's wrong with me…" he choked. It felt good to say it out loud, but it also seemed to make it real. Something *was* wrong with him.

He hated himself. A minute ago, he had felt noble, even good, about taking the fall for his friends. Now…now he felt he deserved everything that was coming to him.

"I'm sorry," he told his father.

Owen squeezed his shoulder, then grabbed the back of Keigh's neck and pressed his shaved head to Keigh's brown locks. They sat like that for a minute, just father and son, quietly feeling all the things they were always too busy to feel. Hurt and disappointment. Love and appreciation. Fear and doubt. Gratitude and hope.

"Owen! You need to leave!" the voice from outside called. "The elders will be here soon!"

"Look at me," his father said, pulling his head back.

Keigh lifted his face and looked at him through blurry eyes. His father's bearded face showed no more signs of anger, and when he spoke, his voice was tender but resolute.

"We are going to get through this." Owen nodded, as if convincing himself with his own words. "Your mother and I will be with you every step of the way. You may lose a lot today, but you will never lose us."

His father smiled compassionately and stood, looking down on him. When Keigh didn't say anything, he bent back down and hugged him, muffling the sobs Keigh had been fighting so hard to suppress. Then he stood again, turned, and walked out without another word.

Keigh sat in the stillness of the room and allowed himself to cry freely. The tightness in his chest released some, but didn't go away entirely.

Wiping his face, he took a couple deep breaths, forcing himself to return to the present, wondering what would happen next. Braddock had said he could potentially be given over to execution. Would he be allowed to talk to his family first? To Misselli? If that happened, would he even want to? The thought of having to see people for the last time was too overwhelming. Surely they would never execute someone so young. Surely the elders would see that it was just youthful foolishness to blame and dismiss the charges.

An hour later, the doors flew open again. This time the sound of agitated voices filled the room, followed immediately by Bjorn's elders. The three men walked across to a long, polished table at the far end of the room. Braddock and the small, pucker-faced man didn't look at Keigh as they passed him.

Only the ancient man, with snow-white beard and hair, peered at him with crystal-blue eyes as he crutched his way to the table's center chair. Once the senior elder had taken his seat, Braddock and the short man took their places on either side of him.

The door opened again, and two canes entered. Victor Giles, who had marched him back to town the night before, stood guard at the door with—to Keigh's dismay—Vicerous Wulf.

Victor kept his eyes up attentively, showing no emotion. Vicerous made no such attempt at hiding his bias as he curled his lip scornfully at Keigh.

Bang! The old man slapped the table with his hand. "Keigh Anders! You are here before us today to answer for the crimes with which you have been charged. Crimes you have unofficially admitted to and will have a chance to bring more clarity to today. You will speak only when asked. Any outbursts will be considered evidence of a rebellious and unruly spirit, something that will not help you when sentencing is decided. Have I made myself clear?"

"Yes, sir."

The elder folded his hands on the table. "My name is Cato Boman. I am chief elder in Bjorn and am burdened with its safety. To my right is Oliver Connell." Cato nodded to the small man with the silver goatee. "And I believe you already know Braddock Fortier."

Braddock looked at Keigh then, for the first time that day, giving him the same contemplative gaze as he had the night before.

"First," Cato continued, "the charges and your pleas. Respond with either 'guilty' or 'not guilty.'"

Braddock interrupted, "Understand that if you plead guilty, Keigh, you will be given no opportunity to defend yourself, while if you plead 'not guilty,' you *will* be given opportunity to explain your situation."

Oliver gave Braddock an annoyed look, like a cat who had just had its prey scared off.

"To the charge of mishandling fire," boomed Cato, "how do you plead?"

Keigh hesitated. What could he say that wouldn't incriminate his friends? He wasn't a good liar. Braddock had easily contradicted each of his lies last night. He needed to explain, but resolved to do so in as few words as possible.

"Not guilty," he answered.

Oliver smirked, but Braddock gave him a small nod of approval.

Cato continued. "To the charge of destruction of kingdom grounds, how do you plead?"

"Not guilty."

"And to the charge of endangering the people of Eden, how do you plead?"

"Not guilty."

"Very well! We will begin with witness accounts."

The first witness was Braddock, who opted to allow Victor to speak in his stead, since he was judging the case and the elders would know his thoughts in deliberations. Victor's testimony was short and as unemotional as his expression, simply stating that Keigh was the only one found at the scene and that Keigh had told him and Braddock that he alone had been at the tower.

That could have been worse, thought Keigh as Victor finished his account. He assumed he would be the next to speak.

He was wrong. At Oliver's insistence, open complaints were to be heard against him.

For the next two hours, a parade of people entered the room one at a time, accusing Keigh of all manner of wrongdoings. From endangering life and property with the fire all the way to *"always looking like he's up to no good,"* he was accused by people he had known his whole life as well as people he had never met. Some were even the same ones who had shaken his hand and clamored to meet him less than a week ago. Most barely knew him, but they all had two things in common: none of them knew the truth of what had happened at the tower, and they *all* wanted to see him bleed.

Finally, after a particularly nasty woman with a beak of a nose and thin, patchy hair had just finished accusing him of ruining a good night's beauty sleep, Victor announced: "That's the last of them, Master Boman."

"Good. Are you satisfied you have heard every complaint, Oliver?" Cato asked.

Oliver nodded begrudgingly.

"Well then, Mr. Anders, if you would please stand, we will hear your account now." Cato's chair creaked as he settled back and gave his beard a thoughtful stroke.

Keigh stood. "Elders of Bjorn, I was at the tower last night—"

"What more do we need to hear?" interrupted Oliver. "The boy openly admits to being there. The men found no one else at the site. The fire didn't start itself!"

Keigh heard a small sniff and looked over to see Vicerous grinning wickedly.

"Actually," said Braddock, "if you would indulge me on this, I would like to know a bit more about *how* the fire started." His eyes narrowed as he waited for Keigh to begin.

"I set my lantern down before starting to climb, and I fear I must not have set it in a clear enough space. I don't know if the wind blew it over or how the flame escaped, but I did not intentionally light any fire."

"And you say you were there to climb the outside of the tower, correct?" Braddock questioned.

"Yes, sir. I was only going to climb to the top window and come down, but while I was on the tower I saw the flames start at the bottom of the building. By the time I got down, the flames were too large for me to put out."

"Interesting...but now I'm curious." Braddock cocked his head. "Why are you lying to us?"

Cato gave Braddock a look of warning, as if he had just breached etiquette in some way.

What did I say wrong? "I...I don't know what you mean? That's what happened."

"Are you a thief, Mr. Anders?"

Braddock's calmness unnerved him. "No! No, sir."

"Have you come into some money recently that your parents are unaware of?"

"No, sir. What are—"

"Did you borrow anything yesterday? Is there someone else who knew you had gone up there that we need to question?"

"No! Nobody! Sir." Keigh cursed himself for letting his refusal come out so adamantly.

"You know, Keigh, lying to us will only add to the severity of your punishment. If you wish to change your account of events, now is your last chance."

"It happened like I said." Keigh glared at Braddock. What was he playing at?

"Unfortunately for you, Keigh, I happen to know your father—quite well, in fact—and one thing I know him not to be is a liar."

"Seems the boy is, though," Vicerous spat from the door.

Braddock's face darkened as he pointed a warning finger at Vicerous, silencing him. "I spoke with your father this morning, Keigh. He told me that you had told him you were going to meet friends last night. And, more relevantly, that you and your family do not own an oil lantern and never have."

Beaudy. Keigh hadn't anticipated Braddock would ask his father about that part of the story. "I...um...I misspoke is all. I meant candle, not lantern."

"And you say you left it at the foot of the tower while you climbed?"

Braddock was cornering him, but into what? Keigh thought frantically, trying to undo the damage. "Yes, in the dirt. I'm always very cautious with fire."

"Then perhaps you can explain why I found this..." Braddock reached under his cloak and produced the charred wire frame of Beaudy's oil lantern. "...inside the tower."

Oliver's face lit up. "There were others there with you! Tell us their names and your punishment will be lessened!"

Keigh was furious. Furious with himself for not thinking his story through. Furious with Braddock for cornering him like this. Wasn't it enough that he had turned himself in? Why did Braddock seem so intent on getting Keigh to admit others were up there with him—and if he knew that, why hadn't he and his men gone looking for them? How had they not found Deacon unconscious in the bushes fifty feet away?

"I was the only one there." Keigh spoke to Oliver, but his eyes were locked on Braddock.

The battle master sat back, pressing the tips of his fingers together, seemingly weighing Keigh, just as he had when Keigh had asked him to grant him an agoge duel. "Understand that your punishment will be more severe if you insist on this," Braddock warned him. His tone wasn't threatening. Rather, it contained a hint of intrigue—and, Keigh thought, maybe even respect.

"I insist," Keigh stated.

Braddock smiled. Keigh had never wanted to punch someone so badly in his whole life.

"Is there anything more you would like to add before we deliberate?" Cato asked.

"Nothing, sir."

"Then remain where you are until we return. Victor, Vicerous, see to it that nobody enters or speaks to Mr. Anders while we are absent," ordered Cato, before hauling himself out of his seat with his staff and following Braddock and Oliver into an adjoining room.

As soon as the door closed behind Cato, Vicerous spoke, his voice eager. "When they find you guilty—and they will find you guilty—I hope I'm the one who gets to carry out your sentence."

"Quiet yourself, Vicerous," said Victor. "Nobody speaks to the boy until the elders return."

"Fine, then. I'll tell you, Victor." Vicerous faced his partner. "This boy is a poison. A poison that must be expelled from the body before it corrupts the whole. He has already corrupted the minds of his classmates and the hundreds of peasants who celebrated the passing of his agoge duels." Vicerous grimaced. "I don't know how he passed, but I know he must have had help. What he did was unnatural, a sick perversion. Nobody gets stronger as they fight. I'm telling you, Victor, sorcery was involved. Probably learned it from his witch mother! Wouldn't be the first spell she's cast. The whole family is filth!" He returned his glare to Keigh. "I just hope I get the pleasure of pruning the family tree."

Keigh matched Vicerous's glare the whole time, unwilling to let the man best him in anything. Now wasn't the time to start a fight, not with his hands and feet tied and men deciding his sentence in a room next door. But right then, Keigh decided that Vicerous Wulf would pay for what he had said about him, about his family, about his mother. He glared at Vicerous long after the man had averted his gaze from Keigh, pouring all his anger and frustration into this one small act of defiance while he waited to hear his fate.

*

An hour later, the three elders emerged from their deliberations and took their seats at the long wooden table. Oliver and Braddock both seemed upset, while Cato seemed at peace.

"Rulings have been rendered concerning the three counts to which you have pleaded 'not guilty,'" Cato began, "as well as a verdict on a fourth charge: perjury."

Keigh felt like throwing up. He was grateful his stomach was empty. If he were going to be convicted, he would receive it like a man, he wouldn't emerge from the hall covered in his own sick, looking guilty and pathetic. He couldn't control the verdict, but he could control how he took it.

"On the first three charges, no consensus was made. As the ranking member, I have decided that your youth, ignorance, and previous good standing should be taken into account. That being said, on the charge of mishandling fire, this council finds you...guilty. For this you will receive five lashes with the cat o' nine tails."

Keigh knew that this was the lightest sentence he could receive for the crime, but his heart nearly stopped at the thought of it. He had seen people whipped before. The cat o' nine tails was a particularly nasty whip, taking chunks of flesh with every strike. How much skin would he have left after five lashes? Who would do the lashing? *As long as it's not Vicerous,* he thought, clenching his teeth.

"On the charge of destruction of kingdom grounds, this council finds you...guilty. For this you will receive another five lashes. On the charge of endangering the people of Eden, this council finds you...guilty. For this you will receive an additional five lashes. Lastly, on the charge of perjury, this council *did* reach a unanimous decision...guilty! For this crime you will receive the maximum sentence of twenty days' imprisonment at the Capital."

Fifteen lashes and twenty days in a cell. Could he even survive the lashes?

The ancient elder's blue eyes never blinked as he addressed Keigh. "Your sentence shall be carried out tomorrow at dawn. Until then you will be tied to the whipping post. Your family may feed you there if they wish." Cato waved to Victor and Vicerous. "Vicerous, please see that Mr. Anders is tied securely to the whipping post outside. Victor, see to it that a sign outlining Mr. Anders' crimes and his sentence is posted above him. And Mr. Anders..."

Cato waited until Keigh met his gaze.

"I do hope to never see you in front of me again for reasons such as these. There is no growth without pain...but it is possible to have pain without growth." Cato paused, tapping the tabletop with a finger. "See that you grow."

He nodded to the two canes by the door, and they moved immediately to take hold of him. Each hooked an arm under Keigh's armpits and unceremoniously dragged him out of the hall and into the gravel street, where a small crowd had gathered, waiting for the elders' verdict.

Keigh kept his gaze fixed on the ground, afraid of what he might see if he looked up. His mom or Misselli crying? His father and brothers turning their backs? Or even worse, would he see that no one had come in his defense at all?

The crowd was silent, apparently waiting for the canes to announce the verdict. When they said nothing, people started murmuring. Keigh caught bits and pieces as he was dragged around the side of the building:

"...must be so ashamed..."

"...what he deserves..."

"...hope he gets the sword..."

When they got to the whipping post, Victor brusquely dropped his arm. The extra weight on Vicerous gave him more than enough reason to drop Keigh. His hands still bound, he was unable to catch himself, and his face smashed into the gravel. Victor departed to fetch what he needed to make a sign, leaving Keigh alone with Vicerous.

The whipping post was a tar-covered knob of wood with a thick iron loop on its top used for fastening prisoners' ties. At two feet tall, it kept whoever was tied to it from standing up straight. A prisoner would have to remain on the rocky gravel or stand uncomfortably hunched over the post.

"Your hands!" Vicerous barked.

When Keigh didn't offer his hands immediately, Vicerous kicked him in the ribs. Keigh heard a gasp he recognized. Misselli was there.

Vicerous leaned down and put his face next to Keigh's ear. "Please, test me again and see if you don't regret it." He stood up straight again and repeated, "Your hands!"

Keigh remained still, hoping Vicerous's inability to control his prisoner would shame him.

This time Vicerous kicked him in the ribs, then grabbed the hair on the back of his head and lifted him off the ground before dropping him onto the post. Keigh narrowly missed hitting the iron loop with his front teeth. Instead, the iron struck his throat, rendering him unable to breathe. He writhed on his back, desperately gasping for air. Vicerous let out a short, mirthful laugh.

"Just do what he says, Keigh!"

The sound of Misselli's cry broke him. He didn't want to fight Vicerous anymore, not if it meant hearing her cry.

Keigh held his hands out.

Vicerous grabbed the rope that tied them and twisted it, wrenching Keigh's wrists painfully, then quickly fastened his ties to the loop using a second section of rope.

"Good little boy," sneered Vicerous, leaning in close to whisper in his ear again. "Listen to your girlfriend."

Immediately, Keigh was reminded of the stranger in the woods. *I see your girlfriend knows the man...* He'd hated it then and he hated it now. Why did men who wished him harm always bring her up? He didn't want her name on their lips, now or ever.

He threw his head back and caught Vicerous in the nose with a satisfying *crack!*

"You little—"

Someone in the crowd laughed, and Keigh turned his head just in time to see Vicerous pull a hand away from his stunned face, revealing the crimson blood dripping from his newly crooked nose.

Vicerous kicked him in the ribs again and fled into the crowd to clean himself up.

As soon as he was gone, Misselli rushed to Keigh's side, earning another round of murmurs from the crowd. Kneeling beside him, she hissed in his ear, "What were you thinking?"

"It was worth it," wheezed Keigh, trying to curl up in a ball as much as his bound hands would let him. "He talks too much."

"I'm not talking about Wulf! I'm talking about you letting yourself get caught last night!" Her fingers gently brushed the locks of hair from his face. "You could have made it into the trees before anyone saw you!"

She wanted a reason. Everyone wanted a reason. "I couldn't make it to the trees carrying Deacon. I was too tired. And I couldn't let Deacon get caught."

"Why not? He would have tossed you to Mace just to see her slap you around! You should have heard the awful things he said about you when he came to!" Misselli huffed. "Said you were too slow, and he wasn't surprised you got caught, since you're the only one he knows dumber than Beaudy."

Hearing that Deacon hadn't appreciated being rescued didn't surprise him, but it still hurt that no matter what he did, the Wulfs seemed bound to hate him. "Did you tell him it was only because of me that he wasn't burned to a crisp?"

"Well...no..."

"No? Why not?" Keigh gave an ill-humored laugh. "There's probably nothing Deacon would have hated hearing more."

"Because," Misselli retorted, "I was the only one who stayed and waited for him to wake up. The first thing he did was blame you! So I slapped him as hard as I could and left him in the dark."

"Oh. Well, he probably didn't like that much either." Keigh winced. He could feel a knot forming on the back of his skull where he had headbutted Vicerous. "Am I bleeding?"

A shiver ran through him as Misselli's smooth hands slid up the back of his neck, her fingers running through his hair, feeling for a cut.

"Why did you do it, Keigh?" she asked him, still cradling his head.

"It was the only way to make sure Deacon didn't get caught. You know as well as I do that if Deacon got caught, he would have given up all our names, and..."

"And what?"

"And..."

Keigh was back with his dad at the family dining table in the dark morning hours after being attacked by the stranger in the forest. He could hear his father's words again: *"I want you to be good to 'em..."*

"And an eye for an eye and a tooth for a tooth would leave all of Eden blind and starving."

"What? How hard did you hit your head?"

He smiled at Misselli's confusion, remembering his own reaction to his father's advice. "It's just something my dad told me."

"Yeah? Is that why you headbutted Vicerous?" asked Misselli.

"I'm working on it. I'll start with Deacon and work my way up to his father." He chuckled, sending pain shooting through his ribs all over again.

"This isn't right!" She pulled back from him. Cupping his head, she lifted his chin so they were face to face. "You can't take the fall for all of us."

"Watch me." He smiled at her. Why had he never noticed how blue her eyes were? That the freckles, high on her cheeks, never quite made it onto her nose? Why was he noticing now?

"I can't let you do this, Keigh!" Her eyes began filling with tears. "I'll go to the elders. I'll tell them we were all there."

"Don't—"

"I'm serious! You can't take the fall for this! You of all people. If not for you, only Tarin and Conrad would have made it back to their families." She pressed her forehead to his shoulder. "You saved our lives...now you want us to watch you take our punishment?"

He didn't like this. She was making him feel resentful. He needed to know what he was doing was right if he was going to survive this. "Don't watch, then," he said. "Go home."

"I'm not leaving."

"Then stop threatening to turn everyone in and undo everything I'm trying to save them from!" Keigh snapped.

"Okay, I won't." Misselli seemed taken back by the sudden venom in his voice. "What if I tell them it was just me and you up there?" She took hold of his hand. "I can't let you do this for me. We'll do it together!"

"Misselli, please, you can't. You have to let me do this."

"No, Keigh! Either we suffer together, or you condemn me to a fate far worse! I can survive my flesh being torn, but if you make me watch—" Her words cut off abruptly. "...watch you suffer for my sake, then you'll have wounded me in ways worse than whips!" Tears fell from her cheeks like spring rain dripping off tender new leaves.

As Keigh looked into her eyes, an image of Misselli being whipped flashed into his mind. It made his blood boil. That could not happen. That would *never* happen.

If she was bent on following him into misery, he had to become someone she wouldn't follow anywhere. Someone she would be glad to see whipped.

"Shut up."

Misselli sniffed. "What?"

"I said, shut up!" he shouted, loud enough that everyone around could hear: "Stay away from me! I don't need your pity and I don't want your company!"

"You don't mean that." Her voice quivered.

She wasn't sure. He had to convince her. Had to get her out of here.

He would press on her greatest fear. Something she had shared with him in confidence. Something that should never be used to hurt her. But if it saved her...

"You know why I tested to be a cane?" he said. "I want to be out of here! Away from Bjorn! Away from this life! Away from *you!* And now, because of you, I'll probably never get to leave. You think I want to be around the person who cost me my dream? I hope you're happy, Misselli. You got what you wanted! I'm not going anywhere. Except now, I don't want anything to do with you."

Misselli collapsed backward as if the words had been a literal hammer to the chest. Her whole body shivered. She shook her head, eyes darting around as if searching for an explanation in the dirt.

Keigh couldn't look at her anymore. While the thought of Misselli being whipped enraged him, the sight of her heart breaking made him physically sick. The knowledge that his lies had caused it disgusted him.

What's wrong with you? Just tell her it was a lie. Just be honest with her and tell her you never want her to leave.

He couldn't do that, though. His life was headed for destruction, and he would not allow her to follow him there. This had to be done.

The two of them sat there, not speaking a word, until Victor returned. He hammered a piece of parchment to the side of the town hall behind Keigh, took one look at the two miserable teens in the dirt, and left.

"What's it say?" Keigh asked quietly as people started to approach the parchment.

Misselli's voice was calm and unbroken when she spoke. "Only what you are." And without another word, she picked herself up and walked away.

*

Keigh went the rest of the day without looking at the notice. He didn't want to know what Misselli thought he was. People stopped to look at him, muttering accusations and cursing him. Some went so far as to spit on him. No one else from the tower came by, though he thought he spotted Tarin leaving one of the few times he lifted his head. After seeing the hate and contempt in a hundred strangers' faces, he had seen enough. The ground was safer. The ground wouldn't curse him, spit on him, or accuse him.

As he stared at the dirt in front of his face, he understood better than ever why his father loved farming so much. The ground was simple: care for it and it would care for you. Provide for it and it would provide for you. People were dangerous. Love them and they'd leave you. Give them your best and they'd hate you for not giving them better.

His father returned midafternoon. He told Keigh that he had forbidden his mother and siblings from coming down, but they had all wanted to come sit with him too. Owen explained that it was his job to shield them from the lies and hate that would be directed toward Keigh.

"Shields don't remove people from harm," he said. "They stand in harm's way and take the blow so those behind it don't have to. I can't stop all of what's coming, son, but I will shield you from all that I can."

"What about Mannie?" Keigh asked. The messenger was set to arrive that day. Mannie had a higher view of Keigh than maybe anyone but Misselli. The thought of his friend seeing him publicly humiliated weighed heavy on him.

His father just shook his head. In that moment, Keigh felt like he had never understood his father better. They had both rejected people they cared for in order to protect them. If they had to suffer so that others didn't, so be it.

They sat like that for the remainder of the day, Keigh never speaking a word. When the sun went down and the last of the hecklers left, his father took off his cloak and rolled it up for Keigh to use as a pillow.

"Sleep, son," he said.

Keigh wanted to object, but there was something different about allowing his father to help him. It wasn't like Misselli; he didn't feel he needed to protect his father. In fact, he felt like his father could handle anything. Like the highest of mountains, Owen Anders couldn't be brought low.

Keigh fell asleep believing, for the first time that day, that everything was going to be okay, as long as his dad was there.

*

The next morning, he woke to find his father sitting guard next to him, exactly as he had been when Keigh fell asleep.

He raised his head and nudged his father's cloak toward him. "Thank you."

His dad grabbed the cloak and hastily put it back on. "I was happy to see you slept well. And..." He pulled at his cloak and inspected the cloth. "I'm grateful you're not a drooler like your mother." He gave Keigh a wry smile.

Keigh allowed himself to smile back. "Mom drools?"

"Just when she sleeps next to me." His father winked.

"Ugh!" Keigh hated when he joked like that.

"Owen!" Braddock's voice brought them back. "It's time."

"Will you be the one to carry out his punishment?" asked Owen nervously.

"I will." Braddock untied the strand holding the cat o' nine tails' knotted cords. "I thought it would be best if we did this early, before people start gathering."

"May I be the one to do it?" his father asked furtively.

Braddock sighed. "I can't allow that, Owen. No one would trust that you hadn't held yourself back in your strikes—"

"Can I trust that you won't put more into them?" Owen shot back.

"I would never," Braddock assured him.

"There was a time I would have believed that without reserve," Owen stated flatly. "But that was a long time ago."

Braddock pursed his lips. His eyes betrayed his desire to attack Keigh's father, but the elder mastered his tongue. "I assure you, I fought to be the one to perform Keigh's lashes. Vicerous was adamant that he be allowed to execute the penalty."

"I'll give you that." Owen shrugged, his whole body seeming to relax. "You're definitely the lesser of two evils."

"I'm the one to blame?"

Owen's' reply was bitter. "Well, it wasn't me that went anywhere."

"True Owen. You didn't..." He shook his head. "Didn't go *anywhere*."

Owen's nostrils flared, muscles knotting in his forearms.

Braddock seemed to regret angering him and quickly changed the subject back to Keigh. "We can begin as soon as Elders Boman and Connell arrive to bear witness."

The three of them waited quietly. Keigh found the silence of the vacant street unnerving. He would almost welcome the slurs and accusations that came with a crowd if it meant he wouldn't be alone with his thoughts.

Cato arrived shortly after Braddock, but Oliver Connell didn't come for another hour—and when he did arrive, he did so at the head of a mob of people shouting slurs at Keigh.

"I thought it was agreed that we would meet here at sunup, Connell." Cato's voice was calm, but his anger was only thinly veiled.

"Yes, of course, but when I saw only the three of you standing here, I took it upon myself to gather those affected by the boy's crimes." Oliver straightened his cloak, his silver goatee jutting out. "They deserve to see justice carried out. Don't you agree?"

Braddock bristled. "It will be carried out! Justice has nothing to do with fulfilling people's bloodlust, Oliver!"

"Of course, Braddock, but what you call bloodlust, I call a passion for righteousness," Oliver explained contemptuously. "The people deserve to know what the boy has done and see him pay for it!"

Braddock huffed. Glaring at Oliver, he argued no further.

"Let us begin," ordered Cato.

Braddock turned to Owen and said in a low voice, "Will you remove your son's shirt, please?"

Keigh felt his father's hands lift the bottom of his shirt and pull it up over his head. His skin tightened as the cold morning air hit his exposed back.

"Do you want me to leave it there, so it hides your face?" his father murmured.

Keigh nodded, grateful for the covering. He wasn't going to give his enemies a chance to see the pain on his face.

He heard his father's footsteps withdraw as a second person approached.

"I need you to know...I take no pleasure in this, Keigh." Braddock's voice was somber and loud enough for only Keigh to hear. "Justice must be done. Every wrong must be paid for. You shall receive what is just and nothing more. You have my promise." Braddock stepped back and called out to the crowd, "Fifteen lashes, to be completed in succession! Should the guilty lose consciousness, lashes will be held until he regains consciousness!"

Keigh's heart pounded faster than ever. His breathing grew quick and shallow as the moment before the first blow seemed to stand still. Would he pass out? Would it feel like fire? Would it feel like knives? Would every blow hurt worse than the last?

From beneath his shirt, he heard a scuffle and the growling of men.

"Restrain the father!" Oliver Connell commanded.

"Owen, please!" Braddock pleaded. "Do not interfere. It will be over soon enough."

Silence again. Keigh watched as a drop of sweat ran down his nose and hung ready to fall, fall as surely as the whip would fall on his back. He watched the droplet, feeling the blood pounding in his ears—

"Wait!"

The voice was distant but urgent.

"Wait!"

It was getting nearer. The crowd began to stir and mutter.

"Wait! Hold your whip!" Whoever it was had arrived. "Elders of Bjorn, a missive from the Capital!"

"What's that to do with this?" spat Oliver.

The crowd's murmuring grew louder as the elders apparently read the message.

"It can't be! No word was even sent to the Capital!" rattled Oliver. "Even if it had been, nobody, not even on horseback, could cover the distance in that time. This must be a forgery!"

"The guilty is *not* to be punished!" Cato's voice boomed with the same unnatural volume Keigh had heard him use at the agoge duels. Shouts of protest went up from the crowd. Cato's voice came again: "Go home!"

"Justice must be served!" Oliver pleaded. "You can't let him get away like this!"

"Justice *will* be served, Connell!" Braddock responded. "You read the missive."

Keigh listened as the three men entered into a muffled, but urgent, argument. A minute later, Cato's voice echoed loud in the street once more.

"I said, go home!" Then, in a softer tone, he added, "Braddock, please unbind Mr. Anders and return him to his father. I must leave. I will verify the authenticity of this letter, and in the unlikely case it's a forgery, we will execute judgment on the boy. But until then, he is to have all the rights and freedoms of any free citizen of Eden. See to it that this is not violated."

Keigh heard people walking away, and his father talking urgently with Cato.

Calloused hands began untying the bonds at his wrists and ankles. Then his father pulled his shirt back down and scooped him up to his feet. Keigh promptly collapsed as the blood rushed to refill his legs. His father picked him up again and held him against his chest.

Braddock stood in front of him. Normally clean-shaven, his dark stubble had grown out, giving him an uncommonly disheveled look. Braddock put a hand on Keigh's shoulder and searched his face as if looking for answers or a confession, but when Keigh remained silent, the cane simply patted his shoulder and walked away.

"You're free, son!" His father's voice was a whisper, but his joy was evident.

Keigh smiled, allowing himself to believe he wasn't dreaming. His dad gave him a hearty squeeze in his arms. *What happened? How am I set free?* The joy of the moment was too much. He wanted to shout at the top of his lungs with relief. Nothing could dampen the victory of the moment—

Or so he thought, in those glorious few seconds before he looked up and read, for the first time, the parchment on the wall. The parchment that listed his crimes and his penalty. The parchment Misselli had told him said *only what you are…*

At the top, above his crimes and the penalties assigned, was one word, written larger than all the others.

LIAR.

CHAPTER 13

CATCHING PUNCHES

20-22-6

For the next week, Keigh stayed at home with his family. He had gone to town once, hoping to find Misselli. He wanted to apologize for what he'd said to her, but Misselli's mother had dismissed him coldly.

The people in town were even more hostile. Like bats waiting for the cover of darkness to fly out and drink their fill of blood, people glared at him from shadows of every storefront and alleyway. Nobody dared spit at him, not now that he had been cleared of his charges, but the bitter looks of contempt he received were enough to tell him that they would if they could.

Midway through the week he received the crushing news that despite his charges being cleared from his record, the cane slated to mentor him had withdrawn. The man told Braddock that he believed the highest ideal of any cane was to live blameless in regard to the law; Keigh had showed obvious contempt for the purity of the position, and was therefore an irredeemable prospect for apprenticeship. Braddock had at least attempted to soften the blow by telling Keigh that he didn't personally agree with the man, but he also admitted that he understood how the cane felt, and that he was unsure if he would be able to find another willing to take Keigh as an apprentice.

How had trying to do the right thing turned so terribly against him?

Keigh pondered his situation one morning from the garden wolves' den. Sitting in the dirt, he threw another twig down the hill, toward the sun-drenched valley, for the pups to fetch.

I didn't even hurt anyone. Why do they hate me?

He still hadn't seen anyone from the night at the tower. He didn't expect anyone to thank him for rescuing them or for standing in their place and taking the blame, but he certainly hadn't expected to be avoided and forgotten. *Have they turned on me too?*

His body tensed as he suppressed a roar of anger. He was mad. No matter how many times he told himself he wasn't, or that he didn't need them to thank him, it was a lie. He welcomed the anger, for it was the one thing that seemed to ease the disgust he felt toward himself for how he had hurt Misselli. *Better mad at them than mad at me.*

The four garden wolf pups, who had been no bigger than field mice when he had moved the den, were now the size of young rabbits. After retrieving a few twigs for Keigh, they lost interest and instead set themselves to harassing a large black beetle.

He watched them play and wished he himself could go back to when he was Jessie's age and life was simple. "I wish the biggest thing I had to worry about today was what game to play," he muttered despondently, snapping a stick over his knee. A black pup looked up from the beetle, cocking his head quizzically at Keigh.

It had been a week since his last attempt to apologize to Misselli. Each day he stayed at home, he worried she would only become more bitter with him. Today, he decided, he would give it another try. Perhaps this time her mother would hear him out and help mediate.

Standing up and stretching, he took off down the hill to his house. After patting the bear head on the door, he entered to find his mother alone in the great room, scraping a pot into the chickens' feed bucket.

"Where's everyone else?" Keigh asked.

Sabriya looked up from her task and smiled warmly. "Your father and brothers went to go see a man about a mule. They hope he will be willing to trade it for labor. They'll need it if they hope to clear any more ground this year. Tree stumps will have to be pulled, else there's no sense in cutting the trees down in the first place...Oh, and your sister is playing in your room."

"What? Why do you let her in there?" Keigh whined. "She's the only one in the house with her own room and she insists on messing with my stuff!"

Closing the door behind him, he stomped toward where his sister was sure to be ruining his things.

"Leave your sister be," said Sabriya gently, stopping him halfway across the great room. She set the pot down and wiped her hands on her apron, then moved to the table. "Come. Sit down and talk with me." She patted the tabletop.

Keigh exhaled, releasing his need to protect his stuff from his sister's sticky little hands. With exasperated effort, he sat down at the table across from his mother.

"How are you, Keigh? You've hardly said a word to anyone since you got home from that dreadful ordeal. I miss my happy boy." She smiled fondly, having said the type of thing only mothers get away with.

"I don't know. I'm fine, I guess," Keigh lied. "I miss my friends, though. None of them have said a word to me since the fire. None except...except Misselli." Keigh hadn't told his parents about the terrible way he had run off his best friend.

"It's a difficult age," his mother explained. "Everyone is starting their apprenticeships soon and your lives will start intersecting less and less, until one day you end up like me and your father—raising a family and spending your time with your children instead of your friends."

Keigh laughed. "Yikes, I hope that never happens!"

"And why would you hope that?" His mother's proud smile disappeared, looking offended.

"I don't know...I just don't want to be done having fun, you know?" Keigh shrugged. "I don't want to give up my dreams and never see my friends again."

"Is that what you think your father and I did?" Sabriya raised an eyebrow. "Gave up our dreams?"

"No!" Keigh laughed at how annoyed she was getting. "I just think we have different dreams."

"It may surprise you to hear this, dear son, but your father and I had many dreams before we ever met each other, before we ever had children. Did you know, my dream was to become a merchant? I wanted to travel to the lands outside of Eden. See the world! Experience new places, new people, every day." Sabriya smiled at the dumbfounded look on Keigh's face. "And your father, he...he..." Her voice trailed off and her expression grew somber.

"What was Dad going to be?" he asked, excited to hear a rare tidbit from his father's past.

"That's not for me to tell. You'll have to ask him."

"Come on, Mom!" Keigh begged. "I feel like I don't know anything about your lives before I was born!"

She winked. "That's because we want our children to like us."

Keigh groaned. "Whatever, Mom." His parents were the two most likable people in all of Eden as far as he was concerned. It was part of what made the Wulfs' mistreatment of their family such a painful reality to swallow. "Seriously, what was Dad going to be?"

She gave Keigh a sympathetic look. "Your father passed his agoge as a cane."

Keigh burst out laughing. "No, he didn't!" he objected, but even as he was saying it, pieces started falling in place. *Is that why the men in town thought he had a sword?* "Dad never even sparred with us when me, Jobey, and Jotham used to play Canes and Criminals!" he said. "I can't even imagine him holding a sword."

"Not only could your father hold a sword, but he was the best in his class with one, too." His mother grinned, clearly pleased with the look of disbelief she had elicited from Keigh. "And that's saying something, since he was in the same class as Braddock and Vicerous."

Keigh realized his mother wasn't teasing him. "Dad could have been a cane?" He shook his head. "So you two *did* give up on your dreams! Why? You both could have been rich!"

"We did *not* give up on our dreams," his mother said resolutely.

"Then what do you call this?" Keigh snorted, gesturing to the simple house they called home.

"A better dream."

"What!"

"You act as though your father and I settled for something lesser." Sabriya smiled tenderly. "Nothing could be farther from the truth. We traded our good dreams for a better one...a shared one."

"How is *this* better?" asked Keigh incredulously.

"My husband and my children have brought more joy and fulfillment into my life than all the adventures and money in the world ever could!" she answered, not skipping a beat. "Every day, I wake up to my favorite people in the world." She inclined her head toward Keigh. "You may not understand this now, but someday you will. The true love of a partner who's willing to commit their whole life to you...It can't be bought or earned, and it's not worth trading away for anything."

Keigh was stunned. "But wouldn't you rather be with someone who wants you to pursue your dreams? Not someone who makes you give them up?" He was still wrestling to make sense of why his parents being together meant they couldn't have still pursued successful careers in their fields.

His mother chuckled. "Really? You think your father and I forced each other to give up their dreams until neither one of us had what we wanted?"

"Well, when you word it like that it sounds pretty stupid, but yeah, kind of..." Keigh drummed his fingers on the tabletop.

If his mother was insulted by the insinuation, she didn't show it. "Your father never once asked me to abandon my dreams and I never asked him to abandon his. You know how I knew he was the one for me?"

Keigh shook his head.

"Because when life forced him into a corner and made him choose between me and his dream of being a cane..." Sabriya's eyes glazed over, as if she had left the room for days long past. "He chose me, without ever being asked." She said wistfully before returning her focus to Keigh. "But that's the easy part. Would you like to know the hard part?"

Keigh nodded.

"The hard part is knowing when and if *you* are the right one."

"What do you mean?" He felt like his mother was talking in riddles.

"You won't know you're the right one for someone until you're ready to lay everything down for them. Until you're ready to do that, you're not the right one for anyone." She patted the table gently, pausing to let the hard truth sink in. "If you aren't ready, then you aren't the right one...and if you aren't the right one, then you aren't ready."

Now she was definitely talking in riddles. Maybe it was curiosity about his parents' pasts, or the fact that he was so confused by his current standing with Misselli, but Keigh wanted to know more. "Can I ask you something?" He had never asked his mother about girls before, and hoped she may know something that could help him. "Is it ever okay to lie to someone to protect them?"

"When would you have to do that?"

"Say Jessie wanted to follow me on a bear hunt. The truth is that it's dangerous and I don't want her to get hurt. But no matter how much I tell her that, she insists on following me. So, the only way to get her to leave is by telling her I don't want her there, that I don't want to be her big brother anymore. It's a lie, but getting her to believe I don't love her is the only way to keep her from following me into danger..." Familiar nausea washed over Keigh, as it had every time he'd thought about the terrible things he had said to his best friend.

"We aren't talking about Jessie and bears, are we?" his mother said knowingly.

Keigh shrugged, refusing to meet her gaze.

The corners of her mouth lifted, having confirmed to herself that her son was asking for relationship advice. "In regard to lying, I'll say this—and this is especially true in a romantic relationship: it's better to hear a painful truth than a sweet lie. Relationships demand honesty and vulnerability. The pain caused by a lie can cause more damage than whatever harm you hoped to save them from by telling it."

"But what if you know they are headed for hurt?" Keigh pleaded. He needed his mother to tell him he'd done the right thing.

"Assuming we are not talking about your six-year-old sister and instead talking about someone old enough and smart enough to find themselves mixed up in whatever you would rightly be involved in, I would tell you to speak the truth and trust them to make their own decision."

Keigh scoffed. "Even if you know they will choose something that will hurt them?"

"Yes!" his mother insisted. "You have to trust others to make their own decisions! Someday, you'll be a parent, and you will be responsible for directing your children in the way they should go—but, with the exception of children, you have to learn to trust people to make their own decisions. If the only time you *trust* people is when they see things the same way as you, that's not trust, that's just agreeing." Sabriya pursed her lips. "And if you base your relationship on agreement, instead of on trust, then it will all fall apart when you inevitably come to a place where you disagree. Trust can survive disagreements, but if what you want is conformity, everyone will eventually fail you."

"So—if you trust people, they will never fail you?"

"Absolutely not! The people you trust will fail you at some point, and when they do, it will hurt like you can't believe," she said, with a tenderness that could only come from experience. "It's unproductive, though, to worry about the trustworthiness of others. Concern yourself with being someone worthy of another's trust. If you can't trust, then you aren't worthy of trust, and if you aren't worthy of trust, then you'll find it impossible to trust anyone else." She smiled at the confused look on Keigh's face. "I speak from experience. Your father is a perfect example of what I'm trying to teach you. And I..." Her posture wilted. "I am the example of what it looks like when you fail to trust."

"What do you mean?" Keigh could tell she had crossed into a sensitive subject, so he had to tread lightly. "What did Dad do right?" he asked, then paused before following with, "What did you do wrong?"

His mother took a deep breath and gathered herself. "Your father would be so mad if he knew I was telling you this." She pulled at her apron, straightening it. "But I want you to know what a good man your father is—what a good man does, so that you can be one someday."

She paused, seemingly trying to decide what words to use.

"When your father...decided to marry me, he did so against the will of his parents, and at the cost of his inheritance. He was from a cane family, and I was a thrall. I never trusted his decision to marry me. I felt unworthy, that he had chosen poorly, given up too much to be with me. That insecurity hurt him—hurt us...hurt you."

"You never hurt me!" How could she say that? How could she believe she was unworthy of his father? Even if he had given up an inheritance to be with her, Keigh still felt like his father had married up.

His mother gave him a grateful smile. "You're a sweet boy, just like your father. Learn from my mistake: if someone chooses to love you, don't doubt it and don't test it." She reached across the table to hold his hand. "Trust they made the right decision. Doubting it will only serve to poison you and the bond between you." She gave his hand a squeeze, then abruptly stood up and straightened her dress. "Weren't you going into town today? You'd best be going if you want to make it before Misselli leaves for home."

"Who says I want to see Misselli?" Keigh asked, annoyed at her perceptiveness.

"Sweet like your father, but simple like him too."

His mother was smiling so kindly at him that her jab almost felt like a compliment. Keigh just shook his head. He let her hug him, then dashed out the door to town.

Running down the road, he savored the rich smell of fresh-tilled earth. The smell of a new crop, of new beginnings. The air was thick with it. Today was a new day. Today he would mend what he had broken. He would tell Misselli the truth, and trust her to make her own decision.

Once past the giant totem poles at Bjorn's front gate, he skidded his sprint to a brisk walk, accommodating for the leisurely pace of the busy street. He made a beeline to Mrs. Labelle's bakery, intent on patching things up with Misselli. He would wait there all day if he had to.

Keigh strode his way through the crowded main street, ignoring the glowering townsfolk. They parted in front of him as if he carried some infectious disease, acting as though they could contract it simply by being near him.

Reaching the bakery, he swung the door open to go in, but found himself forced back into the street as Beaudy and Theo exited the shop, each carrying a loaf of bread.

"Keigh!" Beaudy exclaimed, dropping his loaf and lifting Keigh off the ground in a tight bear hug.

"Hey—ugh!" Keigh wheezed as Beaudy squeezed the air out of his lungs.

"Where have you been?" An excited Theo punched Keigh in the leg as Beaudy continued to hold him off the ground. "We've been coming to town every day looking for you! Thought we might find you here." He tossed his head toward the bakery. "Been coming so often, Mrs. Labelle made us actually buy something today!" he chuckled.

Beaudy set Keigh back down, allowing him to breathe again.

"I was in town," said Keigh coldly, still hunched over, trying to catch his breath.

"When?" Beaudy asked. "We didn't see you."

Keigh stood up straight and looked into his friends' smiling faces. Somehow their happiness at seeing him made his resentment for them even worse. *How can they stand there and talk to me like nothing's wrong?*

"I was in town," he repeated, "for a full day and a half after the fire!"

Theo and Beaudy's smiles vanished.

"You couldn't have missed me!" he spat. "I was the one tied to the whipping post, remember? Or maybe you don't. Couldn't even bother yourselves to come see—" Keigh dropped the volume of his voice so only the two boys could hear. "...see what I went through for you."

"I'm sorry, Keigh," whimpered Beady, now dewy-eyed.

"I'm sorry too, man! But you have to understand, they wouldn't let us," explained Theo.

"Who wouldn't let you? As I remember it, everyone in town was allowed to come see me be humiliated! And they did! Everyone did!" he fumed. "Except my friends..." Keigh shook his head, too mad to say what he felt.

"Our parents stopped us!" Theo insisted. "We both got in huge fights with our folks trying to come see you! They aren't stupid, man. When we came home reeking of smoke, with the watchtower blazing away in the distance... they knew. And they didn't want us anywhere near the trial for fear we would get convicted too!" He paused. "They thought...They thought maybe you might tell the elders we were there..."

"But we told them you would never do that!" Beaudy interjected. "Right, Theo?" His diminutive friend nodded in confirmation.

Keigh took a couple deep breaths, trying to recover from the sudden burst of anger that had caught him by surprise, probably as much as it had his friends. "So...it's just your parents that hate me?" he asked cynically.

"No! Never!" Beaudy objected. "My parents LOVE you!"

"Seriously!" Theo gave Keigh a look of mock disgust. "I think they love you more than us, honestly. We told them what you did, getting us out of that tower alive. Then Misselli explained to us why you let yourself get taken, and..." He shook his head in amazement. "We owe you, man. We know that." Theo dropped his eyes to the dirt and kicked a rock further into the street. "It's just, our parents...They don't want this to be something that follows us, you know?" He looked down the street to where a group of people stood muttering and pointing at them.

"So what? Now you've got to keep your distance from me? Don't want to be stained by the law-breaking thrall boy?"

"No! You're our friend, Keigh, no matter what!" Beaudy seemed on the verge of tears again. "I don't care what anyone says."

"Not at all, Keigh." Theo's voice was solemn. "You're not *dirt*. Being your friend doesn't stain us...You're the best of us! And I'll tell that to anyone who says otherwise." He stood a little straighter, like a cane standing at attention before his commanding officer. "We owe you our lives, man. We should have been there for you." Theo stuck out a hand. "You're still King Keigh to us."

Keigh allowed himself a slight smile, his anger slowly melting away in the face of his friends' apology. "Well, for friends like you two...I would do it all over again." He grabbed Theo's hand and pulled him into a quick hug.

Beaudy gave an animated grin and excitedly scooped Keigh up in another massive bear hug, bouncing him around as he jumped up and down.

From up there, Keigh could see down the street. Misselli was walking his way, talking with Tarin.

His blood boiled again. He had spent a lot of time in the last week trying to think of an explanation for what had happened to Tarin the night of the fire. Where had he gone? Why had he disappeared when his friends were still inside a burning building?

No matter how he looked at it, he kept coming back to the same answer: Tarin was a coward.

"Put me down," wheezed Keigh. "I've got to go talk to Misselli."

Beaudy plopped him back down.

"She's coming this way," Theo pointed out. "Talk to her when she gets here."

"No, it can't wait. It's already waited too long," he explained. "I need to apologize." Keigh patted his friends on their shoulders as he passed between them.

"Yeesh! What did you do this time? Not save her from *two* burning buildings?" Theo teased, apparently unwilling to believe Keigh owed anyone anything at the moment.

Keigh smiled at the support. "Let's just say I burned more than a tower this week." And with that, he turned to make his way back down the street.

Before he had gone even ten feet, the familiar, sneering voice of Deacon Wulf called out from behind him.

"Look who it is! Criminal Keigh!"

Keigh stopped in his tracks, torn between being reconciled with Misselli and confronting the ungrateful snob behind him.

Misselli will have to wait.

He turned and headed back up the street toward Deacon, who had stopped next to a disgruntled-looking Beaudy and Theo.

Deacon shook his head at Keigh. "Unbelievable. Simply unbelievable," he mused. "How is it that you keep managing to roll yourself in dung only to emerge smelling better than before?" He circled Keigh. "Are you lucky? Skilled? No, I think not. I think dung doesn't stick to you because you're lower than dung. Even dung doesn't want to be associated with you!"

"Deacon," Keigh greeted his nemesis with feigned courtesy. "I see you're... *alive*," he jabbed.

"Yes," Deacon sneered at him. "Your faithful followers tried to tell me I owe you something," he sniffed. "Unfortunately for them, I'm not so easily hoodwinked by a peasant posing as a hero."

Keigh stepped toward Deacon. Their faces only a foot apart. "Tell me, then—how did you get out of that building? Huh? Seeing as how you fainted!"

Deacon's nostrils flared. "I did not *faint*. I happened to inhale more smoke than the rest of you, as I was working harder to escape than you cowards! As for how I got out of the building? I assume Tarin or Conrad threw me to the moat." Deacon broke eye contact, still smirking. "Reckless fools. I could have been killed."

"No, Keigh threw me!" Beaudy put in.

Deacon's lip curled in distaste. "Well, I'm certain no one carried you," he said, looking the large boy up and down.

Keigh was enraged. "*I* carried you down. *I* dropped you to Conrad and Theo. Then *I* carried you up the hill and hid you in the bushes, so that *you* wouldn't get caught!"

This was exactly what he'd known would happen if he followed his father's advice. Doing good to his enemies had gotten him nowhere. They were no respecters of kindness. Deacon was proof. There was only one thing they respected: strength.

"A tall tale for sure," Deacon said coolly. "But I know the truth. You dropped me and tried to save yourself. Know how I know?" It was a rhetorical question. "When a rat's caught in a trap, it will chew its own leg off to escape. Father taught me this. A vermin's only instinct is self-preservation." Deacon picked a fleck of bark off Keigh's tunic and dropped it with a look of disgust. "Why would you be any different?"

It took all of Keigh's self-control to keep from picking up that piece of bark and shoving it down Deacon's throat. "Tell me this, then. If I abandoned you and only wanted to save myself, why didn't I give Braddock your name when he questioned me? Why not throw you under? Huh?"

Deacon didn't even flinch. He smiled wickedly. "Because we both know nobody would believe the word of a thrall in an accusation made against his better." He shook his head in mock disappointment. "You kept your mouth shut because you knew accusing me would only make you look like the bitter, entitled field rat you are."

At Deacon's last insult, Beaudy snapped. "*Liar!*" he bellowed, and aimed a punch at Deacon's face.

Deacon easily sidestepped the blow. Grabbing the back of Beaudy's shirt, he drove his knee hard into the large boy's gut, collapsing him into a whimpering heap on the ground. He stepped back, sniggering.

"That's it!" snarled Keigh. "You can come after me all you want, but you won't hurt my friends."

Deacon glanced at Keigh's clenched fists and scoffed. "Go ahead. Take a swing. Let's see if they don't pull you from your apprenticeship."

"They already have." Keigh shrugged. "I've got nothing to lose."

"That," Deacon smirked, "I do believe."

The realization that Deacon *wanted* Keigh to hit him was just enough to keep Keigh from swinging. He gave Deacon one last glare and stooped low next to Beaudy. "Come on, Beaudy. Let's get you up."

"Thanks, Keigh—ouch! Ow, ow, ow!" Beaudy cried as Deacon's foot stepped down hard on the side of his neck, pinning him to the ground.

"Hey!" snapped Theo.

Without thinking, Keigh swept Deacon's leg off Beaudy's neck so hard, he knocked him off his feet entirely.

The move sent Deacon sprawling in the dirt. He rolled out of the fall, his black cloak flapping as he emerged like an oversized crow from a dust bath. The people near them gasped and backed up to watch at a distance as Keigh and Deacon squared off over Beaudy, still curled up on the ground.

"I said don't touch my friends!"

Deacon pouted in mock apology. "I'm sorry, I didn't know you had friends."

"He does! More than you'll ever have!" Theo shouted.

"I meant friends of worth," sneered Deacon—then, cocking his head back, he spat on Beaudy.

Something in Keigh broke. Whatever thin shred of restraint he'd had before that moment was gone.

He saw Deacon pull back his fist, aiming a punch at Beaudy, but before he could land the blow, Keigh hurdled Beaudy and caught Deacon's fist in his hand. That's when he felt it. Again. That feeling of fiery, liquid strength and energy that had poured into his arm when he'd fought the man in the woods, the same strength that had filled him when Mannie lifted him off the ground during his duel, coursed into his hand and up his arm as he tightened his grip on Deacon's hand.

Deacon's expression morphed from outrage to panic. "What...what is—"

Keigh twisted Deacon's wrist with ease, bringing him to his knees. He wouldn't swing at Deacon. Not now that he had him beat. Instead, he channeled all his anger into crushing Deacon's hand. The energy filling his arm and flowing into his body made him feel awake and alive like he hadn't felt since the duel.

"Stop it, you freak! What are you..." Deacon trailed off, as if he were falling asleep.

"Release him at once!"

A booming voice immediately snapped Keigh from his trance.

He released Deacon's fist. The boy folded like a rag doll next to Beaudy. Turning, Keigh saw Cato Boman. His long white beard blown back over his shoulder as the elder hobbled furiously toward him, pulling himself forward with his long, gnarled staff.

Leaning on the staff, Cato stooped down and felt Deacon's neck.

"He just fainted," Keigh tried to explain.

"Fainted..." Cato scoffed, looking up at him and shaking his head. "Come with me!" The old man grabbed him by the back of his tunic and pushed him toward the town hall.

Keigh's stomach dropped. Why had he allowed Deacon to goad him into fighting? Public brawling was against the law. What would they take from him this time? They had already shamed him publicly and taken away his apprenticeship. He had no money to pay restitution. They would have to take it from his flesh.

He looked back over his shoulder to see Theo and Beaudy's terrified expressions. Beyond them—

Keigh's heart froze. Misselli's beautiful face creased in a sad frown as she watched him being marched away. Tarin shook his head sadly, sliding an arm around Misselli's shoulders.

Keigh whipped his head around. He couldn't bear to see that for one more second. He had come to town to apologize to Misselli. He had come to set things right, and now, he was watching the friend who'd abandoned him comfort her in his arms.

Maybe he deserved this. He had been a fool to believe he could alter his fate. He'd had his one shining moment. One week where everyone loved him. But he should have known that was too good to last. The world would never tolerate him, a thrall, rising to a place of equality. They were better than him, and they would never let him forget his place again.

At the front of the town hall, they encountered Chogan Bald Head debating with Crispin Popplardo.

"Chogan, fetch Braddock for me at once!" Cato ordered.

Chogan gave Keigh a curious look. The cane nodded, then took off down the gravel road at a run, his red cloak flapping behind him.

Cato pulled the door open with the top of his staff and pushed Keigh in ahead of him. "Sit down, Mr. Anders." He gestured to the bench Keigh had sat on only a week before.

Keigh took his seat and watched the old man crutch his way around the long table. His walking staff clacking on the wooden floorboards with each step. Cato lowered himself into the same center seat he had sat in the day of trial. Combing his fingers through his beard, he peered at Keigh searchingly, just like he had the day of his duel. The look was unnerving. Unreadable.

They sat in silence as they waited for Chogan to return with Braddock. The whole time, Cato never broke his piercing stare—except the one time he caught Theo peeping in one of the windows, and stuck the boy with a warning glare that sent Theo tripping over himself.

Nearly an hour and a half after they had entered the hall, the door opened. Braddock Fortier entered, clean-shaven again, wearing full cane attire.

He gave Keigh a disappointed look, then addressed Cato. "You sent for me? I apologize for my delay. Mace and I were running off a mountain lion that has been lurking around the Koppens' farm."

"Your delay is of no concern. I realize my calling you was unplanned and… irregular."

"Irregular indeed." Braddock stole a quick glance at Keigh. "May I assume it concerns the boy?"

"You may." Cato returned his gaze to Keigh. "I had to pull Mr. Anders off of young Master Wulf today."

"They were fighting? In public?" asked Braddock, looking agitated.

"Yes, they were. Though admittedly not much of a fight," Cato mused, his expression still unreadable.

"What would you have me do? Shall I take the boy to his father for punishment? Or do you wish me to correct him?"

"Neither." Cato turned to face Braddock. "I want you to train him."

Keigh's jaw dropped. *Train me?*

Braddock's jaw dropped too. Apparently, he was just as caught off guard as Keigh. It took the seasoned warrior five whole seconds to find his tongue again.

"Train him? But Cato, I am retired. It is not customary for students to apprentice under canes who are not actively in the king's service."

"No, I suppose it's not. But you are no *customary* cane, Braddock." Cato smiled for the first time. "And young Mr. Anders is no common student."

"How do you mean?" demanded Braddock.

"I mean the young man is more than he seems." Cato grinned, looking deeply satisfied. "You see, Mr. Anders here…is a potent."

CHAPTER 14

A LOT TO LEARN

20–12–1

A potent! Surely Cato was mistaken. Potents were fairy tales! Myths! Legends! Like mages, they were the concocted fantasies of children and bards. They were supposed to be men and women of superhuman strength and durability, not fifteen-year-old farm boys who had, just yesterday, had to ask their father for help getting the ax unstuck from a tree stump.

"A potent! How do you know?" asked Braddock.

"Wait! They're real?" Keigh interrupted. Braddock shushed him with a hand.

"They are easy enough to spot if you know what to look for, and I do," Cato explained. "I've seen the boy use his power with my own eyes twice now. Tell me, Mr. Anders: in a moment of desperation, fear, or panic, have you ever felt a surge of energy pulse through you? More than adrenaline or nerves—a feeling that your body was unexplainably fresh and rested?"

Keigh had experienced that feeling. Three times now. "Yeah…um…when I fought the stranger in the forest, during my agoge duel, and then again today with Deacon."

"Can you remember exactly when you felt it?" Cato continued. "Were you touching anything? Anyone?"

"Um...yeah. The first time I was grabbing the stranger's neck when he tried to stab me. Then at the duel, I felt it when Mannie helped me off the ground. And today, I felt it when I caught Deacon's fist."

"You caught his punch with your hand?" blurted Braddock, looking astonished.

"He did. It was quite impressive, really," mused Cato. "But that's beside the point. In addition to feeling energy, did you feel anything else?"

Keigh thought for a second. "Yeah, I think so. I felt strong. Like, really strong. Like I could lift anything. In the forest, I tossed the man off me as though he were no more than bed covers." He gaped at his own account, as if until that moment he had convinced himself he had embellished his own memory.

"That's how you broke my sword!"

Keigh flinched, expecting to see anger on Braddock's face, but instead he saw what he thought might be awe. "I'm sorry about that. I didn't know that would happen."

"Already have a new one." Braddock patted the sword on his hip, his eyes glazed as if lost in thought.

"So, Fortier, I would like *you* to begin training Mr. Anders as soon as possible...that is, if you accept." Cato turned his attention back to Braddock, who was still staring at Keigh with a vacant expression. "Will you train the boy to be a cane?" Cato pressed.

"Yes..." Braddock said absently before shaking his head and addressing the old man properly. "Yes. I will take the boy as my apprentice." Turning back to Keigh, he added, "We start tomorrow. Be on my doorstep at dawn." And without another word, Braddock swept out of the hall.

Cato leaned back in his chair, twiddling his thumbs happily, a satisfied grin on his face. He shook his head "Canes. All go and no slow." He turned his bright blue eyes back to Keigh. "Run along, Mr. Anders. Go tell your family the good news. Just...please avoid young Master Wulf, will you?" The old man smirked. "I'll cover for you with his father. *You* just stop yourself from breaking the law again, if you can manage it."

*

The following morning, Keigh woke extra early so he could get in some time on the sparring tree before heading down to Braddock's. He hadn't practiced at all since winning his duel with Vicerous.

His family had been elated to hear he would be given another chance to apprentice as a cane, though his parents did seem a bit wary when he told them Braddock would be his master. As far as Keigh was concerned, he felt like he had been given new life. All his dreams were back on the table. He would become a cane the same way he had passed his duels: with pure hard work and desire.

After finishing his routine at the tree, Keigh fed the still irritable Mrs. Schaffer along with the chickens. He collected their eggs, then tossed the garden wolves the dried liver of a deer he had felled earlier that week. Grabbing his bow and quiver from the tool shed, he stooped to tighten the laces on his leather boots.

Today, everything changes for me.

He stopped to rest his hand on the rough carved bear's head on his front door, promising to be back. Then, with a skip, he was off, jumping the gate and running down the dirt road to Braddock's house in the ashen pre-dawn light.

On his way, his mind raced, imagining what cane apprenticeship would be like. What sword would Braddock give him? Would he get to duel with Braddock every day? Would he accompany the battle master on his official duties? How long would it be before he earned his red cloak in the Queen's Climb?

Keigh arrived on Braddock's doorstep just as the first golden shafts of light broke over the snowcapped peaks of the Ursus Mountains behind him. The brilliant beams slowly illuminated the dark slopes of the Bullhorn Mountains of Eden's western border, top to bottom. Keigh took a second to appreciate the intricate carvings in the side of the massive tree trunk that was Braddock's home before knocking on the door.

As he waited, he looked to the northern end of Eden. The Queen's Veil was truly beautiful this time of year; June snowmelt had doubled the falls' normal width as they plunged off the Garden Wall. He took a deep breath.

This is my ticket out. I will pass my training. I will become a cane and pay my family's debt. Then, I will leave this town forever.

Braddock opened the door behind him.

"Give me your bow." Braddock took the weapon and deposited it inside the door. "Here." He thrust a shovel into Keigh's hands. The cane closed the door behind him and stepped onto the front step, holding a steaming cup of tea.

Keigh gaped at the tool in his hands. "What is this for?"

Braddock looked down his nose at him. "Surely you're familiar with this tool's uses?"

Keigh nodded dumbly. "Yes, sir."

"So long as you are my apprentice, you are to address me as Master Fortier, or Master alone will suffice. Is that understood?"

"Yes...Master."

"Good. Today you will be doing an important task for me." Braddock took a sip of his tea. "Mace has left several deposits too near to the house. Find them and bury them."

"Deposits? Sir?"

"Master," Braddock corrected him. "Yes, deposits. Defecations, if you wish." He took another long sip of his tea.

Keigh's eyes widened as he understood what he was being asked to do. "You want me to bury bear poop?" He waited for a sign that Braddock was joking, but none came.

"Yes," Braddock said, still stone-faced. "And you had best get started. It will likely take you all day."

"All day?" laughed Keigh—but when Braddock raised his eyebrows at him, it hit him. "Wait...How big are Mace's...*deposits?*"

Braddock shrugged. "About your length." Then, with a skeptical glance at Keigh's bare arms, he added, "Quite a bit thicker, though. Best get started. I don't want any mounds left out there. Dig your holes deep!"

Keigh nodded and stepped off the front porch away from the house, but was stopped by a disgruntled cough from Braddock.

"Keigh Anders. You will respond to commands with 'Yes, Master.' Do you understand?"

"Yes, Master."

"Come back to the house when you're finished." Braddock raised his cup toward the rising sun and, without pausing for Keigh to respond, disappeared back inside, closing the door behind him.

"Yes, *sir*," said Keigh to himself, looking at the shovel in his hands where he had, only minutes ago, expected a sword to be.

*

Braddock hadn't lied. Keigh found and buried six of the large deposits in eight hours. Digging was easy in the soft loam of the river valley, but it was *a lot* of digging. Each deposit required a hole at least five feet in length and nearly three feet deep. His work was slowed by Mace insisting on following him around to each of the "presents" she had left for him, as if proud to show him her work. Keigh had even wasted a half hour trying to communicate to Mace that she should dig a hole for him. But whether she didn't understand or was just unwilling to help bury her pride and joy, she never so much as scratched the dirt.

While her deposits were rancid, Keigh did find them intriguing. Each one was a collection of bones and brush from the bear's hunting and foraging in the forests of Eden. In the third pile, he even found what looked to be the skull of a large mountain lion—reminding him once again that the goliath red bear was much more deadly than she seemed, sitting there on her haunches, panting like an overgrown sheepdog.

Braddock had brought him some dried beef and a small barley loaf with a bladder of water for his noontime meal. But when he finished the job, with only four hours of daylight left, he was exhausted and starving again.

Braddock handed him another barley loaf as he opened the door for Keigh to enter his home. Keigh followed him to the two seats in front of the hearth where, nearly two months ago, he had asked to be admitted to agoge duels.

Braddock grunted as he dropped himself into the seat across from Keigh. "Did you finish the assigned work?"

Keigh nodded, his mouth full of bread.

"And was the work done to the best of your ability?"

Keigh cocked his head at the question. "Yes, I think so…Master."

"You think so?" Braddock asked. "If *you* don't know if you gave your best, who does? I did not ask you if you did well enough or if you did the job to *my* satisfaction. Your answer would be sufficient for either of those questions, as you could not possibly know my expectations of you. What I asked was, 'Was the work done to the best of *your* ability?'"

Keigh was confused. *What's the difference?* "I'm sorry, Master, I don't understand."

Braddock pressed his lips together, seemingly in a bid for patience. "You, and only you, know if you did the work to the best of your ability. I, and only I, know my standards and expectations for the job that I assigned you. So, you can answer the question of your effort with absolute certainty. By answering my question with uncertainty, you tell me that you believed I was asking if you thought I would be satisfied with your work…which I was not asking."

Keigh shook his head. Why did everyone have to talk to him in riddles? "I'm sorry, but I don't understand the difference."

"It's all the difference in the world!" Braddock gave an exasperated sigh. "And it will tell me a great deal more about you than you think." He leaned forward in his chair. "If I found your work to be unsatisfactory and you had told me you did your best, then I would know I am dealing with incompetence. While, if I found your work unsatisfactory and you told me you had not done your best, then I would know I was dealing with laziness."

"Why does it matter if it's incompetence or laziness? Isn't the only thing that matters whether the task was done correctly or not?"

A corner of Braddock's mouth lifted in amusement. "The answer to your first question is simple. Both incompetence and laziness are issues that must be fixed, but the solutions to them are far different. Incompetence being the easier of the two." Braddock rose from his seat and fetched them both cups of water. "With incompetence, proficiency with the task must be practiced. An individual who gives himself fully to a task may be great at many things and poor at the few tasks they are unpracticed in. A lazy individual, however, will never be as proficient at anything as they could be. With laziness, the problem is not the task but with the person doing the task. Practice fixes incompetence; only discipline fixes laziness."

"You were testing me?" Keigh asked, befuddled.

"Everything in life is a test, Keigh. People will test you, trials and hardships will test you, and if the world isn't testing you, then you better always be testing yourself." Braddock took a long drink from his cup. "And if you do it right, the tests you put to yourself will yield the sweetest fruit." He grinned for the first time all day. "Although the test I put you through at your hearing may still bear fruit just as sweet."

The memory of Braddock's cornering questions, and the injustice of the whole embarrassing ordeal, came flooding back to Keigh in an instant. "That was a test, too?" he snapped, jumping to his feet.

Braddock calmly motioned for him to take his seat again. When Keigh obeyed, Braddock started digging in a pouch on his belt. He tossed Keigh something shiny.

Keigh caught it, gaping at the gold in his hand.

"That," Braddock announced, "is Russo Conri's watch. But you knew that already, I'm sure."

"When did you find it?" Keigh asked.

"I found that before I even said a word to you that night. I also saw Miss Labelle, fighting the urge to come join you from her hiding place in the trees." Braddock raised his eyebrows, challenging Keigh to deny it. "In short, I knew you were lying from the first time we spoke that night."

Keigh shook his head at the timepiece in his lap. "Why did you let me take the fall? Why didn't you just present the evidence and call them in?"

"Did you know a rat caught in a trap will gnaw its own leg off to escape?"

"So I've heard," Keigh said bitterly.

"That's what an animal would do." Braddock paused. "You, however, not only made no effort to save yourself—you seemed to have intentionally triggered the trap on yourself, so that none of your friends could get caught in it."

"Again," Keigh scowled, "why didn't *you* produce the evidence? Why withhold the truth?"

"Because, Keigh..." Braddock set his cup on a small table and leaned in. "I suspected—correctly, I might add—that you *wanted* to offer yourself up so that your friends could escape. An action that I'm not afraid to tell you I admire greatly."

"Then why press me again in front of the elders? Why did you have to push me to lie, knowing you were only going to make my punishment more severe?" Keigh's voice rose as his blood began to heat.

Braddock gave a short sigh. "I desired to test your resolve, Keigh. I wanted to see what lengths, what costs, you would endure for your friends. You stuck your leg in the trap—would you stick your neck in? Would you give your life or turn them in to save your own skin? I was very pleased to see you did not seek escape for yourself."

Keigh's anger dissipated with his master's words of approval. "So, you knew I wasn't guilty? Was it you who waived my punishment?"

Braddock's face soured. "Not guilty? After all you went through, you walked away believing you aren't guilty?"

Keigh balked at his sudden rancor. "I mean to say, I wasn't the only one who was there, is all..."

"Hear me clearly on this, Keigh Anders." Braddock pointed a warning finger at him. "If all of Eden had participated in setting that tower on fire with you, it would not absolve you of your guilt. An action is never judged right or wrong by the number of people who participate in it. The merit of a deed is undiminished by popularity or practice. Wrong is wrong, no matter how many people participate in it. Sacrificing yourself for your friends does not absolve you of guilt. In fact, it places their guilt on your head as well, making you doubly guilty." Braddock shook his head. "To answer your other question: no, it was not me who waived your penalty. Though I did advocate that you only receive the minimum number of lashes, I'm afraid I still believe you deserved every lash you were sentenced to."

The sting of Braddock's rebuff wasn't enough to curb his curiosity about his unexpected pardon. "If not you, then who?"

"That is a mystery." Braddock's posture relaxed as they changed topics. "We only received word from the Capital that you were to be cleared and acquitted of all charges and penalties. The letter did not indicate how the matter was being dealt with, only that it *would* be dealt with." Braddock rested his chin in his hand, pressing a finger to his lips. "It did give me one more piece to the puzzle of your mystery assassin, though."

Keigh still felt there was something crucial he was forgetting about that encounter. Why had someone been sent to find him? Sent to kill him? What had Braddock figured out?

"Your attacker's body was sent to the Capital for inspection, along with the gun. If the king's men were able to discern his identity, or his origin, they have withheld the information from me. I still know nothing of who the man was, or where he comes from, only that his possession of a gun likely ties him to Draiden. But I think we can safely assume this: after your release…you are not a nobody." The retired cane's eyes narrowed. "Someone wants you dead, and someone else wants you saved. But why?" Braddock's chair creaked as he sat back to ponder the answers to his own questions.

It wasn't the missing piece that had been bothering Keigh, but it did bother him. If he was important, he wanted to know why. Up until two weeks ago, he had never done anything noteworthy. How had his name made it out of Bjorn, when he himself had never done so?

Braddock pulled himself out of his quiet contemplation with a sharp exhale through his nostrils. "That will be all for today." He rose to his feet. "Be back here again at sunup tomorrow." And before Keigh could say "Yes, Master," Braddock ushered him out of the house, closing the door behind him with a bang.

Keigh looked at the sky. He had about three hours before sundown. He wound his way up the dirt road toward his home, lost in thought. After today, he had more questions than answers. This morning, he had thought Braddock would be teaching him more about combat. How to wield a sword, shoot a bow, ride a horse…Really, he had hoped for answers about Cato's assertion that he was a potent. What abilities did he have? How could he use them?

Anxiety gripped him as he thought about Braddock's conclusion. Why did people outside Bjorn know his name? And why were they taking steps to have him killed—and protected? There was still something about the encounter with the man in the woods that wasn't adding up. It was like an itch on his brain he was unable to scratch.

He was so consumed in thought that he nearly didn't see the large man in a brown cloak walking on the road ahead of him.

"Mannie!" Keigh broke into a run to catch up with the old messenger.

"Hello there, Master Keigh." Mannie clasped him on the shoulder as Keigh arrived by his side in a cloud of dust.

"Where have you been?" asked Keigh, beaming up at his tall friend. "I feel like I haven't seen you for weeks!"

"Ah, yes—I would have loved to come sooner, but unfortunately, love has demanded my time." Mannie squeezed Keigh's shoulder and resumed his walk toward the house.

"Wife wouldn't let you come, huh?" Keigh knew precious little about Mannie's home life, but he did know he was married and that the two of them made their home in Sentinel, where they served in the king's court.

Mannie smiled at the question. "I would give her every moment of my time if I could."

"So do you have news for us today, or are you just visiting?"

Mannie's expression grew grim. "News, and not the good kind, unfortunately."

"What is it?"

"I'll tell you when I tell your folks." Mannie threw an arm around Keigh's shoulders. "Why don't you tell me what you've been up to since beating the pride out of Vicerous Wulf two weeks ago?"

They walked the rest of the way home like that: Mannie with his arm around Keigh, Keigh recounting the last two momentous weeks of his life. His five seconds of fame after the duel, the climbing and subsequent burning of the old watchtower, how he had taken the fall for his friends and then had his punishment mysteriously waived. Mannie seemed to think that piece of information was particularly interesting, asking Keigh who had sent the missive and what the Capital planned to do about it. Keigh didn't know the answer to either of those questions, but shared Braddock's thoughts with him.

Lastly, against Cato's instruction not to share his ability with anyone, he told Mannie how the old man had deduced that Keigh was a potent. Mannie deserved to know, considering Keigh had nearly drained him at his agoge duel. Plus, he trusted Mannie with everything, even stuff he would never tell his parents. Mannie just chuckled at Keigh's description, saying, "Well, that explains why I slept so well that night, then!"

Upon finally arriving home, they found Keigh's family still sitting around the dining table, the remnants of dinner still visible. There was a plate and cup set out for Keigh in his usual spot, and by the surly look on his brothers' faces, they had been kept from finishing off the food before Keigh had been given a chance to eat.

"Mannie! What a surprise!" Keigh's father rose from his seat, throwing his arms wide to greet his friend with a hug.

Mannie threw out an arm, stopping Owen from getting any closer. The family fell eerily silent at their friend's irregular behavior.

"Forgive me." Mannie's grimace faded into an apologetic smile. "Not feeling well. Wouldn't want you to get what I got."

Owen took a step back, still eying him suspiciously. "Okay, no need to tempt fate." He grinned and returned to the table. "The Anders are already down one set of hands. No need to make it two."

"We didn't know to expect you tonight." Sabriya pulled a chair out from the table. "Please have a seat. I can cook up a fresh loaf for your stomach."

Mannie looked at the empty chair Sabriya offered him as if it were a snake waiting to strike. "I appreciate it, but I'm sorry—I cannot stay. I've only come to say hello and share some news...news I'll be needing to share with Cato. Tonight."

"What news?" Owen crossed his muscular bare arms. "War?"

"No declaration of war yet, no. But earlier this week—"

"Hi, Mannie!" squeaked Jessie, interrupting the messenger and earning herself a pair of stern looks from her parents.

Mannie's features softened. "My dear Jessie! Is that you?" He squinted at her. "You must be at least...a foot taller than the last time I saw you! Is that a new tooth?"

Jessie giggled, rocking back and forth where she sat cross-legged on a stool. "*Mannie!* I just saw you! Remember?"

"Oh yes! At Keigh's duels!" He clapped a hand to his forehead. "You're just growing so fast I can't keep up! I'm sorry I didn't say hi to you when I walked in. Can you forgive me?" Mannie put his palms together, pleading for her mercy.

Jessie giggled even harder. "I forgive you!"

"Thank you, sweetheart. Now, can you go play in your brothers' room for a bit while I talk to the big kids?"

The Anders boys groaned at Mannie offering their room, but Jessie nodded excitedly and dashed off down the hall.

"This is probably not news for the ears of those too young to process its implications." Mannie straightened himself, pulling on the hem of his cloak. "Earlier this week, one of the king's reconnaissance patrols returned, bearing alarming news of Draiden's most recent movements. One of our canes was able to intercept a missive from Abaddon." The messenger grimaced. "Draiden is taking a census of all the people under his rule."

"Well, that's not that bad, is it?" Keigh asked.

"There's only one reason Draiden has ever counted his people before," Owen grunted.

Mannie's brow furrowed. "Yes. We believe he gathers for war."

*

For the next hour, Owen and Mannie discussed all the possible implications of the news, as well as what they thought the king may do in response. In the end, it was all conjecture. Nevertheless, Mannie appeared troubled—so much so, Keigh noticed, that he refused to sit down the entire time he stayed. It was unlike Mannie to not make himself at home in the Anders house.

At the end of the hour, Mannie thanked Sabriya for the loaf of bread she had baked fresh for him and left for Bjorn.

Keigh barely slept that night. As if he didn't already have enough things to ponder, now war? Would Eden be attacked? If not, would the king send canes to assist whoever Draiden did attack? Perhaps now, Braddock would accelerate his training. Surely, tomorrow he would learn more of his abilities as a potent—or maybe, at the very least, practice swordsmanship.

But the following day, and the four after, were the same for Keigh. He rose early, did his chores, then reported for training with Braddock. Each day, he expected to learn something useful from the former cane, but Braddock only gave him new chores to complete, each day's more pointless than the last. The whole week he had tried to keep in mind Braddock's words: *everything in life is a test*—but by the time he'd finished sorting all the rocks in a fifteen-foot stretch of riverbank by color, and then again by size, he had come to a new conclusion.

I'm not being tested. I'm being punished.

At the end of the fifth day, Keigh burst through Braddock's front door without knocking. He found the retired cane reading a scroll. Braddock didn't even flinch. It was almost as if he had been expecting Keigh's outburst. The thought only further upset Keigh.

"Are you punishing me?" he blurted. "I know you think I deserve those lashes, and honestly, part of me does too, but if you're mad at me..." Keigh threw his hands up. "Just say it! I can take the punishment if I know that's what's happening, but don't look me in the eye and tell me I've been training for the last week!"

Braddock calmly rolled up his scroll before addressing Keigh. "First, you will apologize for that insolent outburst. Then, when you've done that, sit down."

Keigh stood there, breathing heavily. Somehow, Braddock's calmness only agitated him further. He didn't dare push the man's patience again, though. Gathering himself, he exhaled deeply. "I'm sorry," he said. "Forgive me, Master Fortier."

Braddock gestured to the simple wood chair across from him. Keigh slid into it, locking eyes with his mentor.

"Do you really feel like you should have to pay for what you did?"

This was not the question Keigh expected. "Um...yes. That's justice, right? If you do something bad, then bad things should happen to you."

Braddock pursed his lips, then asked, "When I had you released from the whipping post, what did I tell you the letter from the Capital ordered?"

Keigh shrugged. "That I be released, and my record be cleared. That the Capital would deal with the penalty."

"Yes!" Braddock agreed, an excited glint in his eyes. "Now, let me tell you something very important to remember about me and about our king. Justice will be served. Every broken law must be paid for, without exception. Neither I nor the king will compromise on that. When the Capital says they will deal with a penalty, they mean it. Your crimes were paid for, Keigh Anders." Braddock shrugged. "How? I don't know, but we have no cause to believe the king is slacking in his justice. So, if your record has been cleared...why do you still feel like you need to pay for it?"

"It just doesn't feel right that I should get off free when it was me who broke the law."

"Have you ever heard of the town of Skarseld?"

Keigh shook his head.

"Skarseld lives under the king's law as all people of Eden do, but their community teaches that when you commit a crime, you pay for it for life. So even after the required payment for a crime is completed, the town has a special gathering every year where all those who have ever committed an offense against the king's law punish themselves again with whippings and public shamings."

Keigh gaped at the thought of having to be whipped every year. "But why?" he asked.

"For the same reason you still feel the need to pay for your crimes, even after they have already been dealt with...pride."

"Pride?" Keigh nearly choked. "It's the farthest thing from pride! I feel bad for what I did. I just want to make it right!"

"But it's already been made right!" Braddock shook his head. "When the king's requirements for justice are met, the debt is paid." He pointed a finger at Keigh. "*You* just want to be the one to pay for it. To insist on further payment is to insist you know better than the king. As though you have something more to offer that the king has not required. That *is* pride. Foolish pride at that!" Braddock huffed. "I will not question the king's justice. Your guilt has been dealt with and I will not charge you for what's already been paid for... so, to answer your question, I am not punishing you. I will never punish you. You have my word on that."

"What? What if I do something terrible? Wouldn't I deserve to be punished then?"

"You will most certainly be disciplined," Braddock said coolly—a little too coolly, like he already expected Keigh to mess up again.

Keigh rolled his eyes. "Okay—discipline, punish, same thing!"

"Actually, they could not be more different." Braddock took a deep breath, seeing confusion wrinkle Keigh's face. "While punishment and discipline are very similar in appearance, their objectives are entirely different. Punishment has to do with making someone pay or hurt for what they have done. An eye for an eye, a tooth for a tooth."

Keigh smiled as he remembered his father's saying.

"Discipline, however, is always redemptive and instructive in purpose. So, let's take the lashes you deserved, for example. They could be delivered with the intent to cause you harm, to make you hurt for the hurt you caused. That would be punishment. But if *I* gave you those same lashes for the same crime, it would be because my desire is that you learn from your errors and never repeat them again...because I want you to grow, not because I despise you."

Talking to Braddock was like talking to his father. The two were so similar. Keigh realized that was probably why the two were so surly toward each other. He shrugged. "So it's only different for the one dealing out the sentence? The person being whipped gets the lashes either way."

Braddock seemed to consider his point for a moment. "Yes, you are right. A person's perception of why they are being whipped matters just as much.

That is why I need you to know I will never punish you. I will only discipline you. If you know what I do is to protect you, and teach you, then you will grow from it, but if you believe it is because I hate you…" His brow creased. "Then it will only serve to embitter you against me and teach you nothing."

"Can't you just tell me what I did was wrong and teach me the right thing to do?"

Braddock suppressed a laugh. "Unfortunately, no. It doesn't work. Wise people will learn and obey without ever having to fail. But, just as some small children will keep their hands out of the fire simply because they are told to, some will still insist on touching the flames. While a child never burned avoids the pain of rebellion, it is the one burned who learns the wisdom of the command much deeper."

"Sounds like it's better to rebel, then," Keigh pointed out. "I mean, if that's the only way to know the full value of a lesson." He smiled to himself, having caught Braddock in such an obvious contradiction.

"Depends on what you value and what you see as wisdom," Braddock admitted. "To trust the king and obey his commands, in the absence of understanding, is far wiser, and far more noble, than any wisdom that can be gained through understanding. If all people simply obeyed, we would have no strife in Eden. Unfortunately, the hearts of men pay little attention to wisdom spoken. The heart listens best to its cruelest instructor."

"Cruelest instructor?"

"Pain," answered Braddock.

"Pain?"

"Yes pain." Braddock sighed. "The truly wise have no need of it, but for common men such as you and me, it is a necessary teacher. I tell you the truth: you will never know the true value of a harvest until you've lost a crop to famine, you will never know the value of loyalty until you've been betrayed, and you will never know how deeply you love someone until you've lost them." Braddock paused as the two of them reflected on his words. "No one is glad for the pain, and I will never enjoy bringing it upon you, any more than I would enjoy seeing a child burn their hand in a fire. But when you fail to trust and obey, as is true wisdom, I will allow pain to teach you wisdom."

"That just—doesn't seem...kind."

"Doesn't it?" Braddock gave him an amused look. Standing, he made his way over to the door, where Keigh's bow and arrows had sat untouched since his first day of training. Braddock pulled one of the long wooden arrows from the quiver and held it up for Keigh. "Tell me, what is the most painful part of getting shot with an arrow?"

Keigh balked at the question. It was so off-topic, he had to shift his focus before answering. He remembered how the stranger had howled when his arrow had struck the man in the thigh. "I suppose, when the arrow hits you and cuts your flesh."

"It is not, in fact." Braddock shook his head. "Truthfully, pulling the arrow out will hurt more than the arrow going in. But would you ever allow the arrow to stay in your body just because it was going to hurt to have it removed?"

Keigh laughed at the absurdity of the question. "Of course not! If I leave the arrow in, it will kill me."

"Consider this, then." Braddock settled back into his chair, holding the arrow. "Getting shot with an arrow is like suffering the natural consequences of failure." The cane pressed the tip of the arrow to his arm. "It hurts, and left unaddressed, it can kill you. Discipline is the practice of removing the arrow." He pulled the arrow back. "It hurts, but if you let it, it will heal you. So, as you fail—and you will fail—I will pull the arrows out."

"If that's discipline, what's punishment?"

Braddock grinned at the question. "Punishment says 'Shoot him with another arrow!'"

Keigh chuckled at the dark joke. "So then, do you ever punish anyone?"

Braddock's smile faded. When he spoke, he did so somberly. "Yes. When we strike down our enemies in battle, when they raise their weapons in defiance of our king, or to harm his people...we punish them. No lesson is learned after losing your life. It is the king's desire that all the people of earth find refuge under his rule, but there will always be those who oppose him... even to their dying breath."

Braddock's words reminded Keigh of the news Mannie had delivered earlier that week. "Why hasn't the king punished Draiden, then? He opposes the king, and Mannie said he's gathering forces even as we speak!"

"That...is a topic for another day. For now, I want you to consider what we discussed today. Will you submit to the true wisdom of trust and obedience? Or will you choose the hard path of wisdom through understanding, whose teacher is pain?" Braddock rose to his feet, motioning for Keigh to do the same. "Stay home tomorrow. Catch up on whatever work your parents have for you. I do not wish for them to suffer on account of your training. We will resume our work on Monday."

Keigh left Braddock's feeling as though his brain had been churned like cream to butter. Punishment? Discipline? Pain? Wisdom? How would any of that help him do the work of a cane? He couldn't *wisdom* someone to death. He needed a sword, and he needed to learn how being a potent could give him strength to win in battle! He didn't need lectures about morality like some toddler. If Draiden was preparing for war, he wanted to fight. Braddock's pointless tasks and frivolous lectures weren't going to help with that. He resolved to bring it up with Braddock on Monday.

As Keigh got nearer to Bjorn, he saw Theo sitting on the wooden paw of one of the totem-pole red bears that stood guard on either side of the city gate. When Theo saw Keigh, he jolted as if waking from a deep sleep. Hopping down from the paw, he descended on Keigh like a bird on a bug.

"Keigh! Where have you been?" Theo looked nervously over Keigh's shoulder. "Nobody has seen you since Cato snatched you off Deacon a week ago! Are you in trouble?"

Keigh felt a twinge of guilt. He hadn't told anyone what he'd discussed with the two elders, and realized his friends had probably assumed the worst. "I'm fine. I've been down at Braddock's all week."

A look of horror filled Theo's face. "What are they making you do?"

"It's not like that," he said, then he thought about all the frivolous tasks he had been assigned all week and added, "Well, it's not exactly like that." Keigh smiled at the look of foreboding on Theo's face. "I'm not being *punished*, if that's what you're thinking." He emphasized the word, still not fully believing it, no matter what Braddock said.

Theo's fear morphed into excited curiosity. "Oh, phew! What did they say, then?"

"Ha! You change tune faster than Misselli spoils a punchline to a joke."

Theo's tone shifted again. "Do you like Misselli, Keigh?"

Keigh fidgeted uncomfortably at such a personal question. "Yeah...I mean, we're friends."

Theo raised an eyebrow at him. "Just friends?"

Keigh had been asking himself that same question for a month now. Why did Theo care? Why was he digging at this? *It's none of his business,* he thought. "Yeah...just friends."

Theo shrugged. "Oh, okay. So, you don't care that she's spent nearly all week with Tarin, then?"

Immediately, Keigh remembered Tarin slipping his arm around Misselli as he was being dragged away by Cato. He had been in town that day to talk to her, to apologize to her. Something he still very much wanted to do. But every day since then, he had been at Braddock's from dawn till dusk. Keigh's jaw clenched so hard he nearly chipped a tooth. Apparently, he had clenched his fists too, which Theo seemed to notice.

"Well, I just thought, maybe you should talk to her. You know...*if* there is more between you two." Theo grinned knowingly.

"If Misselli wants to spend time with Tarin, that's up to her," Keigh spat. "She can make her own decisions."

Theo raised his hands in surrender. "Just thought you would want to know. Anyways, what did Cato say to you?"

It took Keigh a second to shake the image of Tarin and Misselli out of his head before he could answer. "Um...not much. Just that I'm to do my agoge under Braddock." It was half the truth; Cato had ordered him to tell no one that he was a potent, saying people in Eden wouldn't react well to someone in their community having abilities that were so...unnatural.

Theo's eyes widened. "Braddock? *The* Braddock? I thought he was retired?"

"He is, but Cato insisted."

"Is that all he said?" There was a hint of pleading in Theo's voice.

"Yeah, why?"

"I just thought, you know...Seeing Deacon melt the way he did when you grabbed his fist, maybe there was more..."

"More what? You think I should have been punished?" snapped Keigh, back on the defensive.

"No, man." Theo sighed and tossed a rock he'd been holding. "It's not that...I'd just hoped..."

"Hoped? Hoped what?"

"I hoped maybe I wasn't the only one."

"The only one? The only what?"

Theo dropped his voice and glanced around to make sure nobody was near enough to hear what he had to say. "I'm a potent." He grimaced like he thought Keigh might laugh at him. When Keigh didn't, he continued, "I thought maybe you might be too. That's why I've been sitting here all day waiting for you to pass by." Theo picked another rock up off the ground and chucked it. "Cato told me not to tell anyone, so please don't tell anyone I told you. I thought you might already know anyway, since I pulled so much energy from you when we nearly fell off the tower." He dropped his gaze.

"That's what that was?" Keigh blurted. "I nearly passed out! I felt so tired!"

"I know! I'm sorry! Cato told me it's a huge violation to pull energy from someone without permission. I didn't mean to, I swear! It just sort of happens sometimes, when I panic. Like my body is trying to protect itself, so it starts pulling energy."

Theo was a potent too! If Braddock wasn't going to teach him anything, maybe Theo could. "Wait! So, you can pull energy from people and things?"

"No, I don't think so. Cato made me try pulling from some objects once, but I never got anything out of them."

"Oh…but you can pull from people?" Keigh could barely hide the eagerness in his voice.

"Not great…I don't know. I've only ever done it by accident."

"How do you feel when you pull energy from someone? Strong? Like, really strong?"

Theo's brow furrowed. His eyes narrowed to study Keigh. "No. I just get…I feel really…alive. Like, I'm alert, more alert than ever, and my mind gets super clear." Theo grinned. "I can't tell you the number of times I tried to use it when we were being tested at instruction. Figured Beaudy wouldn't miss a little strength."

Keigh knew what he meant. When he had pulled energy before, he too had felt the heightened sense of clarity. His thinking in those moments had been quick, vivid, and accurate. Maybe Theo was onto something. If he could figure out how to pull energy before talking with Braddock, maybe his brain wouldn't feel like butter afterward. But Keigh had felt strength, unnatural strength, whenever he had pulled from people. He was disheartened to hear that Theo's experience wasn't quite the same as his own.

"You know, Keigh, you're asking a lot of the same questions Cato asked me when he discovered I was a potent."

If Theo was a potent, surely Cato wouldn't mind Keigh sharing his ability with him. "Yeah, well, that's because…I'm a potent too."

"I knew it!" Theo jumped and pumped his little fist in the air. "Seriously! I'm surprised everyone else didn't see it too! You deflated Deacon like a popped waterskin!" He laughed, then grew sober. "I guess it makes sense, why Cato wouldn't want people to know. If you knew people around you could suck the life out of you with a touch…" His eyes grew wide. "You wouldn't trust anybody! And you'd probably want to burn anyone you knew who could."

Keigh nodded at the grim reality, remembering just how quickly the people of Bjorn had wanted his blood when he'd been accused of starting the fire. "Well, at least we have each other." He smiled at his tiny friend.

Theo was still buzzing like a wind-up toy. "So, has Braddock taught you how to use your gift? How to pull energy on command?"

"No, actually, I was hoping you knew how," Keigh confessed.

Theo shook his head. "Cato said he didn't know anyone who knew how to teach me. Just told me to be careful, and to let him know if anything strange ever happened."

A sudden bitter thought occurred to Keigh. *Maybe Braddock wasn't meant to teach me? Braddock probably doesn't know anything about being a potent. What if Cato just wants him keeping an eye on me, so I don't hurt anyone?*

"Well, bud…" Keigh clapped a hand to Theo's back. "I guess we'll just have to figure it out together."

CHAPTER 15

PRACTICE IN PURPOSE

20-19-21

K eigh spent the next day at home helping his father and brothers tend to the fields. By this time in June the potatoes were up, but so were the weeds. Keigh partnered with his father, switching back and forth between pulling weeds and hauling them out of the field to the burn pile. At the end of the day, they had rid five acres of potatoes of all their weeds. He felt a pang of guilt as he looked at the remaining fields. His father and brothers would be left to do the work without his help while he trained with Braddock.

His guilt only worsened when he thought about how pointless Braddock's tasks had been. At least when Keigh worked in the fields, he knew his purpose. Every job had a clear objective and benefit. Braddock's "training" accomplished nothing. After a week of it, the only thing Keigh knew about it was that it *wasn't punishment*.

"Tomorrow, I'll ask Braddock why he hasn't begun training me to fight," he told himself. Somehow saying it out loud made him feel more obligated to follow through on it. He couldn't let his family continue to labor for their survival without his help if he wasn't doing anything productive with Braddock. Plus, he wanted answers.

That evening he made sure to spend time playing with Jessie. They played a couple quick rounds of hide-and-seek before he took her out to see the garden wolves. He gave the pack a dried deer ear to chew on and Jessie attempted to give all twenty of the dogs names, most of which were just a variation of "Fluffy."

The following morning, when Braddock opened the door for Keigh, he handed him the shovel. "Mace had a big week! I think I saw eight out there."

"Yes, Master, but may I ask you a question?" Keigh waited for the hardened warrior to refuse.

Braddock did not. "You may," he said.

Keigh gulped down the knot of anxiety that had formed in his throat. He didn't want to offend his mentor, but he had to know. "Why haven't you taught me anything about warfare? How to fight? How to use my abilities as a potent?"

Braddock gave him an amused look. "You have a knack for making one question sound like three. After our discussion last week, do you still not see the purpose of these tasks?"

Keigh tried to think of all they had talked about. Most of what Braddock had told him last week had seemed more like riddles than instruction. "I...I do not, Master."

"Well then, you shall continue with them until you do." Braddock pressed the shovel into Keigh's hands and closed the door.

Keigh stomped off the front porch toward the river. "So now I have to teach myself? What's the point of even having a teacher?" he grumbled under his breath. Arriving at the first dung pile, he threw his shovel. It landed short, its metal tip catching the ground and flipping the handle straight into the rancid mound of bear scat. "Great!" he shouted, his whole body quaking with the effort of containing the tantrum that threatened to burst out of him.

Was it all another riddle like Mrs. Labelle's? *Here, Keigh, have some sugar bun!* Then giving him sourdough...Why couldn't adults just speak plainly?

Anger fueled his digging, and he finished three holes in under two hours. On the fourth hole, he encountered a particularly stubborn rock that he was unable to move. "This is pointless!" he shouted at the sky. Gripping the shovel with both hands, he brought the handle down hard over his knee, snapping the tool in two.

He stared at the broken halves in his hands, realizing he would have to tell Braddock what he had done. He contemplated lying, but only briefly. Lying to protect others was one thing, but lying to protect himself was not something he was willing to do.

Stepping out of the hole, he made his way back to Braddock's front door. He held the evidence of his lapse in control in front of him like a bag of waste that needed to be taken to the burn pile. Why had he snapped? Everything seemed to anger him more than usual recently. He didn't like how fragile he felt or how easily he lost control of his temper.

The question that had dug at him his whole life came back to mind again: *what's wrong with me?* When he was younger the thought had rarely crossed his mind, like a sick festival decoration that only came out once or twice a year—but in the last few weeks, ever since he had shamed his family by insulting Braddock in their home, it seemed to come to mind at least once daily. Why couldn't he just do the right thing, the safe thing, or the smart thing? Why did he always have to do something to screw things up?

Knocking on the door, he waited for Braddock. When the cane opened the door, Keigh offered him his broken shovel. "I'm sorry, Master." He hung his head, preparing to be scolded.

"Sorry for what?" asked Braddock.

"I'm sorry that I broke your shovel."

"Don't be sorry for that. I am well compensated by the king. Buying a new shovel is a small matter."

Keigh lifted his head, confused. "So, you aren't angry?"

"No." Braddock took the two halves of the shovel from Keigh and wagged them in front of him. "It appears *you* are."

Keigh hung his head again as his face grew hot with shame.

"Come in. Sit down."

The two of them took their seats in the usual chairs by Braddock's fireplace.

"So, tell me, Keigh—*why* are you so angry?"

Keigh's face was still burning. "It was just a stupid rock. I couldn't get it out and I lost my temper."

"No, the rock is merely the thing that tipped you past the point of self-control. I think your anger goes much deeper. What's really bothering you?" Braddock stood and walked over to the counter, where he began filling their water cups.

Keigh briefly debated telling Braddock he thought his training was a waste of time, that his family needed his help more than Braddock needed him burying bear scat, but he decided on a more tactful approach. "I guess I'm just upset because I thought training to be a cane would be different."

"Oh?" Braddock looked curious. "Different how? Are you familiar with the process of our agoge training? I was under the impression we canes kept that a secret."

Keigh admittedly knew nothing of what canes did in their training, only that they were warriors, and warriors trained to fight. "I am not. I just assumed you would be preparing me to fight for Eden."

"That is exactly what I have been doing," said Braddock, straight-faced.

"You have?" Keigh accepted the cup of water from his teacher and Braddock made his way back to his seat. "Sorry...I don't see how burying scat, sorting rocks, or any of the other pointless tasks I've done here in the last week are preparing me to fight!"

"Then, as I told you this morning, we will continue with them until you do. Your character must be molded before your sword will be of any use to the king."

"But we don't have time for that! I don't get it—I may never get it. Draiden is gathering forces right now! When it comes time to fight, I want to fight. And I can't do it with a shovel..." Keigh trailed off, fully expecting to be reprimanded for his outburst.

Braddock studied him for a long moment. "Perhaps you are right. The current situation may call for a deviation from the normal course of training."

He scratched his temple. "Do you wish to know the purpose behind completing such seemingly meaningless tasks?"

"I do."

"Even knowing that if I tell you, and you gain the understanding cheaply, you may endanger yourself or others?"

Keigh thought about this. He was willing to risk danger to himself, but hated the idea of becoming a risk to others. "What could you possibly tell me that would make me a risk to others?"

Braddock smiled. "I'm glad that you are struggling with that. There are a great many things I could tell you that would make you a danger to those around you, but this isn't one of those things. It's not what I tell you that will make you a risk, only that, by telling you and not making you learn through experience, you may not learn the lesson, and every lesson not learned through controlled experience risks being learned through uncontrolled experience."

"Wasn't it you who told me that the truly wise person trusts and obeys? Why make me learn this lesson through pain and experience?" Keigh tried to trap his teacher with his own words. "Let me be wise. I will trust you at your word. I will trust that what you tell me is important."

"Even if I tell you to trust my timing and keep digging holes?"

Keigh hung his head. He had tried to box Braddock into a corner, but ended up trapping himself. "Yes, Master. I will trust you, even if you give me no answers."

Braddock's eyebrows flew up. He looked both pleased and surprised. "Good! Because trust *is* the lesson."

"What?" Keigh's gaze shot up. "How do these pointless tasks teach me trust? And why is *that* more important than wielding a sword or learning my abilities as a potent?"

"Tell me, Keigh: what makes the king's canes the most effective warriors on earth? I will tell you our weaponry is not superior to that of our enemies—in fact, oftentimes our weapons are lesser. Nor is it our style of combat. You will never learn a technique from me that our enemy doesn't know themselves."

Keigh had never really thought about it before. He had always been told that a single cane was as good as ten soldiers from anywhere else. He himself had used and broken Braddock's sword, so he knew that what Braddock said about the weapons was true. Maybe it was the red bears, but very few canes had those.

"I don't know," he said finally. "I have always been told the canes of Eden were just better. I thought maybe I would learn why in my agoge."

"We *are* better, just not for the reasons most assume. Why do you think you were able to prevail over your attacker? We know he was very well funded due to his possession of a gun, so it stands to reason that he was also a highly skilled mercenary. People do not spend huge sums of money or entrust sensitive missions to people they believe to be incompetent or untested. The gun itself was a better weapon than your bow. So again: how did you win when you should have died?"

"I don't know. Luck, I guess," Keigh admitted, knowing he really had been lucky to survive that day.

Braddock smiled. "Luck may have had a part to play in it, but I believe the primary reason you survived is the same thing that gives canes their advantage in battle. Trust. Trust in your cause. Every cane trusts that his cause isn't just right, but that it is good. When you not only have a cause but wholeheartedly trust that it is of greater value than your own personal desires, you have purpose. When you believe in the king's message and the promise of Eden, when you trust that they aren't just one good among many but the single greatest good for any citizen of earth, your every swing of the sword will carry not only the might of your arm, but the might of your purpose." Braddock spoke with the conviction of a true believer. "Superior purpose will allow you to prevail. Your mercenary's purpose was to collect payment or perhaps build his reputation, but your purpose was more than that: to protect the innocent lives of others. Your purpose was greater, so you prevailed."

"I also wanted to survive," Keigh admitted, embarrassed by Braddock's assumption of the purity of his motives.

"No doubt you did, as everyone does. But survival is a poor purpose, for your opponent will share it. Self-interest is just as likely to cause a man to flee as to fight. Our purpose, our noble purpose, drives a man into the fight, unafraid to trade his life for what he believes in."

Keigh understood what Braddock was saying, but he was still confused. "So how do pointless chores teach me trust?"

Braddock gave him a sympathetic smile. "Why did you do the chores I assigned you last week? Was it not because you trusted I was here to train you? That I knew more than you? And how could I know if you trusted me if I only gave you tasks that obviously prepared you for war? I couldn't! All I could know is that you agreed with me, not that you trusted me. So, the chores were testing your trust. A test I feel you are quickly losing patience with."

Keigh hung his head. He hadn't trusted Braddock. He'd thought the battle master was punishing him, not preparing him. "I'm sorry. I should have known you wouldn't ask me to do something for no reason...but how does this help me trust our cause?"

"It helps," reassured Braddock. "Because until you can learn to trust someone you *have* met, you will never be able to trust a king that you have never met. Learning to trust me, and the other canes you will serve alongside, is crucial to your ability to trust the king. If you don't trust him, and by extension the purpose he gives us—and I mean *really* trust him with everything you have to give...then you will shrink back in battle and become a danger to those who fight beside you."

"I never thought of it that way."

"No doubt you haven't. These are philosophical principles that usually aren't discussed until much later in an apprentice's training. *Why* you wield a blade will always be more important than *how* you wield it...but due to current circumstances, we will have to accelerate your learning." Braddock shrugged and sat up in his chair. "So, let's begin. What do you know about potents?"

Finally! Braddock was getting to the stuff he wanted to know. "Nothing, really. Only what I've heard in stories. That they have super strength and can withstand challenges that would kill a normal person."

Braddock wagged his head. "Yes and no to varying degrees. In short, potents are just people who have the ability to channel energy in ways different than the natural way. Not all potents are the same, not in ability or capacity. Think of the various heroes of Eden."

"Were they potents?" asked Keigh eagerly.

Braddock nodded. "Nearly all of them. Are you familiar with Barrett the Brave?"

Keigh nodded enthusiastically. "They say he once collapsed an entire section of city wall with his bare hands, when Eden laid siege to a Substonian stronghold, and that he slayed a Nephilim who had sworn an oath to destroy him!"

Braddock chuckled at his excitement. "Yes, Barrett was a potent who was able to convert raw energy into increased strength of body. And what of Dara the Wise?"

"Dara is said to have memorized every book and scroll in Eden, and could remember every word of every conversation she had ever had."

"True, Dara was a potent who was able to infuse her mind with energy in a way that allowed her incredible memory. A skill I would most like to have myself," Braddock mused. "What about Kwan the Messenger?"

"They say he could run for days! That he even ran to both oceans, east and west, without stopping."

Braddock nodded. "Just another potent with the ability to sustain his body without allowing fatigue or muscle damage to set in. These are all examples of potents with extraordinary abilities." He pursed his lips. "The truth, however, is that potents are rare, and getting increasingly more so with every generation that passes from the Great Collapse. And the potents who still exist are very limited in our abilities."

Keigh's jaw dropped. "Wait, did you just say *our*? Are you a potent too?"

Braddock inclined his head. "I am. But only just so."

Keigh nearly flew off the front of his chair. "Then you can teach me how to use my abilities!"

Braddock grimaced. "As I said, potents are rare these days, and most of what I know I have had to teach myself. I will teach you what I have discovered, but you should keep your expectations low. Every potent I have ever met has been similarly diminished in their abilities. I'm afraid the gifts of the heroes of old are no longer among us."

"When can we start?" Keigh asked, hardly hearing what Braddock said, only that he would teach him what he knew.

"We will begin now. Do you recall the times you felt yourself draw energy before?"

Keigh nodded as he remembered the powerful sensation of energy and strength that had coursed through his veins like liquid fire.

"What did all those instances have in common? How did you feel?" Braddock pressed his fingertips together as he often did when questioning Keigh.

Keigh could remember being afraid when he'd fought the stranger and dueled Vicerous, but he hadn't been afraid when he'd caught Deacon's fist. So, it wasn't fear, neither was it anger. He hadn't been angry when fighting the stranger, just... "I was desperate," he said at last. "I think."

Braddock considered this for a moment. "Desperate is a decent word for it. That is why so many potents first discover their gift in moments of crisis. Desperation will definitely coax the ability out of you, but it's more than that. Elsewise, you would only ever be able to use the ability in emergencies. The thing I have found that allows me to use the gift most readily is *need*."

"Need?"

"Yes, 'need.'" Braddock nodded. "A necessary component of desperation, but something that can exist apart from crisis as well. The trick is differentiating between 'want' and 'need.' It's a fine line, but your powers will know the difference. If all you are able to do is focus on something you want, even if you want it desperately, the energy will not respond to you. But if you can focus on a need—something beyond a want, something you cannot live without—you will be able to draw upon an energy source." Braddock extended an arm to Keigh. "Here. Clasp my arm."

Keigh reached out and grabbed his mentor's arm, noticing how much thicker and more muscular it was than his own.

"Now, you must never pull energy from someone without their permission." Braddock squeezed Keigh's arm, forcing him to pay attention. "And never more than they permit. Is that understood?"

Keigh nodded.

"To do so is a violation of a person, the same as it would be stabbing them with a knife. You can cause great harm, even death, if you do not restrain yourself." Braddock's eyes bored into Keigh with all the gravity of a man who had seen death come at his own hands.

"Yes, Master."

"Good. Now, I want you to focus your mind on a need. Something you cannot live without. Focus on it to the exclusion of all else, letting the need flow out from your mind and into your very heart. When you have centered yourself on that one need, pull from my arm as though what you need lies locked within it. I will warn you, though: this is no easy task. I myself was unable to pull energy on command until months after I started practicing."

Keigh searched his mind frantically for a need. What did he need? He *wanted* a lot of things, but need? This was why his family always had such a hard time giving him gifts at Winter Festival—he didn't feel like he needed anything. Maybe a sword? He would love to have a sword, but did he need one?

It was the closest thing he could think of at the moment, so he set his mind on it. "I've got it," he said, trying to remember exactly how wielding Braddock's sword had felt like an extension of his arm. How it had somehow made him feel complete.

"When you're ready, then, pull. But if I release you, do not continue to pull from me."

Keigh nodded. And when he felt as though the sword was all he needed, all he cared about, he pulled. Pulled so hard that he jerked Braddock out of his chair onto the ground between them.

"Let go of me, you fool!" Braddock shook his arm free of Keigh's grasp and stood up, veins bulging in his arms and neck. He brushed the dirt off his knees. "Pull the *energy* from my arm, don't *pull my arm!* Addle-brained child," he grumbled as he sat again, his head and neck now as red as his iconic cloak.

Keigh's face grew unbearably hot at his boneheaded mistake. "I'm sorry, Master. I wasn't thinking."

"That much is clear," snorted Braddock. "This ability will do you little good if you are unable to focus on a need without losing your wits." He offered Keigh his arm. "Now try again."

This time, when Keigh centered his mind on needing a sword, he tried to channel his desire into his hand, as if the solution to his need were locked away inside his mentor. Gripping Braddock's arm tight, he attempted to leach the energy from him. He felt nothing at first...but then, a small tendril of heat pricked his palm like a hot iron.

Keigh released his grasp in alarm. He checked his palm for a mark.

Braddock grinned. "I had not hoped for so much today, and on your first attempt, no less!"

"You can feel when energy leaves you?" Keigh asked, astonished. Thinking back to when Theo had pulled energy from him on their descent from the tower, he didn't remember feeling anything other than extremely tired—that and Theo's fingernails clawing into his neck. Perhaps he hadn't noticed the energy exiting his body due to his own adrenaline.

"You can," Braddock confirmed. "You should know what it feels like in case you are ever attacked by someone intent on draining you of your strength. Take my arm again."

Keigh did so, Braddock's hand clasping around his forearm in return. Soon, underneath Braddock's palm, he felt the odd sensation of cold water trickling off his skin. Not uncomfortable; subtle, but noticeable. *Noticeable to anyone not falling off a burning building,* he thought.

Braddock released his arm. "Did you feel it?"

"Yes. Does it feel different if they take more?"

Braddock shrugged. "I do not know. I have never had more than a small amount pulled from me, and am not capable of pulling greater quantities than I did from you just now." A mischievous smile crossed his face, and he said innocently, "If you're really curious, you could always ask Deacon. Cato tells me you drained enough from him to render him unconscious."

"Does this mean I'm able to access more energy than you?" Keigh's eyes opened wide at the implications if that were true.

Braddock only splayed his hands questioningly. "Based on Cato's observations and your own account of your experiences...yes, I believe your capacity for pulling energy far exceeds my own. But until you master the ability to gather it at will, the gift will never serve you outside of the most dire situations."

*

An hour later, Keigh was exhausted. The mental effort it took to isolate a single thought and hold onto it without distraction had left him sweating like he had just worked a day in the fields. To his dismay, he was unable to replicate his earlier success. No matter how hard he focused on his need for a weapon, the flow of energy evaded him. Braddock seemed unconcerned, merely suggesting that his focus was lacking, or that he needed to consider using a better need.

After they had practiced extracting energy, Braddock sent him outside into the hot June sun. Braddock emerged from the house shortly after, holding two thick, perfectly proportioned sparring swords.

"Here." He tossed Keigh one of the swords, which Keigh clumsily fumbled and dropped in the dirt. "We will practice with these. I watched your duel with Vicerous. He is an excellent swordsman, and your reflexes and intuition are as good as I've ever seen in anyone yet to earn their red cloak."

Keigh's chest swelled with the praise. "Thank you, Mas—"

"But!" Braddock cut him off. "Your footwork and your technique are sloppy." He slapped Keigh's thigh with the flat of his blade as he walked a circle around his student. "Had you dueled someone more levelheaded and not so blinded by hate, you likely would have lost your duel in short order."

The certainty in Braddock's voice stung Keigh's pride.

"So today, and every day, we will work your form and flow." Braddock whipped his blade up in front of his face and began demonstrating poses and stances, intertwined and combined in elegant motion. "*I* will teach you how to remain light on your feet, yet able to strike with power at any moment. *I* will teach you the most efficient and stable progressions and sequences for defending yourself from swift attacks. But first, we will have to rely upon the most reliable instructor."

"What?"

"Pain!"

Braddock lunged at him, striking him on the ribs before he could bring his sword around for a block.

Keigh yelped in pain and retreated. "I wasn't ready!"

"Your enemies will not wait for you to be ready either. Now defend yourself!"

Braddock lunged again, but this time Keigh was able to deflect the blow. However, his pleasure at having blocked his mentor's strike was short-lived. Braddock pulled his blade back and landed a jab to his gut before he knew what was happening. Keigh dropped to the ground, unable to breathe, fighting the urge to vomit.

"What was that for?" he wheezed, trying to gather himself enough to stand.

"Do you want to feel that again?"

"No..."

"Then do something about it!"

Staggering to his feet, he raised his sword. *Fine, old man. I will.*

Instead of waiting to be attacked again, he went on the offensive. Swinging and cutting, thrusting and stabbing, in as quick a succession as he could muster. Braddock had to work hard to evade the wood of his blade, but he was able to ward off or avoid every single one of Keigh's attacks. Finally, Keigh struck his mentor's sword hard enough to send it bouncing back into its owner's knee. Pain seemed to teach the old warrior as well, because in three quick strikes, he was able to beat Keigh back and land a hard blow on his upper arm.

For the next two hours, they dueled under the hot summer sun, churning up the black soil around Braddock's home. Braddock shouted instructions at Keigh and periodically paused their clashing in order to show him a more efficient way of moving his blade from position to position. Keigh was a quick learner, a fact which seemed to please Braddock greatly. He completed movements at full speed that his teacher had taught him only minutes ago. In that whole time, though, Keigh never once got as close to striking Braddock as he had with the blow to his knee.

When they finished, both of them were dripping sweat and panting heavily. Keigh rubbed the knots from his muscles with his knuckles. He examined his arms and legs. Bruises were already starting to blossom purple and brown where Braddock had struck him.

Braddock reached out and took the sparring sword from Keigh. "Go wash off in the river. The cold water will keep you from bruising too badly. I want you to be ready to resume tomorrow, and I won't accept any excuses about how sore you are."

Keigh winced at the thought of how he'd feel after his limbs had had a full night to stiffen up. "Are you going to soak too?" he asked.

"I would..." Braddock smiled and threw his hands wide. "But I have no bruises to soothe, thanks to you!"

CHAPTER 16

No Going Back

23-43-19

The days and weeks of summer passed, each following the same pattern. Monday through Saturday, Keigh would spend his mornings developing his abilities as a potent. At first he struggled to pull even the smallest amount of energy from Braddock, mostly due to his inability to focus. This led Braddock to assign him long hours of silent contemplation on the riverbank, where his only task was to practice centering his mind on one specific need while keeping his eyes open to all that was happening around him.

Keigh found this especially difficult to do. The river was teeming with life and movement. Barn swallows collected mud for their nests off the bank; deer came to drink their fill of the river's cold, clear water. The calm surface reflected images of clouds and the distant Bullhorn Mountains, the mirror broken only when the river's numerous trout rose to snap up a bug, or when an eagle dove to snap up a trout. Occasionally a red fox or a garden wolf would trot down the bank, looking for rodents.

The task was all but impossible when Mace visited. The massive red bear enjoyed playing in the water more than she liked drinking it. Sprawling out on her belly in an attempt to escape the summer heat, she would roll about in the cool waters, sending huge waves up the bank and soaking Keigh on more than one occasion.

Despite the distractions, by the end of summer he was able to summon the ability on command. Partly because the meditations had helped him fix his heart on a singular need, and partly because he had found a stronger desire: he *needed* to make his family proud.

Still, even with all his progress, he had yet to tap into the ability in the same powerful way he had before. His experiences pulling from Deacon, Mannie, and the assassin had been rivers of energy compared to the trickles he was pulling from Braddock in his studies. Despite his personal disappointment with the dismal advancements he had made as a potent, his mentor still seemed quite pleased with his progress.

True to his word, Keigh made sure to pass the lessons on to Theo, but no matter how much Theo tried, he was unable to pull even the smallest amount of energy from Keigh.

The evenings were spent training with the sword. From the very beginning, Braddock had been impressed by Keigh's speed and intuition with a blade. At the start of the summer, Keigh would return home each night with a collection of new bruises from where his mentor had thwarted his defenses and stuck him with his wooden sparring sword. But by the end of August, he hadn't been touched by his mentor's blade for a month—a feat he was particularly proud of, even if he had still yet to land a single blow on Braddock.

Mannie had altered his random visits so that he was now visiting the Anders every other Sunday—a fact that Keigh loved, since he always had more time to spend with the old messenger than he would have if Mannie came on a day that he trained with Braddock. Mannie hadn't brought them any more dire news since the report of Draiden's census, but even when new things weren't happening in Eden, Mannie was a wealth of stories and information. Keigh was particularly eager to hear everything he knew about potents, but Mannie either didn't know much or was intentionally avoiding the topic. Every time Keigh asked about it, he managed to magically answer the question without giving Keigh any useful details.

Besides spending time with Mannie, Keigh's Sundays were spent at home, working with his family, at Braddock's insistence. The Anders men rose before sunrise and worked long, sweaty hours in the fields till just past midday, when the summer sun drove them to seek shade's relief. His father and brothers used their afternoons to rest, knowing the long, hard days of the harvest season were coming. Keigh spent his afternoons hunting, playing with Jessie, or hanging out with his friends at "club."

It had been three agonizing weeks after his awful words to Misselli at the whipping post before Keigh had finally gotten an opportunity to speak to her again. He had apologized profusely, expecting Misselli to be grateful or relieved to hear he hadn't meant a word of what he said. Instead, she had been nonchalant, saying she knew he hadn't meant it and to forget about it.

Keigh would have loved to forget about it, but no matter what Misselli said, she was definitely treating him differently now. She had resumed gathering their group of friends for "club," but avoided one-on-one conversations with him. At first he had assumed it was because Theo had told him she was spending time with Tarin, but to Keigh's relief, she seemed to be avoiding Tarin as well—though Keigh noticed Tarin was making no such avoidances of her.

Keigh still hadn't confronted his friend for fleeing the scene the night of the fire. He had decided not to bring it up with him. Tarin was upper-class, wealthy, and most likely the future King of Eden. Keigh feared that if he made trouble over this offense, Tarin may just decide he didn't need a thrall friend anymore. Tarin did in fact have far more to lose than he did, but his friend's abandonment irked him still, even if he wasn't willing to confront him about it.

On the last Sunday in August, Misselli had organized a picnic by Tepee Falls on Morrell

Creek near her home. They were sitting in an alcove between two giant roots of a pine, eating their lunches, when the last member of their group, Kervyn, arrived.

"Sorry I'm late for club," Kervyn sputtered as he panted for air. A dark circle had formed on his gray tunic above his round belly where sweat had soaked through.

Keigh rolled his eyes. "Don't call it 'club.' Makes it sound like we're ten years old."

"I'm still waiting on *you* to come up with a better option." Misselli did her best impression of the annoyed look on Keigh's face, to the amusement of everyone. Keigh complained every time they called it "club," but for the life of him he couldn't think of anything better.

"The reason I'm late..." Kervyn leaned on his knees for support, then pointed an accusing finger back down the hill. "Other than that...ridiculous hike...Really, I don't see how anyone lives on the mountain...Torture, pure torture..."

"Get on with it, Kerv." Theo threw the top of a carrot at the late arrival. "Why are you late?"

"Right...let me sit down." Kervyn climbed over a root and wedged himself between Tarin and Conrad.

Tarin scooted closer to Misselli and put his hand on hers, but before Keigh even had time to get upset, she pulled her hand free, placing it in her lap. Neither Tarin's nor Misselli's face betrayed anything, both keeping their eyes on Kervyn.

"Next weekend is the Selection Festival," Kervyn began.

Groans went up from the group.

"That's not news, Kervy! We've known that for months!" said Conrad.

Keigh took another look at the sweaty state of his friend's tunic. Even for Kervyn, it seemed like a lot. He knew of only three things that caused his friend to sweat like that: exercise, the thought of exercise, and juicy new bits of town gossip. All three must be plaguing him today.

"Calm down, calm down. Let me finish," said Kervyn, obviously enjoying the attention. "As you *all* know, next weekend is the Selection Festival. The three elders will select three canes, *ooooorrrrrr* cane apprentices, to go to Sentinel for the Refining Trials."

"Seriously, get on with it!" Theo turned to Beaudy. "I'm going to kill this kid. Can I kill him?"

Beaudy shook his head vigorously, as if he thought Theo might be serious.

"Patience, Theo! I'm getting there!" Kervyn couldn't control the smile on his face at having knowledge everyone wanted. "There hasn't been a Refining for twenty years, and this year our class is being included in the nominations."

"We know!" blurted Addy. Theo gave her a grateful look for her solidarity.

"Anyway, my father received word this morning that Bjorn's Selection Festival...of all the Selection Festivals in Eden...will be attended by...none other than...ouch!" Kervyn wiped the dirt off his tunic where Theo's pinecone had struck him.

"Spit it out, man!" Theo brandished a second pinecone.

"The king!" exclaimed Kervyn. "The king and queen are coming to Bjorn for the Selection Festival!"

The group went silent with shock. The pinecone toppled out of Theo's hand.

"The king? The king will be here? In a week?" Tarin's face was pale. He looked as though he were about to throw up.

"What's the matter, big guy? Afraid to meet your father?" Keigh teased his friend. The group chuckled.

"He could be Deacon's father," offered Addy. "If you believe Deacon, he says Councilman Slate always makes a point of telling him how much he looks like the queen when he comes to visit Deacon's father."

This was true. Deacon had long used his father's relationship with the head of the Queen's Council as proof that he was the blood son of the king. Keigh didn't blame Addy for hoping it might be Deacon. He too would be glad to see Deacon go, but he wasn't so desperate to be rid of Deacon Wulf that he would stoop to wishing he'd become the next King of Eden.

"Okay, none of us have ever seen the king, but rumor is, he's huge! Like an actual giant!" Conrad shook his head. "No way Deacon is his kid. It's got to be Tarin."

"There are other members of the Consecrate outside of Bjorn, Conrad," argued Misselli. "Who's to say one of them isn't bigger than Tarin?"

The group dismissed her argument. Tarin was a big fifteen-year-old by any standard. The chance that another boy in Eden matched his size was slim.

Misselli downplaying the possibility of his lineage seemed to be all the cure Tarin needed for his stupor. "Why do you always insist it could be someone else?"

"I just don't want you to count your chickens before they hatch, is all," Misselli said, avoiding Tarin's eyes. "There are more important things than being king," she added under her breath, making eye contact with Keigh briefly before snapping her head back down to look at the food in her lap.

"Good one, Misselli! And maybe poor is better than rich, or crying is better than laughing, or being hungry is better than being full!" Tarin laughed at his own joke, shaking his head. "Honestly, sometimes you say the cutest things."

They spent the rest of the picnic sharing stories of the king's exploits and rumors of his appearance before dispersing back to their homes. Keigh had wanted to walk Misselli home, but after waiting five minutes for her to stop talking with Tarin, he grew frustrated and walked home alone.

He found Mannie talking with his father and mother in their home's little great room. Keigh told them the news about the king's visit to Bjorn, but Mannie already knew. Because the king had decided to visit Bjorn, he was going to have to attend Vaderkirk's festival as the king's representative instead. Keigh was disappointed Mannie would not be joining him for the Selection Festival, but understood his friend was the king's thrall and had to go where he was sent.

*

In the days leading up to the festival, the town was packed with people eagerly preparing for the king's arrival. Eden's colors of sapphire blue and white were hung on the front of every building, while hundreds of Eden's flags hung from cords that spanned the width of the road, high above. The edges of the community grounds were filled with booths and games run by various well-off families. Keigh had noticed Kervyn's family setting up a barrel for apple bobbing, and Russo Conri had set up a booth where Tarin's mother would do face painting for children. Braddock had enlisted Keigh's help with the construction of a large stage at the rear of the community grounds, where the king and queen would sit with the elders for the nomination ceremony.

Keigh had begged and bribed Braddock incessantly for the name of the person he would be nominating, but the retired cane wouldn't give him so much as a clue. Keigh was sure that both Deacon and Tarin would be nominated since they were both members of the Consecrate, but he was curious about who would receive the third and final nomination. He hoped desperately it wouldn't be Vicerous. Sure, he would be glad to see the man shipped off to Sentinel, but he didn't think he could survive having to watch Vicerous Wulf's smug face as he walked across the stage, receiving the praise of Bjorn and the acceptance of the king. Then to have to listen to him give a speech? Keigh would walk out before he sat and watched Vicerous exalt himself with a self-aggrandizing monologue. He was pretty confident Braddock and Cato would never select Vicerous, but Oliver Connell might. The two seemed to be cut from the same cloth.

Finally, the day of the festival arrived. There had been no official word on when the king and queen would reach Bjorn, so Keigh and his family rose early and went to town to secure a good spot to watch the royal procession. As far as he knew, nobody in Bjorn, other than Braddock and Mannie, had ever seen the king in person. This may be their only chance to ever see their monarch, and they weren't going to risk not getting a good look at him.

Apparently, the rest of Bjorn felt the same way. By the time the Anders arrived at Bjorn's front gate, there were lines of people on either side of the road, stretching from the entrance all the way up to the town center. Keigh's family made their way up the hill until they found an opening large enough for all of them to stand side by side. Before long, the lines of eager townsfolk were three or four people deep nearly all the way up and down the road.

Braddock and Bjorn's other canes had been tasked with keeping the street clear enough for the king's procession to pass unimpeded. Occasionally one of the red-cloaked men walked by, asking everyone to take a step back. Keigh was relieved Vicerous had kept himself to regulating the other side of the road. He was sure to be upset that Keigh had never been punished for embarrassing his son.

As he watched Chogan make a round on the far side of the street, he noticed Emerson crouched low in the third row of people, trying to find a gap between the bodies through which she could view the procession. Sympathy for the shy girl welled up in him.

Keigh darted across the road. Crouching down low to get on Emerson's eye level, he waved for her to join him. "Come on! I have room for you to stand with me in the front!"

Emerson's face lit up with so much joy, she didn't even attempt to hide her crooked yellow teeth like usual. Groans went up from those around her as she wriggled her way to the front.

"Out of the road, Anders!" Zale Woodman yelled at him.

"Sorry!" Keigh waved at the surly cane and led Emerson back across the street to where his family stood pressed against the tar-stained boards of the butcher shop.

Keigh introduced her to his family and asked his dad if he would let Jessie sit on his shoulders so Emerson could take her place and get a good view of the king. The Anders received the homely girl warmly, as Keigh had known they would. If his family was one thing, they were hospitable. The irony had always stood out to him. Despite being one of Bjorn's poorest families, they always seemed to be the most willing to go out of their way for others. It used to bother him that his parents were always giving away their precious time and resources to people who seemed better off than they were, but over time, he had grown to admire it.

They stood there for another three hours, baking under the rising sun and talking amongst themselves. They would have gladly talked with their neighbors, but time had not yet washed the townsfolk's memories of the tower incident, and it seemed their contempt was not reserved for Keigh alone but to anyone who would stand by him.

Keigh and Emerson were watching a group of ants drag a dead dragonfly through the gravel when the rapid sound of footsteps closed in on them.

"The king approaches!" a runner in a simple white tunic shouted, sprinting his way toward Bjorn's center. "Make way! The king approaches!"

"That's the herald," Owen stated as the runner passed by.

"Who's Herald?" asked Jessie.

Keigh and Emerson chuckled, but Keigh nearly fell on his face laughing when Jobey asked, "Yeah, Dad, how do you know his name?"

Every head and neck in Bjorn craned toward the road, trying to be the first to catch a glimpse of the king's entourage—but it would be another hour before the king arrived.

They heard the procession before they saw it. Trumpet blasts and a ripple of excitement made their way up the street from Bjorn's front gate, like a wave on a pond. Shocked yelps of alarm and stifled shrieks sounded as six massive red bears rounded the corner. The behemoth animals were an intimidating sight. One alone was enough to cause a person to go into nervous sweats; six together looked like they could level the town if they had a mind to. The bears' shoulders passed a good seven feet above the tallest men's heads as they walked through the gawking crowd. Four were various shades of red, iconic of their breed, while the final two were blonde and black respectively. The bears lumbered their way up the road, swaying their giant heads side to side as they walked.

Keigh wondered which was the king's bear, Gorr. You couldn't hear a legend about the king without hearing Gorr mentioned. He was said to be furious as a tornado and strong as an earthquake in battle. His claws and teeth disposed of enemies as easily as a child blew the seeds off a dandelion. Gaping at the mighty animals as they passed by his family, Keigh thought that might just be true of all red bears.

Behind the bears followed two rows of six trumpeters, followed by six rows of flutists, all wearing white tunics with one vertical and one horizontal blue stripe that intersected on the chests. The flutes played a joyful melody, while the trumpeters merely held their instruments at attention. Small children danced in the street in front of their parents as the musicians passed.

Following the musicians, twelve canes marched in a "V" formation. They wore dark gray tunics and breastplates of burnished bronze. Their iconic red cloaks lay flat and spotless on their backs. In addition, they all wore open-faced bronze helmets, the third item awarded in the Queen's Climb. The helmets' sides and nose guards extended down to sharp points and much of their bright, polished surfaces had dozens of small bear fangs etched into them, signifying each warrior's litany of accomplishments. Atop each was a narrow plume of red bear hair. This alone would have been an impressive sight, but each of the canes also wore an adamantine of burnished steel, so polished and well-crafted it appeared as though liquid silver coated the left arm of each warrior.

Keigh's mouth dropped open. If there was one piece of cane equipment that was better than their enemies', it was the adamantines: single-arm metal armor that was made with such expertise that it allowed a cane to absorb a direct blow from a sword without even suffering a jolt. Adamantines were extremely precious and marked a cane as having completed the Queen's Climb, cementing their rank as the most experienced and qualified of their order.

Keigh did not have long to gawk at the muscular warriors, for inside their formation was the queen's carriage. Two flawless white stallions pulled the gold-covered chariot, which he expected to see the queen riding in. To his surprise, she was walking behind it. The queen was beautiful—tall and slender, with veils of raven hair framing the flawless white skin of her face. An elegant yet practical dress of red and white flowed like rippling liquid over her slim figure. She was grace in motion. Atop her head was a silver three-pointed crown that sparkled with the light of a thousand inset diamonds.

As the queen walked, she touched the hands of dozens of people. Between her and her attendants, no one was missed. She looked people in the face and spoke quick words to all she could. They made their way up the road slowly and methodically, being sure to grant each person, on both sides, a brief interaction. People clamored to get close to her. Several times, one of the canes had to step in and push someone away from her. Keigh wondered what she was saying to draw such frantic attention.

Then he saw it. Between every greeting, they each would dip their hand into a large velvet bag at their waist and pull out a gold coin to give to the next person. She was giving away money! And not just money—gold! To everyone! No wonder people were coming undone to speak to her.

His awe at the queen was interrupted as a white bull moose, twelve feet tall at the shoulder with antlers nearly as wide as the street, stepped around the bend in the road. On its back sat the king.

He was an impressively large man, though not the giant Keigh had heard described in stories. He was dressed in white pants and a silky white shirt under a vest of deep sapphire blue, decorated with gold filigree. But as impressive as the king's clothing was, it was his helm that drew all the attention: burnished gold of flawless artistry. Painstaking detail had been taken to give the helmet the look of a natural head, with flowing gold hair and curling beard. A gold crown with three prominent points topped the helmet. The face bore an inscrutable expression, holes for eyes and mouth presenting only black voids behind them. The way the helm was sculpted gave the king the appearance of being able to see all things at once—yet Keigh still felt like the eyes had lingered on him.

He shook his head, returning his attention to the queen, who was now before him. She greeted the Anders with a voice as smooth and warm as sun-soaked honey. Her silk-soft hands touched Keigh's as she pressed a shiny gold coin into his palm. Keigh stared at it as the people behind him thrust their arms forward to receive their gold. He had never held so much money in his life! Briefly, he wondered if all his family's coins would be enough to pay off their debt to the Wulfs.

He looked at Emerson, who was equally in awe of the queen's generosity. She covered her coin with both hands and pressed it to her chest as if she were afraid it may fly away.

Just then, a body slammed into the back of Keigh, and an old man stumbled out into the street in front of him. The man fell to his knees in the dust in front of the queen.

"Please, my queen! Another coin! My son is ill, and I am too old to work the field." The man buried his face in his hands. "We will not survive the winter with no crop this year. If you would, save us from our calamity! One more coin would see my family fed."

The cane closest to them grabbed the man by the back of his neck and stood him up. "Off the road!" he growled. "The queen has given you your share!"

"Please, my queen!" the old man begged, tears choking his voice.

The cane drew back to shove the man into the crowd when the queen's hand grasped his arm, halting him.

She reached back into the velvet bag of coins and pressed another gold piece into the old man's hand. "May this be a blessing to you and your kin." She smiled at him, then made her way to the people waiting on the other side of the street.

The old man cried over the two gold pieces in his hand for a moment. Then, without warning, he took off after the queen. "Thank you, my queen! How can I ever thank you?"

Keigh saw what would happen before it did. The cane who had removed the old man from the road raised his metal-coated arm to strike the man down and keep him from touching the queen.

Quick as a flash, Keigh lunged out into the road and inserted himself between the cane and the old man. Bracing for impact, he held up his arms to catch the hit.

He took the full force of the blow. The cane's adamantine arm may as well have been a tree trunk. The strike caused Keigh's outstretched arms to collapse back down on his head, sending him crashing into the old man. They both crumpled to the ground in a jumble of flailing limbs.

"Do not interfere, boy!" The cane raised his arm to strike Keigh again, but before he could, Owen stepped over his son. A hush fell over the town as all eyes fixed on the altercation.

Face down, hands up in a posture of submission, Owen pleaded with the cane. "Forgive him, please! He does not know his place. I am the boy's father. Let me see to his punishment!"

The cane considered Owen's plea for a moment before lowering his arm slowly. "See that you do," he growled, then he turned and followed the queen, who had already resumed greeting the townspeople as if nothing unusual had happened.

Owen jerked Keigh up off the ground, then gently helped the older man back to his feet. They took their places on the side of the road without speaking. If the Anders hadn't been outcasts in Bjorn before, they were now.

As the king approached, his gaze lingered on Keigh.

There was no mistaking it this time. The golden helm peered directly at him. The eyes, black caverns of emotionless focus, bored into him until the great white moose took the monarch past the Anders.

"Have you no sense?" Keigh's father chastised him as soon as the king had departed. "Why must you always insert yourself into trouble that isn't yours?"

Keigh didn't answer. He hadn't intended to embarrass his father. He'd just seen a strong man about to strike a weak one, and something in him had compelled him to intervene. He hadn't put any thought into it at all. It had been like a reflex, propelling him into the fight.

Behind the king, twenty more canes followed. Among them were the canes of Bjorn. Keigh nodded to Braddock as he passed. Braddock nodded back politely, but kept his focus on the king ahead of him. As the canes passed, one of them detached from the procession and made their way over to the Anders.

Vicerous Wulf stood in front of Owen with his palm out. Owen glared at him, but Vicerous' lips were pulled back in an evil smirk.

Without a word, Owen turned to Sabriya and took her coin, then placed both his and hers in Vicerous' outstretched palm.

Vicerous pocketed the coins, then put his empty hand back in front of Owen.

"Let the kids keep their coins, Vicerous." Owen's voice was exasperated, lacking the authority Keigh was used to hearing from his father.

"I won't allow it. You've already let the boy start getting ideas," Vicerous sneered, giving Keigh's mother a glance of utter disdain. "I would hate for his siblings to form any similar...*delusions*."

Owen started to protest, but bit his lip instead. Turning to his children, he put his hand out. "Your coins," he said, then, seeing the hesitation in their faces, snapped, "Now!"

"That's a good boy, Owen," mocked Vicerous as Owen deposited the coins in his hand. "If a wretch like you can learn his place, maybe your children won't all be lost causes."

Owen hung his head as Vicerous walked away cackling, bouncing the Anders gold coins in his hand.

Keigh couldn't remember ever seeing his father so cowed. His father was strong and courageous! He had never backed down to anyone or anything the way he had just submitted to Vicerous. The Wulfs were his family's betters, but what could Vicerous have done if Owen had denied him? They were already thralls—what worse could he do to them?

Keigh knew better than to ask. His family silently fell in with the crowd as it followed the king's procession up to the community grounds.

At the grounds, people dispersed to the various booths around the space. Keigh took Jessie to play all the different games and get her face painted like a tiger by Tarin's mother. He ran into Misselli in the crowd, and they talked just long enough to agree on finding a place where their families could stand together for the ceremony.

While the townspeople milled about the grounds, the king and queen, along with the elders, took their seats at a long table that had been set up on the stage Keigh had helped build. Three red bears sat on either side of the stage while kids threw them bits of food that couldn't possibly be big enough to tempt bears that size.

In front of the stage, the twelve canes with helmets and adamantines stood guard, brandishing their polished swords in front of their chests. They were an impressive sight. Keigh envisioned himself one day standing guard for the king. He would complete the Queen's Climb and be awarded his cloak, sword, helmet, and adamantine, becoming a cane in full—someday...

He was jerked out of his daydream as Jessie pulled him off to go bob for apples again.

*

An hour later, the king's trumpets blasted once more, and Cato instructed the people to find their seats for the ceremony. Keigh hustled to find his parents.

He told them the Labelles wanted to sit by them, but by the time Misselli and Keigh had collected their families, the only room for them was in the back. The Anders and Labelles took their seats on the ground, with Misselli and Keigh sitting next to each other in the middle. Jessie plopped herself into Keigh's lap with a giggle and they waited for the ceremony to start.

The ceremony was a rather simple one. Cato delivered an opening statement, thanking the king and queen for coming to Bjorn and explaining the historic nature of the Refining Trials. He went on to outline the qualities the elders considered when making their selections, then introduced the canes of Bjorn along with their apprentices. Keigh wasn't surprised he hadn't been announced, since neither had Braddock. The only reason apprentices had been included in the Refining selection was so they could include the members of the Consecrate. Members of the Consecrate had all been born in January; Keigh had been born in December, and his family weren't canes.

The first nomination was made by Oliver Connell. He selected Deacon Wulf to represent Bjorn. Keigh had gotten so used to seeing Deacon glare that he was a bit shocked at how pleasant his enemy looked when he was smiling sincerely. Deacon was as happy as Keigh could ever recall seeing him. Maybe that was why Keigh now noticed the alarming resemblance he shared with the queen, who was smiling and applauding regally behind him. Keigh couldn't help pantomiming a gag as Deacon heaped profuse praise on his father, Vicerous.

Braddock was the next to submit his nomination: Tarin Conri. Keigh noticed the queen looked extra pleased by Braddock's selection, further confirming his suspicions. There was no way another member of the Consecrate was the heir, no matter how similar to the queen Deacon looked.

Keigh was happy for his friend. Tarin was the Bear today. He and Misselli cheered loudly as Tarin took the stage to give his speech, which Keigh was particularly impressed with. He had expected it to be insufferably diplomatic, but instead it had been unexpectedly sentimental, thanking his parents for all they had done for him.

For the first time, Keigh really pondered what it must be like growing up with parents you knew weren't your own. Knowing that you were someone else's child, but having a childhood full of memories with people who shared no blood with you, yet loved you and raised you as their own. He really was proud of his friend.

Last to make a nomination was Cato. Chogan Bald Head was his selection. Keigh approved. He liked Chogan from the few times they had interacted, but mostly he was just relieved it hadn't been Vicerous.

Misselli tugged on his elbow. "You want to stick around and listen to this?" she whispered in his ear. "We could go explore the town. Everyone is here—we'll have the place to ourselves!"

Keigh noticed the familiar gleam in her eye she got anytime she was planning something fun—a look he hadn't seen in a regrettably long time. He nodded, lifting Jessie off his lap and telling his mother he would meet them at home.

Crouching low, Keigh and Misselli slipped out the back of the grounds and disappeared from view. The two of them wandered the vacant streets of Bjorn, laughing and chatting like they hadn't done in months.

Misselli had just finished a particularly funny and uncannily accurate impersonation of the queen when she asked him, "So what will you do now?"

"What do you mean?" asked Keigh, confused.

Misselli clasped her hands behind her back, swaying slightly in her white dress. "Well, you train with Braddock six days a week, right? And now Braddock is headed off to the Capital with Deacon and Tarin for the Refining Trials. So, what are you going to do while he's gone?"

Her eyes, which had been locked into his, suddenly darted to the ground. *She's afraid,* he thought. Keigh didn't know what to say. He hadn't even thought about it. His life for the past two and a half months had been so consumed with training that he wasn't quite sure what he would do when all that time was suddenly freed up.

"I suppose I'll probably just help my parents around the house. Final harvest of the year is coming up, and Dad will want the field prepped for next spring before the ground gets too frozen."

Misselli gave an uncertain smile. "So, it will be like old times, then? I mean, your schedule, that is..." She dropped her gaze to the ground again, seemingly too nervous to face his answer.

Keigh felt heavy all of a sudden. The insecure girl in front of him wasn't the Misselli he knew. This was his fault. She had tried to hide what she was asking, but Keigh knew her too well. He sighed to himself. *How could I let this happen? My best friend acts like she doesn't know me anymore. I need to fix this.*

"Yes," he said, "it can be just like old times."

When Misselli lifted her face, her lips were stretched wide in a goofy grin. "Oh, thank you, thank you! Finally!" She grabbed Keigh's hand and started jumping up and down like one of the wind-up toys Crispin Popplardo sold in his shop.

"There you are," said Keigh, overjoyed to see her happy and full of hope.

They grinned at each other for a long moment before the sound of approaching footsteps pulled them out of their reverie. Tarin was jogging toward them. He was grinning from ear to ear, too, like someone who had just found out they were about to be king. Keigh noticed that he looked particularly happy to see Misselli.

"Did you guys see it? Braddock nominated me!" He gave Keigh a slight look of sympathy. "I know he's your mentor, but don't blame him. It's just politics, you know. But still, he made the right choice, did he not?"

Keigh and Misselli nodded.

"You did great!" beamed Misselli.

"Seriously, bud, I thought your speech was excellent," Keigh added. "You're the Bear, once again!"

Tarin looked pleased with the praise. Then his eyes dropped to where Misselli still had Keigh's hand clutched in her own. He took a step back, his smile fading into the grim look of a man who had just been given a piece of bad news.

"Yes...the Bear, am I?" Tarin straightened himself and looked over Keigh from head to toe. He tugged on his tunic and gathered his composure. "So, why is it then, that I still feel like you are?" Tarin reached out and gave

Keigh's shoulder a gentle squeeze. He nodded, then turned on his heel and walked away.

Keigh started to chase after his friend, but Misselli held him back.

"Let him pout." She waved Tarin away dismissively as he disappeared around the corner of a vacant shop. "You don't have to apologize to him for anything. He's been weird about you ever since I told him he owed you for taking the blame for the tower." Misselli shook her head. "He just hates the idea that he would have to owe anyone anything." She took his hand again. "Come on. He'll get over it. Don't let his issues become your issue."

They walked the whole way to Misselli's front door like that. Hand in hand, talking and joking, in the amber light of sunset. Just like the old days. Just like Keigh had promised.

Keigh waved goodnight as he dropped her off at her front gate and set off on the path back to his house. He was saddened to see that the once well-worn path had grown grass over the summer due to lack of use. The nostalgia of the trail and of times spent walking it with Misselli was still worn deep into his heart. Even if the path itself had faded, his memories hadn't.

Just a few months ago, all he had wanted to do was become a cane and leave Bjorn. He still wanted both those things desperately, but tonight, for the first time, he allowed himself to consider that maybe a life in Bjorn wouldn't be the worst thing ever.

Keigh crested the ridge. Below, the windows of his family home were aglow with candlelight under a pink sky that refused to give way to night. He stopped to appreciate the scene. His life in that small house hadn't been easy. They worked hard and had very little to show for it. But his life there had never lacked love. He grinned as he saw Mrs. Schaffer chasing a pair of garden wolves out of the yard, white wings spread wide, neck stiff as a spear.

Sure, there would be places to see, adventures to have—but if this was home, he was okay with that.

Keigh rested his hand on the bear head carved into his front door. "Told you I'd be back," he whispered. He opened the door, smiling to himself.

The smile quickly faded when he saw his parents and the worried looks on their faces. Braddock was sitting with them at the table, wearing a grave expression.

"You need to come with me." Braddock stood up, grabbed his arm, and marched him back out the door.

"What's going on?" asked Keigh. He caught a glimpse of his parents looking longingly after him before the door closed behind him.

Braddock released his arm and waved for Keigh to follow. "We will talk when I get you back to town. The other elders will want to hear everything you have to say."

The two of them walked at a brisk pace all the way back to Bjorn without talking. The town that had only hours ago been bustling with the festival now rested, quiet and still. Braddock marched him up the main street past the darkened shops. The residences above, spilling light and the muffled sounds of laughter onto the street below.

When they reached the town hall, Braddock pushed open the door and gestured for Keigh to enter in front of him. Inside, Cato and Oliver sat at a table, their faces illuminated by the light of a single candle. Braddock pointed for Keigh to sit at the table across from them. Oliver looked disgruntled, while happiness seemed to be flitting about the features of Cato's wrinkled face.

"What did you do today?" Braddock shouted. "Did you say anything to the king?"

Keigh was dumbfounded. What was Braddock talking about? Why would he think Keigh had spoken to the king?

"N-no, Master. I didn't say a word!"

Braddock turned on Cato. "Do you have something to do with this?"

Cato twirled his long white beard with a finger. "I assure you, I have not had a hand in this. Though…I'm beginning to be less and less surprised by the events surrounding young Mr. Anders."

"The king is mistaken." Oliver pulled angrily on his goatee, his face as puckered as ever. "He must have meant someone else. Surely, he could not have meant this…" His nose wrinkled. "*Boy*."

Braddock pursed his lips and clenched his jaw. "No. I don't believe the king was mistaken."

"Nor do I," said Cato.

"I'm sorry, but…what's going on?" Keigh's head swiveled as he tried to address his teacher, who was pacing the floor behind him.

Braddock stepped to the table and snatched a piece of parchment from in front of the other two elders. He handed it to Keigh.

Keigh laid the letter flat on the table to catch the light of the candle. On the parchment was a red wax seal with the king's crest pressed into it: a dove with outstretched wings, carrying a pine sprig in its beak. Above the seal, he read the words etched on the parchment:

Keigh Anders is to enter the Refining Trials as my personal nominee.

—King Thiamtaim

CHAPTER 17

LEAVING HOME

5-28-6

Keigh's parents took the news fairly well. His mother hadn't stopped hugging him since he told them. Any time he resisted, she would guilt him with comments like, "You never know when it could be the last hug you get from your mother," or "How would you feel if you left for a year, and this was how you treated your mother?"

His father had been proud...for all of one second. As soon as Keigh mentioned that the king had nominated him, he acted as though he had just been shot with an arrow, visibly deflating. Keigh had asked him multiple times what was wrong, but his father dismissed it, saying it was nothing more than a stomach bug or that he was imagining things. In the end his father resigned himself to quiet acceptance, preferring to poke at the coals in the fireplace while his wife chased Keigh around, trying to feed him extra dinner.

Jobey and Jotham had congratulated him enthusiastically—a little too enthusiastically, he thought. He was sure their excitement had more to do with having the bedroom to themselves and extra food at mealtimes, so he had not so subtly reminded them that while he was gone there would be no new venison, a realization that sobered them up quickly.

Jessie was the one he had feared telling most. At six years old, she wouldn't realize the importance of what he was doing, how special it was to be invited to the Refining. All she would care about was that her big brother wasn't going to be around to play with her. After a few tears from Jessie, Keigh had offered to play Canes and Criminals with her, and five minutes later she was a giggling whirlwind. All was right in her world again.

Braddock had informed him that the nominees from Bjorn would be leaving for Sentinel on Monday morning, a week from the night of the festival. Braddock had also given him the week off from his training so he could rest for the Trials, but Keigh spent most of the week working the fields with his family anyway.

The evenings were Misselli's. He had promised her that things would go back to how they used to be. The joy on her face in that moment had sent a thrill through Keigh that he wanted to experience over and over again, so all week long he had done everything in his power to make his best friend smile as often as he could. She smiled and laughed all week, but none of it gave him the same thrill as it had that first night, because he knew it was a lie. A taste of something that couldn't last. He was leaving, and Misselli still didn't know. What she saw as a sunrise on a brand-new day in their relationship, Keigh knew to be a sunset.

He was just about to leave for Misselli's the evening before he was to depart for Sentinel when Mannie showed up at the Anders' house.

"Good evening, Anders family!" The king's messenger ducked through the doorway as the family greeted him.

Keigh's father crossed the room, embracing his friend in a firm hug. "Wasn't sure we would be seeing you this week," he said, releasing Mannie and pointing him toward a seat at the table.

"You know I never miss a chance to see my favorite family." Mannie winked at Jessie as she wriggled with joy at being called someone's favorite. "But it is the king's business that brings me to Bjorn this week."

"Is there more news?" Keigh asked excitedly. "Has Draiden made a move against the king?"

"No, no, nothing like that. No news to deliver—just a certain young warrior who needs safe passage to the Capital tomorrow." Mannie grinned proudly, clapping a large hand to Keigh's shoulder.

Keigh's eyebrows lifted. "You know?"

Mannie shrugged. "Am I the king's messenger or not? Of course I know! And he has sent me to ensure that you make it to the Capital unhindered."

Keigh's mother and father both blurted questions at Mannie.

"One at a time," he said gently. "Sabriya?"

Keigh's mother was wringing a dry washcloth in her hands so hard her fingers had gone white. "Does the king expect another attack on Keigh?"

"No." Mannie gave her a sympathetic touch on the shoulder. "Eden is secure. How the lone assassin gained access, we still don't know, but we are confident that no force of any size could have entered undetected. We can safely assume he acted alone. I will admit," Mannie scowled, "not knowing how Keigh's name came to be known to Draiden is vexing. If Draiden has set himself against Keigh, there will always be the risk that he will make another attempt on his life."

Keigh's mother gasped.

"Take courage in this, Sabriya: if the king has set his mind to keeping your son alive, no one can kill him. Not even Draiden." Mannie took a deep breath, adopting a cheerier tone. "Besides, Keigh is to travel in the company of Braddock and Chogan. That's the greatest warrior to ever serve our king... and Chogan."

Mannie winked at Keigh, who was the only one to chuckle at the joke.

"Also, do not consider my presence as proof the king anticipates an attack on your son. He would not send me to deal with a violent threat. You have no cause to worry, Sabriya—I was merely sent as a precaution against... *other* obstacles." Mannie grinned and wagged his head playfully, moving his gaze to Keigh. "Plus...I may or may not have twisted the king's arm to let me come and accompany Keigh on his journey. Three days on the road with my favorite troublemaker seemed to me a great use of my time."

The family laughed, Mannie having sufficiently waylaid their fears—all except Owen, who remained unsoftened. "Now answer my question. Why is the king doing this?"

Mannie pursed his lips, twisting his neck as though trying to wring out a suitable answer. "If the king commands it, that should be all the reason any of us need." He addressed the family, but his words seemed pointed at Owen. In a softer tone he added, "All I know is that the king has his reasons for everything. He does not move in the lives of his people lightly. Not in your life, Owen, or Keigh's. After the assassin's attack and Keigh's interference with a cane at the royal procession last week, it should surprise no one that our king knows his name."

Keigh's father shook his head, apparently unsatisfied with the answer.

Keigh sank lower in his seat. "He told you about that, huh?"

"He did indeed." Mannie's lips curled in a mischievous grin. "I think I'm not speaking out of line when I say he was quite proud of you...Both of you." Mannie looked back at Keigh's father, who stood a little taller at the compliment.

"I'm actually about to leave," said Keigh, standing up and moving toward the door. "Will you still be here when I get back?"

"It's unlikely that I will. I would like to talk with you privately before you go, if that's okay?" Mannie looked at Keigh's parents, who nodded.

Mannie motioned for Keigh to head back to the room he shared with his brothers.

Keigh sat down on the edge of his bed and Mannie followed him in, closing the door behind him. The messenger sighed as he sat down next to Keigh.

"This is a good home, Keigh," he said softly, his eyes journeying around the room.

"Yeah, it's alright," Keigh agreed.

"I wanted to talk to you privately because, over the years, you have made it known to me at every opportunity that you desire to leave Bjorn and make a name for yourself—something I am assuming you don't bandy about so freely in front of your parents."

Keigh squirmed uncomfortably. Mannie was right; he hadn't talked often, or ever, with his parents about his desire to leave Bjorn. Even now, imagining the look on his mother's face as he walked away from home made his stomach churn.

"They would only worry," he explained, "and I don't want them to think it's because of them I want to leave."

"I don't disagree. No parent wants to be separated from their children, and even less would they like knowing their child's greatest desire is to leave."

"It has nothing to do with them, though!" Keigh defended himself.

"I wouldn't say that to them either," said Mannie, resting a hand on Keigh's shoulder. "No parent wants their child to leave but if their child does leave, they would hate to hear that their thoughts and feelings hadn't even been factored into the decision."

"Would you have me stay, then? Just so no one misses me?" Keigh asked, not believing Mannie, a thrall, would be the one to try to talk him out of chasing his dreams. "I won't let people tie me down just because *they* are scared. I need to do this for me! I won't continue to be a nobody just so everyone else can feel comfortable about their own lot in life."

He was startled by his own sudden outburst, but if Mannie was too, the messenger didn't show it. "Nobody is asking you to stay, and I'm not even suggesting you do," Mannie said. "All I want is to encourage you not to get lost."

Keigh snorted and crossed his arms. "Lost? How would I get lost?"

Mannie took a deep breath before he spoke. "There is greatness in you, Keigh. I have always known it. It will likely take you far away from here. Tomorrow is just the beginning. You will go to the Capital, and they will see the greatness in you too. Sentinel is a perilous place. There are many wonderful people who make their home there, but there are also those who would use you for their own purposes. Some will seek to control you and others still will seek to silence you. If you don't know who you are, you risk getting lost in who others want you to be."

The tightness in Keigh's chest released as a warm wave of appreciation washed over him. "Thanks, Mannie. I won't forget who I am."

"Oh, yeah?" Mannie brought his eyes back from surveying the room to look at Keigh beside him. "And just who are you, Keigh Anders?"

"I'm a potato-farming thrall from the quiet little town of Bjorn."

Mannie chuckled. "That reminds me. What's the difference between a thrall and a potato?"

Keigh shook his head.

"Eventually someone will want the potato to come out of the dirt."

Keigh just smiled and shook his head as Mannie laughed at his own joke.

"You will always be more than what you do or where you're from, Keigh. That's as true now of the potato farmer from Bjorn as it will be of the cane from Eden you will someday be."

"Then what do you mean when you say not to forget who I am?" asked Keigh. "Obviously I'm not going to forget my name."

"No, I doubt you will. Such a simple name, 'Keigh.'" Mannie nudged Keigh with his elbow. "I suppose for now, just remember you are loved. If you can remember that, it will be enough to keep you from chasing after lesser things."

Keigh clasped Mannie's shoulder. "Thanks, Mannie. I'm not sure what all that means, but I will."

Mannie laughed and pinched the bridge of his nose. "Strong as a man but still simple as a boy. It means you're worth all the potatoes in the world to us, and you'd do best not to forget it!" He turned around and looked at the shelves above Keigh's bed, lined with his treasures. "Which reminds me...you should take something to Sentinel to remember your home by."

Mannie grabbed several items from the shelves, looked them over, then put them back.

"Aha! This will do!" He grabbed the small metal orb off the shelf and bounced it in his hand. "This is neat and small enough to keep with you at all times. What do you think?" He tossed the orb to Keigh.

Keigh caught the little ball and rolled it around his palm. He liked the idea of having something to remind him of home. As excited as he was to leave, there was still a part of him that knew he would miss his family and friends. "That's a good idea. Thanks, Mannie."

"Good. Hopefully you will find it gives you strength when you need it most." Mannie clapped his hands to his thighs. "Well, I'll let you get going. You'll be seeing more of me in the coming days. Spend tonight with the ones you're leaving." He embraced Keigh. "I'm proud of you, Keigh."

At that moment, Keigh couldn't think of anyone he would rather have accompany him to Sentinel.

The two made their way back out to the great room where Keigh's family had remained waiting for them. Keigh said his goodbyes and dashed out the door to Misselli's, leaving Mannie with his family.

He sprinted down the path. The running distracted him from how hard his heart was pounding. Tonight, he had to do what he had been putting off all week. He wasn't sure if Misselli would cry or punch him, but he was certain she wouldn't be happy to find out he was leaving.

When he finally arrived at the Labelles' home, he found Misselli sitting on the front gate, waiting for him.

"You're late," she said, slipping down off the gate.

"Late?" Keigh scoffed. "I didn't know there was a specific time I was supposed to be here."

"You're supposed to be here at the time when I want you here." She grinned, giving Keigh a shove.

Keigh chuckled. "I suppose I'll always be late by *that* standard."

"Yes. Yes, you will," she said, adopting a very formal tone, like a judge ruling on the fate of a poor soul. "I'm prepared to forgive you, however."

"Oh yeah?"

"If..."

"If what?" Keigh laughed.

"If...you dance with me." Misselli smiled triumphantly.

Keigh rolled his eyes. "Of course it's dancing. Guess you'll just have to stay mad at me, then."

"Oh, come on! Please? It's so easy, look!" Misselli grabbed his hands and began spinning herself around Keigh, lifting his limp arms and twirling under them in her faded white dress.

Keigh thought she looked as beautiful as a fresh bloomed petunia when she spun. Her smile was radiant every time she turned to face him. He smiled back, content to let Misselli wrap herself in his arms as she danced to the music only she could hear. Keigh did not, however, join her. He would rather fight a red bear than embarrass himself trying to dance with his two left feet. His mother had tried to teach him many times in the great room of their little home, but something about dancing sent his feet into a clumsy confusion. He could learn and execute new footwork for fighting easily, but with Misselli in his hands instead of a sword, he could barely walk, let alone dance.

"Look how good you're doing!" she teased him. "Come on, Keigh...just one spin?"

Keigh shook his head. "No...I don't think so. I'm not any good. I'm more likely to trip you than I am to spin you."

"Don't be silly!" She backed away, pulling his arms out straight, pleading for him to join her out on the invisible dance floor. "Dancing isn't something you do to be good at. It's supposed to be fun!"

"Fun for you, maybe," he laughed.

She raised her eyebrows. "Is that not reason enough?"

"It is...and I will dance with you. Just not tonight."

Misselli cocked her head at him, seemingly weighing the promise. "Okay, Anders, but I will collect that dance. Don't presume I'll forget." She dropped his hands. "Anyway, I was thinking tomorrow we could go back up to Morrell Creek and swim by the falls. We need to take advantage of this warm weather before it starts getting too cold to swim."

Keigh's chest tightened. *Tomorrow.* There would be no tomorrow, not for them, and there she stood, excitedly planning their next adventure.

"I can't..."

Misselli shrugged lightly. "No problem, we can go Tuesday."

"I can't go Tuesday either," Keigh said, hanging his head.

"Wow! Busy guy! There isn't a new best friend I need to worry about, is there?" she joked, punching him in the arm.

Keigh lifted his face. "We need to talk."

Her smile faded, her face suddenly nervous. "I'm only teasing. I know you have other stuff going on. We'll find a time that works for both of us."

"We won't, though," he said dejectedly.

"Sure we will! Don't be such a downer!"

"No, Misselli. I'm leaving tomorrow."

"Leaving? What do you mean, *leaving?*"

"I'm going to participate in the Refining Trials."

"Ooh! Ha, ha. Very funny!" She grinned, but only for a moment. When the heaviness in Keigh's face remained unchanged, she argued, "But...you can't be! Deacon, Tarin, and Chogan are the nominees. You're staying here, with me..."

"They are," Keigh said. "But before the king left town, he told the elders that I am to be his personal nominee."

"You can't be serious..."

Keigh nodded glumly.

"Why? Why would the king do that? How does he even know your name?"

"Mannie thinks it's from the incident with the stranger, or possibly the incident with the cane from the queen's guard."

"Don't go." Misselli's jaw clenched, like that of a soldier standing their ground.

"Don't go?" blurted Keigh.

"Yes," she repeated, "don't go. Tell them you aren't ready...or that you have too much to do at home...or that you're sick. Or...or..." Her eyes darted about as if she hoped to find a solution hidden somewhere in the fields around them. "Ugh! I don't know! Just please...don't leave."

"I'm going, Misselli," he said, his voice calm and steady. "This is my chance. I'm not going to pass it up."

"Chance to what?" she cried, finally looking him in the eye. "Chance to leave? Chance to get out of Bjorn and never look back?" Tears were beginning to fill her eyes.

"A chance to be something! To actually be someone people respect! Not just some thrall spending his life digging in the dirt," he snapped back. "I'm not leaving forever. The Refining only lasts until spring, and that's only if I make it to the end." He took a breath. "Braddock says most canes get eliminated pretty early," he offered, trying to soften the blow. "I'll probably be back before Winter Festival…"

"No, you won't." She shook her head, still clenching her jaw in a clear effort to keep from crying. "That's exactly what you said before your agoge duel. You doubted you would pass that, and you only went on to win the most epic duel in the history of Eden! You are more than you think you are, and way more than you think people think you are…" She lowered her gaze, embarrassed of the tears now spilling down her cheeks.

Keigh's insides were on fire. Why were the things he wanted most in this world at war with each other? Why did becoming a cane have to mean leaving Misselli? Why did staying with Misselli have to mean never becoming a cane? He wanted both, but fate seemed intent on making him choose one. He ground his teeth. Misselli would have to understand. She would have to wait. He would return, but the Refining Trials were his one shot at being someone.

"I will come back. No matter how it goes. I promise."

"You promised it would be like old times. Baylor promised to come back…" Misselli spoke softly, her words punctuated by soft sniffs. "Nobody keeps their promises."

"I'm not Baylor!" Keigh bristled at being compared to her older brother. He used to really like Misselli's brother, and Misselli had adored him, but ever since Baylor had left home—and especially after he'd inexplicably stopped writing to his family—Keigh had grown to resent him. Misselli had cried for weeks after Baylor left to start his agoge as a cane. His disappearance thereafter had crushed her. Keigh eventually had to stop asking her about her brother, because it never failed to spark a fresh wave of tears. He hated Baylor for that. He would not do the same thing to her.

"I'm not going to hope," she whispered. "It will hurt less if I just accept you aren't coming back."

Keigh stuffed his hands in his pockets, unsure of what to do with the sad girl in front of him. His hand closed around the smooth metal orb Mannie had told him to take as a reminder of home. He pulled it out of his pocket, an idea forming in his mind.

"Here, take this." He held the metal ball out to Misselli.

She eyed it cautiously. "What is it?"

"It's a trinket from home. Mannie said I should take something to Sentinel so I wouldn't forget where I'm from and who I am."

Misselli shook her head. "Then you should keep it. If it helps you remember us, I don't want you to be without it."

Keigh sighed. "The point of it is to remind me of home, but...my home is where you are." He paused. He meant what he'd said, but saying it out loud frightened him, like he had just sunk a pair of massive, barbed hooks deep into the two of them, tying them together forever.

Misselli must have felt the hooks too, because she lifted her face, eyes wide, trepidation clear on her features. Slowly, cautiously, she reached out and put her hand on top of Keigh's, enclosing the orb between them.

Keigh suddenly felt weak in the knees, the orb cool in his palm.

Misselli closed her hand around the orb and brought it close to her face. "It's a heavy thing," she said, rolling the metal ball in her fingers, studying its polished surface.

Unsure of whether she meant the ball or the gesture, Keigh kept silent.

Misselli tenderly deposited the orb into a pouch at her waist. "If I am to keep this, then you'll need something else to remind you of home." She bent over and began ripping the thin white fabric of her dress.

Keigh watched as she tore off an eight-inch strip from the bottom hem. "What are you doing?"

She approached him slowly, twisting the fabric in her hands. She reached down and grabbed his right hand, lifting it so it was palm up between them. "Hold still," she whispered. Gently, her soft fingers looped the fabric around his wrist, and she tied a knot in the ends. Taking his hand in both of hers, she examined her work. "Will you wear it?" she asked quietly.

"I'll never take it off," Keigh said, a little too emphatically.

Misselli's lips curved slightly in a tender smile. "Hopefully it will remind you of what you're leaving behind." She paused, tilting her face to the ground again. "And hopefully...it will make you want to return to it."

Keigh pulled his hand free of hers and, before she could be offended, pulled her close to him, wrapping her in his arms and pinning hers between them. She rested her head on his chest as he set his chin on her hair.

"Will you write me?" she asked.

"As often as I can," he promised.

"What if I can't wait for you to get back?"

"Uh...what do you mean?" Keigh was taken aback by the question. Was she really suggesting she would forget about him and move on?

"It may be too much for me to handle, sitting here while you're off having some grand adventure without me."

He gave her a reassuring squeeze. "It won't be that grand, and it's hardly an adventure without you there."

"I think I will come visit you. I think...I think maybe Baylor wouldn't have stayed gone if I had just done more."

"Baylor leaving was not your fault. And I will come back. This isn't the end. Not for us."

Misselli hummed, "I'm trusting you, Keigh Anders.".

"Good," he said. "I'm going to make a name for myself. I'll come back someone you can be proud of. Someone people respect."

"You don't have to leave for that." Misselli pulled back far enough to look him in the eyes. "I'm already proud of you. Your family is already proud of you."

"My family? The Wulfs' thralls?" he scoffed. "My family would love me no matter what! It's everyone else that needs to know."

"Know what?" she snapped.

"Know I'm not just another worthless nobody they can ignore! That I'm someone worth their respect, not just some potato digger they can laugh at."

"Nobody's laughing at you, Keigh, and nobody is laughing at your family."

Keigh gave a short, bitter chuckle. "Oh yeah? Tell that to the Wulfs, or Zale Woodman, or Oliver Connell, or Tarin—"

"Tarin is your friend," Misselli reminded him. "And who cares what those other people think?"

"I do!" He took Misselli by the shoulders and held her at arm's length. "You don't know what it feels like to be looked at like you're worthless!"

She stared at him for a moment before slowly shaking her head. "No. I may not know what it's like to be treated like I'm worthless, but I'm starting to get used to being treated like I'm worth *less*."

Keigh paused, weighing what she'd said. She didn't get it. She had never understood why he needed to break out of the life he had. She may never understand, but that didn't mean he was okay with her feeling like he didn't care about her. He wasn't going to argue with her. Not tonight, not about this. He knew what he needed to do, even if nobody else agreed. Someday she would get it, but not tonight. Tonight, all that mattered was reminding her that he would be coming back. He would not abandon her as her brother had.

"I will come back. I promise." He lifted his wrist, showing her the cloth bracelet she had just tied there. "I won't forget."

Misselli closed her eyes and shook her head, burying her face back into his chest. "Ugh! Boys!"

Keigh smiled, resting his chin on top of her head again. "You wouldn't want me any other way," he teased.

"Oh yes I would!" she retorted, her voice muffled.

"That would be boring."

"I'll take boring Keigh over absent Keigh any day."

He squeezed her again. "You'll just have to start making a list of all the fun adventures we can have when I get back."

"Don't think I won't." She wiggled her arms out from between them and wrapped them around him. "Can we just stay here like this forever?"

Keigh's only answer was to hold her closer.

The two of them stood there like that, saying barely a word, until the stars came out, shining like a million shards of crystal broken over a sheet of black velvet.

When it came time for Keigh to return home, he slowly released her. Backing away toward the path to his house, he lifted his right wrist and tugged on the bracelet with a finger. "I will think of you every day."

"You better." She smiled sadly after him. Patting the pouch on her waist where she had stashed the orb, she called, "Don't forget where your home is!"

"Wherever you are, Missy!" He winked and turned toward home, laughing to himself as he imagined the look of outrage on her face at being called her least favorite nickname. He didn't turn back, unsure if his resolve would hold if he saw her blue eyes one more time.

Before long, he crested the last ridge between their homes where he would still be able to see the Labelles'. From the top of the ridge, he looked back. He had expected to see candlelight coming from Misselli's window, signaling that she had gone inside to sleep off the night's emotions, but there was no light there. Just the ghostly figure of a girl in white, who had dropped to her knees outside, blonde hair and pale skin illuminated by the light of the stars as she watched him leave.

"Nothing," he said to himself. *Nothing will keep me from coming back to you.*

CHAPTER 18

BEYOND BJORN

49-5-15

Keigh arrived at the assigned meeting place just outside the gates of Bjorn to find most of the travel party already there. The group was busy checking their gear and adjusting their horses' saddles in the patch of sunlight between the two long shadows cast by Bjorn's totem poles.

"Here." Mannie handed Keigh the reins of a shaggy gray donkey. "Her name is Rose. She's been my ride to Bjorn for more than ten years now." He stroked the ancient animal's mane affectionately. "She will be your ride to Sentinel."

Keigh looked at the disheveled beast. He wouldn't have been surprised if Mannie had said he had been riding her for a hundred years, let alone ten. As Keigh took the reins, Rose narrowed her eyes, apparently displeased with being handed off to one so unworthy to ride her.

"I didn't know you rode to Bjorn," said Keigh, still eying the surly-looking pack animal.

Mannie chuckled and shook his head. "You thought I walked the whole distance from Sentinel every time?"

"Well...yeah, I guess," Keigh admitted.

"I'm flattered you think me so physically capable, but alas, it is not so. Bjorn is two days on horseback and at least three on foot for a man in a hurry."

"How many days on Bag-o-Bones' back?" asked Keigh, exchanging a dirty look with Rose.

Mannie ignored the dig and kept affectionately petting his steed. "Rose has journeyed this road with me faithfully probably more times than any other steed in the history of Eden." Rose leaned her head back into Mannie, as if thanking him for the vote of confidence.

"I believe it," said Keigh, looking at the curve of the old donkey's spine. It looked as though it had naturally contoured itself into the shape of a saddle. It couldn't have been easy carrying the massive messenger all those years. "I've never ridden a horse before," Keigh added.

A laugh sounded from where Tarin, Braddock, and Chogan now sat on their horses in front of Mace, waiting for the last of their entourage to arrive.

"And after you ride that mangy animal, you will still have not ridden a horse!" Tarin joked.

Mannie scratched Rose under the chin and moved his mouth close to her ear as if to tell her a secret. "Don't you listen to them, sweetheart. They're just jealous they don't get to ride you."

The men on horseback all got a laugh out of that. Even their horses snorted.

"I wish I loved anything as much as you love that dusty nag," chuckled Chogan.

"Oh, I'm sure you'll find your own faithful steed someday," Mannie responded without taking his eyes off Rose. He turned to Keigh and created a foothold with his hands. "Alright, let's get you up and ready to ride."

Keigh stepped up and swung a leg over Rose's back. To his surprise, she didn't object.

"Aren't you a little old to still be playing Canes and Criminals?" the sneering voice of Deacon Wulf called out as he and Vicerous rode up to the group on two sleek, beautiful black horses.

"Ah! Good morning, Master Wulf, Vicerous," Mannie greeted them pleasantly.

Vicerous didn't even bother to look at the thrall. Instead he glared at Keigh for a brief moment before rounding on Braddock. "What is the meaning of this?" he snarled, pointing an accusing finger at Keigh.

Braddock leaned forward in his saddle. "Young Mr. Anders here has been nominated to participate in the Refining," he said coolly.

Vicerous's horse stomped in the dust as its rider's grip tightened on the reins. "I was at the Selection Festival, Braddock, and I don't recall hearing his name called." He paused, eyeing Keigh up and down. "Besides, the Anders are my thralls, and I have not consented to his release from service. As worthless as *his* services are," he drawled, curling his lip.

"I think you will find that circumstances warrant his release, at least for the duration of his participation," Braddock continued, unflustered.

"I doubt that," Vicerous snorted. "What circumstance do you believe would cause me to relinquish my hold on any one of the Anders? Least of all the boy?"

Braddock's calm veneer cracked. His eyes and nostrils flared. Keigh appreciated his teacher's protectiveness. He had been called worse things by the Wulfs, and no doubt would be again, but it was reassuring to know Braddock was in his corner on this.

"The king himself has chosen Keigh as his personal nominee for the Refining," Mannie intervened, his demeanor as pleasant and friendly as ever.

Deacon looked like he was going to be sick as he choked back the insult he had no doubt intended to launch at Keigh.

Vicerous' eyes narrowed as he chewed on the new information. "Perhaps the king is unaware of Keigh's station. Surely, he would have asked me for his release had he known."

"The king is aware and has sent his request with me," said Mannie, giving Rose another pat on the neck. "Will you grant Keigh Anders leave of his duties and debt for the duration of the Refining?" he asked, then politely added, "At the king's request?"

Vicerous sat a little straighter in his saddle as he peered down at Keigh, obviously delighted to have something the King of Eden wanted. "No."

The air rushed out of Keigh. "Can he do that?" he asked Mannie.

Mannie nodded sorrowfully.

"Be reasonable, Vicerous!" Braddock objected. Mace issued a low growl at his distress.

"*You* be reasonable!" Vicerous spat, his hair flying as he rounded on Braddock, his eyes wild with outrage. "Your indulgence of this child's fantasies has done nothing but cause chaos and harm to this community! Every day the boy becomes more arrogant. You allowed him to make a mockery of the agoge duels, which led to him burning down a historical structure that could have set fire to the whole town. And how does he pay for his crimes? You let him walk free, without so much as a single lash!" Vicerous paused, breathing heavily. He smoothed back his greasy blonde hair, regaining his composure. "Now you wish to further promote this menace? I won't allow it."

"You would deny the king?" Chogan challenged unexpectedly.

"I would protect the king," said Vicerous, sounding wounded. "He is obviously unaware of the taint that comes with dealing with an Anders." He spat on the ground, as if the name were poison in his mouth.

Braddock shook his head. "Look at yourself. A bitter shell of who you could have been. We used to be friends. Best friends…We loved you, Vicerous. Owen loved you."

For a brief second, Vicerous looked to be on the edge of shame, then quickly pulled his face into a condescending sneer. "Owen is weak. I was naive in my youth and regrettably less discerning in whose company I kept. It's a mistake my son Deacon won't repeat." He shook his head at Keigh in disgust, then turned back to Braddock. "If I recall correctly, though, it was *you* who walked away from *me*. Not I from you."

Keigh's heart was already on the verge of blowing up at Vicerous' refusal to let him leave Bjorn, and now, his head was about to explode with this new revelation. *My dad was friends with Braddock and Vicerous?* Sure, his mother had told him that his father had been in the same class as the canes—but *friends?* His father had only ever talked about Vicerous and Braddock in the most disconnected of ways, referring to them by their titles more often than by their names. Even the times he had seen his father interact with either man, Owen had treated them with a neutral detachment or slight defensiveness that Keigh had assumed was due to a lack of familiarity. Certainly nothing about their behavior had ever indicated they had been friends, especially *best* friends.

"You know what came between us, Vicerous." Braddock's voice was calm, but Keigh could see the muscles knotting in his arms. Bjorn's battle master was squeezing the horn of his saddle hard enough to force the color out of his knuckles.

"Yes," chirped Vicerous, "I do recall. You sided with weakness then, just like you're doing now...and how has that repaid you? You and Owen still thick as thieves?"

"The falling out between me and Owen has nothing to do with you and certainly nothing to do with weakness, as you see it. Our division was of a more...personal nature." Braddock looked mad enough to throw his horse at Vicerous. How had three such different men been friends? And what could possibly have happened to make them all so distant now?

Before Vicerous could respond, Mannie chimed in. "I'm sure the king appreciates you looking out for him, but his heart is set on having Keigh present at the Refining."

"Does the king no longer have any regard for the law?" asked Vicerous, feigning incredulity.

Mannie pursed his lips and shook his head. "I assure you he has no intention of circumventing the law or your rights as the Anders' better."

"Well, then, you can tell him I refuse. He can find some other worthless peasant to show charity to."

"Vicerous!" growled Braddock.

"Remember your oath!" shouted Chogan.

The two men were beside themselves. Vicerous was a cane. Canes did not refuse the king anything.

Mannie held up a hand, quieting the disgruntled warriors, then addressed Vicerous. "Yes, the king had a suspicion you may feel this way." He straightened his brown cloak and smoothed the front of his tunic. "What will your price be?"

Keigh's eyes widened as he stared at Mannie. Was he really offering to pay off Keigh's debt and free him from the Wulfs? In Keigh's wildest dreams he'd thought maybe, *maybe*, he could pay off his family's debt if he were ever permitted to serve as a cane—but never had he imagined someone would outright pay for him.

"The king wishes to buy out the Anders' debt?" Vicerous asked. "What if I refuse to sell?" he said, stiffening his neck. His confident demeanor was only betrayed by the fear in his voice. The fear of a man who believed he was being tricked.

"No, not the whole family. Just Keigh, and just for the length of the Refining."

Vicerous didn't respond immediately. He seemed to be pondering the potential pros and cons of this deal. "What if I still refuse?"

Braddock and Chogan bristled again, but Mannie remained unflappable. "The law states that a person and their dependents only remain thralls so long as a debt remains between the parties, and that an indentured person can pay their debt off at any time during their service." He turned and started digging through one of the bags slung across Rose's back, producing a fine purple velvet sack. "Admittedly, I searched the town records for the amount and nature of the Anders' contract, but to my surprise, there seems to be no record of a legal indenture between Vicerous Wulf and Owen Anders." Mannie fixed Vicerous with a questioning stare. "Yet when I ask Owen about it, he swears he is your thrall, and you are his better. So, in the absence of clear documentation..." Mannie shook the bag and the metallic sound of coins filled the silence. "What's your price?"

Vicerous clenched his jaw, clearly seeing no way to refuse payment. Then his features eased, and with a victorious smile he said, "One hundred justicia."

Keigh nearly fell off Rose. The number was absurd!

"The whole Anders family doesn't produce that much profit in a year! Give a real number," demanded Braddock.

"It's my price. Pay or stay."

Keigh looked to Mannie to object, but the messenger was calmly pulling money out of the purple sack. When he had pulled out ten large gold coins, he handed them to Keigh. "Pay him."

Keigh couldn't help but stare at the stack of gold. He thought he had been rich when the queen had handed him a single gold coin. Now he had ten in his hand, and Mannie had handed them over like Vicerous had asked for nothing more than a cup of flour! What could his father's debt possibly be that Vicerous could ask for this kind of money for a temporary release of one member of the family?

Keigh shut his mouth, realizing it had fallen open. He looked at Vicerous, who was now waiting smugly, leaning over the front of his saddle and holding a hand out for Keigh to put the money in.

"Um, Mannie..."

"Yes, Keigh?"

He looked questioningly at the back of Rose's head. "How do you make her...go?"

"Oh, sorry." Mannie grinned, realizing he had yet to teach Keigh anything about riding. "Just a little squeeze with your knees should do, then just steer her to one side or the other with the reins."

Keigh gave Rose a gentle squeeze with his knees. The ancient animal calmly walked toward Vicerous's glossy black stallion, nearly twice her size. Keigh reluctantly handed the coins up to his better.

Vicerous plucked the gold from his palm as if Keigh's hand were the waiting mouth of a viper and hastily deposited it into a pouch at his waist. "Fine. The boy can go, but don't come to me when he embarrasses you at the Capital. I expect he'll be disqualified in the first week."

"I have every confidence that will not be the case," Mannie said politely, stashing the sack of coins back in the bag at Rose's side. He walked over to the only remaining horse without a rider, a handsome paint horse of cream and brown that matched Mannie's cloak and tunic perfectly. "Shall we go, then?" he asked, mounting in one fluid motion that defied his age. He raised his eyebrows and looked to Braddock for the go-ahead.

Braddock gave Vicerous one last glare before pulling his horse's reins to the side, spurring his mount down the road toward Sentinel.

*

The road from Bjorn went straight south, following the King's River for most of its length. They rode along in a line: Braddock and Chogan in the lead, followed by Deacon and Tarin, Vicerous riding alone behind them. Mannie and Keigh brought up the rear of the group, except for when Mace opted to walk on the road, though she regularly went bounding off into the cover of the forest's looming pines, only to reappear an hour later, waiting on the roadside ahead of the group. Several times in the first few hours, Vicerous made a show of pulling out the gold coins and inspecting them, no doubt in an attempt to rile Keigh and Mannie into another war of words.

After five steady hours, the group came to the city of Brickor. Like all of Eden's settlements, it was a fortified community. Its walls were not as tall as the pointed timbers of Bjorn, but what they lacked in height, they made up for in strength. They were fifty feet high and twenty feet thick, with five-foot merlons spaced only far enough apart to allow a single defender to wage war on those below from relative safety. The walls themselves were constructed of speckled white-and-black granite, polished so smooth that the sun reflected off its surface, nearly blinding Keigh.

Approaching the city, Keigh noticed a group of people at the river's edge, watching a cane in his red cloak coat another man's entire body in mud. "What are they doing?" he asked Mannie.

Mannie looked to where he pointed. "You are familiar with the Kaste ritual, yes? I was at yours, remember?"

"That's Kaste?" Keigh couldn't help but stare. In Eden, nearly everyone observed Kaste. In Bjorn, individuals would smear mud across their forehead when they were old enough to start working. The mud was usually worn for a day, then washed away by a parent or other elder in the presence of witnesses. The washing away of the mud was a symbol, meant to illustrate that a person was willing to wash away their personal ambitions and desires in favor of the king's mission and will.

Not everyone participated, but most people did. Keigh had done his at the age of thirteen. He had just finished hearing Mannie tell a story of one of the king's legendary victories, and in his passion, Keigh had poured water on the bare earth in front of him, eagerly smearing the mud across his forehead. He had worn the mud on his face to instruction that day. Deacon and Cecilia had put dabs of mud on their own foreheads to mock him, but the rest of his peers had been supportive, if not excited. That night his father had taken a skin of cool, clean water and washed the dried mud from his face in the presence of Misselli, Mannie, and his family, finishing the ritual.

"Yes, that's how they do Kaste in Brickor. They believe that if a person is not fully covered in mud, then the Kaste didn't count. Also, they believe a cane must be the one to wash the mud from you." Mannie sighed.

"How did they come to believe that?" asked Keigh, still gawking at the strange scene.

Mannie smiled at the question. "They might ask you how you came to practice Kaste the way you do in Bjorn."

Keigh paused, considering the implication of Mannie's question. "Good point. But who is right?"

"Knowing the king like I do, I can tell you he is far more concerned with the *why* of Kaste than the *how* of it. If a person is sincerely willing to lay down their own life's ambitions and desires in favor of serving his, he is honored by it." Mannie shook his head as he watched the man caked in mud. "But regardless of what the king says, there are still plenty of individuals who will tell you that if you don't observe Kaste the *correct* way, what you did was of no value."

"Is Brickor the only town that practices Kaste this way?"

Mannie laughed. "No, no, far from it. Many people do it this way, even if their city ordinances don't require it like Brickor's."

"Brickor actually requires it by city law?" Keigh asked, shocked that a town would dictate something he had always believed was voluntary.

Mannie's lips stretched thin. "Yes, they do. Unfortunately, if a citizen of Brickor does not participate in a city-sanctioned Kaste by the time they reach the end of their agoge, they are not permitted to live within the walls of the city until they do." He patted his horse, earning him a jealous glare from Rose. "Every settlement in Eden has its own beliefs, practices, and customs that are unique to their community. As long as a city's practices and traditions don't contradict or circumvent the king's laws or attempt to elevate any authority over the king, they are generally not an issue." Mannie reached down and scratched Rose behind the ear, having registered the dusty donkey's looks of abandonment. "Though I will tell you, Keigh, it grieves the king when his citizens believe that their rules and customs are what earn them his favor. He already favors them. They are his people, after all."

"What are some of the other traditions you've seen in Eden?" Keigh asked, curious. "I've never been outside of Bjorn." Even as the words left his mouth, it hit him...*He was outside Bjorn!* Everything he would see, hear, and experience from here on out would be new and better.

Mannie spent the next two hours telling Keigh of Eden's many settlements and their unique traditions and practices. He told him about the city of Vaderkirk, where people set up statues of Eden's past heroes and spoke to them, asking their spirits to bless the king and influence him to help them with various needs. There was the city of Warten, which didn't believe in potents, and the city of Dawnus, where everyone was expected to be a potent. Keigh had been enthralled by the idea of a city with so many potents like himself, but Mannie explained that nearly everyone in Dawnus faked the ability in order to belong.

The villagers of Predannost tattooed the king's seal on their palms, symbolizing all the work of their hands was for him; the city of Taofi believed tattoos were an act of rebellion against the king who had saved them from mutilation. Then there was the city of Sutni, where all the men were expected to be canes. Keigh thought he might like to live there someday. The town of Modesta was the most humorous, however. Its citizens covered every inch of their bodies in clothing, for if the king hid his face, then they should have to hide their entire body.

That night they made camp by the King's River, nearly halfway to the Capital. Keigh spent the evening fishing with Tarin while the rest of the men gathered around the fire. By the time Mace ruined the fishing by flopping into the river like a fat toddler being dunked in a bucket, Tarin had caught three fish to Keigh's one. Keigh acknowledged Tarin as the Bear of the evening as they took their catch back up to the fire.

Mannie fried the fish, along with some sliced potatoes the Anders had contributed to the journey, in a skillet he had packed in one of Rose's saddle bags. After their shared dinner, they laid out their bedrolls under the stars to fall asleep to the sounds of the river and its wildlife.

Keigh, however, was far too excited to sleep. This was it! This was the beginning of the dream he had wanted his whole life! He was outside of Bjorn, seeing the world, and tomorrow he would be in the legendary city of Sentinel for the Refining. He stared up at the clear night sky, focusing on a star that outshone all those around it. *May I shine as you do one day. I will bring light to my family's darkness. I won't leave Sentinel a nobody.*

From there his mind drifted to fantasies of winning duels fought in front of the king and queen. He saw nobles and canes applauding his skill, cheering his name. The king bestowing him with a red cloak, filling his bag with the gold winnings of the Refining that he could use to buy out his family's debt. The shocked looks on the people of Bjorn's faces when he returned home, honored and promoted by the king. His days of being a nobody were behind him.

*

The following morning, the group was packed up and headed down the road to Sentinel before the sun had even crested the peaks of the Ursus Mountains. The September air was clean and cool, leaving its moisture deposited in millions of drops of dew that sparkled in the early morning light from every blade of grass, twig, and leaf.

Mannie spent the first hour of their ride humming gently to himself and gazing at the scenery like it was the first time he was seeing it all. When his eyes finally settled on Keigh, he furrowed his brow. "What's that on your wrist?" he asked.

Keigh showed him the thin cloth bracelet Misselli had tied there. "Misselli gave me this to remember her while I'm away from Bjorn."

Mannie grinned, allowing his body to roll side to side with his horse's steps. "Things are getting a bit more than friendly between you two, huh?"

Heat radiated off Keigh's face. "No—I mean—I don't know...She's my best friend, you know that. I don't want to screw that up." He would admit at least that much to Mannie.

"I married my best friend, and I don't ever regret it." Mannie looked out toward the distant tiered city of Sentinel, where Keigh knew his wife was waiting for him.

"Will I get to meet her?" he asked, excited to know more about his friend's mysterious home life.

Mannie bobbed his head back and forth noncommittally. "I'm sure you will at least get a chance to see her, though I cannot promise I'll be available to make the introduction." He smiled gently at Keigh. "I think you will like her. After all, she is the love of my life."

Keigh laughed. "You're as sappy as my dad! He nearly melts whenever he talks about my mom! Does old age make you that way, or marriage?"

"It's neither old age nor marriage that softens a man. It's love."

Keigh shook his head. "I hope love never strips me of my strength."

Mannie snorted. "I said softens, not weakens. Neither I nor your father have been stripped of our strength. In fact, our love for our brides only strengthens us. I can tell you that the last place on earth you would want to be is between me and my wife. I would tear down mountains to protect her."

Keigh thought of his own father and knew he would do the same for his mother.

"Besides..." Mannie fixed Keigh with a quick grin. "It looks like you're already there." He nodded toward the cloth bracelet and chuckled as Keigh stuffed his hand under his overshirt where the old man couldn't see it anymore. "Oh, come on now, Keigh! This is nothing to be ashamed of! Misselli is a uniquely wonderful young woman, bright and friendly. Why shouldn't you take notice?"

Keigh shrugged, but declined to answer.

"I hope you at least gave her a token of your affection as well," Mannie said wryly.

"It's not about...*affection*," he said, keeping his wrist hidden. "But yeah...I gave her the metal orb you told me to bring as a reminder of home. I figured the bracelet would be reminder enough for me."

Mannie pulled back on his reins, stopping his horse. "You did what?"

Keigh tried to stop Rose, but the stubborn donkey diligently plodded along after the group, ignoring his commands. Turning back to look at Mannie, he was surprised to see the messenger's ever-present smile missing. "What's wrong?" Keigh laughed, still wrestling with Rose.

Mannie shook his head and snapped the reins, trotting his horse up next to Keigh. "That orb was a gift that was given to you when you were very young. You should not have regifted it."

"I'm sorry," said Keigh, still laughing, expecting his friend to say *"Gotcha!"* at any moment. "I didn't know it was a big deal."

Mannie's intensity was only increasing. "Just promise you'll get it back as soon as you can."

"Okay! Fine, I'll get it back!" Keigh conceded, not appreciating the messenger's cryptic disappointment with him. "What's so special about it anyway?"

"Just get it back," Mannie demanded, then sped off to ride alongside Braddock and Chogan without another word.

Keigh spent the next two hours brooding over being kept in the dark on yet another topic. *If it's such a big deal to him, he should have told me beforehand. How am I supposed to know he's emotionally attached to some trinket?*

Keigh's brooding was interrupted when he noticed Tarin and Deacon had turned their horses to face each other up ahead, and were staring at something on the ground. As Keigh got closer, he saw there was a turtle on the road that the boys were trying to get their horses to smash with their hooves.

Keigh jumped off Rose's back and sprinted ahead to Tarin and Deacon. He carried his momentum into two, hard, open-palm slaps that he landed on the horses' rumps, sending both mounts galloping away. Deacon cursed at him while Tarin shouted, "What the heck, Keigh!"

Keigh stooped down and scooped up the young painted turtle, relieved to see that they had failed in their attempt to squash it. He inspected the animal thoroughly for injury. Misselli loved turtles. She never missed an opportunity to try to catch one just so she could hold it and name it. Occasionally, when they would see a turtle by the river, Misselli would even wave to it, calling it by name as if she were hailing an old friend.

"What are you doing out here on the road, little guy?" he asked the turtle. Looking around, he saw it had come from a tranquil pond surrounded by reeds and cattails, and appeared to have been heading toward a large muddy puddle that had accumulated along the far side of the road. Keigh wrinkled his nose at the puddle, which had a lump of horse manure floating in it. "You don't want that. Your home is far better than whatever you think you'll find in there."

Keigh jogged down to the edge of the pond and set the ambitious creature down. Without hesitation, the turtle scuttled back into the smooth water of the pond, disappearing into the dark mud and leaves at its bottom. As Keigh watched it go, he realized he'd forgotten to name it. *Misselli would be so disappointed with me,* he thought, smiling to himself.

When he returned to the road, he found the entire group gathered there, watching him.

"Explain yourself," Braddock demanded.

"I was just putting a turtle back out of harm's way."

"And you thought you needed to startle your friends' horses into a full gallop to do that?" Braddock's temper was quickly worsening.

"You could have killed Deacon!" snapped Vicerous.

"I'm sorry for assuming your son was a competent rider." Keigh inclined his head to Vicerous in mock apology. "I won't make that mistake again."

"Stop your tongue, Keigh Anders!" bellowed Braddock. "What you did was reckless! Even a skilled horseman can still be killed by a frightened horse!"

"They were trying to kill that turtle!" Keigh argued. "King forbid any lower life forms be permitted to live in peace, unchallenged by the *Kings of Bjorn!*" he jabbed, surprised by the new level of contempt he felt for Tarin and Deacon.

Tarin looked hurt by the accusation. Deacon just glared back at him.

"As unnecessary as their destructive behavior was, it is no excuse for threatening their safety in return," thundered Braddock. "They threatened the safety of a turtle, and you threatened the safety of two men. There is no comparison and no justification for it! Now apologize!"

Keigh had felt justified in what he had done, but when Braddock framed it like that…he felt foolish. His actions had been rash. "I'm sorry, Deacon. I'm sorry, Tarin…I wasn't thinking. I could have gotten you both hurt."

"Water under the bridge, bud," said Tarin readily. "I was being stupid. Plus, the excitement of a runaway horse was actually kind of fun!"

"Speak for yourself," Deacon lashed out, his normally slick hair still tangled from the unwanted sprint. "My father warned all of you this is what would happen if we allowed him to come. We should have never let the stray dog in the house. It's only a matter of time before he wrecks everything." He spat on the ground toward Keigh, much like his father had done the day before.

"Enough of that talk, Deacon!" Braddock's eyes locked on Deacon so fiercely that he physically recoiled. "I'll tolerate it to an extent from your father, but I won't have any of it from you."

"Fine—then allow *me* to repeat myself," Vicerous hissed. "The boy is a menace. His proper place is in the dirt!" He pointed a finger at Keigh. "If he threatens the safety of my son again, I'll make sure the dirt is where he stays."

Just then, the horses began to shift about nervously. Keigh felt the ground begin to shudder.

He saw her before anyone else. Mace was sprinting out of the forest behind the horses. She soon rounded the group, shredding the earth with her claws and placing her entire hulking mass between Keigh and Vicerous. Mace bared her teeth and issued a low rumbling growl at the Wulfs.

It was all the men could do to keep their horses from bolting away. Keigh couldn't see much from behind Mace's gargantuan body, but did notice Rose lazily chewing on a mouthful of grass, eyes half closed as if Mace were no more threat than a rabbit.

Soon, Mace stopped her growling and the horses' panicked cries quieted, along with their riders' attempts to settle them. Keigh could hear Braddock talking softly to his bear. His mentor came around Mace's side, into Keigh's view. The old warrior continued to speak soothing words to his bear, but he studied Keigh intensely, just as he had the night of the fire.

After a minute, Braddock shouted, "Everyone back on the road! I want to reach Sentinel before nightfall!" Then, without a word to Keigh, he turned and strode back to his horse.

When Keigh clambered back onto Rose, he looked up to see Mannie back beside him. Mannie didn't say a word, only smiled proudly and gave Keigh one of his signature winks.

*

At midday they got their first clear sighting of Sentinel. Keigh had seen it from the mountainside above his home before, but seeing it this close took his breath away. The whole city appeared to have been constructed of pure white marble, rising away from the earth to its towering center, where the only structure not made of marble stood. The king's palace was constructed of dark polished granite and massive cedar beams. It sat at the apex of the city like a dark jewel set in a ring of white gold.

Mannie must have noticed the look of wonder on Keigh's face. He leaned over and said, "Wait till you get close."

"We aren't close?" asked Keigh, hardly believing the structures of Sentinel could possibly look any larger than they appeared right now.

"Look at the city gates." Mannie pointed to the white pine doors set into the outer wall. "See the size of the people and wagons entering?"

Keigh watched the miniscule figures streaming in and out of the gateway. They were no larger than gnats. "Those gates must be...a hundred feet tall! And the walls at least three hundred!"

"Close, actually...The gates are a hundred twenty feet tall, and the wall is three hundred fifty feet high." Mannie looked admiringly at the city he called home. "You see the curtain?" He pointed to the towering white wall that made up Eden's southern border. "It's five hundred feet high on the Eden side. Seven hundred on the outside."

"How can you build a wall taller on one side than the other?" Keigh asked, marveling at what he was seeing.

"When the curtain was constructed, the stone was quarried from the ground immediately outside the wall. So technically the wall is still five hundred feet tall on the outside, but it sits on the edge of a two-hundred-foot-deep pit." Mannie smiled at Keigh. "You see now why we were all so shocked someone had entered Eden?"

"Well, he certainly didn't come over the curtain," Keigh said, still entranced by the size and beauty of the king's city. "He must have crossed over the mountains."

"I agree. Though that is hardly less impressive," said Mannie, looking east then west at the jagged peaks soaring thousands of feet higher than the top of the curtain wall. "A remarkable feat for even the most capable of warriors." He turned back to Keigh. "Only he hadn't bargained on running into someone more impressive than himself."

Keigh let his friend's kind words wash over him, ridding him of the last scraps of bitterness that had clung to him from the conflict earlier that morning.

"I know why you saved that turtle, and I'm proud of you," Mannie said warmly. "Someone has to look out for the little guy!" He winked at Keigh again and rode ahead to join Braddock.

*

Seven hours later, the group was finally less than a mile from the outer walls of Sentinel. They were nearly there when, suddenly, a large creature appeared at the side of the road. The horses bucked and panicked at the beast's abrupt appearance. Keigh barely saw the odd creature before Mace galloped past him toward the threat, blocking his view. But before the bear could reach it, the animal disappeared just as swiftly as it had appeared.

Mace tore at the ground where the animal had been standing, sending sand and rock flying dozens of feet into the air. The horses continued to panic. Keigh shielded his eyes from the falling sand, flinching as a rock the size of his head nearly struck Rose, who, true to form, never so much as blinked—a fact he appreciated at the moment, but one that he was pretty sure would get him killed if he ever needed to flee from a real threat.

When everyone had settled their horses, Mannie rode back to join Keigh again.

"What was that?" asked Keigh.

"That was a prairie dog."

"A prairie dog? It looked more like a huge mouse than a dog."

"Yes, many creatures still retain their old names from before the Great Collapse," chuckled Mannie. "Even though they've changed drastically since those ancient days."

"Before the Collapse, could they not disappear?" asked Keigh.

Mannie laughed harder. "No, they couldn't disappear then, and they can't disappear now. They live underground for the most part. The one we saw simply dove down a hole in the ground." He pointed to where Mace sat panting over a mound of dirt. "You've never seen one because most of Eden has exterminated the animals. Their tunnels and holes often trapped or hurt livestock, so they had to be removed. They only still exist near Sentinel because there is very little agriculture near the city, and the people of Sentinel believe the task of hunting prairie dogs to be beneath them." A wry smile crossed the messenger's face. "Though occasionally they are reminded of the danger the animals present when a road or house caves in where the prairie dogs excavated too close to the surface."

"Do you know all the animals of Eden?" asked Keigh. "Which ones are different than they were before the Great Collapse?" He loved hearing stories of the Collapse, especially the many mysteries it had produced in the world afterward.

"I know much of what was and what now is, but I suspect there may still be things out there that would still cause me to wonder." Mannie swept his eyes back across the wide river valley. "In Eden, the primary animals that underwent drastic changes in the Collapse were red bears, prairie dogs, ebonies, flower hawks, and garden wolves...not to mention about a hundred different plants."

"Seriously?" Keigh leaned forward on Rose to try to see the prairie dog hole. "What changed?"

Mannie took a deep inhale. "For starters, they all changed in size. It's the most common change that occurred in the various life forms that were exposed to the strong growth chemicals countries bombed themselves with in an attempt to create stronger, more deadly soldiers for their armies. Red bears branched off of a species called grizzly bears, drastically increasing in size and intelligence. It was uncommon for grizzly bears to ever be anything other than brown, while red bears can be any number of colors, if not their usual red. Prairie dogs primarily only changed in size. They used to be as small as a common squirrel. Flower hawks used to be the size of other butterflies before they grew to be the size of eagles. Ebonies are an offshoot of ravens that have not only grown in size but, like the red bears, also experienced a radical increase in their intelligence. So much so that it is said Draiden uses them to deliver messages as well as scout for his soldiers."

Mannie gestured to the empty sky.

"That's why you'll never see one land in Eden. The birds know they'll be shot on sight." He drew an invisible bow and loosed an arrow. "Let's see, what else? Garden wolves are another example, but they seem to have drawn the short straw. Before the Collapse, wolves were an apex predator the size of a large pet dog or bigger—intelligent and able to work in packs to take down prey much larger than themselves. Now they've been reduced so dramatically in size that people dispose of them as they would a rat."

Keigh was silent, imagining a world where wolves were big and bears were small. "It must have been so cool to live back then."

"The world of old had many wonders of its own. Many are a regrettable loss, but much of what was lost in the Collapse needed to be erased. The world and its people are better for it."

Keigh pondered what things Mannie could possibly be referring to, but those thoughts soon evaporated as they passed into the dark shadows cast by the walls of Sentinel.

Braddock raised a hand, bringing their entourage to a stop. His horse snorted as he turned to address the group. "I am not permitted to instruct or aid you in any of the ways you will be tested. I can, however, tell you this...the second you pass through these gates, and every second afterward, you *are* being tested." His piercing gaze lingered on Keigh. "The Refining has begun."

CHAPTER 19

CAPITAL COMFORTS

45-6-16

The king had given the Refining's nominees the first three days in Sentinel to rest, prepare, and explore the city. They had also, each been given their own quarters on the third floor of the king's barracks, which was more like a luxury inn than a housing place for warriors. Keigh's room there was larger than the one he shared with his two brothers at home, filled with the most comfortable furnishings he had ever experienced.

The first night he didn't even make it to bed; instead, he fell asleep in a large, sumptuously cushioned armchair in the corner of his room. He had been looking out the window over the ornate marble buildings of the terraces below, fantasizing about one day living in one, when he had slipped into vivid dreams of fame and grandeur. When he woke in the morning, he had moved himself over to the lavishly covered bed and found it to be even more comfortable than the chair. So comfortable, in fact, that he debated staying in bed all morning—but his curiosity and excitement for the day ahead wouldn't allow it.

He had made it! Keigh Anders, thrall from Bjorn, potato farmer, was in Sentinel! Living in the king's barracks on the king's coin. He was there to compete in the most prestigious competition against the best warriors in the world, as the king's personal nominee. That fact alone still baffled him. He believed he had what it took to be a cane, but had never imagined the king would know his name or single him out for special recognition. Whatever the case, he could get used to living like this.

Keigh quickly dressed himself in a simple tunic and sandals, then hurried to the room next to his to rouse Tarin. Tarin was reluctant to leave his bed, but before long, Keigh had his friend up and out the door. They made their way to the mess hall, across the street from the barracks. A long, rectangular building with high ribbed ceilings, it was filled with wooden tables adorned with fresh white tablecloths. Tarin and Keigh quickly set about filling three plates each with the finest foods Keigh had ever seen. Fresh fruits and vegetables, cut and displayed so artistically he wasn't sure if they were supposed to be eaten or looked at; trays of biscuits, sausages, bacon, and eggs cooked in every way. When they had finished with those items, they treated themselves to a number of sweet breads. Rolls covered in rich buttercream frosting and honey glazes, still warm from the ovens, melted in their mouths. Tarin had to stop Keigh from stuffing his pockets with them. Keigh wasn't sure if they would be fed like kings every day or just the first day, so he was reluctant not to secure himself a private stash of the delicious breads to take back to his room.

When they were finished, Tarin departed to meet with Deacon. They had already made plans to get together with the other boys of the Consecrate, all of whom had been nominated for the Refining. Tarin had invited Keigh to join them, but he had opted to spend the day exploring the city on his own. Tarin was great by himself, but whenever he was with Deacon, and even more so since they had set out for the Capital, their speculations and verbal daydreams of what they would do when one of them was king were insufferable. The prospect of hanging out with three more members of the Consecrate was as appealing to Keigh as babysitting five crying infants.

Once Tarin departed, Keigh stacked their used plates and spoons and cleared them from the table. He walked the edge of the room, looking for a place to deposit dirty dishes.

There was a soft tap on his shoulder. He turned to see a sandy-haired woman of about thirty smiling kindly at him.

"I can take your dishes, sir," she said, tucking a dirty washcloth into the rope tied around the waist of her plain tan tunic and holding out her hands.

"Um, thank you," said Keigh, handing her the plates. "And there's no need to call me sir." He smiled at her and turned to leave.

The woman reached out with her free hand and grabbed his arm. "I'm sorry, sir, but are you Keigh Anders?"

"I am…" Keigh answered cautiously. "How did you come to know my name?"

The woman's smile widened. "I knew it!" She bent her knees as if she were about to jump with joy. "The others are going to be so excited. We have heard many great things about you!"

"Wait…Who is *we*?" Keigh gave a furtive look around the room for anyone else who might be watching him. "And who told you about me?"

"Mannie, of course!" said the woman, radiating pure delight. "Every thrall in the Capital knows your name! He's told us all about how you fought off Draiden's man in the woods, how you won your agoge duel against your better, even how you defended a man from a cane who was about to harm him." She shook her head, her lips pressed tight together in a poorly suppressed grin. "We are all so proud of you! You're one of us, and the king sees you! It gives us all hope."

Keigh blushed at the woman's praise. He also felt a renewed gush of appreciation for Mannie. *He must be king of the thralls here,* he mused, smiling at the thought of Mannie sitting on a throne of mop buckets and brooms.

"Thank you," he said, inclining his head toward the woman, grateful for her kind words. "I hope to live up to Mannie's expectations of me."

"Oh, you already have! He loves you so much. The way he talks about you makes us all love you." She smiled gently, reminding him of his mother. "I do want to warn you, though…" The woman's face became serious as her eyes darted nervously back and forth, checking that she would not be overheard. "While the thralls in the Capital know you and support you, there are many who would be greatly upset to learn a thrall had been admitted into the Refining. Do not reveal your station if you can help it. Many of those who would oppose you wield a heavy influence here in the Capital."

Immediately Keigh's mind went to Vicerous and Deacon. If they knew he could be compromised so easily, he had no doubt they would reveal he was a thrall without hesitation. "Those who came with me already know. What should I do?"

The woman pursed her lips. "If there are ones you trust, ask them not to speak of your station, and if there are those you believe wish you harm…hope their pride prevents them from disclosing that they are in the same group as a thrall." She must have seen the concern on his face, because she added, "I wouldn't worry about it. It's only a precaution. You'll be fine."

"Thank you. I'm grateful for the heads-up." Keigh inclined his head again. "What's your name?" he asked, realizing they hadn't even truly been introduced yet.

"I am Sanya. Myself and my children serve in the palace kitchens. My husband Bard is the foremost thrall in the dungeon master's employ. He basically runs the place himself."

"I look forward to meeting him. And it was a pleasure meeting you. Is there anything I can do to help you clean up after everyone?" Keigh looked around at the tables covered in used dishes, knowing his mother would be disappointed if he ever walked away from a mess like that without helping.

Sanya shook her head, the dimples on her cheeks deepening as her smile broadened. "You are everything Mannie said you would be. I couldn't possibly ask you to help. When one of us finally gets a reprieve from his labors, I will not be the one responsible for putting him back to work serving my betters." She set the stack of dishes down on the table next to them and pointed to several other people in tan dresses and tunics. "Plus, there are more than enough of us to take care of this mess in no time."

"Well, one more set of hands will only make the work go faster." He took the plates off the table. "Just point me where to go and tell me what to do."

Sanya grinned, and didn't stop grinning the remainder of the cleanup. She was obviously pleased to have him stay, but also seemed a bit uncomfortable at giving him things to do. As a result, Keigh had to take most of the initiative in finding himself things to clean up.

While they worked, Sanya introduced him to what seemed like every thrall in the mess hall. The many names passed in and out of Keigh's ears in such rapid succession that by the end he still only remembered the names of Sanya and her husband Bard, who he had yet to meet.

When they finished gathering all the plates and waste, a number of carts were wheeled out of a hidden doorway at the far end of the hall.

"Whoa! I didn't even know there was a door there!" exclaimed Keigh.

Sanya sighed. "Yes, that is the builder's intention. The Queen's Council decided many years ago that the nobles of Sentinel should not have to walk the same passageways as thralls, so the council commissioned the construction of an extensive series of hidden passageways that the thralls of Sentinel must use when serving the needs of their betters."

"Wow. And I thought it was bad in Bjorn."

"Unfortunately, it seems the higher people rise in Eden, the less they believe they have in common with thralls, and therefore the less they feel the need to be involved with them." Sanya wiped her hands on the front of her tunic. "Many of the nobles here believe that we deserve our indentured service for allowing ourselves to get into such debt, so they have no sympathy for us." She stared at the hidden doorway as it opened again. "If our betters spent half the amount of time and resources getting to know us as they do attempting to avoid us, I doubt they would see us as the filth they do now."

At the despair in Sanya's voice, Keigh's indignation and hatred for the system he had lived under his whole life burned hot inside his chest. Then he had a thought he hadn't fully considered before. Did the king he revered treat his thralls like filth too? Wouldn't Mannie have said something?

"How many thralls does the king have indebted to him?" he asked.

The distant look in Sanya's eyes disappeared at the question, and a look of affection warmed her face once again. "All of Eden is indebted to the king," she said, "but the king and queen have only Mannie officially. The king does not hold our debt—he is the one who pays our debt!" She tossed her washrag on the table and planted her fists on her hips. "We serve in his palace, and he pays us for our labor every day. Often our pay is more than what we need to pay our betters monthly quotas."

"If the king has so much money, why doesn't he just buy all your freedom outright? Why settle for paying you daily wages?" Keigh argued, more with himself than with Sanya. He hated that there were people subjected to the whims of others who believed themselves better. Even the title given to debt holders, 'betters', irked him.

"Surely the king is wealthy enough to do that, and I'm sure he could release any number of us in full at any time, but we are grateful." Sanya picked her rag back up and began scrubbing at a spot on the bench. "He gives us what we need for each day. Day in and day out, without fail. Truly, to serve the king and queen is better than serving any other master."

"But isn't it best to have no master? Wouldn't you rather be free to do as you wished?" Keigh asked, beginning to feel bad he wasn't helping. He just had so many questions.

Sanya ceased her scrubbing. "This I have contemplated many times." Standing up, she brushed away the hair that had fallen into her face. "Everyone serves someone. No one is ever truly free. You will be a slave to yourself, if not another. The question we in the palace have to ask ourselves is, 'Am I a better master than the king?'" Sanya shook her head again. "I don't believe that I am. My family were their own masters once and we fell into debt with Councilman Slate. If I were to go back and advise my parents before their failure, I would counsel them to serve the king. He is good to us, Keigh. Always good to us."

Keigh felt a bit better knowing that at least the king was benevolent, but still..."I can't imagine wanting to serve anyone if I had my freedom."

"Mannie tells us you wish to be a cane?"

"I do," Keigh admitted.

"Is a cane not a servant of the king? Does a cane not answer to his commands and march to his orders? Does the king not supply his canes with everything they need to live?"

"Well, yeah, but that's different, because I chose it."

"Just as I told you I would *choose* to stay and serve in the king's kitchens." Sanya smiled her sweet, motherly smile again. "Though I wield a brush and mop and you wield a sword and shield, we have chosen the same master." She attacked another spot on the bench with her rag. "It is a good choice. We are the same in that."

Keigh had to admit that she made a good point, but it still felt different to him. Not wanting to argue, he changed the subject. "Can you show me the passageways the thralls use?"

Sanya exhaled and wiped the sweat from her brow with her forearm. "I would be delighted to, but there is still much to be done to prepare for lunch. I will have to ask another to guide you, if that's okay." She stood up straight, placing her hands on her hips as she looked about the hall. "Ah! There she is!" Sanya set out across the hall, weaving between the tables and benches toward a lone girl sitting at a table, writing on a small roll of paper with a feather quill.

Sanya leaned close to the girl and whispered something in her ear. The girl's braided brown hair whipped over her shoulder as she turned and looked across the room to where Keigh had been left standing by himself. Her eyes widened in what looked like terror, then she whipped back around to face Sanya. He could see her shaking her head quickly at whatever Sanya was saying.

Without warning, Sanya grabbed the girl by the back of the dress and stood her up. She whispered one last thing in the girl's ear and marched off.

The girl stood in place like a statue for a long moment. Then she scooped up her quill, inkwell, and paper. Turning, eyes to the ground, she started across the room toward Keigh. Even when she arrived in front of him, she didn't lift her head.

Her voice was quiet and shaky when she spoke. "Sanya has asked me to show you the passageways the thralls use to navigate Sentinel. Would you allow me to guide you?"

Keigh smiled. She reminded him of his friend Emerson and her nervous way of communicating. "I would be honored if you would, but first I would like to know the name of my guide," he said, trying to ease the girl's nerves. "And maybe even see her face too? I'm Keigh."

He offered his hand for her to shake, but when the girl lifted her face, both his hand and his jaw dropped involuntarily. She was the most stunning girl he had ever seen. Every feature of her face seemed to have been carved by a sculptor commissioned to create a bust that embodied pure beauty. Her skin was a rich caramel and her hair shone with the luster of freshly oiled wood. She even smelled pretty; the faint scent of lilacs seemed to cling to her.

"I'm Tabitha." Her eyes barely connected with Keigh's before nervously returning to the floor. "Sir."

Her voice snapped him back into motion. Closing his gaping mouth, he raised his hand again for her to shake.

As Tabitha reached for his hand, she dropped her quill and paper, then nearly dropped her inkwell as she tried awkwardly to catch the falling items. Before she could bend to pick them up, Keigh stopped her with a wave of his hand. He was actually glad to hide his face from her now, as it had suddenly become quite warm. Kneeling, he retrieved the quill and fallen pages.

As he handed the items back to the girl, he noticed the cloth bracelet on his wrist Misselli had tied there. In a flash, his beauty-induced stupor lifted as his heart began thumping for the girl back in Bjorn.

Back to his senses, he started again. "Please don't call me sir. I'm nobody's sir."

Tabitha laughed, still quiet as a mouse. "Follow me. I'll show you the Centipede."

"The Centipede?"

"It's what we call the hidden passageways. They are long and narrow, with hundreds of arms, just like a centipede."

Keigh followed her to the wall, where she showed him how to identify the hidden doors.

"Every one of the Centipede's doors are marked and opened by one of these." Tabitha showed him a tiny engraving of a lupine bloom. "Press on it and the door will pop open. Try it." She stepped back and let Keigh press the carving of the small flower.

It pushed in ever so slightly, and the stone wall panel next to him swung open. He jumped back in surprise. "Whoa! How does it do that?"

"I'm not really sure." Tabitha shrugged. "All the thralls know how to operate the doors, but I'm not sure any of us understand how they work. But still, that's more than the higher-ups of Sentinel. They don't even know how to open them. Why would they want to know how to get closer to the people they avoid?"

"This is so cool!" Keigh stuck his head through the opening, already thinking of ways to prank Deacon with the secret doors.

Tabitha entered the dark passageway and waved for Keigh to follow. The tunnels were lit with small oil lanterns that hung from hooks in the ceiling. The light was dim, but more than enough to see where you were going. Tabitha took him to every room of interest she could think of. At each door she showed him a small lens that a thrall could look through to make sure they didn't disturb anyone. Most of the rooms they came to were already occupied, so Keigh had to settle for seeing them through the lenses.

The first room they were able to enter was the queen's ballroom. Tabitha opened the door to the deserted room and strode out onto the polished expanse of the dance floor. The floors were a sapphire blue and heather-gray granite with subtle veins of caramel, giving Tabitha the appearance of walking on water.

"This..." She gave an elegant spin, displaying the most confidence Keigh had seen in her yet. "...is where I work."

"What do you do here?" he asked. "Do they make you scrub the floors?"

Tabitha smiled sweetly and shook her head. "No. I teach the nobles and wealthy ables that attend the queen's balls to dance."

"You know how to dance?" Keigh asked, the beginning of an idea forming in his mind.

Tabitha looked at him like she would a confused child. "Yes...I teach it," she said again, more slowly this time.

"Could you teach me?" he asked excitedly. If he could come back to Bjorn knowing how to dance, Misselli would be so impressed.

"I could..." Tabitha's eyes narrowed in suspicion. "But what need do you have for dancing? Mannie tells us you're a promising young warrior. Canes do not typically attend the queen's balls."

Heat rose in Keigh's face again as he debated how to answer. "I—uh... There's this...It's..."

"You have a girl you would like to impress?" An understanding smile spread across Tabitha's perfectly sculpted lips. "Mannie has mentioned you have a friend...Misselli, isn't it?"

"Uh...yes." Keigh exhaled, relieved to not have to explain himself, although he now had a bone to pick with his loose-lipped friend.

"Must be a pretty special girl to make you take time away from your practice with a sword to practice twirling a girl instead."

Keigh looked at the girl standing before him, and again saw his beautiful best friend twirling in her white dress, begging him to dance with her. "Yes, she is. She loves dancing and I always refuse her because I'm so bad at it. I don't want her to think I'm a klutz."

Tabitha smiled sympathetically. "I will be happy to teach you. It was my boy who taught me to dance..." Her head dipped sadly. "We haven't danced together for months, but I am hopeful that we will be reunited again someday."

Keigh was so busy imagining himself dancing with Misselli, he barely heard a word Tabitha said. "Great! Thank you! When can we start? I mean... when is a time that works for you?"

Tabitha giggled at his eagerness. "We can start right now if you wish."

Keigh nodded, excited to cure himself of this weak area in his life.

She beckoned him to join her out on the floor, then took one of Keigh's hands in her own and placed his other on the small of her back. Keigh began to sweat.

His nervousness must have shown, because Tabitha tried to cover her laugh with a sniff. "Relax. We're just going to start with the basics."

The roles had changed so swiftly. An hour ago, Tabitha had hardly been able to look him in the eye; now he was the one sweating like a pig on a spit. She may have lacked confidence in a room full of people, but out here, on the dance floor, she was queen. All signs of insecurity washed away from her as she guided Keigh through various steps and routines, smacking him on the leg when he stepped out of turn and praising him when he got something right.

They spent an hour dancing to the rhythm of the songs Tabitha hummed. When they finished, they made plans to meet back in the ballroom each day after breakfast.

Leaving the ballroom, they continued to explore the many winding passages of the Centipede. When it came time for lunch, Tabitha bid him farewell, explaining that her afternoons and evenings were filled with dance lessons but promised to see him tomorrow for their first scheduled lesson.

Keigh thanked her and sped off toward the mess hall, visions of a blonde girl from Bjorn dancing in his head.

CHAPTER 20

KNOCKED OUT

19-3-3

K eigh spent the afternoon of that first day in the Capital, and the next two days exploring the city. He used the Centipede to get most places. The secrecy of the hidden network of passages intrigued him; plus, it was exclusively for use by thralls. The idea that for the first time he had something the upper classes didn't gave him an odd sense of pleasure, even if it was just a system of dark, damp hallways.

As much as he was committed to the Centipede, he couldn't help spending hours wandering the open white cobblestone streets of Sentinel. Every tier of the city was beautiful. The lowest tier and most outer ring was purely residential. Even the smallest estates were mansions to Keigh. The largest seemed like palaces themselves. All the buildings were made of the same white stone as the city wall; only their trimmings and design set them apart from each other. Keigh spent hours walking the streets of the outer tier, imagining himself living there one day. The city was spotlessly clean— the only blemish he could find were two places where crews of men were repairing holes in the road, where, he assumed, prairie dog tunnels had caved in under the cobblestones.

The second tier of the city sat twenty feet higher than the first, and the two were separated by a short interior wall of thirty feet. The gates in the interior walls were kept open at all hours, while the gates of Sentinel's massive outer walls were closed every night.

The second tier was the city's business district. Its buildings were taller than the mansions of the first tier, but still constructed of the same white stone. Here there were more shops and stores than Keigh thought could be supported by all of Eden. He had always been fascinated with the many treasures and technologies Crispin Popplardo sold in his shop in Bjorn, but here it seemed all the world's advancements were on display and on sale. He found a pair of boots that had a bottom made of a substance as durable as hardwood but supple as oiled leather. The merchant called it "rubber" and told Keigh how old-world people used to make it from liquid oil somehow—a story he didn't fully believe, but found fascinating nonetheless. Another merchant had a special quill that held ink inside of it without dripping or bleeding; only when pressed against parchment did it release the ink for writing.

The most interesting thing he saw for sale, however, was a metal carriage that sat low to the ground on metal wheels. It was very different than the multitude of high, brightly colored wooden carriages clacking up and down Sentinel's streets on their tall wooden-spoked wheels. This carriage had a low, open front end where the driver's seat was mounted in a hollow enclave. The carriage itself had four metal doors painted in glossy enamel that reminded Keigh of glazed pottery. The compartment was surrounded by large clear windows. Inside, all the seats faced forward out the huge front window that was set at a diagonal.

The merchant explained to the crowd that the carriage was a relic from before the Great Collapse. People of the distant past once called them *automobiles*. He went on to describe how they used to have a contraption in the front, where the carriage driver's seat was now mounted, that burned special oil and converted it into power that drove wheels of air-filled rubber, without any pull from a horse! If that weren't fantastic enough, the crowd got a good laugh when he told them automobiles used to be able to move at speeds faster than any animal, faster even than the strongest wind. Keigh laughed too. The more fantastic the story, he knew, the higher the price the merchant could get for the carriage.

The markets didn't just sell luxuries and curiosities. There were also hundreds of shops selling basic items: jewelry, dishware, clothing, and other home goods. The market was particularly full of produce, as Eden and its neighbors were still at the peak of harvest. Every time he passed a bake shop, Keigh thought of Misselli. Mrs. Labelle's shop produced breads as good as anything he saw here. If he was asked to stay in Sentinel, maybe the Labelles could make a living here too—or at least Misselli might be able to apprentice in one of the shops.

The third tier of the city was again separated by a twenty-foot rise and a thirty-foot wall. This was the public works and monuments sector, where the king's barracks were located, along with the city's most impressive structures. Many of the nobles and authorities worked in this sector, but most of the buildings were for public use and enjoyment. There was a stadium, a zoo, an art museum, and hundreds of statues and monuments depicting great events in Eden's history. Between every place of interest were gardens and fountains so lush and beautiful they looked as though they were at the height of spring and not the beginning of fall.

The fourth and final tier was the palace compound, constructed of dark gray granite and red cedar. Colorful banisters and tapestries hung from the walls. Everything about the palace was the height of opulence. There were only certain days and hours when the gates to the highest tier were opened and the king took audience with the public. The rest of the time, the palace and its many courtyards, gardens, and buildings were closed to all but the king's innermost circle...and, as Keigh found out, to the thralls that served there. For it was inside the palace that he met with Tabitha each morning for dance instruction in the queen's ballroom.

At the end of his third day in Sentinel, Keigh was exhausted. He felt as though he would never be able to see all of the city. He had given it his best try, but still, he had seen perhaps only a quarter of what Sentinel held. *I could live my whole life here and never uncover all its secrets,* he thought, his feet aching.

*

The following morning at breakfast, a hulking man in dark green robes presented himself to the nominees of the Refining. The mess hall had fallen reverently silent as the nominees hung on the man's every word. He introduced himself as Damien Rowe, a member of the queen's council and former cane. Damien congratulated the men and instructed them to meet in the stadium in an hour's time, giving them no more instruction than "Wear something you can fight in."

Keigh hustled back up to his room. He grabbed his bow and changed into the buckskin pants and boots he had worn for his agoge duel. He knew that most the men would wear tunics, but he didn't care. He had killed the deer his clothes had been made from, and he had bested the assassin, Zale Woodman, and Vicerous Wulf while wearing them. He didn't really believe in luck, but why change now?

He, Tarin, and Deacon met in the hallway outside their rooms and walked to the stadium together. Deacon and Tarin speculated what awaited them, while Keigh remained silent, focused on acquitting himself well, no matter the task.

As they approached the stadium, Keigh stared up at the building's lofty summit, its exterior walls filled with arches and adorned with thousands of full-size stone statues of canes armed for battle. When they reached the base of the structure, they were directed by a number of canes toward an open gate that led them down a flight of stairs. At the bottom, they were again ushered down a torchlit hallway to a large, circular underground chamber, where they found many of the other nominees waiting. Braddock stood against the far wall, talking to several older men in red cloaks. Keigh assumed they must either be retired canes or guild masters from the various cities and towns of Eden.

Deacon and Tarin split off to join a group of young men Keigh assumed were the other boys of the Consecrate. Keigh made his way across the bustling room toward Braddock.

Braddock saw him coming and gave a subtle jerk of his head, indicating he didn't want Keigh to approach him directly. Keigh altered his trajectory to a well-lit, unoccupied section of wall further down. While he waited for Braddock to come to him, he observed his new surroundings. The room was large but quite plain. Its floor was a mix of sand and straw, with walls constructed of common brown brick. Blazing torches and black doorways were the only breaks in its facade.

Besides the group of older men standing with Braddock, he counted forty-eight men, some of whom were impressively large and muscular. He noticed Chogan was one of the only canes to not be fully arrayed in the armor of the Queen's Climb. Nearly every cane had an adamantine arm, plumed helm, and red cloak. Chogan only had the cloak, and Keigh and the boys of the Consecrate didn't even have that.

How am I going to beat forty-eight others? How am I even going to survive? Keigh gulped as he saw a dark-skinned cane loosening the straps on the back of his gleaming adamantine to accommodate the imposing girth of his muscle-bound arm.

"Are you well rested?"

Keigh ripped his eyes away from the hulking cane and found Braddock had joined him against the wall. "Um, yeah...I mean, I think so."

"Good. Now grab my arm and pull from me." Braddock shuffled slightly closer to him. "Just like we practiced."

"Am I allowed to use my powers here?" Keigh asked, remembering how his mentor had told the boys he would not be able to help them once the Refining started.

"Your powers as a potent are more a part of you than any of their adamantines are." Braddock swept his hand around the room at the dozens of fully armed canes. "You'd be foolish not to." He offered his arm again inconspicuously.

"Can I pull energy from others?"

"In the arena and in battle you can. Outside of that, you must never pull from someone without their consent." Braddock shook his arm again. "You have my permission. Now hurry up and take what you can!"

"Hurry?" Keigh scoffed, remembering his disappointingly slow progress with his potent abilities over the summer. "It will take me five minutes to pull enough energy to actually help."

"Are you going to make excuses or take what I'm offering you?"

Keigh grasped his mentor's forearm, mad at himself for how easily he had let doubt distract him from his goal. As quickly as he could, he settled into the familiar headspace of focused need. Today he needed energy, needed to be strong, needed to *win*.

Soon he felt the familiar spark of energy enter his hand. It remained a steady tingle in his palm until, three minutes later, Braddock was tapping his hand. Keigh released his grip and flexed his back. His body felt full of fiery power and his thoughts had an intense clarity.

"That should be enough." Braddock sighed and blinked rapidly. "Any more and I won't be able to climb the stairs to my seat." Smiling exhaustedly, he added, "That was a good pull. What did you focus on?"

"Winning."

"You really want this, huh?" Braddock sounded surprised by the determination in Keigh's tone.

"More than anything," said Keigh, meeting his master's gaze without blinking.

Braddock returned the look with a hint of pride. "You'll need to, if you hope to win. Just don't lose yourself in the pursuit," he said, echoing Mannie. Braddock looked around to see if anyone was watching, then leaned close and whispered, "This is the only clue I'll give you to winning the Refining. Be the man your parents raised you to be and you'll do well here...You already have."

He withdrew, giving Keigh a squeeze on the shoulder, then frowned and reached over to snatch Keigh's bow off his back.

"This you won't need. Not today, anyway." Braddock gave him a nod, wobbling as he made to walk away in his weakened state. "I'm off to speak with Tarin and Deacon. Good luck today. Use what I gave you wisely."

Keigh waited alone for the next five minutes in silence. He felt a little less himself without his bow, but after flexing his muscles and feeling the extra strength from Braddock coursing through his veins, he decided the bow wasn't anything to worry about.

A door on the far side of the room opened. Ten canes carrying dark, oiled barrels of sparring swords and racks of shields entered and stood on either side of the doorway. One of the old men Braddock had been talking to called for silence, then instructed the nominees to line up single file and follow the guild masters through the door, each grabbing a sword on the way out; the shields were optional.

Everyone was quiet as they filed out of the room. Keigh got in line behind Tarin and grabbed a sword and shield. Neither was remarkable, but both were adequate. The edges of all the metal blades had been dulled drastically, but they could still break bone easily enough.

Outside the room, they entered a long dark hallway with a stairway at the end. From the front, the old guild master called out, "Alright then! You lot will follow us out. Stay in line until you're told to do differently. And don't any of you act a fool and wave to your grandmas and aunties."

A sputter of guttural chuckles echoed from the line of warriors.

"Act like you've been here before! Let's go!"

With that, two broad doors at the top of the stairs swung open. Blinding beams of sunlight and the deafening roar of applause poured into the hallway. Keigh tried to swallow, but his mouth had gone dry. He was prepared to fight, but he hadn't considered the crowd. The prospect of thousands of people watching him terrified him more than the prospect of getting stabbed with a dull blade.

Soon the line was moving and he was walking up the stairs, up into the sunlight. When he exited, he found himself on the floor of the stadium. A wave of sound crashed into him so hard he felt it in his bones.

"Every person in Sentinel must be here!" he shouted to Tarin, barely hearing his own voice above the roar.

Tarin turned and called back to him, "Not even close! Only holds twenty thousand!"

Twenty thousand people! Keigh gaped at the number as the roar of the crowd continued to wash over him in waves.

Soon they stopped and turned to face the north side of the stadium. At the edge of the arena sat four giant red bears. Keigh recognized Mace and another he thought might be the king's bear, Gorr. The other two were beautiful shades of crimson and maroon.

"Why only four bears?" Keigh asked Tarin.

"They won't let any of the nominees' red bears in!" Tarin shouted in response. "They fear they may lose their nerve if their partner starts losing a duel!"

"How do you know so much?" Keigh shouted back.

"I'm the king's son, remember?" Tarin winked at him and turned to face the stands as a chorus of trumpets blared repeatedly, signaling the crowd to be silent.

As the last murmurs quieted, Keigh noticed a platform above the bears, where a row of men in dark green robes stood. He recognized Damien, who had greeted them in the mess hall that morning, and assumed the men must be the Queen's Council. Above them sat the king and queen. The king's golden helm shone brilliantly even in the shade of the platform, where flowing purple curtains with gold trim hung across a canopy of cedar lattice. The queen, dwarfed by her husband, appeared as magnanimous and gracious as she had when Keigh had seen her in Bjorn. Today she wore the sapphire blue of Eden's flag, while the king wore his usual white.

A man of the Queen's Council with long, shiny black hair stood up with arms raised.

Tarin bumped Keigh with his shield. "That's Councilman Slate," he said out of the corner of his mouth.

So that's the one always visiting his good pal Vicerous, Keigh thought, noting the man as someone to treat with caution. Anyone who got on well with Vicerous Wulf couldn't be expected to do him any favors.

In a voice that seemed unnaturally loud, Slate addressed the waiting crowd, a self-satisfied smirk spreading under his pointed nose. "Welcome! It is the king's pleasure to present to you, the good people of Eden, the contestants of the first Refining Trials in nearly twenty years!"

The crowd erupted again in raucous applause.

Slate's chest swelled at the reception of his words. Turning his palms down, he signaled the crowd to quiet. "Your nominees have been selected from all over the kingdom and will compete in a myriad of tasks, tests, and duels for the right to be elevated above every cane in Eden, to be awarded the Sword of Silver, and to earn enough gold to buy their own palace!"

The crowd erupted again. Keigh even allowed himself a cheer of his own at the prospect of winning enough gold to release his family.

"Throughout the year, your contestants will be awarded points for their victories and deducted points for their failures." Slate pointed to the arena floor. "Their scores will be tracked and displayed next to their names on the walls of the king's arena!"

Keigh noticed for the first time the dozens of names, written in six-foot-tall letters, ringing the arena floor. He didn't see any he recognized, but noted that all the names had a large zero next to them.

Tarin nudged him with his shield again. "What did you do?" he asked through gritted teeth.

Keigh didn't have a clue what he meant until he saw Tarin nod to the far end of the stadium. There, his name was written in big, bold letters—and next to it, equally as large, the number *15*. Keigh took another quick glance around the wall. He was the only one with points! But how had he earned them? This was the first event of the Refining, and it hadn't even started.

"Your canes will compete in hand-to-hand duels three times a week, every week, all year! Starting today!" Slate announced. "Nominees! Take your seats, and know that you all have the king's favor!"

The crowd cheered as the contestants took their seats against the wall on the far side of the arena.

"First up: Christian Olson and Walton White!"

One of the other guild masters led a confident-looking cane with blonde hair and smooth features out to the center beside a boy Keigh recognized as one of Tarin's Consecrate pals. The guild master lined them up several feet apart and had them face each other. As soon as he stepped away, a trumpet blared. The crowd roared as the duel began with a clash of steel on steel.

The first duel was a short affair: the older cane knocked the sword out of the younger boy's hand in under a minute, then proceeded to punch the boy in the mouth, even as he was obviously yielding.

Keigh gulped and clutched his shield tighter. If members of the Consecrate could be disrespected so blatantly, he would be a fool to expect any sort of quarter from any of his opponents.

As soon as the duel ended, a thrall ran out of a doorway with a long number *1* and hung it in front of the *0* after Christian Olson's name.

"Seriously?" groaned Tarin. "We only get ten points for a win?"

Keigh laughed at his friend's dismay, knowing it came from Tarin's realization that he could not pass him in points today. "Guess you better just admit I'm the Bear right now, then!"

"Fat chance!" Tarin rolled his eyes. "Not when you don't even know how you scored those points."

"I guess the king just knows a winner when he sees one!" Keigh said. Somehow teasing Tarin was helping to settle his nerves. Tarin continued to shake his head as Councilman Slate called out the next two names.

The morning rolled into afternoon. Most of the duels were hard-fought, competitive affairs lasting five minutes or more, though the Consecrate members' duels were much shorter—the exception being Deacon and Tarin. Deacon had actually won his duel against one of the few older canes who did not have all the armor of the Queen's Climb. Tarin battled his fully armored cane for nearly ten minutes before losing his footing, allowing the cane to press the edge of his sword to the back of his neck. However, his performance still garnered him five points, even though he had lost.

After twenty duels, Keigh's name still hadn't been called—a fact that bothered him for two reasons: first, the energy he had gained from Braddock was slowly ebbing away from him; and second, the dark-skinned cane who could barely fit his muscular arm into his adamantine still hadn't been called either.

Three duels later, it was confirmed. The only two names yet to be called were his and the strongman's. As the second-to-last duelers got up to take their place at the center of the arena, Keigh looked down the row of nominees toward the cane he would soon be fighting, only to find the man already grinning back at him, his white teeth stretching from jaw guard to jaw guard of his beautifully polished steel helmet. A helmet covered in etched bear fangs.

"He seems confident," Tarin pointed out as Keigh slumped back against the wall.

"If I die, tell Deacon he's a git for me," sighed Keigh.

Tarin chuckled. "Tell him yourself. After all..." He elbowed Keigh gently. "You're the Bear today."

Keigh smiled, but shook his head. "You're just saying that 'cause you think I'm about to lose."

Tarin grinned. "Why ruin a good compliment by reading into it?"

"Next up, for the final duel of the day: Keigh Anders and Faraji Aboiye!"

The crowd cheered as loudly as they had all day as Keigh made his way to the center of the arena. The whole way, he could feel Faraji's eyes on him. Nervous sweat began to run down his back as the enormity of the moment threatened to overwhelm him.

Soon, he and Faraji were lined up across from each other, waiting for the crowd to quiet so the horn could blast...but the crowd didn't quiet.

"Silence for the start!" Slate bellowed.

Keigh couldn't help but look up to find the cause of the commotion. Up in the highest rows of the stadium, a whole section of people wearing identical tan tunics and dresses continued to cheer. *Thralls,* he realized with a rush of affection for his fellow servants. In the foremost row of the group, he could even distinguish Sanya and Tabitha, cupping their hands around their mouths as they cheered right through Councilman Slate's protests.

Eventually, Slate relented. With a look of disdain, he signaled the trumpeter to start the duel.

The horn blasted and the fight was on.

Keigh shuffled his feet into the shallow sand of the arena floor and waited behind his shield for his opponent to attack. Gripping the hilt of his sword, his fingers closed with a strength greater than normal. Some of Braddock's energy still remained in him. He was grateful for the strength, but even more relieved that his mental clarity had remained as well.

"Attack me, child!" Faraji roared.

"You first, big guy!" Keigh called back. He wanted to start on the defensive so he could get an accurate idea of his opponent's strengths and possible tells in his movements. Why Faraji wanted him to attack first he couldn't imagine. All he knew was that if that was what his opponent wanted, it was the last thing he was going to do.

"Don't be afraid, boy! Start the fight and I'll go gentle on you."

"I'm good over here, thanks!"

Faraji growled. "I'm losing my patience with you, little one!"

The crowd started to boo. They had been standing there for fifteen seconds and still hadn't moved an inch.

"You hear that? Look! They're booing y—"

Keigh's taunt was cut short by his own sudden inhale of shock. He watched as his sword sailed through the air. He had made to point at the crowd with his blade and, in his sweatiness, had accidentally thrown his weapon halfway across the arena. Mace flinched as the sparring sword landed with a poof in the soft sand next to her paw.

The crowd gasped. Keigh looked back at the man he had just been taunting to see him grinning at his good fortune.

"Don't suppose you still want to wait for me, do you?" He gave Faraji a furtive smile, then dashed toward his sword as fast as he could.

Faraji roared a battle cry and took off after him.

Keigh was fast, but Faraji was faster. Halfway to his sword, Keigh took a look back at his pursuer to find him only ten feet behind and closing quickly. In a flash, he envisioned a dozen different scenarios of how he could grab his sword without Faraji pinning him to the ground as he did it. He could roll into it and pop up blind. He could duck under his shield and hope Faraji committed too much to his initial blow. No matter what he chose, he needed more time.

A distraction! That's what I need! Just enough to buy me a second.

A memory of Jessie throwing a stick for the garden wolves to fetch so she could sneak a pet of the puppies popped into his mind. In an instant, he pulled the shield off his arm and spun around, flinging it with all his might at his attacker in an attempt to slow him down.

He had no time to see if his ruse worked. Continuing his spin, Keigh fell right back into the sprint for his sword. He guessed it must have worked, at least in part, because the crowd gasped in unison. Apparently they had never seen someone throw their shield before. Keigh allowed himself to smile at his own recklessness, then dove for the handle of his sword and popped up as fast as he could, bringing his sword up to block the incoming strike from Faraji.

Keigh winced as he prepared for impact...but none came. It was then that he noticed the stadium had gone silent. Opening his eyes, he looked in the direction of his attacker.

There in the sand, twenty feet back, lay the hulking mass of Faraji, face down in the sand, motionless.

The thralls in the upper rows were the first to recover. The small band of servants cheered with an enthusiasm that made them sound like a group of three times their number. Soon the crowd joined in, in a much less enthusiastic fashion.

The guild master who had lined them up for the duel finally hobbled his way over to Faraji's side. Taking a knee, he checked the warrior's pulse. The old man smiled in relief and nodded to the platform where the Queen's Council sat.

Councilman Slate stood again, his dark green robes looking like wings as he raised his arms for silence. He fixed Keigh with a look of disdain even Vicerous would have been proud of as he announced, "Winner...by knockout! Keigh Anders!"

CHAPTER 21

THE WEIGHT OF GOLD

42-16-10

That evening in the mess hall, Keigh's improbable victory was the talk of every table. Apparently, Faraji, sensing victory, had looked to the king's platform to confirm that the king was watching his performance right at the time Keigh had turned to throw his shield, which had struck Faraji square in the side of the head, knocking him instantly unconscious. Many of the canes told Keigh how impressed they were by how hard he had thrown the shield, even if most of them still believed his win was little more than dumb luck. Keigh knew he had leveraged his unnatural strength from the energy Braddock had given him, but he wasn't about to disclose that. It would only cause the men to resent him, if not outright distrust him.

Deacon was predictably bitter about Keigh's victory and subsequent popularity among the other competitors. Keigh didn't mind, though; he was used to the Wulfs' contempt. In fact, today he almost appreciated it, for it was Deacon's overreaction that seemed to pull Tarin out of his sulking over Keigh's mystery points. Tarin still hadn't acknowledged Keigh as the Bear (aside from the charity designation he had given him before the fight), but Tarin repeatedly throwing food at Deacon's head and shouting "Duck, Faraji!" was almost as good in Keigh's eyes.

As the dinner was winding down, Damien Rowe, of the Queen's Council, informed the contestants that the following day, they would be called in to have a private audience with the king and queen in the palace throne room.

Keigh hoped his interview with the royals would be in the afternoon so that he could get in a dance lesson with Tabitha in the morning. He had only had three lessons so far and already felt more confident in his abilities. Every time Tabitha complimented him, he imagined the shocked look on Misselli's face when he swept her off her feet—a thought that excited him, but also left him feeling anxious. How long would it be before he returned to Bjorn? The Refining Trials could last all the way through spring. What if Misselli didn't want to dance with him when he returned? Hopefully his letters would keep her from forgetting him. He had sent one on his second day in Sentinel, but didn't expect to hear back from her for at least a week. In the meantime, he had to battle his own doubts.

She will wait, he told himself.

*

The following morning, all the nominees were back in the mess hall. Faraji had rejoined the group, his head heavily bandaged but not noticeably injured otherwise. Tarin and Deacon were back with their Consecrate friends, leaving Keigh free to sit with Tabitha.

"That was incredible yesterday!" she exclaimed in a whisper, talking to the table rather than Keigh.

Keigh chuckled as he set his overly full plates on the table, taking his seat across from her. "Better to be lucky than good sometimes."

"You were amazing!" Tabitha insisted, still avoiding eye contact. "Every thrall in the Capital was talking about you last night." She nodded at Sanya, who was waving at them both from across the room. "You're all they're still talking about this morning, too."

"Thanks for coming to watch. I could hear you all down in the arena."

Tabitha smoothed the tablecloth in front of her. "Sanya went to Mannie and he was able to get us in. None of us thought we would be able to attend. But I think Sanya said Mannie will get us seats to every duel, so long as you're still in the competition." Tabitha looked directly at Keigh for the first time since he had sat down. "So, you'd better keep winning." She smiled, then dropped her eyes to the tabletop again. "I got to skip lessons with Sir Rodney to come to your duel. You saved me from an hour of having my toes stepped on while his wife badgers me about my weight."

"What's wrong with your weight?" Keigh laughed. As far as his eyes could tell, there wasn't a single thing wrong with her.

"Nothing!" huffed Tabitha, still quiet as a mouse. "Just 'cause she never met a muffin she didn't like doesn't mean I need to stuff myself full every meal."

Keigh looked at the mounds of food on his plates, then across the table to the meager meal Tabitha had grabbed for herself. An apple, one slice of bread, and a small handful of huckleberries were all she had served herself. "I mean, you could eat *more*..."

Tabitha shook her head. "If only boys' brains were as big as their stomachs... My boy likes his food too. Never saw him leave anything on a plate." She smiled, apparently remembering the meals they had shared together.

Keigh was about to ask her more about him when the doors to the hall flew open and Councilman Slate swept into the room with four other green-cloaked men.

"Good morning, nominees," Slate addressed the room in a tone as oily as his black hair. "My name is Scipio Slate, and I am the most senior member of the Queen's Council. Today you will meet with the king and Her Majesty the queen."

Slate's voice reminded Keigh of someone, but he couldn't put his finger on who.

"Today will undoubtedly be the highest honor of your lives thus far, and for some of you..." Slate's gaze drifted to a particularly unkempt cane who was still chewing his breakfast loudly with an open mouth. "...the highest honor of the rest of your lives," he drawled. "You are to remain here until your name is called. You will walk *alone* to the throne room, and once you have been dismissed by the king, you will walk *alone* back to the barracks. Do not return to the mess hall. Food will be brought to you by the kitchen." Slate sniffed, seemingly not wanting to acknowledge the people who worked there.

Keigh looked at Sanya and was shocked to see her glaring daggers at Slate. No thralls overly liked the people who bossed them around, but open hatred was a dangerous thing to show—especially in the Capital, Keigh imagined.

Slate handed a list to one of the men behind him and, in a swirl of green, left the room without another word.

"Keigh Anders!" shouted the man with the list. "Make your way to the king!"

"You're first!" squeaked Tabitha. "What are you going to ask him?"

"I don't know," said Keigh, standing up, the beginning of a knot forming in his stomach. "I'm pretty sure we're the ones being questioned."

"Good luck!"

All eyes were on Keigh as he weaved his way toward the door.

Tarin grabbed his arm as he walked past his table. "Don't say anything to get yourself in trouble."

"Right," said Keigh. It was a genuine attempt at encouragement from his friend, but the irony of the advice wasn't lost on him. It had been what Keigh *had* said to the elders of Bjorn that had kept Tarin from getting in trouble in the tower fire fiasco. But, if Keigh were truly honest with himself, his friend had a point. Nearly every time he had been in trouble growing up, his smart mouth had been to blame.

When Keigh got to the door, one of the men in green pointed him in the direction of the palace and told him there would be signs directing him on the path he should take. He made his way up the cobblestone street toward the palace. An excited buzz filled the air as he passed through the crowded city. Everyone seemed to be talking about the previous day's duels; some even recognized Keigh and pointed him out eagerly to their peers.

There was an odd assortment of people in the Capital's third tier. Farmers dressed in simple tunics walked the same streets as nobles and rich merchants dressed in their fine robes and cloaks of deep reds, purples, and blues. Most of the people were there for pleasure—very few, other than thralls, actually made their living in the public works sector. Regardless of their differences, everyone seemed united in their common interest in the Refining Trials.

On his way, Keigh rehearsed what he intended to say. *My king, my queen. I am honored to be in your presence. My sword and my shield are yours...*

"No, no, no..."

Your Majesties! What a privilege it is to be granted an audience with you...

Keigh rolled his eyes. Everything he thought he might say sounded exceedingly dumb. *Maybe they will talk to me first,* he hoped.

Lost in his thoughts, he turned a corner toward the palace and ran straight into a lavishly dressed man carrying an armful of scrolls. Cursing, the man tossed his load as he stumbled. Scrolls flew in the air and his coin purse burst open, raining gold coins off the hard cobblestones.

Keigh scrambled to catch the man before he fell as awkwardly as his scrolls had. He apologized for the collision, but the wealthy merchant was too busy cursing him to hear.

"Stupid boy!" he fumed. "No sense to watch where you're going!"

"I'm sorry, sir. Please, let me help." Keigh dropped to the ground and began gathering the gold coins the man had spilled.

"It's the least you can do! You're the cause of this mess," the merchant snorted. "Should be you who cleans it up! Unbelievable!"

"Cornelius, my friend! How are you?" another man in fine clothing called out as he approached the scene of the collision.

"Quite well, Murphy," said Cornelius, stepping over the mess toward his friend. "That is, at least until this buffoon tried to break my neck. Clumsy oaf," he huffed indignantly. "Probably never been to the city before."

"Come now, Cornelius. Let the boy gather your things. I must ask you something quite urgent." Murphy looked down his nose at Keigh, who was still on the ground, trying to roll a scroll that had come unbound. "Privately, if you would."

Cornelius gave Keigh a disdainful look that Keigh was all too familiar with. "See that all my things are gathered neatly. I will fetch them from you in a moment," he said, turning to join Murphy across the street, then calling back over his shoulder, "Try not to dirty anything, will you? I can practically smell the poor on you."

Keigh clenched his fist around one of the gold coins so hard it bruised his palm. This man was no different than Vicerous. Just another man of means who would see him wallow in the dirt for the rest of his life.

"Yes, *sir*," was all he could manage to reply through his gritted teeth.

With that, Cornelius and Murphy disappeared around the corner to have their conversation in private. Keigh cursed himself for not being more aware of his surroundings. This delay would certainly not earn him any favor with the king.

Each of the scrolls had been tied with a strip of ribbon attached to a small metal seal. The seal bore the letters *CW*, which Keigh assumed were the man's initials. He retied the scrolls that had come undone, then bundled them and collected the spilled coins as quickly as he could. With his arms full, he hurried around the corner to find the merchant.

Cornelius took the scrolls and coins without thanks. Keigh issued a final apology, but as he turned to leave, Cornelius reached out and seized his elbow.

"Wait!" Cornelius fixed him with an accusatory glare. "Stay until I count my coins...I know how your type like to *help themselves*."

Keigh bit back the words that nearly came flying out of his mouth. He didn't have time for this, but he also didn't want to make any enemies if he could avoid it, especially enemies with influence. Sanya's warning came back to him: people in the Capital had no love for thralls, and some of them could cause trouble for him.

"...twenty-six, twenty-seven, twenty-eight." Cornelius raised his eyebrows, surprised to have been returned all of his coin. "Well, then, what are you still here for?" he spat at Keigh. "Be gone!"

Keigh didn't need to be told twice. He inclined his head to the two men in an informal bow and took off around the corner, this time being careful to keep his eyes up for other potential collisions. But before he had gone more than ten paces past the scene of his collision with Cornelius, he saw on the ground two more large gold coins next to a scroll with the letters *CW* on its seal.

How could I miss this? He clenched his fists, furious with the rising cost of his own carelessness.

He scooped up the scroll, then collected the two gold coins in his other hand. They were heavy—the same pieces worth ten justicia the queen had handed out on her visit to Bjorn. The same pieces Vicerous had taken from Keigh's family moments later. The same pieces Mannie had paid out for him to come to the Capital. These two coins could do so much for his family, and Cornelius didn't even value them enough to know they were missing...

Wait...Cornelius doesn't know they are missing! He could take the coins back to Bjorn and nobody would ever be the wiser!

As he was about to pocket the coins, he heard his father's voice in his head, speaking one of the old proverbs he loved to quote: *No one ever steals more than they lose in the act.* It was his way of reminding his children that you couldn't put a coin value on integrity.

Keigh looked at the lustrous gold in his hand again. How much was char-acter worth when others didn't think your life had any value to begin with? He ground his teeth, knowing the money in his hand was more than anyone would ever pay his father for anything. He imagined how excited his father would be when Keigh gave him the money, but even in his imagination, Keigh couldn't see a scenario where his father didn't immediately ask him where he'd got the coins. He could lie, but that would only deepen the offense...

No, his parents had raised him to do the right thing. This was not his money. He would become a cane the right way and pay off his parents' debt with gold earned in the king's service. The Corneliuses and Vicerouses of the world could rob him of gold, possessions, freedoms, and a great many other things, but they couldn't rob him of his character. He needed to hold on to that, even if it meant letting go of the gold.

He sprinted back around the corner and found Cornelius and Murphy still standing where he had left them. Keigh briefly explained how he had found the additional items, then handed them to Cornelius. For a brief moment he thought he saw a glimpse of appreciation, maybe even admiration in Cornelius's eyes, but he knew that was wishful thinking when the man snatched the items out of his hand and spat on the ground at Keigh's feet.

"Filthy swindler is what you are! Found them indeed…Probably stole them from the beginning and just let your nerve get the better of you."

Keigh wanted to punch him in his throat. He probably would have, too, if he had not so recently been contemplating the value of character and imagining the looks of disappointment on his parents' faces. Instead, he gave Cornelius another wordless bow and left, racing back up the busy street toward the palace.

This time, there were no more collisions or lost items to delay him, and five minutes later, he had followed the remainder of the makeshift wooden signs to the massive timber doors of the throne room. At his arrival, six thralls in white wool tunics greeted him warmly. Keigh smiled as the servants seemed torn between performing their duty or breaking decorum to introduce themselves to him. In the end, duty won out over their personal intrigue and the six men asserted their combined strength toward the burdensome task of opening the enormous doors. For a moment Keigh thought the doors would hold out, but slowly the gap in the center began to expand as they groaned inward.

Seeking to end the strain on the men as quickly as he could, he slipped through the thin opening into the throne room. Once he cleared the doors, the voice of an unseen herald called his name with a triumphant shout.

Light flooded the expansive room through seven high arching windows on each side. Flecks of crystal in the dark granite walls and floor refracted the warm morning sunlight, giving the room a dreamlike lighting, like so many drops of dew on a clear summer morning. Three opulent thrones stood at the far end, where Keigh could see the king seated between the queen and his red bear, Gorr. Even Gorr seemed small in the oversized hall, and if not for his proximity to the king and queen, Keigh could have mistaken him for a regular bear.

The extensive length of the room gave him too much time to think as he walked, smoothly as he could, toward the monarchs awaiting him at the far end. Why hadn't he asked Braddock how to greet the king and queen? Was he supposed to kneel? Should he speak first, or wait to be spoken to?

It was too late now. He was standing before the most powerful man on earth and his bride. Keigh dropped to one knee and bowed his head. He waited several painfully silent seconds. Then the queen spoke.

"Oh! I like him!" She sounded pleased. "Please, Keigh, stand."

Keigh stood and viewed the powers before him. The king sat straight-backed in his throne of white marble etched in gold and silver lightning, his golden helm as unreadable as ever. Gorr looked at Keigh in much the same way Mace often did during his days spent training at Braddock's: with a mixture of curiosity and playful anticipation, as though the giant bear expected Keigh to throw a stick for him to fetch at any moment. The queen was much easier to read. Her features exuded the same motherly affection he saw in Sanya and his own mother.

"You have the approval of both my bride and my bear, it seems." The king's voice was powerful, yet filled with warmth. The golden helm that covered his face lent a mellifluous quality to his words. "I too must admit a certain fondness for you already."

Keigh had a mental stammer. Of all the ways he'd envisioned his audience with the royals might go, Keigh had not imagined it would start with the king and queen showering him with compliments. So it came as a total shock when Keigh heard the king's next words.

"Search him."

Two canes he hadn't noticed detached themselves from the wall and marched over to him. The first grabbed him by the shoulders with vicelike strength and commanded him to remain still. The second unceremoniously patted him down from his hair to his toes.

"Nothing, Your Majesty," reported the second cane. Both soldiers marched briskly back to their stations by the wall.

"I do hate that part, Thiam," the queen fussed, looking at Keigh apologetically.

"I take no pleasure in it either, Vanitas, but all must be tested," said King Thiamtaim.

"That was a test?" Keigh asked, his mind grappling to understand what they could possibly be testing for with a search of his body. Would someone actually be so bold as to try to sneak a weapon in?

"No, the test was earlier," said the king. "This was only verification of the report."

"Report?" Someone had reported to the king about him? What had they said?

"Bard! Please, join us," the king called without turning away from Keigh.

A small door behind the thrones, which Keigh recognized as an entrance to the Centipede, swung open, and into the room walked the man he knew as Cornelius.

Cornelius, or Bard, as the king had called him, stopped next to the queen's throne. "Hello, Keigh. Sorry for all the rudeness earlier. I hope I wasn't too cruel with my words."

Keigh was dumbstruck. The vile man from only minutes ago was standing in front of him...apologizing.

"Keigh, this is Bard," the king said. "I believe you know his wife, Sanya?"

"I...I do...but I thought he—I thought you worked in the dungeons?" Keigh stuttered, not sure whether to address the king or Bard.

"He does. Both he and his wife are faithful servants of mine, and seeing as how my dungeons are gloriously empty at the moment, I enlisted Bard's help in staging this test. A test you passed most successfully, I would add."

It unnerved Keigh that he couldn't see the expression on the king's face, only the blank, unmoving canvas of gold. "What was the test? Returning all the dropped items?" Now it made sense why the canes had searched him. They'd been looking for coins.

"Yes, in part." Bard took over the explanation. "The test was twofold. One facet you were better equipped than most to pass; the other, you were probably least equipped to pass."

"What do you mean?"

"I mean that as a thrall, like myself, you are more accustomed to being disrespected. So, when *Cornelius* ridiculed you and insulted you, you did not respond in kind, but rather responded meekly, allowing yourself to be slandered and mocked, not taking vengeance into your own hands."

"Yeah, but I wanted to punch you in the throat," Keigh admitted.

Bard smiled, subconsciously giving a grateful touch to his own Adams apple. "I understand. I wanted to punch myself when I called you a 'filthy swindler.'" He laughed. "And that was right after you returned the secondary items I planted for you to find, no less!"

"You planted them?" asked Keigh. It now made sense why he hadn't noticed them when he'd first collected Cornelius's items.

"Yes, that was part of the second phase of the test. The phase you, more than any of the nominees, were susceptible to failing."

"What do you mean?"

Bard sighed. "You and I know the life of a thrall does not afford us the opportunity to acquire wealth for ourselves. Everything we earn must first have a cut taken out of it by our betters. So, when you had the opportunity to take the gold coins for yourself, you faced a more tantalizing prospect than those who are accustomed to having and holding wealth of their own." Bard smiled again. "I was proud to report to my lord the king that you did not take any of the spilled or planted coins for yourself."

"Well done, child!" The queen clasped her hands together in front of her chest.

"What if I hadn't passed? What would have happened?" Keigh asked.

The king answered him this time. "If you had stolen coin, you would have been immediately removed from the Refining Trials. If you had accosted Cornelius for his rudeness, you would have lost points from your score." His voice was unflinchingly serious, but then he added in a more amused tone, "A score I'm proud to see is the highest of all the contestants at this point, too."

Keigh's ears burned as blood rushed to his face. Keigh Anders, thrall from Bjorn, had made the King of Eden...proud!

"Thank you, Your Majesty." He gave another awkward little bow.

"And as a reward for your honesty..." The king reached into a purple velvet sack on the floor next to his throne, much like the one he had given Mannie to bring to Bjorn. He pulled out a large handful of gleaming gold coins. "Ten pieces of ten." Thiamtaim counted out ten coins and proffered them to Keigh.

Keigh stepped forward cautiously, unsure if this too was a test. Only when the king gestured again for him to take the coins did he decide it was safe to do so. Cupping his hands, he allowed the king to deposit the gold in his palms. He croaked his thanks, his throat too tight with emotion to speak clearly. *One hundred justicia!* The same price the king had paid Vicerous for his time at the Refining Trials, more money than his family had ever possessed at one time, was now in his hands. Was now *his*!

"Because you were trustworthy with the two coins that were not yours, I think I can trust you with a few more of my own." The king tossed him a smaller bag for Keigh to put the coins in. "Perhaps in your hands they will do some good."

"Yes, Your Majesty," Keigh answered as he began stuffing the large coins into the little bag.

Just as he dropped in the last piece, another of his father's proverbs came to him: *A debt unpaid by coin is paid in toil; the lender owns the borrower.* One hundred justicia was exactly what the king had paid for him to come to the Refining, and one hundred justicia was what the king had just given him. Was this a test?

Keigh stepped forward and offered the bag of gold back to the king. "For my debt," he said. "The one hundred justicia I owe you for buying my release from my better."

The king sat motionless in his throne. "Did my servant Mannie tell you the coin paid for your release was a loan?"

"No, bu—"

"Then do not treat my gift as some common exchange!" The king's voice rumbled off the walls.

"I only—"

"Only what? Wanted to repay me?" he scoffed. "Look around you, child! All of Eden is mine! There is nothing I need and nothing I can't freely give to those whom I favor." The king leaned forward on his throne. "Do you wish to insult me?"

"No!" Keigh blurted. "Never!"

"Then accept these gifts." The king held a hand up, cutting off Keigh's attempt to explain himself. "And accept them *freely*."

Just then, Gorr huffed and rocked forward onto his feet. The bear stretched, and, with one giant step, brought his head down in front of Keigh. Gorr fixed one of his brilliant golden eyes on him for a moment before rolling the side of his head into Keigh's chest, seeking a scratch behind the ear, much the same way Mace often did.

Keigh scratched the giant bear, grateful for a break in the conversation. Animals were easy; people were difficult. He knew what Gorr wanted and was happy to give it to him. What the king and queen wanted from him, and why they favored him, was still a mystery.

"Well, it appears Gorr has a new best friend," said Bard, cutting the tension.

"I don't know about *best* friend," the king replied.

"True," Bard laughed, "Gorr doesn't know you don't have food to give him." Then, with a clap of his hands, he said, "Anyway, I must be leaving if I am to be in position for the next contestant. I'm not looking forward to running into Faraji. Or calling him foul names, for that matter," he grimaced. With a slight bow to Keigh, he added, "I see for myself today that my wife and Mannie have not oversold me on you, Keigh Anders. The king was wise to select you for this honor. I do hope our paths cross again soon."

With a low bow to the king and queen, Bard exited the throne room through the hidden door, off to test the next unsuspecting nominee.

"Gorr! Sit down!" the king's voice thundered.

The massive bear pulled his head away from Keigh reluctantly, backpedaling to his place next to the throne and flopping down onto his haunches.

"We have time for you to ask us one question," said the king. "Then you will be escorted back to your room, where you are to remain for the rest of the day."

"We will happily answer anything you ask of us," Queen Vanitas agreed.

One question? How was he to pick one question when he had a thousand? How could they move on when he still had more to say on the matter of the gold? He could ask why Eden allowed the thrall system, he could ask why the king covered his face, he could ask a million questions about the world outside of Eden—but there was one question that had been eating at him more than them all.

"Why me?"

The queen tilted her head, apparently confused.

Keigh clarified, "Why did you choose me as your nominee? Why was I spared the whipping post? Why did an assassin know my name and try to kill me?" The questions rolled out of him like snow rushing downhill in an avalanche. "Why me?"

The queen seemed a bit taken aback, as if some of what he was saying was news to her as well. "Whipping post? What on earth could a sweet child like yourself have done to merit such a punishment?"

King Thiamtaim raised a single hand. The queen pursed her lips, as if catching the words that had been about to fly out of her mouth, and smiled graciously at her husband.

"I will answer your questions, for the answer to all of them is the same," said the king.

Keigh wanted to know that answer so badly he felt like he was going to throw up. How could they all possibly have the same answer?

The king's voice rumbled like a distant thunderstorm. "You, Keigh Anders, were selected for the Refining, saved the lashes of the whipping post, and, I believe, attacked by an assassin, all for one reason..." He leaned forward in his throne, his golden face inscrutable as ever. "Your father."

CHAPTER 22

CRAZY TALK

42-6-35

Keigh spent the rest of the day sequestered away in his room in the barracks. His father? What did Owen Anders mean to anyone? As far as Keigh knew, his father was less known than even he was. But there were things from his father's past that he knew very little about. His mother had told him that his father had nearly become a cane before marrying her. Braddock and Vicerous had alluded to being friends with him when they were younger. Owen Anders was a simple farmer now, content to spend his days in the field and his evenings with his family, but it was becoming increasingly clear to Keigh that his father had more of a history than he yet knew.

The king and queen had been of no further assistance. After telling him his father was the reason for the mysterious and momentous events of the last few months, they had declined to answer any of his follow-up questions. Instead, they bade him farewell and good luck in tomorrow's duels.

The next time the king or queen granted him an audience, he would use his question to find out what was so important about Owen Anders. If Braddock had grown up with his father, then why was Braddock also confused each time something significant happened to Keigh? Surely if the answer was solely explainable by his father's past, Braddock would have connected the dots. It had to be something more.

Something about his father was a secret. A secret so well kept that neither his best friends nor his family knew it. How, then, did the king know?

Keigh pondered the mystery until he gave himself a headache. Satisfied that he had exhausted every angle of everything he knew about his father, he allowed his thoughts to return back to the present.

Sitting in the generously padded chair in the corner of his room, he counted his gold coins a dozen times. Each time, he gave them a fresh polish, scrubbing the fingerprints off their smooth faces as tenderly as a mother cleaning the face of her newborn. As soon as he finished, he hid the bag of gold in a drawer of the large, intricately carved wardrobe at the end of the room. He didn't think anyone would come to his room looking for anything valuable—he was still a thrall, after all—but there was no point being careless with his newly acquired riches.

Keigh flopped onto his bed, sinking into the plush covers. He spent the next hour quietly daydreaming about the look on Vicerous Wulf's face when Keigh paid off his family's debt, in full, and in gold. He knew one hundred justicia wasn't enough to cover the debt, but now that he knew he could win coin for passing the king's tests, he was determined that today's winnings would not be his last.

Soon Tarin and Deacon barged in. They were in each other's faces, arguing about "Cornelius." Keigh found out quickly that both boys had lost points, but had not been given a reason why. It also became clear to Keigh that Bard had not revealed his true identity to either of them. Keigh assumed it was because they had both gotten into verbal altercations with the pompous, scroll-carrying merchant.

After listening to both boys tell their stories of their encounter with the king and queen, Keigh didn't feel he could tell them of his own experience without causing them to resent him. Tarin had felt the king was cold and aloof toward him, while the queen had been warm and inviting. Deacon's account of the royal couple had been the exact opposite, sounding particularly disheartened that the woman he hoped to be his mother had been so callous toward him. How could Keigh tell them that both the king and queen had not only been friendly toward him, but had given him one hundred justicia? To keep the peace, he told them only the bare details. How he too had run into Cornelius, then made his way to the throne room for a short conversation with the king and queen.

Before they could dig for details, Keigh quickly changed the conversation to teasing Tarin about seeing his dad. This led to Deacon pointing out that, while Tarin was tall like the king, nobody knew what the king actually looked like, and that he himself bore a resemblance to the queen, whose face they *could* see. Both Tarin and Keigh were forced to admit Deacon looked more like the queen than Tarin did, but both still insisted that they were the king's blood, despite what they lacked—Deacon in stature and Tarin in resemblance.

They chatted for a few more hours, eating their dinner together, before they agreed it would be best to get some rest before tomorrow's duels. When the other boys left his room, Keigh found himself surprised to have no deep feelings of loathing for Deacon. His nemesis had spent the entire evening in his room and hadn't made a single direct attack on him or his family—nothing more than friendly teasing among friends. *Maybe Deacon's just terrible when he's around his father,* he thought. *Maybe there's hope for him after all.*

That hopeful thought was quickly dashed the following morning in a suspiciously empty mess hall as Deacon rudely shouldered Keigh away from the tray of bacon he had been helping himself to. "How are you still here when so many better men didn't make it?"

Deacon had clearly intended it as an insult, but truthfully, Keigh had had the same question. *How am I still here?* Nearly half of the initial forty-eight nominees were gone, including every member of the Consecrate other than Deacon and Tarin.

Even though the number of nominees had been drastically reduced, the number of spectators for the day's duels had not. Deafening cheers rained down on the thirty remaining contestants as they filed into the stadium for the second time that week. Slate gave the crowd an explanation of the previous day's test and spurred them into a renewed frenzy as he waxed eloquently on the virtue of the remaining nominees.

Keigh nervously kneaded the sand of the arena floor between his fingers as he sat behind his shield, waiting for his name to be called. Braddock had been inexplicably missing from the gathering room beneath the stadium that morning. Without Braddock lending him his strength, Keigh's confidence in his ability to win his duel was decaying rapidly.

An hour later, it had only gotten worse. He had hoped that maybe he would duel Deacon or one of the other younger nominees, but their names had all been called. Deacon had beaten a young cane by the name of Andrei Antonov in a closely contested duel, and Tarin had fought to a draw with Chogan Bald Head.

To make matters worse, Tarin had intentionally sat away from Keigh, refusing to look at him, after seeing that Keigh had received thirty points for the previous day's test, ten more than anyone else had been awarded. Keigh didn't even know if Tarin was upset because he felt like Keigh wasn't telling him something, or if he was just jealous of the unfathomable favor Keigh seemed to be receiving in the Capital.

Keigh was disappointed, but not mad, acknowledging that he too would have been upset if his friend had been receiving preferential treatment without any explanation. Right now, before he had even had a chance to earn more points in his duel, Keigh had fifty-five points next to his name, fifteen more than the next highest score and thirty-five more than Tarin. He smiled to himself as Theo's words came to mind: *haters gonna hate*—a phrase Theo used nearly every time someone disagreed with him. There were always going to be haters, Keigh thought. *Just wish my friend wasn't one of them.*

His eyes ventured up to the top rows, where he saw the group of Capital thralls gathered once again to cheer him on. *At least some people are happy for me.*

"Keigh Anders and Lin Guo!" Slate shouted before the crowd drowned him out in hungry applause.

Keigh picked himself up out of the dust and studied his opponent as they paced to the center of the arena. Lin was abnormally tall, but not as muscular as Faraji. Through the open face on his warrior's helm, Keigh could see his black hair and sharp eyes. He looked neither angry nor worried, but had a contemplative expression on his face, as though their duel were more puzzle than brawl. Lin, like most of the other canes, had every piece of armor you could earn in the Queen's Climb.

Keigh sighed in resignation. There were only a few left who didn't have adamantine arms or intimidating plumed helms. He would have to duel everyone eventually, but he had still hoped he would draw a less experienced opponent today when he was missing Braddock's strength.

When Slate signaled the start of the duel, Keigh went on the offensive. Not overly aggressive, but just enough so he could get a feel for the man's fighting style. He needed to be wary of the cane's impressive reach, but if he could get past Lin's defenses, he would have no shortage of body to strike.

Soon after the duel began, it was obvious that while Lin was proficient in technique and skill, his movements were long and drawn-out to the point of offering Keigh windows in his defense. Keigh took advantage of these windows to strike body blows with impunity. Lin tested him to the limits of his ingenuity and technique, but in the end, Keigh's advantage in speed and agility won out over the tall cane's advantage in reach. Lin was nothing if not tough; it took nearly forty body blows with Keigh's blunt sparring sword before the man finally yielded.

The stadium erupted with pent-up elation at his victory—more than at any of the duels before him. Still, he could hear the roar of the thralls in the midst of the noise. Their joy at his victory was unmatched. Keigh looked to the podium where, above the green-cloaked figures of the Queen's Council, the king was clapping slowly and purposefully next to the queen, who had risen from her seat, cheering as if to lead the whole crowd with her example.

A thrall ran out with a large number six and replaced the five next to Keigh's name with it. *Sixty-five points!* Keigh grinned the whole way back to his seat against the wall. He tried to make eye contact with Tarin, but his friend seemed to be overly interested in a piece of straw that he was rolling between his fingers.

∗

That evening at dinner, Keigh sat alone. Tabitha was giving lessons in the queen's ballroom and Deacon and Tarin had squeezed into a table that was already a bit too crowded.

As Keigh was pushing the last bits of food around his plate, Sanya settled onto the bench across from him. "How are you?" she asked, in a tone that suggested she knew something was wrong.

"Uh, good...I'm fine," Keigh lied. Once he had left the stadium and his twenty thousand admirers, he had felt more isolated than ever. At home he always had his family or Misselli there with him, but today he felt alone.

He knew he shouldn't feel that way. The Refining Trials were going better than he had ever imagined. He was ahead in points, richer than he had ever been, and popular among thralls and ables alike, but he still felt like an outsider with the canes. They were the ones he needed to prove himself to. It was a brotherhood he had wanted to be a part of since he was young, yet it seemed the more he did to show himself a warrior, the less accepted he became among the red cloaks.

"Did you see the duel?" Keigh asked, trying to redirect the conversation.

"I did! Bard and Tabitha were able to come as well. They wished me to congratulate you on your win." Sanya smiled. "Bard says he was really impressed with you yesterday. Apparently, you were the only one not to threaten him with physical violence." She laughed nervously.

Keigh chuckled, remembering the worry on Bard's face as he departed the throne room. "Did he mention how things went with Faraji?" Keigh couldn't imagine the manicured merchant Cornelius faring well in a collision with the hulking cane.

Sanya sighed. "Yes...Faraji actually had to be restrained by several canes in disguise when my husband called him, quote, *A meathead, with more muscle in his little finger than between his ears.*' In fact, they were lucky one of the canes was a potent, otherwise Faraji would have escaped their grasp and pummeled my husband's handsome face!"

"One of the canes was a potent? Which one?" asked Keigh excitedly, before realizing it had probably just been Braddock.

"I'm not sure." Sanya's eyes narrowed at his obvious excitement. "I wouldn't go seeking him out. Potents are a treacherous lot, stealing the life from others to feed their own needs."

Keigh was caught off guard by her sudden bitterness. "Aren't there rules? I thought potents couldn't pull energy from someone without permission?"

"Since when have rules ever stopped the powerful? The weak and the vulnerable follow the rules out of fear, and the lawful follow them out of respect for authority, but what of the strong and the lawless? Rules hold no sway over them. Especially potents! Even if you were to make a claim against someone for stealing your energy, how would you prove it? It leaves no mark, no evidence to convict the offender. Just the word of a thrall versus the word of the Queen's Council."

"What?" Keigh asked. Sanya's words had been oddly specific.

Sanya leaned across the table and whispered, "I've had the life leached out of me against my will before. A long time ago, the night the king's son was born, a member of the Queen's Council drained me nearly to the point of losing consciousness as I tried to serve him tea. I haven't gone near the man since, and I won't if I can help it."

"That's terrible!" gasped Keigh, realizing he had done the same thing to Deacon. The terrified look in his nemesis's eyes was still clear in his memory. They had been fighting, but still...he couldn't imagine having the life pulled out of him without knowing what was going on. It would be horrifying to feel like you were dying and not even have the comfort of knowing how. No wonder it was reserved for enemies in battle and those who knew what they were giving. "Who was it?" he asked Sanya. "You must really hate him."

"I won't say." Sanya's eyes flicked to the door of the mess hall. "The Queen's Council has enormous influence, and they could make life very difficult for anyone who tried to make trouble for them." Leaning back from the table, she resumed her normal volume. "And no, I don't hate him. I used to," she admitted with a shrug, "but I've learned better ways of thinking. I won't let the misdeeds of another ruin my peace and happiness."

"But what about justice?" Keigh continued, forcing himself to whisper. "The man needs to be punished!"

"The king has provided me a life here. A good life. I work at a job I enjoy, live with a husband I love, and go to sleep each night under the protection and shelter of four sturdy walls. What need have I for the blood of others?" Sanya was reminding Keigh of his mother more than ever. "For all I know, the man is ignorant. He had no idea how terrible his actions made me feel, but if I go and seek his life as payment for my discomfort, I would never be able to claim as much, for I would know exactly the pain and suffering that I would be bringing. Not only that, but I would have to hold on to my hate for as long as it took to get my justice. My offender may have had a lapse in judgment for one minute that led to my pain, but I'm going to seek his suffering day after day? Night after night? For weeks or months or years?" Sanya shook her head. "Keigh, everyone loses themselves for a moment. Only the truly evil constantly pursue the destruction of another with all their heart."

"But that's the law! It's not your fault he broke it! He should get what he deserves!" Keigh shook his head. How could she not see that she had the right to seek vengeance for the wrongs committed against her?

Sanya frowned in a way that was almost as sweet as her smile. "Mannie told us you yourself had some trouble with the law, and that you yourself did not have to pay the penalty for it. Is this true?"

Keigh blushed, ashamed at having been called out. *How much has Mannie told these people?* "Yes...I mean, sort of, but that was different!"

"Why? Because it was you and not someone else?" Sanya crossed her arms and raised her eyebrows as if challenging him to deny it.

"No...not that," he sputtered. "I didn't mean to hurt anyone."

"Those who break the law seldom do," said Sanya. "In fact, most of the time when people break the king's law, it's for no reason greater than they just thought their way was better than the king's way. Very rarely are things done with the direct purpose of causing another harm. Hurt and harm are just byproducts of selfishness."

"Would you at least agree that people who cause intentional hurt should get what they deserve?"

"Think about that question, Keigh. Do you really believe that? Have you ever hurt someone before? Do you wish to be punished for it?"

Immediately he was reminded of the tears in Misselli's eyes when he had told her he didn't want her, didn't care for her. He had hurt her that day, and he had done it intentionally. "Yeah, I have," he admitted. "But that was different."

"Of course!" Sanya let out a burst of laughter. "It's always different when it's us! Don't you see? We make excuses for ourselves, and justify our wrongs, because deep down we know why we did what we did, and still, even after the hurt and the pain we cause, we have the audacity to defend ourselves! Don't you think everyone could produce an excuse for why they did what they did? Of course they can! The only thing that seems to stand between a person wanting justice or wanting mercy is what side of the exchange they're on."

Sanya set her hand gently on top of Keigh's.

"The greatest wounds I have ever inflicted on another person have been inflicted on my husband, whom I love. There is no law against breaking the heart of a loved one, but I can tell you, it's a hurt far worse than having the energy pulled out of you. I've felt both, and would gladly let a potent strip me of my life a dozen times before I chose to experience the smashing of my heart by the one I love...Do you think I should be punished for hurting my husband's heart? Should he be imprisoned for hurting mine?"

"No, that's just...just...part of life. Everyone hurts someone they love at some point. You just gotta work through it and hope they forgive you."

"So then, if you can admit the greatest hurts we cause are to the ones we love, and that in cases of hurt we would want forgiveness for ourselves, what case can you make for not forgiving others when they hurt you?"

"'Cause I don't love them," stated Keigh, as if it were the most obvious answer.

"Why shouldn't you?" Sanya's eyes pierced Keigh like eagle talons digging into a trout, refusing to let him escape. "We've already concluded that both our enemies and our loved ones wound us, so the dividing line isn't hurt or offense. The only difference seems to be your assumptions about a person's deservedness. Friends and family *deserve* forgiveness and mercy when they hurt us, and our enemies don't. Am I right?"

"Kind of..." Keigh scowled as he thought of Vicerous. That man wasn't deserving of love or forgiveness. "Loved ones deserve a second chance. Our enemies don't."

"Are you nobody's enemy?" Sanya looked across the room to the table of canes Keigh had been excluded from. "There are undoubtedly people who still think you should be in prison for what happened in Bjorn. Aren't you glad they don't get to condemn you?"

"Obviously," Keigh admitted sourly, remembering the glares he had received in Bjorn ever since the incident at the watchtower.

"Then don't be the one to condemn another. If you want mercy from others, you should be willing to give it to others in return."

"What if they don't deserve it?"

"Nobody deserves mercy," Sanya said, squeezing his hand. "Mercy is literally not getting the punishment you *do* deserve."

"Maybe, but some of us deserve it more than others," he said. Surely Sanya could concede that much.

"Ugh! *Deserve*," she groaned. "If the king said he would buy out the debt of any thrall who could throw a rock the length of the King's River, which of us would be free tomorrow?"

Keigh shrugged, waiting for her to make her point.

Sanya shrugged back. "Neither of us, Keigh. You may throw it twice as far as me, but neither of us could meet the standard. Neither of us would *deserve* it, no matter how much more *deserving* your throw was than mine." She squeezed his hand again and released it. "Leave judgment to the king and his officials. Let go and live at peace. Comparison will only steal your joy, Keigh. And I would not see you robbed of yours."

He smiled at the kindness of her words. "Thanks," he said. "Where do you learn all this stuff, anyway? You talk like my dad." Keigh remembered his father's insane expectation that he do good to his enemies—an expectation he had tried to heed, only to end up tied to a whipping post.

"Funny you should ask, because I never used to think this way." Sanya stood up to return to her work.

"What happened?" he asked, genuinely curious what on earth had made this woman and his father so radical in their kindness to people who deserved none of it.

"I started spending time in the presence of the king."

Sanya's answer was affectionate and light, but it hit Keigh like a boulder tumbling off a mountainside. The king had said his father was the reason for the unexplainable events in Keigh's life. He himself had said his father was like Sanya, and Sanya had said she was the way she was because she spent time with the king.

Did Owen Anders know the king?

CHAPTER 23

ANIMALS

48-1-10

The days of the following month went by like clockwork. Mondays, Wednesdays, and Fridays, Keigh dueled in the stadium, and in that time he was still undefeated. He still hadn't dueled Tarin or Deacon yet, each of whom had winning streaks of their own going. The people of Sentinel had affectionately dubbed the three of them "The Bears of Bjorn." Since then, none of them could go anywhere without being swarmed by adoring spectators.

Keigh's friendship with Tarin was the strongest it had been since the watchtower incident. He was unsure why Tarin had ceased to begrudge him his victories, but he suspected Tarin's own winning streak and newfound popularity had done much to settle his friend. That, and a healthy dose of flattery from Keigh. Every duel day, Keigh acknowledged Tarin as the Bear and complimented him on a duel well won. When the day came for them to duel each other, the whole of Sentinel would know who was better. For now, Tarin could think what he wanted. Keigh was happy his friend was happy—and, selfishly, he thought Tarin's unchecked pride might even help him beat Tarin when the time did come to cross blades.

Tuesdays, Thursdays, and Saturdays, Keigh danced with Tabitha in the mornings and explored the city in the afternoons. Tabitha had limited the dance styles to waltz, foxtrot, and swing. Keigh liked the waltz and the foxtrot well enough, and he thought he would like dancing them with Misselli when the time came, but it was swing dancing he found to be the most fun. During every lesson with Tabitha, he insisted that at least part of their time be spent practicing swing. In an odd way, the movements reminded him of fighting with a sword: two bodies pressing toward each other, then pulling away; heads ducking under arms; spins, bends, and presses, all in time with the rhythm of another's movements.

The city continued to reveal fresh secrets. Every time he went out, he discovered something new. His most recent discovery had been the Sleuth, a dead-end alcove in the public works sector that was home to whatever red bears were currently in the Capital with their canes. The bears each had their own giant, man-made cave where they rested when not with their canes. Keigh only found it because he had followed Braddock and Mace one day when he spotted them leaving the palace gates. Braddock spied him before they had even gone a quarter mile through the winding stone walkways of the Capital's third tier. To Keigh's surprise, Braddock hadn't been upset, but rather had invited him to join them as he saw Mace back to her shelter.

Even though Keigh had now seen dozens of red bears, he still felt a deep foreboding at the thought of entering the Sleuth. If Braddock felt any such trepidation, he didn't show it. The retired cane strode into the midst of the massive bears as if they were no more than a herd of dairy cows. As they walked among the giants, Keigh noticed that most of the bears paid them little to no attention, preferring to chew on piles of sugar beets and scraps brought to them from the kitchens.

Keigh asked Braddock if the bears could survive on old vegetables and table scraps alone. He remembered all too well his days burying Mace's droppings, and knew her diet was robust. His question earned him a laugh from the grizzled veteran, who walked him over to the shelter at the end of the alcove, showing Keigh that it was no shelter, but a tunnel, dark and deep. At its very end was a pinprick of light.

Braddock explained that the tunnel allowed the bears to come and go as they pleased; most used it at night to exit the Capital and hunt in the forest beyond. When Keigh asked if the tunnel presented a security risk to the city, Braddock shrugged, explaining that the only people inside Sentinel that even knew of its existence were the few canes who actually had red bears—and besides that, the tunnel terminated in a particularly nasty series of rapids on the King's River. They were no trouble for the goliath-sized bears, but would pose a serious danger to any human trying to cross the angry waters.

"Plus," he added, "even if an enemy could traverse the rapids, they would have to have a death wish to pop up in the middle of a bunch of red bears."

Keigh and Braddock both had a good laugh at that. The idea of an unsuspecting enemy poking their head out of the tunnel like a ground squirrel from its hole, only to find themselves surrounded by a gang of bears fifty times their size who had been eating nothing but scraps, was as comical as it was outlandish.

Keigh appreciated the time spent with Braddock. They weren't what he would call friends, but the old cane was good to him and a comforting reminder of home. Tarin and Deacon spent most of their time with the other canes, and Mannie had only stopped by to see Keigh three times in the five weeks he had been in Sentinel. As exciting as his time in the Capital had been, he still found himself feeling as though all his experiences were running right through him like water through a sieve, his mind catching and holding very little of his adventures. The things that stuck with him were his interactions with people. Mannie's wink at the end of a joke, Sanya's motherly lectures on kindness, Tabitha bopping him on the head for trying a move he'd invented without telling her, Tarin and Deacon doing impressions of each other after their dinners with the king and queen.

The letters from home stuck with him, too. Both his parents and Misselli had written him twice in the last month. If he closed his eyes and tried to remember the sculptures of Orvyn's Garden or relive a duel he had fought, the memories were vague and blurry, but if he thought of the letters, he could see them as clearly as though he were holding them in his hands: the curves of Misselli's words, the smooth flow of his mother's lines, and the choppy slashes of his father's scrawl, all laid out in his mind's eye.

Today he received his second letter from Misselli.

Dear Keigh,

Can you please hurry up and flunk out of the Refining? I promise to tell everyone you did it on purpose—nobody will think you weren't good enough. I mean, you're not as fierce as I am, but certainly better than whoever else showed up to the king's silly little contest. You could tell people your dad needed help on the farm, or just tell them the truth, that you just missed your best friend Misselli too much to stay!

I'm sorry you haven't made friends with the other canes. Probably wouldn't like them much anyway, since they can't hope to compare with my funny jokes and super big brain! Haha Just kidding. Are you sure you don't want me to come down there and beat them up for you? I could make them be your friends.

Anyways, I miss you. We are still doing club, even though it's not the same without you. Addy wanted me to tell you to go try to lift Orvyn's helmet? I'm not sure what that means, but I told her I would tell you. Everyone here says hi and they can't wait to hear all your stories when you get back. Honestly, I'm not sure I can wait that long. I hope to see you soon, but I also want you to reach your dream.

You better write back fast! The mail takes too long on its own to have you slowing it down too. I could probably deliver a letter faster than they can. Maybe I'll find out.

Your forever best friend,

Misselli

P.S. If you see Baylor, please tell him we aren't mad. We just miss him.

It was the third time he had read the letter since it had been delivered that afternoon. He folded the paper and stuffed it in the front pocket of his pants. He would write her a reply when he got back to his room. He finished the last few scoops of the mashed potatoes and beef gravy on his plate, then began collecting the dirty dishes from his table that the other diners had left for the thralls to clean up. Helping Sanya and the kitchen thralls with the dishes had become his practice since his first day in the Capital.

As Keigh deposited the last armful of dishes onto one of the kitchen carts and made to leave for his room, he heard his name being called from the far side of the hall.

"Keigh! Keigh, come on and join us!" Tarin was waving him down from where he sat with Deacon and a group of six other canes.

Keigh wound his way back through the tables over to Tarin. He had a few minutes to talk. His reply to Misselli's letter wouldn't be delivered before tomorrow anyway.

Tarin shoved a young cane Keigh recognized as Andrei Antonov, making room for him to sit down. He clapped Keigh on the back as he sat. "'Bout time you joined us!"

"Why *haven't* you joined us?" asked the blonde-haired cane who had fought the very first duel of the Refining. His steely blue eyes assessed Keigh from across the table. He looked as though he had just spent hours grooming himself in front of a mirror; nothing in his appearance was out of place, and he seemed unnaturally clean. "I mean, we've been feeling a bit like you don't like us." He looked up and down the table as the other warriors nodded and grunted their agreement.

"I'm sorry." Keigh struggled to lift his eyes off the table. "I just felt like maybe I didn't have a lot in common with the rest of you."

"That's because you don't," Deacon said with a huff.

"Hey now, Deacon. I think we will be the judge of that." The clean-looking cane reached his hand across the table toward Keigh. "I'm Christian Olson, one of Vaderkirk's nominees."

Keigh shook the man's hand. "I'm Keigh Anders. I'm from Bjorn, same as Tarin and Deacon."

"Don't ever say you're the same as me." Deacon glared, still seemingly stung by Christian's rebuke of his last jab. "We are *not* the same."

"Believe me, I'm glad of that too," Keigh clapped back before Christian could intervene again.

"So! We've got some bad blood here, eh?" Christian smiled, looking up and down the table again like a bard about to launch into a new performance. "Don't tell me...it's over a girl." The canes all chuckled. Keigh and Tarin both began to shake their heads, but Christian continued. "Don't lie to me, Keigh! I know why you haven't been eating with us. I've seen your pretty little friend over there. What's her name? You know what, it doesn't matter. She's a thrall. Not sure why they even give them names."

The men laughed again. A demented, knowing grin spread across Deacon's face while Tarin squeezed Keigh's thigh, warning him not to lose his temper.

"Anyways," Christian continued, "normally I would tease you for making friends with a thrall, but I must admit, she is a pretty little thing! If I were your age, I would probably be tempted to eat from the garbage too for a morsel like that!" He guffawed at his own joke.

Tarin continued to look uncomfortable with the crass way his friend was talking, but Deacon seemed to revel in it. It was apparent in that moment that Tarin and Deacon still had not shared with the men that Keigh was a thrall.

He stood up from the table violently, glaring at Christian.

"Whoa, whoa, whoa there! I didn't mean to upset you!" Christian apologized, but the smile on his face betrayed the fact that he thought the whole situation was amusing. "Please, sit back down. She's your friend. I can at least respect your loyalty." He slapped the table. "Wish I had a friend that loyal! Theres not a one of you that wouldn't shoot me in the back with an arrow to win the Refining."

The canes laughed uncomfortably.

"Don't be sour about it! I'd do the same to any one of you." Christian let out a peal of forced laughter as the rest of the table caught onto the joke and joined in.

Keigh sat back down as Tarin pulled on the back of his shirt. He was still angry, but he allowed his passion to subside rather than alienating a whole group of canes he still wished to befriend. *They don't know I'm a thrall. They aren't acting any different than anyone else in Eden does behind closed doors.*

A bearded cane in his thirties changed the subject. "You've done mighty well for yourself here, son. Who taught you the sword?"

"Well, I'm mostly self-taught. The first time I ever held a sword was four months ago," Keigh admitted, not sure if it would impress the men or just further solidify any beliefs they had that he shouldn't be there.

"Self-taught?" Christian gaped, looking like a trout out of water. "Can you believe this kid?" He gave a high-pitched cackle that seemed too absurd to be real. "I like you! That's funny! You're funny! Seriously, though, we've all watched you. Some of us have even lost to you." He pointed at the four men who weren't laughing. "Who's your teacher?"

"Braddock Fortier."

"Really? I've heard some wild stories about Braddock. Suppose most of them can't be true. Any matter, whatever he's teaching you seems to be working. You're winning your duels, leading in points, and the whole stadium loves you." Christian's eyes narrowed as if challenging Keigh to deny it, then his face relaxed again as he changed the subject. "What shall we do tonight, boys?"

The men grumbled and murmured various things, but none offered any ideas.

"I know! Have you been to the king's zoo, Keigh?" Christian asked.

Keigh nodded.

"Okay, but have you been after dark? The whole area is deserted! We'll have the place to ourselves. Plus, most of the really dangerous animals the king's collected only come out at night anyway. Let's go!"

The group of canes and the three boys from Bjorn stood and made their way out of the mess hall and into the dark streets outside.

Walking beside Keigh, Tarin whispered in his ear, "Sorry about Christian. He doesn't know you're a thrall. Figured you would appreciate an invite to hang with us, though."

Keigh nudged his friend with his elbow. "It's not your fault. Besides, I'm over it. Thanks for the invite."

Tarin smiled and let it be.

At the king's animal enclosures, there was a barricade across the entrance with a sign attached that read, *The King's Wonders of the Natural World. Daytime visitations only.* The canes vaulted over the barricade without so much as a second glance at the sign.

"Are you seriously going to go in there?" Keigh whispered to Tarin.

"Yeah! Come on, it will be fine. We've been in here loads of times after dark." Tarin put a hand on top of the barricade and leapt over.

Keigh stood where he was. Breaking the rules never seemed to go well for him. He didn't have the cover of being a cane or having family with influence. If they got in trouble, he was sure to get the worst of the blame. He watched as his fellow nominees laughed and punched playfully at each other, making their way deeper into the zoo.

"Come on, Keigh! It's not like Beaudy's here to set the place on fire or anything." Tarin beckoned him from the other side. "You want to be a part of the group, then you've got to go with the group."

Keigh sighed. Tarin was right. He would never belong as long as he held himself apart.

"I guess you can't make an omelet without breaking a few eggs," he smiled.

Tarin grinned. "That's the spirit. Now get in here!"

Keigh hopped the barricade and he and Tarin sprinted to catch up with the group. Christian had been right: while most of the herbivores were bedded down in their enclosures, the predators were all up and roaming around. Their first stop was the big cats where they saw the king's lions and white tigers along with a pair of regal-looking lynx. In another area, they saw a pine marten crush the skull of a deer carcass it was chewing on, and a lizard big enough for a man to ride.

As the group approached the next enclosure, Keigh leaned over the edge to get a look at whatever creature the king had trapped there. After a moment of seeing nothing, he noticed none of the others had joined him at the edge of the pit. Turning around, he saw the group looking at him while Tarin and Christian had a heated, whispered exchange.

When Christian saw Keigh looking at him, he silenced Tarin with a wave of his hand. "So, Keigh, are you ready for your initiation?"

"Initiation?" Keigh asked, suddenly feeling sick to his stomach. The worried look on Tarin's face only added to his trepidation.

"Yes, initiation. The guys and I decided that since the *Bears of Bjorn* weren't formally canes, we should have each of you do a little test to prove your mettle." Christian smiled. "Deacon and Tarin have already completed theirs. I'm sure you'll find it to be no trouble."

Just barely, Tarin shook his head.

Does he really think I can't do whatever he and Deacon did to get in the group? Keigh didn't need Tarin's protection. If Deacon had survived it, then so could he.

Rejecting his friend's silent protest, he answered, "Fine, then. What is it?"

The group grinned in unison, circling around him and nodding their approval. Only Tarin remained grim.

"It's simple, really. All you have to do is retrieve an item from the pit. Easy as that." Christian gave a cavalier tweak of his head. "Go quick and the animal probably won't even know you're there."

"What's in the pit?" asked Keigh.

"This is the badger pit. I'm sure you've seen one before?" said Christian.

Keigh had. Badgers were vicious little critters that seemed to be perpetually angry. He had once had to kill one that kept digging holes in his father's potato fields. It had taken five arrows before the animal finally stopped thrashing about, trying to snap at anything unwise enough to come close. A badger might not be able to kill a person, but they could certainly bloody up a person's limbs.

"What's the item?" he asked.

"That's what I like to see!" Christian lifted his hands as if presenting Keigh to the group for the first time. "See here, boys? This is what courage looks like! First, he stands up for his friend, now he accepts the challenge of initiation!"

He approached the edge of the pit where Keigh stood. "The item doesn't matter. Anything will do."

"Stop!" Tarin yelled. "That's enough, Christian! Keigh is not doing your stupid test." Tarin grabbed Keigh's elbow and made to march him back out of the zoo.

Keigh shrugged off his grip. "Tarin, it's fine! I can do it! I'm not scared of a badger."

"Keigh, it's not what you think! It's—"

"It's time you stand back, Tarin!" Christian bellowed. "Keigh obviously has more backbone than you."

Christian took another step toward Keigh, only to have Tarin step between them. "He's not going into the pit. I won't let you do this."

Keigh shoved Tarin out of the way. Why was he so insistent that Keigh be kept out of anything that could earn him respect? And to act like he was saving him? Keigh didn't need his friend to coddle him. He needed Tarin to finally respect him as an equal.

"Enough, Tarin! I don't need you to help me! I've got this, just like every other scrap I've ever been in. I'm not as weak as you think." Keigh stared unblinking into his friend's eyes.

Tarin's lips tightened, then he took a step toward Keigh and whispered, "It's a trick, Keigh. They're trying to make a fool of you."

"You're the only one embarrassing me right now. Stand aside and have some faith in me for once," Keigh growled through gritted teeth, earning a few heckles from the men at Tarin's expense.

"I won't let you kill yourself trying to prove something to these idiots."

"Idiots, are we?" Christian chimed in menacingly. He began to pace slowly toward Tarin. "You know, boys, come to think of it...I don't remember Tarin completing his initiation." He stuck a finger in Tarin's chest, backing him toward the pit.

Keigh noticed that Deacon now looked worried for the first time. Anything Deacon thought had gone too far was definitely something Keigh wasn't comfortable with. But before he knew it, Christian had seized the front of Tarin's tunic and drove him over the edge, into the pit.

"There's your item," Christian smirked. "Better go get him before the badgers do."

The men roared their approval and clambered to the edge to watch the show.

When Keigh finally recovered from the shock, he swung at Christian, trying with all his might to blacken one of the blue eyes in the man's pompous face.

Christian deftly avoided the blow. "Tut, tut, tut...Control yourself, young man. Won't do you any good to waste your energy up here when your friend needs you down there."

He pointed over the edge to where Tarin lay, groaning in the dirt where he had fallen. Keigh quickly searched for any sign of the small predators making their way toward his friend—but what he saw was worse than he feared.

Two badgers with black-and-white faces and shaggy silver coats were creeping cautiously toward the new arrival in their pit. Keigh was relieved the king only had two of them, but to his dismay, they were not two of the bread loaf–sized creatures he was used to seeing in Eden.

They were the size of black bears.

"They'll kill him!" roared Keigh.

"Guess you had better stop them, then." Christian nodded to the farthest badger, which had increased its speed. "After all, what's a badger to a *bear?*" He jabbed a finger at Keigh and grinned the same deadly grin of flawless white teeth the assassin had just before attacking.

Keigh's mind scrambled frantically, trying to find a way to distract the badgers before they got to Tarin. Looking around, he saw nothing he could throw at the animals. For a second he considered trying to throw Christian over the edge, but dismissed the thought. Tarin didn't need three threats in the pit with him.

I need a weapon, he thought as the badgers closed in on his friend. The one closest to Tarin let out a raspy growl that grated against Keigh's nerves. He had to act, and he had to act now.

I'm the weapon. He remembered Braddock telling him he could use his powers in combat, and if this didn't qualify as combat, then he would answer for it later—but right now, he needed to save his friend.

Keigh grabbed the wrists of the two men closest to him. They tried to shake him off, but the flow of energy had already begun. Energy rushed into Keigh like it hadn't done since catching Deacon's fist in Bjorn, filling his body with liquid fire and unmatched strength. As the two men fainted, he released his grip and dove over the edge of the pit.

Keigh landed chest down on the closest badger's back. He looped an arm around its neck, thinking he could bring the beast into submission by choking off its airway the same way he would in a wrestling match with one of his friends. But this wasn't a wrestling match, and this wasn't one of his friends. Immediately the badger dropped to the ground; reaching back with its two forepaws, it dug its claws into Keigh's back and threw him ten feet forward.

Keigh scrambled to his feet, his back burning where the badgers claws had raked deep furrows in his flesh. He gritted his teeth, determined to block out the pain. He had the energy of three men and strength to match. He had never felt this much power. Even his mind was sharper than the usual uptick in clarity he experienced when pulling energy from Braddock.

Both badgers had fixed their attention on him, but neither made a move toward him. *I've got to lead them away from Tarin, then I can worry about taking them out.*

He took one step toward the furthest badger—and jumped just in time as the badger snarled and swiped a paw the size of a sparring shield through the air where he had just been. Keigh landed behind the badger and stumbled. Even with his increased strength, the sensation of landing from eight feet in the air was still new.

Chase me! Forget about him and chase me! His plea never left the inside of his head, but nevertheless, it worked. Both badgers rolled back their lips, exposing white fangs the length of hunting knives. With guttural growls, they tore after him.

He was faster and nimbler with the extra energy in his limbs, but the badgers were still formidable predators. If the small ones could catch and kill rabbits, these ones were sure to be able to catch a human, no matter how swift.

Keigh ripped around a boulder, trying to keep as many obstacles in the animals' path as he could. His eyes scanned for anything he could use as a weapon. He found nothing. Everything was either too large or too small.

Still running, he grabbed hold of a small tree to aid his change of direction. Halfway through his turn, he felt the tree give way ever so slightly.

His hands moved nearly before his mind knew what they were doing. Grasping the trunk with both hands, he pulled up, lifting the tree's entire root ball out of the ground. Then, in the same fluid movement, he swung the ball of dirt and roots at the lead badger's head.

The root ball exploded in a burst of dirt and rocks, sending the first badger flying to the side, where it collided with the wall of the enclosure and lay limp on the ground.

Keigh's strength and energy was fading at a prodigious rate. He was still stronger than normal, but pulling and swinging the tree had used up much of the energy he had taken from the two men. The tree felt heavy in his hands now, partly because of his decreased strength and partly because it had wrapped its roots around a rock the size of a human head, giving Keigh a weapon that resembled a bushy-ended mace.

He squared off with the second badger. *I need more strength.* His eyes darted to Tarin, who was beginning to come to. Keigh shook his head, dismissing the idea. He wished he could get his hands on Christian.

He looked up at the canes who had conspired to trap them. He expected to see faces smug with confidence, gloating over their prey, but they weren't. If anything, they looked terrified. He knew they weren't worried about his or Tarin's life, so the only explanation was that they were scared of him.

Good. Be afraid.

An idea struck him. Throwing the tree at the remaining badger, he turned and ran to where the body of the first lay crumpled against the wall. Diving onto the creature, he began to dig his hands into its thick fur.

It didn't take long for the second badger to recover from the shock of having a tree thrown at it and it was now bearing down on him.

Keigh's fingers dug even deeper into the badger's fur. Still, he couldn't find the skin he needed.

Time was up. He pulled his hands back from their desperate search for skin and raised them to defend himself from the fast-approaching predator.

The badger stopped five feet in front of him. Baring its fangs, it unleashed another demonic growl. Keigh stood, preparing to try to grab the animal by the jaw. Perhaps he could get his thumbs into its eyes or snout and deter it enough to get it to leave him alone.

Right as he saw the badger gather itself to lunge, a rock struck the animal in the side of the head.

"Over here!" yelled Tarin in a voice slurred enough to tell Keigh his friend was not all there. Tarin's ruse had worked, however, and the badger now turned its attention to its new threat.

Quickly, Keigh dropped back to his knees next to the first badger. "Please, please, please, please work!" He placed his palm flat on the underside of its paw. *Tarin needs help!*

The trickle of energy started slow, then came in greater and greater currents. He pulled as much as he could in the few seconds he had, then sprang after the animal stalking toward his friend. The badger contained shockingly potent energy. Even though Keigh had pulled for only half as long as it took him to drain the men, he felt as though he had gained as much energy, if not more than he had in his first pull.

He caught up to the badger just as it reached striking distance of Tarin. Grabbing the animal by the neck and back, he turned on his heel and began to spin like a discus thrower. On his second rotation he released the badger, sending it flying up out of the pit and into the terrified canes. The men's screams mixed with the rasp of the badger's yowl.

Keigh allowed himself a smile as he imagined the creature chasing after Christian. Then he turned his attention to Tarin. "You okay?"

Tarin blinked repeatedly. "Did you just throw a badger...into the sky?" He wobbled and sat down in the grass.

A chuckle escaped Keigh at the absurdity of what had just happened. "Yeah...I guess I did."

"Oh." Tarin rubbed his head. "Thought you might have; I just wasn't sure." He squeezed his eyes shut. "I don't feel too good."

"Don't worry, bud. We'll get you back to your bed right away."

"What about the others?" asked Tarin, still slurring his words.

Keigh could still hear the men shouting and the growls of the angry badger. "I think they'll be up for a bit longer still," he said, smirking. "For now, let's just worry about getting ourselves out of here."

The walls of the enclosure had been constructed to keep large, dangerous animals in. Getting out would be a trick, and the prospect of waiting until morning to be rescued by one of the zoo's attendants was too humiliating to consider. Keigh paced the confines of the pit, looking around for anything he could climb or lean up against the wall. Stooping, he picked up the tree he had used to strike the first badger in the head. Leaning it against a boulder in the center of the pit, he tested his weight on it. The tree was much too thin and springy to be of any use.

As he hopped back to the ground, a jolt of pain racked his back. The adrenaline of the fight was wearing off and the deep lacerations the badger had left began to assail him with fresh waves of agony.

While the pain in his back occupied most of the attention of his senses, he was also able to sense something else: the faint tingle of lingering power. Throwing the badger out of the pit had consumed a lot of the energy he had pulled from its unconscious mate...but not all. There was still some left.

He strode over to the limp beast. Placing his palm on the pad of the badger's paw again, he attempted to pull the energy, but no matter what he focused on, he couldn't seem to extract more than the smallest trickle. After a few minutes, he abandoned the effort. *What I have will have to be enough.*

Returning to the wall they had come over to enter the pit, he waved at Tarin to join him. Tarin stared up at the rim fifteen feet above them.

"I'm going to boost you up there. Do you think you can pull yourself out if you can get your hands on the ledge?"

Tarin grimaced. "My brain hurts, but my arms are fine."

"Great," said Keigh. "Then you'll have to find something to pull me out with once you're up there."

Tarin nodded and gestured for Keigh to give him a foothold. Keigh cupped his hands and let Tarin step into them. He lifted Tarin's foot chest-high, then, rolling his wrists, he rotated his elbows under his forearms. Tapping into the energy lying latent in his muscles, he pressed Tarin up over his head.

"Got it!" yelled Tarin.

The weight of Keigh's tall, muscular friend left his hands as Tarin pulled himself up and over the edge, disappearing from sight.

"Go find something before this badger wakes up again!" Keigh called after him.

Content that he now had help on the way, he slumped down at the base of the wall, exhausted. Lifting Tarin had been a heavier task than throwing the badger. Though the badger looked as big as a black bear, it must have been predominantly fur; Tarin, however, was mostly muscle.

Just as he was beginning to grow concerned that Tarin had failed to find anything to pull him out with, a rope flung over the edge, its end dangling a foot off the ground.

"'Bout time!" Keigh called out good-naturedly, taking hold of the rope. "Help pull me up. I don't think I can pull my own weight right now." The gouges in his back had tightened unbearably.

Without a word, his friend began to pull him up out of the pit. It was all Keigh could do to hold his own weight. When his hands reached the ledge, he shouted for Tarin to stop pulling so he could transfer his grip from the rope. But the ledge proved harder to grasp, and as soon as he tried to pull himself up, his hands slipped. His stomach lurched as his fingertips left the anchor of the wall, grasping at air.

Before he had even fallen an inch, a hand reached out and grabbed his wrist.

"Thank you," he wheezed gratefully, but whatever relief he initially felt at being saved disappeared as he looked up into the face of not Tarin, but Christian.

Christian pulled him unceremoniously over the edge, letting him tumble in a heap on the cold stone walkway. Rolling onto his belly, Keigh assessed the scene. He was surrounded by the six older canes he had come in with, all of whom had tears and rips in their clothing; several were bleeding. Tarin and Deacon were nowhere to be seen. Looking through the canes' legs, he saw the bloody, matted fur of the badger's lifeless body lying on the walkway a dozen yards away.

"Look what you've done, you worthless whelp!" Christian loomed over him, bearing a fresh, deep cut across his left cheek.

"Personally, I'm impressed," Keigh chuckled. He knew his situation was dire, but he couldn't help himself.

"Impressed? You should have known the badger was no match for six armed canes," spat Christian.

"No, no…obviously I knew *that*." Keigh groaned and pushed himself up to a seated position. "I'm impressed because I didn't think you could get any uglier, but I see I've underestimated you."

Keigh didn't have time to enjoy the outrage on Christian's face before a foot kicked him in the ribs. He curled up in a ball, clenching the spot.

"If you're going to kill me, you had better do it quick." Normally he wouldn't have goaded anyone into killing him, but he had just seen something his attackers had yet to notice. A glint of gold in the darkness. A ray of hope.

The King of Eden was approaching!

With his rescue imminent, Keigh continued to throw verbal jabs at his assailants. It was all he had; there was no fight left in his limbs.

"We won't be killing you, Anders," Christian sneered—then, bending low, he said in a whisper, "We just want to make sure you remember to stay in your proper place." He rejoined the ring of canes surrounding Keigh. "Your victories have come to an end. If you so much as land another blow on one of us in the duels, we will repeat this lesson again." Christian nodded at the men. They nodded back. Stepping toward Keigh, Christian said, "Do try to learn quickly. A dog that can't be taught obedience will eventually have to be put down."

Keigh chanced a glance back to where he had seen the king approaching. The king had stopped in the shadows no more than twenty feet away.

Why did he stop? What is he waiting for? Act now! Protect me!

Christian flicked his fingers at Keigh, signaling for the other canes to begin the beating. "Don't touch his face. No wounds that his clothing won't cover."

Keigh fixed his eyes on his unmoving king. The monarch looked at him through the empty eyes of his mask, his visage stoic as ever.

He isn't going to stop them.

Keigh's heart began to race as reality set in. A shiver of fear wracked his body. "Please, Christian, don't—"

His plea was cut short as a fist struck him in the gut, knocking the wind out of him. It was followed by a stomp on his thigh. Then a kick to the ribs.

He curled up in a ball, covering the back of his head with his hands. He cried out to the king for help as the men closed in on him, raining down kicks and punches in rapid succession. *Why is this happening to me? Why is no one helping me? Does nobody care?*

He cried out for Tarin, for Braddock, even for Deacon. But there was no answer. He cried for help until he just began to cry. Strands of spit flung from his mouth as kick after kick struck him in the gut. Tears muddied on his face as he rolled and writhed on the ground, trying to shield himself from the next hit. Blow after blow landed on his body. None so hard as to break bones. The men weren't trying to kill him. This beating was to send a message. One he was meant to survive and carry with him.

You don't belong here, he thought, sobbing bitterly as the lesson sank in. *You should have stayed at home in the dirt.*

The worst part wasn't the pain of the kicks and punches. It wasn't the cuts to his back. It wasn't Tarin abandoning him again. It wasn't even being hated by the men he had wanted to impress earlier that evening. He had survived those things before. It was the crushing reality of his worthlessness. The king was there. Doing nothing. He could save Keigh at any moment with a single word. Was he worth so little? Could not a single word be uttered on his behalf?

He could have withstood this beating, or any other, as long as he knew the king was on his side. His whole life he had believed that if the king only knew his hurts, his family's troubles, he would have delivered them. For a few glorious weeks he had allowed himself to believe that he had the king's favor. The ruler had even said as much to him...Now, seeing the king do nothing to aid his suffering, Keigh knew: he had broken the rules of the Capital to win the favor of the men beating him, and in so doing, had lost the favor of the king.

What's wrong with me? The familiar question was back, strong as ever, for the first time in months. *Why am I so desperate to belong with these men? Why did I break the rules again? Why?*

Right as he was about to unfurl and surrender himself to his attackers, a roar shattered the night.

The men surrounding him stopped their attacks and looked up. Seconds later, Keigh felt the familiar tremors in the ground that signaled one thing: a red bear was running.

There was a flash of light in the darkness. Soon it showed itself to be the sword of Braddock Fortier, gleaming in the moonlight as the retired cane sprinted toward the group, Mace lumbering behind him. The white scars on the bear's face glowed ominously in the light of the moon.

"Time to go, boys!" shouted Christian.

The canes bolted in every direction. Only Christian paused to give Keigh one last kick to the gashes on his back.

"See you in the arena," he hissed before disappearing into the shadows.

Keigh rolled over, looking for the king. There had to be an explanation. Why abandon him? Why come so close only to hold back at the last moment? But the king too had disappeared into the night.

A moment later Braddock was at his side, kneeling next to him. Mace loomed over his body like a massive furry dome, her eyes and nose working frantically to trace Keigh's attackers.

"We need to get you to a healer," said Braddock.

Keigh didn't have it in him to respond. He didn't have it in him to heal. He just wanted it to be over. The pain was too much. The pain of his body, the pain of being a thrall, the pain of the canes' rejection, the pain of his king's abandonment. All he had left was pain.

He looked into Braddock's face and, for a moment, saw the face of his father. Braddock wore the same expression of loving protection his father had worn the day Keigh had been tied to the whipping post.

The knowledge that he had not been completely abandoned burrowed into his heart like a needle on a thread, stitching together the last shreds of hope he had left.

I'm not alone, he thought, then allowed himself to quit fighting.

CHAPTER 24

THE ANSWER

23-55-9

The following morning Keigh's body began to look like it felt. Brown and yellow bruises covered him from his knees to his shoulders like dirty grease splotches on water. Every breath pained him, and the bed that had once been so comfortable was now barely tolerable. So far as he could tell, nothing was broken inside of him. The men had followed Christian's orders. All his injuries were superficial, but they had wounded nearly every inch of his surface.

He must have passed out after Braddock found him, because when he awoke in his bed, his back had been stitched together where the badger had raked him with its claws. As bad as his beating had been, the badger had still dealt him the worst wound.

Braddock came into his room to check on him, informing him that he would be excused from any physical testing and duels for the next two weeks. Mannie visited shortly after. He was as upset as Keigh had ever seen him, and for the first time, Keigh saw his usually jovial friend cry. Mannie's concern for him was strangely comforting; it did nothing to soothe his cuts and bruises, but the damage done to his heart was quieted a bit, knowing that there was someone who hurt with him and for him.

He asked Mannie not to tell Sanya, Bard, Tabitha, or any of the other thralls of the attack. He had no reason to be embarrassed. Six fully minted canes had ambushed him and won; nobody would have fared better. Yet somehow, he had become a symbol to them, a symbol of hope, and seeing him forcibly put back in his place like this would only serve to snuff out that flame.

Keigh didn't dare ask Mannie about the king. He knew the king had Mannie's absolute loyalty. Hearing his friend defend him would only serve to anger Keigh and tarnish his feeling of solidarity with the messenger.

*

Later there was a knock on his door, and Bard's voice sounded, asking to enter. Keigh tucked his arms under the covers so that only his face was visible before beckoning him in.

Bard had brought him his breakfast and a list of questions from Tabitha and Sanya, who were quite worried he had been sent home from the Refining and not told them goodbye. Keigh explained that he was quite ill and wouldn't be back down to the mess hall for at least a week. Bard seemed to accept the story without suspicion. He wished Keigh a swift recovery and bid him farewell without any further questions.

Tarin and Deacon didn't make an appearance till later that night. The boys brought his dinner and made themselves at home in two of the plush armchairs for the evening. Apparently, Braddock hadn't shared any of the details of what happened after they had left; unlike Bard, they did have a lot of questions. Keigh told them he was just recovering from his badger wounds—an excuse Deacon accepted, since he had fled the moment the badger flew over the wall. Tarin, however, had run for help as soon as the canes stopped him from lowering a rope down to Keigh, so he wanted to know how Keigh had gotten out.

The other question Tarin wanted answered was how Keigh had thrown the badger out of the pit and then, later, pressed him up over his head like a sack of potatoes. Keigh told him it must have been a combination of adrenaline and bloodlust, explaining that the badgers were mostly just fur anyway.

To his surprise, Deacon backed up his explanation. Keigh was under no illusion that Deacon Wulf had any interest in protecting him. In fact, he was sure Deacon knew exactly what he was by now. How could he not? Keigh had drained Deacon to prevent him from bullying Beaudy, then last night he had left two of the canes unconscious before diving into a pit of badgers and throwing one of the creatures fifteen feet in the air! No, he suspected it was pride that kept Deacon quiet. To admit Keigh was a potent was to admit that Keigh had something that he did not, a fact no Wulf would ever admit publicly.

After their initial grilling of Keigh, the two recounted the day's duels to him in hilarious detail. Keigh was especially glad to hear that Christian had been paired with Deacon that day and that Deacon had won in less than a minute. He might not like Deacon, but at least Deacon had never organized a group of men to beat him to a pulp.

*

The week passed in much the same way. Braddock and Mannie visited sporadically, Bard brought him meals and warm wishes from the other thralls, and Tarin and Deacon came by in the evenings to recap the day's events with him.

It took Keigh three days to be able to write Misselli. She would tell him to come back home if she knew what had happened. She would tell him that he didn't need to be a cane, that he could have a better life in Bjorn with her and his family...but he didn't want to hear any of that, especially now that he might actually be tempted to believe it. He was in a vulnerable place, and he wasn't going to let her exploit it. He would fight through. It wasn't over for him. This was only a setback, something to get over and through. Misselli would have him quit, but she would see—everyone would see: he wasn't going to be a nobody.

When he finally did write, he kept it short and positive.

Dear Misselli,

The Refining continues to go well. I am still undefeated in my duels and leading everyone in points. The people here love me, and I can't go anywhere without people recognizing me. Everything seems to be going just how I hoped. I think you would be proud if you could see me now. Wish you were here. I do miss you.

Keigh

Misselli would be upset with how short his letter was, but he promised himself he would make up for it with an extra-long letter when he was feeling better. For now, she would just have to be happy hearing from him at all.

After a week, his body finally felt good enough to begin walking around his room. But half the time when he sat up to work his joints, there was a pressure, an insurmountable weight in his chest, holding him down, refusing to let him move. His heart still ached with rejection. His whole life he had wanted to be a cane, but nearly every cane he had met had deemed him unworthy. He used to believe it was just because he was a thrall that people looked down on him, that if he could get free of that title, people would accept him. But the canes who'd beaten him had no idea he was a thrall. It was him they had rejected, not his class or station. Not a thrall, just a nobody they could abuse and cast aside.

Mannie suggested he start taking longer walks into the city to help take his mind off things and speed his recovery, but it was the middle of the second week before he felt up to that. When he finally did summon the courage to venture out, he knew exactly where he wanted to go.

By now he had reread Misselli's last letter dozens of times. Addy wanted him to go to Orvyn's helmet and try to lift it. He wasn't feeling great, but still, how heavy could a helmet be? Assuming it *was* the mythical helm of Eden's founder Addy had once tried to convince him was real. It could be the name of a building or some other point of interest for all he knew. She had never set foot in the Capital, but Keigh didn't doubt she knew more of its secrets than he did. All her reading had left her with a vast amount of knowledge—knowledge that was mostly useless in Bjorn, but invaluable in Sentinel. He would have loved to have her with him today.

Leaving the barracks, he entered the bustling streets. Hobbled by his injuries, he had the odd sensation of feeling as though the world was in double time, moving unnaturally fast around him. Even aged nobles in their bright robes and walking canes seemed to zoom by him as he walked straight-legged down the cobblestone street, feeling as rigid as the countless marble statues that adorned the gardens and fountains of the public works sector. Many people recognized him and stopped to tell him how they had missed him in the arena. Their encouragement and well wishes helped soothe some of his feelings of rejection. Even if they weren't the warriors he longed to belong to, their acceptance reminded him he wasn't altogether unwanted in Sentinel.

It didn't take long for Keigh to find someone who knew where to find Orvyn's helmet. In fact, it seemed like everyone knew, but it wasn't until the third person he asked that he found someone willing to show him. The kind stranger led him back to a narrow alleyway in a low-traffic area of the public works sector. The buildings there were largely windowless and void of any artistic stylings. Keigh thought it may have been the least impressive area of the Capital he had seen yet.

The stranger pointed to an open doorway set into the side of one of the buildings, wished him good luck, then departed, leaving him alone in the eerie stillness of the vacant alley.

He approached the arched doorway, shuffling stiffly through the shadows. Beyond the dark doorway, a long set of stone stairs led down into the ground. The smell of damp earth hung thick in the air. He groaned. Why did there have to be stairs?

Gritting his teeth, he began to lower himself down the steps, one by painful one, deeper into the darkness. A hundred feet later, he still hadn't heard a sound or felt the slightest stir in the air, but it was there that he got his first glimpse of a light. His hands ran along the clammy stone walls as he delved deeper underground.

At the bottom was a short, flat stretch of hallway, tiled in beautiful mosaic patterns of white, gold, and blue. Following it, he entered a circular domed room twice as tall as it was wide, surrounded by fluted pillars of veined marble. A single luminous shaft of sunlight pierced the darkness, descending from a hole in the ceiling to fall upon a polished bronze altar. The altar was in the shape of a man stripped of his clothing, muscles tensed as he struggled to bear the weight of the plate resting on his shoulders.

Keigh's breath stopped in his chest as he beheld the item atop the plate. An open-faced golden helmet with elegant jaw plates and a fierce, pointed nose guard shone brilliantly in the beam of sunlight. Its entire surface was etched with gracefully flowing vines and flowers, detail of which Keigh had never seen the like. Atop the helm was a short plume of white hair, not unlike the red plumes of the canes' helmets.

He approached the altar reverently. Could this really be the helmet of King Orvyn? Were the legends true? Was there really a set of armor out there that had been imbued with magic? Even if the helmet *wasn't* magic, it was still the most beautiful piece of military equipment he had ever seen.

Keigh looked around for a guard. Seeing none, he placed his hands on either side of the altar. There was writing on the plate in front of the helmet:

To receive this helm

Bring only your shield

And ask the question

Of the answer.

The question of the answer? Keigh wasn't sure what that was supposed to mean, but he didn't have a shield anyway, so he would have to figure that out first. For now, Addy wanted him to try to lift it. He walked around the altar, looking for places where the helmet might be tied down or otherwise connected to the plate. When he found no such anchors, he took a deep breath and placed his hands on either side of the helmet.

"Okay, Addy, here goes nothing."

He began lifting, slowly. The helmet rose an inch off the table with no more difficulty than any other helmet. Keigh peeked underneath to make sure there were no cords or chains attaching it to the altar. When he saw that there were none, he smiled to himself. *Magic helmet! A children's bedtime story was all that was.*

He continued to raise the helmet cautiously. While beautiful beyond compare, it was just a normal helmet—or so he thought. When it reached seven inches off the altar, it slammed back down into its original resting place with such force that he surely would have lost a finger if his hands had been under it. The clang of gold striking bronze echoed through the chamber.

Keigh chewed on the inside of his cheek. There was no such thing as magic; there had to be a trick. Even the stranger's gun, the one piece of magic he'd thought he had seen, had been easily explained by someone who knew information he didn't. He was just missing a piece of information, and if he could figure it out, he would be able to lift the helmet.

For the next ten minutes Keigh tried everything he could think of. He tried sliding the helmet off the side of the altar rather than picking it up; he tried wrapping his hands in his shirt to avoid directly touching it; he tried prying it off with an old extinguished torch handle he found. Every time, the result was the same. The helmet slammed home with supernatural force, leaving his ears ringing with the sound of clashing metal.

Right as he was winding up to donkey-kick the helmet off the altar, a voice in the darkness stopped him.

"That won't work."

The voice was musical and warm. A voice he had heard before.

The voice of the king.

You, he thought, glaring into the darkness. The king's colossal frame stepped out of the shadows just far enough for the light in the center of the room to glitter off the gold of his helm and the filigree on his chest.

"Have you not read the instructions written on the altar?" the king asked, his tone more curious than accusatory.

"I have," Keigh answered curtly. How could the king address him so casually? As if he'd seen nothing of his beating!

The king paused. "What troubles you? Surely you didn't hope to achieve what no other before you has ever achieved in donning the Helmet of Orvyn."

"I don't need the helmet. I can get another one." Keigh kept his eyes set on the king. The ruler of Eden could hide from a fight, but Keigh wasn't about to.

"Of course you could," the king conceded kindly, dismissing his abrasive tone. "But I can tell you, only this helmet will protect its wearer from death."

"Death? All death? That's not possible." Keigh crossed his arms, mad at himself for having allowed his curiosity to override his anger.

"It shouldn't be, I agree, yet it is." The king took another step toward the light.

"Everyone dies, though."

"Indeed they do, though it would appear I haven't." His helm, which had been facing the altar, turned to look directly at Keigh. "And I should say, that's saying something. Over two hundred years I've walked the earth. Fear not, however; I'm still as fit for battle as ever."

Keigh could hear the smile in the king's voice, yet neither that nor the revelation of his unbelievable age could shake Keigh from his bitterness. "If you're so invincible, why didn't you rescue me the other night? Huh?" he shouted, pointing an accusatory finger at the king's unfeeling mask. "Why did you just stand there and do nothing?"

"Ah...thank you," said the king, his voice still smooth as honey.

"For what?"

"For finally answering my question, of course."

"At least one of us is answering questions," Keigh muttered under his breath, crossing his arms again.

"I don't owe you anything," the king stated. "Was it so long ago that you felt like you owed me? And now, you feel I owe you something more?"

"No...I don't know."

Keigh hoped the king hadn't sensed the crack in his confidence. He remembered well the two hundred justicia in gold the ruler had paid out for him and to him. He had been so good to Keigh. But it was his former kindness that drove the knife of his abandonment so deep into Keigh's heart. The king had lifted him to peaks of joy and hope he had never known, just to drop him from those lofty heights and watch him break on the unforgiving rocks below. Why be so kind just to turn around and let him be crushed?

Keigh shrugged. "I just feel like you could have helped me. I would have stepped in if I saw someone getting picked on."

"I know you would have," said the king, his voice returning to its former positive hum. "I was privileged enough to see you do exactly that when I visited Bjorn." His golden head nodded slowly. "I was very proud of you that day. I am still very proud of you."

"Then why didn't you rescue me?" Keigh shouted, his voice heavy with tears. "You could have stopped those men before they ever hurt me!"

For a moment, the echoes of Keigh's words reverberated around the room. When it was silent again, the king answered. "I can't tell you why, only that it was for your good that I didn't."

"My good?" blurted Keigh, aggressively wiping a tear from his cheek, almost mad enough to laugh. "How can getting beat up possibly be for my good?"

"Do you trust me?"

This time Keigh did laugh. "Trust you?" he shouted indignantly. "How can I? You had a clear chance to rescue me, and you didn't! All you had to do was speak one word!" he sobbed, tears flowing freely now. "Was I not worth *one word* to you?"

There was a long pause as Keigh waited in silence for the king to answer him. He thought he heard the king sniff from behind his mask before saying, "Sometimes what we need rescuing from isn't the danger we see, but the one we are blind to."

"Enough with the riddles!"

"Then trust me." His calm voice cut through the echoes of Keigh's shouting.

"Trust you to what? Run from the fight? Leave me alone when I need you most?"

"Trust me to pick the right fight." The king stood tall, unresponsive to Keigh's taunts. "You're in more fights right now than you are even aware of…" He paused, seemingly weighing whether or not to say more. "And I did not abandon you, Keigh Anders. I was there *with* you. Believe me when I tell you I took no pleasure in witnessing your pain, but I never *once* turned my face from you. It grieved me to watch, and my anger burned hot against your attackers."

"Then do something about it!" Keigh flung his arms wide, racking himself with a fresh wave of aches.

The king remained collected. "I already have. Their sentences will be carried out soon."

"When? How soon?" Keigh demanded hungrily. "I want to watch them suffer."

"Don't!" the king said, raising his voice for the first time. "Do not become like them, reveling in the misery of others. If you do, I promise you the payment for their crimes will not heal you, but only drive you deeper into your anger. Release them to me and you will find yourself released in the process."

"Released from what?" Keigh sniffed. "I'm no prisoner."

"Alas, there's more than one kind of prison, and the bars that hold you now may not be made of iron. But bitterness and hate have ruined more lives than all the dungeons of the world ever could."

"You sound like my father," grumbled Keigh, finally lowering his voice.

A warm chuckle resonated from the king. "More than you know, but it is he who actually sounds like me."

"So, when will they be punished?"

The king shook his head, seemingly disappointed. "Do you want answers, or do you want my word?"

"Both!"

"My word will have to be enough for now," said the king, straightening his shoulders.

"Well, it's not." Keigh shook his head. Why did everyone want to keep him in the dark on everything? He deserved answers.

"You won't feel better until it is." The king walked backward, melting into the shadows. "Trust me, Keigh. I will not fail you. You have my word."

Trust. Why did everyone want him to trust? His mother wanted him to trust. Braddock wanted him to trust. The king wanted him to trust. Trust was the last thing he felt like giving anyone at the moment. At least Braddock and his mother had earned it. He knew them, knew he could rely on them. The king was a myth, a legend, one that now seemed too good to be true. Keigh had idolized him his whole life. *As long as the king lives, Eden cannot be conquered,* went the popular refrain. A phrase once full of hope and strength now seemed bitter and insufficient. Keigh wasn't sure if he could, or *should* trust the ruler. Yet everyone he respected in his life did so implicitly...Why?

"How do you know my dad?" he called, but there was no answer.

Hobbling over to where the king had been standing only a moment before, he searched the shadows. There was no door, not even a hidden entrance to the Centipede, so far as he could tell. He walked the circular stone walls, running his hands across their surface, hoping to find any sign of where the king had exited the room. *You won't hide from me! Not today! Not till you've answered my questions!*

He searched the room obsessively, unwilling to accept that his audience with the king had come to a close before getting the answers he wanted... answers he *needed*...When he finally gave up an hour later, it was clear: the only way in and out of the room was the door through which Keigh had entered. Yet somehow, the king was gone.

CHAPTER 25

No Good Deed Goes
Unpunished

A week and a half after his quarrel with the king, it was finally time for Keigh to return to the duels. He had been meant to return the week prior, but upon inspection of the wounds on his back, Braddock had decided further healing was necessary.

Keigh hadn't objected. It gave him more time to explore the city, and more urgently, to continue to make attempts at lifting Orvyn's helmet. He had even brought a shield with him on each of his subsequent attempts, but it seemed the solution was in the second part of the riddle: *Ask the question of the answer.* Keigh had spent many hours pondering that part, but was no closer to understanding it. He knew his best chance was to ask the king for help—but if King Thiamtaim had made one thing clear, it was that he didn't owe Keigh Anders anything. Besides, it wasn't as if the king had a great track record of answering Keigh's questions anyway. He would earn the helmet on his own, same as every other cane. It was a matter of pride. He would never get credit for the helmet if he didn't find a way to lift it himself.

In addition to the hours he spent being bested by the helmet, he also resumed dance lessons with Tabitha. They were a much-needed reprieve from his frustrations with the helmet, the king, and his own slow healing. Tabitha and the other thralls continued to treat him with kindness, even as the rest of the Refining's canes had essentially shunned him.

Christian and his goons had made the most of the week he had spent lying in bed recovering, sowing resentment among all the nominees toward Keigh, who was now somehow seen as having been given an unfair advantage. Nobody seemed to care that he was the youngest, the poorest, and the least trained of all the nominees. In the narrative Christian had created, he was the king and queen's charity project—a poor boy upon whom the royals could pour undeserved favor for the sake of their own moral superiority.

What Keigh hated most about the new narrative wasn't the resentful looks and bitter cold shoulders he received from the other contestants; he was used to being treated like dirt. What bothered him most was that it actually made sense. Maybe he was just a stray dog the king had brought in to feed table scraps—meant to have a taste of the life other thralls could only dream of, but never meant to truly sit at the table.

Sure, not everything had gone his way, but a large number of unexplainable favors had been granted to him. Most recently, the day he was supposed to return to the duels, he had received another sixty points by his name, essentially giving him points for a win in each of the six duels he had sat out. Why? Not even he knew. Even Tarin, his only remaining friend among the contestants, had been bitter about that particular show of favor.

That morning, as he sat eating his breakfast with Tabitha, it was no blessing when the queen visited the mess hall. Clothed in a resplendent red dress, she made her way straight past the tables of nominees clambering over each other for her attention, and right to Keigh.

"Keigh, my dear. How are you?" she asked, lowering herself gracefully onto the bench next to him. Her guards created a perimeter around her. "My husband has told me all about your ordeal. I wanted you to know you have my support."

Keigh could feel the angry stares of the rest of the men in the room boring into the back of his head. "Um...thank you, Your Grace. You are very kind," said Keigh. While his feelings about the king were fragile at best, Keigh had never had any reason to dislike the queen. She had always been gracious and benevolent toward him. If he had any complaint at all, it was that he could no longer look at her without seeing Deacon's smug face smiling back at him, gloating about their royal resemblance.

"Kindness has nothing to do with it," she said, resting a gentle hand on his forearm. "You *deserve* to be here. I want you to know that." Her lips spread in a knowing smile. "Here. I'm blessing the nominees with some coin from the royal vault today. Everyone will get ten justicia, but I want you to have twenty. For your hardships." She pressed two gold coins into his hand and closed Keigh's fingers around them. "Keep fighting, Keigh." And with that, the queen stood and swept her way around the mess hall, stopping to speak with each of the contestants and giving each of them large gold coins.

Keigh took one of the coins and slid it across the table toward Tabitha, hiding it under his hand. "Here. For the dance lessons."

Tabitha covered his hand with both her own. "It's not necessary. Really, I'm happy to help you," she said, trying to push his hand back across the tablecloth.

Keigh didn't budge. "You've done more to deserve this coin than I have," he said. "I received it freely—why shouldn't I give it freely?" He pulled back his hand, leaving the coin with Tabitha. As always, the smooth touch of her hands on his made his heart ache for the day he would see Misselli again. It seemed like years ago that he had stood alone with her, holding her close to him as the sun set over their homes...over their plans of returning to the way things had once been.

"Thank you, Keigh. You are too generous." Tabitha moved her small treasure onto her lap. She sat staring at it, one hand attempting to cover her grin.

Keigh hadn't felt much when the queen pressed the gold into his palm, but he felt a surge of satisfaction seeing the excitement spill out of his new friend as she held his gift. "Dance tomorrow morning? After breakfast, like usual?"

Tabitha nodded. "Wouldn't miss it."

"Me either," Keigh chuckled. "Misselli isn't even going to recognize me when she sees what you've taught me." He stood up, slowly stretching his new scars. "Wish me luck! My back is still pretty sore."

Tabitha looked up for the first time since taking the coin. "We'll all be there, cheering you on. Always."

Keigh left her tapping her toes excitedly under the table and began his lonely walk to the stadium early. He would need the extra time to stretch and pull some much-needed energy from Braddock.

He stepped out into the street and was immediately confronted by a frigid blast of air that blew his wavy locks in all directions and threatened to take his cloak. It was November, and the temperatures had begun to drop. The brilliant blue skies of autumn were gone, replaced by the cold gray of impending winter. The once radiant white of Sentinel's marble buildings seemed to have taken on the color of the sky, giving the streets a dreary and lonesome feel. Keigh pulled his thin cloak tight and turned his face to the wind, letting it blow his hair back into its proper place.

Not far from the mess hall, he encountered a sight as downcast as the weather. A pathetic-looking figure sat on the edge of the street, shivering in a tattered tunic. The man had one leg and a sign saying he was blind, crippled, and in need of help. A beat-up tin cup sat on the ground in front of him. He appeared to be asleep, despite the violent shivers that racked his body.

The sight struck Keigh as odd, and for a moment he couldn't figure out why. Bjorn had several beggars at any given time, many of whom suffered some sort of physical ailment or disability. Then he realized: this was the first and only beggar he had seen since coming to Sentinel. Until that moment he hadn't even noticed their absence, but now that there was one here in front of him, he stuck out like a sore thumb.

Keigh approached the man and looked in his cup. It was empty. He glanced up and down the street at the many wealthy ables making their way to and fro, wrapped in their thick, luxurious garments. Keigh's jaw clenched, stopping the chattering of his teeth. Surely they could see the poor man, and surely they, more than he, had the means to help him.

Maybe it's a test? he thought. Keigh searched the cold, unforgiving gray street for anyone who might be watching. Seeing no one, and noticing what looked to be an infection above the man's amputated limb, Keigh decided that not even the king was callous enough to subject one of his servants to loss of limb, loss of sight, and what looked to be the start of a nasty infection, just for the sake of testing his nominees. No, this was a real man in need of real help.

He stuck his hand in his pocket, feeling the smooth edges of the gold the queen had just given him. The words his father had spoken to him so long ago, after giving one of Bjorn's beggars half the loaf of bread they had bought for dinner, returned to him: *It is the poor who have the easiest time giving the most, for our pockets empty far quicker.*

Keigh smiled at the memory, missing his dad. Owen Anders was always able to speak hard truths in a way that left you happy to have heard them. He knew what his father would do. Taking a knee in front of the blind man, Keigh pulled the coin out of his pocket and placed it gently in the cup, being careful not to wake him.

Keigh stood slowly to leave, fighting the cramping of his back. He gave one last satisfied look at the gold coin glittering happily in the sad cup and departed again for the stadium. But he didn't make it two steps before the image of the man's violent shivering invaded his mind. Perturbed by his own conscience, he turned on his heel and went back. Keigh rubbed his arms for warmth one last time under his thin cloak, then took off the garment and draped it around the poor man's shoulders.

"There," he said, sniffing back his own runny nose. "That ought to help."

He turned to leave again, only this time, it wasn't his conscience that spoke.

"Food, sir!" the beggar croaked. "Spare some food, fer me achin' belly." He moaned so pitifully it stopped Keigh in his tracks.

I don't have time for this! If I don't get to the stadium soon, I won't be able to get my back loose for my duel. Keigh's fingers balled into tight fists. *Why today? Why now, on my first day back?*

He returned to the poor wretch huddled under his cloak. "If I help you up, can you make it somewhere to buy food?"

The blind man took a second to point his face in the direction of Keigh's voice. "'Fraid not, sir. Can no longer get about on me own, sir. Must rely on the good graces o' me countrymen fer all me needs." He seemed to wither as he spoke the words.

Keigh looked at the man, imagining him once young and able. At one time, this man had probably had dreams like Keigh's own; now some cruel twist of fate had left him blind, lame, and helpless...

Helpless like Keigh had been the night the king abandoned him.

Keigh remembered the hurt of being seen but not helped. The claim he'd made to the king echoed in his mind: *I would have stepped in if I saw someone getting picked on.*

He took a deep breath and noticed the putrid smell of the beggar for the first time. Scrunching his nose, Keigh made up his mind. This man wouldn't be helpless so long as he could help. While no person was picking on the man presently, Keigh was familiar with the bullies of cold, hunger, and abandonment.

He took one last longing look up the street toward the stadium. If he hurried, he could help the man and still get there in time. He wouldn't be early enough to stretch his back like he needed to, but he wouldn't miss his duel. Kneeling next to the man, Keigh slipped an arm around his bony shoulders. "Grab your cup," he reminded him.

The beggar felt around for his cup before his hands found his sole possession and grabbed it off the ground. He looked confused by its unfamiliar weight, but realization of what that weight meant soon flashed across his filthy features. "Did you...Is this—?"

"Ten gold justicia." Keigh grinned, seeing the joy his generosity had bought for the second time that day. "Doesn't matter where it came from; it's yours now." Keigh stood the man up to his one good foot, lending his own body as support in place of the missing limb. "Now, let's get you something to eat."

The two made slow progress back down the street. Keigh wasn't sure if he was allowed to bring the man into the mess hall, but he was going to try.

A painfully slow quarter of an hour later and they had made it back. Just as Keigh was about to open the door, it burst open from the inside. A wave of red cloaks, led by Christian and followed at a distance by Deacon and Tarin, exited the hall, laughing and shoving each other toward the stadium.

Keigh held his breath, hoping the group would be too distracted to notice him standing with the one-legged man like the world's saddest three-legged-race pairing. But his hope was short-lived. Christian's blue eyes found him almost immediately.

He let out his high, weaselly laugh, pointing Keigh out to the group. "Look who it is, boys! Oh, and he's made a new friend!" Christian did a quick impression of a one-legged man stumbling around, adding, "I must admit, it's a step up from the thrallskin trash you usually pal around with." He dropped the derogatory name for Keigh's people like he'd said it a million times. "This one's more in your league at least, Anders! Play your cards right and maybe he'll give you a kiss!"

Christian gave them a mocking wave goodbye as the canes fell about, laughing their way up the street, blowing kisses back at Keigh.

Tarin and Deacon waited a moment before following the group. They didn't appear eager to get in close with Christian again, but neither did they want to be associated with Keigh, especially in his current state.

Tarin just shook his head and said, "You can't set them up like that, man."

Deacon seemed more suspicious than anything, giving Keigh a scowl that was less vicious than his usual glare.

"Sorry about that," Keigh apologized to the man waiting patiently on his arm.

"No sense 'pologizin' fer the mockin' o' fools. S'like 'pologizin' fer the rain fallin'," the beggar explained. "Way I sees it, yeh can either curse the sky or grow yer crops, but only one o' em puts food on yer plate."

"What do you mean?" asked Keigh.

"I means, hard times either grows ya or makes ya bitter. S'up to you!" The man bared his rotted teeth. "Wha' one man calls a storm another calls a blessin'. All hows ya looks at it, I s'pose."

"Okay, friend." Keigh patted the man on the shoulder. "The hunger's officially gone to your head. Let's get you inside."

He pulled open the door and found the man a seat at a clean table, instructing him to wait while he talked to the kitchen workers about feeding him. Sanya was more than happy to accommodate, telling Keigh she would feed the man till he was so full he would have to grow a new leg just so he had somewhere to put it all. Keigh thanked her for her kindness and promised to help with extra kitchen work to make up for the additional work he'd brought them. Stopping by the man, Keigh explained he could stay and eat as much as he wanted, then apologized again for having to leave him all alone.

Keigh raced out of the mess hall toward the stadium as fast as his stiff muscles would let him. He arrived at the entrance at the same time as the rest of the nominees. He pulled up next to Tarin, who seemed to be waiting for Christian's crew to clear the narrow hallway leading into the gathering room.

"What'd you do with Deacon?" Keigh panted, noticing the absence of his rival's usual arrogant aura.

"He peeled off right after we left the mess," said Tarin. "Said he left something in his room." He paused, then grinned. "Starting to like him, huh? Now you miss him when he's gone?"

Keigh snorted. "Not even close," he said, but there was some truth to Tarin's joke. The last two months spent with Deacon had shown him another side of his "better": a human side. Perhaps there was something redeemable there, but Keigh wasn't about to admit that to Tarin.

When he finally entered the gathering room under the stadium, Braddock waved him over to a spot by the wall. "Good to see you back." The old veteran clasped his shoulder. "You ready for this? How's your back?"

"It's fine," Keigh lied, curling his shoulders to stretch his muscles. They protested the movement with a fresh stab of pain.

"Alright, quick, then. We're running out of time." Braddock looked over his shoulder, then rolled his sleeve up and offered his forearm to Keigh. "Let's get you some extra energy."

Keigh reached for his arm, but before he could grab it, a hand slapped his down.

"Not today," Deacon sneered.

"Don't interfere, Wulf." Braddock glared at the young man presuming to tell him what to do.

"Shall I inform my father?" Deacon's lip curled in a distasteful grin. "You know he sups with the king and queen every night now. I imagine they would find it interesting to learn exactly how their little charity project has been able to outperform expectations so consistently."

"There's nothing illegal about being a potent," hissed Braddock, eyes darting around for anyone who might overhear. "Keigh is well within his rights to use his...abilities in the arena."

"Perhaps he is, but I know at least two canes who would be *very* interested to learn how they ended up unconscious the night of your little fight with the badgers. They may feel Keigh...*overreached*." Deacon smirked triumphantly. "I've done some checking; the king's law does not allow potents to pull energy from anyone other than enemy combatants and willing friends." Deacon placed a hand on Keigh's shoulder and dug his thumb into the muscle. "I'm sure the canes involved would consider themselves to be neither to you," he said, before turning to Braddock. "I don't want to have to go down that route. Personally, I would rather beat him in the arena where everyone can witness his downfall, but if you two insist on tipping the scales in your favor, I will see to it that Bjorn's best little escape artist does not escape the just prosecution he deserves. Not this time."

The lines in Braddock's face hardened as he glared at Deacon. "What has Vicerous turned you into?"

Keigh shook his head. "I guess you are who you're raised by."

Deacon looked down his nose at Keigh. "Yes, true. Most unfortunate for you, I'm sure...My father prepared me to win. There is no weapon I won't use to win the Refining. I am the king's heir and no thrall from Bjorn is going to upstage me." He released Keigh's shoulder. "It's not personal—in fact, I would almost consider you a friend after these last two months. Tarin has pleaded your case quite convincingly, but alas, what Tarin doesn't see yet is that those born to rule have no true friends, only greedy beggars trying to pull themselves up by dragging us down." Deacon smiled and patted Keigh on the back. "So, stay down."

With that, he strode away, head held high, like a rooster in a house of hens.

Keigh looked at Braddock, who was seething like a boiling pot trying to keep its lid from blowing off. It was clear Braddock was unaccustomed to being spoken to the way Keigh had grown up being treated by the Wulfs. Keigh still hated nearly everything Deacon or Vicerous said to him, but it gave him an odd sense of pride to know that the years of abuse at their hands had given him thicker skin and a stronger defense to verbal manipulation than even the great Braddock Fortier.

"It's okay," Keigh offered. "I can get by without."

"Are you sure?" asked Braddock, his anger thawing into concern. "I'll vouch to the king himself that what you did was done in self-defense. The charges won't stand."

"Even if they won't, he will still be able to smear my name and discredit any victories I have in the arena." Keigh shook his head and pulled an arm across his chest, stretching his back. "I'll be fine. Even if I duel without your energy, I'll still have one huge advantage in my favor."

"What's that?" Braddock asked, still glaring daggers across the room at Deacon.

Keigh grinned. "I was trained by *the* Braddock Fortier."

The hard lines creasing Braddock's face softened. "I hear you've never beat him, though," he said with a smirk.

Keigh shrugged and switched arms. "Someday I will."

"That will be the day." Braddock sniffed and rolled his sleeve back down. "Good luck, Keigh. Stay safe. Yield if you must. No sense in getting hurt again."

"Thanks," Keigh said, as his mentor departed for the company of the older canes.

Keigh spent the remaining minute of the waiting time stretching the muscles he had hardly used in a month. When the time came to exit, he grabbed his shield and sparring sword from the rack and waited to be escorted out into the arena.

Upon entering, he was excited to see that the colder weather hadn't deterred anyone from attending. The stadium was as full as always and roared louder than ever when he stepped out of the shadows and onto the sands for the first time in almost a month. Slate bore a particularly sour look as he had to wait longer than usual for the crowd to quiet, the section of thralls being the last to die down.

Standing in the center with the others, Keigh scanned the wall, looking at the scores. *No wonder they all hate me,* he thought, seeing the *240* next to his name. He hadn't dueled in three weeks and was still in first place by twenty points. Tarin had two hundred twenty, and Deacon was in fourth with two hundred five.

Taking his seat across the stadium from the red bears, Keigh began to picture his upcoming fight against his faceless opponent. His visualizations were cut short when Slate's voice echoed across the sands, announcing the first duel of the day.

"First duel! We have our first contest between two of the Bears of Bjorn!" The crowd roared as Slate stoked their intrigue with the boys' fan-given title. "Welcome back Keigh Anders as he faces...Deacon Wulf!"

Keigh rose to his feet as the crowd erupted into a renewed frenzy. *Perfect timing.* He grinned with giddy anticipation at the thought of embarrassing Deacon in front of twenty thousand people. *Can't ride on your father's coattails today.*

Squaring up in the center of the arena, Keigh dug his boots into the sand in preparation. Deacon stood loosely across from him, a smug look on his face. Deacon was nothing if not confident, but bravado alone wouldn't be enough to win this duel.

"Good luck," said Keigh as one of the old canes placed an arm down between them.

"*Luck* won't be necessary," sneered Deacon.

Keigh raised his sword to the ready. The old cane threw his arm upward and the trumpet blared.

Keigh wasted no time. Lunging forward, he swung at Deacon's hip.

Deacon parried the blow lazily and smacked Keigh on the forearm with the flat of his blade. "Appears you're a bit out of practice," he scoffed.

Keigh spun quickly, his arm smarting from the hit, and launched a sequence of feints and blows at Deacon's torso—all of which Deacon blocked without so much as a change in facial expression.

"Or maybe you've always been this bad." Deacon smiled, then dove into an offensive of his own.

Keigh struggled to defend himself from the onslaught. Deacon was the fastest swordsman he had ever faced. He was just barely able to keep Deacon's sword from striking him. Keigh felt as though he were fending off a ten-headed rattlesnake, and Deacon swung his blade with such ferocity that Keigh almost wished he *were* facing the snake.

Finally, Deacon relented, breathing heavily. "Fight as long as you want, Anders. The longer the duel, the more impressed everyone will be when I inevitably beat you."

"*Inevitably*...That's a big word for you," Keigh jabbed.

"Never short on jokes, are you? No matter. I'll be the only one laughing soon." Deacon's jet-black hair whipped around as he leapt back at Keigh, stabbing furiously.

Once again, it was all Keigh could do to hold him at bay. He dodged the first two stabs and blocked a cutting blow to his thigh with his shield, then, seeing a gap in Deacon's defense, he struck out in his own offensive.

Deacon blocked the first cut with his shield and the second with his sword. Keigh feigned a spinning swing and came back the other direction, nearly stabbing Deacon's shoulder.

He might be fast, but he can still be tricked. He grinned at the reckless thing he was about to do.

Keigh took two steps back in retreat. Seeing Deacon wasn't immediately pursuing, he dropped his shield to the ground, balancing it on its edge.

"You going to throw your shield again?" Deacon smirked.

"Nope," answered Keigh, then, with a heavy kick, he sent the shield spinning like a giant coin right at Deacon's face.

Deacon ducked and growled as Keigh's shield bounced off his own. By the time Deacon had recovered, it was too late: Keigh was on him, battering him with heavy two-handed blows from his sword. Deacon's only option was to retreat behind his shield. His sword hand couldn't hope to stop the muscle behind Keigh's swings.

Then Keigh's sword lodged in the rim of Deacon's shield. Immediately Deacon seized the advantage. Twisting the shield with all his might, he wrenched the sword out of Keigh's hand, throwing it and the shield to the side.

Deacon grinned savagely as he stalked closer to the now unarmed and unshielded Keigh.

"You're all out of toys, thrallskin." He spat on the ground between them.

Keigh had been considering yielding, but when Deacon used that word, something inside him snapped. There would be no yielding today. Deacon would have to kill him before he would submit.

Keigh growled as he charged his nemesis. The crowd gasped in shock.

Deacon swung heavily at Keigh's unprotected abdomen. Keigh jumped back, avoiding the blade, then dove at Deacon, wrapping his arms around his waist and tackling him to the ground. Keigh was both taller and heavier, enabling him to overwhelm Deacon in a wrestling match.

Keigh was just glad Deacon had not turned his sword over and tried to stab him in the back as they tumbled to the sand. It was what he would have done, but for some reason, Deacon seemed more concerned with escaping Keigh's grasp than winning the fight.

He must be afraid I'll drain him of his energy! Keigh realized as Deacon scrambled onto his belly, tucking his bare wrists underneath him.

Keigh let out a bark of laughter, feeling like a dog who had caught a turtle and just needed to figure out how to get past the shell. He seized the back of Deacon's neck and began the pull of energy.

It had barely begun to flow when Deacon growled and wriggled like a hooked fish, breaking Keigh's hold on his neck. No matter; the small boost in energy was enough for Keigh to reach underneath Deacon and pry the sword from his grip. He debated using the sword before deciding to throw it across the arena behind them.

No sooner had he done so than his unstretched back seized tight, immobilizing him. Sensing the lapse, Deacon flipped over. Keigh narrowly avoided the elbow of his left arm, but was unable to avoid the clenched fist of his right hand. It struck the bottom of his jaw like a hammer, and everything went black.

When he opened his eyes, Deacon was standing over him as Slate announced him the victor of the duel.

Deacon knelt in the sand next to Keigh, letting the cheers of the crowd drown out his words. "Oh, good, you're awake. Thanks for giving me just the weapon I needed to win."

"Wha-what?" Keigh's head throbbed, but he was still pretty sure he hadn't given Deacon a weapon.

Deacon put his clenched fist obnoxiously close to the end of Keigh's nose. "This." Rolling his hand over, he revealed a gold coin in his palm. "I took it out of your new friend's cup. Seems you've forgotten. *I* own you. *You* own nothing! You had no right to give that filth my gold." Deacon stood, closing his fingers back over the coin, concealing it from view.

Keigh gritted his teeth and tried to stand. He made it three hunched-over steps before the spinning of the world swept his feet out from under him.

"Tut tut. When will you learn?" chided Deacon. "The dirt is where you belong. It's what you are." He kicked sand onto Keigh. "You never should have left it."

Deacon brushed the dust off his tunic, as if ridding himself of any last traces of Keigh Anders, then walked away, waving magnanimously to the crowd.

Keigh wanted to stand up. To chase him down. To make him pay—but the world continued to spin relentlessly around him.

Braddock was the one to fetch him. Looping Keigh's arm behind his neck, he stood him up and walked him out of the arena. Keigh wanted to protest, but his inability to stand under his own power or even form coherent sentences was all Braddock needed to take him straight back to the barracks.

Braddock laid him in his bed, ordering him to lie down till morning, then disappeared out the door without another word.

Keigh lay for what seemed like hours, watching the lines in the ceiling swirl about. How could he have lost to Deacon? There was no one other than Christian he had wanted to beat more, and now he would have to wait weeks to duel him again. Deacon, who had blackmailed him into not using his gift, who had called him a thrallskin, who had stolen the coin Keigh gave to the blind man and used it to punch his lights out.

He closed his eyes. Even the darkness seemed to spin. *Tomorrow will be a new day,* he told himself. *It has to be.*

*

The following morning he felt much better—physically, at least. The spins were gone and all he was left with was a massive headache. Emotionally, he was still reeling. The optimism he had felt the morning before seemed a distant memory. Reality was much harsher. Deacon, his lifelong nemesis, had beaten him; the canes had rejected him; and the king had abandoned him when Keigh needed him most, challenging everything he believed about Eden. And to top it all off, he still hadn't heard back from Misselli.

He lamented not writing her a longer letter. She didn't deserve to be cut out just because he was having a hard time in the Capital. Keigh wished he had told her the truth about how terrible things had been the last few weeks. He knew she would try to convince him to come home, but he could weather that. She would also encourage him, remind him who he was and who he could be, and that was worth whatever disagreements they had on what he needed to do next.

A low murmur of laughter went up from the canes as Keigh entered the mess hall for breakfast. Tarin gave him an apologetic look as Andrei Antonov did an exaggerated impression of a man fainting. Deacon was in high spirits, gloating shamelessly as various canes patted him on the back as they walked by.

Walking up behind Tabitha with his plate of food, Keigh whispered, "Can we eat in the ballroom?"

She smiled and gathered up her plate. "Of course."

The two of them walked to the queen's ballroom in silence. When they got there, Keigh slumped against one of the polished walls ingrained with silver floral designs and slid to the floor. His plate clattered as he let go of it, sending bits of food spilling out onto the dancefloor's reflective surface. "I don't know what to do, Tabitha," he moaned.

"About what?" Tabitha set her plate down gently, gliding over to take a seat next to Keigh.

"About anything!" He sighed. "Maybe losing to Deacon has just gotten to me."

"You're still winning, Keigh. So what if you lost yesterday? None of us think less of you for it."

"It's not losing that bothers me, it's how I'm losing..." He pinched the bridge of his nose as his head throbbed again. "I feel like I'm losing myself. Back home I had my family and Misselli to keep me grounded. Now that I'm here, I feel like I'm just another one of the king's zoo animals, put on display for the entertainment of the people...and you want to know the crazy thing? I should reject it, walk away, go home, but you know why I don't?"

Tabitha hugged her knees and shook her head.

"Because deep down, I love it. I love the fame." Keigh pulled at his hair. "I love people recognizing me on the street and cheering my name. I love pitting myself against another person and proving *I'm better!*" He slammed the floor next to him with his fist. "And I know I won't be satisfied until they all admit they aren't better than me."

Tabitha put a hand on his shoulder. "Everyone wants to be seen, Keigh. You're not a bad person for enjoying a moment of recognition," she said softly.

"It's like I have these two dogs fighting inside me." Keigh held out a hand. "One wants to be the greatest cane Eden has ever seen, to have my name written in the history books, to have kids listen to stories of my adventures before they go to sleep at night." He held out his other hand. "The other dog just wants to grow old in the company of *my* people, the people who love me for me." He shook his head slowly, his brain aching with every swing. "The problem is...I only feed the first dog. It's the only one I want to win, even though I know the other dog is there. The only solution is to starve one of them...but I can't. I love them both, even though they will never live in peace with one another."

"Maybe you should try feeding the second dog. See how you feel," said Tabitha, absently tracing a line in the floor with her finger.

"How am I supposed to do that now? My family and Misselli are all back in Bjorn." Keigh placed his palms on his temples, attempting to relieve the mounting pressure. "Besides, Misselli isn't even responding to my letters now." He hung his head, feeling pathetic.

"I'm sure she will write you back, Keigh. If she's anything like you've told me she is, nothing will keep you two apart forever. Just like I won't be separated from my boy forever." Tabitha trailed off, then raised her eyes to look at Keigh. "Have you thought about what you'll say to her when you see her?"

"No, not really," mumbled Keigh.

"Typical boy! You've got to practice!" Tabitha stood up, straightening the front of her dress. "If you really care about this girl, you can't just wing it. You have to have a plan!" she extended a hand down to him, inviting him to join her on the dance floor. "Here...you can practice on me. Pretend I'm Misselli."

Keigh took her hand and stood up. They walked side by side to the center of the room. "No, it's not the same. I can't talk to you like that. It's too... personal."

Tabitha put her hands on her hips. "I won't laugh. Girls don't think less of men who are able to express their feelings. We admire them, and every girl wants one for themselves. I hope someone is out there helping my big lug find his tongue. I've hardly heard a word from him since he left." Tabitha reached out and took Keigh by the hand. "Now, I'm Misselli, and you just asked me to dance. Come now! Speak your heart. We can iron out the rough bits later."

Keigh smiled and took her hand, sweeping her into a slow waltz. "I…I've missed you," he said, feeling foolish.

"Oh yeah? What have you missed about me?" replied Tabitha.

Whether she knew it or not, her tone and phrasing had been so near to how Misselli sounded that Keigh was immediately taken back to the night on the trail between their homes. He was no longer dancing with Tabitha, but with his blonde-haired, blue-eyed best friend.

"I've missed…the way you wrinkle your nose when I say something dumb. I miss your snorts when you laugh. I miss the way you blame Tarin for your farts, knowing how upset it makes him. I miss the way you start to skip like a dork when you see me crest the ridge between our houses…"

Tabitha sighed. "Say more nice things."

"I miss your freckles, and the way they spread across your cheeks in the summer like wildflowers in a meadow. I miss seeing the sun in your hair and how it makes me wonder if the light is shining on you or shining from you. I just miss…you."

Tabitha sighed again. "Hmm…I like that."

"I don't ever want to leave you again. Say the word and I'll stay. I…" Keigh paused to choke down the lump that had formed in his throat. "I…I love you."

"Oh, Keigh! I love you too!" Tabitha smiled and laid her head on his chest as they continued to dance.

A sharp, metallic clink pierced the silence. Keigh whipped around to see where the noise had come from.

Misselli stood trembling at the end of the room.

Her teary eyes searched the floor frantically as she attempted to start several words, before finally whimpering, "I'm sorry."

Before Keigh's pain-addled brain could process what was happening, Misselli turned and fled back past a stunned-looking Sanya. Hands covering her face as she began to sob, she disappeared back through the small secret door to the Centipede she had just entered from.

The metal orb Keigh had given her rolled across the smooth floor where she had dropped it.

"Misselli, wait! It's not what it looks like!" He dropped Tabitha's hand and started to sprint after her. He needed to explain. This was all for her! What was she even doing here? How much had she heard? Why hadn't she told him she was coming?

He had nearly made it to the door when his vision began to blur. The pressure in his head had spiked in the short sprint across the ballroom. His vision narrowed to a pinprick of light. "Misselli! Please…"

His voice trailed off. The light around him faded to black and he felt no more.

CHAPTER 26

THE QUEEN'S COUNCIL

35-2-3

Cato Boman pulled on the long white hairs of his beard as he stared up at the three-hundred-foot walls of Sentinel. Their flawless white surface reflecting in his sky-blue eyes. Ironic, he thought, to build such high, impenetrable walls when the greatest threat to Eden already lived inside them.

It had been over a decade since he had last set foot in the Capital. His post in Bjorn had been his sole concern for nearly sixteen years; in fact, it was his post in Bjorn that brought him back to the Capital today. Odd things, momentous things, were happening. To others they may only be coincidence, but Cato knew prophecy was being fulfilled. First, though, he needed to confer with Braddock.

Cato rode his way up the winding stone roads of the Capital, whistling to himself and smiling down at the pedestrians wrapped tight in their cloaks. The people were as doleful as the weather, but there was no reason for him to be. If the outside of a man determined his inside, no one would be any more predictable than the rain. A terrible way to live, in his opinion. He was happy because he chose to be, and no cold wind was going to change that.

Approaching the barracks, Cato spotted the grizzled veteran and fellow elder of Bjorn, Braddock Fortier, exiting the building at a brisk pace.

"Master Fortier!" Cato called out in his unnaturally powerful voice.

Braddock halted, turning to look back. "Cato? What are you doing here?"

Cato dismounted his gray pony with the help of his gnarled walking staff. The two men strode toward each other and extended their arms, clasping each other on the forearm and pulling each other into a quick embrace.

Withdrawing from Braddock, Cato asked, "How's the boy?"

Braddock glowered. "Not well. He just lost a duel to the Wulf boy."

"A single loss is of no consequence. Why are you so troubled?" Cato could see there was more to his friend's clenched jaw than cold weather.

"Apparently Keigh drained two canes he wasn't fighting, and the Wulf boy figured it out." Braddock's nostrils flared. "Now he's blackmailing Keigh into not using his powers during duels."

"Took the poor boy long enough," Cato snorted, suppressing a laugh. "You would think having the life pulled out of you would be clue enough! Anyway, a Wulf's thoughts on an Anders concern me little. I would know what you think. Do *you* believe the boy to have nefarious purposes in drawing from the canes?"

Braddock shook his head. "Both Tarin and Keigh's accounts of the incident line up. In fact, if Keigh hadn't acted, Tarin could very well be dead. Not to mention the king and queen would have likely had the canes involved executed, too. Now they mercilessly slander the boy, not even realizing he saved all their lives. Their conduct is a disgrace to our order." Braddock looked down the street, over the Capital's lower tiers. "This city is poisonous. The power and wealth here corrupt even the best of Eden."

"Has it corrupted young Master Anders?" Cato asked, tapping his staff pensively on the cobblestones.

Braddock smiled. "Not in the least. You should have seen him today. The queen gave all the nominees ten justicia in gold, but gave Keigh twenty—and you know what he did with it? He gave ten of it to the thrall girl he's befriended here—"

"A girl? The boy's befriended a girl?" Cato interrupted excitedly, then murmured to himself under his breath, *"Eden's son will have a wife..."*

"He has…but I'm not sure there is anything there. They just eat breakfast together. I actually believe he's quite taken with the Labelle girl. Dane and Rita's daughter."

Cato grinned. "*Though who he'll choose remains unclear…*"

Braddock snorted at the old man. "Not everything is prophecy, my friend. Sometimes teens like each other."

Cato's smile remained as broad as ever. "No doubt, but when added to the other signs?"

"Maybe." Braddock shrugged again. "But I still think the connections you've drawn are tenuous."

"It was you who told me his abilities as a potent are greater than anyone you've ever seen, save the king himself, did you not?"

"I did—"

"And do you still believe it?" pressed Cato.

"I do—"

"And we both know he was the first testee to ever best a cane in an agoge duel in Eden's history."

"Vicerous was out of his mind, he couldn't fight—"

"*The first to ever…*" Cato cut him off with another line of the prophecy.

"That could apply to any number of things," Braddock protested. "Firsts happen all the time."

"Beating a cane in an agoge duel is *not* a trivial first," Cato chided.

"No, it's not." Braddock's lips pursed. "I just think it's too soon to say definitively."

Cato grinned. "See, that's why I am here—to get us a little help confirming what we believe." He rested a hand on the warrior's shoulder. "Now, I'm afraid I cut you off. Please, finish telling me about what the boy did this morning."

Closing his eyes, Braddock shook his head. "What *you* believe. I'm still not convinced." He sighed. "Anyway, Keigh gave ten of his justicia to the girl, and then on his way up to the stadium this morning, put the other ten in the cup of a crippled beggar! It wasn't even a test, but you know the king and queen have eyes everywhere. He even walked the poor soul down to the mess hall for food." Braddock clapped his hands together. "No other nominee here has so much as offered to serve the king, let alone a beggar! Keigh may have lost his duel, but I won't be surprised if the king gives him his largest point earning yet. You know how he is. Not to mention the gold payout he could get." Braddock suddenly became downcast. "My only worry is that the boy will actually earn enough to make a serious offer to Vicerous for his family's release."

"You know there is no sum Vicerous will accept. Not after what we did."

"I know. That's what worries me. What if he starts asking questions?"

Cato sniffed, amused. "Even if he asked the right questions, who would talk? For goodness' sake, who *could* talk? There are more questions surrounding the boy than answers. Our king favors him, and we still have no clue as to why Draiden knows his name. Goodness! Not only knows his name, but sent an assassin to kill him!"

Braddock nodded slowly, clearly reluctant to agree.

A loud roar went up from the stadium, drawing the men out of their respective contemplations.

"I'm sorry, friend, but I have duties to attend to back in the arena." Braddock began backpedaling toward the sound of the crowd. "He's on the third floor, in the most northeasterly room," he shouted over the wind. "My room on the second floor has a vacant one next to it you can use. My door has the bear engraved on it; the open room is the one with the lynx head."

Cato waved his appreciation, watching Braddock trot off toward the stadium, its high arches towering above the other massive buildings and monuments of the public works sector.

Cato resumed his cheerful whistling and retied the belt on his robe. *Let's go pay young Master Anders a visit.*

*

Cato knocked gently on the door to the third floor's most northeasterly room. The barracks were empty, all its guests currently in the stadium for the Refining duels.

There was no answer. Cato gently pushed the door open with the tip of his staff. "Master Anders?" he whispered.

Peeking through the gap in the door, he saw the still form of Owen and Sabriya's son sprawled out on top of the bed. Cato opened the door fully and stepped inside, walking quietly to the edge of the bed.

The boy lay open-mouthed, snoring gently. There was a dark spot on his pillow where drool was already pooling. His wavy brown locks, tangled and frizzy from the wind, made it look as though a bird had made a nest of his head.

Can this really be the one? Cato inspected the boy. *How could he be?* He knew Keigh's parents did not align with the prophecy, yet all the other signs pointed to this child lying before him. *I could be interpreting the prophecy wrong. There has to be something I'm not seeing...or maybe I'm just seeing more than everyone else. That must be it. This boy must be the one!* So what if he didn't have all the pieces of the puzzle? If he received the piece he needed from the Queen's Council tomorrow, that would confirm it.

Cato pulled down the sleeves of his robe, took one last look at the sleeping boy, and left the room, closing the door quietly behind him.

*

The next morning, Cato rose early and crutched his way up the quiet hill toward the palace to get in line for an audience with the Queen's Council. They would be the ones to grant him his request. He needed to be the first to arrive. The council only conducted public hearings twice a week and he did not want to have to stay in this den of thieves another three days.

The council chambers were just outside the palace walls near its gate, allowing the councilmen to be called upon by the royals at a moment's notice. The chambers exterior was the same white marble as the rest of the city, though its two central domes were made of copper, turned teal over the years. The building's front was supported by three rows of fluted pillars, forty feet high. Under the first dome, the floors and walls were a dark green marble with delicate white veins.

Entering the rotunda, Cato peered up at the ceiling of the first high dome. There was the mural of Eden's founding. Eden's first king, Orvyn, the father of canes, approaching Ibrahim, the father of ables. Ibrahim following Orvyn from the ruins of the ancient city Portland, up a mighty river inland, then crossing many snowcapped mountain ranges before resting in the valley of Eden. There Ibrahim cleared the valley and planted fields. There Orvyn built the curtain wall with the strength of his might.

From there the mural depicted the king leading many desperate wretches into the valley. Images of Eden lush with crops, its people sleek and happy. Then dark storm clouds hung over a scene of Draiden's rebellion, where the king cast out thousands of men and women who rose up to oppose him. After this, Orvyn created the canes and the bonding of the red bears. The mural showed rows of warriors in their red cloaks and shining adamantines, Orvyn at their head, now donning his golden helm with its white plume and his silver adamantine with its beautiful etching and clawed elbow spike. In his hand he held the sword Verity, alight from within. After that was Orvyn's departure and the emergence of King Thiamtaim, the building of Sentinel, and his marriage to the queen, Vanitas.

The mural stopped there. Eden's history hadn't been updated in decades, though Cato wasn't sure what they would add if they did. Thiamtaim had kept Eden secure and safe in his reign, and peace wasn't a landmark event.

Shuffling across the rotunda, the clack of his staff echoing off the walls, Cato gave his name to the attendant outside the doors to the chamber where the Queen's Council heard from Eden's citizens. Cato took his seat on a bench outside the doors and waited.

When his name was called an hour later, there was a line of twenty people behind him. He thanked the attendant graciously and entered the room under the second copper dome.

The dome was smaller than that of the rotunda, but no less ornate. Half of the room was circled by a terraced cascade of benches behind short pony walls. The main floor remained open; the king's crest of a white dove carrying a pine bough in its beak was tiled into the center of the green marble floor.

All of this faced a high platform where the twelve men of the Queen's Council sat behind a long table of dark red wood.

"Cato Boman," droned a broad-shouldered councilman with short black hair as Cato took his place at the center of the courtroom. "What is your business before the council this morning?"

The men of the council raised their eyes from the papers and scrolls they had before them, noticing the man standing on the king's crest for the first time.

"It can't be!" squeaked a nervous-looking little man on the end.

"Good morning, Elric," Cato greeted him as the rest of the council began to mutter. "I see you're still drinking too much tea."

Elric nodded politely as he attempted to hold a twitching, toothless smile.

"Absaar." The cold, sneering voice of Scipio Slate quieted the murmurs. "What dark cave have you been hiding in?"

"No dark cave for me." Cato met Slate's stare without emotion. "Unlike you, I prefer the bright sunlight of truth."

"Absaar! We had no idea where you went!" Damien Rowe rocked his muscular figure forward in his seat. "How are you, my friend?"

"You may not know where I went, but surely you know *why* I went."

"Yes, we all know why you fled," drawled Slate. "A little too much sunlight for comfort?" The white of his teeth flashed arrogantly as he twirled a quill between his fingers. "Undoubtedly why you saw fit to change your name, too..."

"Luckily for me, the king doesn't deal in gossip," Cato continued, staring at the man who had upended his life.

"And luckily for me, the fine people of Sentinel do," quipped Slate. "The name Absaar is dirt in the Capital. Tell me, did anyone confront you when you entered the city?"

"No, they did not," Cato said. Slate was baiting him, and he knew it. But he hadn't come to the Capital to rehash old grievances. "People have short memories, especially when those memories are unfounded."

"Know that I believed you from the beginning!" Damien barked. A few other council members nodded their agreement.

"I appreciate that, my friend, but a support kept silent is no support at all."

Damien sank back into his seat. "He has leverage on all of us," he whimpered weakly.

"Oh, Damien, don't sulk," Slate jeered. "Play the game or get out, but don't whine that I play it better than you. At least Absaar had the backbone to do what was necessary." Slate turned his attention to Cato. "We may not have agreed on much, old man, but at least I respected you. You were a worthy opponent while you lasted. So, why *are* you here today? I assume not for the warm reunion."

Cato wanted to confront the snake above him, but bit his tongue. Scipio Slate would be seen for who he was one day; for now, the king knew the truth, and that was enough.

"I've come to make a request for one of the king's nominees," said Cato.

"Oh? And why does the nominee not speak for himself?" asked Slate, eyes narrowing.

"The boy does not know of what I ask, nor of any of the reason why I ask," Cato admitted.

"Boy?" asked Elric. "Do you speak of one of the two remaining members of the Consecrate?"

"I...do not." Cato grabbed the edges of his robe, rolling his shoulders back. "I ask after Keigh Anders, of Bjorn."

"The point leader?" asked Damien. "The boy has performed remarkably. He is a favorite of the people."

"The same."

"What would you ask for the boy that he could not ask for himself?" Slate demanded.

Cato tapped the ground with his staff. "I would ask that he be given the opportunity to pair with a red bear."

A flurry of activity ignited among the members of the council as they talked with each other in hushed tones. The councilman closest to Slate leaned over and whispered something in his ear.

"There are only three cubs in the whole of the kingdom, and I'm afraid they all have a long list of worthy canes lined up to pair with them, each of whom have already finished their agoge training."

"Add young Anders to the list," Cato pleaded. "What harm could it cause?"

"None, I suppose." Slate gave his quill a lazy spin before pointing it at Cato. "But I would still know why it is that *you* want this."

Cato swallowed. He had to be careful with his answer. Slate would oppose him if he felt his reasons were too trivial, and may even harm the boy if he thought his reasons were too legitimate. "I believe he is the fulfillment of a long-forgotten minor prophecy. For the sake of my own curiosity, I would see if it could be confirmed."

The council resumed their murmuring.

Slate dropped the quill and leaned back over the table. "Which *minor* prophecy? You wouldn't be speaking of your own drunken ramblings, now, would you?"

"We were all there, Scipio! His words were not his own!" Damien set a clenched fist on the table and stared down the row of men toward Slate. "No drink could have produced such a spectacle! His words *were* prophecy."

"Then you believe the boy to be the heir to the throne?" Slate raised his eyebrows in mock surprise. "That is no minor prediction, Absaar."

The council members sat still and silent as they awaited the answer.

"I do."

At his answer, the whole council broke decorum in a mix of excitement and bitter refusal. Their green robes flapped and flailed as the men threw their arms about in frantic attempts to gain the attention of their peers.

Slate silenced them with a raised hand. "The boy is not a member of the Consecrate. Do we not know his mother and father?"

"We do, but—"

"Then how can it be that you believe him to be the king's heir? Knowing he doesn't meet the one most fundamental requirement?"

"The king does not have to choose his own son! You know the law!" Cato bellowed, losing his patience. "Will you grant the boy a pairing or not? If he pairs, you can continue to doubt him as you do now, but if he fails, then you will have confirmation that I am but an old fool, and you can go back to slandering my name among the high and mighty of Sentinel."

Slate paused, seemingly weighing his old rival's proposal. "A tempting offer, old man. But why tempt fate when I can squash this silly dream right now?" He licked his lips. "Keigh Anders will not be granted a chance to pair with a red bear. Not now, not next year, not so long as I serve as head of the Queen's Council!" He slammed his palm down on the table, several strands of greasy hair falling into his face. "Your request has been denied. Now remove yourself from this chamber and go back to whatever hovel you call home."

Cato ground his teeth. "Wait till the king hears of this!"

"The king?" laughed Slate. "The absent king? Good luck finding him. Not even the queen knows where to find the king most days. And if you do speak with him, how do you think he will react to you, the man who tried to seduce his bride, trying to crown a child that's not his own?" Slate curled his lip in contempt. "You'll be lucky if he doesn't have you locked up as an insurrectionist."

"The king knows my only loyalty is to the crown!" snapped Cato.

Slate shook his head, smiling like a jackal. "The king *knew* your loyalty. A lot of time has passed since you sat in this chair. You no longer have the king's ear or his authority. I do."

"The king may permit you a measure of authority, but in the end, his word is final."

"Okay, I'll make you a deal. Go, try to approach the king, but you'll have to go through Queen Vanitas first. I'm sure she will be thrilled to see you." Slate glared defiantly down on Cato. "If you get that far—believe me, you won't—and the king wants to further indulge his little charity project, *Keigh Anders*, I'll gladly step aside. But until the king deigns to rule in the day-to-day cares of his people, he's put me in charge."

"The king trusted you to rule as he would! Not spite his people over your own personal grievances!"

"Trust," scoffed Slate. "The king's favorite word...Trust this, Absaar: he will not hear you. He has no real interest in some flea-ridden brat from Bjorn. His real focus is on the boys of the Consecrate. From *them* he will select his heir." He slicked back his long, oily hair. "Your boy...See, I've already forgotten his name." Several of the council members laughed. "He will be forgotten. A trivial interest in a trivial child. Be gone, Absaar...or Cato, whatever you call yourself now."

Cato looked to Damien for backing, but the muscular man was avoiding his eyes. Finding no other support in the faces of the council, Cato stormed out of the courtroom, his cloak trailing behind him. He slammed the door with more force than a man of his age should rightfully be able, causing the attendant to release an involuntary squeak.

He would find another way. Slate wouldn't hold the court forever, and when Keigh turned twenty, it would be Braddock who would grant him pairing with a red bear. The prophecy might not unfold as quickly as Cato hoped, but he was sure of one thing: Keigh Anders was the child of the prophecy. Keigh Anders was the Son of Eden.

CHAPTER 27

IT COULD BE WORSE

19-23-5

K eigh rolled the metal orb around in his palm, then clenched his fingers around it. *Why did she come here? She should have stayed and let me explain.* He turned away from the window in his room and punched the thick cushion of the chair he was sitting in.

Yesterday, when he'd woken up after passing out in the ballroom, he had spent the remainder of the day searching Sentinel for any sign of Misselli. It was four hours after sundown when he had finally concluded that she no longer remained in the city. Every fiber of his being wanted to ride out after her. He could catch up to her before she made it back to Bjorn, but to leave Sentinel would all but guarantee his expulsion from the Refining. Canes needed to be willing to renounce all they had to serve the king, even if the king didn't require them to renounce much of anything in times of peace. Still, leaving Sentinel, missing potential tests and duels, to chase after a girl? That would be a concrete sign that he wasn't yet willing to renounce everything, as disqualifying a trait as there was among canes.

His stomach had been twisted into a knot ever since seeing Misselli. He hadn't eaten lunch or dinner yesterday in his search, and now he sat sulking in his room, skipping breakfast too. *She must think the worst of me.* He tried to swallow the lump in his throat, but it was there to stay. *I'll explain, though. When I see her next.*

There was a knock at his door, and a second later Mannie's scraggly beard poked through. "Didn't see you down at breakfast, so I figured you might be up here. Mind if I come in?"

Keigh grunted, and the old thrall entered the room slowly, closing the door behind him. Mannie fidgeted with the velvet bag in his hand as he waited for Keigh to look at him.

"I see Misselli found you," he said when Keigh remained silent, pointing at the orb.

"You saw her?" said Keigh, tearing his eyes from the window. "Is she still here?"

"I don't know. I just saw her and her mother in passing." Mannie donned a sympathetic smile when he saw his answer was less than what Keigh wanted to hear. "I was sure she was here to see you, so I directed them to the mess hall. Did it not go well?"

"No!" Keigh barked, releasing some of the pressure in his chest. "It could not have gone worse."

Mannie set the bag on the bed and sat down next to it. "Talk to me, Keigh. What happened?"

So Keigh told him everything. His dance lessons with Tabitha so he could impress Misselli when he returned home; the letters he and Misselli had written each other; how Tabitha had convinced him to practice what he would say to Misselli when he saw her, and how Misselli had overheard that conversation and run out without even speaking to him.

Keigh let out a long sigh and sank deep into his chair. It felt good having someone to talk to. Someone he knew would always be in his corner.

Mannie grimaced in solidarity. "I'm sorry, bud. I know how it feels."

"How can you?" scoffed Keigh. "You're married..."

Mannie chuckled. "Yes, I am, which means I know what it is to love someone with all that I am. Do you suppose in all my years of marriage that my bride has never been upset with me?"

"You probably deserved it," Keigh said, allowing a smile to break out on his lips.

Mannie just grinned and rolled his eyes. "I believe *she* believes that," he laughed. "The point is that no relationship escapes hurt, and the more love that exists between two people, the deeper the hurt is when it comes."

"Great pep talk," Keigh groaned.

Mannie laughed again. "No, I suppose it isn't if you think that's the end of the story."

"Then what's the end of the story?" asked Keigh patronizingly.

"The end of the story is that the same love that causes us to hurt deeply also allows us to heal stronger." Mannie smiled. "The relationship I have with my wife is stronger today than it's ever been, and much of that can be attributed to the hardships we've faced together."

"I'm not worried that *I* can't get over this. I'm worried that *she* won't want to!" He tossed the orb up and snatched it violently out of the air, returning his gaze to the window, toward Misselli.

"That's where trust comes in."

Trust. If he heard that word one more time he was going to start throwing things. "Whatever..." Keigh shook his head and nodded toward the velvet bag next to Mannie. "What's in the bag?"

Mannie must have sensed they had gone as far on the topic as Keigh was willing to go because he didn't object to the abrupt change of subject. "This..." He lifted the bag and shook it. The metallic tinkling of coins filled the room. "This is your reward from the king for the generosity you showed with the twenty justicia the queen gave you." Mannie smiled and poured the gold coins out on the bed. "Two hundred justicia!"

Normally such a thing would have sent Keigh jumping and shouting with joy, but today all it did was add a little kindling to the flame. "How much do you suppose I'll need to pay off Vicerous?"

Mannie's smile faded. "I searched Bjorn's records for your father's debt, and no official record exists...but this should be enough. It has to be." The old thrall began scooping the gold coins up and putting them back in the bag. "The king wished for me to inform you that tests of generosity and compassion will no longer receive monetary rewards. He does not wish for you to become accustomed to being rewarded for only doing what is right."

"So it *was* a test?"

Mannie chuckled. "No, actually, at least not in the sense that it was planned or organized," he explained. "The man you helped was in real need, and Tabitha isn't involved in any of the trials. There was no setup and no lesson. Just a young man dealing kindly with his fellow citizens of Eden."

"Then why am I being rewarded?" Keigh scowled. "Just more charity from the king so everyone else can resent me?"

"First off," said Mannie, "I was there when Braddock told you everything is a test. Everything you do here is being watched and weighed, whether you know it or not. Didn't you wonder how you had points on the wall before any of your peers?"

Keigh shrugged.

"Those points were for the help you gave the kitchen workers. The help you still give them even though you expect nothing in return." Mannie smiled warmly. "Now, as for your resentment of the king's favor: I will tell you now—and I hope you believe me, as your friend and someone who cares greatly for you—that it is better to have the king's favor than the acceptance of all of Eden."

"Why?" Keigh mumbled. "Doesn't keep you from getting beat half to death."

There was a long silence. Mannie opened his mouth to speak, hesitating before saying, "The king's heart broke for you that night."

"Well, I didn't need his pity," Keigh clapped back. "I needed his favor."

Mannie paused again. "Sometimes, they're the same thing."

"Not a lot of good it did me!"

"Really?" countered Mannie. "Was the compassion you showed that beggar in no way connected to your own experience of hurt? Of abandonment?"

Keigh wanted to scream "No!", wanted to deny the old man his point—but the truth was that he had helped that man because he had remembered what he'd said to the king. He had helped because he knew what it felt like to be denied help, and he didn't want anyone else to feel what he had felt.

"What's your point?" Keigh asked. He wouldn't deny Mannie's assumption about his motives, but he didn't have to admit he'd been right.

"The point is, the king always has a reason for everything he does." Mannie took a deep breath. "What if the reason the king let you be beaten was so that you would become a defender of the destitute? What if he wanted you to learn from your pain in ways you could never do while being protected?"

Keigh snorted. Braddock had taught him all about the cruel teacher of pain. Its lessons were brutal, but their impact was deep. Maybe the king had intended to teach him something, but Keigh wasn't willing to give up the idea that the monarch should have prevented his pain.

"I wouldn't have just stood there," he said. "I would have done something."

Mannie chuckled. "You probably would have, and it wouldn't have been a bad thing if the king had intervened that night."

"You think?" snapped Keigh.

"But!" Mannie pointed a finger at him. "Our king isn't concerned with what's good—his concern is what's best! He has never made a practice of telling others his plans, but I can tell you he *always* has one."

Keigh merely nodded. He wasn't in the mood for any more lectures on the king's infallibility from those who had devoted their whole lives to serving him. He continued to stare out the window as he waited for Mannie to move on from the topic.

"Anyway, if you still doubt the king favors you, you might like to know you were also awarded one hundred points for your actions." Mannie stood up from the bed and approached Keigh, working his head back and forth like a boxer trying to seek a gap in his opponent's defenses. "Come on, Keigh. Smile! This is good news! You're now so far ahead in points that you could win this without even doing one more spectacular thing!" Mannie spread his arms as if he were presenting Keigh with the best news he had ever delivered. "Though I'm sure you'll continue to impress us all. You've made so many of us so very proud."

Despite his best efforts to keep the old man's kindness from chipping away at his bitterness, some of it had broken through. "Thanks. I'm trying, Mannie." Keigh offered his friend a faint smile.

"I know you are, bud." Mannie took another step toward him. "Now stand up and give me a hug."

Keigh smiled and rolled his eyes, then crunched his way out of his slouch to stand in front of Mannie. The broad-shouldered messenger enveloped Keigh in a tight squeeze, holding him there inside his brown robe for longer than usual.

Mannie released him and stepped back. "Now, I think it's about time for you to head down to the stadium for your duel. I had Sanya hold a plate of food for you in the mess hall. You would do well to eat something. I must go, but I'll be sure to be there watching!" Mannie tousled Keigh's hair, turning it into a frizzy mess. He gave his handiwork a satisfied smile, then turned and left the room.

Keigh collected the gold off the bed and hid it with the rest of the coin he had won. Stripping off his tunic, he dressed in the buckskin pants and boots that he always dueled in.

The hug from Mannie had stirred the little reservoir of hope still left in him. He would win the Refining. Misselli would believe him, or at least forgive him. The canes would see he was worthy of their ranks. The thralls would have their hero. And his family would have their liberty from Vicerous. People would know his name and listen when he spoke. They would just have to wait and see.

*

Keigh made his way from the barracks across the street to the mess hall, where he found the plate left for him by Sanya. After eating an apple and some bacon, he took off through the clean-swept streets and gardens of the public works sector to the stadium. He could hear the dull roar of thousands of excited people as he went in through the contestants' entrance. Soon they would be cheering his name as he stood victorious once again.

Emerging into the torchlit chamber under the stadium, he spotted Braddock and started toward his mentor, but before he could cross the room, a hand grabbed him from behind. He turned to see Bard, wringing his hands and looking very nervous.

"Hi, Bard," Keigh greeted him. "I've never seen you down here before."

"I need to tell you something..." Bard looked around the room at the other nominees. "In private."

Keigh didn't like how uncomfortable Bard looked. Deciding it was best to trust his judgment, he followed Bard back into the shadows of the stairway.

When the two were alone, Bard began speaking urgently in a hushed tone. "You have been expelled from the Refining. You must leave now." He grabbed Keigh's arm and made to lead him back up the stairs.

"Expelled?" Keigh blurted, ripping his arm free of Bard's grasp. "For what?"

"I don't know," Bard hissed, checking to see that no one had heard Keigh's outburst. "All I know is that I have been ordered as the head of the king's dungeons to accompany a squad of canes out into the arena at the start of today's duels to remove *you* from the Refining." Bard put a hand on Keigh's shoulder. "I would spare you the public shaming if I can. Leave now. Leave the Capital. The city is not safe for you anymore. Those in power have made it clear they will no longer tolerate your presence in the trials."

"If I leave, they'll say I quit."

"So what?" exclaimed Bard. "You will have escaped their clutches and avoided becoming a public mockery!"

"But the king nominated me...Why would he send me away now?" Keigh feared he already knew the answer. He was nothing more than a charity project to the king. A trivial interest in the oddity from Bjorn. The gold reward hadn't been proof of his *favor*; it had been to guarantee he went quietly.

Bard shook his head. "The king has nothing to do with it. He hasn't been seen in the Capital for days!"

"Then we will appeal to the queen," Keigh offered hopefully. "She will stop this."

Bard shook his head again. "The Refining is run by the king, and in his absence only the Queen's Council can make rulings in his stead."

"But the queen can talk to them, right?" asked Keigh desperately. "Surely they wouldn't deny her."

"Keigh! Listen to me! If the Queen's Council has moved against you, it's lucky you aren't dead! It is probably only because they know the queen will protest that you haven't been killed already."

"They wouldn't. They can't," Keigh sputtered. "The council would have a citizen of Eden killed?"

"Can and has." Bard gave a nervous glance over Keigh's shoulder. "Count yourself lucky they only wish to shame you."

"Bard," said Keigh, the beginning of a suspicion forming in his mind, "did Mannie tell you I was attacked by an assassin last spring? Could the council have sent him?"

Bard gave a hurried shrug, obviously anxious about how much time they were wasting. "Maybe, perhaps...but Mannie said the man was a foreigner. I doubt the council would have opened themselves up to suspicion by communicating with anyone outside of Eden. Most likely that was the work of Draiden."

"Draiden? But why would he even know my name? Or want me dead?"

"I don't know, you tell me!" Bard tried to dip behind Keigh and push him up the stairs. "All I know is that at this point, it's clear to anyone paying attention that you're not just some thrall boy from Bjorn. Now go! Get out of here!"

"No." Keigh straightened, standing tall against Bard's prodding. "If they want to get rid of me, they're going to have to own it."

"Why?" Bard pleaded. "What do you gain from it?"

"They can tell any number of vile lies about me when I'm gone, but the one lie they won't be able to tell is that I quit!"

"No one who knows you would believe that. It's unnecessary!"

"You would be surprised what people will believe," Keigh said, remembering the way the people of Bjorn still scowled at him. "Every other day that stadium fills with people hoping to see bloodshed. You think they'll stop wanting to see men fail just because it's me?" His lip curled. "No. They can believe what they want, but they *will* witness that I did not quit."

Bard exhaled deeply through his nose. "I think this is foolish, but I understand. We thralls have been stripped of our pride; I will not oppose you holding on to what little you can salvage from this."

"Thank you." Keigh released his breath, heart pounding in his chest. Why was this happening? What had he done other than rise above his station? But maybe that was it. He was never supposed to rise, and now that he had, those threatened by it had to put an end to it.

"Sanya and I will let the other thralls know the truth. That's the extent of our influence, but we will see to it that the name Keigh Anders is not forgotten in our homes." Bard squeezed Keigh's shoulders, then raced up the stairs.

When Keigh reentered the waiting chamber, Braddock was already gone. He went to find Tarin, but before he could capture his friend's attention, the cane at the head of the room called for them to line up and collect their weapons.

Keigh grabbed a shield and sword and got into line behind Tarin. "You have to win this thing," he whispered.

"Me or you, buddy. Someone's got to," Tarin replied cheerfully.

"It's going to have to be you," Keigh said as the line started forward into the dark hallway that led up to the arena floor.

"Shut up," Tarin grunted good-naturedly. "You're the point leader right now. Don't act like you don't think you can win it all."

"Don't think I'm going to get the chance," said Keigh, eying a random cane in the hallway suspiciously. "The council is expelling me from the Refining."

Tarin spun around, facing Keigh in the darkness. "What! What do you mean? What did you do?"

"Guess they don't like the idea of thralls rising too high above their proper place in Eden." Keigh shrugged, but his tone was bitter.

"Nobody hates thralls, Keigh," said Tarin, turning back to face the front.

"Maybe not, but they don't want to break bread with them either."

"There has to be a reason. Think!" hissed Tarin. "Why would they want *you* gone?"

"I don't know!" said Keigh through clenched teeth. "Why did the assassin attack me and Misselli in the woods?"

"Not that again." Keigh couldn't see his friend's face, but he could hear him roll his eyes.

"Believe it or not, someone in the council has it out for me. The only reason I haven't already left is so that nobody can say I quit."

"I know you would never quit," Tarin offered.

"But you don't believe an assassin was sent to kill me?" Keigh jabbed.

"One of those things I've seen, the other just sounds crazy!" Tarin shook his head.

"Crazy or not, it's real. That's why you have to win," said Keigh. "Deacon can't become king."

"Deacon won't," Tarin huffed confidently. "I'm the one with the king's blood."

"Maybe so, but winning the Refining won't hurt."

They walked into the arena. Despite Keigh's loss to Deacon, the crowd still went wild when he entered. Keigh let the adoration wash over him. This would be his last moment in the sun. He looked into the crowd, picking out individual faces of cheering fans and wondering if any of them would say anything when he was marched out of the arena. Would they protest? Or would they condemn him as a failure?

He saw the thralls clumped together on the upper level. Usually, they were as frantic and frenzied as the most boisterous spectators, but today they stood still. Arms that were usually waving or cupped around shouting mouths hung limp by their sides. It was clear that Sanya had told them the news. Oddly, it was comforting to see their sadness. Keigh knew that his pain was their pain, that they stood with him even now as he was about to be shamed. It gave him strength.

"What the heck!" growled Tarin.

Keigh looked down to see what his friend was upset about. Next to Keigh's name on the wall hung the number *340*.

"I'm still at two hundred thirty, and you shot all the way up to three hundred forty!" Tarin complained. "You didn't even win your duel!"

The line of nominees stopped in the center and turned to face the leaders of Eden. Keigh wanted to explain his score to Tarin, but the trumpets blared before he could, and the stadium quieted. Keigh looked to the king and queen's platform, but today their chairs were empty. On the step below were the twelve green-cloaked men of the Queen's Council.

Councilman Slate stood up and ran a hand coolly through his oily black hair. Raising his arms, he called for silence. "Welcome, citizens of Eden, to the Refining!" he boomed. "Before we begin today, I regret to inform you that one of our nominees has disqualified himself from these trials."

A low rumble of gasps and hurried rumor-spreading ran through the crowd.

"Keigh Anders!" Slate bellowed. "You have been found unworthy of your nomination for stealing coin out of the hands of one less fortunate than yourself. You have disgraced the king and the integrity of these trials! Depart at once!"

So that was it? He had been blamed for what Deacon had done? Keigh allowed himself a smile. All he had to do was find the beggar and explain the situation to the council—but that was when he saw him. The blind beggar from the day before was sitting at the end of the council table, clean and shaven, wearing a new set of thick black robes. Next to him sat Vicerous Wulf, smirking arrogantly down at Keigh.

He ground his teeth. *Vicerous!* Of course he was behind it! Good friend of Councilman Slate, father to the real thief, and hater of all things Anders.

The crowd's murmurs grew louder as a squad of canes in red cloaks and adamantines marched through a gate in the arena wall. Keigh never took his eyes off the council. They wanted him to bow his head, to walk out in shame. He would not give them the satisfaction.

"Did you really do that?" Tarin asked as the canes marched closer, a sullen Bard trailing behind them.

"Why don't you ask Deacon if I did?" spat Keigh, still not breaking his gaze at the council's seats.

When the canes reached Keigh, they formed a tight circle, motioning for him to leave his weapons and stand at the center. Keigh laid down his sword and shield. With one last glare at Vicerous, he entered the ring of warriors.

As soon as the group began their march back to the door, the boos started. Keigh only caught bits and pieces, but what he heard devastated him.

"Thief!"

"Imposter!"

"Whip him!"

"Banish him from Eden!"

Not five minutes ago, those same voices had no doubt chanted his name with love. Now they wanted his blood for something he hadn't even done.

It was then that he finally hung his head. He had known it was coming, but the feeling of actually walking through it, enduring the hate of those around him, tore at him like a hungry vulture picking the last good flesh off the bones.

They hadn't gone far, though, when the crowd gasped. The ground shook as a terrible roar issued from the throats of three red bears charging across the sands of the arena toward them. Out in front, leading the charge, was Braddock's scar-faced bear, Mace.

The red bears slid to a stop in front of the canes, enveloping the escort in an avalanche of sand and dust. They bared their teeth, growling at the red cloaks surrounding Keigh, their mountains of fur bristling ominously over the warriors.

The canes ducked behind their shields and raised their swords. Each held their ground, but Keigh was sickly pleased to see the three canes closest to the furious bears were visibly trembling.

A chaos of sound erupted. Shrieks and screams echoed from a thousand spectators; Slate shouted for the bears' canes to restrain their animals; the bears snarled and clacked their teeth; the canes surrounding Keigh barked at each other to hold their positions.

Above the din, one voice stood out—the voice of his mentor. "Mace!" Braddock boomed. "Settle!" The grizzled veteran pushed his way through the canes to stand face to face with his bear. "Not now, girl," he crooned, touching Mace's nose softly with his hand.

Mace's lip slowly lowered, hiding white teeth as big and sharp as butcher knives. She emitted a low whimper and jerked her nose toward Keigh.

Stroking the top of her snout, Braddock looked back at Keigh. He mouthed the words *Not today*, then slowly led Mace and the other two bears back to their places against the wall.

Not until the last bear had seated itself did Keigh's escort begin to move again. This time an eerie silence settled over the arena. Every eye in the stadium was on him. Every mouth closed as they watched Keigh Anders, Bear of Bjorn, escorted out of the arena.

When the procession disappeared into the shadows behind the gate, the canes released Keigh into Bard's charge.

"We will go collect your belongings," Bard gulped after the last cane disappeared, obviously still shaken by the red bears' charge. "Then...then Mannie has asked me to see you safely to the city gates." With a jerk of his head, Bard indicated for Keigh to follow him out of the stadium.

"Glad I did that," said Keigh, trying to convince Bard his insistence on being publicly dismissed had been worthwhile.

"I hope so," snipped Bard, striding at a brisk pace, "because if the council didn't want you dead before this, they most certainly do now."

Keigh stopped. "Why? They got what they wanted."

"Did they?" Bard spun around. "They wanted you gone and forgotten. Now your exit is sure to have made you more popular than ever!"

"Pretty sure I just heard several people call for me to be castrated," joked Keigh, trying to calm his anxious friend down.

"That was before three red bears publicly vouched for you! Red bears are the most revered animals in Eden, Keigh, and nowhere more so than here in

Sentinel." Bard palmed his forehead. "And not just one, but *three* of them were willing to kill *canes* to defend *you*! Can you not see the significance of that?"

"Are you mad at me?" Keigh asked, confused by Bard's nervous anger.

"Mad at you? No, I'm scared for you!" Bard's face softened as he reached out and touched Keigh's shoulder. "You didn't ask for it, but when those bears came to your aid just now, everyone in that stadium began to doubt the council. They were just publicly discredited, and they will blame you for it."

Keigh swallowed. *Even when good things happen for me, it just makes my life harder.* "It's not fair," he groaned.

Bard smiled sympathetically. "Since when have we thralls ever gotten what's fair?"

Keigh knew Bard was only trying to cheer him up, just like Mannie telling his thrall jokes, but being reminded of his station was the last thing he wanted right now. Being a thrall had cost him everything he had worked so hard to achieve. If he had been born into a cane household, he would still be in the Refining now. But as a thrall? Eden would never let him become somebody.

Keigh shrugged. He was done talking. Done trying to make it all make sense.

The two of them hustled through the vacant streets, back to Keigh's room in the barracks, where he hurriedly collected his things. *At least they haven't tried to confiscate my gold,* he thought. But then again, maybe the council didn't know about it.

Slinging his canvas bag over his shoulder, he met Bard back at the front of the building. Bard led him down the hill to the city's first tier, through the Centipede. They emerged an hour later through a small hidden door in the wall next to the city gates. Mannie was already there waiting for him with Rose.

"You can take Rose back to Bjorn. Keep her with you until I come pick her up," he said, his sour steed looking visibly betrayed.

Keigh glumly nodded his thanks and took the ancient donkey's reins. "Can you come with me now?"

Mannie gave a sad shake of his head. "Unfortunately, I cannot, but you'll be in good company." He nodded back up the road.

Keigh turned and saw, to his utter bewilderment, the senior elder of Bjorn, Cato Boman, riding toward him on a gray pony. The spry old man's white hair and beard, blown heavily to one side by the breeze, gave the old man the appearance of a hay mound that had accumulated a snow drift.

Cato's pony clomped to a stop just short of the three men. The elder's blue eyes pierced Keigh in the same searching way they had the day he had pulled Keigh off Deacon to tell him he was a potent.

"Fear not, Master Anders!" Cato flashed Keigh a toothy grin even whiter than his hair. "Your time in Sentinel may be at an end, but today...today, you begin an adventure even more exciting!"

Keigh scowled. How could the old man be so happy right now? "Oh yeah? What adventure is that?"

"Why...training with me, of course." The old man gave a raspy chuckle as he spurred his pony past the group, through Sentinel's towering outer gate.

Keigh looked to Mannie for an explanation, but Mannie just grinned and winked. "You had better catch up!"

CHAPTER 28

JUST MY LUCK

45-8-13

Keigh's family was happy to have him home—a fact he resented. While he had missed them, their joy felt like confirmation that they had not wanted him to succeed at the Refining. Everyone had their reasons for wanting him to fail. In the end it just seemed like everyone in Eden would be happier if he stayed in his place, living in squalor, rooting for tubers in the dirt. The only one he didn't begrudge for this was Jessie. She had no ulterior motives or competing desires; she just loved him for being her big brother. He wasn't the only one in the house harboring hard feelings, though. Jotham and Jobey's initial gladness had disappeared the second they sat down to their first meal together and their mother gave Keigh the extra cutlet of venison.

He knew his parents had spent extra on his homecoming meal, but Keigh couldn't help but stare bitterly at the venison, potatoes, milk, butter, and bread, remembering the tables of the mess hall piled high with choice meats and produce that he could eat his fill from every day. Even his bed held little comfort for him. His mattress was lumpy and uneven, unlike his smooth, plush bed in the barracks. His first night home, he hardly slept, unsure whether it was because of his mattress or the gnawing bitterness he felt toward everyone and everything that had contributed to his expulsion from the Refining.

Two nights ago, he had been a household name and frontrunner to win the Trials. Now he had been reduced back to nothing. He still had his agoge with Braddock and his instruction with Cato to give him hope, but it was a paltry reward in comparison. There were thousands of canes in Eden, but only one winner of the Refining. There might never be another Refining in his lifetime. This had been his one chance, his one opportunity to become something more.

On top of all that, the thing he had been most looking forward to returning to in Bjorn was now the thing that filled him with the most dread. He had imagined his reunion with his best friend a hundred times. In some of his more hopeful daydreams, it had even included a kiss from the girl he loved. But now...now Misselli was more likely to bite him than kiss him. She was wounded and he was enemy number one.

He thought he might go to her parents to help buffer the tension. Rita and Dane had always liked him, but that was before their only daughter had traveled across Eden to see him, only to find him saying "I love you" to a girl of incomparable beauty, and dancing with that same girl—the one thing Misselli had always wanted from him, and the one thing he had always denied her. Rita would beat him black and blue with a rolling pin before ever hearing him out.

Keigh also considered just letting time ease the tension between them. Misselli would come around eventually, but the idea of letting days, weeks, or even months pass without talking to her was unacceptable. Plus, if he kept his distance, there was no helping which direction she would take. She may decide she didn't want to be friends anymore—or worse, she might fall for someone else. No, he had to talk to her, and the sooner the better.

Keigh got his first chance three days after he returned. Club was still meeting, and Theo had stopped in to invite him. The gang was going to make a bonfire in the woods above Misselli's house.

Keigh was the last to arrive at the little clearing carved into the thick, brooding forest of mature pines. A light snow of large, fluffy flakes was falling from gray skies through the gap in the canopy. He wouldn't have been late if he hadn't changed his clothes a dozen times that morning, trying to find something that Misselli would find handsome. But today he needed all the help he could get. In the end he had resorted to wearing his buckskin pants and boots with a long-sleeved shirt of gray wool.

"Keigh!" Addy and Emerson shouted in unison, sprinting over to him through the maze of rotting stumps. They got to him at the same time, wrapping him in hugs, Emerson's arms around his chest and Addy's around his waist.

"Theo said you might come!" exclaimed Addy, beaming up at Keigh as they both released their hold.

Keigh allowed himself a smile. "Wouldn't miss it."

He spotted Misselli supervising Conrad, who was trying unsuccessfully to light a large pile of branches with flint and steel. Stepping past the girls, he started toward her, but before he had even gone three steps, he was lifted off the ground by a pair of long, thick arms.

"Buddy! You're back!" Beaudy swayed back and forth, dangling Keigh's legs like a pendulum.

"Put...me...down!" wheezed Keigh, wondering how he had survived all these years hunting the forests above Bjorn when someone as large as Beaudy Besnik could still get the jump on him.

Beaudy set Keigh down, landing him right in front of Theo.

"Glad you came, man!" Theo clapped Keigh on the chest. "I think Conrad is going to need your help getting that fire started." A curse sounded from behind the pile of branches, where Conrad had likely just struck his own finger with the steel.

"Are you okay, Conrad?" Beaudy called out in concern.

"Fine, Beaudy. I've got everything under control," said Conrad, right before issuing another curse.

Theo raised his eyebrows and gave an exaggerated blow of air. "See what we've been living with since you left?"

"I can't imagine," Keigh said sarcastically. "Can we catch up in a bit? I need to talk to Misselli." He leaned to the side, trying to make sure Misselli was still there.

"Sure thing, man. Be careful, though." Theo grimaced. "She's been super grumpy all week for some reason. Thought she would be happier, with you coming back and all."

"Pretty sure I'm why she's grumpy." Keigh shrugged. "Thanks for the heads up, though." He gave Theo an appreciative pat on the shoulder before weaving his way through the severed stumps of the clearing toward the cursing pile of branches.

Keigh walked cautiously around the pile, where he found Misselli standing disapprovingly over Conrad like a surly class instructor. If she noticed his arrival, she gave no indication.

"Hey, mate!" Conrad stood up from his kneeling position. Brushing his hands on the front of his pants, the stocky cane apprentice offered one to Keigh in greeting. "How was the big city?"

"Good...Fine," Keigh replied, still trying to catch Misselli's attention, but she seemed to be deeply interested in the branches and tinder they had piled for the fire.

"What was it like? Did you meet the king? How are Tarin and Deacon doing?" Conrad rattled off his questions, oblivious to Keigh's lack of attention.

"They're good. Doing fine," said Keigh absently. "Misselli, can we talk?"

Misselli lifted her gaze from the tangle of twigs she had been stuffing into a gap in the branches, regarding Keigh for the first time. "You've said more than enough this week already."

"Listen! I can explain—"

"I don't want to hear it," snapped Misselli. Turning, she stalked away from Keigh toward Addy and Emerson.

"Wait! Misselli!" Keigh made to follow, but Conrad stepped into his path, cutting him off.

He put a hand on Keigh's chest. "Just let her go, Keigh. She'll come around."

"Take...your hand...off of me," growled Keigh.

Conrad dropped his hand, but stayed in Keigh's path. "Listen, mate, let's just hang out. If she's mad, just let her be."

"Get out of my way, Conrad." Keigh's voice was calm, but there was no misreading the threat.

"Come on, man, just let it rest. Please. Nobody wants to watch you two argue."

At that moment, Conrad was everyone who had ever held him back. Every demeaning word from Vicerous, every snide look from Deacon, every punch and kick from Christian's goons. He was Slate and the council, or anyone else who would dare keep Keigh back from becoming who he was meant to be.

He grabbed Conrad by the front of his shirt and shoved him against the pile of branches. "You think you can stop me?"

Conrad put his hands up in surrender. "What's wrong with you?" he scowled.

The rest of Keigh's friends had seen the confrontation developing and quickly rushed over.

"Maybe I'm tired of people telling me my place!" Keigh put his forearm across Conrad's throat, pressing on his windpipe.

"Stop it, Keigh!" demanded Addy.

Beaudy was on the verge of tears. "Please, Keigh! Be nice! Conrad's your friend!"

Keigh heard their cries, but their words would not dissuade him. Slate, Christian, Deacon, Vicerous...They needed to pay for what they'd done to him. What had he done to be so despised and rejected? Was his existence such a crime?

He pressed harder on Conrad's neck. A gurgling choke spilled from Conrad's lips as he desperately tried to pull Keigh's arm off his throat.

"Come off him, man!" yelled Theo.

"Please, Keigh! You're hurting him!" cried Beaudy.

Keigh didn't see it coming. When the slap hit him, it was as though someone had given him the antidote to the poison coursing through his veins. He released Conrad, who collapsed, gasping on the ground.

Keigh stumbled backward, looking first at his hands in disbelief, then to the terrified faces of his friends. Every one of them was looking at him like they had just seen a monster. Except for Misselli. She had been the one to slap him. There was no fear in her face, no revulsion, just scalding, simmering anger.

"Leave," she commanded.

Keigh backed away, mumbling quiet apologies to Conrad. "I'm so sorry...I don't know what—I didn't mean—"

He tripped over a log, landing hard on his back. No one laughed, but he could feel tears forming, hot in his eyes. Scrambling to his feet, hiding his face, he took off running into the forest, tears pouring fast and heavy down his cheeks.

What's wrong with you? he berated himself. *How could you? Those are your friends! They love you and you just attacked them! The council was right to expel you. You're no better than Christian. You're worse than Christian. You were a stranger to him, but you just attacked your friend! You don't deserve what you have. How could you have ever thought you deserved to be a cane? Braddock and Cato will abandon you for this. They should abandon you for this. You ruin everything you touch. The best thing you could do is leave. Stop letting people down and just disappear.*

Keigh ran and ran, plunging deeper into the forest as he fell deeper into despair. Dead branches and twigs scratched and clawed at him, trying to prevent him from entering the dark solitude of the mountains.

When he finally collapsed from exhaustion, he propped himself against a mossy log and buried his face in his arms. Keigh sat there, weeping, until he had no more tears left. No more cares left to give. No hope left to cling to. Only loss.

He took a ragged breath and lifted his head to inspect his surroundings. There were patches of snow on the ground between the shadows of the trees. *How high am I?* he wondered. It wasn't cold enough for snow to stick in the valley yet; he must be above the snow line. The trees were dark and twisted, thick with Spanish moss. Their wispy lengths swayed in the breeze like the tattered robes of desperate men. *I must be deeper into the forest than I've ever been.*

Standing, Keigh held his breath, listening for movement in the shadows. The deep forest was a dangerous place to be. Giant lynx, white tigers, wolverines, and snow leopards made their homes in these haunts; even the moose here could kill a man. When he hunted, he rarely delved deeper than a mile past the tree line, where the only predators were bears and mountain lions—and even then, he had his bow with him. Now, he was miles deep, with nothing to defend himself but his bare hands.

I've got to get out of here, he thought, his nervous sweat chilling on his skin. Quietly but quickly, he started his way back downhill, carefully choosing paths of soft grass or pine needles and avoiding the hard snow and slate. He picked his way down, eyes and ears alert for approaching danger.

He hadn't gone more than a hundred yards when a blood-chilling roar echoed through the ominous creaking of the trees. Then another. The sound of snapping and cracking branches ricocheted off the cliffs above him, filling the air as Keigh hid himself behind one of the massive pines. A group of crows took flight, cawing their protest as the ground began to shake.

Another roar. This time Keigh had no doubt. He had heard a roar like that before, but this time it wouldn't be Mace or any other paired bear.

He peeked around the edge of the tree in the direction of the breaking branches, and quickly ducked back as three red bear cubs the size of Beaudy hurtled past him. With another deafening roar, the cubs' mother, a large blonde sow, backed in behind them, snarling at something in the shadows uphill.

Reds! Wild reds! Keigh gaped, too amazed to grasp how much danger he was in. He edged further around the tree, hoping the mother bear hadn't seen him. The cubs were squalling so loudly he couldn't think straight.

He heard another roar, this one from farther up the hill. He stole another glance at the mother and her three cubs. The cubs had run into an alcove in the mountainside, trapping them from further retreat, and their mother had backed in behind them, barring their only way out. Red blood matted the blonde fur behind one of her giant ears, but she paid the wound no attention; her eyes were still fixed in the direction they had just come from.

Edging further around the tree, Keigh looked that way. In the shadows of the pines, a pair of amber eyes appeared, glowing above a set of bared white teeth. A whole section of forest moved as a mass of shadow detached itself from the trees, revealing a vicious-looking male red bear, its fur the dark magenta of dried blood. The boar burled through the underbrush, breaking deadfall as thick as Keigh without resistance. Emerging from the trees into the small clearing, the male huffed, facing off with the female and clacking his teeth menacingly. Both bears were larger than Mace, but the male was noticeably bigger than the female.

The female growled and retreated another step closer to her cubs. And suddenly, the male charged.

Both bears reared up on their hind legs, snarling and snapping at each other. Keigh had to crane his neck upward to witness the fight taking place twenty-five feet above him. The bears exchanged a series of blows with their forepaws while their jaws sought to clamp down on each other's throats. Their claws, each the length of Keigh's sparring sword, raked huge patches of fur and skin off each other. Snarling, the giants continued to snap at each other's ears and necks. Several times, the bears lost their balance, coming down so hard on all fours that the tremor it produced bounced Keigh an inch in the air.

The cubs cowered behind their mother, bawling desperately as the two adult reds battled. Then, in a flash, the male caught hold of the female's neck in his jaws. With tremendous effort, he flung the blonde bear hard onto her back. The male released its bite, adjusting and coming down hard with both forepaws on the female's chest, pinning her to the ground.

The male roared its victory, rearing back its head to plunge his teeth into the mother's neck—but he suddenly stopped, rigid, as a rock bounced off the back of his skull.

Keigh looked wide-eyed at his hand, not believing it had just thrown a rock at the violent monster, and had already grabbed a second one to throw if the first didn't work. But the shock of his own actions was short-lived. He knew why he'd done it. He was angry. As he'd watched the fight, he had seen himself in the large male. When the male pinned the mother, he'd seen Conrad's pleading face pinned beneath his own arm. Everything he hated about what he had just done to his friend, everything he hated about himself, was in that dark monster before him.

Maybe if he could fight off this monster, he could vanquish the one inside himself.

Stung by the rock, the male turned its massive head, slowly searching his surroundings for the new threat.

"Hey!" Keigh shouted. "Leave her alone!"

The male snarled, whipping its head around and fixing its amber eyes on his new challenger.

Keigh threw his second rock. The chunk of shale skipped off the bear's shoulder without even eliciting a flinch from the beast.

The male bared its teeth and chopped its jaws in a series of loud clacks. Pushing hard off the mother's chest, he readjusted, lumbering toward Keigh.

"Uh oh," Keigh gulped. He had no plan, no idea how he was supposed to best this behemoth bully. He ducked back behind the tree, hiding himself from view, surveying the hillside above him for anything he could use or anywhere he could hide. *Nothing!*

He ducked instinctively as the bear roared again. A huge paw slapped the tree trunk where his head had been a second before. The bear's claws raked back, stripping the bark off the trunk as easily as Keigh might peel the skin off a tomato.

He dashed to the next tree, hiding behind it. *I'll never outrun him. I've got to put as much stuff between us as I can.* He heard a branch snap to his right, so he ran to his left. Luckily, his pursuer wasn't quiet. *If I can hear him coming, I don't have to risk looking back.*

Keigh dashed to the next tree, then the next, each time deciding which way to run based on the sounds of his pursuer, each time narrowly escaping. *I can't keep this up forever,* he thought, panting to catch his breath. Hearing a snap to his left, he bailed to his right—straight into the face of the angry male.

Stumbling backward, Keigh tripped, kicking up a clump of pine needles as he fell. The needles were sucked straight into one of the bear's open nostrils. The huge bear sneezed on Keigh and reflexively batted him with the back of a forepaw, sending him flying into a clump of bushes. The male pawed at its nose, snorting and snarling, trying to dislodge the ball of needles.

The bushes softened Keigh's landing, but the hit had driven the air out of his lungs, leaving him gasping for breath. Panic filled his heart as he rolled around on the ground. *I have to keep moving.* Keigh willed himself to scramble out of the bush just as the bear pounced on the cluster of greenery. The bush flattened under its bulk and was soon reduced to nothing but shreds as the bear ripped through it in search of Keigh.

Finally, Keigh's lungs filled with a full gulp of air. Panting, he chanced a glance behind him. The male wasn't sprinting after him, but even the dark bear's slow trot was enough to keep Keigh from gaining distance.

Seeing a tree with low branches, he jumped, grabbing a low-hanging limb and beginning to climb. *He's too big to climb. These branches will never support the weight!*

Keigh and Misselli had spent many afternoons climbing the pines behind their homes. This one was no different. This time he just needed to climb faster—a lot faster.

He'd made it nearly thirty feet up before the male reached the base of the tree. The bear snarled, glaring up at him with bloodshot eyes.

"Ha! Too fat to come up here!" Keigh taunted.

The bear huffed, then placed its forepaws on the trunk of the tree, walking itself upright onto its hind legs.

Keigh's eyes widened as the bear's face appeared in the branches next to him.

The male snarled, and Keigh raised his arm as the bear snapped toward him. He closed his eyes and braced himself, ready for teeth to clamp down. He hoped it would be a quick death, like the snuffing of a candle.

There was a loud clack, and warm, slimy spit splattered Keigh's arm and neck. Opening his eyes, he saw the bear's head had been restrained by a thick limb across its neck. Keigh was just out of reach—but for how long?

I've got to get higher. Keigh jolted back to action. He leapt for the next branch and pulled himself up onto it. Reaching for the next limb, he heard a crack—and the branch he stood on gave way beneath him as the bear snapped it off with a swing of its paw.

Keigh plummeted back to earth, hitting nearly every branch on the way down. Scraped and bruised, he landed in a bed of pine needles. He limp-sprinted across the hill into a clearing, grunting with pain. The red bear roared its fury, trying to back out of the tangle of thick branches.

"No!" gasped Keigh, realizing he had run himself into a small ravine. He was surrounded by steep stone cliffs. The only way out was the way he had come. Panicked, he looked around for a scalable portion of rock and found none. He could see the male crashing through the underbrush behind him.

At the head of the ravine was a large pile of deadfall. The gray trunks of dozens of long-dead trees lay jumbled together like the bone pile of some great massacre. He could hide in there. If he could just wriggle down deep enough, maybe the male would lose interest—or maybe he could get a hand on the bear's nose and draw the energy out of it! How much energy would he have to drain? Could he even hold enough to deplete a full-grown red? It didn't matter. He would have to try.

Hobbling to the pile, he searched its surface for a gap he could shelter in, but to his dismay, the pile was primarily young trees that had most likely been deposited there in an avalanche. Even if he got into them, the red bear would toss them aside like kindling.

Abandoning the idea, Keigh began to climb the pile. The top was roughly fifteen feet high, eye level with the male, if it stayed on all fours. *If I'm going to die, I might as well put up a fight. Having the high ground can't hurt.*

Keigh worked his buckskin boots into a stable place in the loose logs and looked back to the mouth of the ravine. The male must have realized its quarry was trapped; it had stopped just inside the mouth of the ravine. Its breath, slow and hot in the cold mountain air, billowed past its fangs like smoke from the mouth of a brooding dragon. Snarling, the bear lifted its lip, exposing its teeth. Then, with a roar, it broke into a sprint.

Keigh watched in terror as his death hurtled toward him, huffing and foaming at the mouth. He stepped back, pressing against the rock as he braced for impact. The bear leapt as it reached the base of the pile, throwing itself headlong at its prey. Right as it did, the log Keigh was standing on budged beneath him, his weight pushing the base of the dead tree down while simultaneously lifting the spear-like point at its far end.

The bear crashed into the end of the tree, its point driving into its throat and deep into its chest like a hog on a spit. The base of the tree, braced against the cliff, held firm against the weight thrust upon its tip. Two thirds of its length disappeared into the bear's body before stopping the beast's momentum.

A piercing whine escaped the bear as it collapsed dead on the logs. The putrid smell of blood and carrion filled the suddenly moist air surrounding the bear's fallen body.

Keigh stood motionless, too afraid to believe the bear was actually dead. At any moment he expected the male to rise and kill him with the last remaining beats of its heart. Grabbing a stick, he reached out and poked it in the eye, the same way he would check to see if a deer he had shot with his bow was dead.

It didn't blink.

Keigh collapsed, slumping against the cliff in relief. Releasing the air in his lungs, he panted heavily, his breaths coming slow and shaky. A second ago he'd been sure he was going to die; now, he had somehow killed a wild red bear without a weapon. *Nobody will believe this,* he thought. *But...we could sell the hide, the meat, the grease!* he realized, studying the dead bear. *This bear has got to be worth more than our house.*

Keigh picked his way back down the pile of dead trees, wrinkling his nose at the stench. Limping back to the mouth of the ravine, he took stock of its location, being sure to note its relation to the familiar peaks and ridges so he could find his way back to the body when he returned with his father and brothers. When he was satisfied that he had a good grasp on the ravine's location, he began the slow, arduous trek back down the mountain.

He had killed the bully bear and it filled him with hope—not just because he had killed a full-grown red, something he thought no one alive could boast; he knew it had been dumb luck that saved him. No, he was hopeful that the death of the bear was a sign. A sign that the monster in him could be killed too.

As he limped through the forest of giant gnarled pines, he fantasized about the look on his friends' faces when they heard he'd killed a red bear. He froze suddenly; a terrible thought had just occurred to him. *What if they're not impressed? What if they're furious?* Red bears were sacred in Eden, and he had just killed one of the majestic beasts! His excitement quickly spiraled into downright despair. *I can't tell anyone. I can't even sell it. Maybe they will believe I found it—but what if they don't? I'll be even more of an outcast than I am now.*

Lost in his thoughts, Keigh rounded a large mossy boulder on the hillside—and stopped dead in his tracks. Not ten feet in front of him was the blonde she-bear. Keigh looked for a suitable escape route, but he would never make it. This was it. He was trapped.

The mother bear eyed him quietly. The cubs poked their heads out curiously from behind her rump.

Hold still. Don't frighten her, Keigh coached himself, hoping the bears wouldn't see him as a threat—or worse, a meal.

The mother bear stepped toward him, lowering her snout to his chest. Keigh closed his eyes, afraid his nerve would fail him. The bear's hot breath blew back his hair as she sniffed rapidly. The mother bear huffed; the force of which nearly knocked him over. He felt her mountain of flesh withdraw from him. Opening his eyes, he saw her circle behind her cubs and nudge them forward, placing them between herself and Keigh.

His momentary relief disappeared as he realized what she was doing. He had seen the garden wolves do this with their own pups. The adults would wound a rabbit or a rat and give it to the pups to practice their hunting. *I'm practice!*

He started to sweat. The only thing worse than being crushed by a massive red bear was being toyed with by three cubs that didn't even know how to kill.

He could be alive for hours while they got the hang of it. At least the mother hadn't wounded him first—but that was little comfort.

The three cubs didn't make a move toward him. They just sat there, staring at him. Occasionally one would tilt its head as if to view him from another angle. Though only cubs, they were still the size of full-grown ponies. The one on the right was slightly smaller than its siblings, and a different color. The two larger cubs were a dark crimson, much like the king's red bear Gorr, while the smallest was more orange, with a glistening coat that shone like burnished copper.

Without warning, the smallest cub stepped forward. Then, with a couple playful hops, it bounded back and forth, bobbing its head like a happy puppy.

Keigh remained motionless, unsure if the cub was friendly or just giddy with the excitement of an upcoming meal. At his refusal to play along, the cub sat down and tweaked its head to the side. Keigh almost laughed. It was the most emotionally expressive animal he had ever seen, unless he counted Rose, whose primary emotion seemed to be disdain for Keigh.

The other two cubs turned and stood behind their mother, leaving their smaller sibling with its meal. The mother stepped forward again, apparently impatient with how long her cub was taking to subdue its prey. She dipped her head and pushed it forward with her snout until it was within a yard of Keigh.

He remained still, locking eyes with the cub, waiting for any indication of a strike. The mother snorted, then turned and sauntered away, her other two cubs bounding along behind her.

"Don't want an audience, huh?" Keigh whispered to the cub. He knew that even a cub could still kill him easily, but now he at least had a fighting chance.

Suddenly the cub pounced, plowing Keigh to the ground and landing heavily on top of him. Keigh quickly scrambled to roll over, attempting to protect his throat and belly, covering the back of his neck with his hands.

The bear's teeth cut into the back of his skull so smoothly he felt no pain, only the hot, wet blood that now matted his hair and coated his hands. The bear's mouth tugged on the back of his head. Then, as suddenly as the cub had pounced, it was gone.

Keigh felt the back of his head with his hand, assessing the damage. He must be in shock; he still didn't feel anything. Putting his hand in front of his face, he looked at the blood that coated it...but the blood was colorless, and a bit slimy. *Spit?*

He rolled over in the dirt and saw the cub sitting on its haunches, watching him, its mouth slightly open in what looked almost like a smile.

Keigh felt the back of his head again. He couldn't find any cuts or lacerations from the cub's teeth.

"Did you...lick me?" he asked the cub, who took one happy hop as if nodding "yes" with its whole body.

Slowly, Keigh got to his feet and wiped the black dirt and loose pine needles off his sleeves. He stared at the cub. *It can't be...It's not—It's never—*

Keigh cautiously stretched out a hand toward the cub. Before he reached the end of its snout, the cub pressed the top of its head into his palm.

Keigh smiled in disbelief. Chuckling to himself, he scratched the young cub between the eyes.

Had he just paired with a red bear?

CHAPTER 29

THE RICH GET RICHER

40-6-21

Keigh set the scroll down next to the last one he had finished. Squeezing his eyes shut, he rubbed his temples. He had been reading for the last four hours in Cato Boman's study, a room surrounded by dark floor-to-ceiling wood shelves filled with books, scrolls, and an assortment of potted plants, all reaching greedily toward the sunlight streaming in though the large colonial windows.

"I'm done," Keigh announced, still massaging his temples. *Let this be the end. Please let this be the end!* He leaned back in the stiff wooden chair he had been confined to all morning, his legs tingling as blood found its way back into them. It was his first day of instruction with Cato—instruction he had initially been excited for, but now, there was a big, furry problem tied to a tree in the woods above his house.

I probably didn't need to tie him, Keigh thought again, kicking himself for the hundredth time. The small red bear seemed to understand nearly every command he gave it. *It can't understand words, can it?* He shook his head. Of course it couldn't. The bear probably just had a heightened ability to read body language and tone, but still...the cub was incredibly smart. Smarter than Mace, maybe…or maybe Mace responded to Braddock better than she did to him? The bond between a cane and a red bear was special; he knew that much. But how connected could a person be to an animal?

He was sure he would find out, but first he needed to find somewhere to hide the cub. *It can't live behind my house, not yet.* Telling his family about the cub would have to be done carefully. Jessie and his brothers were sure to think it was the best thing to ever happen to their family. His mother would worry about the public pressure it would put on her son, and his father would worry about the increased demands of feeding another mouth. *Oh no. Do I have to feed it?*

His sudden panic was interrupted as Cato's wiry white hair appeared in the doorway to his study.

"Finished the whole scroll, did you, Master Anders?" said the old man, sounding pleased.

"Yes, sir."

"Good." Cato shuffled into the study in his long, gray wool tunic. "Tell me one thing you found fascinating in today's readings."

"Fascinating?"

Cato beamed. "Yes, Master Anders, fascinating! You know—what filled you with wonder, left you asking questions, or was just plain *neat?*" He began searching the shelves as he waited for Keigh's answer.

"About the history of Eden?" Keigh wasn't asking, just stalling long enough for his brain to come back from his red bear.

Cato looked back over his shoulder. "That is the scroll I gave you, is it not?" He smirked, apparently aware of what Keigh was doing, if not why he was doing it.

"I guess I found it interesting—"

"Fascinating," Cato corrected him, giving an excited clap of his hands at having found what he was looking for. He picked up a jumble of metal pieces from the shelf and sat down in the chair across from Keigh to begin untangling them.

"Right...fascinating." Keigh rolled his eyes. "What I found fascinating is the descriptions of the old world."

"Oh? In what way?" Cato grinned as he twisted one of the metal pieces, releasing it from the others with a *plink*.

"I mean, I know that histories and legends can get embellished over time, but the old world really sounds magical. Light without flame? Windows that projected images of people and places far away? Carriages that transported people at speeds faster than an antelope? Even ones that flew in the sky like birds! What an incredible time to have lived!"

"Ah, yes, the old world was full of many wonders, but you might be shocked to know that the people of the time were far from fascinated by it." There was another *plink* as Cato freed a second piece of his puzzle.

"How?" asked Keigh, astonished. "Theirs was a time of magic!"

"I assure you, Master Anders, there is more magic in the world today than there ever was then." Another *plink*; another piece released. "I'm afraid the people of that era were plagued with the same weaknesses as we are now. In this case it's that familiarity breeds contempt."

"What do you mean?"

"What would you do if you discovered a nugget of gold the size of your fist, trapped in a rock?" asked Cato, peering at Keigh over the top of his puzzle.

Keigh laughed. Wasn't the answer obvious? "I would bash the rock with whatever I could find until the gold was free and in my hand."

Cato smiled. "No doubt you would, Master Anders. What do you suppose one of the rich merchants of Sentinel would do in the same situation?"

Keigh's brow wrinkled. "Wouldn't they do the same?"

A bark of laughter escaped the old man. "I assure you, they would not. That amount of gold is a trivial thing to those who have mountains of the stuff in their own vaults. What's rare to you is common to them, and because it's common, they do not treat it with the importance or value it is due."

"That's insane. Who would treat gold as worthless?" Keigh shook his head, wondering what it would be like to be so rich that he could just ignore a lump of gold staring him in the face.

"Insane, is it?" Cato's white eyebrows rose up his wrinkled forehead. "Have you never yelled at your parents?"

Keigh tilted his head, confused by the change of subject. "Yeah...a few times, I guess," he admitted honestly, sinking a little lower in his chair.

"Interesting. Have you ever yelled at me?"

"No..."

"Huh." Cato set the puzzle on the table and locked his blue eyes squarely on Keigh. "Do you love me more than your parents, Master Anders?"

"Of course not!" Keigh blurted—then, concerned he had been a little too emphatic with his answer, added, "I mean, no, sir."

Cato merely chuckled. "No worries, child, no offense taken. Believe it or not, I already assumed as much. So why, then, yell at your parents and not at me?"

"Give me enough time and I'm sure I will," Keigh said, half humorously, half disheartened by his own quick temper.

"I hope not, but yes, you probably will as you become more familiar with me." Cato groaned as he lifted himself out of his chair and shuffled over to stand in the golden sunlight falling through the large window. "The reason you yell at your parents and not at me is familiarity. You know your parents, and the reason you feel free to yell at them and not at me is not because you love them less, but because you are convinced that they love you more than you are currently convinced of my feelings toward you."

He plopped down into a cushioned chair next to the window, forcing Keigh to turn around to face him.

"*That* is fascinating! That it is our utter confidence in the love of another that leads us to mistreat them. It's the same phenomenon that causes the rich merchant to pass on gold he has to labor for, and it's the same thing that caused the world of old to care little for the wonders around them. Anything that we allow to become common soon becomes worthless." Cato thumped one of the chair's armrests, creating a puff of dust that swirled in the sunlight. He ran his fingers through the illuminated particles, watching them flow over and around his knobby knuckles. "For the world of old, it was knowledge; for

444

the merchant, it is gold; and for you, it is the love of your parents. I am afraid, Master Anders, that you are every bit as *insane* as every other person. While you may not be rich in knowledge, or in gold, you *are* rich in love…and that is why you treat it with contempt."

"I don't treat my parents with contempt!" Keigh bristled at the accusation.

"You do, though, and you've already admitted as much." Cato set his hand down, leaving the dust to swirl on its own and returning his gaze to Keigh. "Yelling at your parents for any reason is contemptuous behavior; whether you agree or not, it is. You've admitted to yelling at your parents and not at me. Why?" Cato wriggled deeper into his chair. "I'll tell you. It is because you know that your parents will always love you—that no matter what you do, they will never abandon you. With me, you're still unsure, so to yell at me would mean you risk losing my favor. You spend your parents' love as freely and recklessly as a rich man spends gold, because you both know there will always be more coming in."

Keigh knew what Cato said was true, but he still hated it. It was like the man had just held a mirror up to his heart, and Keigh didn't like what he saw. He was no better than those he thought to be insane, maybe worse. He thought of his family, of all the times he had ignored them and passed on opportunities to spend time with them. Yelling wasn't the only way he had treated them as common. He would do better. His family loved him, and that wasn't something he wanted to take for granted.

Cato must have seen the look of remorse on his face. "Fear not, young master. You are not alone in this insanity, and now that you are aware of it, you are equipped to battle it!" He shook a triumphant fist, then pointed a finger at Keigh. "I teach you this lesson so that you might not be so quick to judge others foolish. Only when we see ourselves clearly can we treat others graciously. We all suffer weaknesses; while some are obvious, others parade around as virtues. Better an obvious illness than a sweet-tasting poison. The person who knows he's dying seeks help and can find new life. The ignorant may live in peace, but their every step is a step toward death."

"What else is wrong with me?" Keigh had asked himself the question so many times; maybe the old man saw him more clearly than he saw himself.

Cato's laughter, as cheery as the sunlight he sat in, filled the room. "My dear boy, I'm sure there is a great deal wrong with you! But I believe there is a great deal right with you as well. Knowing your shortcomings is valuable, as it allows you to address them, but dwelling on your shortcomings never profited any man. Your mother and father have done a fine job with you. I should say that if I had a son of my own, I would wish him to be cut from the same cloth, so to speak." Cato clapped a hand to his knee. "That's enough for today, I think. Go home to your 'gold.'"

Keigh froze, thinking of the gold hidden in his room at this very moment. Did he know? Then he relaxed, realizing Cato was referring to the love of his family. "Right...yes, sir," he said, relieved.

The two of them rose from their seats, and Cato walked him to the front door of his home. Keigh stepped out into the cold street, still unthawed by the sun, and had begun walking toward home when the old man's voice called after him.

"I am for you, Master Anders! Someday you'll know that so well that you'll yell at me too!" Cackling at his own joke, Cato shut the door.

Keigh smiled to himself. He was going to like lessons with the old man, even if it meant reading all the books and scrolls in Eden.

He owed his parents an apology. He had treated them as common in so many ways. Hopefully paying off their indenture to Vicerous would help them understand how much they really meant to him.

But they were just one of the things on his list. The most pressing thing right now was finding a place to hide his cub. Conrad, Misselli, his parents... They would all have to wait just a little while longer. He looked at the cloth still tied around his wrist, no longer white but brown with sweat and dirt.

Please wait.

Being careful not to come within sight of his house, Keigh snuck through the barren fields and into the forest behind. Staying concealed in the trees, he made his way to where he had tied the cub that morning. When he arrived, he was pleased to see the cub lying on its back, batting at the air toward an angry squirrel, who was chittering angrily at him from the safety of the branches above.

"Hey...um...boy?" Keigh greeted the cub, realizing awkwardly that he needed to give the bear a name.

The young red bear sat up, excited to see him. Like a dog shaking itself dry, he shook off the dirt and pine needles he had picked up lying on the ground.

"What should your name be?" Keigh asked, studying the cub. All the red bears he knew had short names. Should he name him something that inspired fear like *Gorr*, or something nice like *Mace*? But Mace was the name of a weapon, he realized. He had always assumed it was short for Macey for some reason.

Keigh untied the rope from the cub and then the tree. The cub closed his big amber eyes and pressed his large, fluffy head against Keigh's chest. Keigh rubbed him behind the ears and was pleased to hear his happy little grunts of satisfaction.

"We're going to find you somewhere safe to live," he said, speaking right into one of the bear's furry ears. "Just for a little while, okay?"

The cub sat back on his haunches and bobbed his head.

Did he just nod? Keigh wondered, watching to see if he would do it again. In any case, the cub was in a good mood and obviously happy to see him.

"I've got a place in mind, but it's kind of a long walk. Here." He dug a few pieces of jerky out of his pack and tossed them to the cub. The bear snatched a piece out of the air and began chewing the tough meat, then did the same with the pieces that had fallen to the ground. When the cub was finished, Keigh walked past him, heading north. "Let's go," he said, and the cub fell in, bouncing along happily behind him.

As they walked through the shadowy woods, Keigh contemplated what Cato had said to him. He really was rich in love. His family didn't have much of anything, but they did have love. At the moment, Keigh actually had both, but he knew which gold he would gladly trade for the other.

He turned and observed the young bear padding along contentedly behind him, his shimmering copper fur glistening in the shreds of golden light that managed to find their way through the tangle of branches overhead.

"I already have my gold, but you can be my copper," he teased the bear.

The cub lifted his head, eyes wide.

"You like that?" Keigh asked. The cub's tongue lolled out of his mouth as he looked at Keigh with something like a smile. "Then it's settled," he grinned. "I'll call you Copper." The cub did a quick spin in place, chasing after his short tail, confirming the name was a good fit.

*

An hour later, the pair exited the shadows of the forest onto the sun-drenched slope above their destination. A short stroll through the sagebrush and they were there.

"What do you think, Copper?" Keigh asked. "Can you stay here while I figure out what to do?"

Copper approached the edge of the water and took a drink.

"You can hunt for yourself in the forest, there's water in the moat, and there's enough left of the building that you'll have some shelter from the weather—at least until you're a bit bigger, that is." Keigh looked at the shell of the old watchtower, its stones caked black with soot. Nobody ever came up here when the tower was whole—why would anyone come now that it was destroyed?

Keigh and Copper crossed the logs he and his friends had laid over the moat only months earlier. Copper's weight caused the logs to bend comically low, threatening to swamp Keigh's boots with icy water. The doors and stairs inside had all been reduced to ash in the fire, but the stone remained standing, making a nice open room for Copper inside the first level. There was a burnt-out window at the far end, but it would still give Copper some much-needed shelter from the worst of the winter elements.

Keigh spent the next hour cleaning out the space. First, he rid the room of the nails and charred timbers that hadn't been totally disintegrated in the fire. Then he gathered armfuls of dead grass and sage boughs from the field to give Copper a place to bed down.

"Thanks for the help," he said as he dropped his last load of grass on the pile and waited for Copper to drop his mouthful of brush. He scratched Copper behind the ear, then began spreading the grass out into a makeshift bed. Eager to help, Copper started pushing the grass around the floor with his paws too.

When the grass was spread to his satisfaction, Keigh stood up and leaned against the stone wall.

"This will have to do for now," he said, surveying his handiwork. "I've got to get home before my parents start to get curious about where I've been."

Copper rose on his hind legs and pressed his paws against the wall in an imitation of Keigh.

"You're more copy*cat* than bear," Keigh chuckled.

Copper huffed, pushing himself off the wall, then falling back into it in rapid succession.

Keigh smiled and shook his head at the excited animal. *How did I get so lucky? I'm paired with a red bear! I must be the only non-cane to ever pair with one. How is this my life? Nothing could be cooler than this.*

There was a sharp crack of splitting stone as Copper pushed off the wall again. Before Keigh could react, the young bear hit the wall, pressing against it with all his weight.

With another loud crack, the wall they were leaning on collapsed.

Keigh and Copper plunged through, tumbling head over paw with a wall's worth of rubble down a wide, steep stone stairway. Their descent came to an abrupt stop in a heap of fur and stone at the bottom of the stairs.

Copper recovered first. He tugged Keigh upright by the back of his tunic.

"Didn't take you long to start trashing the place," Keigh teased, brushing himself off. Standing up straight, he assessed his new surroundings.

He and Copper had fallen fifteen feet below the tower floor into the mouth of what appeared to be a long, narrow cave. A gentle breeze from within rustled his hair. He stared into the depths, waiting for his eyes to adjust to the darkness. When they did, he noticed a faint glow coming from the back of the cave.

"It must open up to the outside back there," he whispered. "Let's go check it out." Keigh stepped into the darkness, motioning for Copper to come along, but for the first time since pairing with Keigh, the cub seemed apprehensive about following him. Keigh turned back to look at the whimpering giant, silhouetted against the light from above. "Scared of the dark?" he asked.

Copper gave one final whimper before hustling up next to Keigh's side.

"Don't worry, boy, we'll be okay." Keigh looped an arm over Copper's neck as they walked side by side into the darkness.

Water dripped from the ceiling as they passed under where Keigh assumed the moat must be. The cave was more than tall and wide enough for both of them to walk upright and abreast, and showed no sign of narrowing the farther they went. As they progressed, the light became stronger, but still wasn't as bright as Keigh expected from daylight. *Must be a small opening. Maybe a section of the cave collapsed and that's why they walled it off.*

Suddenly the floor dropped. Before Keigh could fall forward, Copper snatched the back of his tunic in his teeth, pulling him back to safety.

"Thanks, Copper." Keigh swallowed, waiting for his stomach to descend from where it had lodged in his throat.

Moving forward again cautiously, he tested the ground in front of him with his foot. *There!* His foot traced the edge of a ledge in the floor. Squinting, he noticed the light seemed to be coming from below, not above. Holding onto Copper, he reached a foot over the ledge and, to his relief, found flat ground only inches below.

"Stairs," he breathed. *But who would carve stairs into a cave?*

Navigating the stairs slowly, checking each step with his foot before proceeding, they descended another twenty silent feet below the earth. As they reached the bottom, Keigh could clearly make out an archway spanning the width of the cave. The light behind it was much stronger now. Approaching the arch, Keigh could see it had been constructed of smooth finished stone. *This is more than a hole in the ground,* he realized, wondering what the old watchtower's purpose had really been.

Walking cautiously through the archway, Keigh entered a room finished floor to ceiling with brick. At its center was the source of the light. He gaped as he beheld it. A sword unlike any Keigh had ever seen stood upright on a stone pedestal twenty feet away.

Looking around the room for clues, he found nothing but a single rock figure in the shape of a sparring dummy. Keigh slid his feet carefully over the surface of the floor, watching and listening for anything that may be a trap. After traversing the room without incident, he paced a circle around the sword. *How?* He squinted at the flawless blade. *Where does it get its light?* Stepping up to the pedestal, he noticed an inscription at its base:

To wield you must know

To know you must wield

He looked back at the sword. On the flat of the blade, the word *Verity* was inscribed. Wonder and dread filled him as the realization hit him. *This is Orvyn's sword!*

The sword was flawless; not one chip, chink, or defect existed in the glowing blade. Its hilt was silver with a straight, strong cross guard and coiled handle. The pommel was in the shape of a spade with a hole at its center. The blade was a metal unlike Keigh had ever seen, both translucent and reflective. Even the light that shone from within it was one of a kind, making all around it visible without blinding the one who looked at it.

As incredible as the sword was, Keigh was sure of one thing. If this was Orvyn's sword, he wouldn't be able to pick it up until he figured out the riddle. Orvyn's helmet had been too heavy to lift, and try as he might, Keigh had never been able to accomplish more than he had on his first attempt, even after bringing a shield.

Keigh reached out a hand and grasped the handle. *Only one way to find out,* he thought, and with a mighty heave, he tried to lift the blade from its stand.

To his surprise, not only did he lift the blade, but he pulled so aggressively that he fell over backward, landing hard on the brick floor with a *whumph.* Keigh coughed as dust billowed around him. *I did it!* He grinned like a fool at the iridescent blade in his hands. *I was able to lift the sword!* He must have solved the riddle without even knowing how!

Keigh picked himself up and held the sword out in front of him. Not only was it visually perfect, it was also perfectly balanced. He ran his fingers over the edge, testing its keenness. The blade was as sharp as any of the thin knives he used to fillet fish with.

I wonder...

Grabbing a pinch of Copper's fur, he lifted, then carefully put the edge of the blade to it. Copper let out a disgruntled groan as the blade cut through the hairs with almost no pressure.

Keigh smiled and looked at the stone sparring dummy. "Could it be...?" he asked himself, walking over to the stone figure. The dummy was covered in chips and grooves just like a regular wooden dummy, but who would use stone for sparring? That would flatten a blade's edge in seconds—*unless...*

Carefully, Keigh took Verity and tapped it against the stone figure. He checked the blade for any sign of a scratch or ding. There was none. So he did it again, this time a little harder. Still no blemish was made on the blade. He repeated this over and over until, finally, he took a full-strength swing at the dummy.

Copper ducked as shards of stone ricocheted around the room. "Oh no!" Keigh yelped, convinced he had gone too far. But upon inspection of the blade, he found that once again it had not been harmed. *It's unbreakable!*

He grinned, stabbing its point into a brick in the floor. All his life he had wanted a sword of his own, and now he had one. And not just any blade, but Orvyn's sword! *All these years I thought Orvyn's armor was a fairy tale, and now I've seen two pieces of it in the last month!* Not only had he seen it—he possessed a piece himself.

"Let's go, Copper," he said excitedly to the still wary bear. Holding Verity out in front of him to light the way, he skipped back toward the stairs, hardly able to contain his excitement.

Reaching the entrance to the room, he nearly cut himself in half when the blade suddenly halted in place under the archway. Keigh narrowly dodged the sword as his body kept right on moving past the frozen blade. The stop was so sudden and firm that Keigh lost his grip and the blade fell to the ground with a clang.

"No, no, no, no! Not the sword too!" he begged. Grabbing it again, he tried to pull it past the archway, but he could do nothing to get it through.

A leafy vine carved into the underside of the arch had illuminated when the sword tried to cross the threshold. *There must be a barrier here, some sort of trick that's triggered by the special metal of the sword.* Whatever the trick was, it was working. Every time he tried to take the sword through the arch, it was stopped just as surely as Orvyn's helmet could never be lifted more than a few inches.

"Think!" he barked, startling Copper. "*To wield you must know, to know you must wield...*" He turned the phrase over in his mind. "Know what?"

Keigh paced back and forth inside the brick-lined chamber, twirling the perfectly balanced blade in his hand. It was getting late. He didn't have time to figure this out today.

Placing the sword back on the pedestal, he backed away from it. "I'll be back for you," he promised.

As he passed through the archway, he gave Verity one last look. He'd been meant to find this sword, he was sure of it—as sure as he was that Copper had been meant to pair with him.

With a red bear and an unparalleled sword, he might still be somebody yet.

CHAPTER 30

SIGNED, DRAIDEN

20-21-2

"Unbelievable." Owen Anders pulled on his thick beard, shaking his head as he said the word for the twentieth time since he and his sons had arrived at the body of the monstrous red bear Keigh had killed two days prior.

Keigh knew that if they were to salvage anything from the bear, it would have to be done sooner rather than later, but he had other motives for bringing his dad and brothers up here today. He wanted to gauge their reaction to the death of a red bear. That, he hoped, would give him the insight he needed to decide whether to tell them about Copper or not.

Unfortunately, they had been far more interested in Keigh than in the bear, asking him to retell the story several times as they inspected the massive carcass. As much as Keigh emphasized that it was luck, not skill, that had saved him from a sure death, his father and brothers still looked at him with a new sense of respect, bolstering Keigh with a confidence he hadn't known he needed.

"Your mother is never going to let you go hunting again after this," Owen laughed, ruffling Keigh's hair affectionately. The burly farmer shifted the heavy pack on his back and took one last look at the dead bear splayed out on the weather-bleached pile of deadfall. He gave one more amazed shake of his head before turning to follow Jotham and Jobey out of the ravine.

"Will we come back for more later?" Keigh asked, kicking through a drift of fresh snow and nearly falling under the weight of his pack as he struggled to keep pace with his father. They had only taken one of the bear's tenderloins today; each of them carried a quarter of one loin on their backs, and even that was a burdensome task. Keigh had hoped his father would see the value in the bear and make plans to sell as much as they could.

Owen snorted at the question. "We will be eating the meat we harvested today for the next year! Anything more we couldn't hope to preserve."

"But we could sell it, right?" Keigh pleaded, hoping to plant a seed of opportunity in his father's mind. "Just think what someone would pay for a red bear rug! Some rich merchant in Sentinel would give a fortune to have a red bear skull in their estate! We could use the money to pay off the Wulfs!"

Owen paused his descent. "I'm already rich in all the ways that matter, son." Resting his hands on his hips, he gave a contented sigh and looked over the fog-covered valley below. "I've made peace with the fact that Vicerous will never accept our release. We will use the parts of the bear that serve our family. Anything that would draw too much attention must be left."

"Are you afraid people will hate us for cutting up a red bear?" Keigh asked between gasps of cold mountain air. "Or just afraid Vicerous will take all our gain for himself? We can't possibly owe him more than the bear is worth," he said, unsure of the truth of his own words. He knew nothing of his father's debt. And after his time in Sentinel, Keigh had more questions about who his father had been than ever before.

"Unfortunately, Vicerous has taken a liking to having our family, specifically me, subjugated to him." Owen rolled his eyes, working his thumbs under the straps of his pack. "I think he would always claim we owed him more. As far as what people think about the red bear..." His bushy beard lifted as the corners of his mouth curled upward. "There is no animal more precious than my son's life." Owen reached out and gripped the back of Keigh's neck, giving it a gentle squeeze. "If I had to kill every red bear in Eden to keep you safe, I would do it without apology."

Keigh chuckled, envisioning his father fighting off a team of snarling red bears wielding nothing more than a sack of potatoes. He matched his father's tender gaze and let the warmth of his love permeate every bit of him. "I bet you could do it, too," he said. His father would do anything for him; he was sure of that.

Vicerous was an unreasonable monster, but Keigh was still going to attempt to buy his family's release the next opportunity he got. He just couldn't tell his parents until the deed was done. If his father would face a red bear for him, then he was sure he would never let Keigh spend the small fortune of gold he had acquired on freeing him. His father would insist he use it to create a life for himself when the time came for him to leave home. But how could he live free while his parents remained indebted to the Wulfs?

No, he would not allow it. But his family couldn't know until it was too late to interfere. If all went well, they would be celebrating their first Winter Festival of his lifetime as a free family of ables.

*

Hours later, when they arrived home, the whole Anders family gathered in the warmth of the firelit great room to set about butchering the meat into usable sizes. Long, thin strips were cut for smoking, thick slabs were salted and placed in a barrel of brine for later consumption, and several weeks' worth of roasts and steaks were hung in the attic, where the winter cold would keep them from spoiling long enough for the family to eat them.

That evening they enjoyed steaks with their potatoes, cooking enough of the fresh meat that not even Jotham and Jobey complained of having too little. The meat was tender and sweeter than the venison Keigh had grown up on. It reminded him more of the pork Mannie had gifted them one year for Winter Festival. As delicious as it was, Keigh still had trouble swallowing his meal. Someday Copper would be a big, ferocious red bear too, and the thought of anyone eating him was enough to make Keigh sick.

After dinner, his mother surprised them all with a pumpkin pie. "I decided my boys could use a little something extra after climbing in the mountains all day," said Sabriya, pulling the covered pie from the pantry and sweeping back to place it on the table.

"And I helped! Didn't I, Mommy?" Jessie tugged on the front of her mother's dress.

"I couldn't have made it without you, sweetheart." Sabriya ran her fingers through Jessie's long brown hair. Jessie displayed the few teeth she had in a grin so tall and so pleased that it forced her eyes shut.

Owen stood and stepped toward his wife. He took her hands and spun her into his arms. Keigh recognized the move from his lessons with Tabitha. She called it the "Hey Babe."

"You, my dear, are all the sugar I need," said Owen, planting a kiss on his wife's lips.

Keigh joined his brothers in feigning fits of gagging. Jobey even went so far as to fall off the bench, clutching his throat. While Jobey rolled around on the floor, Jessie clapped approvingly at her parents' public display of affection.

A few days ago, Keigh had resented being back home. Home had felt like failure, but now it felt like the goal. *This is gold worth digging for,* he thought, remembering his lesson with Cato. Keigh doubted Vicerous would ever have the joy and love in his home that the Anders had this night, and he was willing to trade all his coin to keep it going.

*

The following morning, as Keigh made his way to Cato's in the chilly gray of an overcast day, he encountered Conrad, Theo, and Beaudy huddled together at the base of one of the town's towering totem poles.

Theo watched Keigh warily as he approached the group. "Which of us will you be beating up today, Keigh?" he scoffed, placing himself between Keigh and Beaudy like a mouse defending a cat.

Keigh squirmed, feeling like a fox among hens. But before he could apologize, Conrad shoved Theo back into Beaudy's belly.

"Come off it, Theo. Have you already forgotten how Keigh saved your life? Or how he took the fall for all of us? What did we do when Braddock showed up?"

Theo opened his mouth to answer, but Conrad cut him off.

"We hid in the woods! And how about the days after, when Keigh didn't give up a single one of our names and the whole town hated him? Huh? We kept our distance, didn't we?"

"Our parents made us stay away!" objected Theo.

"There were a hundred reasons not to stand up," exclaimed Conrad, "but none of them are a good reason to leave a friend high and dry like we did. If I were Keigh, I would have beat our hides. He doesn't deserve our contempt. He deserves our thanks." Conrad removed his scowl from Theo and faced Keigh. "I'm sorry, mate. You deserved better from me."

Keigh was stunned. He felt he deserved all the scorn and more for his behavior. He was the one who needed to give an apology, yet now he found himself on the receiving end of one.

"I—but—still..." Keigh stammered awkwardly. "Thank you," he said eventually. "I still owe you an apology. I should never have come at you like I did. There's no excuse for it."

"Water under the bridge, champ." Conrad grinned and extended his hand.

Keigh shook it, sealing the peace.

This time he saw it coming, but no sooner had they shaken hands than Keigh found himself lifted off the ground again, pulled tight against Beaudy's belly. "I'm sorry, Keigh!" Beaudy blubbered. "We've all missed you so much! Theo talked about you all the time while you were gone." He dropped Keigh back to his feet.

"Is that true, Theo?" Keigh poked a finger at his small, scowling friend's ribs. "Did you miss me, buddy?"

"No," Theo denied weakly, ducking a shoulder to avoid the next jab of Keigh's finger.

"I don't know," Keigh said, smirking. "Sure sounds like you missed me." He turned to Beaudy and Conrad, who nodded in confirmation.

"You guys are idiots," dismissed Theo. "I never said I missed Keigh."

"Yes you did," Beaudy argued. "It was your idea to write him letters, remember?"

"Shut up, Beaudy." Theo crossed his arms, clearly feeling emasculated.

"I would have loved that," said Keigh, nudging Theo. "Truthfully, I didn't have anyone to talk to most of the time. It would have been good to hear from you."

"Yeah?" Theo's face relaxed. "I guess I might have mentioned you a few times."

"A few times?" Beaudy exclaimed. "You talked about him like he was your best bud! I remember, 'cause I thought I was your best bud?"

"You are, Beaudy." Theo rolled his eyes. "Okay, fine. We talked about you. Happy now?"

Beaudy brightened immediately at being affirmed as Theo's best friend.

"I am happy, Theo," Keigh beamed. "Thanks for asking."

Theo opened his mouth to respond, but both his and Conrad's smiles faded as their eyes flashed over Keigh's shoulder. Keigh turned just in time to see Misselli stomp by, eyes to the ground, a scowl clouding her usually bright demeanor.

Keigh gave his friends a *wish me luck* grimace and hurried to catch up to the little dark cloud storming away from him.

"Misselli, wait!" he called, chasing her through the portcullis. "Let me explain! Please!"

Misselli whipped around to face him and Keigh was sure, by the look in her eyes, that if she could have cast lightning at him, she would have.

"You want to explain?" she asked, exasperated. "Want to tell me why I'm too stupid to understand what I saw? Too dumb to know what I heard?"

"It's not like that—"

"Not like what? Not like exactly what I thought would happen? Not like I knew you would forget about me the second you left home?"

"I didn't forget about you—"

"No, you know what? You're right. What you did was worse! You gave me hope! Made me believe you missed me! Wrote me letters." She bit her lip, teetering between rage and tears. "Made me think that even though you were living the life you had always dreamed of, there was part of you that still wasn't happy without me by your side."

"I did! I wasn't!" Keigh protested.

People in the street were now staring openly at the two quarreling teens, but Keigh didn't care. They could think what they wanted, but Misselli could not go one more day thinking he didn't love her. That he would ever trade her for anyone else.

"Maybe you did miss me. Maybe that wasn't a lie. But you couldn't wait, could you? You had to go and replace me." Her angry scowl softened to a teary-eyed sob. "What about me isn't enough for you?"

Keigh was too taken aback to speak. How could she possibly think that? He gritted his teeth. If he ever saw Baylor again, he would punch him in the mouth for the damage he'd done to Misselli.

Misselli must have taken his hesitation as confirmation. She set her jaw, nodding to herself. "I begged you to stay. Begged you not to go. You made your choice. It should have been clear to me then. I should have never chased after you to Sentinel. My mom always said, 'When someone shows you who they are, believe them.' I'll always be the lesser of two dreams to you, Keigh. The fallback, in case you don't get what you really want."

"Will you just listen to me?"

Misselli's scowl darkened. "There is nothing you could possibly say to me that will undo what you did."

"How can you—"

Keigh was abruptly cut off by a hard tug on the back of his tunic, nearly picking him off his feet and dragging him up the road, away from Misselli.

"Hey! Get off me!"

"You can play house with Miss Labelle later. Right now, you need to come with us."

Keigh took one last desperate look into the glistening blue eyes of his girl before angrily twisting his neck to see who had stolen him from her this time.

At the end of the muscular arm gripping his tunic was Braddock Fortier. The retired cane marched him purposefully away, up the main street toward Cato's. Braddock released him as soon as he saw Keigh had given up his attempts to break free from his grip.

Free from one grip, he was immediately pulled into another as a hand landed on Keigh's shoulder, drawing him close into a dark brown robe.

"Mannie?"

"Hello, Keigh. How's home been?" The tall messenger gave him a friendly smile. "I see you and Misselli haven't quite patched things up."

Keigh was angry. Angry at being torn away so suddenly from Misselli. Angry at her for not letting him explain. But mostly angry at himself: once again, he was asking her to wait, asking her to understand. Some things in life could wait and others couldn't. He was pretty sure Misselli couldn't. But there was no controlling Braddock. Duty called, and he had been forced to leave her in the lurch again.

At least Mannie was there. His presence always had a calming effect on Keigh. It didn't matter what was happening in his life, if Mannie was by his side, he felt somehow everything would be okay.

"It's been...complicated," Keigh said at last.

"Bjorn is a special place, isn't it?" Mannie looked about the street in a satisfied way, taking in the busy people and shopfronts of Bjorn's main thoroughfare. "How's your family?"

"They're good," Keigh admitted, allowing himself to take his mind off Misselli and feeling the warm reassurance of his family well up in him again. "Really good, I think. Will you come up to the house and visit?"

"I suppose I'll have to! You've got my girl, after all." Mannie winked.

"What?"

"Rose," Mannie clarified with a chuckle. "I'm sure she misses me something terrible."

"I don't know about that," said Keigh. "She seems to have taken a shine to Jessie, actually."

"Huh..." Mannie snorted. "I guess I should have seen that coming."

They soon made it to Cato's home. One of the few buildings in Bjorn that had been built into the town's exterior wall, the cedar-shake hut looked much smaller than it actually was. Braddock opened the door without knocking and led Mannie and Keigh to the study, where the trio waited for the wispy-haired elder to join them.

"Would any of you fine sirs be interested in a cup of tea?" Cato's voice piped from the kitchen. "I'm trying a new brew of hibiscus, lemon balm, and echinacea." When no one answered, his face poked around the entrance to the study, his blue eyes darting among his guests.

"I would love a cup. Thank you, Cato." Mannie inclined his head graciously.

"Me too," said Keigh, following Mannie's lead.

Braddock just waved the old man off, apparently eager to get on with business.

"Why are you back in Bjorn?" asked Keigh. "Is the Refining over?"

Braddock grunted. "The queen has granted myself and Vicerous leave to tend to our homes for a week. We won't be here long."

"Vicerous is in town?" Keigh never thought he would be so happy to hear his enemy was nearby. Perhaps he could buy his family's freedom sooner than he had hoped!

Braddock squinted at him inquisitively. "Don't get any ideas, Keigh. Just because you've been removed from the Refining doesn't mean you don't have more to lose. Vicerous will not hold back if you provoke him and I'm not there to intervene."

"I won't provoke him," promised Keigh.

Braddock let slip a wry grin. "Your very existence provokes him. Keep your distance if you can help it. He's been particularly insufferable lately."

A minute later, Cato shuffled into the study, bearing a silver tray with four steaming cups of tea on it. "I made you a cup anyway, Master Fortier. You could use a little warmth in you."

Braddock gave a disgruntled shake of his head as he accepted the hot beverage from Cato.

When they all had their tea and Cato took his seat, Mannie cleared his throat to speak.

"What has Draiden done now?" Cato asked, cutting him off before he could begin.

"How do you know Mannie brings news of Draiden?" challenged Braddock.

Cato merely smiled into his teacup. "News of Draiden is the only thing that causes you to forget your manners in my home, Master Fortier."

Braddock sat up straight, removing a dirt-covered boot from where he had been resting it on the coffee table. "My apologies, Elder Boman."

"No apology necessary. Now, out with it, Master Raya. What news of Draiden?" Cato took a long sip of his tea.

Mannie grinned at the white-haired elder, but his expression soon turned serious. "Scouts have returned to Eden with grave news. Draiden has secured the loyalties of all the eastern kingdoms and currently has his disciples dispatched with gold and weaponry to the southern kingdoms. It is expected that they too will align themselves with him."

"Has no one refused him?" asked Cato.

"One king did." Mannie sighed. "The city state of Marsough rejected his offer. So Draiden marched on the city with his legions and razed it to the ground. Word is that he made the people of Marsough witness their king's execution in exchange for their release."

"That doesn't sound too bad. He only killed the king?" Keigh asked.

Braddock and Cato pursed their lips and Keigh wondered what he'd said wrong.

"Yes, only the king was slain," Mannie responded. "But it is the method and purpose with which Draiden executed him that is most disturbing. Draiden had the king tied to a post before the whole assembly of the people. Then he handed each member of the king's family a small dagger and gave them a choice: stick the dagger in the king and live, or refuse and die. His poor children were faced with the choice of torturing their father by sticking the blade somewhere non-fatal, or ending his pain quickly and having to live with the knowledge that their father died by their hand."

Cato sighed. The muscles in Braddock's jaw knotted.

"What did they do?" asked Keigh.

"The king had thirteen children, all of whom failed to muster the courage to either refuse Draiden and forfeit their own life, or mercifully end their father's suffering with a fatal cut." Mannie scratched his cheek. "Fortunately for their king, his queen used her blade to end his suffering."

Keigh's fists clenched. What sort of senseless evil could even concoct such a thing? "Why? Why not just kill him? Why involve his children?"

"This is why." Braddock dipped his head toward Keigh. "Are you angry?"

"Furious! The man is sick!" Keigh fumed.

"Draiden knows our king will feel that same anger. Marsough wasn't a threat to Draiden." Braddock shook his head, stirring his tea. "It was a message to our king."

"What message is that? *I'm an evil lunatic, signed, Draiden*?" Keigh looked to the older men, hoping to see that they were as outraged as he was.

"No," said Mannie. "Draiden is saying he will destroy our king, and that he will use his children to do it."

"The king's son? How could he possibly get Tarin or Deacon to betray the king?" Keigh asked, confused.

"No, not the king's son, the king's *children*," Mannie explained. "King Thiamtaim has always lovingly referred to the people of Eden as his children. Draiden does not merely wish to conquer our king, but to utterly destroy him by wielding those he loves most against him."

"How do we know all this? Did we have a scout present?" Cato asked Mannie.

Mannie sighed. "No. The people of Marsough showed up at our gates three nights ago. Our information comes directly from them."

"Have they come to seek refuge? Or did Draiden send them?" asked Cato.

"Both," answered Mannie, setting his teacup back on the silver tray with a clink. "Draiden sent them to deliver his message and told them the king would take them in. Which he knew wasn't entirely true."

"What do you mean?" asked Keigh. "Why wouldn't the king let them in? Aren't Eden's gates open to all?"

Mannie shook his head. "The king and the king alone decides who can enter Eden. Everyone who comes here seeking refuge is given a choice. They can live in the city of Sebya just on the other side of the curtain wall and keep their old ways and customs. There, our king will provide for the needs of the city, but should the city come under attack, they will not be protected. The other choice they can make, if they wish to enter the protection of Eden, is to submit to the king's authority and live by the laws he gives, and yes, he will take all those who choose that option. But..." Mannie turned his palms up, seemingly disappointed with what he had to say next.

"But what?" Keigh pressed.

"But...the people of Marsough are hedonists." Mannie's usually cheery face saddened. "Their lives revolve around the pursuit of their own personal pleasure. They may bend the knee for a moment, but few of them will ever submit to a life governed by an authority not their own. However...in the king's absence, the Queen's Council has begun selling entrance into the kingdom. Only those with desirable skills or deep coin purses are being admitted."

"Slate!" growled Cato. "The king would sooner let enter a poor cripple who loves his edicts than a wealthy man of many skills who spurns his commands."

"The king is still gone?" asked Keigh, remembering how he had been inexplicably absent when Keigh had been wrongfully kicked out of the Refining. *Not like he would fight even if he was here,* he thought bitterly.

"It is presumed the king is outside Eden's borders," said Braddock.

"Why?" asked Keigh.

"We must trust that he has a reason. He has never failed us before," Cato offered, earning nods of agreement from Mannie and Braddock.

Trust. Always trust. Keigh stiffened at the word. Why was everyone so ready and eager to trust the king?

The room was quiet for a moment. There was only the soft plinking of Cato's fingers strumming his half-empty teacup as everyone in the room seemed to be wondering for themselves just what the king was doing outside Eden.

"Seems to me like he's failing us right now," said Keigh, breaking the silence.

Braddock sat up so quickly he nearly flew out of his chair. "What did you just say?" he shouted. "I will not tolerate one more careless word about the king!"

Cato also looked displeased, but Mannie settled the men, holding one hand up and placing the other on Keigh's chest. "I believe I can shed some clarity on young Keigh's frustration with our king."

"It won't be justified," said Braddock, gripping the end of his armrests so hard they creaked.

Mannie inclined his head. "No, it won't justify his words or his feelings of bitterness, but it will help you understand how our *youthful* friend has arrived at this fallacious conclusion."

"If it's understandable, how am I not justified?" asked Keigh, sulking at his mentor's reproach from under Mannie's massive hand.

"Because no matter how you arrive at a wrong conclusion, you are still wrong." Cato smiled, now twiddling his thumbs in his lap. "If I were to bake you a cake of mud from the stables and tell you it was chocolate, it may be explainable or even understandable that you would take a bite. But tell me, Master Anders, is there any explanation I could give you that would convince you to take another?"

Keigh shook his head.

"Good! Well then, you're not totally devoid of wisdom." Cato cocked his head to the side, looking at Braddock as though he had just settled the argument.

Mannie leaned forward in his chair so he could face Keigh directly. "Listen, Keigh. There are a thousand reasons I could point to for why you should trust the king, but for now, if you have any respect for us, you should trust him because we do." He waved a hand at the two elders of Bjorn. "For now, that will have to be enough. Someday you'll see for yourself: the king was always worthy of your trust."

Keigh shrank into his chair as his mentors watched him, awaiting his response. The truth was, he did respect these men. If he could one day be as strong as Braddock, as wise as Cato, or as good as Mannie, he could hold his head high knowing that he, like them, was a great man. So what did they know about the king that he didn't?

The wrestling match in Keigh's mind must have been visible on his face, because Cato didn't wait for him to speak. "Would you have any respect for a king who only knew as much as you?" he asked. "Don't you desire your king to be wiser and more knowledgeable than you?"

Keigh bit the inside of his lip. He knew the right answer, but it felt like the old man was just setting him up for another lesson—one that would no doubt be aimed directly at his pride.

"Yes," he said reluctantly.

Cato grinned. "Well, I'm pleased to report that that is exactly the kind of king we have in Eden. Our king is considerably wiser than any man I know, and that's really quite something, because I know these two men here." He gestured to Braddock and Mannie.

"The king's never done something you've disagreed with?" asked Keigh skeptically.

"Goodness, yes! Many times!" Cato cackled. "That's how I know he is wiser than myself! If the king always saw things my way, then I could only assume he was exactly as wise as me. It is only because the king has done things I didn't agree with or understand that I *know* he is wiser than I."

"What do you mean?" Keigh liked Cato, but he wished the man would speak plainly for once.

"If two men walk the same path to a destination, how can you know if another trail might have been faster? Only when two paths are traveled is it clear which way is superior. Differences create distinctions. Distinctions allow us to determine superiority. Namely, the distinction between right and wrong and the ability to know that right is superior to wrong."

Keigh nodded. It made sense. Without seeing the outcome of two reasonable options, it was hard to know which was better.

Satisfied, Cato continued. "So when the king and I have had different opinions on a matter, or taken different paths, so to speak, I have been able to see who was right and who was wrong. Admittedly, some of those took years to determine, but in all my many years—and I assure you they are many—do you know how many times I have found the king's way to have been the lesser path?"

Keigh shrugged. "I'm guessing not many."

"Never! Not once!" Cato grinned.

Keigh had never seen someone so happy to be wrong.

"You know how often the king has agreed with me?" Cato pointed a knobby, wrinkled finger at himself.

"I don't know. Probably pretty often."

"Never! He has never agreed with me!" Cato chuckled merrily. "Any time the king and I have seen things the same way, it was because I agreed with him, *not* because he agreed with me. The king takes counsel from no man, nor should he. None possess his insight." He sank his head back into the cushion of his seat and stroked his white beard. "I have seen it firsthand, Master Anders. Give it time…You will see it too."

Cato was acting like the conversation was over, but Keigh still wasn't buying it. He ground his teeth, debating whether to say what he felt. "That just seems like blind devotion," he said after a moment. "Only thralls submit themselves to such mindless servitude."

Cato raised an eyebrow. "Are you not a thrall?"

Not for long, thought Keigh. Soon he would deliver his gold to Vicerous. Then, he and his family would be able to chart their own destiny, no longer bending to the will of a better.

"I am," he admitted, once again feeling like he was being set up.

"Perfect! Me too!" Cato clapped his hands together jovially.

"You're a thrall?" Keigh gaped at the old man. How had he not known? "But—you're an elder of Bjorn!"

"Everyone is a thrall, Master Anders," said Cato, picking up his cup again and taking a sip. "We all submit to something or someone, whether there's documentation or not. Some serve the king, like the men in this room; some serve themselves and their own interests; some serve coin or glory, work or wives. There is no escaping servitude, Master Anders. The wise choose their master instead of letting a master claim them." Cato spread his arms, again indicating Mannie and Braddock. "We surrendered our servitude to the king. There is no better master."

The other men nodded their agreement.

How can these intelligent men be so blind? So trusting? Keigh was incensed. "I'm sorry," he sneered, "but I can't see a single good reason the king abandoned me the night I got jumped in Sentinel. He was there! He could have stopped it! Could have rescued me! All he had to do was speak—just say the word and I would have been saved. But he didn't." Keigh sat upright in his chair, breathing heavily. The injustice of that night infusing him with fresh anger.

Cato's cheery expression softened. "You are correct. One word from our king and you would have been spared that horrible attack. I have discussed this with both Master Fortier and Master Raya, and none of us are certain why the king didn't intervene that night. But we are all certain of one thing... He did what was best. It's not blind devotion. We have heard great things about our king, about his mighty feats of valor and strength, as I'm sure you yourself grew up hearing."

Keigh had heard the stories. He had once possessed a reverence for the king that bordered on worship. He still remembered the sense of peace and protection that enveloped him when he saw the king approaching the scene of his beating. Keigh *had* trusted him. Maybe that was why it hurt so bad to see him do nothing.

"You're young, Master Anders. In time you will see that the king had a reason for not intervening that night." Cato stood. Hobbling over to Keigh, he knelt in front of him. "While you wait for your own answers, may I encourage you with a story of my own? It's a story of perhaps the most bitter disagreement I ever had with the king. One that I only recently saw his wisdom in."

Keigh nodded, still wrestling with the bitterness in his chest.

"What I am about to tell you does not leave this room. It is not common knowledge, and I would not have it become so."

"He doesn't need to know this!" Braddock objected.

Cato merely waved off his protest and continued undeterred. "Fifteen years ago, I sat on the Queen's Council. I had a different name, different dreams, and a different life. One day, I discovered treachery of the highest kind was taking place in the council. But before I could tell the king of his betrayer, my fellow council members ousted me from their ranks with a most vile lie. I appealed to the king, fully expecting to be reinstated—but do you know what the king did? He did the farthest thing from what I expected, from what I wanted. He sent me away. No trial, no witnesses, no chance to clear my record…He just sent me out of Sentinel to start a new life in Bjorn under a new name. I asked him why. Why was I being banished when my enemies retained their titles and their power? You know what he told me?"

Keigh snorted derisively. "Trust me?"

Cato clapped a hand to Keigh's thigh. "*Trust me*, he said. Can you believe it? I'd never been so angry in all my life. The king was upending everything I had ever known and didn't even see fit to tell me why. No explanation, just the command: *Trust me*…For the last fifteen years I've been in Bjorn, wondering if the king got it wrong, wondering if there was any reason why my life had been turned upside down." Cato paused. "Then, a few months ago, it started to make sense. And today, I know why the king sent me here, and I know he was right to do it. Fifteen years of anger and doubt and the joy of discovering my purpose here has washed it all away." The old man grinned and patted Keigh on the knee, looking like a father who could hardly wait to present their child with a gift. "Any idea what that reason is, Master Anders?"

Keigh's eyes narrowed suspiciously. He shook his head.

Cato sighed. "I'm here because of you. *You* are my purpose in Bjorn. You will play a vital role in the history of Eden. I know it now, but our king has known all along. Trust him."

CHAPTER 31

MORE THAN BARGAINED FOR

28-3-1

Snow was falling lazily on the hill beside the old watchtower, giving everything it landed on a rounded cap of white powder.

"Unbelievable." Braddock stood slack-jawed, watching Copper smack his lips noisily on a burnt loaf of bread Keigh had *accidentally* forgotten to take out of the oven for his mother. "You killed…a full-grown wild red bear? And then another full-grown wild red just…just…gave you one of her cubs?"

"Like I said, it was sheer luck—"

"Or fate," Braddock interjected, still staring at Copper.

"Fate?" asked Keigh. Why were his mentors, men of high repute and distinction, suddenly talking about him as if he were special? His whole life, nobody had even noticed his existence outside his small circle of friends and family, and now he was supposed to believe the king had known about him since he was born? That his father had once been someone important enough that Draiden had sent an assassin to kill him? That Cato's whole life had been directed to intersect with his? And now, that Braddock was suggesting he was always meant to have a red bear?

"Forgive me." Braddock's eyes sharpened from their glassy-eyed stare at Copper to focus on Keigh's face. "You're right: sheer luck. It had to be." His words backed away from his previous reverent wonder, but Keigh could tell by the way the man was studying him up and down that the old warrior was deflecting.

"Why did you say *fate*?" Keigh pressed. "And why is Cato suddenly so enthralled with me? A year ago, Mannie was the only one of you who even knew I existed." He hoped that Braddock would give him some answers now that they were alone. Back at Cato's, the men had been so cryptic that he'd walked away feeling like he'd been given more questions than answers. What were they hiding from him?

"Forget I said it." Braddock bent down and packed a ball of snow in his hand. Standing back up, he tossed it up in the air for Copper, who caught the ball in his mouth, bursting the snow back into a thousand bits. Master and apprentice both chuckled, watching the young bear stand up and begin frantically searching the ground for the ball.

Braddock wiped his hands dry. "Cato was wrong to say what he said to you. It's just that..." He paused and looked about the ground, as if he hoped to find the words to say written there. "None of us have sons of our own. And..." Braddock shuffled his feet in the snow. "Well, we...You're family to us now."

Braddock looked deeply uncomfortable in his vulnerability. It was an odd look on him. Awkward or not, Keigh couldn't help himself from pressing the subject. He maneuvered himself in front of Braddock so his mentor couldn't ignore him, like a puppy tugging on the ear of an old gray-haired dog that just wanted to be left in peace. "So, you guys love me, huh?"

"I didn't say we loved you," grumbled Braddock. "We just have a responsibility to take care of you now."

Keigh didn't know many intimate details of Braddock's life, but he had spent the whole summer training with the man, so he knew enough to be sure he was making his mentor uncomfortable. "It's okay, Braddock. Mannie tells me he loves me all the time."

Braddock raised his eyes and fixed them on his apprentice. "It's *Master* to you, and that's Mannie. He's always been one to speak freely."

"I free you, Master!" Keigh said with mock authority. "Speak freely!"

The corners of Braddock's lips curved upward, ever so slightly. "Fine, I shall."

Keigh grinned like an idiot as he awaited his mentor's affirmation.

"You keep this up and you'll wish the bear *had* killed you."

Keigh merely shrugged. "Sorry, Master, you're stuck with me. The son you never had but love regardless."

Bam! Braddock punched his shoulder so hard his whole arm went numb. Chuckling, Keigh tried to shake life back into his fingers. "Hey! What was that for?"

"That," Braddock said, inspecting his knuckles as he held a clenched fist in front of his face, "is a Fortier hug. It's how the men in our family show our *love*." He grinned, lowering his fist.

Keigh grinned in return. "I accept." Then, without warning, he leveled a punch at his mentor's shoulder—a punch that never landed. Braddock brushed it away with one hand, cuffing Keigh in the side of the head with his other. "Ouch!" Keigh laughed, his feet slipping on the snow underneath him as he tried to regain his balance and nurse the freshly smacked side of his head.

"Keep it up, Anders. I'm happy to show you just how much I love you." Braddock smiled, looking like a friendly merchant selling fresh knuckle sandwiches.

"Okay, okay, you don't have to say it...but I'm writing in my journal that you did," Keigh teased, making sure he was out of arm's reach this time.

"That settles it," said Braddock.

"What?"

Braddock shrugged. "You can't be my son. No son of mine would ever keep a diary."

"It's a journal!" Keigh argued. "And I don't—it's just a joke—who keeps a journal? Not me..."

"Sure," Braddock said sarcastically. "There is no denying one thing, Keigh..." The warrior pulled his red cloak tighter to his body shielding himself from the cold. "You seem to be the center of a great deal of uncommon events, and for that reason alone, I think you should tell no one else of Copper or

Chapter 31

the bear you killed." He gave Keigh a sympathetic grimace, clearly knowing that wasn't what he wanted to hear. "At least not until Copper is big enough to defend himself. Though he's as large as a full-grown black bear, he is still a cub in his mind. There's no telling how he would react to a threat. Come, let's talk inside." Braddock nodded toward the skeleton of the old watchtower and began walking up the snow-covered hill.

"No!" Keigh blurted.

Braddock stopped in his tracks, tilting his head at Keigh. "And why not?"

"It's…um…it's filthy in there," he improvised. "Smells terrible! Copper doesn't know to poop outside, and I haven't gotten around to cleaning it up." Copper whipped his head around to face Keigh's false accusation, looking as indignant as a bear could.

The truth was that Keigh was sure Braddock would notice the gaping hole in the wall and the steep stone stairway that led down to Orvyn's sword. A sword he still very much wanted and needed. He wanted to find out more about the weapon before sharing its discovery with anyone else.

"Odd. Red bears are very intelligent—it's not like them to soil their own living space." Braddock narrowed his eyes at Keigh, then relaxed. "Copper is a wild red, though…Perhaps they differ in ways."

"When's the last time someone paired with a wild red? Maybe we could ask them for advice?"

Braddock gave a short guffaw and shook his head. "Keigh Anders, you are the first and only person to pair with a wild red bear since Orvyn paired with Cye. It wasn't until the formation of the canes a hundred years after Eden's founding that Orvyn captured and domesticated seven of the animals. Canes have paired and bred the offspring of those original seven ever since. In order to pair with a cub, canes have to receive a pairing appointment from the Queen's Council for an opportunity to meet with a cub, and even then, being chosen by a cub is no guarantee. The council only selects canes after they have successfully completed their agoge training. So…" Braddock shook his head and smiled at Keigh. "Not only are you the only person to pair with a wild red since Orvyn did it hundreds of years ago, you're also the youngest to ever pair with a red bear of any kind."

Keigh and Braddock spent another ten minutes standing in the snow, talking about red bears. Throwing the leg bone of a deer Copper had managed to kill earlier in the week, they watched the young animal slide down the hill on his belly after it. As excited as Keigh was to be spending time with Braddock and Copper, he was still most excited for tomorrow. Tomorrow he would track down Vicerous and pay for his family's release.

Braddock and Keigh walked together through the snow-covered sagebrush back to the city gates, making sure to take the long way around the town's fortifications and disguise their tracks, just in case anyone was curious enough to try to piece together where they had been. They found Mannie waiting dutifully outside the portcullis, telling riddles to a group of eager twelve-year-olds.

"The answer is...a silver!"

A boy with sandy hair that fuzzed straight out like a blooming dandelion complained, "But you said one of the coins wasn't a silver piece!"

Mannie smiled. "Yes, so I did, but the other one was!" He winked, leaving the poor kid scratching his head. "Ho there!" he called, standing up to greet Keigh and Braddock. "You two have a nice father–son outing?"

Keigh burst out laughing. The messenger could not possibly have known how poignant the jab was. Braddock groaned. Rolling his eyes, he waved Mannie away and turned down the snow-packed road to his home.

"Not good, huh?" Mannie called after his friend, earning another dismissive wave from Braddock. "Was it something I said?" he asked Keigh.

"No," said Keigh, still laughing. "He's just afraid to admit how much he loved it."

Mannie frowned, apparently still confused by his friend's curt goodbye, then turned his curiosity to Keigh. "Why are you holding your arm? Did you fall?"

"No," Keigh chuckled. "I just had a good time too."

"Good. I'm happy to hear it." Mannie gave Keigh a pat on the back. "He really was a mess when you got removed from the Refining. His mind goes to such a dark place. Took everything I had to convince him you would be safe at home with your father." He pointed up the road toward the mountains hidden in the falling snow and the two of them started out for the Anders' home together.

"What do you mean?" asked Keigh. "I'm out of Sentinel. What does anyone there care about me now?"

"The council might not care *for* you, but they certainly still care *about* you." Mannie sighed. "You embarrassed them in front of thousands of people. You didn't do anything wrong, but they still blame you for it, and with the king out on a mission, there isn't the usual safeguard for you against the council's scheming."

"Do you think they would they try to have me killed?" asked Keigh.

Mannie shook his head. "The council would never be so bold as to seek your life, but there are other more devious ways in which they could harm you and your family. That is what Braddock was so worried about. He's been better since we started back to Bjorn, though. Likes to think he can protect everyone while he's here."

"If anyone could, it would be Braddock." In all the sparring and duels Keigh had participated in, he had still not met anyone as skilled or strong as his mentor.

"Indeed," Mannie agreed. "Speaking of protection, do you have the metal orb with you?"

Keigh pulled the shiny sphere out of a pouch at his waist. He carried it with him everywhere now, not only because Mannie had been so adamant that he keep the little oddity, but because it reminded him of Misselli. Several snowflakes melted on the trinket as he held it out to Mannie. In the summer, the orb felt a bit cooler than it should, but in the winter, it was much warmer than its surroundings. Keigh had convinced himself that its warmth was the result of Misselli holding it for two months; and right now, that was the only warmth he could expect from her.

Mannie took the orb from Keigh and wrapped his fingers around it. "Keep this with you at all times, especially when your father, Braddock, or myself aren't around," he said, shaking it in his fist. "If you find yourself in need, take hold of it and you'll find the help you need."

"Why are you making such a big deal about this?" asked Keigh. Mannie was rarely so adamant about anything as he had been about this little ball. "What's so special about it?"

Mannie opened his hand, balancing the sphere in his palm and looking into its reflective surface as snowflakes continued to melt on it. "All you need to know right now is that this sphere is more valuable to *you* than to anyone else in Eden, so do not part with it."

Keigh took the orb back and stuffed it in his pouch. "So, instead of an answer, you want me to trust you?" he asked, feeling bitter at being left in the dark again.

"I promise, as soon as the king is back in his throne room, I will tell you exactly what it is. But for now, if the information got out, there would be those who would try to take it from you, so the less you know the better." Mannie gave him a sympathetic smile. "Loose lips sink ships, you know."

"What's a ship?"

Mannie let out a hearty laugh, tossing free the snow that had settled in his wavy brown hair. "Sometimes I forget the world you know is so small. There is so much you have left to learn and experience. Ask Cato what a ship is if you have two hours of your life you don't care to lose, but for now: a ship is just a very large boat. People used to traverse great bodies of water in them, withstanding waves and storms that would turn Eden's fishing skiffs to splinters!"

That night, Mannie ate dinner with the family, staying late into the evening swapping stories with Owen by the crackling fire while the Anders children sat cross-legged on the worn wood floor, consuming each tale with eager ears and interrupting often to ask questions. Keigh felt as though the two men had lived a hundred lifetimes. Their storytelling reminded him that the king knew his father, and somewhere in his father's past was the story of how.

Afterward, Mannie collected his faithful steed, Rose, and rode off into the dull darkness of a snowy night. Keigh withdrew to his lumpy bed, pulling the thin blankets tight around his shoulders. But before he could drift off to sleep, his mother entered the room.

Sitting on the edge of his bed, she gently swept a wavy lock of hair out of his face and cradled the side of his head tenderly with her palm. "How's my boy?" she asked.

"Good, Mom. Just tired." Keigh gave her a reassuring smile.

"You've had a lot on your plate lately, and I'm worried your father and I haven't done enough to help."

"Help?" Keigh sniffed. "There's nothing you can do. Pretty sure everything that's happened to me is out of your control."

"You sure?" Sabriya gave her son a mischievous smile. "Your father and I are pretty tough, you know. I noticed you haven't been seeing much of Misselli since you've been back. What's happened there? You want me to talk to her for you?" She ruffled his hair, obviously knowing that was the last thing her son would want.

The familiar sinking feeling that emptied his chest when he thought of Misselli these days returned. "No, Mom, I need to fix that on my own. It's just...just a misunderstanding."

"Well, your father and I have been married a long time, and we've learned a lot over the years. If you ever want advice, you can ask us." Sabriya set her hand on top of Keigh's and gave it a squeeze. "We've weathered some pretty tough storms, you know. It hasn't always been this paradise you see in the Anders home today."

As if on cue, Jessie started crying for Sabriya from down the hallway.

"I'm going to go see to your sister, but I want you to know how much your father and I love you." She kissed him on the forehead and stood to leave.

"I love you too, Mom," Keigh said, the warmth of his mother's kindness doing battle against the chill of his situation with Misselli in his chest.

"Always and forever, son."

"Always and forever, Mom."

Sabriya made to leave, then slowly turned back around. "Also, your father and I haven't forgotten it's your birthday in two weeks. Be thinking about what you would like me to cook for you. Whatever it is, we'll make sure you get at least that." She smiled again and disappeared through the doorway.

Keigh grinned to himself, pulling his blankets back up and rolling onto his side. He hadn't forgotten. In fact, he would be the one getting his parents a gift: the gift of freedom from the Wulfs. He closed his eyes and imagined the looks on his family's faces as he rehearsed exactly how he would surprise them with the news. He hadn't been this excited since the day he'd been told he could test to be a cane—the first day of his life he'd been given reason to believe he wouldn't have to be a thrall forever. Now, his excitement wasn't just for himself; it was for his family. Tonight would be the last night he slept with that lump under his back, for tomorrow he would spend the gold that caused it. Tomorrow, the Anders would all be free.

*

Keigh found Vicerous early the next morning. Although he had never been to the Wulfs' home before, he knew where it was. The clouds continued to drop their big, fluffy flakes over Eden, blanketing the entire valley in flawless white.

Blonde-haired, red-cloaked Vicerous sat on his glossy black horse, a scorch mark on the otherwise clean world. The Anders family's better watched from a distance as a group of men packed the contents of his two-story house into wooden crates that they loaded onto horse-drawn carts.

Keigh approached the unnecessarily large timber home cautiously. Adjusting the rucksack on his back, he reminded himself that Vicerous was still a dangerous man, even when doing nothing wrong.

"What do you want?" Vicerous asked contemptuously, not taking his eyes off the workers.

Keigh had expected to be the first to speak, and this slight deviation, mixed with the fear of having his offer rejected, caused him to hesitate.

"Spit it out, boy. My horse shouldn't be made to breathe the same air as you for longer than absolutely necessary. It's beneath her."

Keigh stiffened. Everything in him wanted to smack the man's horse and send Vicerous sprawling in the snow. But today wasn't the day to fight. Today he needed to keep his temper.

"I want to pay my family's debt to you," stated Keigh firmly, just as he had rehearsed two dozen times on his walk from home that morning.

Vicerous finally turned his horse to face Keigh. "Are you sure?" he drawled, sounding a little too pleased. "The price is more than you think, boy."

"I'll pay whatever it is. Just hear me out."

"Will you, now?" Vicerous gave Keigh a very curious study before shaking his head and turning his horse back to face the workers. "Sorry, I'm not interested in whatever worthless trinkets or pinecones you've collected."

Keigh swung his rucksack off his shoulder and pulled out the velvet bag with the king's crest on it. "How 'bout gold?" He bounced the sack in the air between them, the coins inside emitting their metallic song.

At the sound, Vicerous turned his horse to face Keigh once again. "I accept." Leaning forward in his saddle, he snatched the bag from Keigh.

"Aren't you even going to count it?" Keigh asked, surprised. Surely the man who had opposed his family at every opportunity was not about to lie down now.

"No need." Vicerous appeared impressed as he hefted the bag in front of his face, feeling the weight of the gold. "You're all worthless. Any amount of gold is an upgrade." He loosened the drawstring on top of the bag to peer inside.

Keigh ground his teeth. His family's freedom from this monster couldn't have come soon enough. "Then why did you haggle with Mannie so hard when we left for the Refining?"

Vicerous cackled. "'Cause that old fool *does* think you're worth something! And he's got the king's resources to pay with." He cinched the top of the bag shut and stuffed it into one of his saddle bags. "Truth be told, I only kept your family in my service because your *parents* needed to be kept in line... Well, that's not entirely true." He smirked. "I did enjoy seeing Owen grovel, but I have no need of that anymore. I won't be returning to this backwoods cesspool again."

"Wait…You're leaving Bjorn for good?"

"Yes," sneered Vicerous, obviously taking issue with the hopeful tone of Keigh's voice. "The council has recognized my true value is wasted here. Really enjoyed the little switch I pulled on you, they did." He grinned, seeing Keigh's clenched fists at the reminder of his sabotage at the Refining. "I would think you'd be glad I did what I did, though. Your little one-legged friend from the gutter has never had so much gold! A fortune to him, but really, a small price to the council for his silence and your removal." His smile fell into a scowl when Keigh didn't react further. "Anyway, in the Capital, I will be of great value to the council, and when Deacon is named heir to Eden, I will be given a prominent position in the palace."

Evil! Wicked! Liar! Keigh fumed inwardly. Vicerous wanted him to react, wanted him to blow up the deal. But he wouldn't. Not today. What was done was done. Vicerous had accepted the gold, released his family, and was about to leave Bjorn forever.

Keigh slung his rucksack back onto his shoulder. "Well…good luck, then," he offered, scared to say more as he turned to leave.

Before Keigh had even gone five steps toward his newly bought freedom, Vicerous called after him, "You mustn't blame yourself, you know."

Keigh froze. *Just walk away. Don't take the bait.*

But he turned to face his antagonist. "Blame myself? For what?" he snapped.

Vicerous adopted a tone of mock sympathy. "For failing. For being a failure…It really is a miracle you got as far as you did, growing up in that home with Sabriya and that cuck, Owen," he spat, words dripping with contempt.

Keigh tensed. Every muscle in his body flexed, fighting the urge to lunge at the man insulting his family. "Say what you want about me, but keep my parents' names off your lips."

Vicerous smiled viciously, satisfied to have finally struck a nerve. The pompous cane straightened in his saddle. "Interesting choice of words," he drawled.

"What do you mean, snake?"

"Snake..." Vicerous sniffed, his lip curling. "Me, a snake? When it was *your* mother who slithered into my arms and put herself on my lips?"

"Shut up!" screamed Keigh, taking a threatening step toward Vicerous. "I'll report you to the elders for slander!" He dug his fingernails into the palms of his clenched fists. Vicerous would not talk about his mother that way and get away with it.

Vicerous let out a bark of laughter. "Your father would never allow it!" he said, smile widening.

"Why's that?" Keigh couldn't believe the man's arrogance. Even canes couldn't slander people with impunity. The king's law forbade it.

"For the same reason he hasn't ever told you why your family are thralls—the reason Mannie can't find any documentation of his indenture, and yet your father still maintains he owes me a debt..." Vicerous grinned like a cat who had finally trapped its mouse. "Because it's true."

"You lie!" Keigh shouted. His mother would never—not with anyone—especially not with this monster.

"So sorry to be the one to have to teach you this," Vicerous drawled. "But seeing how Owen and Sabriya would rather lie to you than tell you the truth, it falls to me to do so. Not all debts are financial, boy," he sneered. "Your mother's family were my parents' thralls before she ever married Owen. Guess she must have missed me, because even though Owen had already freed her of her indenture, your mother soon came running back, into my arms...into my bed."

He smiled, sitting a little straighter in his saddle as his black steed stomped in place.

"Once your mother's spell wore off of me—I never would have touched her if I were in my right mind; she was beneath me, thrall *filth*—she went running back to Owen, who, being the weak man that he is, took her back and begged me to keep her secret. And, being the fair man that I am, I agreed, of course—on the condition that he abandon his agoge as a cane and enter into my service for as long as he wished me to keep their secret."

"Lies!" bellowed Keigh, a hard knot forming in his throat. *Not my mother, she couldn't...She wouldn't...She loves us...*

"Search your heart, boy. You know it to be true."

Sweat beaded on Keigh's brow. Why were there no records? Why hadn't his parents ever told him what the debt was? His mother had been a thrall... Was this what she'd meant when she told him she had nearly destroyed her relationship with his father because she didn't trust that she was worthy of him?

Keigh's guts were trying to force their way up to his throat, and the knot that had formed there was the only thing keeping his heart from leaving with them. Tears filled his eyes, but he refused to blink. He wouldn't give Vicerous the satisfaction of knowing he had hit his mark. Vicerous hadn't even had to lift a hand to crush him more completely than Christian and his canes ever had. Everyone and everything he'd ever wanted or loved had rejected him. The king, Misselli, the Refining, and now...The two people he could always rely on to love him and be there for him had been lying to him his whole life.

If his mother had been willing to walk out on his father, she would certainly be willing to abandon him too. And his father...his father would let his family rot in the fields to protect his image and the image of a woman who had disgraced him? Owen was weak, just like Vicerous said. His father hadn't quit his agoge to be with his mother; Vicerous had forced him out, forced his whole family into a life of servitude! All to protect Keigh's traitorous mother. How could she? How could they? Keigh's whole life had been completely unnecessary. He could have grown up a cane's son and trained with the best equipment, eaten the best food, never had to endure the constant mockery and belittlement of his peers.

Keigh felt as though he could cry and not stop for weeks, but that would have to wait. Anger, burning hot anger, was all that could dry his eyes right now, so that was what he would be. Angry.

"Give me back my gold!" he demanded, reaching a hand out to Vicerous.

"The deal is done," said Vicerous casually, as though he had just gotten a loaf of bread at half price. "Your family has their freedom! What more could you want?" His smile was poison, eating away at the last of Keigh's resolve.

Keigh stretched his arm out further. "My father never owed you money, and now you've spilled his secret. Give me back my gold."

"Your *father*," Vicerous scoffed. "And no, not *exactly*. Yes, I told *you* his secret...but only you," he smirked. "In exchange for the gold, I'm promising to keep my mouth shut. Only you will have to live with the burden of knowing what scum your parents are."

Keigh lowered his arm, still simmering with anger at the smug snake before him, at his mother, his father, at everyone who cared nothing for him. "Why should I trust that you won't just take the gold and go tell everyone?"

Vicerous snorted derisively. "Please, don't insult me. I've kept their secret for nearly seventeen years and never told a soul. You have more cause to trust me than you do either of them. I, at least, told you the truth; Owen and Sabriya continue to lie to you. They've lied to you your whole life, and when you go home today, they'll continue to lie to you." Vicerous slicked back his blonde hair, wiping it free of snow. "I never wanted to hate *you*, you know," he said, his tone losing some of its menace. "But my hand was forced. I don't expect you to understand. I only ever treated you poorly because I knew the truth...Quite unfortunate for you that what you told my son *is* true." His lip curled, the menace in his voice returning as he looked Keigh up and down. "What was it again? You are who you're raised by?"

Vicerous huffed and turned his horse back to face the house.

"Now, get off my property. Come near me again and you'll pay in more than gold."

CHAPTER 32

BIRTHDAY BLUES

42-12-2

"Still burning, I see?" said Cato, opening the door to his home for Keigh to enter.

Keigh stepped in out of the cold as the old man closed the door behind him. "What? Um, yeah," he mumbled absentmindedly. He had almost forgotten he had told Cato the reason for his red eyes was that his family had been burning slash piles at the edge of their fields. In truth, he had been crying again. He felt bad for Copper. The poor animal had had to sit there and listen to him cry or watch him practice with Orvyn's sword every day while he avoided being at home. *Tomorrow, I'll take him exploring in the woods,* he told himself.

"Interesting," Cato mused. "You never smell of smoke." He watched Keigh out of the corner of his eye as he flipped the cushions on one of his armchairs.

"I...I change my clothes before coming here." Keigh flopped into a chair, hating that his parents' secrets had forced him to lie. Truth was, he hadn't changed his clothes more than three times since Vicerous had upended his entire world. Just taking his boots off to get in bed each night felt like a monumental accomplishment. Getting out of his clothes was asking too much.

"I didn't say you don't smell," said Cato, lowering himself slowly into a chair across from Keigh. "Only that you don't smell like smoke."

Keigh sank a little lower. "I'm sorry. I'll wash before coming back."

"Please do." Cato grinned. "If not for my sake, at least do it for Miss Labelle's."

Keigh winced at the stabbing pain in his chest. "Misselli? Why would she care? We've hardly said a word to each other in weeks."

"Oh?" said Cato, acting surprised. "Well, she dropped this off for you this morning." He produced a small glazed cake from behind a stack of worn books and set it on the low table between them. "Naturally, I invited her to stay and tell you happy birthday in person, but she insisted she had to help her mother with preparations for Winter Festival."

Keigh stared at the cake on the table. Maybe Misselli didn't hate him entirely? Or maybe her mother had made her deliver the cake. Either way, it was better than the silence that had occupied the void between them for weeks now, the one exception being the dressing down she had given him two weeks ago in the street. The last time he had seen his best friend, she had verbally slapped him, and the time before that, she had physically done the same. Even though he had made up with Conrad and the guys, Keigh hadn't had the courage to show up to club again looking or feeling as disheveled as he did.

"Tell her thanks for me, will you?" he asked.

Producing a small knife seemingly out of nowhere, Cato cut the cake and took a piece for himself. "You will tell her yourself, I think." He took a bite and chewed with exaggerated fervor. "Ah! Rita Labelle has worked her magic once again," he said, holding the piece of cake up to his eyes as a jeweler might hold a gem up for inspection.

"I don't know if I can do that," admitted Keigh, sounding as pathetic as he felt. There was so much he wanted to say to her—the first words out of his mouth couldn't be *Thanks for the cake*...

"You must," Cato insisted. "When people love you, the very least you owe them is gratitude." He turned the piece of cake around in his hand, apparently attempting to decide where to bite next.

Keigh sniffed. "She doesn't love me. She's mad at me."

"What more proof do you need?" Cato gave Keigh a brief glance, looking at him as though he had just said something very stupid. "Love *is* madness."

Keigh sighed. Perhaps Cato had a point. He loved his parents, but was still furious with them. He had hardly said a word to either of them in two weeks. They hadn't pushed him on his silence, no doubt because they thought he was upset about any of the other terrible things in his life.

"Eat a piece of cake, Master Anders." Cato nudged the knife across the table. "It will help you with your grumpys."

"I'm not *grumpy*," Keigh said, crossing his arms.

Cato snorted. "Oh, of course not. Not you, Master Anders," he sniggered at the sullen teen slumped in the chair across from him. "All I'm saying is, I've seen children look happier after receiving a paddling than you've looked the last two weeks."

"Can we just get on with the lesson?" Keigh groaned.

"Very well." Cato set what was left of his piece of cake on the table and brushed the crumbs out of his scraggly white beard. "Since today is your birthday, I thought I would allow you to ask me a few questions on whatever topics you desire. I don't know everything, but I do know a great deal. I can give you knowledge that many men would pay dearly to obtain."

Keigh perked up slightly. This was a good gift. He had a thousand questions for the elder, starting with: "Where is the king? Why do you think he's absent?"

Cato nodded and leaned back in his chair. "A worthy topic, though it's one where my answer will mostly consist of speculation and rumor. Firstly, though..." He wagged a finger at Keigh. "The king is never absent; he is always precisely where he is. As for where *that* is, he is rumored to be outside of Eden, on the front lines."

"The king is fighting back?" Keigh asked, leaning forward in his seat. "Has he declared war? Will he rally the canes?" He could hardly suppress his eagerness. This sounded more like the king he had grown up hearing about: mighty and strong, unbeatable in battle, the greatest warrior on earth.

Cato chuckled at Keigh's excitement. "No. His task is rumored to be a rescue mission, not a military offensive."

Keigh relaxed slightly. He had hoped the king would fight and that he would be called into service. As many issues as he had with certain people in Eden, Draiden was the real enemy. Draiden was the one who had tried to have him killed—not even the Queen's Council or Vicerous had gone that far...yet.

He leaned forward and cut himself a slice of cake. "So, if the king isn't fighting, how is he rescuing people?" he asked, stuffing the whole piece in his mouth.

"Simple, really: he presents himself to those outside of Eden and asks them to follow him back to safety."

"Will people come?" Keigh mumbled, his mouth full of cake. He swallowed it all in one dry, painful gulp. "What happens if he shows up with more people than Eden can hold? Wouldn't it be easier to just defeat Draiden and let people stay where they are? Why bring them back here?"

Cato inclined his head. "Another good question. No, not many will follow the king back to Eden. The journey is arduous, and the king only offers them the promise of a better life."

"So why don't they take it?"

"You know at least part of that answer." Cato smiled wryly. "To follow the king requires a great deal of trust, something you yourself are still wrestling with; and secondly, the offer of a better life is really only appealing to those who believe there is something wrong with the life they live now. There are those outside of Eden who live in comfort and plenty that you can't even imagine. They almost never accept the king's offer of rescue."

"Don't they know Draiden is coming? Sure, they might have it good now, but Draiden will strip them of everything. Just look at what he did to Marsough!"

Cato let out a long, heavy sigh. "Yes, I know, and you know, but you must realize that Draiden has been lord of the lands outside of Eden for many years—years of comfort and plenty for many of his subjects. When the king tells them that Draiden is coming to collect his dues, they seldom believe it, and if they do, they convince themselves that they can always just get to Eden on their own when they see Draiden coming." Cato closed his eyes for a long moment. "Little do they know that by that time, it will be too late."

"So why doesn't the king just kill Draiden?" Keigh asked again.

"The king cares deeply for all people, and because of that, he is not satisfied in giving them what is second best. Life in Eden under his rule is the best life available on earth, so he invites them to enter into it, rather than just solving the threats that plague them where they are." Cato gave his beard a pensive stroke, then added, "Besides, if it wasn't Draiden, it would be someone else. There are a thousand other kings outside of Eden, every one of them a lesser king than ours."

It made sense, at least for the king his mentors described to him. Still, Keigh thought it wouldn't hurt for the king to take out Draiden. "Will he ever confront Draiden?"

"If you believe in prophecy, then you know he will, for it has been foretold that *only one shall reign supreme, one shall win only to lose, and the other shall lose in order to win.*"

Keigh gaped at his teacher. "There's such a thing as prophecy?" he asked, forgetting his sadness, momentarily captivated by wonder.

Cato laughed. "Of course there is! Most prophecies concern the king, but some pertain to others..." He trailed off, fiddling with his hands in his lap. "New topic! What else would you like to know?"

Keigh wanted to know more about prophecies. Who made them? Were they all recorded somewhere? How did you know the difference between a prophecy and some madman's ranting? But he could tell Cato wanted to move on, so he resolved to bring the subject up again another day. "What do you know about Orvyn's armor?" he asked instead. He had now seen two pieces of it firsthand, and if the sword and helmet were real, why wouldn't the adamantine, belt, breastplate, and boots be real too?

Cato leaned back in his seat and eyed Keigh curiously. "Interesting topic...I take it you saw the helmet when you were in the Capital?"

"I did," said Keigh, "but obviously you know I couldn't lift it."

"No, not you or any man, for that matter."

"Is it true it makes its wearer immortal?" Keigh asked. "At least...the king told me it did."

Cato raised his eyebrows. "The king spoke to you about Orvyn's armor?"

"Well, not all the armor," Keigh admitted, "just the helmet. He was there the first night I tried to lift it."

Cato's smile widened. "The King of Eden met with you, one on one, in private?"

Keigh paused at the old man's curiosity. "Yeah...I mean, we just happened to both be there at the same time. It's not like it was scheduled or anything."

Cato's grin became even more satisfied. "Of course, just *coincidence*... To answer your question, there is some information I can give you on the armor, but most of its secrets are still that: secret. In all, there are six pieces of armor upon which Orvyn is said to have bestowed magical properties—"

"Magic?" Keigh blurted, nearly chopping off his finger as he cut his second slice of cake. "But magic isn't real."

Cato scowled. "Magic is real! Why shouldn't it be?"

"Well..." Keigh's mind raced to find a valid objection. His real objection was that it just seemed childish to believe in magic. It wasn't something rational adults put any stock in.

"Well what, Master Anders?" Cato was clearly amused by watching the wheels spin in Keigh's mind.

"Well, because...because it doesn't make sense! How does it work? There's no explanation for it!" Keigh could feel himself beginning to blush, but it was the best he could come up with on the spot.

Cato shook his head. "Might it be that there's something more to this world than what Keigh Anders can explain?" He looked down his nose at Keigh. "Assuming you knew half of everything there was to know in the world, might there be room for magic to exist in the half you don't know?"

Keigh was speechless, feeling even dumber than he had two seconds ago. Once again, the wizened old man had worded things in a way that left his arguments null and void.

"Not to mention, if you've seen Orvyn's helmet and failed to lift it, then you have witnessed magic firsthand."

"So Orvyn was a real-life—"

"Mage, yes."

Keigh looked around the study at the rows of shelves lined with books and scrolls. Cato was the most knowledgeable man he knew, aside from maybe Mannie, and if he was saying magic was real...then it must be. Keigh shot forward excitedly, leaning over the edge of his seat. "Are there other mages? Do you know any?"

"Do you want to know about the armor or about magic users?" Cato began braiding the unruly hairs of his beard into a single thick plait. "You know, I'm surprised that you are so shocked by this. As a potent, there are many who would believe what you can do is magic."

"But what I do isn't magic." Keigh locked his hands together and wondered for a second what would happen if he tried to pull energy from himself. Releasing his hands, he dismissed the idea as pointless. "It's just...moving energy around."

"Maybe so," conceded Cato, "but why, then, can you take energy and convert it to unnatural strength, and young Master Pipps can only pull energy and store it?"

"What? Theo's a potent too?" Keigh asked, doing a rather poor job of feigning surprise.

"Please, Master Anders. I know you know he is. Theo may be able to hold limitless amounts of energy, but he has little to no ability to hold his tongue." The old man shook his head. "Another attribute you two have in common."

Keigh's cheeks warmed. He could no longer look Cato in the eye.

"But back to my original question. If there's nothing magic about what you boys can do, and it's just a natural process, why are your abilities so different?"

"I don't know..." Keigh shrugged. "Why are some people short and others tall? People are just different."

Cato pursed his lips and nodded. "A fair point. Now, back to your first question: the armor." The elder continued to braid his beard as he began his rundown. "The helmet is located in Sentinel. Orvyn wrought magic in it to make its wearer unkillable, but protected it with a magic that also makes it unliftable. The rest of the pieces of armor are lost or hidden. It is said that when Orvyn left Eden he wore only his belt, breastplate, and boots, leaving the sword, adamantine, and helmet behind. The sword was held in Sentinel, much like the helmet, for many years. Unlike the helmet, people could lift the blade and wield it, but any time someone tried to leave its chamber with it, the sword would halt itself at the door. Much like the helmet, it was a popular attraction for quite some time.

"I myself visited both the sword and the helmet in my younger years. The blade was said to be sharper than any other sword and never dulled or broke. It also shone with a light from within that illuminated the sword's surroundings without blinding its wielder. However, its light was visible only to those who had held it before. Those who visited the sword often claimed the light got brighter the more often they held the blade. But after years and years with no evidence that the sword could be taken from the room, people lost interest and forgot about it, just as they have the helmet."

"Wait—go back." Keigh's heart was pounding. "Did you say the only people who could see the sword's light were those who had held it before?"

"Yes, that was one of its qualities."

Keigh had seen the light of Verity before ever picking up the blade. What did it mean? Why could he do what no other had done?

Cato looked up from his beard, hands full of hair. "Why do you ask?"

"How did it get moved?" blurted Keigh, hoping to deflect whatever suspicions the old man might be forming.

Cato eyed him. "Who said it was moved?"

"Well, I—you—you said the sword *used* to be in the Capital," Keigh stammered. "So, it's not there anymore, is it?"

"True, I did." Cato resumed his braiding. "King Thiamtaim took it, of course."

The king took it? Why doesn't he still have it? Why is it sitting in a hole in the ground next to Bjorn? Keigh's mind whirled with questions, none of which he dared ask Cato for fear he would reveal too much. "What about the adamantine?"

"That piece was never on display. The only reason it's believed to still be in Eden is that Orvyn wasn't wearing it when he left. It was said to be unbreakable like the sword, and infused with a magic that allowed it to capture the energy of any blow it sustained and transfer that energy to the wearer. So, the more an enemy struck at the adamantine, the stronger the wearer became." Cato tied a knot in the end of his beard and happily dropped the braid onto his chest. "I think we've got time for one more question before I send you home to celebrate with your family."

Keigh frowned. He didn't want to go home—not just because he was distraught about his parents, but because he still had so many questions for Cato. "What do you know about red bears?" he asked.

Cato grinned. "Fascinating animals, red bears. Fearsome in battle yet gentle enough to play with children. It's said they can understand spoken commands after only months of being paired with a human. The largest reds are a hair over thirty feet when standing upright, with the smallest of them still standing at over twenty. Unshakably loyal—nearly every red bear who doesn't die of old age dies defending its partner. They also have an innate ability to sense innocence and guilt. Many elders will request the presence of a red bear when trying particularly weighty crimes for that reason. If the red bear likes the accused, elders are much less likely to convict, while if the bear becomes agitated or angry, it is all but certain the accused is guilty."

"How do they do that?" asked Keigh. He knew Mace and Copper were intelligent, but how could they possibly know a person's inner being?

"Magic, obviously," Cato said with a wink, then shrugged. "Who knows? Many mystifying things happened in the Great Collapse. Some wondrous, some terrible. How the red bears sense innocence I do not know, but I do know they can. You should, too—hasn't Mace defended you twice now?"

Twice? thought Keigh. "She and the other reds tried to defend me when I was removed from the Refining, but the night I got beat up, Mace wasn't really defending me. She got there after I'd been attacked."

Cato shook his head. "I'm not referring to the night you were attacked in Sentinel. I'm referring to the night the tower burned. She had every authority to kill you that night, but she didn't. She knew you weren't guilty in the way you claimed to be. That, more than anything, is what persuaded Master Fortier to stay his hand and investigate the incident more thoroughly."

"Some investigation," Keigh grumbled. "I still ended up on the whipping post."

"If I recall correctly, that was at your own insistence, was it not?" Cato wagged a finger at him. "Do not blame Braddock for your suffering. You don't get to play the martyr and the victim. You chose martyrdom. Even though I didn't know what you were doing at the time, Master Fortier did. He allowed you to take the fall for your friends. Do you now wish he hadn't? Or do you merely wish he would have persecuted your friends for you so that you didn't have to be the villain?" Cato's blue eyes began their familiar practice of piercing through Keigh's facade, right to his innermost thoughts.

Keigh's tongue was frozen. Had he wanted his friends to pay for leaving him to face punishment alone? No, that wasn't it. Misselli had tried and he would never have allowed it. He had done what he did for the right reason, but Cato had touched a nerve he hadn't expected. Did he regret saving his friends?

"I never wanted my friends to suffer any harm, I just..." He paused. "I just expected a bit of gratitude, maybe..."

"You did a noble thing, Master Anders." Cato stood up with a grunt. There were a dozen little snaps as his back straightened. Flattening the front of his tunic, he brushed off the remaining cake crumbs. "Don't ruin it by feeling bad for yourself. A hero for the sake of recognition is no hero at all, and one who seeks thanks, deserves none."

Keigh hung his head, feeling foolish for harboring bitterness toward his friends. "You're right," he said, slouching back into his chair.

"Of course I am! Why be wrong when you can be right?" Cato extended a hand to Keigh to help him up. "Come on, now. Head on home to your family and enjoy the evening with them." He pulled Keigh to his feet and gave him an encouraging pat on the back as the two made their way out of the study toward the front door. "I know they are proud of you, just as I, too, am proud of you."

They might be proud of me, but I am not proud of them, thought Keigh, opening the door and stepping onto the front step. The hard knot in his throat had returned at the mention of his family. "Thanks," he croaked, hoping Cato would assume he was choked up over hearing how proud of him everyone was.

Keigh took his time going home. He spent nearly an hour lingering in front of Rita Labelle's bake shop, pretending to be interested in items on display in the windows of various other shops, hoping Misselli might see him. But when it became clear that nobody inside was going to come out, he gave up hope and started the lonely trek home, shuffling through the snow, watching his tears disappear as they fell into the white.

He stopped at the gate in the rail fence that circled his home. Taking a moment to regain his composure, he looked at the house that had been his home all his life: windows glowing, smoke rising from the chimney in the gray light of dusk. *A home built on lies,* he thought, tightening his grip on the fence. He scowled at the building as if it were a monster there to consume him.

Today was the day he had planned on telling his family of their freedom from the Wulfs. Today should have been the happiest day of his life, but instead his heart tore even wider between his sadness at the loss of the parents he had known and his anger at the ones he now knew. Mostly he was just sad, though. More than anything, he wanted that warm feeling he got each time his mother pulled him close or his father told him how proud he was, but now everything they did felt like salt in the wound. Every hug was a lie, every praise a deception meant to keep him and his siblings in the dark.

"Gold," he scoffed, remembering Cato's lesson. *More like fool's gold,* he thought, kicking open the squeaky gate and trudging up the hill.

When he opened the door, he was met with a blast of noise as his family shouted in unison, "Happy birthday!"

Jessie scuttled across the room and wrapped herself around his legs. "Happy birthday, Keigh!" she squeaked, looking up at him adoringly with her big brown eyes.

Keigh hugged his little sister. There was still warmth there. He released the breath he hadn't realized he'd been holding. Maybe he wouldn't always feel so cold. Maybe he could come to trust his parents again. He smiled down at Jessie. This home wasn't *all* a lie. His heart wasn't beyond repair. If only Jessie knew the hope she gave him.

"You've got a present, Keigh! Open it! Open it!" She tugged on his hand, pulling him toward the wooden table where his family sat waiting for him.

His mother and father stood up from the bench to greet him as he got to the table. "My boy! A man! Officially a man!" Beaming at Keigh, Owen wrapped him in a tight squeeze before passing him off to his mother.

Sabriya took his hands in her own and tried to meet his eyes. "I made you your favorite meal." When Keigh didn't respond, she pulled him into a hug. "Today is a good day! We have much to be thankful for, and today, we are all thankful for you." She gave him a tight squeeze, then let him go and sat back down.

Keigh took his seat next to Jessie and looked at the plates steaming on the table before him: beef steaks grilled to perfection on the fire, mashed potatoes, sweet cream butter, pickled asparagus, and honey-glazed sugar buns. All his favorite foods, yet the sick feeling in his stomach stripped him of his appetite.

Jessie tugged on Keigh's sleeve and pointed to a long, rectangular package wrapped in brown paper at the end of the table. "Mommy, can he open his present now?"

Sabriya giggled at her impatience. "It's up to your brother, sweetie."

"What is it?" Keigh asked, careful not to sound too interested. "Vicerous won't be happy if he finds out you spent money on a gift for me." He knew the threat was idle. His parents had entered them into the monster's service; they could live in it a little longer.

"Bah! Vicerous won't tell me what I can and can't do for my kids," huffed

Owen. "Anyway, it's not from us. Someone left it at the post hall for you. Nobody there recognized the man who left it. He told them it was for 'Keigh Anders, the rightful winner of the Refining'!" Owen clapped a hand on Keigh's back and squeezed his shoulder. "Whoever the stranger was, he sounds like a right smart man to me."

Keigh nodded for Jobey to pass him the package. He wasn't sure what to think about a gift from a stranger. Last time a stranger had showed up in Bjorn, the man had tried to kill him.

"Careful, it's kinda heavy." Jobey handed Keigh the package. "We've been trying to guess what it is all afternoon."

"Jobey thinks it's a roast," Jotham offered. "I think it's dough for cinnamon rolls."

"Either way it's food, you think?" Keigh asked sarcastically.

His brothers both looked offended. "Those would be great gifts!" Jobey argued.

"I'm sure you think so," Keigh conceded as he began to tear the brown paper off the long box. Beneath it was a polished wooden chest five times as long as it was wide.

"What's in it?" squealed Jessie.

Keigh turned the chest around so he could lift the lid. Slowly, he opened it.

"Whoa!" Jessie exclaimed, standing up on the bench to look into the box. "What is it? It's so shiny!"

Keigh stood dumbfounded at the gift that lay before him: an adamantine of such exquisite beauty that he had never seen its like.

Lifting the metal arm out of the box, he raised it for everyone to see. His mother gasped and covered her mouth.

"No way!" his brothers chimed in unison, mirroring each other's slack-jawed awe.

The adamantine's bright burnished silver was covered with intricate etchings of vines and flowers of every kind. Keigh bent the arm at its elbow. A sharp, dagger-like protrusion extended ten inches out of the forearm plates. *A weapon and a shield,* he marveled. Inside the cuff was a metal handle; Keigh assumed it was what the wearer gripped when throwing punches. The end of the gauntlet portion had large metal knobs that were braced back into the forearm for extra support. He rotated the adamantine, marveling at how light it was. The wooden chest weighed more than the metal arm itself.

"Put it on!" shouted Jessie, hopping up and down on the bench beside Keigh.

"Yeah! Let's see if it makes you actually look like a cane and not just some skinny little brother!" Jotham teased.

Keigh slid his arm into the armor, feeding his hand down through the top of the sleeve. Cinching the leather ties tight, he flexed his elbow. *It fits perfectly!* Keigh grinned as he tested his arm's full range of motion. It was as if he wore nothing more than a linen sleeve. The armor was so light and comfortable he felt he could probably sleep in it. Then he remembered the sharp protrusion at the elbow and thought he better not try it.

"This is incredible!" Keigh grinned, throwing a punch at the air over the table.

"I'm just happy to see you smiling again," his mother said.

"We should sell it."

His father spoke for the first time since Keigh had opened the present. He was staring at the silver armor, strumming his fingertips nervously on the table.

"What?" Keigh snapped. "You can't be serious."

"Owen!" chided Sabriya.

"I am serious," Owen confirmed, staring at the silver on Keigh's arm. "The armor is worth more than our house. The money from its sale could feed this family for years." Owen took his eyes off the adamantine and looked Keigh in the eyes. "You understand, right, son?"

Keigh gripped the handle inside the armor, a volcano of anger threatening to erupt inside of him. "Understand?" he spat. "You want me to understand... *now?*" He glared at his father, who no longer looked nervous, but concerned. "Why don't you help me understand this, Father...Why are we thralls? Huh? Mannie said there are no records of our family having any debt with the Wulfs.

Why don't we go down to town tomorrow and bring it to Cato's attention? I bet he would love to release us!"

"We can't do that, son." Owen gave Keigh a look, a plea for him to stop.

But Keigh had no intention of stopping, not now. His father had deprived him and his siblings their whole lives to keep his secrets, and now he wanted Keigh to sacrifice the most valuable thing he had ever owned so that he could keep covering for Keigh's mother? No. He was going to force his parents to be honest with him.

"Why not? Help me *understand*," Keigh drawled, glowering at his father. Never had he had less respect for the man before him than right now.

Owen stood. "Sabriya, take Jessie to her room," he commanded, looming large over his youngest son.

"Jessie can go. She stays," said Keigh, pointing an accusatory finger at his mother.

Owen inhaled slowly though flared nostrils. "It may be your birthday, but do *not* try to control your mother."

"Maybe if you had, I wouldn't have to!" snapped Keigh, matching his father's intensity.

Owen's eyes quivered, the blood draining from his face as he started to piece together what Keigh meant. "Who told you?" he asked calmly.

"Jessie, go. Now!" Keigh barked at his sister, not speaking again until he heard her sad little whimpers fade as she ran down the hall to her room. "Who do you think told me?"

"Vicerous! That viper!" Owen punched the tabletop, clattering all the dishes of hot food.

Keigh shook his head, disappointed. "Don't be mad Vicerous had the courage to do what you didn't."

Owen redirected his outrage. "Oh? And what would you have done in my shoes? Let your wife be sentenced to death?" he shouted.

Keigh bit his lip, too angry to respond at first. "No!" he said eventually. "But I wouldn't have let my whole family go down with her either! You didn't have to let Vicerous order you around. You could have been a cane. But you chose *her.*" He pointed again in the direction of his mother, unwilling to even look at her.

Owen's nostrils flared. "Yes, I did! And I would choose her again, and again, and again! Anders don't *ever* walk out on family!" he yelled, slicing a hand through the air.

"Why not?" Keigh clapped back, disregarding the muffled sounds of his mother sobbing behind him. "She walked out on you! Walked out on us!"

"When I married your mother, I promised to love her for the rest of my life with all that I am, and that's exactly what I've done." Owen slapped his own chest in emphasis.

"Well, she obviously didn't promise the same!" spat Keigh.

Owen exhaled. "Your mother made a mistake. Would you have her die for it?"

The tears that had been held back by rage broke through as Keigh allowed the sound of his mother's weeping mix with the image of her dying. "No," he choked, trying to hold strong. "But I wouldn't have made my children pay for it either."

His father's expression relaxed. "Son...what would you have had me do? Shame your mother? Tell her children, who rightfully adore her, that their mother isn't worthy of their love?"

"She's *not* worthy, and neither are you." Keigh wiped a tear off his cheek aggressively, his whole body shaking. He faced the ground, fearing that if he looked at his father for one more second, he might lose what little control he still possessed.

"None of us are, son. Deal with it. Everyone lets you down at some point. It's how you love people through their faults that defines you. Nobody gets through life perfect." Owen took hold of Keigh's trembling shoulders. "You might have asked for a better father, but you could not ask for a better mother."

"Well, maybe I want both," said Keigh, lifting his face to stare defiantly into his father's eyes. Tears had started to form in their corners, giving his father a pitiful look. This wasn't the strong, confident man Keigh knew; this man was broken, weak, just like Vicerous said. Would he fight or just lie down? Keigh was going to find out.

"You don't mean that," Owen mumbled, his bottom lip beginning to quiver. "You're just angry, that's all."

"Angry? You think I'm angry?" Keigh roared, his blood boiling again. "You're right! I'm angry! I gave Vicerous three hundred justicia in gold to buy our release...and you know what I got in return?" he asked with a bitter laugh. "Not the happiest day of my life, but the worst day of my life! I wanted to surprise you for my birthday, but instead you surprised me. Congratulations! You're free, but now I have to live with knowing the people I thought were my heroes were actually my captors this whole time."

Keigh shrugged his father's hands off his shoulders and stalked back to his room. Slamming the door behind him, he pulled out his rucksack and started stuffing it full of clothes. When the bag was full, he flung the door open and stomped back out to the great room, where his father sat consoling his mother, who was weeping uncontrollably.

"Son..." Sabriya tried to grab Keigh's arm, but he ripped it out of her grip.

"Where are you going?" asked his father, eyeing the rucksack on Keigh's back.

"Anywhere but here!"

"Son," Owen pleaded, reaching a hand toward Keigh. "It's freezing outside. Don't do this."

"Somehow it still feels colder in here," sneered Keigh, looking at his parents' tear-streaked faces. He stalked the rest of the way to the door and flung it open, letting in a swirl of snow. "Enjoy your new freedom. You'll just have to enjoy it without me." He nodded to his brothers who had been struck silent by the exchange, then looked at his parents one last time. "Don't come looking for me."

Keigh slammed the door behind him, silencing their cries. Reflexively, he raised his hand to place it on the weathered bear head carved into the door like he always did. He considered the image: gray, cold, unfeeling. He lowered his hand. He wouldn't promise to come back. He couldn't this time.

He could still hear his parents crying through the door. His hand drifted toward the latch. *Just go back in,* he thought. *You can get through this.*

Shaking his head clear, he tore himself off the front step and began trudging through the snow toward the gate. Every fiber of his heart yearned to run back to his parents, to hug them and be hugged by them, but it was too late. He had said too much; they had lied too long. There was no fixing this.

Whatever they had been to him was broken now.

CHAPTER 33

SNOW DANCING

46-15-49

Keigh lowered Orvyn's sword, panting. He punched the stone figure in front of him with the metal knuckles of his adamantine, leaving four powdery dots where the metal had ground the stone to flour.

The sparring dummy was barely more than a knob now. In the week since Keigh had left home, he had spent nearly every waking moment he wasn't with Cato practicing with the sword, or exploring the forest above the watchtower with Copper. His duels with the stone man and his hikes with Copper were the only things that seemed to dull the hurt he felt.

How could they? Another shard of rock ricocheted off the stone as he struck what used to be the neck. *I thought they loved me!* Another blow, and another chip in the block. *Liars!* Stab. *Cowards!* Hit. *Cheater!* Cut.

Keigh turned a full revolution, putting everything he had into a swing he hoped would cleave the stone dummy in half. A burst of dust and rock shards flew into the air. Verity sang in his hands like a bronze bell, its clean ring filling the chamber. Breathing heavily, Keigh let the sword fall from his fingers. Its melodic ringing degenerated into a jangle of metallic pings and dings as the blade clattered on the hard floor.

Keigh slumped to his knees. *What am I doing here?* He clasped his hands over his face. The cool metal of his adamantine wicked the heat from his forehead. He wanted to go home, but if he went home now, his parents might think they had won. They had certainly not won. He wanted them to beg for his forgiveness. They owed him that much. All his life a thrall? A mockery? So that they could keep their secret?

He loved his parents. The constant, debilitating ache in his chest was confirmation enough of that—but they were the ones who needed to make it right. He would not go groveling back and let them think he was the one who was sorry. What did he have to be sorry for? Exposing their lies?

Keigh cringed, hearing his own words echo back to him in his mind. He had said some terrible things, awful, untrue things, the night of his birthday. He wished he could take them all back. He hadn't meant them; he'd just been so angry. Hopefully they knew that.

He screamed at the ceiling, releasing the pressure in his chest and startling Copper awake. The bear sauntered over and planted his warm nose on Keigh's forehead, trying to nudge his hands off his face.

Keigh straightened up a bit, taking Copper's head in his arms. He hugged his friend's furry face and gave him a few good scratches under the jaw.

"You'll never let me down, will you, boy?" Keigh said, allowing Copper to pull away.

The bear sat down on his haunches and observed Keigh with big amber eyes. After a moment his mouth dropped open as he breathed excitedly.

"I'm taking that as a no," said Keigh, appreciating the simple nature of their relationship.

He stood up and patted Copper on the side. Picking Verity up off the ground, he performed a couple more progressions and poses. The sword could not have been more perfect. Every time he picked it up, it fascinated him all over again. From its flawless weight and balance to its impossibly sharp edges, it was an unparalleled weapon. The thing that intrigued him most, however, was the light. At first the blade had resonated with a dull glow, but now it seemed a bright light—probably a side effect of Keigh having lived underground for a week. But whether his eyes had adjusted or the sword shone brighter, he could now see his surroundings with absolute clarity, better than if the room had been ringed with torches.

"Oh no!" Keigh whirled around. "What time is it? Cato is going to kill me if I'm late again!" He darted to the pile of clothes strewn against the wall and grabbed his thinning wool cloak. "I gotta go! See you after, boy!"

He sprinted out through the archway, only to be violently halted as Verity hit the magic barrier, preventing the sword from leaving the hall.

"Oooof!" Keigh's feet flew out from under him as he landed hard on his back. He stared up at the illuminated vine carved into the underside of the arch. *At least I didn't run into the edge of the blade,* he thought, exhaling his relief and scrambling back to place the sword on its podium. "Let's try this again," said Keigh, raising his eyebrows at his clearly unimpressed red bear. "Bye, Copper," he shouted, sprinting out the door successfully this time.

Keigh jogged as fast as he could across the crusty patches of snow and ice that covered long stretches of his path. Arriving at the portcullis, he checked the sun. *I'm not late!* Bending over, he rested his hands on his knees while he caught his breath. That was when he saw something he had not expected to see that day, or any day in the near future: Deacon Wulf was striding down the main street out of Bjorn, closely followed by Cecilia Giles.

"Did he ever mention me?" asked Cecilia, following so closely after Deacon she nearly stepped on his trailing black robe every few steps.

"No," said Deacon, looking more unpleasant than usual. He didn't appear interested in slowing down for the beautiful redhead. He stomped toward Keigh, sounding exasperated as he said, "Why would Tarin talk about you when he could have any girl in Eden?"

Cecilia stopped, clearly stung by Deacon's bluntness. Then, with a subtle shake of her head, she appeared to change tactics. "I'm glad you're back." She smiled and resumed chasing after him. "I was only asking about Tarin because it's wonderful to think that one of our friends is going to be the next King of Eden."

She must have said the wrong thing, because Deacon's face soured dramatically. Keigh thought he might be about ready to scream at her when Deacon finally noticed him.

He stopped and looked Keigh up and down. "Keigh," he said, his voice sounding a hair less contemptuous than usual.

"Deacon." Keigh nodded, adding a scowl for good measure. The last time he had seen Deacon, the sleaze had bested him in front of twenty thousand cheering fans using a coin he would later blame Keigh for stealing. The memory of Deacon's unique ability to rob him of things he wanted stayed his tongue.

"I suppose you aren't surprised to see me here," said Deacon, straightening his stance. "You always knew it would be Tarin and not me."

Cecilia put two hands on Deacon's shoulder and sidled up close to him. "I'm surprised, baby! I just knew you were the king's son!"

"Stop, Cecilia!" Deacon barked, looking annoyed at the flattery that had always left him looking smug and arrogant before.

"Actually, I am surprised," Keigh admitted. "Not because I thought you would win, but I did at least think you would make it to the end."

"I did!" snapped Deacon. "The Refining is over, Anders."

"What?" asked Keigh, taken aback. "But the Refining lasts till spring..."

"It's *supposed* to." Deacon seemed to be trying very hard to keep his composure. "But the king has been gone for a month now and the queen has called an end to the competition, naming Tarin heir, and my..." He paused, nostrils flaring. "My *father*, the Queen's Shield."

Keigh couldn't find words. He had expected Tarin or Deacon to be named the heir of Eden, but not until the end of the Refining, and not by the Queen. And Vicerous was a snake—why would the queen want him anywhere near her? It must have been the council and his good friend Slate that had appointed him. They were just as slimy as he was. *Good riddance,* Keigh thought.

"So why are you back? Didn't want to stay with Daddy?" he teased. Deacon hadn't provoked him yet, but it was only a matter of time. He might as well get in the first barb.

Deacon tensed, once again visibly waging war to keep his composure. Keigh grinned, sickly delighted. But to his surprise, Deacon seemed to be winning that battle.

"My *father*," Deacon sneered, his eyes shifting uncomfortably, "has sent me back to look after his things here."

"Not even sixteen and he has his own house," gloated Cecilia.

"Well, congratulations." Keigh gave a slight bow. "Even the king of nothing should have his own castle."

Deacon bared his teeth, but once again refused to clap back.

"He got closer to being king than you ever will!" said Cecilia, grabbing hold of Deacon's arm.

"Guess I was just born one month too soon." Keigh smiled disdainfully at Cecilia. "So, what now? Does that make you the queen of nothing?"

Deacon ripped his arm from Cecilia's grasp and stormed off. Cecilia gave Keigh a dissatisfied huff then turned her nose up and chased after her king.

Satisfied that he had finally gotten a rise out of one of them, Keigh set off up the main street toward Cato's. Bjorn's dirt streets and tar-stained wooden buildings were all decorated with pine boughs and candles. Red and green tapestries hung from ropes strung across the main road. Winter Festival began tonight.

A sharp pang wrenched at Keigh's chest. Winter Festival was his favorite holiday. Not just because it was the only holiday where gifts were exchanged, but because it was the one that celebrated family. Every night of the festival, his family would come to Bjorn to drink fizzy wine and eat sweet breads with the rest of the town. They'd listen as traveling bards told stories and sang songs of epic adventures and heroes of Eden at the common grounds. When all the epics had been told and songs had been sung, his family would go home and sit in front of a blazing fire to hear their father and mother tell stories of their families. Stories they were meant to learn and pass on to their own children someday.

Had those nights been real? Were all the love and memories just part of one big elaborate lie, meant to cover the ugly truth? Or had it been genuine?

Was the love who his parents really were, and the ugly bits the lie? Keigh shook his head, trying to rid himself of thoughts of family. He wouldn't be seeing them tonight and there was no point trying to figure it out until they apologized.

He walked past the Labelles' bakery, salivating at the pile of sugar buns stacked high in the front window. It reminded him that last year had been his favorite festival ever, even though it had arguably been the worst. Misselli had been sick the whole time, so instead of going to town each night with his family, Keigh had brought the festival to her. He cut fresh pine boughs and filled her room with them, a gesture Misselli's parents hadn't been particularly happy about. Then, each evening he would bring fizzy wine and an assortment of sweet breads for them to snack on. While their families were both in town celebrating with everyone else, the two of them had spent the time reliving their favorite memories from their friendship.

Keigh smiled even as his insides wrenched. His favorite memory of Misselli was the time she had tried to catch a small painted turtle that had ventured too far from the water of Mueller's pond. In her excitement she had sprinted down the hill after the turtle, but it was too fast, making it back into the water before Misselli could get her hands on it. As funny as seeing her get out-run by a turtle was, the best part was when she tried to stop her momentum and stepped in a fresh cow pie. Her feet flew out from under her, landing her squarely in the dung. She slid all the way into the pond, coated in mud and wet cow pie. Keigh had laughed so hard he thought he would pass out. Then, when he finally got down to the edge of the water to help her out, she pulled him in with her.

He grinned, remembering how Misselli had thrown a sugar bun at his head for saying that was his favorite memory. It was a good memory, but it wasn't actually his favorite. His favorite wasn't really a memory at all, more of a compendium of moments shared with her. The way she laughed when she got hiccups, or smiled at him when he was angry about something stupid. The way she made a wish every time she saw a bluebird or weaved dry blades of grass into golden flowers that she would tuck behind her ear. Every moment with her was his new favorite memory, because they were in it together.

Still smiling to himself, he rounded the corner to his teacher's house and saw the mountain of black fur that was Mace, sitting dutifully outside the elder's cedar-shake home.

If the Refining is over, that means Braddock is back! Keigh realized, brightening at the thought of resuming his lessons on combat and furthering his abilities as a potent. Maybe the retired cane would even let Keigh stay with him? He wouldn't have to sleep another night underground with Copper and Verity.

"Hey, Mace!" Keigh said, approaching the black giant. "Thanks for defending me. You might have saved my life, you know."

Mace lowered her head to Keigh's level. A low thrum emanated from her throat as though she were thanking him for his recognition.

Keigh reached up and gave her a few vigorous scratches on top of her head. Suddenly she snorted and pointed her gigantic nose straight at his chest. Sniffing in and out rapidly, she reared back and gave him a puzzled look.

"She smells Copper," stated Braddock from Cato's doorway. Before Keigh could greet him, Braddock barked, "Now get inside!"

What did I do now? Keigh wondered, confused.

Entering Cato's study, he found the old man sitting in his chair, smiling happily as usual. "Hello, Master Anders," Cato chimed.

"Sit down," commanded Braddock.

Keigh took his normal seat across from Cato while Braddock stalked the room, glowering at him.

"You left home?" Braddock asked. It wasn't a question, but an accusation. "What were you thinking? Go home, Keigh." The warrior's arms flexed menacingly as he gripped the back of a cushioned chair. "Tonight."

"No," said Keigh, locking eyes with his master. He could glare too, and he scowled with all his might at the man presuming to tell him how to live his life. What did Braddock know about family?

Braddock raised his brows. "Excuse me?"

"I said no." Keigh gripped the armrest of his own chair. "You don't know what they did."

"You think I need to know what happened to tell you what you did was foolish?" Braddock pointed a finger at Keigh's chest. "Your father and mother would do anything for you, and how do you repay them? By storming out? They're worried sick!"

"Maybe they deserve it," grumbled Keigh.

"Deserve it? What on earth could they have possibly done to deserve such disrespect?"

Keigh glared at Braddock as he debated telling him of his mother's indiscretion and his father's cowardice. "You wouldn't understand," he said, crossing his arms and staring out the window.

"Try me!" Braddock walked around the chair and sat down in it. "You think I've never been mad at your dad?"

Keigh turned to face him. Braddock had been best friends with his dad and Vicerous. Did he already know? Was this the scandal that tore them all apart? "No...I know you used to be friends."

"He was my best friend," Braddock corrected him. "We were going to conquer the world together! He was the most impressive cane apprentice in Eden before he quit. You know, he was actually supposed to have a pairing appointment with Mace before I did. He was almost there! Six months from earning his cloak. Then he gave it all up...for family. Where do you think you get it, Keigh? You're great because your father is great." Braddock inhaled slowly. "But I didn't think you would quit like him."

"I'm not quitting," said Keigh.

"Yes, you are. Your father may have quit on our dream, but he never quit on his family. Make it right. Go back home."

"What makes you so sure he wouldn't?" Keigh asked bitterly. His father had quit on their family the day he bent the knee to Vicerous.

"Because I know!" snapped Braddock. "When your father quit his agoge, he devoted himself to your mother like no man I had ever seen. I couldn't even get him to come to Sentinel with me for my cloaking ceremony. I didn't like it, and I didn't agree with it, but the man chose what he thought mattered and never backed down from it. Owen Anders had never doubted our destiny, and overnight he decided to throw it all away. He's the best friend I've ever had, but he didn't quit on our friendship. I did."

Braddock paused to take a breath.

"I convinced myself it was your father's fault. He abandoned our plans, then refused to accept my help when Vicerous suddenly claimed a debt over him. He wouldn't fight! The best fighter I ever met, and the man just wanted to lie down and take it! I could see it tearing him apart. He wanted to explain it all to me, but he could never bring himself to do it...I wanted our dream more than I wanted my friend, so eventually I gave up on him. I hated Vicerous for how he treated your father, and I hated your father for protecting him."

Silence prevailed as Keigh digested what Braddock had said. Cato continued smiling happily at the two angry men arguing in his study.

"He does that," Keigh responded at last. "He protects people who don't deserve it." Vicerous and his mother were the last people who deserved loyalty from his father.

"You should know," said Braddock flatly. "Remember when you were tried and convicted for burning the watchtower and endangering the lives of everyone in Bjorn? Did you *deserve* saving then?"

"You know why I confessed to that," snapped Keigh.

"Yes, *I* do, but your father didn't." Braddock rapped his knuckles on the coffee table. "As far as he knew, his son had set the tower on fire as a joke, but you know what he did? He got on his knees in front of me and begged to take your place. He begged a man who had quit on him to allow him to rescue a son who had shamed him." Braddock's eyes began to water. "He didn't care if you were the guiltiest man on the planet. He would have gladly taken your lashes to save you."

Keigh had to choke back his own tears. "Well, I'm his son—what father wouldn't? Still doesn't mean he should have covered for Vicerous. He should have listened to you. He should have fought back! What's so noble about falling on your sword for someone like that?"

"If you only knew the half of it!" said Braddock, leaning forward in his seat. "Many people would die for their family, but would they give their life for a stranger? Or even an enemy like Vicerous? Many a man could be convinced to lay down their life for king, country, or loved ones, but few would dare lay down their life for a stranger—even fewer for an enemy."

"That's 'cause it's foolish," Keigh retorted. Was Braddock really going to try to convince him someone like Vicerous was worth shielding?

"No, not foolish. Selfless. To lay down your life for someone who has done nothing to merit your favor *is* the more noble cause. Sacrifice without payment is the most selfless thing a person can do. To defend someone because of who you are, not because of who they are...There is no more noble a trait."

"If it's such a noble thing, why doesn't everyone do it?" scoffed Keigh.

"Because it's also the most costly thing." Braddock leaned back in his chair. "There is nothing special about doing what everyone else would do. Doing what no one else would dare do...That is worthy of recognition."

Cato, who had been quietly observing the exchange, cleared his throat. "Would you cover for young Master Wulf if he were guilty of a crime?"

"I *did*, remember?" snapped Keigh, once again seeing himself hiding Deacon in the bushes outside the watchtower as Braddock and Mace bore down on them.

Cato smiled cheerily. "See, then? You are no different than your father. You were willing to shame your family and have your back torn open to save a boy who has never done anything but torment you. So, tell me now, Master Anders..." Cato's piercing blue eyes cut straight to his core. "What don't you get about the heart of your father?"

"I haven't shamed my family like he has," mumbled Keigh, realizing how tenuous his position was becoming.

"No?" asked Cato, his white eyebrows shooting upward. "Maybe you don't remember all the spit and vegetables hurled at you, hunched there at the whipping post, because it was your father they hit! His body covered you! He absorbed your shame even if he wasn't permitted to take your lashes. Your actions deserved it, but your father took it upon himself to shield you. You are Owen's son, Master Anders. To hate him is to hate yourself."

A familiar nausea rose in Keigh's stomach. The regular side effect of thinking about how his parents had hurt him—only this time, he was the villain. Had his father really done all that? For Keigh's mother, who was unfaithful to him, for Vicerous, who betrayed him...for Keigh, the son who had shamed him? His father's only crime was loving people who failed him. How could Keigh have been so blinded by anger to treat his father with such contempt? Owen Anders wasn't a coward—he was the bravest man Keigh knew. And if his father could love his mother after what she had done, then why shouldn't he?

Keigh couldn't imagine admiring anyone more than he did his father right that moment. Cato and Braddock obviously admired him too, even if they didn't know the whole story. *If I want to be like my father at all, I'll have to start with forgiving my mother,* he thought, resolving to make things right.

"I'll go home tonight," he said.

"Go home now," Braddock suggested, giving Keigh a sympathetic smile. "If you hurry, you can catch them before they leave for the festival."

Keigh thanked his mentors and hurried from the house out into the falling snow. That morning, he had been certain he would not be the one to repair things with his parents. He had thought them weak, but now...now he understood: his mother had made a terrible mistake and his father had loved her enough to pay the cost, just like Keigh himself had been willing to pay the cost for his friends at the tower.

It still blew his mind that his father had been the top of his age in his agoge training; even Braddock admitted it. His father had given up a life of honor, recognition, and adventure, exchanging it all to keep his wife and kids together. Not so long ago, Keigh would have thought that an unreasonable trade, but if the heartache and tears of the last two weeks were anything to judge by...maybe family was more important, not just to Owen, but to him too. Sure, he had cried when he thought he had lost his apprenticeship, and even more after he had been removed from the Refining, but the deep hurt? The constant ache of a broken heart? Those had come from broken relationships, not broken dreams. The abandonment of the king he revered, the rejection of the girl he loved, and now his own self-pitying spurning of his parents.

He wasn't sure there was anything he could do to fix the first two, but the divide between him and his parents was his fault. All he had to do was take a page from his father's book and choose to stay when others would walk away.

Keigh stood tall and proud for the first time since paying off Vicerous. He was the son of the greatest man in Eden. No title or riches could change that fact. Even the king knew his father was important, even if Keigh still didn't know why. Keigh was grinning like an idiot as he passed under the portcullis, already imagining the feeling of being wrapped in his parents' arms once again.

He was just beginning to break into a sprint when a familiar voice called his name. He turned to see Misselli standing nearby in a thick beige wool robe. Her hair was braided in a crown around her head. She held a lit candle with one hand and shielded the flame from the falling snow with the other.

"I'm...Can we...Will you walk with me for a minute?" she asked nervously. The anger that had filled her voice the last time Keigh heard it was undetectable.

Keigh looked up the road toward home, then back to his best friend. He had time for a short walk. Besides, he would see his family at the festival if he didn't make it home before they left. He would still apologize today. If he was careful, and didn't choke one of his friends in front of her, he might even be able to make things right with Misselli too.

"Yeah. I can do that," he answered, marveling at how the snow made her blue eyes even brighter.

"Did you get the cake I left for you?" she asked.

Keigh nodded. "Yeah, I did. Thank you for that. Honestly, I wasn't expecting to get one this year."

Misselli studied the candle in her hand, its tiny flame flickering under the protection of her palm. "This was the first year since we were seven that we didn't spend your birthday together."

"That's my fault. I was completely out of line that day at club." He held out his hand and watched a large fluffy snowflake melt in his palm. Was that the fate of all delicate things in his hands? Was he even capable of not wrecking what he loved? He gulped, uncomfortable with the battle between doubt and hope taking place inside him. "I'm sorry I was such a jerk to Conrad."

"You were a jerk," Misselli agreed, falling in alongside Keigh as they walked back into town. "That's not you. Not the you I knew, anyway..."

"I know," Keigh said, hanging his head. "I was in a really messed up place that day."

"Was?" Misselli turned to face him. "I went to your house this week, Keigh. Your parents said they haven't seen you in days! They're worried sick about you. Poor Jessie asked me to bring you back." She smiled slightly. "I didn't have the heart to tell her you ran away from me too."

"I didn't run away from you!" Keigh objected. How could she think that? She was the one mad at him.

Misselli looked at him disbelievingly. "You were the one to leave our last conversation, and you *literally* sprinted away from me the time before that."

Keigh smiled. "Well, maybe you don't recall the scary lady who slapped me."

"I do remember her." Misselli smiled in a self-satisfied way. "She was right to slap you."

"That's probably true, but at least now you understand the running," said Keigh, risking a playful nudge with his elbow.

Misselli didn't hesitate to nudge him right back. "You made the safe choice. No telling what that crazy lady would have done next." They both laughed at that.

The two of them walked to the common grounds, catching each other up on the last few weeks of their lives and commenting on the colorful decorations that seemed to be multiplying by the minute. People were already starting to show up for the evening's festivities. Keigh and Misselli snuck a glass of fizzy wine and a honey bun from a table and escaped to a back alley, where they continued reminiscing about past Winter Festivals.

"Remember when Addy accidentally set Mrs. Feldman's hair on fire?" Misselli laughed, holding a hand to her mouth so as not to spit bits of honey bun everywhere.

"Tarin nearly cried!" laughed Keigh, taking another sip of fizzy wine before passing the cup to Misselli. "He was already terrified of her even without her head covered in flames."

"He still is!" Misselli exclaimed. "I think that night sealed it, though. Remember how she put it out?"

"Oh yeah!" said Keigh, through another fit of laughter. "She pulled up Braddock's cloak and smothered her head in it!"

"I honestly thought we were going to see a murder that night." Misselli set the cup down next to her candle on a recessed windowsill. "If looks could kill, she would have died."

The two of them laughed until their stomachs hurt. Braddock had been a mystery to them at that point in their lives. For all they'd known, he might have killed their teacher that night.

Catching his breath, Keigh attempted to ask something he'd been itching to know for months. "Did anything...Did Tarin...Were you two..."

"No! Never!" scoffed Misselli. "Tarin's only interested in the things he doesn't have yet and the things he's told he'll never have."

"So that makes you—"

"*Very interesting.*" Misselli said, finishing the sentence for him. She snorted Tarin's name to herself and reached for another drink of fizzy wine.

Keigh exhaled, relieved. He would have understood if she had taken an interest in the tall, strong, handsome heir to the throne. Cecilia wasn't the first girl to swoon over the newly named prince. Most girls would, if they weren't already. But Misselli wasn't most girls; never had been. Taking the win, Keigh braced himself for the change of subject he knew he had to make.

"Listen, Misselli, I need to talk to you about...about...what you saw in Sentinel. Nothing ever happened with Tabitha."

"I know."

Keigh nearly inhaled a chunk of honey bun. He had prepared himself for anything: yelling, finger pointing, cursing, even another slap. But he had not expected that. "What do you mean *you know*? I thought you said there was nothing I could say to you?"

"*You* didn't." Misselli shrugged. "Mannie told me what happened."

"He did?" Keigh smacked his forehead. "I could kiss that man!" he shouted, never having been so grateful to have the big messenger in his corner.

"I don't think you were interested in that girl...at least, not anymore." Misselli sniffed. "But you still scared me, Keigh."

"Scared you?" Keigh chuckled. "How?"

"Seeing you that day made me realize how much you meant to me." Misselli fidgeted with the cord that tied her cloak shut. "*That* scares me."

"What do you mean?" asked Keigh, still grinning like a dummy. "Sounds like a good thing to me."

"Don't joke, Keigh," Misselli pleaded. "Not about this. I can't lose you, and I don't think I could survive if you left for good. Baylor leaving really messed me up. I'm not enough. Baylor put that in my head, but seeing you happy and dancing in the city of the king, with the whole of Eden cheering your name... It was just..." Misselli raised her hands, then clapped them down hard to her sides. "How can I compete with that? I'm scared to love you because someday I know I won't be enough. There will be a new adventure, another challenge to conquer, and I won't be able to hold your heart. You're meant for more than this." She waved a hand at their surroundings. "I've always believed that, but seeing you actually do it, actually break out of Bjorn and win the hearts of everyone in Sentinel...What's my heart when you have everyone else's?"

Keigh and Misselli stood there looking into each other's eyes for a long moment, the distant sounds of the festival floating over the snow-covered rooftops. Keigh's brain scrambled for words. It was true. He didn't ever see himself settling down in Bjorn. He wanted to be a somebody. He liked hearing the crowd chant his name, and he liked proving himself against worthy opponents, and someday he did want to serve the king as a cane. But right now…right now he would trade it all for the girl in front of him. Just like his father had.

"You know what my time in Sentinel taught me?" Keigh asked, taking a step toward Misselli.

She shook her head.

"I always wanted to be a cane, to be someone important—"

"You will be," Misselli interjected, lowering her eyes. "I know you will."

"That's what I *knew*," Keigh continued. "What I know now is that I don't want to be anything like them. I won't trade who I am for a red cloak, and I definitely won't trade any of the people I love for it." Keigh took Misselli's hands in his own and lowered his face toward hers, trying to coax her blue eyes back out from hiding.

"Did you…Did you mean it? What you said in the Capital," Misselli asked timidly, as if afraid the question would startle him away, like a bird off a fence post. "Do you…love me?"

Keigh gulped, momentarily grateful she was still fiddling with the cord around her waist and not looking at the panic on his face. He'd had a hard enough time saying it when it was just pretend, but this was the real thing. If he said it now, it would change everything about their friendship.

"I…" Keigh bit his lip. "It's…"

"It's fine," said Misselli, pulling her hands out of Keigh's. "It was silly of me to bring it up."

Keigh grabbed her by the shoulders and placed his face directly in front of hers. "I love you, Misselli Labelle." The blue jewels he'd been looking for finally rose to meet his gaze. He searched them, looking for any hint, any sign that she loved him too. *She's not saying anything*, he thought, panicking. *Quick! Explain yourself!* "You—you're—my best friend," he stuttered, "the one I want to see every day—"

Misselli closed her eyes and pressed her lips against his, shutting him up.

All the worry, all the hurt, all the weight of the last month of his life melt-ed away faster than the snow falling on their faces. They stood there, lips pressed together, as the sound of voices singing the songs of Eden carried on the breeze.

Misselli pulled back—entirely too soon, Keigh thought.

She smiled innocently. "You made me do that."

Keigh snorted. "I? Made you...do that?" he asked, grinning like a toddler with a mouth full of sugar.

Misselli batted her eyelashes as a snowflake fell on them. "Well, I couldn't let your first kiss be Mannie." She grabbed his hand and stepped away from him. "Now, come, Master Anders. Show me what you learned in Sentinel." She spun, sweeping the snow on the ground with the bottom of her cloak.

Keigh followed her out onto their dance floor for two. "Only if you promise me another kiss."

She smiled wryly and offered her hand. "That, Master Anders, will depend on your dancing."

CHAPTER 34

GOING HOME

45-5-8

They danced. From the back alleys of Bjorn, all the way up the road to their homes, they danced. This was what he had been missing all those times Misselli had begged him to dance with her before. What a fool he'd been to turn her down. The light of the full moon reflected off the snow-covered earth, bathing the whole valley in a silver glow that shone off Misselli's braided crown like a halo. They had made hundreds of snow angels on the ground as kids, but seeing her tonight, Keigh was convinced that this was what a real angel would look like.

As he spun her once more, she slipped on a patch of ice in the road. Keigh caught her and held her there, halfway to the ground, cradled in his arms, giggling. Keigh didn't laugh. *How can this be real?* he marveled. *This can't be my life. It's too...perfect.*

"Well, are you going to stand me up or just hold me here forever?"

"Can I?" asked Keigh.

"Stand me up?" Misselli tittered. "I would hope—"

"Hold you," Keigh cut her off, "forever?"

Misselli stopped giggling and smiled so warmly at him he thought the sun had risen in his arms.

"That," she said, laying a hand over his heart, "is not a question for me. Ask yourself." She patted his chest and looked away.

"I would!" he blurted, then with more reserve, amended, "I will."

Misselli smiled, returning her blue eyes to his brown. "It's not that simple, Keigh. Your answer isn't one given in a moment. Answer me in minutes and months. Answer me in seasons and sick days, in triumphs and trials." She touched his cheek. "I want your words, but I *need* your will."

Keigh stood her up and pulled her close. "You have it," he said. "You'll see."

Misselli laid her head on his chest. "Then start by showing me you have what it takes to make peace."

Keigh's brow wrinkled. Hadn't they made up? He thought the kiss was pretty firmly in the peace category. "What do you mean? Aren't we good?"

"We..." Misselli squeezed him, "are good."

"Really good," he said, squeezing her back.

"Yes, really good," she hummed, "but I'm not talking about us. I'm talking about you and your family."

Keigh pulled back. "I'm going back. I was going to apologize even before you said anything, I promise. But...you don't know what they did."

"Doesn't matter," Misselli countered confidently.

"Doesn't matter?" Keigh nearly choked. If she had even the slightest clue what his parents had done, she wouldn't be so cavalier about it.

"Doesn't. Matter," she emphasized. "My mother taught me that a real man, a *good* man, will humble himself to make peace in his home. A real man isn't just one who would die to protect his family. A good man dies to himself every day in order to give his family what they need. And right now, your family needs their son back. Can you humble yourself, Master Anders?" challenged Misselli, her grin returning as she tugged on his cloak strings.

Keigh knew she was right. How many times had he seen his father do exactly that? Even when he had overheard his parents arguing and *known* his father was right, it was always his father who extended the first apology.

Keigh leaned his head over Misselli's, shielding her upturned face from the falling snow. "Maybe for another kiss I could," he bartered. He was going to apologize no matter what, but if he could steal another kiss in the deal, why not?

Misselli leaned in. Keigh did too, eager to meet her halfway, but she abruptly mashed four fingers against his lips. "Make peace first," she whispered. She gave him a devilish grin and pushed his face away, then spun out from his arms, dancing with an invisible partner on the snow-covered road toward her home.

"I'll walk you home," Keigh called after her.

Without stopping, Misselli called back over her shoulder, "You can walk me home tomorrow after you take me on a proper date."

Keigh shook his head, but he couldn't shake the grin off his face as he watched Misselli dance into the distance. How had his life turned around so gloriously? Maybe this was magic. This morning his heart had been colder, harder, and in more pieces than the stone sparring dummy he'd been hacking at for weeks, and now it was warmer, softer, and more whole than he could ever remember it being. Magic didn't just make swords glow, and its wielders weren't all mages. Braddock, Cato, and Misselli had worked a miracle in him today, whether they knew it or not.

Leaving the road, he pushed open the front gate in the rail fence surrounding his home. He crossed the yard, floating across the snow, feeling lighter than ever. There were no candles lit in the house, just the dull glow of a slowly dying fire in the fireplace. *They must still be at the festival,* he thought. He stomped the snow off his boots on the wood steps outside the front door and eyed the gray wooden bear head carved in its timber. He rested a hand on it. *I promise I won't leave like that again.*

He stayed there a minute, pondering the simple reliability of the bear. His home hadn't gone anywhere; he had. It was here, and now he was too. He took a deep breath of cold night air. *As soon as I walk through this door, I'm choosing to release all my bitterness, all my anger. My parents are not perfect, nor am I...but they love me, and I love them.* Exhaling, he breathed out the last shreds of anger that still resided in him.

He opened the door and stepped into his home. His nose wrinkled as he was confronted with a strangely familiar stench. He had smelled it before… right before—

There was a loud *crack*. Blinding pain shot through him as something hard struck the back of his head. Keigh fell face first, hard, on the great room floor, and his whole world went black.

*

When Keigh came to, he was lying face down on the floor with his wrists and ankles bound. He winced at the splitting pain in the back of his skull.

"About time you woke up," said a voice from the shadows—an oddly familiar voice.

"What…Who…" Keigh's mind was still fuzzy as he tried to catch a glimpse of his assailant.

"I wanted you to be awake for what happens next." Heavy boots clunked on the wooden floor as a tall, blonde figure, wearing pants and a jacket in mottled patterns of white and black, stepped into the glow of the embers.

"You…" Keigh gulped, not believing his eyes. "But you're dead! I killed you!"

"No, you did not. Unfortunately for you." The handsome face of the assassin in the woods leaned toward him, lips stretched thin in disdain.

"But I saw you die!" shouted Keigh, trying to make sense of what he was seeing. "Braddock said you were dead!" He rolled onto his side, fighting the ties on his wrists.

"No, you did not, and no, I am not," the man sneered. "Like I said, unfortunate for you." The man knelt in front of him and smiled, his chipped tooth no longer boyish or charming as it had been the day Braddock had escorted him from town.

Just then, Keigh realized the thing that had always bothered him about his interaction with the assassin, the thing he had never quite put his finger on…The man in town, the man Braddock had sworn he escorted far out of Bjorn; this man in front of Keigh now—he had a chipped tooth. The man in the woods, the one he had seen *after* the man in town…That man's teeth had been perfect.

Twins, he realized. The dead assassin's words echoed in his mind: *They told us…*

That man hadn't been the only one sent to Bjorn. The twin brothers had both been here last spring.

"Draiden told us you were important. He did *not* tell us you were dangerous." Bitterness dripped from every word his captor spoke. "You may have succeeded in killing my brother, and you may have convinced Draiden not to have you killed…" He jabbed a finger hard into Keigh's forehead. "But I'm going to make you watch as I burn your home to the ground."

"Don't you touch my family!" Keigh growled, resuming his fight against his bonds.

His captor chuckled. "I won't. Me and you are leaving. Draiden wants you delivered to him alive, and quickly." He rose to his feet and walked to the fireplace, leaning against the mantle and peering into the embers. "You'll have to live the rest of your life knowing your family thinks you burned their house down and ran away. They'll hate you more than they miss you."

"They wouldn't believe that!" Keigh shouted, flopping onto his back.

"Oh?" The mercenary gave him an amused look. "Perhaps it was some other boy I heard shouting at them? Something about them being unworthy? That they shouldn't come looking for you?" He sniffed contemptuously. "Don't worry, boy. They won't."

A sharp pain pierced Keigh's chest as he remembered the horrible things he had said to his parents. *Those can't be the last words they ever hear from me!*

"Anyway, story time is over," the man said coolly. "Time for us to be going." He stretched a leg into the fireplace and swept the glowing hot embers onto the wood floor with a kick of his boot.

Keigh winced and wriggled as an ember landed on the exposed skin of his neck. "Stop!" he begged. "Don't do—"

The man stuffed a balled-up rag in Keigh's mouth, muffling his shouts.

"Say goodbye, boy. You won't be coming back." The man stooped down and scooped Keigh up in his arms, then threw him over his shoulder.

Keigh squirmed with all his might, trying to get the man to drop him, but instead his captor spun, slinging Keigh's head violently into the wall and dazing him all over again.

"I have to deliver you alive, not well," the man growled. "Don't test me."

Was this it? Was there really nothing he could do? He had escaped every close call before this. Smoke was already filling the room as the embers burned into the dry wood floors. He mustn't quit.

Keigh resumed squirming, only to have his head bashed against the wall again. This time his vision blurred, and his thoughts slowed to a snail's pace. Cold air blew up his cloak as his captor opened the door and carried him outside. *BAM!* He was hit again, but this time he wasn't being hit against something; something had plowed into them, sending him and his captor sprawling across the snow-covered ground.

He heard a growl. His brain tried to make sense of the collision. It was like being mauled by a...a...

A bear.

Copper!

Keigh rolled over, blinking, trying to focus on where his bear was now. But he didn't see a bear, and the growls he was hearing weren't animal.

"Keigh!"

His mother's voice.

Keigh's eyes slowly adjusted as he looked toward the source of the commotion. His vision finally clearing, he saw, not Copper, but his father grappling with the assassin in the snow next to him. Owen had the man pinned down and was attempting to press a muscular forearm against his throat.

Snarling and growling, the man pushed his hands against Owen's face, pulling at his beard, trying to pry the much larger man off of him. The intruder managed to get a leg free. Bringing his leg up toward his face, he hooked

Owen's head in the crook of his knee. Flexing his hips, the man pried Owen away enough to roll out from under him.

Owen grabbed the man's jacket as he attempted to flee. Pulling the assassin back within striking distance, he landed several punches to the man's already chipped front teeth, turning them red. While his face took a beating, the man managed to pull a short dagger from his waist and plunge the blade deep into Owen's shoulder.

Owen bellowed. Rising to his feet with the dagger still sticking out of him, he grabbed the scrambling assassin by the front of his jacket with both hands and lifted him bodily off the ground. Then, just as swiftly as he'd picked him up, Owen slammed him back down to the ground.

Keigh was too delirious to fully comprehend what was happening, but he could see enough to know Braddock hadn't been lying about his father being the most impressive cane apprentice in Eden. He was a force of nature. Keigh doubted Copper would even be able to hold his own against him.

Draiden's mercenary coughed and choked, spitting mouthfuls of crimson blood onto the white snow as he desperately tried to claw his way away from the fury of Keigh's father.

Owen straddled the man he had just slammed to the ground. Seizing the front of his jacket, he picked him up again. This time he carried the man to the side of the house and pinned him against it with a forearm to the throat, leaving his feet dangling above the ground.

"Who are you?" growled Owen.

A wet gurgle issued from the man, before he spat a mouthful of blood in Owen's face.

Owen snarled and wiped the blood away with his free arm. "Jotham, Jobey, get in the house and put out whatever's causing that smoke!" he ordered.

Keigh heard his brothers' footsteps thumping toward the house behind him.

Owen pressed harder against the man's throat. "Start talking!"

The man winced, his hands pulling frantically at Owen's arm, trying to take the weight off his throat. "I'll...die...first," he choked.

"Oh, you will die," Owen promised, "but it won't be first. You think you can come after my boy? My son!" He slid the man a few inches higher up the wall. "Now talk!"

The man winced again, blood spilling from his mouth where his lip had been split by a punch. He dropped his hands from trying to take the pressure off his throat and hung suspended by his neck.

"'Bout time you gave up." Owen gave a satisfied grunt and turned to face his son.

As Keigh locked eyes with his father, the battle rage drained from Owen's bearded face. It was replaced by a look of sheer tenderness, wholly out of place for the situation. The corners of his lips began to lift—

Three blasts shattered the night in rapid succession.

Owen's face went blank. Eyes wide, he toppled backward into the snow.

"Daddy!" Jessie screamed.

No! The air was gone. Keigh had heard a blast like those before. A mounting pressure in his chest refused to let his lungs fill or his heart beat. *Not him. Not my dad. Not now!*

His father lay motionless in the snow, staring up at the sky.

This isn't—It can't—

He waited. Any second now his father would get up. Would shake it off. Would get back in the fight.

Nothing.

But I came home…Everything's going to be good again…I CAME HOME!

Keigh screamed. Shouted and sobbed incoherently into the rag in his mouth. Thrashed frantically on the ground, rolling and squirming, trying desperately to move closer to his father. *I have to be with him, near him…If I can just get close, everything will be okay. I just need to get close. He'll make everything okay. I know he will. He can fix this. He's fine. Nothing can hurt my dad.*

But even as he told himself that, he knew it wasn't true. *He* had hurt his father.

Before Keigh could get to Owen, the gunman recovered.

He pointed the short, silver gun at Keigh as he staggered over, his blonde hair askew, blood splattered all over the front of his mottled clothing. The man kicked Keigh in the ribs to stop his writhing, then picked him back up and slung him over his shoulder.

"Call for help and the boy dies!" he yelled at Sabriya, who was standing at a distance, shielding Jessie.

As the mercenary threatened his mother, Keigh could see his father lying wide-eyed in the snow, fingering the spots where blood was soaking through his tunic.

He's still alive! He'll get up. He always gets up.

"C'mon," the man growled through clenched teeth, then turned and started marching up the hill toward the tree line.

His mother had dropped to her knees in the snow, pressing Jessie's face against her shoulder as she wailed loudly.

As they passed Keigh's father, Owen reached out to him. Keigh screamed through the rag in his mouth. His father's final flickers of life, still concerned with protecting his son. Keigh let his head drop. Tears poured from his eyes, spilling up his forehead into his hair as he hung limp and defeated over his captor's shoulder.

"Guess you'll have a slightly different memory to live with," said the mercenary, spitting another mouthful of blood into the snow. "Serves you right! Your father for my brother."

He was right. This was all Keigh's fault. Why couldn't he have just died that day in the woods and saved his family all the heartache that came from him living? Was it too late? Couldn't this man just kill him now and end his misery? Why should he live when his father didn't?

The world darkened as they entered the forest. The snow caught in the branches high above, leaving the forest floor bare and black. An owl hooted eerily. Keigh's head pounded, the pressure unbearable.

His luck had run out. There would be no more miracles. He'd had his miracle earlier that day...

Misselli! There was still a reason to stay. A reason to live.

Keigh began to thrash violently again. He couldn't let himself be taken.

The man growled and dropped him. "You really want to do this the hard way?" he snarled. Hunching over Keigh, he pressed the gun against the side of his head. "I could make it look like an accident. Draiden would be furious, but he'd get over it. You can't be that important to his plans."

Keigh threw his bound feet upward, collapsing one of the man's legs, dropping him to the ground. Keigh rolled onto his side and attempted to reach out and touch the man's skin. If only he could pull enough energy from him to break his bonds—

But the man was too quick, smoothly rolling out of reach. "Nuh-uh-uh." He stood, wagging a finger. "I've been told not to let you touch me." He pointed the gun at Keigh. "Better be safe about it."

Keigh rolled over just before the gun blasted again. A metallic ping rang like a bell. Keigh registered the impact to his arm, but felt no pain.

"What the—"

The man's curse was cut off as a lonesome howl sounded in the trees. The mercenary spun to face the direction of the animal. Another howl cut through the night behind them. Soon the sound was echoing from all directions. Keigh's attacker spun wildly, pointing his gun in the direction of each call.

A growl issued from his left. Keigh looked into the shadows and saw a pair of golden eyes glowing in the darkness. Soon there were more, flashing in the undergrowth.

The garden wolves.

The man fired his gun again. A wolf whimpered in the shadows. He fired once more and another wolf whined. He pointed the gun again, but this time it clicked. He jerked it a couple times, each time only accomplishing a click. He began to look worried as the growls grew louder and the eyes wove through the trees around them.

"Back! Stay back, you filthy vermin!" the man threatened, still spinning frantically.

A single howl pierced the night. Barks and growls emanated from the pack as twenty of the small dogs closed the gap. They pounced on the mercenary in unison, overwhelming him with their numbers.

Four went flying through the air as the man ripped them off of his body, their sharp teeth ripping bloody furrows in his skin. In his panic, he tore one of the wolves away from his throat. Blood gushed from his neck.

The man paled and clasped a hand to his throat. He sank to his knees as the remaining wolves continued to tear at him. He writhed on the ground a minute longer, never once screaming or crying out.

When his body finally went limp, the growls and barks stopped. The garden wolves jumped off him and walked away, apparently uninterested. Several circled around Keigh, licking the abrasions on his head and nuzzling him with soft whimpers.

Keigh lay there, panting, trying to convince himself that what he had just seen wasn't a hallucination. If the mercenary was real, then his dad—

I've got to get free! My dad might still be alive!

Keigh strained, every fiber of muscle working to break the cords that bound him. He struggled in the dirt for a minute before trying to communicate to the wolves to chew through his bonds. They simply stared at him and pressed their furry heads into his hands, trying to get a scratch from him.

He lay on his back, panting. Closing his eyes, he desperately tried to think of a way out. Maybe he could worm his way over to a tree and rub the cords against the trunk until they snapped.

He was wriggling his way toward the closest pine when his hand brushed against the pouch at his waist. *The orb!* Uncinching the top of the pouch, he dug it out with his fingers. "Mannie said you could help," Keigh pleaded, clutching the orb in his palm. "Well, I need it now!"

He could see his father's face. See his hand reaching out. Keigh flinched as a familiar, yet unexpected, spark of energy passed from the ball into his palm.

He clasped his hand around the orb and focused on his need. He *needed* a father. He *needed* to save his father.

A current of fiery energy flowed into him, stronger than any before. It coursed through his veins, filling him with strength. He flexed his arms, snapping the cords. Reaching to his ankles, he pulled them free as well. Keigh stuffed the orb back into the pouch at his waist and raced down the hill toward his house, heart pounding, limbs strong.

As he got closer, he saw his mother crouched over the prone figure of his father, holding one of his hands against her cheek. Jobey and Jotham stood at a distance, shielding Jessie.

Keigh dropped to his knees, sliding up next to his father. He was alive! His skin was as pale as the snow around him, but his eyes were still sharp. Their green fixated on his mother's brown. The two of them seemed to be saying everything without saying anything.

His mother was the first to break their gaze and look at Keigh. Eyes red and glistening, lines down her cheeks where her tears had burned paths across them. She grabbed Keigh's hand in one of hers.

Owen slowly rolled his head around to look at Keigh. The faintest smile touched his lips. "I...I thought...I thought I'd lost you." His words were barely more than a whisper.

Keigh's chest began to heave. His throat tightened painfully as he fought back tears. All he could do was shake his head.

His father's blinks were becoming more drawn out. Each time he closed his eyes, Keigh feared he had looked into them for the last time. "F-for..." His father struggled to part his lips. "Forgive...us?"

Keigh nodded, the knot in his throat squeezing his vocal cords into silence.

Owen Anders smiled. His face relaxed. His relief was so visible, so profound, that Keigh worried he might be witnessing his father's life leave him.

Owen slowly lifted his other hand toward Keigh's face. His eyes drooped and his hand began to fall back. Keigh grabbed it and pressed it to his cheek, letting his tears wet his father's calloused palm. Owen's eyelids lifted, but his eyes lacked focus now. "Remember..."

His father whispered the word so quietly Keigh had to lean in and put an ear next to his lips.

"You...you are my son. I...I am your..." Owen inhaled, his breath ragged as he tried to fill his lungs. Exhaling, he breathed, "Your father."

Owen's eyes closed. His arm pulled away from Keigh's face, but Keigh refused to let it fall. *He's tired, that's all. Just needs to rest.* He watched his father's face intently, waiting, *needing* to see those green eyes look on him with love as they had countless times before.

Sabriya broke. Pressing her face into her husband's chest, she began to weep.

"He's okay, Mom," Keigh told her, his throat finally freed of its paralysis. "He's just resting...Right, Dad?" He gave his father's shoulder a gentle shake. "Come on, Dad. We gotta get you fixed up." He sniffed, still waiting, eyes locked expectantly on his father. "Anders don't get hurt, we get better...Remember? Remember you said that to me?"

His father's hand was getting cold now, his always rosy cheeks blue above his dark beard.

"I'm home now, Dad. Everything is going to be okay. Just like it used to be. Right?" Keigh tried to hold a smile, but it was too heavy. "You forgive me, right?" he asked, no longer hoping, just begging. "Please, Dad...just one more word? Please say yes...Say yes, Dad. Say you forgive me. I need to know—*You* need to know...I'm sorry, Dad, I'm so sorry! I didn't mean any of it! I was wrong! I should have never left. I should have never doubted you. Forgive me? Please, Dad. I need to hear you say it."

The pressure in his head was unbearable as he forced the sobs to stop in his throat. If he opened his mouth again, there would be no holding them back.

"Please, Dad," he begged as the dam broke, unleashing pain enough to stop his own heart. "Anything—one more word? A look? A smile? Yell at me! Tell me to leave! Anything! Just say something! Please, Dad, you can't go...I'll do anything, just don't leave me..."

He couldn't bear to say anymore, not if his father wasn't going to answer him. His father always answered.

Sabriya crawled her way around Owen to Keigh's side. She pulled him close, rocking him gently. Two hearts breaking over the one they both had broken. Two hearts breaking over one that would never break again.

CHAPTER 35

MAN OF MERCY

19–27–10

on't come looking for me. Those were the last words his father had ever heard him say. *Don't come looking for me.*

His father hadn't listened. Apparently, Owen had searched tirelessly for Keigh ever since he hadn't returned home the morning after their fight.

"Cato knew I wasn't at home before Braddock told him?" Keigh asked his mother, who was sitting on the bench next to him in the great room of their home.

His mother nodded sadly. "Your father wanted to stay. He would have waited for you at Cato's. Cato told him he could, but warned him that if you returned home because you felt forced to or guilted into it, the wounds might never heal." Sabriya rubbed his back gently. "He wanted you home so desperately, Keigh. He loved you more than I could tell you, but he wanted you to want to be home." His mother laughed softly, sniffing back a tear. "You should have seen his face when he saw the tracks in the snow leading up to the house. He just knew you had come back. He was only able to hit that man so hard when you first came out of the house because he was already sprinting to see you."

She had told him all this before. He wasn't sure why he kept asking. Maybe if someone else was to blame he wouldn't feel so bad. He had tried being mad at Cato for not insisting his father stay, or for not calling him out on his foolishness earlier, but the truth had already etched itself on his soul. His father was dead because of him. If Keigh hadn't left home, neither he nor his father would have had to face Draiden's mercenary alone.

If he hadn't been born, Draiden wouldn't have sent anyone to begin with.

It had been a week since the fateful night that claimed the life of his father. The funeral had been a small, intimate affair. Only Braddock, Cato, and the Labelles stood with the Anders family in front of the headstone on the hill as they laid Owen Anders in the earth. They had buried him above the potato fields he had spent so much of his life nurturing. The headstone read: *Owen Anders, Devoted Husband, Loving Father, Man of Mercy*. Mannie had been unable to attend, but Keigh knew the messenger couldn't have been expected to receive the news and travel to Bjorn on such short notice. A year ago, Keigh wouldn't have thought any of the town elders even knew his father existed; now two had come to mourn his passing. Keigh might never know all his father's secrets, but he knew Owen had been a great man. Nothing would change that, not for him.

Misselli started placing bowls on the table where Keigh sat with his mother.

"Please tell your parents thank you again for the soup." Sabriya laid a hand on top of Misselli's. "Keigh will be going to town tomorrow to collect our papers of provision."

"It's nothing you wouldn't have done for us," Misselli said, giving Keigh's mother a gracious curtsy.

"Thank you for being here too. It helps…" Sabriya nodded silently toward Keigh who had buried his face in his hands. "More than you know."

"Nowhere else I would rather be." Misselli smiled softly, setting a hand on Keigh's shoulder.

Keigh's mother sighed quietly and blinked her gratitude.

Misselli lifted her hand from Keigh's back and gently ran her fingertips from the top of his head to the bottom of his brown curls. Singling out a long, wavy hair, Misselli plucked it sharply from his head.

"Ouch!" yelped Keigh, sitting up straight to scowl at her. "What was that for?"

"It's time to eat," said Misselli, planting her hands on her hips, her dimples deepening in a bossy grin. "And you can't have any of my mother's famous leek and onion soup with that handsome face buried in your hands."

"She called you handsome!" Jessie giggled, skipping into the room from the hallway.

"That's because I am." Keigh winked at his little sister and turned around to face the table.

"I'd call it...rich man homely," pitched in Jobey. He and Jotham had just come through the front door carrying armfuls of split firewood.

"Or poor man passable," chirped Jotham, setting the wood down by the fireplace and sauntering over to the table.

"Beauty is in the eye of the beholder," rebutted Keigh. "You're both just mad nobody *be-holding* you!"

Jessie erupted in a fit of giggles at the stung look on her eldest brothers' faces. Misselli tried to hide her grin behind her hand, but her cheeks gave her away.

"*All* my boys are handsome," Sabriya intervened. "Just like their father..."

All eyes went to the empty space at the end of the table, where the smiling, bearded face of Owen Anders had looked on them with pride for so many years.

Their moment of levity over, the family ate their lunch in silence. Only the crackle of the fire and the tinkle of their spoons dipping into their bowls filled the air that should rightfully be full of the sound of Owen Anders' deep baritone laughter.

After lunch, Keigh and Misselli left the house together. Misselli had organized another group get-together for their friends and convinced Keigh it would be good for him to get out of the house for the first time since the Winter Festival.

Copper bounded up to them, his fur glistening as the sun shone down on him and reflected off the snow. A wave of powder hit Keigh and Misselli as the giant cub slid to a stop beside them.

Keigh had brought Copper home the day after his dad died. He didn't care what anyone thought of it. He wouldn't go anywhere without him again, if he could help it. Things might have been different if Copper had been with him that night, instead of waiting up at the tower because Keigh had been too afraid. Even as a cub, Copper was more than any lone man could handle. *Unless they have a gun,* he thought, growing bitter again.

Keigh gave the big cub a pat on the neck. Copper and Misselli had been invaluable in helping him and his family survive the week. Misselli had practically lived with them, spending morning till evening helping his mother with chores around the house and taking care of Jessie. Keigh didn't consider himself someone who needed another person to console him, but he would be lying if he said Misselli hadn't been a tremendous comfort to him in his grief. Copper seemed to know something was wrong, too; the bear had been extra affectionate that week, nuzzling up to Keigh at every opportunity. He had also proved his worth to the family by allowing Jessie to ride on his back, an experience Jessie loved and such a whimsical sight that it brought everyone else some much-needed joy.

"You know you don't have to come." Misselli looked at him seriously. "I think it will be good to see people, but I understand if it's too soon."

Keigh inhaled the crisp winter air, letting the cold burn in his chest. It probably was too soon. He was still a wreck, and he didn't want to risk snapping at anyone again like he had with Conrad, but if he stayed home, his mind would end up wandering back to the same dark thoughts that had plagued him all week.

My father is dead because of me. I abandoned my family.

"Come with us, boy," Keigh told Copper. He took Misselli by the hand and they walked off together, traipsing through the snow.

When they arrived at Mueller's pond, they found their group of friends had beat them there.

Kervyn dropped the snowball he had aimed at Theo, his jaw falling just as fast. "It's true!"

"You paired with a red bear?" shouted Conrad. He and Beaudy dashed out from behind a makeshift wall of snow they had constructed.

Addy pushed her foggy glasses up with a mittened hand. "I thought only cloaked canes were allowed appointments with red bear cubs?"

The whole group gathered in front of him, staring at Copper.

"That's true," admitted Keigh, breathing a sigh of relief that Copper had successfully stolen the attention away from the fact that he was now fatherless. "But he was the cub of a wild red, so...no appointment necessary."

"Is he safe?" asked Theo from behind Beaudy.

"Can I pet him?" asked Beaudy, already reaching a hand toward Copper's nose.

"He's very friendly." Stepping aside, Keigh motioned for them to approach Copper. Discreetly, he looked at his bear and mouthed the words *I'm sorry* as the group descended on the cub.

Rather than being perturbed, as Keigh worried, Copper seemed to bask in the attention. *I guess being isolated for weeks in a tower will do that,* he thought, watching Copper push his head into Beaudy's belly, then give the large boy a quizzical look when he found he couldn't budge him.

"What's his name?" Conrad asked as Copper gave his face a wet lick.

"Copper," Misselli answered.

"Don't feel bad, Keigh," Theo quipped, "creativity isn't everyone's strength."

Keigh felt a tug at his sleeve. It was Emerson Bardwick.

"I'm sorry to hear about your father, Keigh," she said, shuffling her feet under her fraying gray robe, unable to look him in the eye. "He was a good man. Helped my father once—you know, when we couldn't make our debt payment."

"Thanks, Emerson. He was."

"I…" Emerson shook her head and pulled on the front of her robe. "With…" She turned as if to walk away, then pulled herself back around to face Keigh. "Can I tell you something?"

Keigh could see she was nervous. "Of course, Emerson. What is it?"

She winced, looking almost as though she had hoped he would refuse. "Do you remember the day my dress ripped last year?"

Keigh did remember. He remembered the laughter. He remembered the horrified look on Emerson's face. He remembered his anger.

"I do," he said, not wanting to elaborate for fear of embarrassing her again.

"I've never told anyone this before, but…" Emerson wrung her hands and looked around to make sure no one else was listening. "I…I was going to the Queen's Veil that day." She bowed her head in shame.

Keigh didn't understand. What was the big secret? The Queen's Veil was a beautiful place; many families went there to look at the falls and swim in Lake Grebe. Of course, it also had the unfortunate reputation of…

Keigh's heart wrenched as he finally understood what she was saying. "No, Emerson…" He bent down on a knee, bringing himself into her field of vision.

Emerson nodded and wiped the corner of her eye. "I had already decided to do it when I came to class that day. Then my dress tore. I was so embarrassed. I had never felt so worthless…Everyone laughed." She inhaled deeply. "Everyone but you."

It was true. Keigh hadn't laughed that day. He had been far too angry to laugh. Emerson had been the only other thrall his age, and that had given them a sort of kinship. In truth, he had always seen her as more of a little sister than a friend.

"Do you remember what you did?" asked Emerson, sniffing a tear off the end of her nose, still talking to the ground.

Keigh nodded. He had nearly fought Deacon. If not for Tarin interfering, he would have.

Emerson started sobbing quietly. "If you hadn't been there that day, if you hadn't given me your cloak, I…I…"

Keigh's eyes filled with tears. How could someone so close to him have been that low without him even knowing? Had he been too absorbed in his own self-pity to see what had been right in front of him?

"I'm so sorry about your dad, Keigh." Emerson looked at him with bleary eyes. "It's just...you never know when life can be over, and I don't want to leave anything unsaid, in case...in case..."

"In case I die?"

She bobbed her head.

"I'm not going to die," Keigh reassured her. "Probably ever," he teased.

"How can you say that?" Emerson asked in an urgent whisper. "If the rumors are true, the man who killed your father was there for you." Her lips puckered and she shook her head as a new round of sobs threatened to break free. "You saved my life, Keigh. I would have done it...I would have drowned myself if you hadn't stood up for me that day. You're the reason I'm still here, and I...I needed you to know." She stepped forward and wrapped her arms around him. "Thank you."

Keigh hugged her back. Had she really wanted to end her own life? He could still see her cheering and dancing in the common grounds for all to see, the day he won his agoge duel. *That* girl had wanted to end it all? How could he not have seen it?

Still, as troubling as Emerson's revelation was, what really bothered him was that she had just done what he had failed to do. She had told him how much she appreciated him and was thankful for him. Something he had not done with his father, and now something he could never do. He both admired and resented her for that.

Emerson let go of him and stepped back, wiping her eyes. "Thank you, Keigh. I just... just wanted you to know."

"Anytime," said Keigh, unsure what else to say.

Emerson smiled weakly and walked over to join Misselli and Addy as they rubbed Copper's belly.

"Look who it is!" Theo called out. "If it isn't Lord Wulf!"

The group turned to face the lone, dark figure walking cautiously toward them.

"Keigh is here, and I don't think he would appreciate *you* hanging around," Conrad challenged.

Deacon raised his hands in surrender. "I'm not here to fight. I promise."

Next to Vicerous, Deacon was the last person Keigh wanted to see right now. How could he show his face here, today? *After my father...after Emerson!*

But something was off. Hating Deacon usually felt so good, so right—but there was something in the other boy's voice, something desperate...Or did everything just sound sad today?

"Are you here to be a wanker? 'Cause you're already doing that," Theo jabbed.

Beaudy sidled up behind Copper, who was now sitting up, watching the confrontation.

"You shouldn't be here, Deacon. Just go home." Misselli edged around Keigh, placing herself between the two boys.

Deacon looked pleadingly at Keigh, his hands still raised. "I just want to talk."

Keigh wasn't hearing things; something was definitely different. He couldn't put his finger on it, but Deacon didn't seem his usual arrogant, insulting self. He opened his mouth to accept Deacon's truce when a snowball suddenly drilled Deacon in the side of the head, exploding into a thousand pieces and knocking his black hair awry.

The group cheered Conrad's throw and began throwing snowballs of their own. Deacon spun, holding up his cloak to block the volley of ice.

Then Copper charged, the muscular cub galloping toward Deacon at a breakneck pace.

"No!" yelled Keigh, his stomach dropping. Was a wild red really this unpredictable? Sure, Deacon was no friend, but he wasn't an enemy that needed to be killed! *Don't hurt him!* Keigh hoped silently, too stunned to speak. What would happen to Copper if he hurt Deacon?

Everyone froze. Deacon paled and threw his hands over his head.

Copper growled menacingly, then spun around in the snow, placing himself between the group and Deacon. He flashed his teeth and clacked his jaws together, daring someone to throw another snowball.

The girls gasped. Everyone dropped the snowballs they were holding.

"What's wrong with your bear, man?" asked Theo accusingly. "Can't he tell Deacon's the bad guy?"

Keigh didn't respond. Calmly, he edged around Misselli and walked over to his bear. Copper was no longer growling or baring his teeth, but his eyes stayed fixed on the group. Keigh rested a hand on Copper's neck, looking at Deacon.

What do you know, Copper?

Deacon brushed himself off angrily. "Never mind! I'll leave. You're all children!"

Normally Keigh would have had something to say to that, but it was as if his nemesis were only playing the part of Deacon Wulf. There was no conviction in his voice. Why was Deacon *pretending* to be a jerk?

Deacon gave Keigh one last look, then whipped around in the snow, his black cloak billowing like the wings of an ebony as he stomped away.

"Go back to your den, you viper!" Theo called after him. "Too cold out here for snakes!"

The group chuckled at the insult, but Keigh remained conflicted.

"You okay, mate?" Conrad asked as Keigh and Copper walked back to the group. "Never known you to hold back on Deacon."

"I'm fine." Keigh shrugged. "Just felt like you lot had it handled."

"We did until your bear lost its mind," said Kervyn, jerking his chin toward Copper.

"He's fine, I promise." Keigh scratched the side of Copper's jaw. The red bear was panting happily again. "Just his first time around so many people... He must have got confused." But Copper wasn't the one confused; Keigh was. Red bears could sense innocence, Cato had told him—a trait Deacon Wulf had never had before today.

*

The following morning, Keigh was in town early. Braddock had given him the morning off to collect his family's papers of provision. Now that the head of their household was deceased, his family could collect food and clothing provisions at the king's expense. He and his brothers would be covered for a year since they were adults, but Sabriya and Jessie would receive help until either one married.

Stepping out of the cold and into the stillness of Bjorn's hall of records, Keigh closed the door behind him. The hall was a deep, narrow building taller than it was wide. Shelves lined both sides, their ledges packed thick with books and scrolls. Almost every scroll and parchment had been written and recorded right here in Bjorn. Addy had told him there were a few older books, some even predating the Great Collapse, but Master Alden kept them well protected.

A wiry old gentleman in a maroon robe swept up the hall toward Keigh, the candles flickering behind him. "How may I be of service, young sir?" Master Alden asked, peering down his beak of a nose.

"I'm here to collect my family's papers of provision," said Keigh, still distracted by the volumes of writing on the shelves before him. "My father was Owen Anders." He hated saying it out loud: My father *was...*

"Of course." Master Alden gave a shallow bow. "I was shocked to hear of his passing, and under such mysterious circumstances." The man shook his head as though the most tragic thing about it was the disorderliness of it all. "My sympathies." He inclined his head and retreated to a shelf further down the hall.

"Keigh!"

Master Alden shushed a small girl in thick glasses who had just emerged from a nook in the shelving with an armful of scrolls.

"Hey, Addy," Keigh greeted his friend as she laid the scrolls down on a table next to them. "How's your agoge going with Master Alden?" he asked quietly, not wanting to be shushed.

"It's great!" Addy rose onto her tiptoes, delighted. "Can you believe I get to read all day and call it training?"

Keigh glanced around at the piles of parchment in the soft candlelight and smiled, happy for her to be happy. "Just the thought of that makes me sleepy."

"Not me," Addy beamed. "There's nothing more exciting. You know there's a book here from before the Collapse about a boy who can do magic? They called themselves witches and wizards. The boy even had a cloak that made him invisible! It's really fascinating stuff. Master Alden said it's a work of fiction, that it's not any more history than stories of the fat man who used to deliver presents for Winter Festival, but I don't know. If Orvyn's real, then maybe these people were too!" She took her first gulp of air since she'd begun speaking.

Keigh let out a short laugh. "I take it there isn't a lot of talking during your day?"

"Master Alden says where words are plenty, so are fools. He prefers books to people, I think. Never really wants to discuss what we do, just likes doing the task quietly. I don't understand it. Everything I read, I want to tell people about. For example, did you know Orvyn is the only person on record to ever pair with a wild red bear? You're the only person other than the founder of the kingdom to do it, Keigh! Don't you think that means something?"

Keigh couldn't help but grin as the words poured out of his diminutive friend like water from a spring. "Actually, I did know that. Braddock told me."

"Braddock would know. He and Cato are in here all the time. They read so much I wonder how they have time for anything else."

"I see you've met Miss Osmond," said Master Alden, laying several pieces of parchment on the table before Keigh. "Here are the papers of provision for the household of Owen Anders. One wife, three children." He tapped the documents with a boney finger for Keigh to take.

"Three children?" asked Keigh, bewildered. "There should be four."

Master Alden scowled as if Keigh had just called him a foul name by suggesting he had made a mistake. He lifted the papers from the table and read the names aloud: "One Sabriya Anders, one Jotham Anders, one Jobey Anders, and one Jessie Anders."

"There should be one for Keigh Anders. Can you look again?" asked Keigh.

Master Alden inhaled sharply, then seemed to decide arguing with a boy who had just lost his father was a bridge too far. He attempted a sympathetic smile and went to check his records again.

He returned a minute later shaking his head. "I'm afraid there is no record of a 'Keigh Anders' in your family's files," he said. "Which is odd, because I checked the birth records for Bjorn, and Keigh Anders was recorded as being born in December of 288 AGC to Owen and Sabriya Anders."

"So, what now?" asked Keigh. "Can you write me a paper of provision?"

"I am afraid I can't." Master Alden shook his head sadly. "Papers of provision are Capital documents. The king funds the provisions, and the palace issues the papers."

"So you lost it?" snapped Keigh.

Master Alden's demeanor darkened. "I did not lose anything. I *do* not lose anything. This record hall keeps and stores its documents with the highest integrity and care. If your paper is not here, it is because it was never issued." He paused and gave a sigh, his scowl disappearing. "I am sorry for your loss, but if you wish to have papers issued to you, you will have to take it up with the Capital." He held out Keigh's family's papers for him to take. "I really am sorry."

Keigh thanked him and said goodbye to Addy. Why did he seem to have the worst luck? He should have known the Capital had something to do with it. It was obvious he wasn't liked there, probably for the same reason Draiden knew his name and wanted him captured. But if the king was right and the reason was his father, why come after Keigh? Why hadn't Owen been the focus of their ire? What had his father done to upset so many powerful people?

Outside, Keigh stuffed the papers under his cloak. "Come on, boy," he called, beckoning Copper to follow him to the back of the butcher's shop to check for any discarded organs or bones the bear could have.

As they walked down the street, people now regarded them with a mixture of pity and awe—a stark contrast to the scorn they had held for Keigh ever since the tower fire. People were fickle. In less than a year, the citizens of

Bjorn had gone from not knowing he existed, to adoring him, to hating him, to pitying him. Bjorn was a small town and rumors spread quickly. By now everyone knew his father had been killed, that an outsider had tried to abduct Keigh, that he had paired with a wild red bear. People even knew he had killed a red bear, no doubt due to one of his brothers trying to impress a girl in town.

Deviating from the main road to the narrow alley that ran behind the shops, Keigh was startled to find another person already picking through the waste littering the alleyway.

"Deacon?" Keigh said. There was no mistaking the dark, handsome, albeit filthy boy in front of him.

Deacon's head whipped up. He looked startled to have been caught. His momentary panic dissipated to a mixture of shame and disgust when he recognized it was only Keigh. "It's you..."

"It's *you*," Keigh retorted, still in shock.

"Yeah, it is." Deacon resumed his search, lifting a crust of bread from the scraps. He eyed the piece contemptuously before throwing it back down. "You come here to gloat?" he asked without looking up from his task.

"No," said Keigh. Truth was, he was totally confused. Why was Deacon Wulf, wealthy cane's son and member of the Consecrate, digging around in the trash? "Did you lose something?"

Deacon appeared to consider the question before answering, "Yeah...I did."

"Need help looking?" Keigh offered sincerely, surprising himself.

Deacon stepped out from the waste and wiped his hands off on his cloak. Keigh noticed the cloak was filthy; bits of food and mud were matted all over its outside. Deacon was lacking in a lot of areas, but hygiene and cleanliness had never been one of them. It was unlike him to be dressed in anything other than the finest, cleanest clothes.

"What I lost can't be found," grumbled Deacon, giving the rubbish pile a scornful glance. "Look..." He faced Keigh, but refused to meet his eyes. "I'm sorry about your dad. That's all I came by to say yesterday. Now if you will, please, leave me alone. I don't need another snowball chucked at me right now."

A bark of a laugh escaped Keigh. "You? *You* came to say...sorry? That's rich! Why did you really come around? Your dad got you spying on me? Well, you can tell him to get lost!"

Deacon hung his head. "I can't."

"Can't what? Can't tell Daddy no?" Keigh mocked.

Deacon looked up, this time locking eyes with Keigh. "He disowned me!" he snapped. His jaw started to quiver. Walking over to the closest wall, he slid down it to sit on the ground. "I don't have a father. I don't have a home. I have..." He lifted empty palms to the sky. "Nothing."

Keigh hesitated. Was this a trick? Vicerous was a heartless monster, but so was Deacon. "You deserve it," he said, looking at Deacon crumpled against the wall, dejected. Keigh didn't really mean it, but he wanted to see if he could coax the monster out. Seeing Deacon sad and weak unnerved him as much as seeing him cocky and cruel.

Deacon hung his head between his knees. "Honestly, I probably do. You know your dad was the first one to realize I was living on the street?"

Keigh's words caught in his throat. "My...my dad did?"

Deacon nodded. "He offered for me to stay at your house."

Keigh shook his head. He knew his father was capable of such compassion, but hearing it from Deacon still shook him.

"And you know what I said?" Deacon laughed to himself. "I told him I'd rather freeze than live in his filth."

Keigh's fists clenched.

"Then," Deacon chuckled, lifting his head, tears now streaming down his face, "then he offered me a loaf of bread he was taking back to your family, and you know what I did?" He gulped back a sob. "I spat on it. I spat on the loaf and threw it back in his face." He sniffed, shaking his head before hanging it between his knees again.

"Why are you telling me this?" demanded Keigh. "Do you want me to hit you?"

"I want you to forgive me!" begged Deacon, looking up at Keigh. "I deserve all of this. Your father...He didn't deserve what I said to him. None of your family deserved what we did to you." He hung his head again. "Hit me if you want. I won't resist."

Keigh wanted to laugh, wanted to be mad, wanted Deacon to suffer every bit of his misery. For years, he and his father had abused Keigh's family, and now he wanted to be forgiven? Keigh wanted to punch him for even asking. The boldness! To trash someone, treat them as less than human for years, then have the audacity to ask them to forgive you?

Keigh's chest was rising and falling heavily with each breath. His blood was boiling, but the longer he looked at Deacon, the more he envisioned the scene of Deacon throwing a loaf of bread back in his father's face, spitting at his offer of a home...The more he thought about it, the more Keigh kept seeing himself slam the door in his parents' face, kept hearing himself say the words *You aren't worthy*.

He had waited years to see Deacon Wulf defeated and humiliated. He'd thought he would enjoy it, but instead he felt like puking. The knot in his throat was back as the pressure mounted behind his eyes. He had wounded his father worse than Deacon ever had.

Keigh considered his enemy again. His remorse seemed sincere, but more than that, Deacon was fatherless—and that was a hurt so deep Keigh wouldn't wish it on his worst enemy. He could sleep at night knowing his father had fought for him, that his life had been stolen. Deacon had to live with the knowledge that his father was still alive and didn't want anything to do with him.

Keigh's fists unclenched as he allowed pity to break down his walls of anger. He knew what his father would do. He couldn't undo his own wrongs, but if he could live like his father, if he could do the things Owen would have done, then maybe his father would never truly die.

Exhaling deeply, he walked over to the wall Deacon was huddled against and slid down next to him. "I'm sorry Vicerous did this to you," he said, pitching a crust of bread to Copper.

"I should have seen it coming," Deacon admitted, raising his head, his tears now under control. "My father didn't reserve his cruelty for just your family."

He pulled down the collar of his tunic to reveal the top of what looked like a much larger patch of white, twisted, scarred flesh.

"Is that a burn?"

"He pinned me against the fire one night." Deacon let his tunic go, covering the scar again. "Tarin bested me in our sparring that day. My father couldn't stand the embarrassment of a *second-best* son." He shrugged. "He beat me or burned me every time I failed to live up to what he called *the qualities of an heir*...He was always careful not to mark me anywhere visible. Never gave me a wound that didn't heal. Not on the outside, anyway..."

Keigh's mouth dropped open. *That's why he panicked in the tower fire.*

"Deacon, that's horrible." Keigh couldn't imagine his father ever attacking him. Sure, he had disciplined Keigh, but that was because he loved him. What Deacon's father had done was against the law. "Why didn't you turn him in? He could have killed you!"

Deacon snorted. "These last few weeks, I kind of wish he had...I don't know. I guess I just thought if I could be better...beat everyone else...then he would be proud of me." He paused, rolling his head. "He was convinced he was grooming the next King of Eden, and I believed him. Then the queen named Tarin heir, and the second it was clear I wouldn't be king, my father was done with me."

Keigh's life had been hard, but he would take hard labor over abuse and abandonment any day. He couldn't imagine either of his parents treating him for one minute how Vicerous had treated Deacon his whole life.

"I'm sorry I didn't make things easier," he offered. "I had no idea."

"It's not your fault. We hid it well." Deacon shrugged. "Plus, you never gave me anything I didn't deserve."

"Come live with us." The words were out of Keigh's mouth before he had even thought of the implications.

Both boys paused, looking at each other in silence.

Deacon balked first. "Thanks...but I couldn't. Your family doesn't need one more mouth to feed."

"It's what my father would want," asserted Keigh, now confident in what he was doing. "It's what I want." He pushed himself up off the cold hard ground and offered Deacon a hand. "Plus, my family came into quite the large supply of meat recently. You won't be a burden, I promise."

Deacon looked at his hand, apparently still unsure if this was a trick. Then, setting his jaw, he reached out. "Okay."

Keigh took his hand, pulled him to his feet, and did something he had never done before, something he never thought he would do. Keigh Anders hugged Deacon Wulf.

Deacon stood stunned, arms limp at his sides. After a moment, he hugged his lifelong enemy back.

"Just one thing you need to know," said Keigh, stepping back.

"What's that?" asked Deacon, looking wary.

"Jessie is boss," Keigh laughed. "If she's happy, everyone's happy."

Deacon sniffed, allowing himself a shaky smile. "Easy enough. What about your mother and brothers?"

"Them," Keigh said, tossing another scrap of bread to Copper, "Them you can't change."

"Oh," said Deacon, his shoulders drooping.

"My mother will love you like one of her own, no matter what you do," he said, throwing an arm over Copper's neck and leading the cub toward the back of the butcher shop. "It's just who she is."

Deacon smiled. "I've never had a mother."

"Well, now you have the best." Keigh clapped Deacon on the shoulder with his free hand, sandwiching himself in the middle of his fellow dumpster divers.

"What about your brothers?" asked Deacon.

"Oh, they'll hate you," Keigh laughed. "But not because of why you think," he added. "They just hate anyone who eats food off *their* table. But don't worry about them. They're harmless—even their jokes are soft."

"Okay." Deacon smiled, following Keigh down the alley.

"Plus, if they do want to fight you..." Keigh turned to face Deacon again. "They'll have to fight me and Copper too." Keigh grinned. "Now let's find Copper something stinky to eat."

CHAPTER 36

A DUTY TO SPEAK

59-4-17

"**N**o," said Misselli, resolutely throwing a handful of feathers to the ground.

She and Keigh were sitting on the front step of the Anders' home, cleaning the carcasses of three pheasants Keigh and Deacon had killed that morning with their bows. The spring sun reflected bright off their white skin as it did off the many snowdrifts that still dotted the valley.

It had been nearly three months since Deacon had moved in with Keigh's family. Whatever fears Keigh had previously had about Deacon moving into his home proved to be unfounded. Deacon had taken to family life like a starved man takes to a honeyed ham. He listened and asked questions of Jotham and Jobey as they droned on about potato farming; he played hide-and-seek with Jessie for hours on cold winter days when they were stuck inside together. But while Keigh's siblings had Deacon's time and attention, it was Sabriya who had his heart.

Deacon didn't know any of Sabriya's history with his father, and Keigh was determined to keep it that way. The boy had never known a mother, and now he had one of sorts. Keigh wasn't going to tarnish it the way he had temporarily tarnished his own relationship with his mother. She didn't deserve that, and neither did Deacon. He would do as his father wished, as his father himself had done. He would put the failures of his mother behind him, forgiving and forgetting.

The last three months had been nearly perfect, which was just enough to dull the constant ache he felt for the loss of his father. His relationship with Misseli was stronger and deeper than ever, Deacon had become the brother he hadn't known he needed, and his family had rallied around him in ways he still didn't quite feel he deserved. If they felt like he did, that Owen's death was his fault, they didn't show it, even in the slightest.

He and Deacon were both continuing their agoge with their respective canes, only now, Keigh didn't have to hack at the old dead tree he had grown up fighting. Now he could spar with Deacon—a practice that improved both their skills tremendously. In fact, between the time spent sparring with Braddock and Deacon and the many hours he was still devoting to wielding Verity, Keigh had become better with a sword than he had ever thought possible. Deacon never bested him now, and while Keigh still couldn't beat Braddock, the legendary cane could no longer beat him outright.

In addition to his training with Braddock, Keigh was still meeting with Cato twice a week. He'd spend hours reading before being grilled by the old man on every matter under the sun. The elder seemed to have a never-ending curiosity for him, but then again, the old man was curious himself.

Copper was a bottomless pit, consuming food as fast as Keigh could find it. His red bear was fully capable of hunting and foraging his own food, but was still more than willing to eat anything Keigh gave him. When he'd paired with Copper, the cub had been no bigger than the size of a common black bear; now he was larger than one of farmer Mueller's prized bulls.

Mace and Copper got along famously, though Keigh still had a mild panic attack each time the bears wrestled. Their grappling matches had left the earth behind Braddock's house tilled more thoroughly than if Keigh and his brothers had plowed it for a new year of potato planting. Copper was no match for the full-grown Mace, but it never stopped him from trying to take her down. Keigh was proud of the young bear's fight and determination in the face of impossible odds, but it still scared him that Mace may one day decide that she had had enough and put the pesky cub down for good.

Keigh leaned into Misselli, nudging her with his shoulder. "No, huh? One of our best friends since the time we started instruction is being named heir to the kingdom and I can't go celebrate with him?"

Misselli scrunched her face at him. "Don't phrase it like that. I'm happy for Tarin too. It has nothing to do with not supporting him and everything to do with the fact that Draiden has now made two attempts on your life, and the Queen's Council is probably still peeved with you for how you exited the Refining." She sighed, setting her bird down and turning to face him. "Your family needs you here. I need you here. I don't know what we would do if anything happened to you."

"I do." Keigh grinned. "You would go mad with grief, hunt down my killer, and avenge me." He nudged Misselli again as he saw her scowl threatening to falter. "People would sing of your love-stoked vengeance for centuries!"

"They *would* be sorry," said Misselli, picking her bird back up and plucking a handful of feathers particularly violently.

"Oh yeah?"

"Yeah, but not as sorry as you would be." Misselli slapped the bird out of his hand.

"Hey," Keigh laughed. "Easy now!"

"If you let someone kill you when we still have so much life ahead of us..." Misselli paused her plucking. "I would find a way to resurrect you just so I could kill you myself."

"Aww." Keigh placed a hand over his heart. "There's the sweet, gentle girl I fell in love with."

Misselli elbowed him in the gut. "I'll show you gentle!"

Keigh grabbed her arm before she could land another blow to his stomach with her pointy elbow. "I won't get hurt or killed," he said, raising a hand as if testifying before the elders. "I promise."

"You can't promise that any more than I can stop you from going." She shook her head and resumed plucking her pheasant.

Keigh sidled up next to her. "I need to go," he said. "Next to you, Tarin is my best friend. He's the only one who didn't look at me as a thrall. We've been dreaming about this day since we were little. I need to tell him he's the Bear, one final time. He would do the same for me."

Misselli stretched her neck. "Will you at least take Deacon with you?"

"Deacon thought he was going to be king someday. It's still a little too fresh for him, I think. He doesn't want to go, and I don't blame him," Keigh explained. "Plus, I would feel better knowing he was here, close to you and my family. And I'll be with Braddock. He's the best warrior in Eden next to the king, and he really wants me to go with him. You have nothing to worry about." He paused. "Well, except..."

"Except?" snapped Misselli. "Except what?"

"Except that you'll miss me too much."

Keigh laughed as she slapped the bird violently out of his hand for the second time. "Hey!"

"Believe me, Keigh Anders, *that* will be the least of my worries."

*

"You're not coming." Braddock looked down on his apprentice from the back of his horse.

Keigh tucked his hands behind his back, swaying awkwardly. "Well...you see, the thing is, I kind of already told everyone I was going with you. So how would it look if I just showed up back at home?"

Braddock sniffed, unamused. "It would look as though you overestimated your welcomeness."

"Come on, Master!" Keigh pleaded. "Tarin is one of my best friends! I should be there to congratulate him when he's crowned heir."

"Perhaps you misunderstand why we are going to the coronation," said Braddock, cocking his head. "Cato and I go to *protest* the naming of Tarin as heir. We do not expect our rebuke to be met with open arms."

"Then why go?" asked Keigh. "If you know they aren't going to listen, why say anything at all?"

"It is our duty!" the unearthly strong voice of Cato Boman called out from behind Keigh. The old man rode up to them on his gray pony, leading a second horse by the reins. "It is our duty to the king to speak to his interests while he is out of Eden. How it's received is not up to us, only that the message is delivered."

Braddock eyed Cato's extra horse resentfully. "Why did you bring that?"

"Yeah," Keigh chipped in. "Master Fortier said he wanted me to ride Mace this time."

Braddock rolled his eyes.

"Why, for young Master Anders, of course!" Cato grinned. "I won't have him walking the whole way to Sentinel. And he can't ride Copper, can he?"

At the sound of his name, Copper ceased his pestering of Mace and turned to face Cato.

"Nor would I," glowered Braddock.

Keigh looked excitedly back and forth between his mentors.

"I *would* have him walk the whole way back to his home where he belongs," Braddock said to Cato, then fixed Keigh with a stare, warning him not to accept the old man's offer.

"Nonsense!" Cato huffed, pulling an odd round object from his pocket. "The boy needs to see the importance of speaking for the king. And he needs to see the right way to do it...Now, look at this." He pulled a string from the round object and fixed its looped end around his finger. He dropped the object and it spun toward the ground, unwinding more of the string as it did. Before it hit the ground, it stopped suddenly and climbed back up the string into Cato's waiting hand.

"Whoa!" said Keigh.

"It's called a 'yoyo,'" explained Cato. "Crispin Popplardo acquired it from a merchant outside of Eden. Apparently, they were quite the popular pastime for people before the Collapse." Dropping the yoyo again, he added, "I can see why. Absolutely delightful!"

"Fascinating," Braddock drawled, unmoved by the old man's levity. "So, you insist the boy comes, then?"

"I'm afraid I do," Cato replied, still dropping and catching the spinning disc.

"Fully aware of the danger it presents to him?" Braddock pressed.

"Fully *aware*," Cato repeated. "Fully aware that we are in the company of Eden's mightiest warrior, save the king himself, of course."

"Even I won't be able to save him if the council decides to have him silenced," Braddock warned.

"If the council moves against him, it won't matter if he's here or there. Better to keep him near us where we can better control the outcome." Cato wrapped his hand around the yoyo and stuffed it into a pocket in his cloak. "Now then, shall we go?"

"Fine," Braddock groaned. He motioned for Keigh to mount the horse Cato had brought.

Keigh bounced up on his toes, excited to have won one over Braddock. He ran over and gave Copper a scratch on the head before sprinting back to mount his ride.

"Tell me," said Braddock, turning his horse as Cato rode up beside him. "When is the last time you spoke with Mannie?"

"Must have been before Winter Festival," said Cato, stroking his wiry beard. "He did tell me the king may be sending him on mission for a while."

"Did he mention what the mission was?" asked Braddock.

Cato shook his head. "Only that he feared it would be a long one."

"Blast!" cursed Braddock. "Our message would be better received if he were with us."

"Ah," said Cato, laying his staff across his lap, "but alas, he is not. A mission's likelihood of failure does not negate one's duty to complete it."

Braddock snorted, causing his horse to snort, causing Keigh to laugh. With a disgruntled kick of his heels, he spurred his horse down the road toward Sentinel.

*

Two days later, the three of them arrived at the Capital. After depositing Mace and Copper in the Sleuth, they stood at the gates to the palace, seeking an audience with the queen.

"The queen holds open court twice a week in the king's stead," explained the cane serving as sentry. "If you wish to be heard, you must come back tomorrow morning like everyone else."

"You can't be serious," Braddock huffed, looking down his nose at the uncooperative cane. "I will see the queen today. It's an urgent matter."

The sentry looked at them, eyes half shut with boredom. "Everyone who seeks an audience with the queen does so because their need is urgent," he said, waving them off. "Come back tomorrow."

Braddock looked as though he were about to accost the sentry, but Cato stepped forward. "Would you oblige an old man and send a runner to the queen? Tell her the one who knows is here to see her."

The sentry's eyes narrowed. "What do you know?" he asked, waving a messenger boy over to him.

Cato smiled charmingly. "If I told you that, I wouldn't be the one who knows. We would be the two who knew," he said with a wink.

The sentry gave Cato a quizzical look before bending and whispering something into the messenger's ear. The boy nodded and took off down the paved pathway, quickly disappearing into the budding gardens of the palace grounds.

Ten minutes later, a pair of canes fitted with all the armor of the Queen's Climb came marching back up the pathway toward the gate.

"Her Majesty will see you now," the bigger of the two informed them. "Follow us."

Braddock flicked his eyes to the sentry as if to say *I told you so* as they followed the canes through the gate into the palace compound.

Keigh had only been to the palace through the outer grounds once before, and even though he had only been gone a few months, he had forgotten the grandeur of it. Every building was constructed of huge, dark gray granite blocks and massive doors, beams, and colonnades of red cedar. The structures seemed to have been built as much as individual works of art as they were functional buildings. Sculptures and carvings of wild animals adorned the corners, spires, and flying buttresses. The gardens and fountains were so dense it made one feel as though they were walking through a lush mountain forest, only instead of rocky outcrops and boulders, there were great stone halls and chambers.

Their entourage entered through the towering timber doors of the throne room as the six attendants forced them apart.

"Keigh!" called Tarin, his shout echoing through the cavernous room from where he sat on an illuminated throne of bright gold at the far end.

"Tarin!" Keigh dashed ahead of his mentors. He and Tarin met and embraced at the base of the steps below the thrones. "It's finally happening!" Keigh blurted. "I mean, we kinda always knew it would, but now it actually is!"

Tarin ran a hand through his hair. He was dressed in fine royal blue pants and vest with a brilliant white, baggy-sleeved shirt underneath. "It's wild, man," he grinned. "I had imagined what it would be like, but honestly, it's so much more." Tarin shook his head, gazing around the throne room. "But the biggest adjustment of it all is realizing who my true parents are." He smiled as the queen approached them in a resplendent red dress, much like the one she had worn the last time Keigh had seen her. "How crazy is it that my mom is the queen and my dad the king!"

"Not crazy at all, my dear son." The queen touched Tarin's shoulder affectionately before turning to Keigh. "Though, if I had a second son, I would have wished that he would be like you." She pursed her lips sympathetically. "I am so sorry for the way your time here ended, Keigh. Know that I argued most passionately for you, but I was powerless to undo what the council put in motion. I hope you can forgive me?"

Keigh had wondered why the queen hadn't done more to defend him. It was encouraging to know now that she had fought for him. It was crazy to think that the council had more authority than she did, but what did he know of politics? The queen had always been especially kind and generous toward him, and he wouldn't begrudge her his misfortune at the hands of the council.

"Nothing to forgive, Your Majesty," he said, giving her a shallow bow.

"A young man as wise as he is valiant." The queen tucked a strand of her glossy black hair behind her ear, then swept Keigh into a soft hug before withdrawing to her throne of intricately carved wood and red velvet.

"Here," Keigh said to Tarin, digging into his wool cloak and producing a small wooden bear that he handed to his friend. "I carved this for you. It's not valuable, and I'm sure you have endless riches now that the palace is your home, but I thought you might keep it as a reminder of our time in Bjorn." Keigh shuffled awkwardly. "I thought you might want something to remember us by…and…just kind of my way of saying that, well…you really are *the* Bear now, aren't you?" He glanced at the gleaming gold throne his friend had claimed. "Never to be outdone."

Tarin held the wooden figure reverently, then gently deposited it in a pouch at his hip. "Thank you, Keigh. This means a lot," he said, fidgeting with the cuff on his sleeve. "You know as well as I do that you would have won the Refining had you not been dismissed." Tarin reached for the pouch again, producing a gold ring and handing it to Keigh. "Here, take this. Let it be a reminder that my ascension to the throne not only lifts me, but all those who have been with me from the beginning. If you ever have need of anything…" Tarin set his hands on Keigh's shoulders. "The king's riches are your riches."

Keigh held his hand up and put on the ring. "Thank you."

Tarin suddenly punched him in the arm, only to pull his hand back, shaking his knuckles. "Seems you've already come into some riches of your own! When did you get an adamantine?" he asked, pulling Keigh's sleeve up to gape at the silver covering his arm.

"Oh yeah!" Keigh had almost forgotten he was wearing the silver armor. It fit so comfortably he almost never took it off. He raised his cloak so Tarin could get a better look at it. "I was actually hoping you or the queen knew about it—someone sent it to me for my birthday and didn't say who it was from."

"Probably just some fanatic merchant you charmed with your heroics at the Refining," Tarin deflected. Then reaching for Keigh's other hand, snatched his wrist. "What's this?" he asked, pulling at the dirty cloth bracelet Keigh had worn since the night he'd first left Bjorn. "Why are you still wearing that?"

Before Keigh could answer, Braddock cleared his throat. "If you two don't mind, we have business to attend to that requires Tarin's attention."

"That's Heir Tarin, to you," a voice Keigh had hoped never to hear again sneered from the shadows. Vicerous Wulf, dressed in all the armor of the Queen's Climb, stepped around to the front of the thrones, glaring at the three visitors from Bjorn before kneeling at the queen's feet.

"Rise," she said, dismissing him to the side with a flick of her hand.

Vicerous rose and stood dutifully beside her. He was clothed in the red cloak of a cane that he had always worn, but the rest of his clothing was even more lavish than usual. Even his new armor was gold; his new breastplate and adamantine must have taken hundreds of justicia to forge.

Hot anger filled Keigh at the sight of him. He had numerous reasons for hating Vicerous Wulf, but this time it was what the man had done to Deacon that filled him with rage.

"Traded your son to be a lapdog?" Keigh jabbed.

"My *son...*" Vicerous' lip curled. "I have no son. Isn't that right, Cato? Braddock?" He shot the elders of Bjorn a particularly contemptuous scowl. "Besides, my loyalties are to the royal line, not some random child given to me who—"

"Silence!" the queen commanded, fixing Vicerous with a warning glare. "I don't want to hear another word."

"Apologies, my queen." Vicerous inclined his head.

The queen addressed Keigh. "Vicerous has been reprimanded thoroughly for his shameful abandonment of the boy. I appreciate your concern for your friend, but I promise you the issue has been dealt with. Now, what, may I ask, brings you here today?" She turned her dark eyes to Cato. "It must be most urgent for you to show yourself in my presence, Absaar."

Absaar? Why did the queen call him that? Braddock and Vicerous looked equally confused.

"Yes, Your Majesty, it is quite urgent," Cato answered, leaning on his staff with both hands. "We received word that you intend to hold a coronation ceremony for young Master Tarin in two days' time. We would caution you to wait for the king's return before taking such drastic action."

The queen accepted Cato's reproach magnanimously. "Thank you for your concern. Your objection has been heard, and I assure you that we would not be moving forward if I did not believe the timing to be absolutely necessary."

"Naming an heir is something only the king has power to do!" argued Braddock. "It's no small thing to overstep your powers in his absence."

Tarin must have sensed the growing tension in the room. Not waiting for his mother's reply, he addressed Braddock directly. "I am in no rush, Master Fortier. I will not object to waiting for the king."

Braddock nodded, accepting Tarin's compromise, then turned his eyes back to the queen.

"I'm afraid the decision has been made," she said resolutely. "My son will be crowned heir of Eden in two days' time. You are all welcome to stay and celebrate this most important day in Eden's history with us, but if you insist on causing dissension…" Her eyes narrowed. "I would graciously ask you to return home *now*."

Braddock's lips tightened. "We can't do that, Your Majesty. We are duty bound to our king to protect his kingdom. Even if that means confronting you."

The queen smiled graciously once again. When she spoke, her words were sweet and smooth, but gave the clear impression that she was not to be trifled with. "Men of the king—for that is what you are—you should be most proud of the way you have defended your lord's honor. But hear me clearly: this decision was not made lightly. Draiden is closing in on our borders. Every day his forces grow stronger and closer. We do not know when the king shall return, or *if* he shall return. Our people need a figurehead, someone they can look to for strength and guidance in the event that he does not. I hope you can see that I seek no power for myself, but I will use what power I have to give the people a leader they deserve. My son is strong, and he is ready. This is my decision, and I will live with the consequences."

Tarin's chest puffed out at his mother's praise. Cato and Braddock bowed.

"We are only servants, Your Majesty," Braddock answered. "It was our duty to speak up for our master. We have been heard. We will return home in the morning knowing we have done what was expected of us."

"Then you will not give your blessing to the coronation?" asked the queen, sounding disappointed, though not surprised.

Cato shook his head and tapped his staff on the floor. "We can do no such thing, Your Majesty. Not so long as the king still lives. For he, and he alone, has the power to grant authority." The old man inclined his head again. "You know as well as I, that *this*..." He glanced briefly at Tarin, "...is not the king's will."

The queen nodded solemnly. "Regrettable, that we cannot be of one mind on this matter," she said. "Understandable...yet still, regrettable. My loyalties are to the kingdom and I must do what's right for Eden. If my husband does not *will* for this to happen, then he should be here. Until such time as he speaks, I am the authority he has left in Eden. My will *is* the king's will."

"Be that as it may, Your Majesty, the king's will is not unknown on this matter," Braddock challenged.

"That is your belief." The queen stood and gave a diplomatic smile. "Enjoy your stay in the Capital. If you have need of anything at all, I will command the palace thralls to see to it." With that, she turned and strode out through the large doors behind the thrones, followed closely by Vicerous.

"I'm sorry, Braddock, Cato," Tarin apologized. "I didn't intend for any of this to happen, especially for it to become something the king hasn't blessed."

Braddock and Cato walked over to where the boys stood. "It's not your fault, Tarin," said Braddock. "The king has given his bride the authority she has. Obey her in all things unless they clearly violate a command of the king's." He gave Tarin an encouraging pat on the shoulder. "We are proud of you. Don't let our objections here today take away from that. I assure you, they have nothing to do with you."

Braddock and Cato walked back toward the doors of the throne room, leaving the boys alone.

Keigh offered Tarin his hand. Tarin took it and pulled him into a tight embrace.

"Congratulations again," Keigh said, pulling out of the hug.

"Thanks." Tarin's finger caught on the cloth Misselli had tied to Keigh's wrist. Looking at the bracelet, he asked, "How is Misselli?"

"Good," said Keigh, unsure how much to tell him. "She's still working with her mother at the bakery. She's also been helping my family out since…" His throat froze. He still had a hard time saying it out loud, like keeping it quiet would somehow make it less real.

"I heard what happened," Tarin sighed. "I'm sorry, Keigh. He was a good man."

"Master Anders!" Cato's voice boomed through the massive hall.

"I'm sorry! I've got to go. These old men don't like to wait," said Keigh with a slight smile.

"They also don't like being referred to as 'old men,'" Braddock shouted.

Keigh grimaced. "I'll try to come visit you soon. Maybe I can convince Misselli to come," he added. "I know she would love to see you."

Tarin smiled. "I would like that," he said, clapping Keigh on the shoulder. "Next time you come, tell the sentry the words 'Son of Eden' and he will know to let you in. It's my personal keyword. Use it anytime you wish to see me in the palace."

Keigh grinned. "I will," he said, taking in the tall, handsome prince before him, the one who, not so long ago, had just been his buddy from Bjorn. Once just one of the gang, now dressed in finery, poised to be the next King of Eden. Keigh was excited to have a friend in a position of influence, but he was going to miss having Tarin in Bjorn.

Keigh shook his friend's hand one more time, wishing him luck, then rushed after his mentors.

CHAPTER 37

EAVESDROPPING

After meeting with the queen, the trio from Bjorn returned to the barracks, where they had left their things before heading to the palace. Instead of going to their quarters with his mentors, Keigh went to the mess hall in hopes of finding his friends from the Refining. He soon found Sanya and Tabitha. Keigh would have liked to have seen Bard as well, but he had just been called out on official palace orders.

After much food and deep conversation, Keigh returned to the barracks to find Braddock attempting to calm an uncharacteristically unsettled Cato.

"Good, Master Anders, you're here," said Cato, looking relieved. The white-haired elder slung his pack over his shoulder and grabbed his staff from the bed. "Grab your things. We should be off."

"Calm yourself, Cato," said Braddock, not moving an inch from where he sat in a plush, comfortable-looking armchair. "We can leave in the morning. They won't do anything to us. We made it clear that our duty was to speak up for the king in his absence. They have no cause to believe we desire further conflict." Braddock spread his hands as though dropping the matter. "We spoke our piece, and now we let the queen do as she will."

"That's the problem," said Cato, walking to the window and checking the streets below. "I know what she will do. She will send people to silence us. We must leave before she makes her move!"

"Is that so?" Braddock fixed Cato with an inquisitive stare. "What does *Absaar* know that I don't?"

"A great many things, my friend." Cato grabbed Keigh by the arm and pulled him toward the door. "I'll explain on the road, but we must go. She will send men in the night, when she believes us least prepared."

Braddock began to laugh, but was silenced by four sharp knocks. The three men fell silent, eyes fixed on the door.

Cato put a finger to his lips and pointed to the tall wardrobe in the corner of the room. Keigh moved quickly and quietly to obey.

Braddock stood. Grabbing his sword from the bed, he crept toward the door. "Who's there?" he called. "State your business."

Cato closed the wardrobe doors, concealing Keigh, right as the voice of a young woman answered, "Food service, sent on behalf of the queen."

Through the small gap between the wardrobe doors, Keigh saw Braddock gave Cato a relieved look. Putting a hand to the door, Braddock answered without opening it. "Tell Her Majesty thank you, but we aren't hungry."

Braddock put his ear to the door, listening for the young woman to leave. Smiling, he gave Cato the okay.

Suddenly the door burst open, kicked in by the muscular leg of a cane in full armor. The door struck Braddock in the side of the head; he dropped his sword and staggered to the ground. Ten canes poured into the room, red cloaks flapping and silver arms flashing. Cato immediately surrendered as eight of the canes fell upon Braddock, pinning the stunned warrior to the ground.

Keigh was too scared to breathe. *Should I help?* he wondered. Cato wouldn't have asked him to hide without believing whatever was coming for them was beyond his ability to fight. Regardless, he steeled himself, convinced of what he needed to do. He took a deep breath and put a hand to the wardrobe door—but just as he was about to throw his lot in with his mentors, another man entered the room.

Scipio Slate swept through the doorway in a sleek robe of deep forest green. His oily black hair was smoothed back behind his ears, revealing his leering, angular face.

Keigh froze. He wanted to hear what this traitor had to say before he attacked.

"I heard my old friend Absaar was back in town causing trouble again," said Slate, disregarding Braddock and moving slowly toward Cato.

"Slate," said Cato, raising his head.

"Tell me, old man." Slate moved about the room, casually picking up and discarding various items. "What did you think would happen when you showed your face here again?"

"This, I suppose." Cato's tone was friendly. "But in my imaginings, I actually cut down five or more of your henchmen."

One of the canes laughed at Cato's joke, earning himself a glare from Slate.

"You're a great many things, old man," sneered Slate, "but dumb isn't one of them."

"Dumb? No, I should think not," said Cato, giving his beard a casual stroke. "Truthfully, I was just craving the little fried sausages they sell down in the market. Truly, it's been too long since I've tasted the greasy goodness of one of Samuel's Savory Sausages."

There was a sudden loud clap as Slate silenced Cato with a swift backhand across the face. A dribble of red streaked the old man's white beard as blood dripped from his split lip.

"Don't touch him!" Braddock growled, thrashing against the men holding him to the floor.

"Ah, yes, the famous Braddock Fortier," said Slate, as if noticing Braddock's presence for the first time. The head of the Queen's Council took a knee in front of Braddock's face and tilted his head to the side, assessing the legendary warrior. "I was told to bring more than ten men when we learned you had come. But I insisted you aren't the man you used to be." He grinned, straightening his head again. "Turns out I was right. Besides, the fewer witnesses the better. Truth can be such a destructive thing when not kept contained in appropriate vessels...Isn't that right, Absaar?" Slate stood and began pacing the room again. "Now, where's the boy?"

"Under," said Cato.

"Under where?" asked Slate, leaning back to peer under the bed.

One of the canes holding Cato let out a brief chuckle.

Slate backhanded Cato again, once in each direction. "Make your jokes," he spat, his hair now askew. "You won't be so glib after a couple weeks in the dungeons!"

"Sir!" one of the canes holding Braddock called.

"What is it?" Slate turned away from Cato, whose eye was beginning to swell shut.

"Sir," the cane slurred, wobbling as though drunk. "Erikson just passed out, and me and Tolson aren't feeling too great."

Keigh noticed Braddock's finger on the man's wrist, but Slate saw it a moment too late. Bjorn's battle master shoved himself off the ground with such force that the remaining soldiers holding him scattered like shards of stone struck by a steel mallet. Four remained slumped on the ground, too drained to lift themselves; two staggered to their feet, only just strong enough to stand; the two Braddock had not managed to pull energy from converged on him, along with the two that had been holding Cato.

"Put him down!" ordered Slate. "Don't let him touch you! Kill him if you must!"

Braddock seized the wrist of the cane closest to him. With a sharp twist, he broke the man's arm with an audible crack. The cane dropped his sword and collapsed to the ground, holding his deformed wrist. Braddock deftly picked up the fallen weapon and swung at the next cane with such force that the warrior's adamantine flew back into his face, knocking him unconscious.

The last two looked at each other before deciding to attack at the same time. Braddock ducked a swipe intended to decapitate him while parrying a stab from the second cane. Lunging, he punched the first man in the chest with unnatural force, collapsing his breastplate so deeply the cane could no longer breathe. In a panic, the warrior dropped to his knees, frantically trying to loosen the ties on his armor.

Braddock now faced only one man. The two squared off and studied each other.

Keigh watched his mentor setting up the poor man. He knew Braddock's skill as well as anyone; he also knew the few tells that gave away his next move, so when Keigh saw the slight hitch in Braddock's left foot that indicated he was about to fake a stab to the left, only to come full circle in a body-severing windmill blow to the right, he knew the fight was over.

Sure enough, a second later, the last man lay in two pieces on the floor between Slate and Braddock.

"Please! Mercy!" Slate groveled. "Surely there's been a misunderstanding."

"No misunderstanding." Braddock wiped the blood from his blade, then cracked the cane struggling to breathe under his dented breastplate over the head with his pommel, rendering the man unconscious. "That was for hitting my friend," said Braddock, glaring at Slate as he stalked slowly toward him. "What, then, do you think I'm about to do to you?"

Slate dropped to his knees and pleaded for his life.

Braddock raised his sword—but before he could bring it down on the man in front of him, a cord dropped down over his head, tightening around his throat. Braddock choked and dropped his sword, pulling at the cord, working furiously to wriggle his fingers underneath. His eyes bulged, every fiber of muscle straining against his unknown assailant. He managed to get a hand under the cord. Pulling with uncommon strength, he gasped as his throat became unblocked. Then, just as he had worked a second hand under the noose and was looking as though he would pull himself free, his eyes began to droop. Braddock went suddenly slack, collapsing in a heap on the floor.

No! Keigh panicked silently from his hiding place. *What happened?* He gently pushed the doors to the wardrobe just enough to broaden his view.

Standing in the space Braddock had just occupied was Vicerous Wulf, panting and holding the cord he had attempted to strangle Braddock with.

"Why didn't you just run him through with your sword?" spat Slate, throwing Braddock's limp leg to the side by the ankle he had been clutching. He rose to his feet, slicking his hair back.

"Why didn't *you* just drain him while you had the chance?" sneered Vicerous. "The way I see it..." He looked around the room at the ten limp and dismembered red cloaks. "You're lucky I came at all."

Slate curled his lip in obvious disdain for his rescuer. "Powerful as my abilities are, I still have to touch a man's skin for several seconds in order to pull enough energy to incapacitate them." He gave Braddock's limp body a contemptuous kick. "I doubt *he* would have waited that long to remove my head with his sword."

"Then it's like I said." Vicerous leaned over Braddock's body. "You're lucky I was here at all."

"You—"

"Silence!"

The command rang out, cutting off Slate's retort. Keigh recognized the voice before he saw its owner. Stepping into the room, dressed in black silks that covered every inch of her body save her face, was Queen Vanitas.

"What happened here?" she asked, surveying the room with horror.

"We arrived just in time, my—"

"Go!" the queen interrupted Vicerous, pointing him to the door. "Leave us."

"Yes, my queen." Vicerous bowed and strode out of the room.

The queen closed the door behind him, then proceeded to nudge each of the bodies on the floor with her foot, checking for consciousness. One of the canes groaned. She rolled her eyes in disgust. Reaching into a fold in her silks, she produced a thin, polished dagger and handed it to Slate. "Make it look natural."

Slate nodded and took the dagger, quickly and efficiently moving about the room, dispatching the canes he had brought with him.

Keigh couldn't believe what he was seeing. The queen had just ordered the executions of her own men!

She walked over to Cato. The old man had sat down on the bed, nursing his swollen eye and split lip.

"I see you two are still...the same," he said.

"As are you, Absaar," said the queen. "Still sticking your nose in places it doesn't belong."

"Truth will win out," said Cato casually, either unaware or unafraid of the danger he was in.

"Will it?" the queen sniffed. "Did it win for you last time? Did my husband believe you when you told him what you saw? Or did he believe me, his bride, when I told him his most trusted advisor attempted to force himself on me?"

"Neither." Cato shrugged. "The king already knew."

"What?" the queen snapped, a flash of panic on her face. "Then why is it you were banished, and I have never for one day been anything but loved and adored by my husband?"

Cato shrugged again. "The king has his reasons. As is true with everything he does."

Vanitas scowled. "You really haven't changed," she said, placing a finger on the old man's forehead and pushing his head back so Cato was forced to look up at her. "Still the king's man. Still believing the fairy tale of the infallible king."

Slate walked up beside Vanitas, wiping the blade of the dagger clean of blood. "Would you like me to finish these two as well?" he asked, taking an eager step toward the old man on the bed.

Vanitas took her finger off Cato's brow and opened her gloved hand for the dagger. "Drain him." She nodded at Cato. "Until we have the boy, these two must live. We need to know what the old fools have told him."

Slate nodded, closing the gap between himself and Cato.

"The boy will fall before he ever surrenders himself to you," said Cato, slapping aside Slate's outreached hand.

What is that supposed to mean? Keigh couldn't see a way out of his current predicament. He was trapped in a room with the most influential woman in Eden and a potent that could strip a man of all his strength in seconds, and if he made it past them, he would still have to face a fully armored Vicerous Wulf in the narrow hallway.

"We don't need him to surrender," scoffed Slate, placing a hand on the elder's neck. Two seconds later, Cato fell back onto the covers, unconscious, drained of his energy. "He's gone. The only one who knew and the only one who would have ever believed him are now both in our custody," he gloated, running a hand through his hair, moving closer to the queen. "They can't harm us now."

"What of the boy?" asked Vanitas. "We must be sure they didn't tell him anything."

"We will find Keigh Anders. It's unlikely the old man told him anything," said Slate, now standing awkwardly close to the queen. "Besides, who would believe a disgraced thrall boy from Bjorn? If our word was enough to discredit Absaar, what chance does the boy have of convincing anyone?"

The queen looked around the room at the dead warriors. She exhaled and turned back to the councilman.

This time Slate put a hand gently on her face—and kissed the Queen of Eden with all the passion of a torrid affair.

Keigh nearly gasped, but clapped a hand over his mouth instead. The queen, the king's bride, was kissing a member of the council! Was this what Cato had known? What he had told the king?

The two separated. Queen Vanitas wiped her lips with all the dignity of her station while Slate smiled like a lovestruck teenager.

"Now is the time, my love," he said, caressing her arm. "The king is gone. Vicerous has been pacified, our opponents imprisoned. Who is to stop us from claiming the throne and installing our own son as heir?"

The queen seemed to consider it for a moment before shaking her head. "No, Scipio. It cannot be." She gently ran a finger through his oily hair. "Eden will never accept it."

"Why not?" Slate recoiled, obviously stung. "Their king has left them alone. We stayed. *We* are here. The people adore you and they respect me."

He pressed a hand into his chest. "Not all will accept it at first, but in time they will see we are the rightful rulers of Eden."

"The shame of it, though," said Vanitas, inhaling slowly and turning away from her lover. "How could I show my face when all of Eden would know of our indiscretion?"

Slate pulled her hair back over her shoulder and spoke softly in her ear. "When we rule Eden, we can make our own laws," he cooed. "If we say what we did was right, then it will be so."

"Those who hold to the king's law will never accept it," she said, flipping a sword over with her slippered foot.

"Which part? Us or our son?"

"Both!" snapped Vanitas. "Eden is a shining light, a beacon of strength and purity in a filthy world. What you're suggesting would prove to our enemies that we are no different than them. Weak, easily corrupted, defiled by baser desires..."

Slate stepped back, clearly wounded. "Is that what you think of me?" he asked, circling Vanitas to find her eyes. "Am I just the man who defiled you? I thought you loved me."

Queen Vanitas grabbed Slate's arm and pulled him to her bosom. "I do love you, Scipio," she said, cradling his face in her hands, "but there is an image to uphold. I am the gatekeeper. The message of Eden is *strength through discipline*. The whole reason I instituted the Queen's Climb for the canes was so that there would be a way of distinguishing the deserving from the undeserving. We cannot let the rabble in. We hold our authority only so long as the people believe we are better than them. No one will follow a king and queen they believe to be susceptible to the same failings and entrapments of the common people."

"So, being with me...having our son...is all just...failure to you?" asked Slate, a quiver in his voice.

"What would you have me do? Give up everything we've earned in the name of love?"

Slate gathered himself. "No, I don't expect you to disgrace yourself or your station as queen. That is selfish of me. But I would have you put our son on the throne in Tarin's stead." He took her gloved hands into his own, holding them between their chests. "For goodness' sake, Vanitas, the boy doesn't have a drop of royal blood in him! Why should he be heir while our son rots away in that backwater, cavorting with peasants and the like?"

Keigh had to stifle another gasp. Tarin was an illegitimate heir and the queen's son wasn't even the offspring of the king? Who was their son? How had they kept him hidden all these years?

The queen drew herself up to her full height. "You know full well why I moved to put Tarin on the throne," she said, adopting a businesslike tone. "He looks kingly. No other boy in the Consecrate is his size and strength. Tarin is a *believable* heir. Deacon looks exactly like us! Vicerous put it together. How long before someone else does?"

Keigh's mouth hung open. The sharp jaw and angular bone structure of Scipio Slate, the tan skin and handsome features of the queen, and the jet-black hair of both. Deacon was their son.

In Bjorn they had always joked about how alike Deacon and the queen looked, but never did Keigh imagine Deacon's father could be anyone other than the king. No wonder Slate had befriended the Wulfs. He'd been there to see his son.

"So what if they do?" Slate pleaded. "We can brand them all liars and lock them up for slander. Deacon deserves to know who his parents are. We can give him a home in the Capital where we can visit him regularly." He clenched his jaw, firm in his demand. "He doesn't have to be the heir, but he has to be brought home."

The queen exhaled softly, pulling her hands free of Slate's. She ran her fingers through his hair affectionately once again. "You are set on this?"

"I am," said Slate, rolling his shoulders back. "If you love me at all, if you love our son at all, do us this one kindness."

The queen continued to caress her lover's hair while she weighed his demand. "Scipio..." Her face softened as she looked into his determined eyes. "I do love you." She lifted his chin. "Let's bring our son home."

Instant relief washed over Scipio's face. "Thank you! Thank you, my queen!" He kissed her on the lips and pulled her close, wrapping her in his arms.

Vanitas caressed Slate's back and spoke softly in his ear. "Yes, my love. We will all be together soon."

She dropped a hand to her side. When she raised it again, her dagger was clutched tightly in it.

Keigh saw it coming, but remained frozen, utterly overwhelmed.

"Forever," she said, her eyes glistening with tears as she sank the blade into the middle of Slate's back, squeezing him tight to her chest.

"No," Slate wheezed. He tried to pull away, but she held him fast against her. "Don't do this!" he sobbed. "Please, Vanitas…"

His voice was muffled against her chest as he started to slump. He began grabbing, searching, reaching, attempting to find skin he could pull from, but the queen had covered herself thoroughly in her black silks. He grasped at her face, but she leaned away, keeping herself just beyond his reach.

Soon Slate's arms fell to his side as the circle of blood around the dagger turned his green robe black. A second later, his legs gave way.

The queen lowered him gently to the floor. "Shhh," she whispered. "This is goodbye, my love. Go where it's safe. No one will hurt you ever again." She laid Slate's lifeless head gently on the floor. Wiping a tear from her cheek, the queen stood, lingering over the body like a mother watching her infant sleep innocently in its crib.

Keigh grabbed the metal orb from his pouch and tried to pull as much energy as he could from it. He had to get out of here. He wasn't about to fight the queen, but he would need to get out of Sentinel quick if he hoped to escape. Hopefully she had not already put the canes on high alert. He squeezed the metal ball, trying to coax the energy from it faster—

But it shot out of his sweaty palm and landed on the wood floor of the wardrobe with a loud *clunk*.

The queen's head whipped up, her eyes fixing on the wardrobe. She took a cautious step backward toward the door. "Is that you, child?" she called to Keigh. "You know, it's very rude to hide from your friends."

Keigh grabbed the orb and stuffed it back in its pouch. He had pulled a good deal of energy from it; he only hoped it was enough.

Kicking the doors open, he jumped out of the wardrobe and faced the queen.

Vanitas smiled graciously at him. "I'm afraid I can't let you go," she said, gripping the corner post of the bed. "Not now. Not after what you just witnessed. I never wanted you to get hurt, Keigh. I liked you. Truly I did. Unfortunately for you, so does my husband. Seems to think your father is really quite important. Slate had you removed from the Refining at my insistence. People would have questioned Tarin's legitimacy if you had been allowed to win. That was all. No other reason." She shook her head sympathetically at Keigh. "You were never supposed to come back here. Never meant to hear, or see, any of this—"

"Well, I did," Keigh spat. "Now everyone is going to know what you've done."

"Who's going to tell them? You?" The queen's voice was sweet, but Keigh knew a threat when he heard one.

He looked at the lifeless body of Scipio Slate. "Guess it will have to be."

Vanitas smiled—then, with a deep breath, screamed at the top of her lungs, "Help! Murderer! Vicerous, come quick! The boy has killed the head of the council!"

Keigh was so stunned by her sudden shift that he didn't even move when Vicerous burst through the door and leveled a bow at him, aiming an arrow straight at his chest.

"Shoot him!" she screamed. "What are you waiting for?"

Vicerous loosed the arrow, but inexplicably missed his target. The arrow flew over Keigh's shoulder, shattering the window behind him.

"Don't let him leave!" she ordered, slinking back behind Vicerous.

Vicerous dropped his bow and drew his sword. "If you want to survive this, for once in your life, boy, stay in your place!" he growled, advancing across the room toward Keigh.

Keigh looked frantically around the room for anything he could use as a weapon. Seeing nothing within reach, he knew what he needed to do. It was the only thing left to do.

Surrender. Vicerous would kill him if he resisted. Surrender and live to fight another day. Surrender—the one thing Cato had said he wouldn't do. The old man's last words came back to him: *He will fall before he ever surrenders*...

An idea came to him. Not a good idea. Not one he was looking forward to, but it was his only one. But how could the old man have known? Or was it just coincidence?

"Come quietly or come in pieces," snarled Vicerous, approaching slowly, as if he thought Keigh might have some hidden attack planned. "You're trapped, boy! There's no way out of this for you."

"I'm familiar with the feeling." Keigh gulped, steeling himself for what he needed to do next. Broken glass crunched under his feet as he slowly backed away from Vicerous. "Lucky for me, I've done this before," he said, flashing the queen a cocky grin. He only had time to see the confusion on her face and the look of understanding in Vicerous' eyes. Now was the moment. He couldn't wait another second.

Turning, Keigh jumped out the broken window.

He grabbed the sill with the increased strength in his fingers. Vicerous bellowed. The queen screamed in rage. Keigh let go of the ledge just in time. Vicerous's blade screeched off the stone sill where Keigh's fingers had just been, showering him in sparks.

He fell ten feet before catching the sill of the window below. Luckily for him, whoever had designed the barracks had made each story identical, lining the windows up perfectly for him to drop straight down.

He dropped again. His fingers and arms were strong enough for the task, but his joints still felt like pulling apart each time he stopped his fall. He dropped once more before landing on the street below. Picking himself up off the cobblestones, he looked up to see the queen hanging out the window, smiling murderously at him.

"Murderer!" she screamed. "Keigh Anders has killed a member of the Queen's Council and assaulted the queen!" Vanitas's voice dripped with fear and panic as she repeated her cry for help at the top of her lungs.

She can't, Keigh thought, before realizing he had just watched this woman kill a man she claimed to love. He hoped nobody would believe it, but in his heart, he knew everyone would.

He gave the queen one last glare, then dashed down a dark back alley, away from the scene. He had to get Copper before the alarm sounded.

When he arrived at the Sleuth, there was already a squadron of red cloaks standing guard in front of the enclosures. By the angry growls behind them, Keigh assumed the bears had already been chained and muzzled.

"I'm sorry, boy," he whispered to himself, hating to leave the cub alone and restrained.

He flung himself back into the shadows of a narrow alley as he heard the alarm. Horn blasts sounded in cascades from the top of Sentinel down to its bottom tier. He needed to get out before the gates to the city were closed. Keeping to the main road, not wanting to waste time navigating the back alleys, he sprinted his way through the city, hoping desperately that he would get there before enough canes arrived to pull shut the massive doors in the outer wall.

Twenty minutes later, horns still blaring over the city, Keigh spilled around the corner into the plaza just inside the outer gates, a pack of red cloaks sprinting desperately after him. He had arrived before reinforcements, but there were still two fully armed sentries stationed in the open gateway.

"That's 'im!" One of the guards pointed at Keigh.

Keigh was the only one on the road, and his headlong sprint toward the gate in front of a host of shouting canes left very little investigative work for the sentries in the gateway.

"Yeah, that's 'im," the second guard confirmed. "Stop, you! Stop in the name of the king!"

"Surrender yerself peaceful like and we won't be 'urtin' you!" called the first guard.

Keigh assessed the situation. He could hear the dozens of canes closing in behind him. Stopping wasn't an option. He could try to evade the two sentries in the gateway, or he could bowl right through them, blocking their swords with his adamantine. Or...

Yes. He grinned. He liked option three the best.

"Hey you! Boy! Stop yer smilin'!" shouted the second guard. Turning nervously to the first, he asked, "Why's 'e smilin' like that, huh?"

Sprinting at the guards, Keigh bellowed, lowering his head to ram them.

"'E's insane, 'e is!" shouted the first guard as the two raised their shields and drew their swords to meet the charge.

Just as Keigh was about to crash into the two hapless sentries, he tapped into the last of the strength he still had from the orb—and bounded clear over the top of them.

The guards watched, dumbfounded, as he flew through the air.

Keigh fell awkwardly as he returned to earth, scraping his knees and elbows on the gravel road. Fortunately, the guards were still too shocked to respond. Scrambling back to his feet, he sprinted off the road and bolted for the tree line. Several arrows whizzed past him, but none found their mark.

A minute later, he disappeared into the dark halls of the forest. On the run. Accused of murder. Alone.

CHAPTER 38

LIGHT IN THE DARK

19-119-105

"Ouch." Keigh grimaced, sitting alone in Verity's brick-lined chamber, dabbing a cut on his thigh with the corner of his cloak. "Stupid!" he chastised himself. He had expected there would be canes stationed at his house—he just hadn't anticipated that one would be hiding in the forest above his home.

The burly red-headed cane had caught him by surprise. The only thing that saved him was that the cane seemed to have been ordered to capture him alive. The arrow shot at his thigh was only intended to cripple him, not kill him. But in the end, he was in Keigh's woods; even a highly skilled cane couldn't hope to best him in the forest of his youth. He had led the man on a wild chase up the mountainside to a cave that he and his brothers used to play in when they were younger. Inside, he lured the man in further by tossing pebbles off the cave's walls from the darkness of his hiding place. Little did the cane know, there was a ten-foot-deep pit on the right side of the cave. Keigh once had to fish Jobey out of the hole when his older brother had ventured too recklessly into the darkness.

A loud curse and the *whump* of a body hitting the ground told Keigh his trap had worked. He'd then wasted hours trying to convince the cane to surrender his sword in exchange for help out of the pit. Keigh had to give the man credit: the honor-bound warrior would not give up his weapon.

Keigh shook his head as he assessed his wound. If only the man knew the truth. He wasn't the enemy—the queen was! She had betrayed the king with Slate; she had ordered the murder of the canes and then killed her lover in cold blood—all to maintain her image and install a false heir on the throne. The king had no son, only the queen's son, Deacon.

Keigh took a deep breath. How was he going to tell Deacon? *Could* he tell Deacon? Would Deacon want to know who his birth parents were if it meant knowing his mother had murdered his father to keep from ever having to claim him as a son? Keigh released the breath. No, it was probably best to let Deacon wonder. At least in his imaginings he could hold on to the hope that somewhere out there, his birth parents loved him and missed him.

Pinching the cut in his thigh together, Keigh was relieved to see the wound wouldn't need stitches. His tunic had deflected the arrowhead just enough so that it had only cut the skin. *I'll go back tomorrow,* he told himself, leaning against the brick wall, bathed in the light of Verity. Maybe the cane would be more agreeable after a night alone in the pit.

He stared at Orvyn's sword on its podium. Its gentle light shone brightest on its sharpest edges. *If I had you, I wouldn't need to take a sword from someone.*

The first thing he had done when he'd got back to Bjorn was try to break into Braddock's house to find a weapon, but he had traveled the distance from Sentinel on foot through the rough forested terrain of the foothills. The Capital's canes had taken the road to Bjorn on horseback, so when he'd arrived it was to find the small town already crawling with red cloaks. Braddock and Misselli's homes, as well as his own, had canes standing guard. Vicerous must have told the queen all about him, because every one of the places he might find refuge was being watched with extra vigilance.

His mission today had been to get a message to his mother or Deacon. The cane in the forest had spoiled that. Now they would be expecting him to try again. The canes stationed at his house would be on high alert. At least he was safe here. Nobody had thought to look for him in the old watchtower when he had run away from home. Only Braddock and Misselli knew where he had been, though even they knew nothing of Orvyn's sword or the chamber beneath the tower. Keigh trusted neither of them would give up any information. He was safe here—and even if someone were to find him now, they wouldn't be walking in on an unarmed fighter, but one armed with the sharpest sword in Eden.

Keigh gave a start at the sound of his belly grumbling. If he hadn't been a potent, he would have collapsed from hunger two days ago. Luckily, he'd been able to pull enough energy from his orb to keep him going, even if it did nothing to satisfy his groaning stomach.

He pulled the heavy ball from his pouch and held it up to the light of Verity. *Mannie knew what you were all along.* Keigh wished his old friend had just told him what the orb was, but mostly he wished the scraggly bearded messenger were with him now. *What could the king possibly have him doing that would keep him gone for so long?*

He missed Mannie, but even more, he missed his dad. His father always knew what to do—and not just what to do, but the *right* thing to do. He had always been the one Keigh could go to with anything; the one who knew him best, faults and all, and still loved him more deeply than anyone besides his mother. Even after Keigh had rejected him and left him, his father had never stopped searching for him, never stopped loving him.

A tear spilled over the edge of his eye, falling into his lap and disappearing into his wool cloak. He hadn't loved his father as well as he should have, and now, he would never be able to. His father was gone, and it was his fault. There was no undoing that. But he still had men in his life who cared for him like fathers, and right now two of them were being held prisoner in Sentinel. He knew what he needed to do; what Owen would have done. Just like he'd refused to leave Deacon because of his father's example, he would not leave Braddock and Cato to their fate in the Capital's dungeons. He would not abandon them like he had once abandoned his own family.

His dreams of being a cane were gone now, but even if they hadn't been stripped from him, even if the queen herself offered him title, fame, and riches in exchange for disowning his mentors, he wouldn't do it. His whole life, Keigh had wanted to be something to everyone. To be famous and known, like he had been during the Refining. That feeling had been intoxicating, but ultimately unfulfilling. The excitement in Jessie's face when he agreed to play tag with her, the embrace of his mother, the pride in his mentors' voices when he followed their instruction, the joy he shared with Misselli...While not as thrilling, these were the things that left him full of purpose, feeling whole and fulfilled. His father had never been anything to anyone outside his little circle. The greatest man Keigh had ever known had been unknown to the world, but he had been the whole world to the unknown.

Keigh jumped to his feet at the sound of a rock clacking as it fell down the stone steps outside the chamber. *Someone's here!*

He tensed, looking toward the doorway. Quickly, he dashed to the center of the room and took Verity in hand. He waited quietly for any clue as to who his surprise visitor was or where they were now. He could just barely hear the muffled scrape of boots on stone—

A lone figure holding a candle stepped into the archway.

"Misselli?" Keigh whispered. He wanted to shout, but what if she wasn't alone? What if there was a cane behind her, his sword prodding her forward as a human shield?

"Keigh?" Relief flooded Misselli's face. She leaned forward and squinted. "Step into the light," she said, holding her candle up higher.

Why can't she see me? he wondered. Verity was shining with enough light to fill an entire house. "Are you alone?" he asked.

She stepped into the room, clearly still straining to see past the dim light of her candle. "Yes, Keigh! Stop playing around. It's creepy down here and I need to see that you're okay."

"Am I invisible?" Keigh joked. "You're looking right at me!"

Then it dawned on him. *Maybe I am invisible? This sword is magic...*

Misselli stamped her foot in frustration. "Anyone would be invisible in this darkness! Now stop playing with me and come into the light!"

Keigh shook his head and walked toward his best friend, still wary that she may be there under threat. As he got closer, her eyes seemed to focus on him. She closed the gap between them, striding quickly toward him.

"Oh, Keigh," she cooed, throwing her arms around his neck in relief.

"Hey!" Keigh yelped. In her rush to embrace him, Misselli had tipped her candle, pouring hot wax down the back of his neck and extinguishing the flame on his skin.

"Oh, shoot! Sorry!" She set her candle on the floor and reached toward his face, groping about aimlessly with wide, vacant eyes like a blind beggar.

"What are you doing?" Keigh chuckled, grabbing her hands and placing them on his cheeks.

"Well, I was going to kiss you, but now I can't see a thing—and by the tone of your voice, I'm not sure you deserve one anyway," she said, stepping back stubbornly but keeping hold of his cloak, as if afraid she'd be lost without it.

Keigh was about to tease her again when he remembered what Cato had said about Orvyn's sword. *Its light was visible only to those who have held it before...*

"Here." Keigh pressed Verity's handle into Misselli's palm. "Hold this."

Misselli grabbed the handle. Keigh immediately ducked as she swung the blade upward, unaware of what she was holding. Misselli gasped at the newly illuminated room. The blade dropped to the floor with a clang as Misselli's hands flew to her mouth.

"What the—? How—?"

Keigh picked up the sword and handed it back to Misselli. She stared at the iridescent blade, then spun in a circle, taking in the brick chamber.

"What is this place?"

"This is where Orvyn's sword has been hiding all these years, and where I've been hiding the last two days."

"This is Orvyn's sword?" Misselli lifted the blade closer to her face, this time being careful not to swing it through Keigh. "How?"

"Magic," said Keigh.

Misselli fixed him with a skeptical smirk. "Magic?"

"You got a better explanation?" he laughed, remembering his own skepticism. "You can see for yourself. As soon as you held it, you saw the light, didn't you?"

Misselli's eyes flicked up and down, marveling at the blade. "Keigh...this is amazing!" she said, grinning at the sword in her hand. "I was worried you were out here defenseless." She handed Verity back and wrapped her arms around him, burying her face in his chest. "What happened in Sentinel? I told you not to go..."

Keigh rubbed her back slowly, enjoying having her next to him. "It's kind of a long story, but the queen killed a guy and blamed me for it."

"Not just any guy!" Misselli pulled back and dug something out of her robe, pressing it into his chest. "You're accused of killing the head of the Queen's Council!"

Keigh grabbed the parchment and lifted it to see a rough sketch of his likeness above the words: *Wanted for murder. Extremely dangerous. Do not approach. Report any information to your nearest cane. 1,000 justicia for any information resulting in criminal's capture.*

"People don't actually believe this, do they?" Keigh asked incredulously.

"Of course they do! People always believe the worst!" Misselli pressed herself back into him. "They are saying the most awful things, Keigh," she whimpered.

"You don't believe it, do you?" he asked. Could his relationship with Misselli survive one more scandal? Would she stay by his side when everyone else thought the worst of him? Before, when he had been tied to the whipping post, he had driven her away. Did he have what it took to do that again, when all he wanted was to keep her close?

"Of course not," she replied. "And even if I thought you had done it, I would still stand by your side."

"Really?" Keigh asked, worried she would feel his heart beating like a war drum inside his chest.

"If anyone comes to take you, I'll have a poster just like yours."

He chuckled. "Okay, crazy."

"I'm serious!" she said, looking up at him. "My life is tied to yours now, Keigh." Misselli worked her fingers under the cloth bracelet she had tied to his wrist months ago. "As you go, I go. Where you go, I go." She leaned away and snatched the wanted poster back from him. "If they put you on a poster, they'll have to put me on one too!"

"Misselli..." Keigh paused, taking in the determined girl in his arms. She was perfect. Better than he deserved. But she didn't know what she was saying. "I have to go back to Sentinel. The queen has Braddock and Cato."

Misselli didn't blink. "Then we go together," she said, as casually as if she were offering to run an errand with him.

Keigh exhaled in disappointment, then inhaled the sweet fragrance of the girl he loved. A little bake shop and a little wild sage, she was tender and tough.

"You can't," he said resolutely. The image of his father falling backward, shot through with the mercenary's gun, flashed in his mind before he could suppress it. Someone he loved had already died because of him. He would not allow anyone else to be harmed for his sake. "It's too dangerous, and I won't put you at risk. I don't even know if I'll be able to pull it off. They have Copper and I still have no sword."

"What do you mean, you have no sword? You have the best sword!" She pointed at the razor-sharp blade as if Keigh were the dullest man in the world.

Keigh groaned. "It can't leave the room. Its magic prevents it from crossing the threshold."

Misselli pondered his words for a second. "Then we get help."

"Get help?" Keigh snorted. "Who is going to help me, huh? You said everyone thinks I'm a murderer."

Misselli held up a finger. "First off, it's *us*, not *you*. Second, not *everyone* thinks you're a murderer." She grinned triumphantly. "I know a few people who would be happy to help."

"I'm sorry, but my mother and Jessie would be no help at all."

"Not them." Misselli blinked. "Better than them."

"Oh yeah?" Keigh threw his hands wide as if to say, *Look around.* "What sane person would sign up to risk their life saving men they hardly know with a guy who's being hunted by the deadliest warriors on the earth...Who?"

CHAPTER 39

BETTER TOGETHER

21-4-12

"I thought you meant you knew people who could help," Keigh whispered out of the side of his mouth to Misselli, as he surveyed the motley group of teens before him. "Like...*adult* people," he added, watching poor Emerson grope around in the dark for a wall to lean on.

Keigh wished Misselli had shown up with Chogan or Victor, canes loyal to Braddock and Cato, but instead she had shown up with the club. Deacon and Conrad were the only two he thought might hold their own in a mission to Sentinel. He feared people like little Addy and big Beaudy might not survive the walk to the Capital, let alone a prison break that was almost sure to result in a fight.

Keigh exhaled slowly. Even though they weren't the help he wanted, they were a much-needed lift to his spirits, reminding him that not everyone had written him off. There were still people who believed in him.

"Misselli, if this is your idea of a joke, I'm not having it." Deacon walked slowly into the sword chamber, testing the ground in front of him with the point of his sword before each step. "How did you find this hole in the ground anyway?"

"Can we watch just a little longer? This is hilarious!" Misselli whispered to Keigh. "Did I look this awkward before I held the sword?"

Keigh chuckled quietly. "Awkward, yes. But not *this* awkward." He nodded toward Conrad, who was squatted down low, shuffling sideways along a wall like some cave crab.

"Ouch!" Theo shouted as Kervyn stepped on his foot. "Back up, ya great goon! You're smashing me against a wall—" Theo felt the surface behind him. "Never mind, it's not a wall. Just Beaudy."

"Why is it we weren't allowed to bring a candle or lantern, again?" asked Addy, polishing her glasses on the front of her dress as if cleaner lenses would help her see in the dark.

"Fire, plus this tower, plus Beaudy, equals everyone almost dying," Misselli said.

Beaudy hung his head.

"Beaudy?" Addy asked. "I thought Keigh caused the fire?"

"Keigh didn't cause anything," Deacon corrected, squinting in Addy's general direction. "He's no more guilty of the tower fire than he is of murder."

"Then why did he tell the elders he did it?" Emerson asked, leaning heavily against the wall she had been groping for.

"Cause that's the kind of guy he is!" Theo stated. "Have you really still not heard what happened?"

"No," said Emerson. "When it happened and Keigh was in trouble, nobody said anything."

Keigh could see Deacon, Conrad, Theo, and Beaudy shift uncomfortably.

"Then when the charges were dropped, nobody brought it up again," said Addy. "At least, not to us, and I didn't dare ask him."

"I caused the fire," Beaudy said quietly. "I was too scared to come forward when Keigh got caught...but I'm not this time."

"We all held our tongues when it happened," said Conrad. "Keigh saved us from the fire, then he saved us from the whip. Everyone who was at the tower that night owes their life and reputation to Keigh Anders."

Keigh started to tear up as Misselli squeezed his arm and the boys nodded their agreement. The cheers of twenty thousand fans couldn't compare to the kind words of a few close friends. As long as he had friends like these, he didn't need fame.

"Same for me," Emerson added quietly.

"Well, he saved my life twice, so that makes me his favorite," Misselli chimed in, clearly trying to lighten the mood.

"Actually, he's saved mine twice too. So we're tied," said Deacon.

"I'm pretty sure I'm still his favorite." Misselli squeezed Keigh's arm again and kissed him on the cheek, knowing nobody could see them yet.

"You think kissing him makes you his favorite?"

"It doesn't hurt," Keigh whispered to Misselli, who giggled. If someone had told him there would be a day where Deacon Wulf would argue with Misselli Labelle over which of them was his favorite, he never would have believed it.

"Kiss him yourself and then you'll know for sure," Misselli teased, earning laughs from the group.

"Enough, you two," Theo interjected. "Bunch of weirdos..." he added under his breath. "When is Keigh meeting us here, and what are we going to do about light? Darker than the inside of a cow's stomach in here." He held a hand in front of his face and squinted at it.

"I think I can answer both those questions for you, bud," said Keigh.

"Keigh!" Emerson and Addy gasped together.

"How long have you been listening?" Deacon asked awkwardly.

Keigh chuckled. "Long enough to know I'm gonna have to guard my lips around you."

The group laughed.

Deacon scowled and shook his head. "That was Misselli—it's not—" he sputtered.

"You're my brother now, Deacon!" said Keigh. "Kisses are entirely unnecessary."

Deacon sighed and shrugged off the joke.

"As for the light…" Keigh looked around the room at his vacant-eyed friends. "Stay where you are. I'll come by and put something in your hand that will help you see."

He spun Verity in his hand. The sword had become a friend to him. It had been with him through his lowest moments, a bright light in dark times, and after hours and hours practicing with it, his arm now felt incomplete when not wielding it.

Keigh approached Deacon. "Just hold it. Do not lift it, drop it, or swing it," he said, shooting Misselli a smirk. She looked away, an embarrassed little smile on her lips.

Keigh pressed the handle of the sword into Deacon's hand. He watched Deacon's eyes go from a vacant stare to focused and clear as the light of Verity shone on his surroundings for the first time.

"Whoa…" Deacon stared transfixed at the glowing blade in his hand, then at Keigh. "What is this?"

Keigh patted him on the shoulder, smiling at the wonder on his face. "I'll explain to everyone when they can all see."

Keigh made his way around the room, giving the light of Verity to each of his friends. Then he took his place in the center of the chamber. All eyes were fixed on him as if they were seeing a ghost. The room was silent save for the sound of dripping water echoing down the dark tunnel.

"Thank you all for making the trek up here in the middle of the night," Keigh said, unsure of how to begin.

"Misselli said you needed help," said Beaudy. "I'll help, Keigh. No matter what."

Every head nodded in agreement.

"We all will," Conrad confirmed. "Just tell us what you need us to do."

Keigh took a deep breath, knowing what he was about to ask was no small thing. He would understand if they didn't want to join him on his suicide mission. "I'm going to break Braddock and Cato out of the king's dungeons and free Copper and Mace. I don't expect you to go with me, but I need help preparing."

"Braddock and Cato are prisoners?" Addy asked. "I heard they had been branded traitors to the throne, but nobody knows why."

Keigh spent the next half hour telling the group all the events of his mission to Sentinel. He left out the part about Deacon being the son of Slate and the queen. Finding out who your birth parents were from the person who allegedly murdered your father didn't seem appropriate. He would tell Deacon when things cooled down a bit and the kingdom wasn't so riled up. In Keigh's version of events, the queen killed Slate for disagreeing with her. It was true enough, but saved Deacon any unnecessary heartache.

When he finished, the group exploded with a flurry of questions. Keigh quieted them with a calmly raised hand.

"This will be dangerous. If you have any way to help, that will be great, but like I said, I don't expect any of you to go with me."

"I'll go with you," said Conrad.

"So will I...brother." Deacon grinned. "I have some unfinished business of my own there."

"I'm with you, Keigh." Beaudy attempted to puff out his chest, but only succeeded in pushing out his belly.

Theo rolled his eyes. "Guess I better come too," he said, nudging Beaudy. "Someone has to look out for the gentle giant."

Emerson said she would help with planning and securing any supplies she could find.

Misselli stepped forward. "Where you go, I go." Under her breath, she added, "Like you could stop me if you tried."

Kervyn committed to supplying the group with food for their mission.

Last to talk was Addy, who swayed uncomfortably when her turn came. "I don't want to get in the way...or slow you down..."

Keigh smiled at her, "It's okay, Ad—"

"But!" she cut him off. "I probably know more about Sentinel than the rest of you muscle-bound sword swingers combined." She grinned. "You need me if you're going to pull this off."

"I know about Sentinel too," Beaudy mumbled.

The group collectively set their eyes on him.

"How do you know about Sentinel?" asked Emerson.

"That's where I'm from."

"How come you never told me that?" asked Theo, looking hurt that his best friend had hidden something from him.

"Nobody ever asks me much about me," said Beaudy, shrugging. "But I know things."

"Alright!" Keigh allowed himself to feel optimistic about the task ahead for the first time. "The way I see it, we have two big advantages. One: they won't recognize any of us, except Deacon and me. Two: we have an inside man."

"Tarin won't help us," Misselli said flatly.

"Yes, he will," Deacon stated.

"I agree with Deacon," said Keigh. If everyone in this room was willing to trust him, he needed to put trust in others too. "You didn't see him when we confronted the queen about his coronation. He volunteered to wait for the king's return. He will do what's right."

"Right for him or right for the kingdom?" asked Theo skeptically.

"Right for his friends," Keigh asserted. "Listen, if we can't trust each other, we've failed before we've even started. I say we can trust him." He looked around the room, making eye contact with each of his friends. "I don't see a way for us to pull this off without a little inside help. So, until someone comes up with an idea for how to get this done without including Tarin, we play the cards we have."

"There's another thing in our favor," said Emerson, raising her hand to speak as if they were in one of Mrs. Feldman's lessons. "Bjorn is crawling with canes looking for Keigh."

"I'm sorry, did you say that was in our favor?" Misselli asked.

Emerson balked slightly, but continued, "Well...yeah. I mean, if the canes are here, they aren't there...Right?"

"Good point," said Conrad. "Kinda makes me wish the queen hated you more, Keigh—then they would *all* be here."

"That's it!" shouted Addy, nearly losing her glasses as she jumped up.

"What's it?" asked Deacon.

"We need to get the queen to hate Keigh more!"

"Great idea, Addy," said Keigh. "Let's just invite all the canes down to Bjorn—"

"Exactly!" exclaimed Addy, beaming. "Let's invite them all here. Then there won't be any left in Sentinel!"

"And how do you propose we do that?" asked Theo, flicking a shard of stone across the brick floor. "I'm afraid me and the queen aren't exactly exchanging letters these days."

"The invite isn't a letter," said Addy, turning in place to speak to everyone. "We just need to kick the hive a bit and the bees will swarm here on their own."

"How do you propose we do that?" asked Keigh.

"Simple." Addy grinned. "You're going to make a speech...in town."

Deacon nodded. "I like it."

"Yeah, mate!" said Conrad, grinning at Keigh. "Bait 'em in, then ditch 'em for Sentinel!"

Keigh looked to Misselli for backup. How had all his friends so readily agreed it was a good idea for him to walk into Bjorn and reveal himself? All the canes would have to do was lower the portcullis and they would have him trapped like a fish in a net.

Misselli just smiled. "It's a good idea, and if it helps keep your friends safe in Sentinel, then you should do it."

"Fine." Keigh cocked his head at Addy. "What did you have in mind?"

Over the next thirty minutes, Addy outlined her plan to the group. Emerson, Theo, and Kervyn made adjustments to a few critical points, potentially saving Keigh from capture. Bjorn was their town, and when everyone had contributed their insight to the plan, even Keigh felt confident they could pull it off.

The group slowly dispersed back to their homes. Everyone had their jobs; some would take days to complete. In the meantime, they all agreed to meet back in the sword room every other night until the plans for both Bjorn and

Sentinel were ready for action. Once the sequence of events was set in motion, there would be no opportunity to pause and recoup.

"Deacon, can I talk to you for a minute before you leave?" Keigh asked, pulling his newest friend to the side, away from the conversation they'd been having with Conrad and Kervyn.

"Sure," said Deacon, joining Keigh by the wall. "What do you need?"

"I need a sword," Keigh confessed in a hushed voice. "Do you think you could get me one? Would Vicerous have left one at your old place, or could you sneak into Braddock's and get one?"

"What are you talking about?" Deacon's brow wrinkled. "You're holding Orvyn's sword, and you want me to find you some bit of steel someone left behind?"

"I can't use it," Keigh explained. "The sword literally can't leave the room."

Deacon laughed. "What do you mean? Who's going to tell on you?"

"Here, see for yourself." Keigh handed Deacon the sword. "Hold it behind you and try to walk out the door with it."

Deacon lifted the sword reverently, examining its blade with an expression of longing and wonder. Giving Keigh a confident smirk, he said, "Easy."

Deacon strode across the room, holding up the sword for all those remaining in the chamber to see. A triumphant *I told you so* smile broke out on his face as soon as he crossed the threshold of the archway unhindered—but as soon as the hilt of the sword hit the invisible barrier, Deacon was abruptly pulled off his feet.

He landed hard on his side. A gush of air escaped his throat in a painful wheeze.

"What was that?" he moaned, still gripping the sword but now staring incredulously at it as if it had just stabbed him in the back.

"That," Keigh said, walking over to help his friend off the ground, "is why I need another sword. Orvyn put some sort of spell on it to keep it from leaving the room."

"Man..." Deacon stood and brushed himself off. "So, the thing's just a glorified torch, then?"

"Until I can figure out how to get it out of here, yeah."

Deacon handed Verity back to Keigh. "I'll find you a sword. Don't worry about it," he said, clapping a hand to Keigh's shoulder.

Keigh smiled at his one-time enemy, grateful to be on the same side. "How's our family?" he asked.

Deacon's smile faded, but he still managed a look of deep appreciation at being included as part of the family. "They're sad," he said. "They miss you and they're all worried you'll get caught."

"Will you tell them I'm safe? Tell them not to worry. I'll be home soon," he said, as much to reassure himself as to reassure his family.

Deacon nodded. "I'll tell them," he said, then pursed his lips. "But are you sure I should? I mean, even if everything goes right and we get Braddock and Cato out, what makes you think the queen will let you just go quietly back to your life as it was before?" He squeezed Keigh's shoulder. "Do you want to make them a promise you might not be able to keep?"

"People need hope, Deacon," said Keigh, putting his own hand to Deacon's shoulder. "I need the promise as much as they do. My father is dead because of me. I won't let anything keep me from them."

"Your father isn't dead because of you." Deacon released Keigh and pushed him in the chest. "You know, if half the things I've learned about your dad in the last few months are true, then I know he wouldn't have had it any other way. If he died to give you life, then he died a fulfilled man." He gave Keigh a sympathetic smile. "Draiden is to blame. And when the two of us are canes, we will go hunt him down and make him pay for what he did…together."

They both chuckled at that—the idea of the two of them storming the gates of Eden's most powerful adversary, alone.

"You know why I find it so easy to believe all the stories about your father?" asked Deacon, serious once again.

Keigh shook his head.

"Because someone once told me," Deacon jabbed a finger into Keigh's chest, "*you are who you're raised by…*"

Keigh shook his head. "Deacon, I was mad. I didn't mean—"

"Nope." Deacon cut off Keigh's apology. "You were right. I was every bit the monster that Vicerous is…and if you are anything like the man who raised you, then he truly was a great man."

Keigh hung his head at the compliment. He hoped it was true. Hoped he was half the man his father had been. He would need to be if he was going to free Braddock and Cato and clear his name.

"We just gotta hope my condition isn't permanent." Deacon chuckled to himself and gave Keigh a jab in the arm. "Ouch!" He pulled his hand back, shaking his knuckles, then tugged up Keigh's sleeve to reveal part of the gleaming adamantine. "Dang! I always forget you have that thing on."

The two of them embraced, then Deacon left, disappearing past the light of Verity into the darkness of the tunnel, leaving Keigh alone in the empty chamber.

This is insanity, he thought. Not even Draiden dared march on Sentinel. Who were they to test the mightiest warriors on earth in their own fortress? What hope did they have? It would take more than perfect preparation and planning; it would take an insane amount of luck and good fortune.

He grinned, remembering his fight with the first assassin, his victory over Faraji in the arena, his narrow escape from the angry male red bear, pairing with Copper, finding Verity, the garden wolves rescuing him from the second twin…Luck had got him this far. Keigh wasn't sure how he felt about that—it stung his pride to admit that so many of his victories had nothing to do with his skill—but there was a peace in knowing he wasn't alone in this next fight. His friends, his club…They were with him, win or lose. With them, he didn't need more luck. He was already lucky.

*

It was two weeks of meeting and scheming before everything they needed was in place. After staying out all night every other day, everyone in the group was looking haggard. But they had a plan, and Keigh was surprisingly happy with it.

Addy and Beaudy had proved themselves invaluable already. Addy had read *The Mysteries of Sentinel* by Dara the Wise twice before and was able to help them plot their route in and out of the dungeons. Beaudy, being from Sentinel, had intimate knowledge of where people lived. He explained, as only Beaudy could, that "knowing where to find trouble is just as important as knowing where to find help."

"Okay! Everyone on board with the plan?" asked Keigh, shoving Verity's point into the floor and leaning on the blade like a crutch. Beaudy and Theo stopped picking wood chips off their tunics and throwing them at each other and faced him. Keigh looked around the group of tired faces and saw each one nodding confidently back at him. "Good. Go home and get some rest," he said, waving his hand for everyone to clear out. "Meet back here Saturday morning."

The tired bunch peeled themselves up off the floor slowly and began shuffling toward the exit. Keigh placed himself in the archway, giving everyone a hug on their way out, thanking each of his friends for all they had done to get them to this point.

Soon only Misselli remained. "They would all follow you straight through Draiden's gates if you asked them to," she said, watching Addy take Conrad's arm as the two started up the dark stone stairway outside the chamber.

Keigh chuckled. "Well, I would never ask them to."

"Nooooo," she drawled, "you only want them to follow you into Sentinel." Misselli threw her hands in the air, exasperated. "What are we doing, Keigh?"

Keigh was stunned. "Where is this coming from? You've had as big a part in planning all this as anyone."

"I know! And I can't shake the feeling that we are asking our friends to risk their lives!" Misselli stepped toward Keigh and grabbed his hands. "Let's just go. We can find a quiet corner of the valley and start our own life. We don't have to put our families or friends at risk. If we leave, nobody will ever come after them. Your family has their papers of provision. My parents will get along just fine without me."

Truth was, Keigh had already had those same thoughts. Why should anyone else suffer trying to protect him or serve in his mission for justice? He'd thought of all the ways things could go wrong, how the queen would surely punish his family and anyone else who aided him. He didn't want anyone to suffer his fate, least of all his friends and family. Their best hope in avoiding the queen's wrath was for the king to return and intervene on their behalf. Keigh soured at the thought. He wasn't about to place any of his hope in the king coming to their rescue; he had already done that once. What they were about to do was what the king would want, but that didn't mean he would lift a finger to help them.

"Misselli," Keigh said gently, dropping her hands and pulling her close against his chest where she could feel his heartbeat. "What would you have me do? Let innocent men and bears suffer and die while I escape and live free? I know you don't know them like I do, but I promise you, if the roles were reversed, they would give their lives to rescue me." He paused. "It's what my father would do. It's what he *did* do." He squeezed her tight in his arms. "I can't ask you to come, but you can't ask me to stay."

"Please?" Misselli reached up and twirled one of his curls around her finger. "I'll bake you fresh sweet breads every morning for the rest of our lives," she offered, pitching him as though she were Crispin Popplardo trying to sell one of his trinkets from outside Eden to some sucker with too much coin in their purse.

Keigh chuckled. "Oh yeah? You come into some money I don't know about?"

Misselli smiled, laying her head on his chest. "We could be bandits. We will just steal whatever money we need to make our meals."

"Right, the notorious sweet bread bandits."

"I'm open to trying out different names," Misselli conceded with a giggle of her own. "I'm just scared for you. Scared for us."

"It's normal to be scared, Misselli, but we can't let fear have the last word."

"Ugh!" She buried her face in her hands and leaned into Keigh's chest. "Why did I have to fall for a boy with integrity? I could have gone for Tarin and been the future queen!"

604

"It's not too late, you know," said Keigh, hoping she was only teasing him. "He still likes you, I bet."

Misselli leaned back and slapped his chest. "Don't ever suggest anything like that ever again!"

Keigh smiled, relieved. She had only been joking, but there was more truth in it than he liked. Tarin would have her if she ever wanted him. She could be queen, but instead she had chosen to slum it with a wanted criminal hiding out in a hole in the ground. Thinking about the choice she had made for him made him feel both guilty and lucky, but he had decided long ago to take his mother's advice and trust Misselli to decide for herself who and what she wanted. She had chosen him. It didn't make sense, but she had. His only job now was to make sure she never regretted it.

"Not a fan of Tarin, eh?" he asked, giving her a little shake. It was a rhetorical question, but he wouldn't have minded if she'd shouted *"NO."* "Well...there's always Deacon. He's come a long way." He laughed as Misselli slapped his chest again.

"It has nothing to do with Tarin or Deacon or any other guy alive," she said, dropping the joking tone and looking up at him seriously. "I've chosen you. You and only you."

She wrapped her arms around him. They stood like that for a full minute, listening to the rhythmic drip of water from the tunnel, appreciating each other in silent nearness.

"Why couldn't you just be the world's best potato farmer?" Misselli teased. "Why did you have to go off and become a fake murderer with a pet bear?"

"You wouldn't want that. Potato farmers make terrible sweet bread bandits." He rubbed her back playfully, feeling her hum at his joke. "Come on, let me walk you out."

Misselli rolled to the side and let Keigh put an arm around her. They walked through the door and started up the stairs together.

"I should probably leave you in Bjorn, you know," Keigh said.

"Oh yeah?" She bumped his shoulder with her head. "You think you could, huh?"

"Well, I mean, you already threatened to get yourself a poster like mine once. I'm afraid if I take you to Sentinel, you're more likely to kill Tabitha than you are anyone else." He laughed, the sound multiplying as it echoed off the cave walls.

"Laugh all you want, but that might be the truest thing you've said in the last ten minutes."

Keigh grinned. "She doesn't hold a candle to you, Misselli. I'm actually more worried you'll love her than kill her."

"I can't be friends with anyone who got to dance with you before I did." She gave him a soft elbow to the side. "Just kidding. I'm sure she's *lovely*."

Keigh didn't even have to look at her to know she was rolling her eyes.

Stepping outside into the cool spring night, he filled his lungs with the fresh scent of pine trees and sage. "Full moon tonight?" he asked, looking to the sky in search of the silver disc that bathed them in its light. "I thought we just had one…"

"Keigh!" Misselli gasped.

"What?" His brow furrowed as he located the thin sliver of the moon through the clouds.

"Look!" Misselli was pointing at his waist. "You have it," she breathed. "You did it!" She jumped up and down like he wasn't the most wanted fugitive in Eden.

As reckless as Misselli's excitement was, Keigh had no words for her.

To wield you must know. To know you must wield.

There at his hip, shining like a full moon, coating everything around them in shadowless light, was Verity.

CHAPTER 40

KICKING THE NEST

49-2-8

K eigh peeked out the bottom of his hood to watch the people of Bjorn milling around the town common grounds like sheep in a freshly plowed field. Today was the day the queen was sending a wagon of free bread to Bjorn—at least, that was the rumor Kervyn and Emerson had been spreading for the last two weeks. After all, if there was one thing the people of Bjorn would trust a thrall about, it was when and where to find the king's benevolence wagons.

Keigh took a couple deep breaths. What he was about to do made him more nervous than any fight or duel he'd ever been in. Luckily, he didn't need to say much. The main objective was to make an appearance that would send canes from all over Eden scrambling to Bjorn. Showing his face would light the fire well enough, but speaking against the queen, exposing her dirty laundry...That would fuel the fire into a raging inferno.

He gulped down the lump in his throat as Emerson gave him the signal, indicating all those going to Sentinel were clear of the town walls. It was now or never. Once he showed his face, there was no going back.

Standing up, he shed the oversized cloak he had borrowed from Beaudy to sneak into Bjorn that morning. A few people gasped as they recognized his face, others at the sight of his gleaming sword and adamantine. In five paces he had reached the makeshift stage and jumped up onto its platform.

"People of Bjorn!" he shouted. "There will be no bread from the queen today."

The faces in the crowd that hadn't been angry to see him were now. The mass of townsfolk seemed torn between stepping back and pressing in.

"The queen has overstepped her authority! Our king is on a mission and our queen seeks to rule in his stead." Keigh's eyes darted to where a pair of red cloaks were now wading their way through the crowd toward him. "It is she who killed the head of her council. I am merely guilty of witnessing it."

"Liar!" several people shouted, but one man bellowed, "Proof! What proof do you have?"

Keigh shuffled toward the end of the stage, knowing his window to escape was running out. Five more canes had just sprinted up the street to the common grounds and were closing in quickly.

"Where are your elders?" Keigh called out. "Surely you have noticed Masters Fortier and Boman are missing."

"Traitors to the throne! Same as you!" snarled the cane closest to him.

Several of the townsfolk screamed, "Traitors!"—but a few became noticeably less rigid, their expressions curious.

"Masters Braddock and Cato love our king and serve his kingdom," shouted Keigh, jumping a swipe at his ankles by one of the canes. "They would never betray our king! Search your hearts! You know it's true! The queen has abandoned her first love and seeks to install an heir of her own choosing! She must stand down!"

An arrow thudded into the wood planks inches from his feet. *Time to go.*

He dashed to his left and leapt off the stage, sprinting out of the common grounds. The crowd parted before him like pigeons before a plow mule, though whether in support of his case or in fear of his blade, he didn't know.

He made it to the edge of the grounds quickly and paused at the mouth of an alley, waiting for the canes to close the gap. For this next bit to work, they had to be closer.

Another *thud* as an arrow lodged into the side of the building next to Keigh's head. His eyes widened, staring at the still quivering bolt. *The capture alive order must have been suspended!* They were willing to kill him now. He had to go. None of the diversions would matter if he was dead.

Keigh turned and sprinted down the alley. He knew the streets of Bjorn better than any of these out-of-town canes. They would assume he was headed back toward the main gate, when in fact he was heading deeper into Bjorn. Any cane who attempted to take a shortcut toward his actual destination would find themselves cut off by the town hall. The alley he was on was the only one that bypassed the town's largest building. Only a cane who knew Bjorn would know you had to go back to the main street to cut him off, and there were only three local canes left in Bjorn: Victor Giles, Zale Woodman, and...

"Chogan!" Keigh blurted as he rounded the corner to find his way barred by the long-haired, russet-skinned warrior.

"Turn yourself in, Keigh," said Chogan, presenting his hands, empty of weapons. "If you don't surrender, they'll kill you."

"You know I didn't do this," Keigh pleaded.

"Doesn't matter what I think. If the queen has ordered that you be arrested, I must honor her authority." Chogan's lips stretched tight in a pained expression. "Please, Keigh. Let me help you. You don't need to get hurt."

"You are only bound to obey the queen so long as she isn't directly undermining the king, and I'm telling you, she is! That's why Braddock and Cato went to Sentinel in the first place!"

"I believe you, Keigh, but we need to let the king sort this out."

"Normally I would agree, but I just watched the queen kill a man who threatened to undermine her scheme..." Keigh drew his sword and took a step closer to Chogan. "You need to let me go."

Chapter 40

Chogan's eyes locked on Verity as if hypnotized by it. The cane relaxed and slowly stepped aside to let Keigh pass unchallenged.

Another trio of canes pounded around the corner behind Keigh. They stopped, shoulder to shoulder, closing off any avenue of retreat.

Their sudden appearance seemed to break Chogan's trance. He gave a startled shiver, his eyes coming back into focus. Drawing his own sword, he squared himself in front of Keigh, once again barring the way forward. "Drop your sword and come quietly," he ordered.

Keigh gave Verity a playful twirl, readying himself. "Sorry for this," he said, then swung the sword at Chogan.

Keigh had no intention of hitting the man, but he needed to swing hard enough to force Chogan into defending himself. The two blades met in a shower of sparks. Verity sounded like a clear bell compared to the screech of Chogan's steel blade.

Chogan recoiled at the impact, allowing Keigh to dash past the stunned warrior as he stared dumbfounded at the deep gouge Verity had just cleaved in his blade. The canes behind them roared their frustration and resumed the chase.

Spilling out into the main street, Keigh took a hard left. Six canes to his right caught sight of him and joined the pursuit. He pounded up the hill away from the main gate, now with nine canes behind him. Coming up on Crispin Popplardo's shop, he nodded to Kervyn as he raced by. Kervyn nodded back and grabbed the reins of a large mule with a rope tied to its harness.

A second later, Keigh grinned as he heard the yelps of a half dozen men behind him. They had been too focused on catching him to notice that the cord that usually spanned the distance between the eaves of Crispin's shop and the tanner's had been relocated to the ground, where Kervyn Popplardo had tied one end to a horse hitch and the other to his father's mule Buckeye. The mule had pulled the loose end tight as soon as Keigh had passed. Keigh hoped the men would be too focused on him to bother punishing Kervyn for his interference.

He took another hard left and raced to the end of the street toward the open door of Cato's house. The trip line had bought him the time and distance he needed to disappear inside without being seen. Keigh dove through the open front door just before it was slammed shut.

"You bring our fee?" a voice confronted him from the shadows.

Keigh rolled over and produced two sticky oat bars from the pouch at his waist, tossing them to his brothers. "Thanks for doing this, guys," he gasped, nodding to Jotham and Jobey. "Be sure to tell Mom and Jessie I'm alright."

"Are you, though?" asked Jobey, peeking out at the street through a crack in the door. "You seem a bit more hated than usual."

"We will tell them," Jotham agreed. "Just make sure you make it back as soon as you can."

"Yeah, I'm not sure we can take another week of entertaining Jessie." Jobey grunted as he helped Jotham slide a heavy shelf holding various pots and pans away from the back wall of the house. "And I don't think she gets our jokes."

"That's because nobody gets your jokes," said Keigh, giving each of his brothers a friendly punch in the arm. Then, stooping behind the shelf, he reached inside the hole that Beaudy and Theo had spent the last two weeks chiseling through Bjorn's outer wall.

"Come out and surrender yourself, Keigh Anders!" a voice cried from the street. "If we have to come in after you, you'll pay for it!"

"Showtime!" said Keigh, grinning at his brothers. "Remember, they don't know what I sound like, but they will notice if you say something stupid."

"I want promises!" Jobey yelled to the canes outside, then looked to Keigh and whispered, "How was that?"

"Good. Just don't ask for honey buns and you should be able to stall them for a few more minutes." Keigh smiled. "Thank you. I love you guys."

"We won't kill you!" the voice from outside called again. "That's all you'll get from us!"

"Go!" his brothers whispered in unison before Jobey yelled, "And I won't kill you if you stay outside!"

Keigh crawled into the narrow tunnel and wriggled toward the slivers of light at the far end. He heard his brothers slide the shelf back into place behind him to cover the hole in the wall, followed by the sound of Jobey shouting, "Tell me your names! I won't surrender myself to a bunch of strangers!"

Keigh crawled the ten feet to where Beaudy and Theo had stopped their chiseling a half-inch shy of breaking through the outside surface of the wall. Keigh punched through the thin membrane of wood with his adamantine arm and crawled through the hole, flopping into the young green grass of spring that had grown up against the warm, sunbaked walls of Bjorn.

He rose to his feet. When he was satisfied nobody had spotted him, he took off at a jog toward the old watchtower. Halfway there he finally stopped and turned to look back at the town he had just escaped. From here, a person would never know it was anything other than an uneventful day in Eden's least eventful town. But Keigh knew the red cloaks were swarming like ants whose nest had just been stepped on.

He snorted. He would have given anything to see the look on the canes' faces when they busted into Cato's house to find Jotham and Jobey having tea in the old man's study. Still, he hoped desperately that the canes would not punish his brothers or Kervyn too harshly for interfering.

After catching his breath, he resumed his trot to the tower. The fresh morning air suddenly smelled sweeter, and the sun felt a bit warmer. They had actually pulled it off! His misfit club of teens had just duped and evaded a town full of earth's greatest warriors. By the time they discovered the hole in the wall behind the shelf, Keigh and his crew would be well on their way to Sentinel. They would spend days trying to track him, but all they would find was an empty tower and some tracks headed into the mountains. Once Keigh had them in the forest, he was sure he could cover their tracks and leave the canes believing he was holed up in some cave. They would spin their wheels searching the Ursus Mountains top to bottom while he and his friends broke into Sentinel and freed his mentors.

Keigh smiled as the tower came into view. Soon he would be back with his friends, embarking on a mission worthy of the bards. He quickened his pace. The sooner he got there, the sooner they could depart—

A figure stepped out from their hiding place in the bushes, blocking the trail.

"I was right," sneered Christian, his appearance as groomed and flawless as always, save for the shiny pink scar across his cheek where the badger had clawed him.

Keigh halted. His eyes darted from Christian to the tower and back.

"Don't worry." Christian smiled, running the tip of his tongue across his front teeth. "Your little girlfriend is fine. I'll be sure to thank her later, though."

"What for?" spat Keigh. His anger at being found out, coupled with the bitter memory of his last encounter with Christian, threatened to thrust him prematurely into a fight.

Christian sighed. "Well, when I couldn't find you, I decided the best course of action was to follow the people you love. No secret you love the girl. Deacon used to mock you for it regularly when he ate with us." He drew his sword and lazily polished a spot on it with his cloak. "A bit boring for my taste, always walking to town or your mother's house—that is, until this morning, when I followed her here," he said, gesturing toward the burnt remains of the tower. "Would have never known this was up here if not for her." He shook his head. "As boring as she is, she really is quite pretty. No doubt she will be devastated when she realizes you aren't coming. But don't you worry." Christian raised his sword. "I'll stop in to comfort her."

Keigh roared. Drawing Verity, he lunged at Christian, raining heavy blows down on him in rapid succession. By the end of his first onslaught, the edge of Christian's blade was serrated with gouges from Verity, leaving it looking more like a saw than a sword.

"I see you've found yourself a new toy." Christian eyed Keigh's blade covetously. "I shall take it for myself when we're done. A blade that fine deserves a warrior to match."

Christian lunged in his own assault, testing Keigh's reflexes with a rapid succession of diverse attacks. Keigh fielded half the blows with his sword and half with his arm.

Christian withdrew, eying the adamantine. "You've got everything but the cloak and helmet, don't you?" he said, scowling. "How'd you get them? You certainly haven't earned them. You're too young, too *worthless*, to have been awarded either in the Queen's Climb."

Keigh's nostrils flared. Christian had just voiced the thing he had wondered since receiving the adamantine for his birthday. Why had it come to him? What right did he have to wear what everyone else had to earn?

Christian must have realized he'd hit a nerve. He pressed harder. "You may look the part, and you've played the part convincingly enough, but face it, Keigh. You're a nobody from nowhere. A thrall that got out of its pen and played pretend. The king may have indulged your fantasy, but that's all it was—a fantasy. You'll never be one of us. Not truly." He lifted his chin, looking down his nose at Keigh like so many other high and mighty men before him. "I personally don't care that you were allowed out of place. It just makes it that much more satisfying to put you back where you belong."

With a growl, Christian went on the attack. Keigh once again fielded the blows between his adamantine and Verity. His shielded arm lived up to everything he had ever heard about the canes' most unique piece of equipment. He hardly felt the impact of Christian's blows—until, with the last stroke, there was a snap of fire in his palm.

Stung, he retreated. Christian seemed content to catch his breath. Keigh looked at his palm, expecting to see a snapped tendon balled up under his skin, but instead saw the handle inside the cuff of his armor glowing a soft red, like an iron poker in a fire.

Could it...

Keigh grabbed the bar and felt a trickle of energy flow into his palm. It was! His adamantine had been collecting the energy of every one of Christian's swings.

He gripped the handle and began the pull of energy. White-hot fire filled his veins as his muscles flexed with newfound strength.

"What are you grinning for?" sniffed Christian.

"This fight is over."

The smooth-skinned cane snorted. "Yes, as soon as I end it."

Keigh closed the gap in an instant, lunging with unnatural speed. Verity struck out like the fang of a viper in his newly energized arms.

Christian's face quickly turned from smug to panicked.

With an upward two-handed swing to Christian's shoulder, Keigh sent his opponent's blade flying through the air. Spinning like a maple seed, it fell back to earth.

Christian watched, dumbstruck, as his only means of defense landed in the bushes downhill. Dropping to his knees, he began groveling for his life. "Please! Please don't kill me! I was only following orders!"

Keigh stood over his vanquished opponent. "Why shouldn't I kill you?" he asked coldly. A vision of Verity removing his enemy's head flashed in his mind's eye. Christian was high on the list of people who least deserved mercy. He could do it. He could end this menace right here, right now. Christian would never be able to attack or abuse anyone ever again.

"Mercy! I beg of you!" Christian bawled. "Please, spare my life. You won't regret it!"

*Mercy...*Keigh remembered the words carved into his father's headstone: *Man of Mercy*. He ground his teeth. Of all the things his father had been, of all the ways Keigh one day hoped to be like him, *merciful* was the hardest trait to swallow. But there was no divorcing Owen Anders and mercy. He couldn't think of one without the other. There would be no honoring his father without surrendering to mercy.

"I'm not going to kill you," Keigh said through gritted teeth. "You were, as you say...only following orders."

"Exactly!" spewed Christian, turning his face upward—just in time for Keigh's silver-backed hand to knock him unconscious.

Keigh knelt and ripped several lengths of cloth from Christian's tunic, which he used to bind and gag the cane. He took the red cloak and set it to the side. Satisfied that his knots were tied well, he pushed Christian's unconscious body into the long grass beside the trail.

"Hope your friends find you before the animals do," Keigh huffed, glad to be rid of him.

He lifted the red cloak to put it on, then stopped. Christian's mocking words rang back to him: *You didn't earn it.*

Keigh rolled the cloak up and stuffed it under his arm. Christian was right. When he donned the red cloak for the first time, it would be Braddock draping it over his shoulders. He could wait for that day. In the meantime, the cloak could still come in handy for what they needed to accomplish in Sentinel.

Keigh sprinted the remaining distance to the tower with the strength he had pulled from his adamantine. Descending into the tunnel, he raced toward the sword chamber to find his friends huddled in the darkness around a dying candle on the floor. Verity instantly washed the room in light, the chamber made even brighter by the relief and joy that spread over his friends' faces.

"He's safe!" shouted Beaudy as the rescue party got to their feet and took turns hugging their de facto leader.

Keigh allowed himself to bask in the joy of success for a minute, but only a minute. They had started the clock. They were now in a race to get into and out of Sentinel in the brief window of time their stunt had bought them.

They had two days to get to the Capital, and only one shot to get out alive.

CHAPTER 41

GETTING IN

9-16-7

"Nuh-uh." Deacon frowned. "I'm not going in there."

"Would you prefer we try to waltz through the front gate?" Keigh jested. "You may not be wanted for murder, but your face is every bit as recognizable as mine since the Refining."

Keigh stood next to Deacon on the edge of a large prairie dog hole dug into the hillside across from Sentinel. Both boys stared down into its inky black depths. Tonight was the night. On the afternoon of their second day traveling through the trees, they had spotted rows of red cloaks marching north from the Capital on the road toward Bjorn. The queen had taken the bait. Her desire to capture or kill Keigh before he spilled her secrets had led her to send an altogether ludicrous number of canes to Bjorn in response to his little show of defiance.

"It's our only way in," said Keigh, "and it may take us a while to find a tunnel that gets us under the walls, so we need to go now. We planned for this. Why are you only speaking up now?"

"I don't like the idea of being trapped in the dark with an animal the size of a horse!" Deacon protested through clenched teeth, loud enough for only Keigh to hear.

"They eat grass, Deacon. They're as harmless as cows."

"So do bulls, Keigh, and you don't see anyone lining up to be trapped in a pen with one of those."

Keigh turned to Addy, who was waiting nervously behind them. "Will you tell Deacon he has nothing to worry about from these prairie dogs? Surely you've read about them."

Addy scraped the dirt with her feet. "I wish I could, but they're actually quite fierce defenders of their burrows."

"What? Why are you just now telling me this?"

Addy dropped her gaze and continued to shuffle nervously. "I don't know...I guess...I just trust you, Conrad, and Deacon to protect us."

Misselli, Beaudy, and Theo nodded their agreement behind her. "We trust you, Keigh," Beaudy said, standing up straight.

Keigh looked at his ragtag group of loyal friends. *What have I done? Why did I let them risk their lives for my mission?* It wasn't too late to go in by himself. They had made it to Sentinel, but so far, they hadn't done anything to break the queen's captives free of the dungeons. Misselli and Addy had already gone into the city that morning to contact Sanya and Tarin, both of whom had discreetly agreed to help them. They could all go home now, though. Sanya and Tarin's assistance would be enough.

Keigh opened his mouth to tell them to go when Deacon suddenly left his side, disappearing into the hole, his cloak flapping as he fell.

"What are you doing?" Keigh drew Verity, casting light down into the hole.

Deacon's white smile shone in the darkness. "I decided I trust you too. No prairie pig is going to best the Bears of Bjorn!"

"Weee!" Misselli dropped into the hole while Keigh was still staring down at Deacon.

Conrad, Beaudy, and Theo joined in rapid succession, followed by Addy, who asked Beaudy to catch her.

Before Keigh knew it, he was the only one left above ground. The expectant faces of his friends smiled up at him, catching the light of Verity in the darkness.

"You coming?" Theo asked.

He couldn't ask them to go home now, not when they were this united. They were ready to give their lives for him, for what was right. To tell them he could do this on his own would be to spit in the face of their sacrifice.

"C'mon, mate, you and that magic sword get down here so we can see where we're going," chirped Conrad, looking nervously down the tunnel, his own sword already drawn.

Keigh locked eyes with Misselli, who gave him a subtle nod as if to say, *I'm with you.* That was all the convincing he needed. He made sure he had his orb, checked his bow was hanging securely on his quiver, gripped Verity's handle, then dropped into the hole after his friends.

For the next hour, the group followed Keigh in the light of Verity through a dozen branches of the tunnels. The air was thick and humid. The strong smell of fresh-tilled dirt and animal droppings gave Keigh the feeling of walking through the world's longest, darkest barn. Only this barn's animals weren't penned in, and may not be friendly.

As they ventured deeper into the labyrinth, they searched for any light in the ceiling that would indicate they were under the collapsed section of road Misselli and Addy had spied while in the Capital's lowest tier earlier that day. The plan was to finish collapsing that section of tunnel, then, as stealthily as they could, crawl above ground and make it into the Centipede, where Sanya would lead them unseen to the dungeons.

They followed a particularly deep section of tunnel in what Keigh assumed was the direction of Sentinel. After a few hundred yards, the tunnel began to climb up toward the surface. Rounding a bend, they finally found what they had been looking for. A hundred yards ahead of them, thin shafts of light fell in columns onto a mound of dirt and rock.

"There!" Keigh pointed Verity at the break in the ceiling. "We found it!"

The group sighed their relief and trotted toward their escape point. Beneath the collapsed section of tunnel, Keigh was relieved to find that the mound of dirt and rock had formed something of a makeshift ramp, granting them the ability to climb to the surface relatively quickly as opposed to having to climb onto Beaudy's shoulders and have Keigh or Conrad lift them out one by one. Only a thin layer of hard gravel and cobblestones separated them from the surface.

"Me and Deacon will break apart a hole for us to climb through," Keigh whispered. "Conrad, watch our rear for any sign of trouble. Beaudy and Theo, make sure the debris gets moved aside and doesn't fall on anybody."

They would need to move quickly. It was late, but there were sure to still be a few people wandering the streets of Sentinel. A group of teenagers crawling out of a hole in the ground would surely lead any common citizen to report to their nearest cane.

Deacon and Keigh climbed the earthen ramp toward the gap in the ceiling, but before they could get to work, a short, piercing squeak echoed from the way they had just come. The group turned as the squeaks continued, increasing in volume and frequency. Keigh climbed back down the ramp and walked the tunnel back, placing himself next to Conrad, between the unexpected visitor and the rest of his friends. He could hear the scuffling of something large coming toward them.

The noise stopped abruptly. Keigh peered into the darkness, past Verity's light. In the shadows he saw two tiny slits of light.

Eyes.

A prairie dog the size of Copper jolted into the light. Its solid black eyes, the size of dinner plates, reflected Verity off their glossy wet surfaces. With a twitch of its nose and an ear-splitting squeak, the prairie dog bowled through him and Conrad, knocking them both to the side.

Keigh dropped Verity as he bounced hard off the wall of the tunnel. The overgrown rodent had plowed through them as if they were no more than toddlers trying to block a full-grown man with a twig. Before anyone knew what was happening, the beast had grabbed hold of Beaudy's tunic and dragged him screaming back into the darkness beyond Verity's light.

Keigh scrambled to pick up the sword and give chase, but Theo had already sprinted past him, unarmed and unprotected, after his best friend.

"Beaudy!" Theo's cry echoed back up the tunnel.

Keigh finally got a handle on his sword. He waved for Deacon to follow him and told Conrad to stay with the girls. It had all happened so fast. They were only seconds behind the animal, yet they seemed to have already fallen miles behind. They tore after the sounds of Beaudy's cries for help, only delaying once to decide which fork in the tunnel the sounds were coming from.

The cries suddenly stopped, filling Keigh with panic and spurring him to new speed as they flew down the tunnel. They were sprinting so fast that they nearly crashed straight into Theo and Beaudy. They skidded to a halt in front of Theo, who was helping his large friend back to his feet. Keigh gaped at the apparently dead body of the prairie dog behind the boys.

"What happened?" Deacon asked before Keigh could find his tongue.

"Did you…?" Keigh looked from Theo to the lifeless mound of fur.

Theo nodded.

"That much? That fast?" Keigh asked, impressed.

Theo shrugged. "I needed to save my friend."

"Thanks, Theo." Beaudy shook the dirt from his tunic.

"You can hold all of it?" Keigh asked, still focused on the skinny little teen in front of him. Cato had mentioned Theo's ability to hold vast amounts of energy, but still, the prairie dog was huge! "How do you feel?"

"Awake!" Theo's eyes widened. "Like…really awake."

"Not strong?"

Theo gave Beaudy an experimental shove, nearly knocking himself over. "Nope."

"What are you two talking about?" Deacon's head shot back and forth between Keigh and Theo. "How did you—Is he…?" Deacon pointed at Theo, but asked Keigh the question.

Keigh nodded. Deacon had a right to know. They were all in this together.

"So can he…?" Deacon flexed an arm.

Keigh pursed his lips and shook his head.

Deacon turned to Theo. "So, you're just a sucker? I mean…" He quickly corrected himself. "You just pull energy but can't use it? I thought all potents were the same?"

"Nope, not a sucker." Theo smiled. "Though maybe I am, following you two down here just to see y'all get bested by an oversized squirrel."

Keigh and Deacon smiled back. "We're glad you're with us." Keigh clapped Beaudy on the shoulder. "Both of you."

A minute later, they rejoined Conrad, Misselli, and Addy where they had left them.

"Are you okay?" cried Addy as both girls rushed Beaudy, pincering him in a double hug and still finding him to be wider than they could wrap their arms around.

Beaudy put an arm around each of them, looking as happy as ever. "A bit dusty, but I'm fine...thanks to Theo."

The girls peeled themselves from Beaudy and rushed to hug Theo. This time they found not quite enough boy for the two of them to hug at once. They tried all the same, though, leaving Theo standing as tall as Keigh had ever seen him.

Deacon and Keigh climbed the mound and used their swords to make quick work of the last layer of dirt and cobblestone separating them from the surface. Poking his head through the hole slowly, Keigh looked for Sanya. She was nowhere to be found—instead, it was Tabitha waiting against a wall not twenty feet from where they had excavated.

Tabitha gave a start at the sight of him, followed by a nervous smile and the signal for *all clear*.

Keigh gulped, half excited to see his friend, half nervous about what Misselli might do to her. He whispered back into the hole for everyone to follow him quickly and quietly, then pulled himself up onto the street and gave each of his friends a helping hand out of the hole.

Addy came first, followed by Misselli. Keigh nearly forgot to help Theo out as he watched Misselli approach Tabitha. He gave Theo his hand without taking his eyes off the encounter. "Please don't say anything," he muttered under his breath as Misselli marched up to a wary-looking Tabitha. Tabitha was the prettiest girl Keigh had ever seen, but that wouldn't do her any good if Misselli decided to claw her face off.

Keigh tensed, ready to sprint over and pull Misselli off of Tabitha if needed. He started to take off as he saw Misselli throw her arm back, loading up a punch—then nearly fainted when she looped that arm around Tabitha's neck in a hug. A hug Tabitha returned.

Keigh breathed a sigh of relief. *One crisis averted.*

Theo joined Misselli and Addy behind the narrow door in the wall that Keigh knew was their entrance to the Centipede. Deacon and Conrad came up next, and together, the three of them helped heave Beaudy from the pit.

Keigh patted his loyal friend on the back and ushered him to follow the others toward the door. But Beaudy was frozen, his eyes locked on Tabitha.

Keigh waved him on again. "I know she's pretty, bud, but you've got to move!" He looked to Tabitha for support and was shocked to see she, too, was frozen.

"Beauds?" she whispered. "Is that you?"

Beaudy nodded, eyes shimmering with tears.

Tabitha sniffed, covering a flash of a smile with her hand. "You're back." She broke into a run and threw herself into Beaudy, who caught her gently in a warm embrace.

He stroked her hair as he held her close. "I'm so sorry, Tab."

Everyone stood rooted in place, slack-jawed. They hadn't been this surprised even when they all held Orvyn's sword for the first time and saw its magic light with their own eyes. Keigh stared. *Beaudy* was the boy Tabitha always talked about?

"Hate to break up the reunion," Theo spoke up, "but, in case you forgot, we are in the most heavily fortified city in the world, with a wanted murderer, trying to break two old farts out of a hole in the ground without getting ourselves killed in the process!" His hushed voice was as urgent as it was salty.

Beaudy and Tabitha each gave each other embarrassed grins. Beaudy took Tabitha by the hand and they trotted to the door. Keigh and Deacon brought up the rear, exchanging looks of disbelief.

Once they were all inside the passageway, Tabitha closed the door behind them and lifted an oil lantern.

"Here," said Keigh, offering her the handle of his sword.

She looked at the sword and shook her head, confused.

"Trust him," Misselli said. "Just hold it for a minute."

Tabitha reached out tentatively and grabbed the handle. Immediately her eyes were opened to the light of the blade around her. She looked at each of them as though she were seeing them for the first time. "How?"

"It's Orvyn's sword," Keigh explained as she handed it back. "Where's Sanya?"

"She's distracting Bard," said Tabitha. "She agrees with you that it's best that he doesn't know anything. That way he can be genuinely ignorant when his two charges are found missing tomorrow."

"So, what Addy told us is true?" Keigh asked. "We can access each cell in the dungeon through the Centipede?"

Tabitha nodded with a smile.

"I told you I knew stuff," said Addy, grinning her satisfaction at being proved right. "They installed the doors so that canes wouldn't have to do the lowly task of feeding prisoners."

"Never doubted you." Keigh smiled back, glad to have her here with him.

"Did she also tell you that the doors to the cells require three people to operate and can't be opened from inside?" asked Tabitha, looking convinced that this at least would be news to the group. But they all nodded. "Huh," she said, eying Addy with newfound respect. "Great. I'll show you what we need to do when we get there. Follow me."

She squeezed her way to the front of the group and led them at a brisk walk through the maze of tunnels that permeated Sentinel like arteries through a body. Keigh had spent many hours exploring the tunnels, but following Tabitha through the maze reminded him again of how completely lost he would have been if he had tried to find the dungeons on his own.

He snorted. How fitting that the desire of the rich and powerful to be separated from the servant class would be the very thing that allowed him and his friends to sneak through the city undetected. It was rare that he appreciated having grown up a thrall, but tonight, all his suffering and work would prove to be the key that unlocked the means to saving lives. *Serves them right,* he thought, envisioning the outrage on the queen's face when she was informed her captives had disappeared.

Tabitha took them on the most direct route possible to the dungeons, but it still took nearly an hour to reach the straight stretch of tunnel lined with solid cell doors. Each door was on the same side of the wall, ten feet apart. They each had one iron lever on either side and one across the hall for a total of three levers per cell.

"Who wants to pick which door to try first?" said Misselli, stretching out an arm as if presenting the doors like cups in a shell game.

"Try one of the middle ones first," said Addy. "That way you'll have the best chance of seeing or hearing one of them, even if the cell you choose isn't the one they're in."

"Right," Keigh agreed. Wasting no time, he led the way to a door about halfway to the end. "This will do."

Tabitha stepped forward and grabbed one of the iron levers. "Misselli, will you operate the handle on that side of the door, and Beauds, will you take the one across from us?"

Misselli and Beaudy stepped forward and gripped their respective levers.

"Misselli, try to push yours down," said Tabitha.

Misselli pulled down on the lever. It didn't move.

"Okay, so that's the lever for the inner door," Tabitha said to herself. "Which means...mine is for the outer door." She pulled her own lever down and the door swung inward with a creak, revealing a closet-sized alcove with another closed door at its back. "Sanya said that the inner door's lever won't operate while these two are up. Beauds, yours can only go down when mine is down, and only up when mine is up. Understand?"

Beaudy nodded. "So should I pull mine down now?"

Tabitha nodded. "Your lever acts as a lock for the two doors. In order for Misselli's door to open, my lever has to be up, and your lever has to be down." Tabitha looked to Keigh. "Go," she said, nodding to the empty alcove.

Keigh stepped into the nook. Misselli gave him a concerned look, mouthing the words *Be careful.*

Tabitha lifted her lever, causing the open door to swing shut again, separating him from the group and sealing him between two locked doors. Keigh could still hear Tabitha giving instructions.

"Now that mine is up and Beaudy's is down, yours will work, Misselli. Once yours is down, Beaudy's won't go up and I won't be able to open the outer door while the inner door is open." Tabitha paused. "Keigh, knock on the door when you're ready to come out."

"Okay," he said, just loud enough for her to hear.

"Misselli, you can pull your lever down now. Leave it down until he knocks."

Keigh heard the metallic clicks of a ratchet, then the inner door swung in toward him. He raised his sword, ready for whatever might be lying in wait for him in the cell. To both his relief and disappointment, the cell was empty. He stepped into the cramped space. A small wooden bucket lay in the corner of the otherwise bare stone room. Locked iron bars separated him from the torchlit hallway outside the cell.

Keigh crept quietly toward the bars, the crackling of torches obscuring the sound of his steps. His vision was limited, but he could see enough of the hallway to know it was unoccupied. "Psst!" he hissed. "Cato! Braddock!"

No response. A jolt of fear gripped him. What if they were asleep? He panicked. *I'll have to search every cell! Or worse, what if they aren't answering because they're dead?*

He shook the last thought out of his head. They wouldn't be dead...They couldn't be. The queen was sick, but she wasn't stupid. If there was any chance of leveraging the men to capture him, she would not have disposed of them yet.

He turned to exit the cell, more anxious than he had been since entering the city. Their plan's success was largely dependent on not being seen, and now that they would have to linger in the dungeons, searching every cell one by one, their chances of going unnoticed had dwindled to near zero.

He had just stepped back into the nook when he heard a quiet voice call to him from the hallway.

"Keigh?"

CHAPTER 42

GETTING OUT

19-55-12

"Last two cells on the end," the hushed voice called.

Even at a whisper, Keigh recognized the sound of Braddock's voice. He rushed back to the bars and pressed his ear toward the hallway. "Which end?"

"The correct one," rasped Cato's voice.

Keigh smiled, too relieved to care that the old man was cracking jokes when all their lives were in imminent danger.

"Furthest from the entrance," Braddock clarified softly. "Stay quiet. Guards on duty. Opposite end."

Keigh went back through the door at the rear of the cell, being careful not to scuff his feet. He knocked gently on the still closed outer door. He heard one of the girls gasp on the other side, then the clicking of a lever being lifted. The door to the cell swung shut. More clicking, and the door to the Centipede swung open.

"Did you find them?" Theo asked.

Keigh nodded, pointing to the end of the passageway. "Last two cells. Stay quiet."

The group rushed down to the cells without speaking. His friends took their positions at the three levers and in no time, Keigh was in the alcove, waiting for the first cell door to swing open.

When it did, Keigh found himself looking at the snow-white hair and electric-blue eyes of Cato Boman.

"Hello, Master Anders," Cato whispered. "I've been expecting you." The old man smiled, patted Keigh on the chest, and stepped into the alcove, squeezing in tight with him in the space made for one.

"You have?" Keigh whispered.

"Admittedly, I thought I would probably see you through the bars of my cell after you got yourself arrested, but this…" Cato traced the frame of the hidden door to the Centipede, then eyed Keigh's sword. "This is much more interesting," he said, with a gratified grin. "Shall we be off, then?"

Keigh nodded and gave the door a light knock. The door to the cell swung closed, cracking Keigh in the elbow on its way. "Ouch!" he yelped, then bit down on his lip, upset with letting the sound escape him.

A few more clicks and the door to the hallway swung open. The two of them spilled out of their cramped quarters.

Cato leaned heavily on Keigh for support, looking positively delighted to see so many of Bjorn's young people there to rescue him. "I see you brought your whole class," he said, giving Keigh a weak nudge.

"Almost," he chuckled. "Conrad, will you help Cato walk? We need to get Braddock and get out of here." Conrad nodded and stepped forward to replace Keigh under the old man's bony arm.

A minute later, the door to Braddock's cell swung in. Keigh didn't even have time to greet his mentor before Braddock shoved him back into the alcove and pressed himself in behind him.

"Get us out of here. Now!" he growled.

As Keigh knocked on the door, he heard a shout from the hallway. "Prisoner missing! Put out an alert!"

Before the cell door swung shut, Keigh caught the eyes of a stunned cane as the guard appeared outside the bars of Braddock's now empty cell. The secret door swung shut, and a second later, the door to the Centipede opened.

"We have to go. We've been discovered," Braddock growled, stumbling into the Centipede like a blind man and bumping into Beaudy. He paused, realizing Beaudy's large belly didn't belong to wispy old Cato. "Who else is here?" he asked, squinting.

Each of the rescuers answered with "Me" or "I am" at the same time.

Braddock scowled at the multitude of voices. "You're kidding."

"Surprise..." said Theo.

Braddock grabbed Keigh by the shoulders. "I assume you have a plan to get us out of Sentinel?"

Keigh nodded, feeling odd to have Braddock looking to him for answers. "But first..." He waved for Tabitha to lead the way. "Let's go get our bears."

Braddock nodded his approval.

"Quick. Take hold of my sword." Keigh pressed the handle of Verity into his master's hand and watched as Braddock's face lit up.

"It can't be..." Braddock stared at the glowing blade. "This hasn't been seen...Where did you...?"

"I'll tell you everything later," said Keigh, taking the sword back. "Right now, I just needed you to see." He turned and made to offer the blade to Cato next, but the old man waved him off.

"I've already known that blade. I've seen its light and I see it now, strong as ever." Keigh's surprise must have shown on his face, because Cato added, "I'll tell *you* everything later."

A door to the Centipede slammed open behind them. A half dozen helmeted canes in red cloaks and silver adamantines stumbled into the passageway, bumbling over each other in the dark corridor.

"There! That way!" bellowed the lead cane, pointing a finger toward the sound of the group's surprised gasps.

"Sorry, sir," Beaudy called to Cato as he ran up behind the old man limping slowly alongside Conrad. Unceremoniously, the large boy scooped the skin-and-bones elder into his arms and sped off after the group without missing a step.

The rescue team sprinted after Tabitha with reckless abandon, trusting her to lead them the correct way to the red bear keep. The canes struggled to catch them as they navigated every tight turn and corner in the dark. Twice Keigh heard a loud yelp of pain as one of the canes failed to see a corner in time and crashed into the unforgiving stone.

Soon they were all spilling into the empty street just outside the Sleuth. They all took a moment to catch their breath before staggering toward the dens.

"They will have shackled Mace and Copper," Braddock stated between gulps of air, obviously weakened by his stint in the dungeons. "What's your plan for that?"

"Tarin," said Keigh. "He promised to stash the keys to their chains in their dens with them."

"You trust him?"

Before Keigh could answer, the door behind them blew open.

The six canes righted themselves in the torch-lit street. The lead cane pointed a finger at Braddock. "It's a dead end, Braddock. You and the kids need to give it up now!"

Keigh took stock of the situation. They were outnumbered, but two of the canes were already nursing bloody noses and seemed unsteady on their feet. He motioned for his friends to keep walking toward the Sleuth. "Stay behind us. Go with Braddock and Conrad. Get Mace and Copper." He looked to Deacon, his lifelong enemy, now brother. "Let's see if that sword does more than shovel dirt."

Deacon smiled and worked around the group to stand with Keigh and Braddock.

Braddock shook his head, glowering at the red cloaks. "No...Deacon, give me your sword."

Deacon hesitated. Just slightly, but it was all Keigh needed to see to know what he had to do.

"Keep your sword, Deacon," he ordered.

Braddock's eyes flashed dangerously.

"I'm sorry, Master, but only you can command our bears. We need them more than your sword right now. Take my bow. Stay with the group. Send the bears. If we fail, the plan was to go down the bears' entrance and have Mace ferry us across the rapids."

At first, Keigh thought Braddock was going to scold him for his insubordination, but after a second of his master's piercing gaze, Braddock snatched the bow off his back and shifted to face Deacon. "Give me your hand," he commanded.

"My hand?"

"Now!" Braddock ordered.

Deacon stretched out his hand. Braddock took it quickly. A second later, Deacon's face lit up. "Am I...a potent?"

"No," said Braddock, "but I am." He let go of Deacon's arm as his posture sagged. "It's the last of my strength. Use it well. Defend your friends."

Deacon flexed his arms and gave an experimental swing of his sword. He grinned at Keigh. "They're going to need more than six to take us."

Keigh returned the grin. "Then let's find out what the Bears of Bjorn can do when we fight together."

Keigh and Deacon sprang into action, going on the offensive and closing the gap between themselves and the canes in a short charge. The two were a whirlwind of silver and light as they rained down sequence after sequence of strikes on the shocked men. Keigh caught most of the return blows with his adamantine, soaking up the energy from the canes and getting stronger as he went. Deacon was a force to be reckoned with, even when he didn't have the energy of two men. This night, he fought with all the speed and fury of a young Braddock.

After their first onslaught, Keigh and Deacon had grievously wounded a cane apiece, but the remaining four were now mounting their own offensive, gaining ground on the pair of them slowly but surely. The clashing of steel and whirling of blades continued, the canes pressing them back, step by hard-fought step, till they were nearly to the arched entry to the Sleuth. Deacon cursed as his foot caught on a cobblestone. He stumbled backward, falling hard on his side.

Keigh swiftly stepped over him. Throwing up his armored arm, he deflected the heavy downward blows of Deacon's assailants. The canes' swords sparked off his adamantine. Keigh quickly pulled the energy from the joint blow to his arm, then threw his elbow back with unnatural speed at his own attackers. The dagger-shaped protrusion on his elbow caught the first cane through the temple, ending his life in an instant. His body swung off Keigh's elbow and crashed into his partner, collapsing the other man at the knees.

Keigh didn't have time to register what he had just done. He wheeled back around to meet the next attack. Throwing his arm out in front of himself, he braced for impact...but none came. The canes in front of him were backing away, wide-eyed.

Surely these men are more battle-hardened than this. One man dies and they retreat?

Just then, a warm, humid gust of air blew Keigh's hair forward into his face. *Mace!* he realized, with a sudden rush of hope. Tarin had come through for them.

A terrifying roar sounded above him as the massive red bear stepped over him and batted the two canes with a mighty swipe of her paw. The canes' bodies hurtled through the air like a pair of caped snowballs before crashing into a stone wall and falling into lifeless piles of armor on the ground.

A snarl to his left alerted Keigh to the presence of Copper, who had taken to eliminating the final fighting cane. The metallic sheen of the young bear's fur rippled in Verity's light as Copper flexed his muscles, pinning the last cane to the ground and crushing his windpipe in his jaws.

For a moment, there was stillness. The bears stood, panting heavily, eyes searching for remaining threats as they came down from their battle rage. When both were satisfied that the danger had been eliminated, they turned back to their partners. Mace lowered her head and let Braddock scratch her behind the ear. Copper pounced on Keigh, knocking him over and licking him vigorously from neck to ear. Finally, the cub backed off, allowing Keigh to sit up.

"Hey, Copper! I missed you, boy!" Keigh said, patting the side of his neck.

Next thing he knew, Keigh was being lifted bodily off the ground as two large arms inserted themselves under his shoulders.

"We did it, Keigh!" Beaudy wheezed excitedly in his ear, still being careful not to shout.

Keigh landed hard on his feet as Beaudy plopped him back down. "Yeah, buddy. We did...together." He patted his friend on the shoulder as Beaudy lifted a protesting Deacon off the ground next. "Now we just need to get home."

Tabitha walked up to hug Beaudy around his waist. He smiled tenderly at her and hung a large arm around her shoulder. "I think Sentinel might be home again for me now," he said. "I'll come back to Bjorn with you so I can tell my parents. My agoge will transfer, and if it doesn't, I can always become a thrall to the king."

Misselli crept up from behind Keigh and worked her fingers into his. The warmth of her hand in his own was unlike anything else. Even the rush of pulling energy, the feeling of liquid fire coursing through his veins, couldn't hold a candle to the flame she lit in him.

"You would really become a thrall, huh?" Keigh asked Beaudy, but he wasn't really asking. He rubbed the back of Misselli's hand with his thumb.

"For Tabitha..." Beaudy paused, looking down into his girl's face. He grabbed her hand and spun her away before quickly pulling her back in close. "Anything."

Keigh had always seen Beaudy as a large, diffident, often clumsy wrecking ball, but with Tabitha, he was confident, poised, and smooth. The world was a funny place. Love had made Keigh a stammering, weak-kneed little boy, but had turned Beaudy into a charismatic man, bold and strong.

Misselli jabbed him in the ribs. Keigh realized he had been staring at Beady and Tabitha with his mouth open. He snapped his jaw shut and extended a hand to Beaudy. "I'm happy for you," he said, shaking his friend's hand and pulling Misselli closer with his other. "And I understand."

"Understand what?" asked Theo, approaching them with an armful of swords Braddock had instructed him to collect from the fallen canes.

Keigh and Beaudy rounded on him, guilt plain on their faces, but before they could say anything, Braddock saved them by insisting the group not tarry any longer.

"Let's get moving. We aren't out of the woods yet." Braddock looked anxiously over their heads toward the street and waved them toward the red bears' tunnel.

"Tell you on the road," said Beaudy, winking at his best friend. He lifted Tabitha in the air and spun her around before setting her gently back on the ground. "This is the last time I leave you, I promise," he said, gently kissing her on the forehead before backing toward the tunnel, his eyes never leaving hers.

Everyone thanked Tabitha, who bid them each farewell. The group followed Beaudy toward the tunnel that would lead them out of Sentinel.

Misselli elbowed Keigh in the ribs again. "Do you think we look that cute?" she asked, watching Beaudy walk backward, blowing a kiss to Tabitha, who reached up and caught it with her hand.

"We're cuter than that," Keigh snorted, still baffled by the odd couple. "Because of you, of course," he added, almost too late.

Beaudy trotted ahead of the group. Stopping at the mouth of the tunnel he turned back for a last look at Tabitha. "Come on, guys! Let's go! I've got missed time to make up for."

Keigh was soaking in Beaudy's happiness when a glint of gold flashed in the shadows behind his friend.

"Beaudy! Get back!" he shouted.

But it was too late.

Beaudy hardly had time to register the panic in Keigh's voice before the bloody tip of a sword sprouted from his chest.

Tabitha screamed. The rest of the group froze, stunned. Beaudy's cheerful face went slack. Blood soaked through his gray tunic like a dark shadow stretching away from a lone tree at sunset.

A dribble of spit dropped from his lower lip as he gingerly touched the steel point at his chest. His face wrinkled in confusion. Swallowing hard, he looked at the bloody metal curiously, trying to make sense of it.

Beaudy dropped to his knees. The sword point disappeared with a squelch before he clapped two hands over the hole in his chest.

He glanced at Tabitha, his eyes giving her one last glistening apology before rolling upward. Beaudy's chin dipped to his chest. His arms dropped limp to his side. He fell forward, his cheek smacking hard against the cold, hard ground.

Out of the shadows, a gold-armored Vicerous Wulf stepped over the still form of Beaudy Besnik, careful not to stand in the blood now pooling around the boy's body. He wiped his blade with a white cloth and dropped the sullied garment on top of the slain teen.

The group's shock turned to anger. Keigh and Deacon readied their swords to the sound of the red bears' deep-throated growls.

"Beauds..."

"Tabitha!" Keigh shouted, trying to grab her arm as she rushed past him toward Beaudy.

Vicerous backhanded her before she could get to Beaudy's side, sending the girl sprawling onto the stones. "None of you," he sneered, "are going anywhere. Not unless you drop your weapons, turn over the prisoners, and bend your knee to the queen." He glared at Deacon and Keigh. "It's not too late for you. The queen has instructed me to tell you that she will forgive your trespasses. Your status and futures will be restored. None of you will be punished for your rebellion. Just bend—the—knee!"

Keigh's friends looked to him. He could see their nerve faltering. They had risked everything to follow him on his mission. They had tried, and now they had lost one of their own forever. Vicerous was offering them clemency, and under threat of death and the loss of whatever future they each hoped to still live out, the group was teetering on desertion.

Keigh swallowed hard. Quaking, his body fought to restrain both new and old hate for the man before him. His anger was threatening to erupt in violence, but if it did, he would be sealing not just his own fate, but the fate of all those who had trusted him.

"Keigh and Deacon," Vicerous continued, "submit to the queen's authority. Hand over these worthless men and you will both find yourselves elevated beyond what you could ever become alone. The queen is gracious, and will give you both paid apprenticeships as canes and a home in her palace," he grimaced, the words seemingly causing him great pain to speak. "This is her offer. Take it and secure your legacy. Refuse it and die nobodies, forgotten forever."

"Keigh," Braddock growled, glaring at Vicerous as he grabbed Keigh's shirt and pulled Keigh behind him. "I'll handle this."

Keigh took one look at the man who had just placed himself in harm's way for him and knew what he had to do.

He seized Braddock's hand and quickly pulled enough energy to drop his mentor to one knee.

Mace whipped her head around and growled at Keigh. Copper growled back at the larger bear. Mace bared her teeth threateningly, snarling her fury at Keigh's betrayal.

Keigh didn't flinch. He held her gaze, sure of what he had done, of what he needed to do.

A second later, Mace's lips lowered back over her teeth. She gave Keigh a huff and returned her attention to Vicerous, as if she already knew.

"Why?" wheezed Braddock, eyelids drooping, hurt plain on his face.

"I already lost one father. I won't lose another."

Vicerous grinned wickedly at the sudden turn of events. "I was hoping you would choose to fight," he said, licking his lips. "Foolish, though."

He whistled. The sound of tramping feet and clacking armor rose from the tunnel. Soon, dozens of red-cloaked canes were filing out in battle formation. The bears snarled and took a step back as row after row of warriors lined up to face them.

Keigh weighed the situation as it changed, cane by cane, before him. "Conrad, Theo," he barked, unable to look his friends in the eye. "Get Braddock back into the shelter of a den. Misselli and Addy, get Cato in there too. Deacon and Conrad will protect you if anyone makes it past me and the bears."

His friends hustled to obey without protest. They would stand behind him till the bitter end.

All except one.

Deacon stood beside Keigh, unmoved and unmoving. "I have as much a right to fight him as you," he said, scowling at his father.

"Together, then?"

Deacon smiled appreciatively; the rising of his cheeks forced a tear from his eye.

Vicerous cackled. "You presume to fight me?" He placed a hand on his golden breastplate. "Good. I'll sleep much better knowing the both of you have been taken care of once and for all!"

Without warning, the older and younger Wulfs lunged at each other, leaving Keigh to catch up. Their blades rang clear as the two collided. Swords locked together at the hilt, father pressed against son in a battle of wills.

Vicerous kicked the side of Deacon's knee, ending the stalemate. Deacon stumbled and nearly fell. Before Vicerous could take the advantage, Keigh was upon him, cutting and slashing with all the speed and ferocity Braddock's strength afforded him.

If Keigh had thought his previous victory over Vicerous was any indication of how tonight's battle would play out, he was sorely mistaken. Vicerous was every bit the renowned swordsman Braddock and Deacon had always claimed him to be, not the belligerent, tantrum-fueled man Keigh had dueled for his agoge. Keigh was striking as quickly as he could and never so much as came close to touching the Queen's Shield.

Deacon quickly gathered himself and rejoined the fight, sending the battle to a new level of intensity. Mace and Copper could watch no longer. Roaring, they approached the dueling trio. The bears attempted to pick Vicerous off without harming Keigh or Deacon, but the three had become a whirlwind of lethal metal.

Vicerous whistled again, and with a unified roar of their own, the rows of red-cloaked canes charged the bears.

Mace bellowed as a dozen arrows flew at her, the canes swarming about her like red ants. Most of the arrows deflected off her thick, coarse fur, but several found their mark, drawing huge drops of hot blood that rained down, splashing off the cobblestones. Mace smashed a cane into a red pulp with a powerful stomp of her right forepaw, then swiped away another six with her left. Their bodies crunched against the unforgiving stone walls.

A group of canes surrounded Copper, prodding the young bear with their sword points. Copper whirled around, then back the direction he came from, so quickly that no soldier dared move closer. One of the canes pulled his bow and loaded it, but before he could draw back the string, an arrow lodged in his chest.

The teens sheltered in the den cheered, seeing Conrad's arrow had found its mark.

The distraction was all that Copper needed. He bolted forward and seized the stunned cane by the ankle. Whipping around, Copper swung the man's body violently into his cohorts, scattering them like glass marbles across the cobblestones. The canes groaned in pain as they struggled to get off the ground before the bear descended upon them to finish the job with teeth and claws.

The arrogant grin on Vicerous's face vanished. The two boys from Bjorn were proving to be more than a fair match. Snarling, he batted Keigh's blade to the side and backhanded Deacon with his golden adamantine.

Keigh and Deacon both recovered swiftly, just in time to field Vicerous's offensive. Keigh had been impressed, if not dismayed, at his enemy's skill in defending himself, but the man was an even better attacker. The two boys mustered all their focus and speed to deny Vicerous's blade any taste of their blood, but to no avail. Soon Keigh had a bloody slice in the side of his neck and Deacon a pair of cuts to his unshielded arm.

Mace roared again. Rising onto her hind legs, she towered over the pile of limp bodies below her. A dozen red cloaks loaded their bows and tilted back, taking aim at the giant bear's exposed belly.

Another roar sounded to their left. The bowmen looked over just in time to see Copper hurtling toward them.

Having dispatched his own canes, he bowled through the archers, sending them skittering across the ground like coins falling from a cut purse. Mace dropped back to all fours and set about ending the last twenty warriors with the copper wrecking ball.

While the bears were now well in control of their battle, aided by the occasional well-placed arrow from Conrad, Keigh and Deacon fought on, still no closer to having defeated Vicerous than when they first started. Their swords connected and sparked, cut after cut, blow after blow.

"I can shoot him!" Conrad called.

"No!" shouted Keigh and Deacon together.

Just then, Vicerous caught Verity in the crook of his adamantine. He pulled down hard, ripping the blade from Keigh's hand, then punched up suddenly, catching Keigh under the chin with the knuckles of his metal arm.

Keigh's vision blackened, and the next thing he knew he was lying on the ground with Deacon standing over him, doing battle with his father alone.

"Thought I taught you better than this, boy!" snarled Vicerous as he hacked at Deacon's side. "With my training, you could have been something. But instead, you sank to his level!"

"There's nothing lower than a man who beats his own child," shouted Deacon, punching Vicerous in the ribs, buying himself a sliver of time.

"Malcontent!" snapped Vicerous. "I gave you everything!"

"Except the one thing I needed," cried Deacon. "The one thing he always had!"

"That again?" Vicerous scoffed. "He's only alive now because I hardened you."

"I wouldn't be here at all if not for him!"

"Give me one more minute and you won't be."

Keigh searched frantically for his sword. Deacon couldn't hold out on his own much longer.

There! He saw the glowing blade ten feet to his left, but there was no time to retrieve it. Vicerous would get through Deacon's defense any second.

Searching for something, anything he could use to help his friend, his eyes fell on the ghost-white face of Beaudy, lying in a pool of his own blood.

Deacon's sword fell to the cobblestones next to Keigh right as Keigh swung his adamantine down hard at Vicerous's unprotected feet. Vicerous deftly dodged Keigh's attempt to crush his feet. Hopping backward to avoid the blow, he landed in the pool of Beaudy's blood. Vicerous groaned as his foot slipped, dropping him hard to one knee.

Swordless, Deacon silenced him with a hard knee to the face.

Vicerous' head snapped backward. His mangled sword clattered on the street as he fell back against Beaudy, unconscious.

Deacon picked his sword up off the ground. Slowly, he raised its tip to Vicerous' chest, readying himself to plunge it into the man who had filled him full of hate and hurt, then abandoned him to a beggar's life in the streets of Bjorn.

"Stop!"

Deacon whirled on Keigh, shooting him a furious look. "Why? Why should he live?" he screamed, his sword arm trembling, fighting back tears. "Give me one reason! One reason, Keigh!"

Keigh picked himself up off the ground and approached Deacon.

"It's exactly what he would do. It's what he wants you to do. But you aren't like him, Deacon...not anymore."

A gurgling laugh emanated from Vicerous's throat. The Queen's Shield raised his head, his nose and mouth red. "Do it, boy," he said, spitting out a mouthful of blood. "I welcome the irony of it." He leaned his head back and cackled, choking on the blood in his throat.

"There will be no irony to your death, only justice," said Deacon, pressing the tip of his blade menacingly against his father's chest.

Vicerous lifted his head, wearing an evil grin. "Won't there?" he asked, looking back and forth between Deacon and Keigh. His eyes lingered on Keigh. He spat, hitting Keigh in the face.

Keigh snarled and wiped the blood away. Quickly, he retrieved his sword and advanced on Vicerous, but Deacon blocked him off.

"That's right, stay on your leash, *boy*," Vicerous drawled, his eyes half closed. "Raised by dogs...you became one."

"Why shouldn't I let Keigh put an end to your miserable life?"

"That would be rich," Vicerous laughed. "But no, Deacon, it should be you. You see, he..." Vicerous pointed a finger at Keigh. "He's the one who killed your father. Your *real* father."

Deacon looked at Keigh, suddenly unsure.

Vicerous cackled. "He didn't tell you he found out who your birth father is? Kept that from you, did he?"

"Liar!" Deacon screamed. "Keigh wouldn't!"

Keigh raised his sword again to finish Vicerous before he could say another word, but Deacon blindsided him, shoving him so hard he lost his feet and fell.

Deacon looked down on Keigh. "It's true?" he asked, hurt clear in his voice. "You found out who my father is?"

"And your mother!" Vicerous laughed. "Then he killed your old man! That's why..." He coughed. "That's why you need to be the one to kill his."

"Keigh's father is already dead!" Deacon growled.

Vicerous slowly shook his head. Laughing, he pointed to Keigh, who was now frozen in place.

Keigh's gut dropped so suddenly his heart paused its beating. If it was true...

He slumped back, lying flat on the ground, his body quivering, too weak, too faint to even raise his head and look at the man. The man who had hated him, enslaved him, tried to have him whipped. The man who had preyed upon his mother and cheated his father.

The man, he realized, who had abandoned him, rejected him, and lied to him his whole life.

"He knows," said Vicerous, grinning at the devastation his confession was wreaking on Keigh. "Don't look so surprised, son. Didn't actually believe you'd gotten your talent from that cuck Owen, did you?"

"What's he talking about, Keigh?" Deacon asked, still shaking his sword. "You know who my parents are? And Vicerous...He's...he's your—"

"Father!" spat Vicerous, as if the word were poison. He curled his lip at Keigh in disdain. "Speak, boy! Don't you have anything to say to me? Sixteen years living a lie under the Anders' roof, and you finally know you aren't the trash you thought you were! You're the son of a cane! That means something! Stand up, boy! Act like a man! Be the Wulf you should have been from the beginning!"

Keigh heard Vicerous, but only as a distant echo.

Why had he stopped Deacon from killing him? If he had only held his tongue...

But that was what Vicerous would have done. Vicerous would have let Deacon kill him...and now Keigh found himself thinking just like him, just like...his *father*.

He gagged, repulsed to have shared the man's mind for even a second. He shook his head, hoping to rid himself of whatever poison Vicerous had planted there. They should be on their way home right now. *Home...* The word evoked images of his mother and Jessie wrapping him in hugs. His brothers arguing over the last scrap of dinner. Long walks with Misselli. Sunset sparring sessions with Deacon...Owen smiling proudly down on him, for doing nothing more than being his son. All in the only place that had ever loved and accepted him regardless of title or station. *Home.*

"Fine!" spat Vicerous. "Hold your tongue, then. I gave up on you years ago! You can't live in the trash and not come out tainted by it..."

"Who's my real father?" Deacon asked, pointing the tip of his sword back into Vicerous's chest.

Vicerous turned his attention back to Deacon, grinning with blood-stained teeth. "Ah, yes. Didn't get to that juicy bit, did we? Well, your father isn't the real news. It's your mother who—"

An arrow zipped past Deacon, piercing Vicerous through the throat, silencing him before he could speak another word.

A sick grin spread across his face. His body convulsed with laughter at the torment he had inflicted on the boys with his last breaths. Slowly, his head drifted back onto the street and his body went still.

"He talked too much," called a voice from the shadows.

Deacon and Keigh spun to meet the newcomer.

"Is everyone alright?" the voice called again. A second later, Tarin stepped into the light, holding a bow cased in gold. A circlet of gold on his brow glinted in the moonlight.

Keigh's body had responded to Tarin's arrival, but his heart and mind were still too stunned and sick to process anything more. Chills and shivers washed over him in waves. Thoughts of home had warmed him momentarily, but there was a sickness in his gut that he felt he needed to vomit out. *Vicerous can't be my father. He's not…human.*

He gagged again. No matter his wishes, Keigh knew it could be true. His mother's affair with the man was real enough. He was tan-skinned and skinny like Vicerous, not broad and thick like Owen and his brothers…

"Fool!" Deacon snarled at Tarin. "He wasn't a threat! Why did you do that?"

"He was threatening my friends," Tarin said, looking wounded. "More than that, he's a traitor to the crown."

Deacon's nostrils flared dangerously. He shook his head and turned back to Keigh. "What he said about my parents—about you knowing…Is it true?"

Keigh lowered his eyes. "Deacon…I—"

"Keigh found out who your parents were just before they were killed," said Tarin, cutting Keigh off. "Vicerous killed your father and tried to pin it on Keigh. Then he tried to spread the rumor that your father and my mother, the queen, had been having an affair. A lie he regrettably told Keigh, then blamed him for." Tarin's eyes narrowed as he looked at Keigh. "Isn't that right, Keigh? Now that Vicerous is exposed and out of the way, you can all go home. I'll see to it that the queen pardons all of you."

Keigh stared at his friend. Was Tarin covering for him? Or was he just trying to preserve his position as heir by not letting Deacon know his mother was the queen? Either way, it was clear to him that Tarin wasn't offering something for nothing. He was offering Keigh a deal. Cover for Tarin and Tarin would cover for him. If Keigh accepted, Deacon could have closure and his friends could be pardoned for the foolish crime of trusting him. Refuse, and the queen's wrath would remain focused on them all. Plus, Deacon would likely spurn both Tarin and Keigh—Keigh for knowing the truth and not telling him, Tarin for outright lying to his face.

"Well?" Deacon stared at Keigh, searching his face for answers.

"Yes," said Keigh, agreeing to the deal.

Deacon let out a long, slow exhale. He gave the body of the man he had once called father a long look, then, without another word to his friends, he wandered off toward the tunnel, the tip of his sword scratching a lonely line across the cobblestones behind him.

Keigh watched him go, full of the same heartache and confusion Deacon must be feeling. But they all needed the pardons. There would be a right time to tell Deacon. Right now, he needed to get them all out of Sentinel.

"Thanks," Keigh sighed. Tarin would do and say anything to keep his position as heir. Now wasn't the time to argue with him, though.

"You bet," said Tarin, grabbing Keigh's arm and pulling him into a tight embrace. "When this is all cleared up, I want you to come back and stay with me in the palace," he whispered in Keigh's ear. "My treat to you. It will be like old times, only richer." He stepped away, grinning benevolently.

The rest of Bjorn's teens had finally ventured out from the shelter of the den. Misselli came running up from behind Tarin. Brushing past the heir, she latched herself onto Keigh, hugging him in a way that made it obvious she had just spent the last ten minutes fearing he was about to die.

"Thanks," Keigh said, still too overwhelmed to be upset with Tarin for being who Keigh had always known him to be. He wrapped an arm around Misselli, feeling a bit of the warmth of home in her presence. "But I'm already rich."

A muscle in Tarin's jaw twitched. "I see that," he said, forcing a smile.

"Let's go," Braddock called, looking restored to full strength. Keigh assumed he must have pulled energy from some of the mortally wounded canes the bears had left in their wake. Braddock pulled an arrow out of Mace as he continued to shout commands. "Deacon and Conrad, take the front with Mace. I'll cover our middle. Keigh, you and Copper bring up the rear."

"Thank you, Tarin." Misselli let go of Keigh and gave Tarin a quick hug. "For everything." She rested a hand gently on Keigh's chest before setting off to obey Braddock.

Tarin and Keigh both watched her go. "Looks like we both got what we wanted," Tarin said, now looking at peace with it. "I'll sort things out here. You get everyone back safe, okay?"

"I will." Keigh stepped forward and the two friends from Bjorn embraced. "You get us those pardons."

"I promise." Tarin crossed his heart with a finger. "After tonight, you'll never have to worry about the queen again."

"Thank you," Keigh said, this time really meaning it. The palace had become a rat's nest in the king's absence. If he had it his way, he would never set foot here again. It wasn't a place for people like himself, Cato, and Braddock. But Tarin could play the game better than most. He knew what it took to survive here, and he was willing to do it. Keigh didn't envy him, but was grateful to have him on his side nonetheless.

"Keigh! We need your help!" Theo's voice pleaded from behind him.

Somehow, in the midst of everything, Tabitha had found her way to Beaudy's body. Theo and Addy were trying to gently pull the weeping girl off of him so that Braddock and Conrad could move Beaudy onto Mace's back. But each time they tried to take hold of her arm, she wriggled free of their grasp and took a white-knuckled grip of Beaudy's tunic.

Keigh gave Tarin a look, asking silently for space. Tarin nodded his understanding and withdrew.

Keigh and Misselli replaced Theo and Addy beside Tabitha. Keigh consoled the heartbroken girl with words of Beaudy's love for her while Misselli stroked her hair and rubbed her back.

Eventually, Tabitha released her grasp on Beaudy's tunic, allowing Braddock and Conrad to move the body away. She was shaking uncontrollably, face puffy and fingers white from holding her favorite dance partner tight for the last time.

Misselli and Addy held her as Keigh joined the men in lifting and securing Beaudy onto Mace's back. Keigh could have lifted his friend himself with a dose of energy from his metal orb, but this task was one he needed to do with his own strength. It was he, after all, who had led the gentle giant into the teeth of the Capital.

Once Beaudy was secure, Keigh wiped a tear from his face and went to give Tabitha one last hug. "Go find Sanya and Bard, okay?" he told her. "You shouldn't be alone right now."

Tabitha nodded. "When you dance with her..." She dipped her head toward Misselli, who was just disappearing into the tunnel alongside the rest of the group. "Will you remember him? Remember my Beauds." She choked down another sob. "He loved to dance."

"No, he didn't." Keigh shook his head. "He loved *you*, Tabitha." He let his own love for Misselli infuse his words. Tears for Beaudy, tears for Deacon, tears for his own loss, welled in his eyes. "Dancing is just an excuse for us boys to hold close what's most important to us. You were his song, the same as she is mine." He tugged gently at the cloth bracelet on his wrist.

"Thank you," said Tabitha, wiping her cheeks dry. Still trembling, she dipped her head goodbye before wandering off into the night.

Keigh watched her go, not wanting to imagine how he might feel if Misselli had been harmed or killed in his mission to save his mentors. To have held your future in your arms one moment then watched it bleed dry in front of you the next...

Copper, who had been waiting patiently, walked up beside Keigh and nudged him toward the tunnel. Keigh had lingered too long. He wiped his face again and raised a hand to Tarin, bidding him goodbye.

Tarin smiled fondly back from where he stood amid the dozens of bodies littering the ground. He returned the wave and turned back toward the palace.

Keigh's delay had put him far behind the group. "Let's go, boy," he said to Copper, stroking the top of his snout affectionately.

He entered the black opening of the tunnel. Verity banished the darkness from around him, but his group was still far beyond its light. His feet jogged to catch up, but his mind was racing. *Beaudy's dead, and it's all my fault. Tabitha is crushed; that too is my fault. Vicerous is...my father? And...Tarin killed him. I lied to Deacon to protect him, just like my own parents lied to protect me. How long will it be before the truth comes out? What if Deacon leaves me the same way I left my parents? I've got to tell him, as soon as—*

There was a simmering hiss in Keigh's ears just before the arrow struck him square in the back.

The force of the impact knocked him forward. He hit the dirt hard, losing his grip on Verity as his face collided with the ground. He gasped like a fish out of water, desperately trying to reactivate his lungs.

"Canes! Reinforcements!" Tarin yelled from the mouth of the tunnel. "Run! Get out quick! Me and Keigh will hold them off as long as we can!"

Keigh heard the frightened gasps of his group farther down the tunnel as Tarin's alarm reached them. "Go, Copper," he wheezed. "Hold them off." He hoped the cub could buy him enough time to catch his breath and fetch his sword. Copper huffed and charged back up the tunnel.

Keigh reached behind to his back and jerked the arrow out of where it had lodged in his quiver. Rolling over, he began to sit up—

A hand closed around his throat and slammed him back to the ground. The cold point of a dagger pressed underneath his chin.

He looked up at his attacker, expecting to find a red-cloaked cane, but instead, he saw a golden crown.

"Tarin..." he wheezed. "What—"

"Quiet!" Tarin hissed. "Thanks for sending your guard dog off. I debated just shooting you...but you deserve to know."

Keigh tried to speak, but Tarin squeezed his throat harder.

"I don't want to hear your voice," he sniffed, fighting back tears of his own. "Do you know what it feels like to have everything? No, of course you don't. How could you possibly..." Tarin's nostrils flared. "I befriended you because I felt like you needed me, that I was helping you out of your misery. And how has my kindness been repaid? With a curse?" He pressed down harder on Keigh's throat.

647

Curse? Keigh's mind worked frantically to understand. He tried to work his arms out from under Tarin's knees, but Tarin was stronger than him, always had been. If he couldn't get his hands on his attacker or the orb in his pouch, he had no hope of escaping. Keigh shook his head, trying to work a wisp of air past the hand blocking his windpipe.

"Don't shake your head. Don't shake your head at *me!*" Tarin growled, tears dripping off his clenched jaw. "You take everything that's rightfully mine...I wanted to give to you, but all I could think about was wanting to *be* you!" He exhaled and swallowed hard, seemingly relieved by the confession. "How does it feel to be the hero? To have people thank you and mean it? To know your friends would take an arrow for you, not because they have to, but because they want to? They give you such blind devotion when they should be devoted to me, their future king! The one with actual authority, actual power...and..."

The scowl on Tarin's face darkened.

"And how could *she* choose *you*...over *me?* Why do I, the one who has everything, wake up in a palace every morning wanting what *you*, a thrall, have?" Tarin inhaled slowly, allowing his tremors to settle. "Not anymore. Not one more day will I suffer your existence." He brought the tip of his dagger up to Keigh's face and pressed the flat of the blade into his cheek. "I will tell them you fought bravely. That you died trying...I can give you that much. You are, truly, the best friend I ever had. Which is why—" He choked back a sob, reaching into his pocket. "You should have this back."

He pulled out something small and dropped it on Keigh's face. It was the little wooden bear Keigh had carved to congratulate Tarin on being named heir.

"Truth is, you've always been the Bear. They see it. I saw it. And I hated you for it. A better man would relish the competition." Tarin sniffed, shaking his head. "But I'm not the better man. I'm just the one holding the knife, and in this world...that makes me better. It's clear to me now: the only way to beat you, the only way to end this curse you've put on me, is to end you. As for Misselli...she will mourn for you, I have no doubt, but when she's finished, when she's *forgotten* you...then, she will see what she always should have seen. Then she will sit at *my* side." Tarin leaned in close and put his lips next to Keigh's ear. "*For one to rise, one must fall.* Fall well, friend."

Keigh's vision flickered. He hoped he passed out before he felt the dagger pierce him. He hoped to feel nothing at all. No more hurt, no more loss, no more betrayals.

But as he was about to pass into blissful nothingness, he felt one more thing.

The subtle rumble in the earth from the pounding feet of a red bear.

Keigh fought with every ounce of his will to stay awake just a few more seconds. "You—talk—too—much." He choked the words out with the last of his air.

Tarin huffed and drew back his knife to plunge it into Keigh's neck. Then suddenly, his weight lifted away.

Copper slammed into the prince like a battering ram, sending him sprawling into the dirt. The young bear didn't waste any time fighting with Tarin. Instead, Copper grabbed Keigh's quiver in his teeth and began dragging him as fast as he could down the tunnel toward the raging river below.

"You're banished, Keigh Anders!" Tarin screamed down the tunnel after them. "You hear me? Don't show your face in Eden ever again! If I so much as hear your name, I'll kill your whole family!"

CHAPTER 43

RIDDLE ANSWERS

43-16-2

*R*emember...*you are my son...and I am your father.*

Owen Anders' last words echoed in Keigh's head for the hundredth time since Copper had dragged him from the Capital to safety on the other side of the rapids. Everything had happened so fast, so suddenly—it wasn't until they had all stopped moving that the full weight of what had happened settled in.

Keigh looked at the faces of his friends. They all sat wordlessly around the crackling fire Braddock had constructed for them, deep in a grove of cottonwoods. Keigh wished someone would speak. That way maybe his thoughts wouldn't be so loud. But as it was, the only signs of life were the soft puffs of breath that escaped each of their mouths and swirled in the misty morning air.

Theo was unrecognizable. His eyes puffy and swollen with tears, he pulled at his hair, tearing out tufts of it between his fingers.

Addy, whose mind was usually sharp as a nail, sat glassy-eyed, the flames reflecting off her lenses as she stared into the fire, as if nothing in all the books she had ever read could explain why the purest and gentlest of people could be murdered so casually.

Deacon and Conrad seemed to be taking their cues from Braddock, who was sharpening the sword he had taken off one of the canes with a whetstone he had also likely pilfered.

Cato held a fern frond in his lap that he was studying intently. His was the only face that could be argued to be north of miserable.

Misselli sat hugging her knees to her chest, rocking back and forth. She alternated staring at the fire with staring at Keigh. What did she want him to say? What could he do now? Beaudy was dead and it was all Keigh's fault. Did they all want an apology? Was he supposed to tell them it was all going to be alright?

Keigh stood abruptly. "I'm going for a walk."

"I'll come with you," said Misselli, looking up from the fire hopefully.

There was a moment of indecision before Keigh could answer. He wanted her company. She, as much as anyone, had been there for him over the ups and downs of the last year. Only Mannie and his parents could claim as much, but they weren't here with him now.

On the other hand, Beaudy had died following him. Misselli wouldn't die following him for a walk, but then again, he couldn't be sure of that either, for she had almost died following him into the woods on a morning hunt once before. Following him anywhere wasn't safe anymore, not when enemies, both inside and outside of Eden, wanted him dead.

Keigh shook his head. Misselli didn't attempt to convince him otherwise. He made eye contact with Copper, who immediately stood and followed him away from the fire.

The two of them picked their way through the thick undergrowth of the foggy river-bottom forest, dew-drenched plants soaking every fiber of Keigh's clothing. Everything around him seemed a mixture of life and death. Tufts of green grass pushed up through the dead stalks of last year. New green leaf buds were unfurling above the mat of dead brown leaves that had fallen last autumn. Last year's life would fuel this year's growth. No new leaf could flourish if the old never fell.

Keigh walked until he came to a cascading stream, full of spring runoff from the snow fields high in the Bullhorn Mountains. He scrambled up a large mossy boulder and perched himself atop it. Pulling out the polished metal orb, he studied his distorted reflection in it. So much of him seemed dead now. The thrall boy from Bjorn who had grown up swinging sticks at the tree in his yard didn't exist anymore. He had swung real blades through real men.

Twigs crunched and snapped as Copper sat down in the undergrowth. Keigh cringed at the sound, remembering the feeling of his elbow dagger sinking into the skull of the cane.

Remember...you are my son....and I am your father.

Keigh clenched his fist around the metal orb, turning his knuckles white. Owen had known. He'd known Keigh was the son of another man. Why had he used his last words to lie to Keigh? The king had told Keigh that the events of his life had transpired because of his father. Had he meant Owen or Vicerous? Who was responsible for all this?

Keigh sat there quietly, listening to the splashing of the stream, contemplating all that had happened and all that would need to happen next. He had never been good at riddles. Now his whole life had become one.

Copper's head suddenly swung back in the direction they had come. Soon, Braddock and Cato emerged, picking their way through the undergrowth, the older leaning on the younger. Braddock's steps became quicker and more confident when he caught sight of Keigh.

"How you holding up?" Braddock asked when he reached the foot of the boulder. Cato watched Keigh as he set about giving Copper a thorough head scratching.

"Okay, I guess." Keigh shrugged. "It's not every day you kill a man, watch your friend murdered by a coward, then find out that *that* murdering coward is your father."

"Owen Anders is your father, Keigh," said Braddock. "No matter what Vicerous says."

"You don't even know," Keigh huffed, tearing his eyes away from his mentors. "Vicerous wasn't lying. He *is* my father. I can't tell you how I know it, but I know it."

"We know about the affair," Cato said gently.

Keigh sighed. Of course they knew. Everyone knew everything before he did. "So how can you stand there and deny Vicerous's claim?"

"We are not denying his claim," said Braddock. "We *are* denying that he is your father by anything more than birth. There's more to being a father than the ability to get a woman pregnant." He paused. "I know you already know that, though..." Braddock looked at the palm of his hand, from which Keigh had pulled his last remaining energy before confronting Vicerous.

"Master Wulf entered into his agreement with Owen before you were born, before he even knew your mother was pregnant with you," explained Cato. "But when he saw that Sabriya had given birth to a healthy son, he came to us and demanded he be granted custody of you, as you were the son of his seed."

"Vicerous wanted me?"

"Yes, very much so," said Cato. "He risked much in trying to claim you, because in so doing, he was confessing both his and your mother's crime."

"Unfortunately for Vicerous, your father knew him too well," Braddock added. "Owen knew Vicerous would try to claim you, and with the consent of your mother, he decided to trust me with the secret, long before Vicerous demanded to have you." He paused. "Your father's sudden departure from our shared dream of becoming canes together suddenly made sense."

"Then why weren't you two friends the whole time I was growing up?" asked Keigh, a bitter edge to his voice.

Braddock sighed. "While I now had an answer for why your father did what he did, I still didn't like it. I thought your mother and Vicerous should pay for their crimes. I thought Owen was a fool for taking the fall for them. At first, I was furious at him for not giving me answers, but I found my anger only deepened when I got an answer I didn't like. I wasn't the only one unhappy with our friendship, though. Your father also wasn't too pleased with my insistence that Sabriya be punished. He argued that if he, the aggrieved party, could see fit to forgive her, then what right did I have to call for her blood?"

"You didn't like my mother?"

"I didn't like anyone who would hurt my best friend," Braddock said, like it was the most obvious answer in the world. "The way I saw it, Vicerous and

Sabriya had destroyed him, and in so doing, pitted him against *me*, the one friend who had never betrayed him."

"So why not give me to Vicerous and free my father from his agreement?"

"Many reasons," Braddock admitted. "One: doing so would have opened up your mother and Vicerous to punishment for their crime—something your father would never forgive me for. Two: I believed any man willing to steal his friend's wife, then enslave him for taking her back, was unfit to have a child in his care. And lastly…" Braddock's face softened as he looked at the wounded boy before him. "Owen loved you. I couldn't take you from him."

"Loved me?" Keigh snorted. "I wasn't even born yet, was I?"

Braddock's lips curled in a thin smile. "You were half Sabriya. That's all Owen needed to know. If he only loved you half as much as he loved her, then I imagine you were more loved than most sons could claim."

"He did…love me, that is. I know he loved me," Keigh choked, trying to hold back tears. He had doubted his father's love many times in the past year, but somehow saying the truth out loud helped solidify it in his mind. His father, his first and only *real* father, had loved him deeply, just like the two new fathers on the ground below him did.

Cato exhaled. "The two points Master Fortier gave me, and ultimately why I rejected Vicerous's petition, were: one, you already had a legal father, and two…Master Fortier insisted that a child could have no finer father than Owen Anders." The old man looked proudly at the seasoned warrior before him as Braddock averted his eyes from Keigh, a bit redder in the cheeks. "However," Cato continued, "Vicerous had fathered a son, though not legally, so that technically made him part of the Consecrate. Did you not ever wonder how Vicerous was given a child from the Consecrate when he himself had no wife?"

"I guess…I guess I never considered that," said Keigh. "But I was born in December, not January."

"Actually," said Braddock, "you *were* born in January. The same month as the king's son."

"Slate's son, to be more accurate," Cato grumbled.

"We recommended to Owen that they report your birth a month early to avoid you being taken up in the Consecrate and given to a family of canes," said Braddock.

Keigh hugged his knees, still soaking wet from his walk, staring at the creek. "So, I'm part of the Consecrate?"

Cato shrugged. "Not that it matters, considering the king has no son of his own seed—I suppose he could technically choose you to become his heir, since you were born to a cane...but he would have no way of knowing you were. Master Fortier and I kept your families secret and will continue to do so."

"Why..." Keigh hesitated. He couldn't believe he was about to ask this; he couldn't believe he actually cared. "Why did Vicerous hate me, then?"

Braddock and Cato exchanged a nervous glance. Cato dipped his ancient white head, deferring to Braddock to answer the question.

"Vicerous..." Braddock began. "Well...he hated your father for winning Sabriya's heart. He hated your mother for choosing Owen over him. He hated you..." He paused. "I think he hated you because you were the physical reminder of everything he had been denied. I think he only doted on Deacon so intensely in front of you because he was trying to convince himself that he didn't actually want you, that you were less of a son than he deserved... but as you matured and continued to do things that defied belief, it became more difficult, to the point where it wasn't enough to try to convince himself that you weren't good enough—he had to convince himself that you were entirely worthless."

Keigh sat in silence, watching the water rush by, churning its way toward the river, the same way his own thoughts and feelings churned within him now. How could anyone hate someone for the sole purpose of not loving them? He remembered how he had felt when he had run away from home. As long as his parents had been liars, being away had been bearable. It was only after Cato and Braddock had made him understand his parents that being separated from them became untenable. Vicerous had done to him exactly what he had done to his own parents. Keigh's jaw tightened. He didn't like having anything in common with that man.

"What about me is real?" he groaned. "Seems like everything in my life has been done to save my mother from the consequences of her indiscretion. Even my birthday is fake."

"So what if it was?" asked Braddock. "What wouldn't you give to protect your mother? What would your father give? Was he a fool?"

"Maybe," Keigh mumbled.

"You know he wasn't." Cato smiled, but his eyes were serious. "You, Master Anders, risked your life, risked everything, to save a couple of old fools last night. And we don't even cook your meals!"

Keigh sniffed. "Yeah, but you were innocent."

"You didn't do it because we were innocent. You did it because you care about us." Braddock gave Keigh a wry grin and punched his shoulder—a Fortier hug. "Just like you saved your friends from the consequences of setting fire to the tower. Did you do *that* because *they* were innocent?"

"No..."

"Don't you see?" Cato stepped away from Copper. Hobbling over to Keigh, he grasped his forearm. "Love is your motivation, and there is no greater love than to willingly offer up your own life for those who don't deserve it. Many people could be convinced to lay down their life for someone good. Few, *very* few, would do it for the guilty."

"Of all that you've done, it's what I'm most proud of you for," said Braddock. "It's what Owen did, and it's what convinces me that you're more Owen's son than anyone's. The true mark of kinship is the son being molded in the image of the father. Your body might not be built like Owen's..." Braddock pressed a finger into Keigh's sternum. "But your heart *is*."

Keigh swiped his hand away. "What does it matter? They're both dead now."

"In a sense, yes," said Braddock, "but in another sense, so long as you live as Owen lived, loving and fighting for those around you...he will never truly die."

Keigh allowed himself to smile. He opened his palm and looked at himself in the reflective surface of the orb again. He noticed the sharpness of his jaw and the ridge of his nose. They were just like Vicerous. He blinked. *Owen is my father. Blood doesn't change that.*

Cato gasped suddenly. "Is that a ruhe?" he asked, pointing at the orb.

Keigh gave his mentor a quizzical look. "A what?"

"A ruhe, Master Anders!"

Cato held out a shaky hand. Keigh placed the metal ball reluctantly in his palm. Cato's hand dipped a bit under its weight.

The old man chuckled excitedly. "Even when I think I know what to expect from you, Master Anders, you find a new way to surprise me."

"What are you talking about?"

Cato skipped in place. "This is a ruhe! Very rare, *very* valuable. In the years following the Great Collapse, when potents were much more common, they used ruhe to store and carry energy. You can fill one with the energy of ten men just by leaving it in the fire overnight. The orbs are made of a special metal that can hold vast amounts of energy without overheating or leaching the energy to its surroundings." Cato tossed the ball from one hand to the other with a dexterity that defied his age. "The early potents could pull energy from inanimate objects as well as living things. When potents, long ago, lost the ability to pull from lifeless items, they stopped making ruhe. After all, what good is a ball of energy if you can't pull from it?"

"I can pull from it," Keigh interrupted. "I have, several times."

Braddock's jaw dropped.

Cato just grinned. "*The force he yields, he's one of one.*" He winked at Braddock.

"Why didn't you tell me this?" Braddock asked Keigh, seeming flustered.

"I don't know. I only discovered it by accident," Keigh deflected. "Weren't you the one to tell me all potents are different?"

"Not that different!" blurted Braddock. "Do you realize what you can do with this ability? To never have to rely on others to give you strength or risk laying hands on an enemy?"

Truth was, Keigh had realized the advantage; he just hadn't known that it was unique to him. "Mannie must have known what it was. He's the one who told me to keep it with me and use it in times of trouble...which means..."

"Which means somehow our friend Mannie knew of your abilities before you did." Braddock shook his head. "I've got questions for that man when I see him next."

Keigh had questions for Mannie too—namely, *Where did you go?*—but for now there was another question that had been eating at him. "Can I ask you a question?"

"You just did, Master Anders," said Cato. "But go ahead, ask two."

"What do you mean?"

"Three is fine too." Cato snorted, laughing at his own joke.

"Just ask your question," sighed Braddock.

He looked desperately to his mentors, hoping they would absolve him of the guilt he had been feeling. "Did...did we kill innocent men last night?"

Vicerous was a monster for killing Beaudy, but was Keigh just as bad? He had killed canes last night. Canes with families and friends. Canes who had just been carrying out orders.

Cato's expression sobered. "It has been foretold that a day will come in Eden when those who bear the mark of the king will drive out his true servants. That day is coming, and perhaps already upon us, when those who seek the lives of Thiamtaim's true servants do so believing they are serving the king."

"Prophecy or not," said Braddock, "good men who allow themselves to march under false authority perish the same as evil men. That is why it is so important to know the king, to trust that he is good. Why do you think we have tried to stress his trustworthiness to you? If he was not good, or if you were unsure that he was the one rightful authority, you would find yourself a city without walls, defenseless and vulnerable."

"But they died for what they thought was true, didn't they?" Keigh challenged. His mentors hadn't answered his question. "They didn't intend any evil."

"They all should have known they were on the wrong side the second they were asked to muzzle two red bears to obey the queen," Braddock replied. "No red bear of one of the king's canes has ever been recorded being in opposition to the king's law or will. They can sense purity and will not raise a claw against an innocent. You know this to be true. Remember how Mace restrained herself when she found you at the tower? Or how the bears came to your defense when you were escorted from the Refining? Even last night, when you attacked me, her cane, her partner, she did not crush you as she did the other men. Why not? Unless she somehow knew your heart, better than even I did."

Braddock looked Keigh up and down, nodding his own approval.

"Besides the bears, which should have been clue enough, every cane swears to serve the king above all others. The king is our only commander; we will only serve *his* will. If a cane dies in service to the king, he dies a noble death. But if a cane denies the king by serving another master, especially one whose commands contradict the king's, then they have crossed over from servant to enemy. There is no neutral ground. The canes last night were willing to kill children and imprison innocent men because they were told to. They are dead to truth; they traded the truth for a lie and are not innocent in their deception." Braddock sighed. "The queen is the king's appointed authority in Eden right now, but he has limited her to only doing what is in agreement with his character. She has gone outside of that."

"But who's to say she doesn't believe she is doing what the king would want?" The queen had killed Slate in cold blood, so Keigh knew his objection didn't apply, but he still wanted the answer.

"This is what we have been trying to tell you," said Braddock. "You have to know the king. Know who he is, why he does what he does. Everything he does, he does for the good of his people. As a cane, you always need to be able to ask yourself 'What would the king do?' and come to the correct answer. If you don't know him, you'll just end up following your own gut. Our king gave us his law that we may know his heart. The queen is not ignorant of that law. She is in willful rebellion to the king. We will oppose her where she is in error and obey her if ever she should submit herself again to the king's will."

Keigh remembered Braddock telling him that what really separated the canes from all other warriors on earth was why they fought and who they fought for.

"So, the king is the *only* rightful ruler in the whole world?" he asked. "Is that why Draiden can't defeat us? Is that why he hates Eden?"

"There is no one more worthy of your loyalty than the king, Master Anders," said Cato. "The world has never seen his equal and I suspect it never will. As far as Draiden goes...he grew tired of bending the knee to the king and instead desired the throne for himself."

"Wait!" interrupted Keigh. "Are you saying—"

Braddock nodded. "Draiden was a cane."

"The king's highest-ranking general, in fact," said Cato. "He was the finest servant the king ever had. He was magnificent, a truly remarkable specimen. Strong and intelligent, charismatic and fierce."

"You talk like you knew him," said Keigh.

"I do know him—that is to say, I did know him. I knew the man he wanted me to know. His true nature he kept hidden until the day of his uprising."

"That would make you—"

"Very old." Cato nodded, seemingly satisfied with the shocked look on Keigh's face.

"He tried to overthrow the king?" asked Keigh. How had he never heard this?

"He did. Many of the king's servants joined him in his revolt. They managed to slay a great number of their brethren, but it all ended the second the king entered the fight. He bound that snake and banished him from Eden in less time than it takes to drink a cup of tea!" Cato gave a clap of his hands. Then he sighed, his smile fading. "Why the king didn't destroy him then and there, I must admit, I don't know. Needless to say, Eden hasn't had a direct attack on its borders since. Not unless you count this little stunt the queen and Tarin are playing at."

"Then I know what I have to do." Keigh hopped down off the boulder and brushed the moss off the back of his pants. There was only one thing that could fix all that had gone wrong, only one answer to his dilemma. If he was the man that Braddock and Cato said he was, then his next move was obvious. "I need to go find the king."

"The king is not *missing*. He is doing what he must...What is best." Braddock puffed out his chest. "But I've never known him to be one to refuse those who seek him out."

"*His feet will take him far from Eden...*" said Cato, shaking his head, looking fascinated.

"You'll watch after my family while I'm gone, won't you?" Keigh asked.

Both men nodded.

"And my friends?"

"No harm will befall them," assured Braddock. "Even if they must join me in hiding."

"Hiding?"

"You don't really expect Tarin or the queen to pardon us, do you?" he said. "Not after last night. Not to worry, though. I have a place we can all go, if need be. They will all be safe there."

*

Keigh returned to the fire with his mentors. By unspoken consent, the group had declined to travel. Instead, after a morning spent silently grieving, they spent the afternoon remembering Beaudy. It was a poor substitute for a funeral, and Keigh still hoped his friends would hold a proper one for Beaudy back in Bjorn, but he couldn't help but believe the gentle giant would have loved nothing more than to know his friends were safe, together, and full of joy because of him.

Keigh remembered Beaudy's faithfulness as a friend. It was Beaudy who'd been the first to publicly believe Keigh had been attacked by an assassin when everyone else thought him a liar.

Conrad told a hilarious story about the time he and Tarin had challenged Beaudy to a two-on-one wrestling match and lost. He had always respected the fact that Beaudy never once brought it up to anyone, as Beaudy knew the story would have embarrassed the two aspiring canes.

Addy told of a time when Beaudy had stopped in at the records hall just to say hi, and when she'd asked if there was anything he would like to read, he had made a gagging noise before explaining that he would rather get to know the people in front of him than the ones he could only ever know in writing.

Misselli had a particularly touching story: she had once watched Beaudy follow his mother around town while she ran errands and talked to friends. Beaudy had looked like he was about to pass out in the summer heat, but never once left his mother's side. Misselli believed there wasn't another boy in Eden who would have willingly subjected himself to something like that, something other boys could use to mock them as wimps or suckling lambs.

Keigh thought she was right about that. It was proof Beaudy had been braver than anyone gave him credit for, that the boys of Eden would rather face death by sword than be shamed by their peers, but that Beaudy cared more about being a good son than preserving his reputation.

Because of his shameful past with Beaudy, Deacon didn't have much to say, only that Beaudy had been one of the first to forgive him for who he had been, when he should have been the last.

Cato surprised everyone by having a memory of Beaudy from when the boy first moved to Bjorn with his parents. He recalled how the large boy had wrapped him in a hug instead of shaking his hand as his parents had. Apparently, Beaudy's parents had been mortified that their son had approached the town's senior elder so familiarly. For that reason, Cato had valued it more than most hugs in his life.

"When someone embraces you, even though you've done nothing to win their affection," he said, "that is when love speaks most loudly of the worth of the giver and not of the value of the recipient. It's quite the thing to be the highest-ranking member of a society and feel that you are in fact the one lucky to be meeting them."

Theo remained too choked up to speak, though Keigh saw the white flash of his smile several times while the others were talking about his best friend.

Keigh decided that if at the end of his life, people spoke of him as they had of Beaudy, that would be better than being remembered for any heroic exploits. Better to be someone people would miss than someone people idolized. Better to be in the trenches with friends than on the mountaintop alone.

He looked around the circle. He hoped these people would be the ones with something to remember him by.

Stories of Beaudy continued, but the one thing they all had something to say about was Tabitha.

"How? Just how?" Conrad's head shook like something had come loose in his brain.

"Of course *you're* confused. You're a boy. Boys don't understand women," said Misselli, to a general round of laughter at Conrad's expense.

Deacon snorted. "Women don't even understand women. You all are knots of your own tying." The boys laughed. Even Braddock had to fake a cough to hide his grin.

That evening they grilled two geese Deacon and Conrad had shot with their bows. When everyone had eaten their fill, Cato entertained them all with stories of Kwan the messenger—his narrow escapes from giants, how he tamed a mastodon and rode it into the far north in search of people King Orvyn had not yet made contact with, and several more tales of the wonders and oddities outside Eden's borders.

When it came time to bed down for the night, Keigh made his way around and hugged each of his friends. He thanked them for all they had done to help him free Cato and Braddock.

Only he knew he was actually saying goodbye.

Braddock took the first watch, just as he and Keigh had discussed before returning to the fire earlier that day. He would watch for threats, but his real duty was to wake Keigh when everyone else had fallen asleep.

Seemingly seconds after Keigh closed his eyes beside the fire, they popped back open. The crackling of slowly dying embers was the only sound. He looked up to see Braddock motioning him to get up. Carefully, Keigh unwrapped himself from his cloak and stood. He checked that he had all the items he needed for his mission and when he was satisfied, nodded to Braddock.

"Be safe," Braddock whispered. "You've got a lot more training to do when you get back."

"*If* I get back." Keigh smiled sadly, wishing Braddock could go with him. "Till then, I look forward to it."

"You'll be back," assured Braddock. "You're going to be on the same side of the wall as the king! Probably safer out there than in here." He smiled and gave Keigh a soft punch in the arm. "*You* definitely will be."

Braddock and Cato's trust in the king matched that of Keigh's father. How these men had come to trust the king with everything still baffled Keigh, but he knew they weren't fools.

He looked around the camp at his friends one last time. Cato's blue eyes sparkled back at him in Verity's light. The two exchanged a silent nod.

Keigh's eyes lingered on the still form of Misselli. Her blonde hair tied up in a bun, she lay under her cloak, facing the fire. Would she forgive him for leaving? No doubt she would have begged him to stay if he had told her. If she had, would he have had the strength to refuse her? Could he tell the girl to whom he'd give anything that he couldn't give her this? She was his weakness. A blessed, beautiful, glorious weakness...but a weakness just the same. She made him strong, too. He was his best self around her. But what would happen when what he needed to do conflicted with Misselli's safety? Could he do what was necessary for others when his heart's deepest affections were reserved for her first?

A vision of Beaudy, the blood-stained blade protruding from his chest, entered Keigh's mind. "*I trusted you, Keigh,*" Beaudy whimpered, looking down at the wound.

When the large boy looked up, it was no longer Beaudy, but Misselli in a white dress. Crimson blood spread through the linen covering her chest. *"This is what I get for following you?"* she cried, her eyes piercing him to his core with the pain of betrayal.

Keigh swallowed, his mouth suddenly dry. He took a moment to allow his eyes to remind him Misselli was still there, still alive and unharmed, sleeping quietly before him. Once he assured himself she would be safe—safe with Braddock, safe in Bjorn—he took a deep breath and set out into the darkness.

Copper rose from where he had been lying in the grass and followed him as silently as a two-thousand-pound bear could. Keigh held Verity out in front of him for light, weaving his way through the shadowy columns of trees toward the river.

Clearing the grove, he scowled at the white walls of Sentinel, looming high above him on the other side of the roaring rapids. The city that was meant to be the citadel of hope had crushed every hope he had. Now it was a symbol of disappointment. Inside its walls he had been given a taste of what he had always wanted: to be a cane, to be famous, to have his name cheered by strangers. But those canes had proved to be men he never wanted to be like. It had only taken a well-crafted lie to change his fame to infamy, and the adoration of strangers had shown itself a cheap forgery of the love his family and friends had for him at home.

Even his flawless image of the king had been tested. If not for Cato and Braddock, he may still harbor bitterness for the king he would never understand. His time at the Refining really had refined him, only not in the way he had expected. He had expected to shine like a nugget of gold among rocks in a miner's pan, but instead he had been melted down, reduced to nothing, all his false hopes and desires rising out of him to be discarded. The heat had not been comfortable, but he was purer now than before. Now his purpose was noble. He would no longer fight for his own ambitions. His sword was not his own; it belonged to the ones he loved. His mission was to bring the king back into his kingdom, a kingdom broken and dangerous without him.

Tarin would pay. The queen would pay. All those who had rebelled against the king in his absence would answer for their crimes. They may have him on the run and banished, but if the king proved to be the man his fathers said he was...then Keigh wouldn't be alone.

Something touched his elbow. Keigh jolted out of his reflection. Spinning, he raised his sword to confront whatever had snuck up on him in the night.

"Don't!" Deacon cowered in front of him. "It's us, Keigh!"

Us?

Keigh looked past Deacon to where Misselli stood, one hand resting on Copper's back.

"What are you doing here?" he asked in a panic. This was exactly what he had wanted to avoid by leaving in the dead of night. "Go back to camp. It's not safe."

"We aren't going back," said Misselli.

"And why's that?"

"'Cause you aren't going back," said Deacon, raising himself to his full height. "Are you?"

"That's *my* business," argued Keigh. "*You* need to go back and make sure our friends make it home safe. How did you even get past Braddock?"

Deacon grinned. "I convinced him it was best for you to have someone with you, watching your back."

"And you?" Keigh asked Misselli, trying to mask his worry.

"I made it clear I was going with you and there wasn't anything he could do to keep me from you, short of killing me."

Keigh's throat tightened as he fought to suppress the tears their devotion evoked. To have their loyalty like this meant everything to him—but they couldn't come. Misselli couldn't come. It was too dangerous.

"How did you even know I was leaving, or where to find me?"

Misselli stepped away from Copper, approaching Keigh slowly. "When you hugged me last night, I...I just knew you weren't hugging me goodnight. I felt goodbye. I don't know how I knew other than that I know *you*, Keigh. I can tell when you're up and when you're down, when you're full of hope or full of fear. When you said goodnight, I felt fear. You held me like you would never get to do it again. You can't mask that. Not from me."

"I thought your hug was fine." Deacon shrugged. "But when Misselli explained her hunch to me, I thought it was at least worth sleeping with one eye open," he chuckled. "Finding you was easy. Ever since I held that sword, it's like following a star around. You couldn't hide from us, not when you're carrying that."

Keigh kicked a rock toward the river. What was he to do? If they followed him, could he live with himself if they got hurt? Deacon, maybe—he, at least, had trained for this. But Misselli? She was a bird leaving its nest for the first time. She might fly, but what if she fell?

"You're right," Keigh admitted. "I'm not coming back. Not tonight, and probably not anytime soon. Tarin banished me and threatened to have anyone close to me killed if I showed my face in Eden again."

"So, you're running away?" Deacon scowled. "To protect us—ouch!" He grabbed his shoulder where Misselli had punched him.

"Keigh doesn't run away!"

Keigh's eyes widened at the sudden aggression. *So much for a baby bird!*

"If he is leaving, he has a good reason. Don't you, Keigh?" Misselli asked, but it was more of a statement, not a shadow of doubt on her face.

"I'm going to find the king," Keigh said. "And when I do, I'm going to convince him to come back and make everything right. He's the only one who can."

"See?" Misselli drew her fist back, causing Deacon to flinch.

"I never doubted him! I was just pressing him is all."

"So, it's settled. We are coming with you."

Misselli opened her clenched fist and reached out for Keigh's hand. But when Keigh went to take hold of it, she bypassed his palm and slipped a finger into the band she had tied there so many months ago. With a sharp tug, she snapped the fabric.

"Hey! Why'd you do that?" Keigh stooped to retrieve the fallen strip.

"You're going to have to settle for the real thing now," she said, placing her hands on her hips. "No more tokens, just me, with you."

"With you," Deacon echoed.

There was nothing Keigh could do now. They were in this together. He was lucky to have them. Both of them. He wouldn't fight it. He wouldn't run them off.

"We'd best set out, then," he said.

Deacon and Misselli grinned at each other. Deacon gave a celebratory pump of his fist. Misselli flung herself at Keigh, wrapping her arms around his neck.

Bringing her lips next to his ear, she whispered, "I don't ever want to feel another goodbye hug again."

"Okay," he chuckled, wrapping his arms around her. He lifted her off the ground and spun her around. "How 'bout that one? What did that hug say?"

She giggled and squinted as if deep in thought. "'Misselli, you're amazing and I can't believe I tried to sneak off and rescue Eden without you'?"

"Can we get going already?" Deacon shouted back at them over the roaring rapids. He had already started making his way toward the curtain wall.

"He was closer," said Keigh, giving Misselli a wink and a wry smile.

"Ugh!" She slapped a palm to his chest. Keigh laughed.

Together, they set out.

Out of Eden.

Out to find the king.

You just finished book 1 in the Son of Eden trilogy!
Thank you so much for reading.

YOU CAN HELP!

If you enjoyed this book and want to continue the journey with Keigh and his friends in books 2 and 3, tell two of your reader friends to buy the book for themselves. This is a self-published work and the process of writing it was time consuming and expensive. The reality is that writing is not my day job and in order to write books 2 and 3 I need to sell enough of book 1 to justify the investment it would take to bring books 2 and 3 to life.

The books are outlined and ready to be written! I hope to be able to bring you the journey in full but at the end of the day, if this book was an encouragement or a blessing to you, if it helped you see life in a new light or gave you the courage to persevere when everything seems to be going wrong, then my time was well invested and I'm happy to have played a small part in your journey.

Also, please leave Keigh Anders and the Bears of Bjorn a positive review on Amazon and Goodreads.com. Every kind word helps!

Until the adventure continues,
Trust the King.

www.ingramcontent.com/pod-product-compliance
Lightning Source LLC
Chambersburg PA
CBHW021928110726
47901CB00003B/751